Hull
Volume I

Hull
Volume I

JT Phillips

---

http://www.jameskryackltd.com/p/contact-us.html/

ISBN 978-1-4848-8762-2

www.jameskryackltd.com

For those who said, "keep going," even when the going got tough.

Contents

A Start to Things

It was both my first and last case with the Newfield Police Department. Here I was, just two weeks after returning home from a two-year deployment in Iraq as a combat medic, and I already had an offer as a medical examiner. Granted, Newfield only had around sixty thousand people and the city was in the center of the Willamette Valley in Oregon. To sum up the location, it was in the middle of nowhere. But it was where my older brother lived with his family, who had generously offered me a place to stay until I had my feet on the ground. I would have been a fool to turn down the opportunity. I also would have been a fool for the fact that, had I not moved here and taken the job, I never would have met Mr. Sheridan Hull.

I sat at my new desk in the forensic investigation department, which just so happened to be in the basement of the police building. Beside the complete lack of natural light, the location was made more unpleasant by the eclectic mixture of odors. Across the hallway was what the other examiners called the "temp morgue." Every body brought in for an investigative autopsy was kept in there. And the number of murder-related crimes in Newfield were abnormally high. There was a good traffic of bodies in and out of the room. Just down the hallway was where any arrested individual was kept until the proper paperwork was filed and a decision on their destination was made. For a basement, the floor received a high level of activity. And my job was to analyze bodies at a crime scene. So far, my presence hadn't been requested at any scenes. So far.

"Walker," the chief examiner at the far end of the room yelled, disrupting the silence that had fallen for almost an hour. "Lennox wants you upstairs."

I looked towards my superior's desk, shocked at having heard my name attached to his statement. "He wants me?"

"Get up there," the examiner said, not bothering to look up from his paperwork. I stood up quickly, grabbing my temporary badge from my desk before leaving the room. Lennox was the head investigator of the department, just below the police commissioner. If he requested you, it meant you were heading somewhere in the field. And since I'd been called, my hopes were high.

I approached Lennox's door with both anxiety and fear. To everyone here, I was the new guy. I'd been given my doctorate after four years in college, one year in medical school, and a sudden demand for medical professionals in the Army. I had no actual experience working in the criminal investigation field, and for that, the chief examiner had been reluctant to even give me a desk. Nonetheless, the opening had been present and the chief of police was a good friend of my brother. Thankfully, the people above the basement had been more open to my arrival.

When I was within a meter of the door, it opened. A tall, black-coated man exited, back-first, his black hair shining and neatly combed. He was almost a head taller than me, but probably the same weight. Despite his leanness, he had broad shoulders, and when he turned, he did so with a sense of pride. His face was both stern and welcoming, his eyes so deep a shade of brown they blended perfectly with his pupils. His face was cleanly shaven, save for a goatee. He smiled and nodded at me before glancing back into the office.

"Busy schedule, Greg? You've already got another visitor," the man said. Another man exited the office, standing eye-to-eye with me. He wore a more business-based attire with a gray suit and dark blue tie. His hair was brown, short but lengthy enough to be visibly combed forward. He had a bit more weight accumulated, but not to an unhealthy level.

"Yeah, well, you know how it goes, get done with a business meeting, have a crime scene to get to." The man, Inspector Gregory

Lennox, clasped the black-haired man on the shoulder before gesturing to me. "Mayor Montorum, this is Dr. John Walker, our new medical examiner. Dr. Walker, this is Mr. Jameson Montorum, Newfield's mayor."

"Pleasure to meet you, Doctor," Montorum said, grasping my hand and giving a single shake with a prominent squeeze.

"The pleasure's all mine, Sir," I replied coolly, giving a nod.

Montorum looked from me to Lennox. "Well, I'd best be off. Good luck with the crime scene."

"Have a good day," Lennox said as the mayor turned from us both and left. The inspector focused on me. "Alright, Walker, let's hope you're as good as your brother makes you out to be."

"Well, Sir, you need to know I have no actual experience with—"

"You're a doctor and you've seen dead people." Lennox shrugged. "That's enough experience in my book." He closed his office door behind him, then started forward. "We just got the call about ten minutes ago. Concerned neighbor found the door to the next house over wide open. Went to investigate and found three bodies, all shot through the head. You, me, and two other officers will be the first ones on location. Ready?"

"As ready as I can be."

"Good. We leave in two."

*

We arrived at the scene after a short fifteen minutes of driving. It was a small house on 4th Street, one story, normal looking, save for the police tape that now barred entry. The two officers who had come with us were now speaking to the neighbors, asking questions about the house. Lennox and I were bound for the home itself. I passed under the police tape to reveal a normal enough home, the living room filled with décor and nothing substantial standing out. It was in all regards a typical home. Except for the three dead bodies in the center of the living room floor.

Lennox crouched over the bodies cautiously, his gloved hands careful not to touch them. He gave a loud sigh after several seconds of silence.

"Definitely a triple-homicide," he said. I stooped to examine the bodies from over his shoulder.

3

"Or so you are to believe."

Both Lennox and I snapped back and spun, the new and unfamiliar voice piercing our concentration. Standing in the doorway that led to the kitchen was a man, about half a head taller than me and fairly lanky. He wore a gray overcoat that reached his knees, as well as a purple scarf. His hair was a blond so dirty it was better described as brown. His face was stern, his cheekbones prominent, but his eyes were most certainly the defining quality. The one on the left was a brilliant blue while the right was a shimmering green. Both had a distinctive glint.

"Ah." Lennox craned his head back a short way, looking at the newly-arrived man. "Hull. Should've known you'd be here already."

"Yes, you should have." The man, Hull, looked at me. "Iraq, then?"

I furrowed my brow. "I beg your pardon?"

"You served in Iraq."

I looked at Lennox, who made a face that suggested both humor and resignation. I looked back at the newcomer with confusion. "I did, yes. How did you know that?"

"Your walk suggested you are attuned to carrying a heavy load on your back. You tend to slouch forward as you move. You have removed the weight, but your mind and mentality has not." Hull's voice was strong and confident, but also almost monotonous. "The way you scanned the home before entering it was the same way one would do so when looking for individuals camped out with weapons, guns trained to fire on anyone who comes too close. The tone of your skin is adjusted to that of a country in the Middle East, and your eyes are less adjusted to darker areas, explaining why you pause after entering an indoor location."

I stared with a slightly ajar mouth. Somehow, this man was accurately describing so much of my life in Iraq. I had no idea how it was possible, but he knew. I looked over at Lennox, expecting an explanation. What I got was not what I'd hoped for.

"He's always like this, too." The inspector stood up. "Dr. Walker, this is our resident Brit, Mr. Sheridan Hull. Hull, this is Dr. John Walker."

"Pleased to meet you, Doctor," Hull said, shaking my hand. It was only then that I noticed the small, subtle accent of a man from the United Kingdom. He stepped back, then to the left, giving himself a better position to analyze the bodies. "No, I would say these were intended to look like murders, and that if you were to take them as that, you would chase the wrong trail entirely."

"Then tell me, *genius*," Lennox retorted, taking a step away from the bodies and spreading his arms to encompass the room, "what happened here?"

Hull appeared to ignore the initial crack. "The scene is designed to look as if it was three people shot, but the wielder of each individual gun, as there were three all fired simultaneously, happened to also be the victim of the bullet. These are suicides, but forced. You can see by looking there, there, and there," he gestured to three different areas on the walls, where the paint had been chipped away, "that the guns were fired with shaking hands through their own temples. Had these been executions, the bullets would have traveled to the ground, but because they travel upward, and we can assume the person behind this is not an extremely short individual, they had to have been fired by the people who are dead.

"It should also be noted that there were five people here originally, and two of them are still alive, one being the owner of this house. You will want to begin your search, Lennox, by finding these remaining people, or better yet, finding out where our house occupant has vanished to. I am certain the neighbors will provide bountiful information."

Hull stooped down over one of the bodies, carefully running his hovering hands only a few centimeters above the clothing. Lennox gave a sigh before walking out. I looked at the new arrival with curiosity abound. Never before had I seen someone so quick to learn so much about everything in a given situation.

"So tell me, Doctor," Hull said, bringing my train of thought to a halt, "what has brought you from the front lines to a state so off the charts as this one? And in a city just as remote?"

"Well, my brother lives here and—"

"No, of course, I was foolish to ask such a question. It is quite obvious of as to why you chose here."

"It, uh... it is?"

"Indeed. Being a retired military member, you would have access to an abundance of resources in finding new employment wherever you preferred. Yet you still picked Newfield, Oregon. You would have preferred to not have to live with your brother, but you were not given much of a choice financially, as you were dismissed from your previous job. Had you not been dismissed from the military, Army, I'm presuming, you would not have ended up here. No, you were dismissed for something, and that put you in a position where you needed to be somewhere as far away from your training base as possible."

Hull looked up at me, eyes still glinting. "Now, why was it dishonorable?"

I took a moment to gather my bearings before replying. "Dishonorable. Somewhat. My squad and I were deployed when we walked into an ambush. Our commanding officer ordered us to leave, that he would handle them. We resisted at first, but he was adamant. Upon returning to base without a commanding officer, we were questioned. They didn't believe us, saying we'd deliberately left a CO to die. All of us were dishonorably discharged."

"Ah." Hull chuckled. "Oh the fallacies." He stood up, walking around to face the three bodies. "Tell me, Doctor, what can you analyze about these three individuals?"

"Uh.." I glanced down at the bodies nervously, feeling as if the man was able to deduce even my thoughts. "Well, not much else besides what you've already seen."

"Seeing and observing, Doctor, are two very, very different things." Hull swept his hand over the three bodies. "What I can observe here are three factory workers, all diligent but none from the same facility." His hand came to hover over the one on my left, his right. "This one worked in some sort of chemical facility as a conveyor belt monitor. If you notice the pant leggings on both other workers, they have dried mud and other particles gained from working outside. This one does not. This tells us he worked inside. The scuff marks on his inner arms show signs of repeated rubbing, the result of resting his elbows against the side of the conveyor and having the belt occasionally catch his sleeves.

"The center one worked in a much more outdoor facility. The pants are dirty, far more dirty than either of the other two, and the mud is much fresher. The gloves in his right pocket coupled with the calluses that line his lower palms show that he worked constantly with heavy, rough material. He has a much stronger upper build, helping to affirm this thought. The very distinct smell of sap tells us that this man worked in a lumber yard of some sort, helping to offload logs as they arrived.

"The third one is more difficult, but not impossible. Similar mud specks on the pants, but not near as frequent nor fresh. His lower body is significantly more toned than his upper, showing he presumably did much more moving of his own self than of other things." He kneeled down, gently pushing the body to reveal the front. "The insignia on his shirt is that of the Boeing Company, a multinational aerospace construction industry. Boeing has an airplane construction and test site one mile north of Newfield. This person presumably worked on the tarmac, helping to direct planes before and after test flights." He stood up, looking at me with some expectancy. I merely stared at him in shock. How could he have possibly figured that all out with just the minor details?

"That's..."

"Deduction?"

"Amazing."

"Ah." He stepped back, glancing down at the bodies one more time before looking back up at me. "I suppose that is one way to describe it." His eyes traveled to something behind me before his head arched back slowly. "It would seem the next part of the case is about to reveal itself." I was on the verge of asking when Lennox entered, phone in hand.

"Just got a call about a hostage crisis, Hilton Hotel on the corner of 20th and Archer," the inspector reported. I looked forward to see Hull, gone. I looked back at Lennox, expecting some kind of surprise. There was none. "They want us there. Chief says he thinks it might be affiliated with this."

"The one taken hostage," I murmured, glancing back at the bodies.

"The boys will deal with those. You and I are going to that hotel."

*

"He's supposedly turning himself in, but we have no idea what happened to the hostage he came with." Lennox hadn't stopped talking since the moment we'd entered the car. Most of my attention was dedicated to him, but a part of me still wondered what had happened to Hull. And I suppose there was a part of me interested in the overall crime, but to me, death was still something very natural and very frequent. Adjusting to normal life would take a bit more time than two weeks. Just a bit more.

"Where is he now?" I asked as we passed through the automatic doors to the lobby.

"Sixth floor, room 636. We have one officer overseeing him until we get there." I nodded, following Lennox into the elevator.

Finding the room wasn't difficult, and the man wasn't all that impressive. He was bald, his face shaved, and his hands cuffed behind the chair he sat in. From just a glance, he didn't look like a man who would force three people to kill themselves. And he certainly didn't look like the choreographer of a hostage situation. He looked up as Lennox and I entered the room, a smile carving its way onto his face. I was no Hull, but I could tell by just a look, we were somehow being played. The smile wasn't one of insanity, as I'd seen on too many occasions. It was humor.

"Oh no, big bad Inspector Lennox is here," the man said, glancing up at the officer to his left, "what am I gonna do now?"

"You're gonna shut up and tell me where your hostage is," Lennox said, his voice more stern than I'd heard before.

"What're you gonna do? Shoot me? Kill me? Don't I have rights against that?"

"Your rights only go so far, now you tell me where the hostage is."

The man smiled. "Why don't you look?" Lennox's eyes shot up to the police officer, who promptly shook his head.

"You're gonna stop bullshitting me right now. Where is the hostage."

Bang.

I spun around, the very familiar sound of a gunshot sending wave after wave of nostalgia through my veins. Lennox charged through the door, the policeman at his heels. I followed the three, subconsciously realizing we had just left the suspected hostage taker alone. Several rooms down was an open door, and inside was a woman, gunshot wound through the forehead. Lennox rubbed the arch of his nose while I looked around the room. Nobody had made an exit through that door, or we would've seen them. So it meant they had to still be here. Didn't it?

"You will now find that both the actual criminal and your supposed hostage taker are gone."

I spun once more, this time to find Sheridan Hull standing in the doorway, hands in his pockets and eyes resting on the now-dead body. Lennox didn't even bother turning; he simply sighed and closed his eyes.

"And just where have they gone?" the inspector said, exasperation in his voice.

"The roof, most likely. Considering the gunman never left this room through the doorway and the fake hostage taker wouldn't have made it too far through the lobby doors with handcuffs. Bravo leaving him alone, by the way. As if a chair is too heavy for a built man to carry." He stepped over to the body as Lennox took out his phone, walking out into the hallway with the policeman. "It seems we have found our fourth individual."

"A shame, just killing them off like this," I said, feeling as if my words would meet his expectations. Of course, they did not.

"Shame? No, this is the game." He leaned over the body, eyes moving so quickly one would almost guess he had astigmatism. "From a metaphorical perspective, of course. It's a living, fluid game. Like chess. And we are all the pieces. She was a pawn to her murderer, and her murderer a rook to an even larger game. This woman was actually far more significant than the other three victims, despite having shared employment location with one of them. Her attire, however, is more official than that of a factory worker. This woman was a supervisor at the same chemical factory as the first worker.

"As well as being a supervisor, it would seem she was the owner of the house that holds three bodies." He kneeled beside her, swiftly reaching a hand into her coat pocket. He pulled out a long, slender key. "This key is a very unique one of a very unique style. The metal used for the key is the same that was used for the lock, an often unused-for-locks metal called rhodium. The lock this key goes to was built into the doorway of the house where three people were forced to commit suicide.

"The clothing inside the house was all from a local tailor, one who does not sell to many consumers. However, the owner of the house was an avid fan of their work and sought to cover their home in the clothes. They also covered their body, explaining why this woman's blouse and scarf are both custom-made by the tailor, affirmed by the lack of any tags from a branch store. It should also be noted that in the house, several pictures lined the mantelpiece above the fireplace. In the majority of them, this woman's face was prominent."

"But why were they all at her house?" I asked, my fascination overflowing. "Three workers from different places and her?"

"That's where it gets interesting, isn't it. From what I can tell, the three workers were acting, and presumably unofficial, representatives of their individual establishments. This woman had a reason for gathering them, something the industries have in common. All of them held positions in where they were directly involved with the main products of their employments. We just need to figure out what product made it to all three of them, and why.

"But yes, she called a meeting of these three to discuss something. Something that had traveled between their industries, possibly something all three of them had handled personally. An outsider, however, did not like the meeting, or wanted to keep the certain traveling something from being discovered, and therefore interfered by killing them. This certain traveling something is now at the center of the case, and our priority. We need to find the correlation."

"Where would we start?"

Hull looked up at me, the glint to his eyes shining. "I would suggest the chemical factory, though I am certain Lennox will have other plans. They will presumably involve going back to the police station and sending out a watch request for the supposed hostage taker. The time wasted to do this will be crucial. I will be going to the chemical factory." He tilted his head slightly. "You are, of course, welcome to join me, Doctor."

I opened my mouth to respond, but stopped when Lennox and the officer reentered. "He's right, both of them are gone. I'm going back, hoping to try and run a scan on the man's face." Hull gave a minute hiccup-like motion.

"If it's alright with you, Sir," I prompted, eyes moving from Lennox to Hull, "I would like to go with Hull to investigate the factory this woman worked at."

Lennox looked at me with wary eyes, then glanced at Hull. "You want to go somewhere with him?" He paused, eyes going back to me. "Voluntarily?"

"I would, with your permission."

It took Lennox nearly ten seconds before he threw his hands up in resignation. "Sure. Keep your phone on hand, I'll call you once we get some real results." With that, Lennox and the officer left, leaving Hull and me in the room. I looked back at the man to find him staring at me with an interested look on his face.

"What?" I asked, glancing down at my attire.

"You aren't like the rest of those blithering idiots in the department, that much is clear. Whether it's from your military background or just natural common sense, you stand above them. Especially Lennox."

"I pride myself in not being stupid, but what you do is amazing."

"So you say. Others are not so gracious."

"Why? What do they say?"

"That I'm insane."

*

The chemical factory was not too difficult to find, considering it was the only one in the entire industrial district that occupied the northeastern part of Newfield. The factory, Warmack Chemical, was surprisingly large, occupying nearly a quarter of the land dedicated to the industrial district. Four large smokestacks rose high into the air from the center of the facility, with buildings varying in size creating a sizable perimeter. Hull and I walked towards the facility's visitor center, the other man a short step ahead of me. I knew that somewhere in his head, he was figuring everything out. Despite physically being a step behind him, I knew mentally, I was nowhere close.

Hull had been relatively silent on the taxi ride over. I hadn't made a move for conversation, but even so, the silence was almost unsettling. He just sat and stared forward; not out the window, forward. And his eyes moved side to side with such speed that I worried if he may have been suffering from a seizure. I'd only known the man for a few hours, but I could see he was different. Very, very different. His ability to see, no, *observe* everything was astonishing. Marvelous. I couldn't even begin to comprehend how he did it. And it wasn't over yet. Now him and I sat in the office of a Mr. Alexander Wygant, one of the head scientists for Warmack.

Wygant was fairly tall for his age, which I put at a little over sixty. His hair was a sleek gray that was combed to the left, probably covering a balding patch. His face was wrinkled and his eyes a deep blue. He wore a white lab coat that was stained in several locations. Behind his desk was a window that looked down at the production line, where dozens of workers moved to and from a central conveyor belt. Hull and I sat looking at him as he softly shuffled some papers from his desk to the garbage bin to his right.

"So you gentlemen are investigating what now?"

"Two of your workers, one more attuned to manual labor, the other a supervisor, did not show up for work today. They are dead." Hull's monotonous tone almost came off as cold as he stared down the scientist. "We are here to gather what information we can."

"Ah. You'd be talking about Josephine Dunphy and Allen Mark. Two great workers, real shame to hear this happened. I'm more than willing to offer whatever information I can to help in the investigation, of course."

"Ms. Dunphy and Mr. Mark were two of four people killed, all of them together at one point and Dunphy killed after the other three. She was taken as a hostage before being executed. It is my belief that something was here that she did not like, something Mr. Mark had handled, and sought to learn its whereabouts. Someone was not appreciative of her curiosity and in turn sought to keep her prying eyes from learning more." Hull stood, walking to the right of Wygant's desk and looking out at the factory body.

"Well, I assure you that all of our contents are cleared by multiple levels of authority before being authorized. If something was out of place, Ms. Dunphy would have reported it."

"Mr. Wygant, can you tell me of some of Warmack Chemical's primary products?"

Wygant looked up at Hull, still staring out at the conveyor area. "As in, our chemicals?"

"Yes, the chemicals."

"We create a wide array of things, from chemicals used for medicinal purposes to farming. Many of our products are shipped across the nation, we have quite the reputation for potent antibacterial components. Something about Newfield's climate allows for better settling with the chemicals."

"And do you only work on a national level?"

"Well no, we do work locally as well. As I said, a lot of our chemicals are used for medicinal purposes, which are sent to pharmaceutical drug development locations, hospitals, whatever they need."

"I see. And what about chemical acquirement? Do you import from out of state, or do you operate locally in that regard as well?"

"We try and support the local economy as best we can. Most of our chemicals are developed from rather simple means."

"Such as?"

Wygant paused for a moment, glancing at me before continuing. "It entirely depends on the chemical. Some we are able to harvest naturally, others are created via mixtures. We do a lot of testing and sampling with a new endeavor called 'green chem' development. Using materiel gathered from shrubbery, moss, trees, those sorts of things, we are able to create chemicals that are environmentally friendly and more easily renewed."

Hull looked over at Wygant before turning completely, taking enough steps to stand beside me. "That should be all. Thank you for your time, Mr. Wygant."

"That's all?" Wygant asked, standing. "But you hardly mentioned the two victims."

"I didn't need to. We know they are dead. We just need to figure out why. That doesn't necessarily require much information about them personally." He started for the door, giving me my cue to stand and follow. Several minutes of silence passed before we reached the taxi, still waiting for us. As soon as we'd both situated ourselves, he leaned forward.

"Take us to the Boeing facility," he said calmly before sitting back.

"What did you get from that?" I asked, my curiosity overwhelming me.

"They work locally. Dunphy became suspicious after a chemical was sent somewhere, and pursued it as far as Boeing, also being efficient to return to its source. Green chem development. Something that was delivered from the lumber yard to the chemical factory made its way to Boeing. And Dunphy didn't think it should have."

"What kind of chemicals go into airplane construction?"

"That's what we're going to figure out, isn't it?"

*

The construction and test facility was truly a sight to behold. At least a dozen hangars stretched off out of sight, with four long runways creating a huge empty space that spanned to the hills of the north. Two extremely large planes were currently moving up and down their respected runways slowly, possibly testing the landing gear or engines. Hull and I were escorted to an office complex next to the hangars, the hub of administration for the entire facility. Sitting before us was a man, Mr. Glenn Radburn, the head of public relations for this Boeing district. He sat with a slight jitter to his hands, not from concern, but more likely from the enormous coffee mug that sat within arm's reach.

"So what can I help with, gents?" Radburn asked, clasping his hands together.

As usual, Hull did the talking. I was along to witness his genius at work. "We are investigating the murders of four people, one who worked at this facility. Mr. Steven Dunkelman was a runway technician, I believe. He was found dead earlier today in a home, which I am sure you were notified of."

"I was. Tragic to hear. We've never had one of our employees die like this. We've sent our deepest condolences to the family."

"Yes, Mr. Dunkelman was among two other bodies found, and a fourth joined them not long after. We believe some kind of product was delivered from Warmack Chemical to this facility and Mr. Dunkelman was somehow involved with it. Not necessarily in a bad way, but somehow involved."

"Well we do get shipments from Warmack, but company policy keeps me from disclosing what and for what purpose."

"Does it now?"

Radburn paused, raising his brows. "You think something from Warmack is what killed them?"

Hull scoffed. "Hardly. I believe something from Warmack is getting people killed." He leaned forward. "Mr. Radburn, it is very important you cooperate. A certain product delivered from Warmack reached here, and one of Warmack's supervisors did not think it was right. She called a meeting of unofficial representatives from three different companies, and now all four of them are dead. Again, your cooperation is very important. I need to know what Warmack has sent as of late that Mr. Dunkelman may have had a hand in dealing with."

"He was a tarmac tech, he didn't handle the chemicals." Radburn sighed. "I can't disclose what we use without proper authority, but I can say that nothing from Warmack is ever used on the runways. There's no way he would have been involved with anything from the factory."

"And what of the chance that something from the factory did make its way onto the runway? Would he have then?"

"What are you suggesting, some kind of toxic spill? We're an airplane construction site, not Chernobyl. We don't deal with chemicals that can kill everyone, only things vital to a plane's construction and testing."

"Such as?"

"I can't disclose that."

Hull stood, breathing in heavily through his nostrils. "Thank you for your time, Mr. Radburn." He turned rapidly, leaving the room before either Radburn or I could speak. I looked at the visibly-flustered man with a look of sympathy.

"I'm so sorry. He's, uh.. well, I don't know if he's like that all the time, but.. I'm sorry." I got up and quickly exited, finding Hull nearly fifty meters away, staring down one of the runways. I ran to catch up, glancing back to make sure Radburn wasn't charging after us in anger. I reached Hull quickly, taking a moment to breathe.

"Now why," I huffed, "did you do that?"

"He was unreliable, only so much information he was willing to give, not for the sake of hiding anything but for the sake of being official."

"Is that bad?"

"It's inconvenient. The more information we can glean from the innocent, the closer we get to finding the guilty."

"And looking down an empty runway is going to help?"

"It just might."

I looked down the runway to see a plane being ushered onto the tarmac. The plane must have recently been put together, as it lacked any kind of detail, even the cockpit windshield. I watched the man leading it back up slowly, calling out indistinguishable commands to the driver of the tug. The plane wasn't too large, nowhere near the size of the two already out on the runways, but it was still sizable enough to hold a significant number of people.

"It just might," Hull repeated before turning away, starting the walk out of the facility. I followed slowly, eyes still glancing cautiously towards the administrative complex. I should have been paying attention to where we were going.

Ahead of me, Hull ducked as a man, garbed in black and wielding a baseball bat, attacked. The tip of the bat caught my arm, sending me spinning to the ground. I struggled to stand, watching as

15

Hull adeptly avoided two more attacks before lashing out, catching the bat in one hand and forcing it back at the holder. The man staggered, his wrist twisted. Hull charged forward, grabbing the bat once more and smashing it into the man's forehead. The man fell backwards, head hitting the ground with a thud. I stood next to Hull, feeling slightly disoriented. Hull stood over the man, panting slightly.

"He's a worker from Warmack," he heaved. "He watched us leave and followed us."

"Why?" I prompted as Hull leaned down, patting the man's pockets. "Is he the murderer?"

"No. But he works for him. The murderer's on to us." He stopped when he reached the man's left coat pocket, reaching in and pulling out a slip of paper. He unfolded the paper to reveal a six-character combination: 210TDC. Hull stood slowly, eyes fixated on the paper.

"210TDC. Is it something scrambled?" I asked, looking from Hull's face to the numbers and letters.

"No, it's.. some kind of.."

He stopped, looking up with wide eyes.

"Oh, of course!" he exclaimed.

"What? What is it?"

"We need to get to Portland International Airport, *now*."

"What? Why?"

"There isn't time! Get the taxi!"

*

We arrived at PDX at almost 2 AM. Hull didn't even stop to pay the taxi, and all the while I wondered why we didn't just take his car, or mine. He rushed into the terminal with me in tow, quickly going for security. Several people made motions to stop him, but I was able to talk them off, telling them why we were here. He pushed onward, not perturbed by anything in his way. He eventually reached a desk and rapidly started banging on the security window. I came up behind him as fast as I could, grasping his shoulder.

"Hull, don't do that, they'll think you're—"

"What they think is irrelevant, we need to intervene now."

"What do we need to—"

"Is there something you need?" a security officer asked, emerging from the office door behind the desk.

"There is a plane departing for Washington, D.C. in approximately twenty minutes. You need to stop that plane now."

"I'm sorry, Sir, what evidence do you have to—"

"The plane has been altered and if you do not stop it, many people will die. Please, for once in your pathetic job, comply with something someone is saying."

The guard first bristled at the crack, but then nodded. He turned to his left shoulder and started speaking, then pointed at the gate to the left of the office. Hull and I passed through it, ignoring the beeps of the metal detectors. The guard exited the office, standing in front of us. "You better be right about this, whoever you are. Follow me."

The guard led us through the terminal to one of the gates. Through the windows we could see a plane, partially moved away from the gate. About thirty people sat in the gate waiting area, all looking disgruntled. The plane had been evacuated, which was good. The guard continued into the gate, taking us to where the captain of the plane was waiting at a metal staircase that took us to the tarmac. We walked down and looked up at the plane, Hull moving around to the front.

"What's this about, then?" the captain called after him. "I've got a timetable to meet." Hull ignored him, eyes glued on the front of the plane. I came to stand next to him, slowly joined by the guard and captain.

Suddenly, the windshield of the plane cracked at the sides, the cracks moving virulently to the center. The glass did not shatter completely, but pieces fell away into the cockpit and out of sight. The captain looked up at the windshield in horror, the guard sharing the same look. I glanced at Hull, who, for just a short moment, offered a smile before returning to his stern look. He looked over at me, or more, the area around me.

"A chemical from the facility used to create an anti-fogging deterrent on the windshields of airplanes. But this one was altered, specifically for this plane." He walked towards me, then froze, eyes looking over my shoulder. I glanced back, eyes traveling down the runway to a small gate. On the opposite side of the gate was a black car, pulled over to the side of the road. The lights of the car flashed to life as the vehicle sped away and out of sight. Hull grabbed me by the arm, pulling me back to the gate. "Come on!"

We reached the parking lot within thirty seconds. Hull immediately smashed away the window of the nearest car, causing me to stop in my tracks.

"Why in the Hell did you just—"

"Get in and drive!" I complied, knowing better than to argue at a time like now. We sped out of the airport parking lot, out on to the main highway. There was only one car on the road ahead of us, and it was the exact one that had been parked. Hull pressed my leg down, causing the car to accelerate. The car was fast, but not faster than us. We were within twenty meters when Hull spoke.

"Go up beside it. Be cautious, but do exactly as I say." His voice was hardened, his eyes glued on the car ahead of us. I continued to accelerate, moving into the lane to the left of the car. I could see it desperately attempting to gain speed, to no avail. After five seconds, we were almost side-by-side with it. Two more seconds, and we were. What Hull did next, I never would have expected.

His hands flew like lightning, gripping the steering wheel and pulling it towards him. Our car lurched sideways, slamming into the black car. The car recoiled away from the hit, front wheels moving left while the back wheels went right. The back end of the car caught the railing at the side of the road, sending the car up into the air. It spun horizontally before sliding along the highway ahead of us, back end smashing into the railing one more time and sending it spinning into our lane. I slammed on the brakes, feeling the steering wheel shudder. Our car came to a halt, as did the overturned black car. Hull jumped from his seat instantly, bound for black car.

I exited our car, coming up just as Hull leaned down and opened the driver door. He quickly wrenched a figure from the car's insides, throwing him out on the pavement. The man's gray hair was ruffled and matted with blood, his wrinkled face cut and bruised. His black coat was torn down the side and his hands were horribly gnarled. He looked up at us with both rage and fear. I felt my breath stop in my chest.

"Mr. Alexander Wygant," Hull said affirmatively. The scientist looked up at him with hatred boiling over.

"You're a rotten ass, Sheridan Hull. You should've kept to your own business," the scientist spat.

"My business is your crime, Mr. Wygant. And what an elaborate crime indeed." Hull stepped back, pointing towards the airport. "All to kill nearly twenty government officials. How charming."

"He what?" I interjected, shock still flowing over me.

"Wygant is a member of a crime organization, one I can't say I'm familiar with. The organization thought it necessary to commit an act of terror, and thus recruited their top scientist of Newfield, Oregon to do something devious. Wygant, being only so creative, devised a plan to sabotage a flight of twenty government officials from the Oregon legislation on their way to Washington, D.C. for an important session of Congress.

"His plan was efficient and brilliant, but so faulted. Using the sap gathered from a certain tree native only to the local area, he created a special coating that would be applied to the windshield of an airplane and, after a certain amount of time had passed, would cause the glass to crack. Had the plane been in the air, moving at its normal speed, the cockpit would have exploded as the glass cracked and imploded, causing a massive burst of air to enter the secure area and kill the pilots, bringing the plane down altogether.

"In order to get the altered chemical to its destination, he had to alter the contents of the order from Boeing. He personally changed the contents, keeping the order forms the same so as to prevent too much suspicion. But one of his employees, Ms. Josephine Dunphy, was not so fooled and noticed the changes to the order. By the time she noticed, however, it was too late. She confronted Wygant about it, showing him the order receipts and acknowledging that the contents had been changed. He dismissed it as a lie and kept the receipts, which he forgot about until our visit yesterday, when he quickly attempted to dispose of them.

"Dunphy, however, was not so willing to give up, and pursued the altered chemicals by first contacting the lumber yard and requesting a log of what they had recently sent, what the chemical factory had worked with, and what it was being sent to Boeing for. She called for a meeting of three informants at her home, which Wygant anticipated. He quickly dispatched one of his men to stop the meeting and kill the workers, but take Dunphy hostage. He intended to have his gunman framed, the very man who attacked us at Boeing.

"His mistakes lied not only in his forgetfulness, but his sloppiness and choice of workers. At the Boeing facility, I noticed a signed order form that confirmed a 'new and improved' type of deterrent for the windshields of the planes, the order signed by

Wygant. He had ensured that the deterrent would be perfect for the plane that had only just been finished, and would soon be on its way to Portland International, where it would take twenty of Oregon's government officials to Washington, D.C. The plane would fall from the sky, and just like that, our state's government would be thrown into disarray.

"His mistake of workers was also evident in their foolish methods of killing and attacking. The first gunman, who ordered the three workers to shoot themselves using the same gun, was foolish enough to keep the gun on him when he was detained at the Hilton Hotel, a gun I instantly recognized. The second worker was foolish in his attack methods, when he attempted to kill you, Walker, and myself. He was also stupid in that he carried a slip of paper to remind him of when the plane would depart and where it was going. 210TDC. The 2:10 flight to Washington, D.C.

"You played the game, Wygant, and you lost." Hull glanced over his shoulder to see three police cars speeding towards them. "And now, you will spend your time in jail where you belong. A criminal, a murderer, and an idiot."

Wygant stared up at Hull for a long moment, eyes trembling. He spit towards Hull, sending a blotch of blood at the detective. Hull side-stepped, the blood landing harmlessly on the ground. Before Wygant could spit again, the police were there, two officers grabbing him by the arms. Another two approached Hull and I, but Hull raised his hands.

"We aren't the criminals, gentlemen. He is. Send him back to Newfield, where Inspector Lennox will deal with him." The cops looked between each other before shrugging, then turning away. Hull spun to look at the flipped car. I looked at him with absolute admiration.

"That was brilliant."

He looked over at me, brows cocked and a subtle smile on his face. "Is that what you would call it?"

"Of course. You figured all of that out? Just like that?"

"It's what I do."

"Absolutely brilliant."

*

It was almost four in the morning when our taxi reached my brother's house. I hesitated before exiting, glancing over at Hull.

"This was.. well, fun, I suppose is how I would describe it. Exhilarating. Thank you for letting me join you," I stated, offering my hand.

Hull shook it firmly. "Of course, Doctor. I'm sure our paths will cross again."

I nodded, opening the door and stepping out. Before I closed it, I glanced back in. "Wait. When we found the supervisor, you said she was a pawn, and her killer was a rook. Did you mean the gunman or Wygant?"

"Wygant."

"But why a rook? Wouldn't he have been the king?"

Hull looked over at me, his eyes glinting from the lights of the house behind me and his voice taking a deeper, more serious tone. "Oh no, Dr. Walker. He was most certainly a rook. The king is someone else entirely."

"What do you mean by that?"

"Have a good evening, Doctor."

With that, he reached over and closed the door. The taxi sped away, turning the nearest corner. I watched until the taillights were out of sight before giving a shake of my head. Never before had I met a man like that. So unique, so intricate. So intelligent in his own way. Not only was I horrified of him, I was fascinated. He was different. In that moment, I did not regret my decision to move to Newfield. I did not regret my decision to take the job as a medical examiner with Newfield Police Department. I would have been a fool to regret it. For had I not moved here and taken the job, I never would have met Mr. Sheridan Hull.

And my life would have remained endlessly boring.

A RETURN TO THINGS

What amazed me most about returning to civilian life was how quickly time seemed to go by now. Where a week once felt like a month, now two months feels like two days. Because as soon as the chemical case had been solved, the next two months of my life just seemed to go by in a blur. I left the police department three days after the case was resolved. Something about being a medical examiner under the department just felt off. I'd started as a call-in nurse for a local clinic near where my brother and his family lived. I didn't make much, but my brother didn't demand rent.

I still felt guilty.

Something about the police department just seemed very dull in those days that followed the case. Maybe it was the slowness of the things that did come through. Or maybe it was that Sheridan Hull wasn't apart of the police department, and he was most certainly what had made the case interesting. His ability to see everything, to just *know*, was amazing. The case itself hadn't even been that intriguing, in hindsight. Hull had been the one to make it something worth paying attention to. I didn't imagine the day-to-day cases that went through the department to reach that level of interest again. So I left.

Now, looking back, that may have been a foolish decision. Because from there, I started as a call-in. And unfortunately, there aren't near enough medical tragedies in suburban Newfield to constitute the usage of a call-in. I spent most of my days sitting and reading, taking walks, writing about my time in service. In other words, I was bored. Really bored. Part of me hoped that Lennox, who had accepted my resignation on friendly terms, would call me up with another job offer. I knew that was pushing my luck, though. I'd been fortunate enough to get the job when I had it. Now, my luck was running thin.

Or so I thought.

"Hey John, you got something in the mail."

I looked up from my stupid magazine about the lives of celebrities to see my brother, Henry, standing in the doorway with an envelope. "Something came for me?"

"Yeah. Pretty accurate addressing, too."

I furrowed my brow before taking the envelope. He wasn't lying. "To Mr. John Walker, the Spare Bedroom, Number 4 12th Street, Newfield, Oregon." I turned the envelope over a couple of times. "No return address... how do they know which room I'm in?"

"Dunno. I haven't really told anyone. Unless it's Mom."

"Ha. Because our mother is definitely going to send me letters while I'm mooching off of you."

"Hey, you know it's not like that." He clasped my shoulder. "You're just trying to figure out what you want to do. She should be happy."

"Yeah. Should."

He sighed. "Alright. Well, that was all." He walked away, leaving me alone with the envelope. I was at first a bit wary to open it, but my curiosity didn't wait long to take prominence. I carefully opened the envelope and into my hand fell a single, thin piece of paper. I turned it over to see it was a ticket for a play. The title "Romeo & Juliet" was artfully sprawled across the top of the ticket, with the date, time, and other information typed on the bottom. The date was set for this evening.

I bit my lip for a moment, opening the envelope again. The rest was empty. I held the ticket in my hand with a slight sense of apprehension. I didn't have many friends, especially in Newfield. I also didn't expect it to be from someone who hated me enough to try and kill me at a college production of a Shakespearean play. I really

couldn't think of who would send me a ticket, unless I'd signed up for a contest in the past two and a half months and forgotten about it completely. Nonetheless, I had nothing better to do besides sit and read stupid magazines that my brother's wife found enthralling. The play was my evening event.

I hadn't been to Newfield University's campus before tonight. While the road layout was atrocious to navigate, the buildings were quite the sight to behold. Most of the older buildings followed a theme that dated back at least a hundred years. Newer buildings looked nice, but they were new. They stood out. The building I was directed to was called Withenhelm. This was, according to the ticket, where the performance was held. After a short wait, I was shown to my seat, a surprisingly nice spot right in the middle-center.

To my right was a man in a black coat and bowler hat. His head was tilted at just an angle to mask his face. To my left was a woman, probably a student at the university. I knew better than to pursue that. I remembered my college days well enough. Within five minutes, the lights dimmed and the show started. It had been a long time since I'd seen any kind of play. In fact, the last play I had watched had probably been Romeo & Juliet, in high school. Plays weren't my thing, but the ticket had been free.

"But soft! What light through yonder window breaks?" the actor playing Romeo bellowed, stepping across the stage to stare up at a prop window. "It is the east, and Juliet is the sun."

"I'm sure it didn't take him long at all to learn that line."

I looked to my right at the bowler hat man, brow furrowed. Even though I hadn't attended a play in forever, I knew talking during one was disrespectful. Especially talking to a complete stranger. "I suppose," I said in as whispered tone I could manage.

"Tell me, Doctor, what aspect of this show intrigues you most?"

I looked at the man with a somewhat-intense glare. "Do I know you?"

"Of course you do." The man looked up, calmly reaching up and removing his hat. I had to fight the urge to gasp.

"Hull! I didn't recognize you."

"Well of course you didn't. Had I wanted you to, you would have."

I gave an awkward nod, looking back at the play. "What are you doing here?"

"Seeing the performance. I do have some appreciation for the arts."

"Shh!"

I glanced behind Hull to see a woman, mid-thirties, glaring at us. I gave an apologetic nod before looking forward. Hull remained silent throughout the entirety of Romeo's speech. I'd lost all interest in the play, though. Here was Sheridan Hull, coincidentally in the seat next to me at a random college play. My curiosity was overwhelming.

"So you sent me the ticket, then," I said in a hushed tone.

"Correct," he replied, making no attempts to lower his voice's volume.

"Which means you wanted me here."

"Correct."

"But I can't figure out why."

"Multiple reasons."

"Shh!"

Hull straightened his neck, looking above the play at nothing. I didn't know him well enough to know whether the woman was truly agitating him or not. We remained silent again for at least ten minutes before I attempted to continue.

"And those are?" I whispered, my voice barely audible over the speaking of the actors.

"One of them is an inquiry. I hear you are without work."

"Well, that's one way to put it... but who told you that?"

"Irrelevant. I have a potential job for you."

"Oh?"

"The last case. I preferred having someone who was medically trained on my last case. I would prefer to keep that preference."

I felt a small part of my insides light up. "What are you suggesting?"

"I am suggesting you work with me. I know for certain you found a sense of thrill in the previous case. And I would like to have someone in whom I can thoroughly rely on."

I had to fight the urge to smile. This was just the kind of opportunity I'd hoped for. The chance to continue working with Hull, to witness his talent, was one I could not pass up.

"I'd love to," I replied, a touch of excitement showing in my voice.

"Excellent."

"*Shh!*"

Hull turned, his eyes wide and fierce. "Ma'am, you can't possibly be so stupid to not know how the play will pan out. It's been written for over four hundred years, and if you haven't heard the plot yet, you've been ignorant." The woman gasped at his claim before standing and shuffling her way down the aisle and away from us.

I sighed. "You handled that well."

"It's not my fault if she's unaware of classic literature."

"And it's certainly not your fault for interrupting a show she probably paid for."

"Irrelevant."

I resisted the urge to chuckle, looking forward at the play. Hull remained quiet again, and it slowly dawned on me that he was just waiting for me to bait the conversation. Why, I had no idea. I wasn't willing to play into the bait.

"If we are to work together," Hull prompted, "it may be of convenience if we, ah.. shared a residence."

"I haven't had a roommate since college."

"Neither have I. Some say I'm difficult to live with."

"Did you have a place in mind?"

"I actually did. A quaint place owned by a woman I know."

"Affordable?"

"With two people, yes."

"Sounds good."

Hull allowed a short smile to appear. "Excellent."

The silence that followed lasted nearly twenty minutes before I recognized the winding down of the act. Suddenly, the situation I was in finally struck me as odd. I clicked my tongue softly.

"Why exactly are we seeing this play?" I asked.

"Because," he replied, watching the lights come to life as the play entered intermission, "it is our next case."

*

After the show had ended, Hull and I worked out our arrangements. He would come by at 10 AM the next morning with a taxi and take us to the new place. From there, we would start work on this case he had created from a simple Shakespeare play. I sat in the taxi at about 10:10, looking at the buildings passing by. Hull hadn't stated where the building was, despite being right next to me. He was still as silent as ever. Now, however, I was curious.

"So what can you tell me about this place?" I questioned, keeping my eyes on the buildings increasing in height.

"It's a cheap, but qualitative, flat towards the center of town. The area is on the second story of a fairly large complex, all owned by a lady I have known since arriving here. Her name is Ellen Hanson, I'm sure you'll like her."

"How many rooms?"

"Enough to be comfortable."

I looked over at him."You really aren't the chatty type in the car, are you?"

He returned my stare. "Not when I'm on a case. I apologize for that."

"Ah." I settled in, returning my gaze to the contents of the street. "You haven't mentioned much about this case. Besides the fact that it's apparently a play."

"It is relevant to the play. It is not *the* play."

"That's beside the point, isn't it?"

"Oh no. It is, in fact, the essential piece to the case." I turned to retort when he leaned forward. "We're here. Please stop."

The taxi pulled off to the side. First Hull, then I exited. We were at the corner of an intersection, cars moving in all directions. Hull took in a deep breath and pointed forward at a doorway.

"We'll be through those doors, up the stairs, to the left. Complex 221B."

I looked over at the nearest stoplight post to read the street signs. The two green signs read "Bay" and "Kerr."

We passed through the door to find a lobby-esque room. An older woman was visible in the kitchen behind the main desk, taking a large black bag to an out-of-sight area. We stood at the desk for about a minute before she came from the kitchen, smiling at the sight of Hull.

"Sheridan! So glad you decided to get the rooms." She came around the desk, giving Hull a large hug. "I was worried you'd stay in that dreadful hotel room for the rest of your life!"

"Now now, Mrs. Hanson, it was merely a place between places." He held her at arm's length before gesturing to me. "This is Dr. John Walker. We'll be splitting the costs for the flat."

"Pleasure to meet you, Doctor," the woman said, shaking my hand with a surprising level of firmness. "I'm glad you decided to stay

with Sherrie here. He's not the most social." The noticeable twitch to Hull's eye on being called "Sherrie" forced me to hold back a laugh.

"It'll be interesting getting to know him, Ma'am."

"Indeed," Hull interjected. "Well, we best get your stuff upstairs. You can unpack later, we need to head on our way."

I glanced out the door at the taxi before a thought clicked. "What about your stuff?"

"Oh, I'm already moved in." He started for the stairs, leaving me to gather my things.

"Thanks for the help," I muttered, turning towards the taxi.

It didn't take too long to get my minimal belongings moved in. The living situation was quite spacious, except for the surprising amount of boxes Hull had already moved in. Many of them were unopened, but from the few that were, I could identify some of the most random things possible. And nothing looked like it was truly organized. In fact, after I'd gotten all of my stuff placed in my room, I quickly realized Hull was a bit of a slob. With a bit being a severe understatement.

"Don't you care about keeping things clean?" I finally asked after sitting down in one of the armchairs. Hull sat across from me, staring blankly into the unlit fireplace. I took a moment to really take in the quarters. The bedrooms were down a hallway that ran parallel with the staircases, their doors facing each other. The hallway opened into a main room that extended away from the stairs, eventually leading into a kitchen. There was also a bit of a terrace through a sliding glass window.

"No."

I looked back at Hull, his delayed response returning my attention. "Don't you think you should?"

"Mrs. Hanson will clean it up eventually, she hates the filth when it accumulates."

"What, she'll just act like a maid?"

"I would say she'd prefer the term 'maternal landlady'."

I sighed. "So when do we get started on this case?"

"As soon as the fire lights itself."

I glanced at the fireplace, then back at Hull. "Are you serious?"

"Always, Doctor." He stood up, pacing to the other end of the main room. He stopped at the bookshelf, sliding his finger along the spines. After several seconds of searching, he stopped. "Ah, there you are, William." He pulled a book from the shelf, then tossed it over his shoulder, adeptly aimed for me. I caught the book, turning it over to read the title.

"'The Collected Works of William Shakespeare'. Why are you throwing this at me?" I set the book down on the small table to my right. "How does this really apply to the case?"

"We have an appointment."

"What?"

"You and I have an appointment with our clients. They just aren't aware of it yet."

*

Hull and I sat in the back of the taxi, currently en route to the more wealthy part of Newfield. He'd been silent since we left the apartment, which was becoming the usual custom. I knew when he went silent, it was to think. I could only imagine how much he was able to process in his mind, how much he was able to know. It astounded me. But even so, the silence was unnerving. Somewhat unnatural, too.

"Why is it we always take taxis?" I asked.

"You don't own a car and I don't possess a license," he replied nonchalantly, eyes watching the traffic going past us.

"You don't have a license?"

"Never required one."

"Alright. Now tell me what we're doing."

He glanced over at me, a pondering look in his eyes. After a moment, he gave a small nod. "You and I are landscapers for a local company looking for work. We are visiting the Medina family, one of the more wealthy families in Newfield. Follow my lead and all will go well."

"We're posing as landscapers?"

"Yes. Are you able to do this?"

"I think so."

"Good. We're here."

The taxi came to a rest. I glanced out my window and felt my breath get caught in my chest. The house that waited at the end of a long, brick path was one of the most luxurious I'd seen in my life. The home stretched three stories high, and from just guessing, it was as wide as a city block. Decorative plants lined the railings of the

multiple terraces, and four large pillars supported a central cover over the entrance. Large hedges bordered the brick path to the double-door entryway. Hull and I exited the taxi, standing at a large, floral archway.

"Rich types always flaunt their money in such useless and trivial ways," Hull commented, starting down the brick path. I followed briskly, my eyes wandering across the scenery. The exterior of the building was made of a very dark wood that almost looked purple. I was so caught up in the scenery that I almost missed Hull purposefully spilling some green concoction of his into the hedge to the left.

"What the Hell are you doing?" I blurted.

He nudged my arm, a way to tell me to keep moving. "Securing us time. Trust me. I was a chemistry major once."

"Once?"

"College bored me. After my second year I left. I'd taken all the classes I saw necessary, and the fluff wasn't worth my money."

"Did you graduate?"

"What, go through the pointless ceremony? No. As I said. I took the necessary classes and left."

We'd reached the front doors. They stretched as high as the second story, despite the handles being at their normal place. Hull reached up to the large, brass knocker and rapped it against the door twice. He took a step away, clasping his hands behind his back.

"So as a chemistry major, what did you learn that constituted what you did back there?"

"You will see."

The door opened slowly, revealing a man, mid-forties with sleek black hair and a thin mustache. He stood with his nose held high, as if Hull or I had a particularly odoriferous scent to us. He looked at Hull, eyes undeniably seeing the consulting detective's dirty pants. He settled on me, a look of minor satisfaction reaching his face. It wasn't that I made a point to dress nice. Hull just cared a little less.

"Yes?" the man said, still looking at me.

"Hello, we're from Garress Landscaping, we received a call about some bad soil?" Hull said. The man looked at him, his nose scrunched.

"I made no such call. I think you have the wrong place."

"Are you sure? The hedge just back there looked to be sick."

Hull pointed back at the exact hedge he'd poured his vial's contents on. I glanced back, then did a minor double-take. The hedge had visibly changed to a dull brown, several tufts of hedge falling off entirely. I resisted the urge to stare at Hull in shock. The man gave a slight gasp.

"My goodness. The groundskeeper must have made the call. Yes, come in." He opened the door wide, allowing Hull and I inside.

The room we entered stretched from the floor to the ceiling, three stories up. A large, glass chandelier occupied most of the space. The lights above the chandelier reflected off the glass shards, sending a brilliant display of lights across the antechamber. The man stopped near the center, turning and extending his hand to us.

"Garth Medina. I hope you gentlemen will be able to correct this issue promptly. I can't imagine what could have caused the tainted soil."

Hull shook his hand. "That's our job, Mr. Medina. We'll be sure to figure it out soon. Perhaps you could lead us to an area where we can discuss financial needs?"

"Yes, of course, follow me." We moved from the antechamber into a long hallway, lined with portrait-style pictures of different people. I tried to take in as much as possible, but I still had no idea why we were really here. Besides Hull's sabotage of the hedge, the place was kept in optimal shape. There wasn't the slightest sign of dust, dirt, or anything that would blemish the perfection of the home. Hull's attention appeared to be directly forward, on Medina's back. I knew that he was somehow taking in far more than I could. What truly amazed me was how little he had to do, to deduce so much.

We arrived at a doorway that entered into an office-like setting, several paper-covered desks arranged against the far wall. Medina moved to one of the desks, grabbing what looked like a checkbook. Hull and I stopped about a meter from the man.

"How much are you going to require?"

"Thirty for additional fees and twenty for labor."

"Done."

"Excellent. I apologize, but I couldn't help but ask. That painting on the wall," Hull pointed at a particularly large piece displaying a country landscape, "is that the Paese Paesaggio?"

"It is," Medina said, a look of surprise on his face. "You have an appreciation for Italian art?"

"I do." Hull took the signed check, folding it and tucking it away in his pocket. "Well Mr. Medina, we should be back shortly. Thank you for your business."

"Thank you for your promptness, Mr... I actually don't recall catching your name."

"So you didn't." Hull turned and walked from the room, turning left and out of sight. I glanced from Medina to the doorway. It was becoming more and more common that Hull would charge out of a place and leave me to clean up. And we'd only known each other for a very, very short while. Medina watched me with cautious eyes. I nodded at him.

"Afternoon," I said before turning to follow Hull.

I found him standing in the antechamber, eyes gazing down another hallway. He was silent, his hands buried in his pockets. I stood at his side, glancing back down the hallway I'd come from.

"Why do you do that?" I questioned, not seeing Medina.

"I observed what I needed."

"Really?" The small hint of sarcasm in my voice wasn't hidden very well. "How is that?"

He smirked. "We should leave. Mr. Medina will not appreciate us lingering." He started for the door with me in tow, perplexed and slightly frustrated with his constant dodging of questions. About halfway down the brick path, he pulled out the check, quickly ripping it in half. He stashed the ripped pieces in the nearest hedge, brushing his hands on his pants after. "Now we visit our next clients. Though first I will probably require a different change of clothes."

"We aren't going to be landscapers again?" I asked, only half-serious.

"No. We get to be more official for our next visit. The Cunningham family. Another wealthy name to the city, half a mile down the road."

"Fantastic."

"Have you pieced things together?"

"We're visiting rich people. Unless you're looking for donations, which I can rule out after you tore a check for fifty dollars, I have no idea."

"Your first analysis was correct. The families we are visiting are extremely wealthy, and are seeking to expand their wealth at the other's expense. The Medina and Cunningham families are currently locked in a legal battle over the ownership of a certain estate located just outside of the city limits. Both families claim they have had ownership of the land since the settling of this valley. Neither family can provide sufficient evidence to win the case. Desperation is becoming more visible in the case.

"This is, however, not the true cause of the tension. The families seem to have disliked each other for a very long time. A small estate out of town is most certainly not the largest concern of theirs. The many financial documents Mr. Medina had on his desks showed that the family would show no significant benefit from receiving the property. Their wealth is far too expansive to be affected. No, this tension has been present for a long time, but something recent has caused a spike, and it is most certainly not the estate debate."

We stepped into the waiting taxi. Hull handed the driver a slip of paper, presumably with the address to the next location.

"So what's this illusive thing?" I asked, glancing back at the Medina house.

Hull smirked."That's what we need to figure out, isn't it?"

*

"I assure you, Ma'am, the case is going well, but we require a few more key points of information from you before we can continue."

Hull's voice was firm and confident, reflective of his new choice of attire. He now wore his black coat and matching pants, the purple scarf tucked in neatly. His hands were clasped behind his back as he stood face to face with the lady of the house, Casandra Cunningham. She was an older woman, probably the same as Mr. Medina. Her hair had started to gray in several areas, but she obviously didn't let that detract from the power she commanded with her presence.

"Well I hope you can keep it quick," she said, her voice having a slight squeak to it. "I have a very busy schedule, you know."

"I'm sure you do, Ma'am." I couldn't quite tell if Hull was being completely serious or sarcastic enough to come off as serious. "I only need you to answer these questions. You need only write them and sign." He handed her a sheet of paper, one I didn't recall him having when we left the flat.

"Yes, yes, fine." She looked over the paper with a pinched nose before rolling her eyes and walking out of sight. She made no offer for us to enter, but Hull didn't seem to care. He stepped through the door, giving me no choice but to follow.

The doors entered to a long hallway that led to a vast family room, couches creating a crescent around a fireplace. Mrs. Cunningham took the paper towards a bar off to the right, grabbing a pen from the other side. Hull walked around the room aimlessly, spinning a few times while looking up. I stood closer to the hallway back, eyes moving from Hull to the woman. Her attention seemed focused on the paper. Until a point of contention arrived.

"Why does this ask for an estimate on the estate worth?" she called back, not bothering to look up.

Hull kept moving around the room, pausing to sit on one of the couches. "It helps us grasp the severity of the situation. Whether we can make a viable plea to the judge in your favor depends entirely on whether the disputed land is worth the effort." He leaned in close to the couch, taking in a heavy sniff.

The woman started to turn, and as she did, Hull shot to his feet, somehow managing to jump back a good meter. She looked at the distance between him and I with a confused look before continuing. "But an estimate on the estate?"

"Technicalities, Ma'am. I don't write the rules, I only abide by them." He walked in front of the fireplace to reach the same wall as the bar, but instead turned his attention to a row of photographs. His eyes glanced over the first two before resting on the third. "Is this your youngest daughter?"

The woman leaned to the side to get a better glance at the photograph before smiling. "It is. Her name is Julia. She truly is our gem."

Hull flashed a smile, one I could identify as fake, surprisingly. "Wonderful. And an actress?" I furrowed my brow, walking to see the photograph. It showed a girl, brown hair to her shoulders and brilliant blue eyes, standing on a stage and holding a bouquet.

Mrs. Cunningham came to stand beside us, a smile still on her face. "She is. And a wonderful one at that. She has a show tonight, actually."

"Oh really?" A certain familiar glint seemed to brighten in Hull's eyes. "Well that is just particularly wonderful for her."

"Yes," the woman replied, her eyes focused on her daughter, "it truly is."

"Well, that should be all from us," Hull said, snatching the paper from Mrs. Cunningham's hand. "Thank you for your time."

"But I hadn't even finished putting down the—"

"Irrelevant, we have all that we need." He marched past us, walking towards the hallway. I didn't even bother looking at the woman as I followed. He'd obviously found what he needed, even if I had completely missed it.

As I closed the door to the taxi, Hull tore the sheet of paper, tucking it away inside his coat. My jaw went slack for a moment.

"Why did you just—"

"As I said, irrelevant. We have all that we need."

"But how?"

"We now know that both families have more wealth than they know what to do with. But they still have this hatred for each other. It's not a matter of the property, it's a matter of honor. The daughter in the picture is the same age as the son in a photograph from the Medina household. The son of that household is also an actor. Both children attend the same school, and both children are acting in a production tonight."

"Romeo & Juliet!" I exclaimed.

"Precisely. Our next case."

"But how does their participation relate to the case?"

"The families are growing desperate in their feud. And both families reign from histories of violence. They are willing to go to very severe extents to send a message to their enemies. No matter the consequence. The children are in danger."

"The families are going to attack each other's children?"

"Tonight, at the play."

"What do we do?"

Hull smiled, an authentic one now. "See the play."

*

The high school's parking lot was bustling with activity. Cars were lined up on the entering road and the lot itself had started to spill into the additional parking, which was essentially a field. A line of high school-age boys were lined up at the doorway to usher people in. Hull and I were led to a large gymnasium and seated towards the center of the audience. The show was set to start in fifteen minutes. Both parents were seated towards the front of the crowd, a good amount of space separating them. It still shocked me that the families would be willing to kill in order to settle a dispute, but if they truly had a history of violence, it wasn't as surprising.

"We must remain vigilant. Any sign of activity from either family or potential threat to the children, we intervene." Hull's eyes were obviously surveying the crowd. "Don't hesitate to interrupt the performance."

"Oh of course not," I replied. "We don't have anything to fight them with, though. If they have guns—"

"They won't."

"How can you be sure?"

"The attackers will be silent. They wouldn't dare draw additional attention to themselves by killing with a gun." His eyes settled on one of the families. "A gun also poses a risk to hit others. They won't take that risk."

"Will the attackers be from the families?" I asked.

"Possibly. We must be cautious."

The play started. Two young men walked out onto the stage. The man on the left spread his arms wide to acknowledge the audience.

"Gregory, o' my word," the boy said, "we'll not carry coals." My attention immediately slipped away from the show. I'd seen the show enough times while I was in high school to have the ability to truly enjoy a teenage representation. My eyes settled on the Medina family. Their heads were all turned to the stage, watching and waiting in anticipation of their son's arrival. I turned to look at the Cunningham family, finding the same result. None of them appeared to care about the other family. They were merely focused on seeing their children perform.

I must have invested a lot of time in merely watching the families, as the next time I looked up, a young man, his hair a dirty blonde similar to Hull's and a build like that of a Medina, walked out on the stage.

"Is the day so young?" the boy said. I watched the Medina family lean forward. And as they leaned forward, Hull nudged me. I nodded, keeping my eyes on the Cunninghams. They seemed disinterested; not planning a death, simply disinterested. I watched them with unblinking eyes until the set dimmed and was instantly replaced with a new group of people. The young girl from the picture in the Cunningham home entered the stage.

"How now! who calls?" the girl cried out. Now the Cunningham family was paying attention. I glanced over at Hull to see him staring intently at the stage. He was waiting for something. I suppose I should've been waiting too.

"No one is making an attempt to attack," Hull whispered, his eyes starting to move in their rapid-like fashion.

"Should we move to a different location?" I murmured, turning my attention back to the families.

"No, it won't change anything. It's almost like they—" He inhaled sharply. "Oh of course. How could I have been so foolish!" His exclamation garnered the attention of the patrons around us.

"What? What is it?"

He stood, starting his way through the people to his left. I followed as he spoke. "We've been waiting for a cue that we won't see. Quickly!" He moved through the seats quickly before reaching the side, dashing off towards the left off-stage doorway. He moved at a slow enough pace to keep from drawing attention. I was on his heels the entire time, all the way to the door. He opened it and moved through, completely ignoring all other people present.

The backstage was fairly dark, with several people moving around. Hull and I traveled close to the wall, keeping in the dark as much as possible. Ahead of us was what looked like a group of dressing rooms. Hull pressed his back against the wall, then reached out and forced me back as well. The darkness was enough to keep us hidden from those standing in the lights. The majority of them were students, but some were faculty assisting with the play.

"What are we doing back here?" I whispered frantically, keeping my voice as low as it would go.

"Watching for the murderers."

"They're here already? I thought they were with the family."

"They are, it's just that..." His voice trailed off. I followed his line of sight and felt a chill go down my spine. Something, or more specifically someone, was moving behind the curtains opposite us and adjacent to the dressing rooms. Below the curtain, I could make out two feet shuffling as slow as they could to prevent making noise. I glanced at Hull, expecting him to make some kind of move. He simply waited. I looked forward to see the young Medina boy step out of the dressing rooms, his costume fluffed and ready.

From the stage-bordering curtain came the Cunningham girl, who rushed to his open arms. He spun her around before kissing her on the cheek and lowering her to her feet. They started speaking, their voices too hushed for me to hear. I did, however, see the feet behind the curtain stop, just at the edge. Hull did too.

He charged forward, his footsteps causing the two teenagers to notice him. I moved after him, but had nowhere near the speed. He slammed into the curtain, a muffled shout of surprise emanating from the other side. I would have reached him had my peripheral vision not caught the sight of a large blur moving towards me all-too quickly. I stopped and spun, pulling back my legs. The blur stopped as well, revealing itself to be a man, about my height with a large, black coat. He charged at me with shocking speed, but not quick enough. I reached out my arms and grabbed his extended hands, pulling him in and side-stepping. The man slid past me, a look of bewilderment crossing his face.

The distraction was only momentary. Instantly he was facing me again, this time bringing a fist across towards my face. I ducked quickly, sending my own fist towards his groin. He backed away, his legs hopping up. I re-angled my fist's trajectory, instead sending it into the man's knee. A very resounding pop confirmed my hopes. The man collapsed backwards, immediately clutching at his dislocated knee. I stood up, surprised at my shortness of breath. I hadn't really exerted myself in this manner since getting home. Of all the emotions I expected to feel, exhilaration wasn't high on the list.

I looked up to see Hull holding a woman by the back, edging her along towards the man and I. The two teenagers had vanished, and now a group of adults were approaching us fairly quickly. I pointed at them, hoping Hull would pay them some mind. Of course, he didn't.

"How coincidental, that we should find the likes of you two sneaking about back here," Hull said, tossing the woman to the ground next to the man.

"Hull..." I said, eyes watching the approaching adults.

"Irrelevant. Tell them to get the police."

"But why would they believe we aren't at fault?"

"Because we aren't equipped with blades."

I glanced down to see the man move to pull something from his belt. Hull's foot smashed down onto the man's arm, pinning it against his chest. The group of adults arrived, some perplexed, others keeping a level of distance. From the dressing rooms, both the Medina boy and Cunningham girl emerged, looks of astonishment crossing their faces.

"Diane?" the boy called out, changing from a walk to a run. The Cunningham girl was at his side, but her attention was fixed elsewhere.

"Arthur!" she yelled. I looked down to see the man and woman watch the advancing teenagers, a mixture of disappointment, horror, and fear in their eyes. I looked up at Hull, who was still pressing his foot against the man's, Arthur, arm.

"Yes," Hull said, his voice hitting his tone of victory. "Diane Medina and Arthur Cunningham. Both attorneys for separate law firms that have been locked in an estate dispute, titled 'Medina v. Cunningham'." A smirk crossed his face. "How clever."

*

Hull and I stood by the entrance of the school as both Diane and Arthur were escorted to a waiting police car. Lennox looked up at us, saluted, and closed the rear door, cutting off view of the attempted killers. Lennox walked around the car, taking his seat in the driver spot. I glanced over to see the Medina family gathered around their son, Ryan, as they watched their oldest daughter, Diane, taken into custody. The woman of the family was in tears. Garth Medina had a look of pure disappointment. Five meters from them were the Cunninghams, all gathered around their daughter, Julia. Casandra Cunningham held her daughter through silent trembles of tears.

My eyes finally fell on the man standing next to me. Hull looked out at the scene with a slight glaze to his eyes, almost as if he didn't care at all. But I knew he did. There was a certain sense of satisfaction radiating from him, knowledge of completion that he felt comfortable with. He glanced over at me, as if he knew I'd been looking at him, and smiled.

"Clever indeed, wasn't it. We were following the wrong trail the entire time." His words had a chipper tune to their usual monotony.

"I haven't followed since you took us backstage."

"It wasn't until you suggested we change locations that I realized where we had gone wrong. The entire time we had spent looking at the case as if the families were behind the plotted deaths. It wasn't the families overall, though. Just the spiteful offspring." He readjusted himself, nodding at the families. "The families have often not liked each other based on their financial rivalry. But a year ago, a budding relationship between their youngest children, Ryan Medina and Julia Cunningham, created a true point of contention. They could never allow their children to be together.

"In order to truly paint the other family as the villain, they first needed to make them look greedy, to prevent their children from making what they believed to be horrible mistakes. So they entered a lawsuit, a trivial lawsuit with no actual beneficial outcome, to defame the opposite. And they trusted their legal powers in their oldest children, Diane Medina and Arthur Cunningham, two up-and-coming legal attorneys for separate firms. The scenarios were perfect for both families."

He adjusted again, now looking in the direction of where the police car had departed. "That is, until Diane Medina and Arthur Cunningham decided they would find immense profit in putting both of their families to shame. They weren't stupid. They knew exactly what to do and how to do it. But because of the persistence from both families, things became difficult. Strained. In order to truly receive the profit they hoped for, they would have to do something so drastic, it would force the families out of the estate dispute and into a battle much more important."

"Killing the youngest children," I said, understanding flowing through me.

"Precisely."

"But their own siblings?"

"That is where the history of violence becomes notable, as well as a deep-running sense of jealousy for both Diane and Arthur in regards to their younger, more 'dramatically-talented' siblings. As Mrs. Cunningham said, Julia is the gem of their family. Both families valued their youngest children over their oldest. And the oldest children intended to use that to their advantage. By killing both Ryan and Julia, it would cause the families to blame each other and enter a new dispute. Diane and Arthur would receive significant pay and, using their family connections, additional funds by selling the disputed estate to the city."

"But why?"

"Ah, yes. The motive." By now, both the Medinas and the Cunninghams had gone to their respected vehicles. The number of people had been reduced to just Hull and I. We walked down the

41

stairs of the school entrance, moving into a cooler, more misty parking lot. High above, a crescent moon shined bright, with uncountable stars shimmering across the sky. Hull stopped in the middle of the empty parking lot, looking up. "'From forth the fatal loins of these two foes, a pair of star-cross'd lovers take their life'."

He smirked. "Many years ago, Diane Medina and Arthur Cunningham were classmates. And, being as young teenagers do, they fell in love. They, however, were smart enough to know their respected parents would never approve of their romance. So they kept it secret. The secrecy, however, became too much to bear, and we can assume one posed an ultimatum while the other devised the plan. Murder their youngest siblings, thus removing their personal points of jealousy. Send their families into disarray. Make off with a formidable sum of money. And spend their lives together."

My jaw slowly fell. "Romeo and Juliet."

Hull looked at me, the smirk turning into a full smile. "Precisely."

"Brilliant. Absolutely brilliant."

"So you could say." He started forward towards the road, hands rummaging through his pockets, presumably for his phone. "You did well back there, too. Haven't lost your soldier touch."

"I wasn't much of a soldier, but I still have my instincts."

"Even so. Had you not been there, I most certainly would have been overwhelmed."

"You're welcome." He stopped. For a brief moment, the thought of regret at what I'd said crossed my mind. Perhaps he hadn't meant to thank me at all.

"Thank you," he said, the words probably forced. He continued forward. As we came closer to the sidewalk of the main road, he turned around, electing to walk backwards. "'For never was a story of more woe than this of Juliet and her Romeo'."

THE CASE OF SILENT STREETS

The police car approached the parked vehicle slowly, the lights on top of the prior flashing and the policeman watching with caution. It wasn't a rarity for officers to find abandoned cars on country roads around Newfield. But this car wasn't abandoned. It was nearly 2 AM and there was someone in the car. Or, at least, someone nearby who had left the headlights on. The officer, Dan Hastings, had been out on these roads all week, and the only thing he'd come across had been a mountain lion that had strayed too far from the nearby range.

He stopped a good several meters behind the car. He looked up at the vehicle, thoughts going quickly through his head. It could be just another drunk driver who decided to pull off before passing out. Whatever it was, he had to deal with it. He exited the police car, checking to make sure he had his gun holstered just in case. He'd yet to pull it on anyone, but you could never be too careful. He was about halfway to the car when he realized he'd left his flashlight in the passenger seat. If he turned back now, the person, if they were even conscious, could become suspicious, or even try to leave. He kept going forward and was somewhat surprised to find an open window waiting for him.

It was too dark to see the upper half of the person sitting in the driver seat, but they were most certainly conscious and alert. From what Hastings could see, the person wore a heavy black jacket that blended in with the natural darkness. Hastings leaned forward slightly, still unable to see the person's face.

"Hi there," he said, looking in the direction of where he assumed the person's head was. "Mind telling me why you're out here so late?"

"Just some business to deal with, Officer," the person, a male by the voice, replied.

"Alright. Just for safety purposes, I'm gonna have to see your license and registration."

"I'm sorry, Officer, but I believe this is a gross allocation of police resources," the stranger said.

Hastings furrowed his brow. "And why is that?"

"There is a far more serious crime occurring at this very moment."

"What crime would that be?"

"Murder."

Bang.

*

I had been living with Hull for almost a month when he got sick. Not a fatal illness, or even a serious one. I recommended he see a clinic doctor, since I was more specialized at recognizing wounds and postmortem situations. He had already given the self-diagnosis of an upper respiratory infection. I say self-diagnosis because he had no desire to "pay someone to tell me what I already know." I knew, however, that if he was right, he would have difficulty recovering without the proper antibiotics. He didn't seem to care. He had been sick for ten days, and I quickly learned that he did not treat being sick like a sick individual would.

After two days of being sick, Hull discovered he couldn't move without severe body aching. This prevented him from continuing his very odorous experiment in the kitchen, which Mrs. Hanson was very prompt to throw out. Hull had claimed he was testing the properties of milk when exposed to diseased cow meat. Why he had sought to test this, I had no idea. I was just glad the God-awful experiment was gone. Now that Hull was restricted to a bed, he spent the next eight days compensating for his inability to move, or even relatively speak. He lost his voice on day four, and even then, his coughing fits kept him from trying to talk.

Without being able to move or talk, Hull was restricted to his laptop and me. He would sit up in his bed for hours staring at the illuminated screen, doing work I didn't quite understand. For anything outside of the flat, he sent me. In the first three days of his bed restriction, I was sent to pick up an orange sweatshirt missing a sleeve, deliver a coffee mug, and tell a homeless individual to "rally 37th street." It was on day five that Hull discovered exhaustion. He would often stay up for days on end when healthy. He attempted it while sick, and verbally expressed his confusion at having slept for sixteen hours.

In summary, dealing with Hull while he was sick was, in fact, *more* difficult than dealing with a sick toddler.

Twelve days after he got sick, Hull was back to his healthy, normal self, who now sat across from me for breakfast, twelve days unshaven and not in a hurry to correct it. His eyes skimmed over the contents of the newspaper cover, pausing at some points and completely ignoring others. Headlines never caught his attention, I had learned. I don't even know what part of the news he cared for. He opened the paper, completely hiding his face. I glanced down at his plate, seeing the eggs to be gone and everything else untouched.

"Why not tell me you only want the eggs?" I asked.

"I don't wish to inconvenience you," he replied from behind a half-cover photo of a soon-to-be-constructed library.

"But then all that food goes to waste."

"No, it goes to your stomach, just like the leftovers from yesterday. I know you'll eat what's left but you feel bad about making more for yourself initially. This way, we're both satisfied."

"I don't know how you do it," I said as I scraped the food from his plate to mine, "but you're right, as usual. Also, if I get sick because of you, you'd better be as good of a caretaker as I was."

"We're going to have a visitor soon."

"Who would that be?"

He put the paper down. "Inspector Lennox," he said, taking a drink from the same mug I'd taken elsewhere. How he'd gotten it back without stepping foot outside of the flat, or receiving a delivery, or having me pick it up, I would never know.

"Why?"

"A police officer was murdered."

"When? Where?"

"Last night, on a country road."

"You read that in the paper?"

"No, I heard it on the scanner."

I paused. He set down his mug, looking up at me with expecting eyes. "Wait, that's the buzzing noise I constantly hear from your room?"

"Last night an officer didn't report in after being paged around four. I suspect they have found his body and have no clues to help them. Thus, they will come to me."

"You seem pretty confident in that mindset."

"Mindset of what?"

I leaned back, clasping my hands behind my head. "Of being the police's crutch."

He smirked. "That's because I *am* the police's crutch."

I started to respond, but the buzzing of the doorbell a floor below stopped me. Hull reopened the newspaper, once again hiding his face. The sound of the door opening, as well as Lennox's distinct voice, echoed up the stairway. Moments later, the familiar inspector appeared, eyes falling on Hull.

"We've got a—"

"Murdered cop," Hull interjected.

Lennox blinked. "Yes, and we've got—"

"No leads whatsoever."

"Yes." Lennox stepped through the doorway. "Did someone call you already?"

"No." Hull stood up, letting the newspaper fall to the floor as he moved into the main room, grabbing his coat from one of the chairs. "Where is it?"

"Out on Parker Lane. We've got the road taped off."

"We'll be along shortly."

Lennox looked from Hull, who was standing and staring out the window, to me, and then, with a nod, departed. I came up next to Hull, grabbing my own coat.

"What do you make of this?" I asked, looking up at his sun-basked profile.

"A dead police officer." He glanced over at me. "There isn't much else we can garner while here."

*

We arrived at the scene within the hour. Several police cars were parked at either end of the lane, and the crime scene itself was simple in looks. A single police car, door open and lights on, was parked towards the side of the lane. Several meters in front of the car was a body, the head disfigured from a gunshot. The body was on its back, arms splayed out. There was no sign of another vehicle, or relatively anything to work off of. Yet this didn't seem to perturb Hull. He walked over to the dead officer slowly, a soft gust casting his coattail out behind him.

"Name?" he called out, eyes fixated on the body.

"Dan Hastings, twenty-four. New to the force, assigned graveyard shift to patrol the outer streets. Didn't check in for his 4 AM shift change. Some tourists called him in, said they found the body and car just like this about two hours ago," Lennox reported, circling the body and looking out at the area. We were in an empty stretch of land, the closest trees being at the mountain range to the east. From here you could see every car driving on the other outer lanes, and the sprawling cityscape of Newfield occupied the entire western horizon. "No signs of who did it."

"Wrong."

"What?"

Hull pointed to the dirt at the side of the road. "Wrong. Look here." He walked to the shoulder of the lane, Lennox and I in tow. "Faint tracks, but defined by some kind of stud in the tire. They quickly return to the road. Most of it has been dusted over, not by nature but by man, probably your own men 'patrolling' the area. The car of the murderer has a flat tire, or will be flat shortly. That's no stud, it's a nail, and a big one by the print."

Lennox pulled out his radio. "I'll get security looking for a car with a flat tire, but that doesn't narrow it down much."

"No, of course it doesn't." Hull turned, eyes on the body. "Run a report on Hastings's activities before arriving at work. See if anything significant comes up." Lennox nodded, walking away. When he was out of earshot, Hull sighed. "Moron."

"Huh?"

"Him. He's a moron. So are the rest of them." Hull stepped off the road, leaning down to look at the dirt about a meter from the tracks. "They look and look for evidence but they fail to observe what's clearly in front of them. Look here." I came up and glanced down, spotting the faint outline of a shoe.

"Footprints?"

"Leading off to the east. Not matching that of the officer, since he has academy-issue boots that have a far thicker heel than these." He stood up and started forward, eyes glued to the ground. I followed carefully, glancing back once to see if Lennox was watching. He, of course, wasn't.

The footprints moved in a straight direction for what I estimated to be one hundred meters before stopping. I suppose it would be better to describe them as "vanishing," though. We reached an area that looked to have been a small orchard at one point, tree stumps littering the ground. The footsteps stopped at one of the larger ones. Hull and I looked down at the stump, and I felt my heart give a louder beat. Etched into the wood was a very definitive "2 MORE." And surrounding the etching was what looked like thick splotches of blood.

"What does it mean?" I asked.

Hull's eyes were focused on the etching. Or the blood. Or perhaps he was looking inward and I couldn't tell. "It's a warning. Left for us."

"Us specifically?"

"Left for whoever would find the body."

"This was all planned for the cop?"

"No."

I took a step away, eyes locking on Hull's back. "Then what body?"

He looked up, then left, then right. He spun around, eyes moving like blurs. "Where is it? We need to find it."

"The body?"

"Yes, the body!" he hissed. He started out, moving in a somewhat-circular motion from the stump. "Find it, or get Lennox."

"You won't have to," a new voice called. I looked back to find Lennox and three other officers. He cast a furtive look at Hull, then me. "What's he doing?"

"Finding this," Hull called out. The group of us saw him behind a row of tree stumps, eyes locked on the ground. We moved to join him and froze. Lying in a haphazardly-dug hole was a body, horribly mutilated in the face and missing both hands. The legs were buried with a light cover of dirt, but it was obvious the body had been left out to be found.

Lennox scratched his chin. "This complicates things, doesn't it." Nobody answered. After a long silence, the inspector coughed. "Alright, you three," he said to the officers, "get him out of there. We'll need to identify him."

"Someone did a good job of working to prevent that," Hull noted. It was true: without facial identification or fingerprints, it made the forensics team's job harder. The officers cautiously pulled the body from the hole, setting it down in the clearing. Hull seemed to hold his chin high, looking down at the body as if he were using his nose as a centering device. Suddenly, he stooped down, hand running over the body's coat.

"What the Hell do you think you're doing?" Lennox shouted, moving to grab Hull's arm.

"Confirming the lack of a wallet," Hull snapped, pulling his arm away before the inspector could get him. He stood up, softly brushing the dirt from his knees.

Lennox sighed, looking down at the body, then back towards the crime scene. "I'll call this one in, tell 'em we've got another body on our hands." With that, he walked away, leaving the three officers to mark the area. Hull started back towards the initial crime scene, first stopping to glance at the etched tree stump. About halfway to the scene, I saw Hull pull a small card from his sleeve.

"What's that?" I asked, even though I knew it was something from the second body.

"A reminder for a now-dead man." He showed me the card. "Time and day for a meeting. Day is today, time is in four hours. Location is near the city center, a diner, by my guess."

"He was going to meet someone?"

"Yes, and now we need to, otherwise another man is going to end up dead."

"What? How?"

"The card had been removed already. It wasn't tucked into the man's pocket, it was folded inside the coat collar. Someone is leaving clues deliberately."

"Then aren't we just following a trap?"

"No, they have no intention of killing the police. They do intend to kill two more individuals, however. That is what we need to stop."

*

"When it said 'two more,' did it include the cop that was killed?"

I kept my voice as hushed as possible. Hull and I now sat in a diner near the city center, with about ten minutes left until the supposed meeting. While I worked my way through a decent burger, Hull kept his eyes on the door. Not in the obvious manner, but well enough to notice anyone enter that matched who he expected. I say he because I had no idea what to expect.

"He was a casualty of timing. The murderer was already there, disposing of the body and planting the clues. The officer had the inconvenient luck of stumbling upon the crime," Hull said, his voice somewhat-distant. I could tell his attention was devoted to watching the door, but he was capable of multi-tasking.

"Why is the murderer leaving clues, though?"

"They're making it into a game for the police. They want to taunt them and laugh in their face when two more people die and the law enforcement is clueless."

"Why?"

Even with the bustling diner creating a constant wave of noise, I could see Hull mouth something and almost hear a faint "why." After a moment, he turned to me. "I don't know."

There was something in his voice that sent a small chill down my spine. Hull had seemed to be the master of his element, no matter the case. The silence to his voice, the way it was more of a whisper. It spoke of true confusion. To think that even the likes of Hull was stumped by this case filled me with an unfamiliar feeling of fear.

"So who are we looking for?" I asked, trying to move the conversation in another direction.

Hull's gaze returned to the diner entrance. "Someone on their lunch break from a business or corporation. The card they used to schedule this meeting was a typical business card size, but blank." He paused. "And it's possible they may be afraid."

"Of?"

"Dying."

"You don't think the murderer would attack them here? Or that the murderer is even after the person?"

"On the contrary, I expect the murderer to attack them here, since the person so conveniently set up a meeting for them."

I would have responded, but Hull's hand flew up to the side of his face, one finger pointed up. I somehow knew this was a signal for silence. Through the diner doors came a man, probably ten or so years older than myself and definitely more worn from time. His skin was pale, his brow arched. His balding head had a slight shine to it from the sun still peaking through the door. He looked around the diner with a small sense of hesitancy before taking a booth seat close to the door.

"What do we do?" I whispered.

Hull averted his gaze, possibly to make it less obvious that he was watching the man. "We wait and observe. He will eventually realize his contact is not arriving. That is when we—"

He stopped, and for good reason. We both watched a man, clad in a black coat and matching pants and eyes hidden by a low-brimmed hat, take the seat opposite the businessman in the booth. Hull was visibly leaning forward, but not yet leaving his seat. I looked from the booth to Hull sharply.

"What do we do?" I repeated, a slight hint of worry in my voice. Hull was silent, but from where I sat, I could see his eyes working furiously. They moved in their side-to-side fashion, speeding up as the seconds passed. I looked over at the booth, unable to see the businessman's face but able to know the black-clad man was talking.

"If we approach him we'll alert the murderer. The man sitting there could be a messenger, but the lengths he's gone to keep his identity hidden... he couldn't just..." Hull's voice trailed off. I could tell something wasn't all right with him. Part of me wanted to blame his recent illness. An upper respiratory infection wouldn't explain an inability to "deduce," but it could definitely inhibit him. Perhaps he wasn't quite over the illness.

I looked back at the booth and stifled an exclamation. The black-clad man had stood and was looking down at the businessman, who was slowly standing and trembling. I could see the black-clad man's hand hovering very close to his hip, and extending from the inside sleeve was the barrel of a gun. The businessman walked with the black-clad man behind him from the diner.

Hull stood abruptly, not bothering to look back. "We have to stop him, *now*!" I didn't object. Hull and I ran from our seats to the diner exit, stopping to look around. Because the diner opened up to the city center, there were far too many people to make finding the murderer and his hostage an easy task. But Hull's eyes must have caught something, for he bolted off to the left with me in pursuit. He ran for nearly twenty meters before turning into an alleyway. I followed him in, finding him stopped. He stared forward at a break in the alley, going off into two diagonal directions.

It only took Hull a moment before he charged to the left. I didn't know how he was doing it but I saw no purpose in complaining. Hull was similar to a bloodhound in some aspects. He found the scent and was on the trail. He continued down the alleyway, easily dodging garbage bins and other pieces of trash scattered about. We were about halfway to the end when a loud *bang* echoed from ahead. Hull stopped, but only for a moment before continuing. We both knew what we would find. I suppose he held hope in finding the murderer before he escaped.

We, of course, had no such luck.

We found the businessman slumped against the alley wall, his forehead contorted by a bullet wound and blood streaked down his face. He was turned to the side slightly, and even without checking I knew it meant his wallet had been taken. This murderer was doing everything he could to slow us down. Even though this man would be identifiable once he reached the forensics lab at NPD, it would take time. And we had no leads to follow the murderer. And all of this uncertainty was taking its toll on Hull.

"Call Lennox," he said, his voice hoarse. "Tell him we've got another."

"What about you?"

"I'm going home. I need to think."

With that, he started away, and I noticed the way he carried himself. He relieved weight from his left leg, giving him an odd limp. Something was most certainly wrong indeed.

*

When I returned to the flat, it took me some time to find Hull. He was unresponsive to my calls, so it became a search. I found him in the bathroom, fully clothed, the sink not quite turned off so that it dripped every second. He clutched the inside of the sink with pale fingers, his left hand trembling. His eyes stared at his reflection in the mirror, moving back and forth at a slow pace. He spoke, too, but it was a rushed whisper that I couldn't make sense of. This case was getting inside his head.

I moved out to the main room and gasped. Somehow, Hull had procured a very large chalkboard and now had it propped up against the wall with the terrace. The chalkboard was at least four feet tall and six feet wide. In the center was a large chalk-drawn "2 MORE," and surrounding the replica of the etching were different notes and tidbits of information, all of them linked with lines and all of them eventually attaching to the central drawing. Above the central drawing was an astonishingly good sketch of a man, top-half of his face hidden by a hat, and the rest of his body gone. Hull had an artistic side to him... when he needed it.

"It doesn't make sense."

I jumped, turning to see Hull sitting in one of the armchairs. The chair was repositioned to face the chalkboard. He sat with his legs crossed beneath him, his hands clasped together under his chin. His eyes were wide and stared at the board, as if he was expecting something to pop out. I stepped to the side, trying to give him a clearer view of the chalk web.

"There isn't enough evidence to work from," Hull said, his voice distant. "The murderer is clearly leaving a trail but the trail has such a vast break somewhere in it. It doesn't make sense." His hands flew apart, slamming to the arms of the chair and gripping tightly. "If he wants someone to solve it, we've missed something. Something important. He wouldn't want to lose us before the final kill... no, there's something else to this entirely." He continued to stare at the board when a distinct ring started. It was Hull's cell phone, sitting on the table to his left. His arm snapped out, grabbing the phone and activating the speakerphone in an instant. "What?"

"We've got a positive ID on the first man," Lennox's voice said. "Steven Washington. Age forty-five, member of the executive board for Plyer Incorporated, a local company that manages production and distribution of solar panels. Didn't show up for work today. Now we know why."

"And the second man?"

"We're still working on him. Shouldn't take as long, but I can't give any time guarantees. Something happened to his hands."

"What do you mean?" I asked, raising my voice to ensure the phone picked it up.

"His fingers look like they were dipped in acid or something. We can't get any fingerprint matches from this mess. We'll be running a DNA test from the hair he's got. I'll keep you boys informed."

Hull clicked off the phone before I had a chance to respond. The maddened look to his eyes was replaced with the familiar glint. "Plyer Incorporated. We need to leave."

"What?"

"We need to find everything we can about this Steven Washington, and once Lennox gets back to us on the second identification, we'll need to find out how they're connected." Hull stood, walking back into the kitchen. He stopped when he reached the table, eyes going to the floor, then back up. "*Oh!*"

I entered the kitchen, looking around frantically for the source of his exclamation. "What is it?"

"Oh we need to get to Plyer immediately," he said, rushing back into the main room and grabbing his coat. "How could I have been so foolish?" He returned to the kitchen, grabbing the newspaper from the floor and moving towards the stairs.

"Hull, wait a second!" I called after him, to no avail. I ran down the stairs, barely managing to catch up to him as he hailed a taxi. "What is this all about?"

"Curse my still-recovering mind, I should've caught this sooner," he said, more to himself than me. He glanced over at me. "The library, Plyer, the threats, oh it all makes sense! We just need to get to Plyer and make sure... oh I can't believe how blind I was to this."

"You're practically speaking Latin to me, Hull," I said as the taxi pulled up.

"Good thing I'm fluent in Latin, then, yes?" he said, stepping into the taxi.

"You're fluent in a dead language and I still can't understand a word you're saying. Yes, that's good, very good," I replied, the sarcasm laid on thick.

"Take us to the corner of Stonewood and Flare," Hull said to the driver before leaning back. He looked out the window, the glaze falling over his face. Usually this was the cue to give up on getting answers, but I was far too confused to let it rest.

"You have to catch me up on this, I have no idea why we're going to this place or what we're even looking for."

"These men are dying because they stand in the way of something, and the murderer wants to have an audience when he reaches his goal. But he's a fool in the fact that he's given us too much to work from, and now we have him."

"*Too much*? Minutes ago you said there was a missing piece, that it didn't make sense."

"My own blindness. The piece wasn't missing, I'd merely ignored it."

"But what piece?"

"Plyer!" He looked back out the window. "Please, Doctor, give me silence, I need to think." I opened my mouth to retort, but instead sighed. There was no use pressing the issue. I'd just have to comply and be alert. Otherwise, like usual, Hull would figure everything out and I'd be left in the dust. Part of me was fine with that, though. I wasn't exactly alone in being completely clueless when it came to Hull's intelligence.

Within twenty minutes, Hull and I stood in the lobby of Plyer Incorporated. We were currently waiting for the receptionist to get us a tour guide, of sorts. One of the executives was on their way down to meet us. We were here in lieu of the police to investigate Steven Washington's office for any potential clues to help with the case. Of course, that was the official reason. Hull more than likely had ulterior reasons for being here.

The elevator to our right opened, revealing a man in an indigo business suit. He had a wide smile and black hair that was cut so evenly, you'd think it had been done moments ago. He approached us, extending his hand. "Pleasure to meet you, gentlemen, George Hickensons, junior executive here at Plyer. You're investigating the murder of Washington?"

"Yes," Hull replied, shaking the man's hand. "We'd like to have access to his office, if that is acceptable."

"Sure, sure, just follow me, I'll take you right to it," Hickensons said, moving back towards the elevator. Hull and I followed quickly, entering the elevator. Hickensons pressed a button near the top, then sighed. "I'll be honest with you, it was damn tragic to hear about Steven. He'd been on the board for almost eight years, and was one of the guys that recommended me."

"Do you know if Washington was doing anything to make himself a target?" I asked.

"Can't say I do," Hickensons replied, glancing back at me with a weird, pout-like look. "He was a good man, never stepped on anyone's toes. Can't think of him doing wrong by anyone to constitute being murdered."

The elevator stopped. We stepped out onto a long hallway, one wall completely glass, the other covered in portraits. As we walked, I noticed each of them being that of a member of the board of executives. Hickensons stopped when we reached a portrait in particular. Despite the mutilation, I recognized it as the portrait of Steven Washington.

"A good man indeed. Can't believe something like this would happen to him," Hickensons said, shaking his head. I looked to Hull, but he was staring down the hallway, away from us. As I turned to nudge him on the shoulder, a flash of light from the windows caught my eye. I looked over, seeing a building with a cleaning crew hard at work. I felt an odd sense of familiarity from the building, and glanced down. Directly next to the base of the building was a small, one-story restaurant. Or, more properly, the diner Hull and I had visited before.

"Hull, that's the—"

"Diner." He glanced down at the restaurant, then back forward.

"Does that mean the—"

"Second victim worked here, yes." Hull took several steps forward, then turned to face another portrait. I came up beside him, looking up into the painted face of the latest murder victim.

Hickensons came up to us, looking at the portrait. "Oh, that's Keith Adams, another one of our board members. He left work early today, said he had some personal matters to get to."

"And he won't be coming back," Hull said, a new spark to his voice.

"What?" Hickensons said, looking at Hull with distress-filled eyes.

"We need to see Washington's office, now."

"What do you mean by—"

"*Now*."

Hickensons hesitated, then nodded, continuing down the hallway. We arrived at an open doorway that led to a group of different rooms. He led us into one on the far side of the group, revealing a desk, several chairs, a bookcase, and other miscellaneous items. Hull immediately went to the desk, rifling through the papers until he found a large stack. He spun to me, flipping through the pages.

"Washington was one of the executives in charge of a new charity project to give back to the city. It was to be a library constructed here in the city center, and the power would be completely solar-provided. Washington was one of three executives fronting the project. The other two were Keith Adams and Richard Jefferson." Hull looked up at me. "Jefferson is the third."

"Third what?" Hickensons piped in.

Hull turned to him. "Where is Richard Jefferson right now?"

"Probably at home preparing for tonight's stockholder's meeting. What is this about?"

Hull ignored his question. "We need to find him now. This is a matter of life and death."

"But.. what.." Hickensons stuttered. "I can.. I can get you his address."

"Please do. Quickly." Hickensons left the room.

"So the murderer is trying to stop the construction of the library? Why?" I asked as Hull started from the room.

"He's not just stopping the construction, he's trying to send a message. Not just to us, but to the company. He—" Hull stopped, looking over at a portrait. Even on just a glance, I knew it was Richard Jefferson. Hull continued. "He wants to show he's above everyone else. Killing three board members doesn't just halt the construction, it cripples the company. And if the police can't catch him, it makes him invincible."

"But you have this figured out, right?"

"As well as I can." We stepped into the elevator. "We need to reach Jefferson." The elevator door closed.

*

We arrived at Jefferson's home. He lived in the suburban area of Newfield, so reaching the home wasn't near as difficult as our infiltrations to the Medina and Cunningham homes had been. We walked up the pathway quickly, Hull not pausing for any consideration.

"What do we tell him?" I asked, keeping in line with Hull.

"Nothing, not yet. We just need to make sure he's safe."

"Do you think the murderer will attack him anyways?"

"I don't think so. The murderer is—"

He stopped. Stopped talking, stopped walking. He stared forward, eyes on the dirt right next to the sidewalk that led to Jefferson's front door. I saw his eyelids spasm ever-so-slightly. "Someone is here."

"What?"

He started forward, quickening his pace. "The murderer, he's already here." Hull reached into his coat, then pulled out a pistol, one I'd never seen him carry before. We reached the door, and rather than knocking, Hull bashed the butt of the pistol into the handle, knocking it loose. He kicked forward, slamming the door open. He stepped in, gun at the ready. I followed cautiously, but soon learned now was not the time for caution.

"*Down!*" Hull yelled, and I complied. One gunshot rang out, shortly followed by another. Hull jumped forward, taking cover behind a wall that divided what looked like a living room from the dining room. I heard a voice cry out in pain, then saw a dark figure move quickly from the living room to a different doorway. Hull followed quickly as I scrambled to my feet, entering the living room and feeling dread sweep through me.

Propped in the only recliner was the now-dead body of Richard Jefferson, the bullet wound passing directly through his left temple and creating a mess on the wall to the right of his chair. The blood had completely covered a picture of what looked like Jefferson and a woman. Jefferson himself looked to be in his late fifties. I rubbed my face in anguish, feeling a sense of guilt pass through me. Hull returned to the living room, breathing heavily and rushing to the front window.

"He made it out, but I got him in the leg. His pants took the blood but he's hurt," the detective said, shutting the curtains and hiding his gun.

"There's a man lying dead right there!" I exclaimed.

"Acknowledging it won't bring him back."

"We should've been here sooner."

"There's nothing we can do now except call Lennox and alert him." Hull folded his hands together, holding them close to his face. "The three are dead, but he has to ensure his success, he has to make sure the message is clear."

I looked at Jefferson's body, feeling something in my head click. "The stockholder's meeting. Hickensons mentioned a meeting tonight."

Hull spun to me, his face lit. "Yes yes, that's it! Brilliant, Walker!" He started for the door. I followed as fast as I could.

"Hull, you don't even know where the meeting is!"

"But I do!"

"How!"

"*Library*!"

*

We arrived at the library just as the sun was beginning to set. Hull was tired, I could tell, but he was determined. The crowd that surrounded the library made it difficult to sift our way through, but eventually we reached the entrance. The stockholder's meeting had begun, and there was a schedule of different speakers. Hull was certain one of them was the murderer. He and I entered the main floor of the library, which currently housed almost two hundred people, as well as an impromptu stage at the far end. The library we were in now was to be closed, the books removed, and the building demolished to make room for the new, solar-powered facility.

Hull and I stopped at the entrance, his eyes scanning the crowd.

"Did you get a good look at the murderer?" I questioned, my own eyes surveying the mass of people.

"No. He was attired the same as he was in the diner. But he wasn't expecting us, or he would've locked the door behind him. Or included another bullet in his gun."

"How could you possibly know he only had one bullet?"

"What other excuse is there for not firing back?"

I paused, then nodded. "Fair enough."

"He won't be difficult to miss, though. Nobody gets shot in the leg and walks the pain off. He won't have received medical attention. He'll stand out."

"How do we find him?"

"We split up. You take the left side of the area, I take the right. He'll be here, either in the crowd or ready to speak." He started into the crowd immediately, his entirety vanishing. I moved into my own section, softly nudging my way past the bustling individuals. The number of people here was astounding, but then again, a company that had stocks was expected to have dozens upon dozens of stockholders in the town. So far, nobody looked as if they had just recently been shot in the leg.

After almost five minutes of searching, I felt a hint of resignation seeping into my thoughts. If this man was here, he wasn't on my side. And since I hadn't heard a gunshot, Hull hadn't found him, either. I turned to start back, my ears casually listening to the current speaker.

"...and now we'll be entering the question and answer portion of tonight's meeting. I'd like to bring up Mr. Benjamin Arnold, the directing assistant for the new library project." A round of applause followed. I continued towards the back of the room, expecting to find Hull there waiting for me. I was halfway to the back when a new voice started.

"Yes, thank you, everyone, thank you. Now I'd like to get right into things, so we'll start with the gentlemen in the front."

"Sheridan Hull, local consulting detective."

I spun, eyes going to the front of the group. Hull stood apart from the rest, a microphone in his hand and a stern look to his face. The speaker, Arnold, had a smile and an expecting face. But there was something else to that face. A wince to the eye that looked all-too familiar to me. One I'd remembered seeing on injured soldiers.

"Yes, Mr. Hull, what is your question?"

"The cost behind the new facility's creation is extremely high, especially for a charitable donation. Are we to assume Plyer had a successful quarter and thus explains the donation?" I started towards Hull, moving slow enough to keep from attracting attention.

"It's no secret that the cost is high with the project. The demolishing of this current building was expensive itself, but we are fully committed to what we are doing and plan to create a new, state-of-the-art, solar-powered facility for the usage of Newfield citizens for years to come." Another applause followed. "Anything else, Mr. Hull?"

"Why is Plyer in such a position to make this new facility?"

"Plyer strives to create a better community through energy efficiency. If we have to shell out some money to build an institution to encourage reading and knowledge, so be it. We'll slip a few books about solar energy into the shelves." Echoing chuckles followed by another round of applause. "Is that all, Mr. Hull?"

"One more question. Why are you limping?"

The blood drained from Arnold's face. He charged away from the stage, Hull jumping up into pursuit. I moved through the crowd faster, gently shoving people out of the way. Hull and Arnold had vanished into a large row of bookshelves. I made it through the crowd, rushing to find them. I heard one gunshot ring out. The crowd behind me screamed in panic, people falling to the ground to avoid further fire.

Another gunshot rang out. The shot was like audible fear, pumping my adrenaline and forcing me to move faster. I couldn't let Hull get shot by some random killer, but I still had no weapon of my own. I turned into a row and stopped. Arnold was at the opposite end, looking back and aiming his gun. I charged forward, grabbing a book from the shelf and chucking it towards the killer. The book slammed into the back of his head, knocking him forward. He spun, an angry look on his face. He aimed his gun at me, firing once.

I slammed my body against the closest shelf, just narrowly avoiding the shot. I knew any second Arnold would shoot again, and this time I wouldn't be able to avoid it.

The next shot to ring out, however, did not come from Arnold's gun.

Arnold fell to the floor, desperately clutching the hand that had moments ago held his own pistol. Hull stood behind him, aiming his own gun forward. He approached Arnold slowly, first kicking the killer's gun away, then slamming the butt of his pistol into the man's temple. The man's head hit the carpet. Hull passed over him and came to me.

"Are you all right?" he asked, looking over my person.

"I'm fine," I heaved, allowing myself to catch my breath. I could see he too was physically exhausted. "Thank you.. for that."

"Nothing of it," he said, turning to look at the downed killer. I stood against the shelf for a minute, letting my heart rate fall before walking to join Hull, who was staring down at the man.

"So why?" I asked, looking down at Arnold and the pool of blood forming near his hand.

"He wasn't just the directing assistant of the library project, he was the financial manager. He knew exactly how much money was going into this project, and he saw a way to make his own profit from it, while at the same time making a fool of the police force and leaving Plyer to be blamed."

"But how?"

"The cost of this project is approximately six million dollars. Not because of the architecture, but because of the location and the solar panel requirement. He was going to take the money, abandon the project, and shift the paperwork to make it look like Washington, Adams, and Jefferson had funneled the money to an outside source, but not one linked to him. It would have put the company to shame, and there would have been absolutely no leads to follow.

"In order to truly get the money, he had to hold a high enough position in the project. Washington was the director and board representative, Adams and Jefferson were the primary funding directors. Arnold became the assistant to Washington, and Washington trusted him enough to give him access to all vital information. Arnold started a relocation of funds, and once the money was securely placed in a separate account, he started his next phase. That would be the killing of the only men left with direct ties to the project.

"He killed Washington sometime last night, and took him east of Newfield to bury the body. But Washington, Adams, and Jefferson had started to become worried of Arnold and his discreet activities. Washington and Adams had planned to meet, then inform Jefferson, who was the primary spokesperson of the board of executives. He found the card for the meeting in Washington's body and knew he would be able to kill Adams then. He sat down and told Adams what had happened, and that Adams was going to die. He told him there was no chance of delaying it.

"From there, he moved to ensure his tracks were covered and that the police were investigating. Thanks to your keeping Lennox informed, he could see that the police had only just discovered Washington's identity and recovered Adams' body. He went to Jefferson's home and gave him the same speech as he gave Adams. He was interrupted, however, by us, and shot the man preemptively before attempting to escape. I managed to hit him in the leg, explaining the limp he had when he took the stage and eventually ran."

"But why make a game of it for the police?"

"The board members' concerns stemmed from Arnold's mental stability. They'd been informed of a history of manipulation. On Washington's desk, there was a dossier filled with information on Arnold. The page he had pulled out told me enough. Arnold sought to be the puppeteer of the entire situation. He could leave the police dumbfounded and the company defamed. And it would have all been by his hand. He would receive some manic level of joy from watching the panic, and then would have vanished just as silently as he had entered the company. With six million dollars, Benjamin Arnold would have vanished from the United States completely."

"Amazing. Absolutely amazing, how you can piece this all together."

He looked at me, smiling. "And you're sure you aren't harmed?"

"Completely fine, don't worry a-a-*achoo*!"

My own sneeze caught me off-guard. I noticed a slight headache had been growing, and my nose was starting to run. Hull looked at me with a devilish smirk. I looked at him, blinking.

"Oh you ass."

PROJECT SUPERMAN

One of the things that came with living with Hull was the idea of shared items. We quickly adjusted to each other's shower schedules, eating times, and whatever else we could keep relatively coordinated. But it wasn't until three weeks after the library case that something had struck me: neither of us owned a television. I suppose it was something that had always been a constant in my home, as well as my brother's. To find that neither of us owned a television meant that we had nothing to do during the stale time. My job at the nearby clinic didn't earn much, but it did make enough to buy a decent flat-screen.

One quirky thing I learned shortly after buying the television about Hull: he has an astonishing wealth of knowledge in regards to Walt Disney animated films. I don't know why, but he is able to remember every little detail from every Disney animated feature. Maybe he's this way with all movies, but in the time we'd lived together, I couldn't recall him going to the movies all that often. Or ever. Nonetheless, I found that he got a true, small sense of enjoyment out of having something as simple as *Snow White* or *The Black Cauldron* playing on the television while I wrote and he did his experiments. Thank God his latest was something without a smell.

Of course, something I also noticed was what he mouthed while said movies were playing. Everyone usually remembered one or two catchy lines from their favorite movie. Some dedicated fans would memorize segments of dialogue. Hull knew every single word to every single movie that we played. I don't even know how that's possible, since there were several dozen movies that accounted for several dozen hours of footage. Several dozen hours of talking. And he would sit and mouth the entire thing, without watching the screen to see who was talking. Sometimes he'd even chuckle at something he'd just mouthed. It was extremely peculiar.

Oh, and despite us having purchased a television that was only a few months old, Hull insisted on somehow plugging in an ancient VCR and watching the movies on videocassette.

In the aftermath of the library case, Lennox made a personal request for Hull to avoid any murder cases for a while. He said that "it looks bad to have people die that you could have saved." I understood perfectly, but I don't think Hull was quite as satisfied. Yet he took to his "punishment" with dignity. At least, that's what I think it was. Had I let him, he would've locked the doors, blinded the windows, and delved deep into his experiments, only stopping to sleep, if even that. I made sure he ate and took in some sunlight, despite the fact that Newfield was in its worst weather phase. Then again, Oregon wasn't renowned for its wonderful weather.

Hull currently stood facing his chalkboard, a very long string of equations written out with words written backwards after the equal sign. I gave it one glance before looking back down to my laptop. Hull's mind most certainly did *not* function the same way as everyone else's. But I wouldn't say that's too bad of a thing. It just made him different, and I don't think he minded. My attention would have remained on my laptop had a buzzing not started from the table across from me. Hull's phone was going off. I glanced over at him, his eyes not moving from the chalkboard.

"Aren't you going to get that?" I asked, nodding at the phone.

His attention remained on the board. "You get it."

"But it's your phone."

"Like they'll recognize the difference."

I sighed, setting my laptop down on the table beside me. I glanced over at him while moving towards his phone. "Where did you get that chalkboard, anyways?" He ignored me. I grabbed the phone, seeing it come up as a local number, and answered. "Hello?"

"Yes, is this Sheridan Hull?"

"No, this is John Walker, but this is his phone."

"Ah yes, Dr. Walker. Is Mr. Hull available?"

I looked at Hull, seeing his attention still focused on the board. "Somewhat."

"I was calling to ask if he'd be willing to meet me at my work. There's been a recent.. uh, event, and I believe it calls for his expertise."

"Ah. One moment." I pressed the phone against my shoulder. "It's for you."

"What do they want."

"Says he has something that calls for your expertise."

"Who."

I brought the phone back up. "Who is this again?"

"My name is Dr. Alan Rodgers, I'm one of the head researchers at Selecan Genetic Studies here in Newfield. There's been an incident at our primary laboratory and I don't particularly trust the police with it. It's something far too valuable to risk having an entire force know of."

"Okay." I covered the phone again. "He's a doctor at a local genetics place. Says he doesn't trust the police."

"Selecan Genetic Studies."

"That's the one."

"Tell him we'll be there."

"We'll be there," I said into the phone.

"Excellent! This is good news. I look forward to your arrival." The click told me enough. I set the phone down on the table, looking over at Hull.

"You couldn't have done that on your own?"

"No, far too busy."

"With what? Your mathematical equations and reversed letters?"

He smirked. "You could call it that, yes."

"Well no, tell me what it is."

"Irrelevant." He stepped away from the board, walking back into the hallway and out of sight. I walked around to find the board completely blank. I gave a sigh, rubbing the bridge of my nose. He came back out, coat in hand. "I'd wear a coat. The rain doesn't look forgiving." He stepped into the stairwell and vanished once more.

I walked around the board again, closing my laptop and grabbing my coat from the chair. As I walked towards the stairwell, I gave a short look back at the board. "Most people choose to live with friends or siblings, but no, I pick the genius sociopath."

*

Selecan Genetic Studies was a surprisingly large facility in the industrial district of Newfield. The central building had two side towers that stretched five stories into the air. But the central building itself was misleading in looks. The facility was seven stories in total, with two being underground. The main laboratory was on the second floor, only one floor between it and dirt. We were escorted there by a young woman, probably a few years younger than Hull and me. The man we met looked to be in his early forties, and well-built at that. He had a full head of black hair, with enough gel used to keep it in a very curious shape.

"Pleasure to meet you both, I heard about your work with Plyer," the man, Dr. Alan Rodgers, said after shaking our hands. "Knew you were the perfect fit for this job."

"And you ruled out the police?" Hull asked.

"As I told Dr. Walker, the contents of this issue are far too fragile." He turned and walked away from us, glancing back after about seven steps to gesture for us to follow. We walked through the outer area of the laboratory before arriving at a large, sealed doorway. Rodgers pressed his thumb against a scanner, then held his eye open for another. He stood straight as a scan crossed his body, then said, "Alan Rodgers." The door hissed before sliding open slowly. Hull and I followed him in.

We found ourselves in a very white, very sterile room, the walls lined with whiteboards filled with chemical formulas and equations. The wall opposite us had a very large refrigerator-like appliance, and a desk of computers was on the right adjacent side. In the center of the room was a vast table with restraints and different slots for vials. Rodgers came to stand next to the table. Hull gave a glance at the whiteboards before focusing on the scientist.

"So what is this about?" Hull asked.

Rodgers leaned down, pulling a manila folder from under the table. He slapped it onto the white tabletop, then opened it. Hull fanned the contents out himself while I watched. The documents looked ancient, some of them faded from time. Rodgers cleared his throat. "In 1942, the United States started a special division of the military to help look for the 'golden bullet' to end the war in the aftermath of the Pearl Harbor bombing. The United States Division of Special Research had many projects running to develop this 'golden bullet.' We were one of them.

"Selecan Genetics was founded as a subsidiary of the USDSR to work on a genetic formula that would manipulate the physiological structure of a human being, enhancing them in almost every way possible. We wanted to make the subject stronger, smarter, faster, whatever you could think of. We wanted to create a super-soldier to help combat the growing Axis threat. The operation was given the name 'Project Superman' and was immediately put to work in this very facility. Since Newfield was founded in 1941 as a potential western foothold in the event of an invasion, they wanted to have the facility as close to the possible front line.

"Selecan Genetics was avidly funded and tested in this very room. The formula was created, developed, and tested here. Their results were, at the time, unimpressive. Either the subject would only undergo very minor enhancements that soon wore off, or they would die altogether as a result of the rapid genetic restructuring. In May of 1945, Project Superman had its funding revoked, as Truman believed the atom bomb would be far more successful than enhanced soldiers. Selecan Genetics was boarded up and left in the dust.

"That was, however, until word reached the United States that the Soviets were developing their own nuclear weapons. Under President Eisenhower's leadership, Project Superman was reinstated as a potential 'golden bullet' to solve the growing communist problem. Eisenhower figured that a battalion of super-soldiers would be enough to strike fear into the Soviet's eyes and prevent war from breaking out. Breakthroughs in genetics helped us to advance the formula, but over the course of the Cold War, we never reached a true breakthrough. By the time the Soviet Union collapsed in 1991, we had made minimal progress, and President Bush, Sr. had us once again shut down.

"This did not stop the progress of Selecan Genetics. Despite our being labeled as unproductive and defunct, the head scientist, Dr. Charles Rodgers, continued Project Superman. He pressed forward on the research, but also had Selecan do other projects to give it a public face. Many of the medical breakthroughs in regards to the H1N1 scare from two years ago came from this very laboratory. Dr. Charles

Rodgers passed away in 2007, but ensured the research would be continued by his only son."

"You," Hull interrupted.

Rodgers smiled. "Yes. Me. And for the past five years, I have been in this room, taking the research from my father, the man who first devised the formula in 1942 and continued to work on it for sixty-five years, and refining it. My father was a genius, but at the same time, his methods were far too outdated. In summer of last year, we found our breakthrough. Using modified genetic strings, we were able to create a stable version of Project Superman. We tested it on chimpanzees to keep from accidentally killing another person. And it worked."

He pointed at one of the whiteboards. "The formula was able to physically and mentally strengthen the body and mind of a human being. With just the insertion of a fluid into the veins, the serum would immediately disperse and travel to every part of the body, infecting the muscles and organs with a growth enhancement gene that would cause near-immediate change. The person would take minutes to become a living super-soldier. A real Superman."

"But." I looked up from the postwar-era documents at Hull, who was practically looking down the arch of his nose at Rodgers.

The scientist sighed. "But two nights ago, someone managed to break into the upper facility and work their way down into this room. They got in, stole the only stable prototype of the serum, and took all of the documents in regards to the genetic codes and formulas. The only copies we have of them."

"Besides that," Hull pointed at the whiteboard, "and these," he moved his pointed finger to the folder, "you only kept one documented source of all of your studies?"

"The completed formula is the gateway to much, much more, Mr. Hull. It could lead us to medical breakthroughs in very positive ways. But at the same time, it could lead to very dangerous paths. Being able to immediately alter the genetic code can result in far more than just enhancing one's abilities." Rodgers stepped closer to Hull, only about twenty centimeters between them. "Can you imagine watching someone shrivel before your eyes as their genetic code is rewritten and their innards are destroyed by a chemical weapon devised from that very formula?"

"I would rather not," Hull said, not budging.

"Neither would I. That is why it is of the utmost importance that the prototype and the documents are found and returned *intact*."

Hull glanced at the whiteboards, then smirked. He looked back down at the folder, then stepped away, putting his back to Rodgers. "What leads do you have?"

"Slim to nothing. The surveillance footage was tampered with and we have no idea how they managed to get into this room. As you saw when you entered, the security is very tight. Not without approved thumbprint, retina, and vocal recognition confirmation can someone walk through that door, the only point of entry to this room. There are eight people who have received that level of clearance, Mr. Hull. And five of them have passed away."

"And the other two?"

"Drs. Seymour Williams and Richard Cain, the two remaining scientists. They were hired in 1965 and have remained since."

"Do you suspect them?"

"No."

"Why not?"

Rodgers leaned against the table. "Because I've worked with these men for fifteen years, and my father worked with them for forty-two. He trusted them that long, why shouldn't I?"

"Why should you?" Hull turned to look at the scientist, the glint in his eye. "If this formula is as powerful as you make it to be, then it would be worth quite a fortune. So much, in fact, that if a man were to say the formula was stable, he would literally have to merely sit back and watch the governments of the world throw themselves at his feet and start piling money. You invest too much faith in your coworkers, Doctor. There is, in fact, a price someone can reach to where they will disregard friendship and settle for a peaceful retirement with a hefty fortune." Hull looked at me and, with a nod, turned.

"But Mr. Hull—" Rodgers started.

"I will find your prototype and documents, Dr. Rodgers," Hull said without looking back, "though I cannot guarantee you will be pleased when I do."

Hull and I walked away from the laboratory, the detective's chin held high as if he were already triumphant.

"So what do we do?" I asked when we were almost to the road and waiting taxi. "And how do you always convince the taxi drivers to wait?"

"Money. We have little to work from, and I have some ideas, but we'll need to investigate so that I can confirm them."

"All of them?"

"Oh yes. This is quite the interesting case. And I wasn't lying when I said he may be displeased with the results."

"Why?"

"Things may come to light that Selecan Genetics would have preferred kept in the dark."

We entered the taxi, and Hull passed a slip of paper to the driver.

"What kinds of things?" I asked as the taxi started.

"Things of the most delicate nature. Curious, isn't it? That it would take seventy years to perfect a genetic growth formula? You'd almost think they delayed it. Or..."

"Or they figured it out and deliberately kept it secret?"

"Precisely. The theft is what's most curious, though I doubt it was a theft at all."

"How so?"

"Three men have access to a room as secure as the safety bunker of the White House, and a petty thief breaks in? Oh no, I doubt that with every genetic fiber in my body."

"So where do we go?"

"We talk with the other two scientists. One of them will know something. I'm certain of it." He turned to look out the window. "And we start with Dr. Seymour Williams."

*

We arrived at the home of Dr. Seymour Williams, a small, one-story home about five miles outside of the city. The house was situated on top of a hill with a large oak tree growing in the front yard. Only one vehicle was parked in front of the house. We exited the taxi and walked towards the house, Hull showing no signs of concern. How he was able to piece everything together with such little details... it baffled me. It was amazing, to watch him enter a room and suddenly know everything that was essential.

He knocked on the door twice, then stepped back. I glanced back at him, realizing he'd made it look more as if I was the one here with him as my companion. I looked forward as the door opened to reveal an elderly man, faint patches of silver hair on his otherwise-bald head and heavy wrinkles on his face. He looked at me, then to Hull with a soft gaze.

"How can I help you?" he asked, his voice hoarse.

"Are you Dr. Seymour Williams?" I asked, knowing that Hull was up to something and wouldn't be the one to talk.

"I am."

"I'm Dr. John Walker. This is Mr. Sheridan Hull. We're here to investigate reports of stolen information from your work, Selecan Genetics."

A quick look of fear crossed Williams's face. "Oh? Come in, better for us to talk while sitting." We followed the elderly man inside to a well-kept house, everything very clean and pristine. He led us to a living room, where a loveseat faced two armchairs with a coffee table in the middle. He sat down on the loveseat and gestured for us to take the armchairs. Once we were all settled in, Hull leaned forward.

"Dr. Williams, what can you tell us about Project Superman?" the detective said, his voice stern.

Williams showed signs of growing concern. "I'm not sure I follow."

"We have just spoken with Dr. Alan Rodgers, and we are aware of what you do at Selecan Genetics. Dr. Rodgers also informed us that two nights ago, the prototype serum and official documents in regards to Project Superman were stolen."

"Stolen?" The aged scientist's bottom lip trembled. "But how could that be possible?"

"That is precisely what we aim to figure out," Hull replied, standing up. He walked around the armchairs, eyes purveying the nearest cabinet. "Are you married, Dr. Williams?"

"I-I was..." he stuttered, watching Hull carefully. "My wife passed away two years ago."

"I'm terribly sorry to hear that, though I am curious, who keeps the house so clean?"

"..I beg your pardon?"

"You are not a man who strives for absolute cleanliness, that was identifiable by the state of the back seats of your car, yet there is not a speck of dust to be found in this room, or any of the others. Even the china in the cabinet has been cleaned on a weekly basis. So, either someone cleans your house, or you do not stay here often, and even then someone would clean the house."

"I clean my own house, what does this have to do with the project being stolen?"

"Why clean the house but not your car?"

"Because she never cleaned my car!"

I watched the scientist bury his face in his hands. He sat there for several moments before letting out a heavy sigh.

"After she died, I would clean the house. It was always what she did, and... I didn't want to lose that part of her. As if it were possible that I could keep the house clean, and it would be like she was still here with me."

Hull returned to his seat. "Thank you, Dr. Williams. That is exactly what I was waiting for you to say." He leaned forward. "Now, what can you tell us about your coworkers? Alan Rodgers and Richard Cain?"

Williams seemed to release some of his inner tension, rubbing his cheeks before responding. "Rodgers is an odd fellow. I worked with his father for too long. And Charles always struck me as selfish, I guess. He was the mastermind behind Project Superman, all the way back in the 40s. I wasn't with the research team then, I joined in the 60s, but I fought in World War II. I was seventeen when they bombed Pearl Harbor. And Charles was an odd man with very odd ideals. Very odd ideals.

"Even when Project Superman was decommissioned, Charles kept it going. Throughout the Cold War, he worked tirelessly on it. But we didn't need super-soldiers in the Cold War. We weren't fighting a guns and blood war, we were standing on opposite sides of the ocean making ourselves look tough. Charles was after something with the operation. Something nobody else cared for. I wasn't sure if it was money or what, but he had his mind on other things. His priority wasn't the safety of the United States."

"What of his son?" Hull prompted.

"Alan is no different. He has the same ulterior motives as his father, like they were just passed down to him. I've been with the operation since before Alan was born, but Charles always kept him close. He taught him everything he needed to know about Project Superman. And Alan has always been very secretive about some of the genetic coding his father worked on. I never pried, it wasn't my place, nor was I overtly interested. But I suspect that both of them had a profit in mind for themselves."

Hull pressed his hands together, holding them close to his lips. He remained silent for almost a minute before giving a rapid series of blinks. "And Richard Cain?"

Williams shook his head. "I've never liked Richard. He's always had a feeling to him, like he didn't care at all for the operation. He wasn't assigned to us, he picked the job. But he's always been disassociated from the rest of us. A loner, I guess. If anyone was going to steal the prototype, it would be him. I hate to point fingers, but it's the truth. Richard isn't an honest man. But this?" He shook his head again. "This is just something unreal. But I guess we should've seen it coming. Nobody bothered telling me it had been stolen."

"So I thought," Hull said, standing up. He gave another look around the room before nodding at Williams. "That should be all from us. Thank you for your time."

"That's all?" the scientist said, also standing. "You're free to check the house if you like, I promise there's nothing from the lab."

"I believe you, "Hull replied as he walked towards the door. I knew better than to expect any kind of goodbye from him towards the scientist, so I turned to the elderly man, gave him a nod, and followed Hull from the house.

Once we were closer to the taxi than the man's house, I spoke. "You believe him?"

"Of course. As soon as he'd shown his willingness to trust us by telling us the reasons behind the home's tidiness, I knew he would be honest enough. He had nothing to hide, and frankly, nothing to gain from stealing the operation. That man isn't after wealth or power. He's an aged man who has dedicated his life to his work, and regrettably so. We will have use of him, but later. Now, we must go meet with Cain." Hull stepped into the taxi.

"Do you think Cain stole it?"

"Not directly, no. Though I do suppose Cain is responsible for something."

"What would that be?"

"The thief's entry. No thief could bypass that level of security. If only three men have access, and we know Williams was completely unaware of the theft, then either Rodgers or Cain let the thief in, on purpose. There's no thief in the vicinity of Newfield capable of doing it on their own, and trust me, I would know. Thieves steer clear of Newfield."

"Why?"

"Because even the best thief leaves a trace, and that is all I need to find them."

*

Cain lived inside the city limits, just near the fringes of the more metropolitan area of Newfield. His home was an apartment on the third floor of a four-story complex. Hull and I stood outside the door patiently, the sounds of families surrounding us. Hull stared forward at the doorway, eyes narrowed and head tipped down. From the front, it probably looked like he was glaring. I could hear the sound of someone approaching the doorway, and as I turned forward, I saw Hull lift his chin. Some things I truly did not understand about that man.

The door opened to reveal a man much younger than Williams but still older than Hull and me. His hair was dyed black, though it was minimal. He stood half a head shorter than myself, putting him a full head shorter than Hull. He looked from Hull to me with quick glances, and I could tell the man was visibly nervous about something. There was a slight shake to his eyelids and a hesitancy to face us. This wasn't good for him at all. Thankfully, Hull had told me before that he would do the talking for this.

"Dr. Richard Cain, I'm Sheridan Hull, consulting detective. I'm here investigating reports of sensitive material going missing from your workplace, Selecan Genetics."

"Something's gone missing?" Cain replied, his voice cracking.

"Yes, and it is not something I would think you would like mentioned in public," Hull said, glancing back at a couple coming up the stairway.

Cain saw them and gave a visible shudder. "Okay, come in. Quickly."

Cain took us into a three-room apartment, the main room horribly messy with papers and easy-bake food trays. The television was on, playing some game show I didn't recognize. Cain walked into a room out of view, then returned with a collapsible chair. He propped it up next to the other two in the main room, then took a seat. I sat down in one of the others, but Hull remained standing, his eyes locked on the scientist.

"Is this about Project Superman?" Cain asked immediately.

"You've been informed of its theft?" I questioned, recognizing the hole the man had fallen in to.

"Yes, we all were. Rodgers sent out the call yesterday when they found the facility had been breached."

"Did he now?" Hull said, eyes leaving Cain. "And at what point did he contact you yesterday? Was it during your outing in the park, the comedy show you saw, or the time you had a young lady over?"

Cain watched Hull with wide eyes, his mouth agape. "E-excuse me?"

"I can't make myself much clearer. At what point did Dr. Alan Rodgers call you yesterday to inform you of the break-in? Because you were not here for most of the time and since you lack a cell phone, he couldn't have contacted you had you been gone."

"I don't know what... what do you mean... are you—"

Hull went rigid, except for his eyes. Those moved from spot to spot across the room. "You aren't tidy enough to clean this room, therefore someone else is. This complex offers a cleaning service on the Tuesdays of the first and third weeks of the month. The number of meals accumulated here would signify you have sat in front of that television for dinner for only four of the five previous nights since the routine cleaning. Since the comedy show you attended was last night, shown by the date on the stub over on the table, you were obviously out last night.

"Granted, that still leaves an opening during the day, but there is a significant amount of mud on your shoes, and it is fresh, but it hasn't rained since yesterday morning. Once the rain had passed, you left your apartment and took a walk, stopping to have a fast food meal provided by a vendor close to one of the parks. You got the food and ate it there, but still managed to spill both ketchup and mustard on the pants you wore, which are, in fact, the pants you chose to wear today, which also have signs of the mud matching those on your shoes by the door.

"The young lady's presence was by far the easiest to find. You're an older man, unmarried, possibly from your lack of cleanliness, possibly from your smoking habits. Yet even older men have a yearning for some level of satisfaction, especially if they lacked it during their younger years. As such, you were able to find a relatively cheap service nearby, cheap because you'd live somewhere other than a pay-when-you-can apartment complex. That service provided you with a woman willing to give you that satisfaction for a price, and as would be customary for her, she wore a very heavy, very alluring perfume that still lingers in the room.

"You also aren't good at attempting to hide her previous presence, as the contraceptive items used are visible in the garbage bin by the door. Disgusting place to put that, by the way, and not a pleasant smell at all. The cleaning service must hate reaching your area. So, you went to the park, you went to the comedy show, and you had a lady with you last night. You do not own a cell phone, nor did you check your messages yesterday, since the answering machine is blinking with a very vibrant, red number seven. Now, when did you find time to learn of the stolen information?"

Cain stared up at Hull with a mixture of both astonishment and pure terror. I'd only seen that look of fear in the eyes of soldiers who thought they'd lost too much blood from a wound. Cain remained silent, though I wasn't sure he'd be able to speak even if he wanted to. He simply looked up at the detective with horror.

"Very well," Hull said, turning away and glancing into one of the nearby rooms. "Walker, you search the bedroom, I'll search the kitchen. The prototype and documents will be here somewhere."

"N-no!" Cain yelled, standing on shaking knees. "I d-don't have the p-p-prototype! I swear!"

"You hardly expect us to believe that?" Hull replied over his shoulder.

"It's not here! I never t-touched them!"

"Then who did?"

"*Chimaera!*"

Cain gasped, collapsing back into his seat and almost causing the chair to fold in on itself. His head lulled to the side, his right eye twitching and his lips trembling. Hull turned, eyes burning with a new intensity. He sat down in the seat next to me, leaning close to the scientist.

"Chimaera?"

Cain took his time regaining his composure before letting out a very shaky sigh. "I'm so sorry. I needed the money."

"Irrelevant. Who is Chimaera?"

Cain licked his lips, and I could see tears rimming up in his eyes. "Rodgers t-told me that S-Selecan would be undergoing a r-r-routine maint-t-tenance upgrade and that all of the s-security would be offline. I knew I c-c-could make some m-money if I told someone, b-but I didn't know w-who."

Hull pressed onward, knowing he had Cain at his weakest. "And so you went where?"

"I'd heard a name before, of a... group who d-dealed in this kind of thing. Inf-f-ormation. B-black market dealings. I was put in t-touch with an informant. I told him about t-the upgrade and he gave me... it was so much m-money I just couldn't believe..."

"And this informant was from Chimaera?"

"Y-yes. He left before I c-could say anything else... and I thought everything would b-be f-f-fine..."

The scientist buried his head in his hands, the only sounds coming from him now being sobs. Hull stood.

"Thank you, that should be all from us," he said, turning.

Cain looked up, eyes puffy. "Y-you're not going t-to arrest me?"

Once I reached Hull, he glanced back at the crying man, a smirk on his face. "How could we? We aren't police."

*

We were back at the flat now, with Hull facing his chalkboard and me at my computer. Hull had written up his usual web of clues for the case while I tried looking up our new, illusive foe.

"Chimaera," I said out loud, eyes scanning the search results. "Nothing stands out."

"No, of course it doesn't, they'd never be that well-known. You'll have to look carefully," Hull said through clasped hands, his eyes scanning the contents of his board.

After several minutes, something did arrive, and its correlation shocked me. "This is odd. It's a news report from when you busted the scientist from Warmack Chemical. It says that during his trial, he mentioned a group by the name of 'Chimaera,' but refused to elaborate."

Hull glanced over at me. "Chimaera was the group that requested the bombing of the plane. Wygant was merely the tool."

"How big can they be?" I asked, my mind racing.

Hull looked from me to the board, probably at the spot that said "Chimaera." After a long bit of silence, he snorted. "Chimaera. A crime syndicate group existing right under the streets of Newfield.

The ones who adeptly coordinate all necessary crimes to continue their job. Oh how clever indeed." He picked up a piece of chalk, drawing a line from one thing to another. "I wouldn't worry about their size, Walker. I'd be more concerned about their reach. Their power. Their influence."

"How do we stop something like that?"

"We don't." He moved away from the chalkboard. "We do, however, capture the informant."

"How do we do that?"

"By letting him come to us."

I leaned back from my computer, a look of disbelief no doubt on my face. "And how do we do *that*?"

A buzzing from below was enough of an answer.

Hull sat down in the chair that faced the doorway and waited. I too watched the door with a slight sense of anticipation. How he'd managed to get the informant to come here was beyond me, but if he'd truly pulled it off, I was once again impressed. What the doorway opened to reveal, however, was not in the slightest what I expected.

A young boy, probably seventeen or eighteen, stood in the doorway, black hair and very pale skin. He wore baggy clothing and had his hands in his pockets. He looked at us with a very smug face before making an odd gesture, like he was pointing at us with his elbow.

"You guys the ones selling something?" the kid said.

"We are," Hull responded, taking a deep breath. "Are you willing to pay for it?"

"I might be," the kid replied, his smug look etched into his face. "What's the information?"

Hull scratched his nose, then glanced at me. "Doctor, would you mind retrieving the package from the kitchen for me?" I looked at Hull for a very long moment, but realized he had something planned. Or, at least I hoped. I stood and walked to the kitchen and found a brown box sitting on the table, no markings, no labels, just a box. I picked it up and learned it was surprisingly light. I brought it back to the main room, handing it to Hull. "Thank you."

"That's it?" the kid said, taking a few steps closer.

"It's inside here, yes," Hull replied, slowly opening the box, but keeping its contents hidden from both the kid and myself.

"What is it?"

Hull pulled the contents of the box out and aimed it at the boy. It was a pistol, his pistol, the one I recognized from him using at the library. "Your decision."

The boy froze, hands coming out of his pockets and flying up to pointlessly protect his face. "*No! Please!*"

"All you have to do is comply, and you will be free to go. I promise." There was a notable sense of difference to Hull's voice, like he was forcing himself to sound truthful. The boy peeked at him through his fingers. "You recently received some very expensive items from Selecan Genetics. I would like to see them."

"It's down in the car," the boy stammered, pointing back behind him.

Hull stood, keeping the gun aimed at the boy. "Good. Take us to it." I stood as well, not entirely happy with what Hull was doing, but still trusting him *not* to shoot the kid. The boy led us downstairs, past Mrs. Hanson, who nearly screamed when she saw the situation. I pressed a finger to my lips, reassuring her things were under control. She watched us exit, Hull being careful to hide the gun inside his coat as we walked outside. A car was parked at the side of the road, with no passengers visible.

The boy opened the passenger rear door, reaching in with shaking hands and pulling out a large, cardboard box. He set the box down carefully on the sidewalk, then opened it. Inside was a rack of test tubes with only one tube present, and a very large pile of documents, as well as several discs and memory drives. The only test tube in the rack was filled with a vibrant green liquid that seemed to glow in the darkness.

Hull hid the gun inside his coat, then leaned down, pulling the test tube from the rack. He held the tube up to the light, then smirked. He glanced at the boy, then at me, and then, with a large smile, threw the vial against the ground. The boy jumped back as it shattered, the green liquid creating a splatter mark across the cement.

"Why did you do that?!" the boy exclaimed, eyes filled with both fear and rage.

Hull kneeled down, running his finger over the top of the spilled liquid. He then stuck his finger into his mouth and made a loud slurping noise. As he stood, he spoke. "Water. Green food coloring. An added chemical to give it a glow. A perfect substitute to trick an idiot into thinking they had the prototype of Project Superman." He kneeled again, this time pulling the documents, discs, and memory sticks from the box. "And these, oh yes, these. Dozens of pages of research, hundreds of megabytes of information on these storage devices?"

He snapped the discs and memory sticks and ripped the papers in half, with an amazing amount of strength, I might add. "All forged and fake. Irrelevant and completely worthless in regards to Project Superman. If I were you, I would return to your employer and tell them the news." The boy stood still for a moment, legs shaking as he attempted to make his decision. Finally, he turned, slammed the car door, and ran around the side. Hull watched with a smile. "Oh, and also tell them that Sheridan Hull sends his regards!" The boy entered the car, started it, and drove off, leaving a black skid mark on the sidewalk curb.

"How did you know?" I said, amazement filling me.

"I've known since the start," Hull replied, turning to enter the flat.

"What?" I called after him. "You have?" Hull moved quickly up the stairs, not bothering to respond. He grabbed his coat from the coat rack, then charged back down with me in tow. He stopped in the main lobby, looking over at Mrs. Hanson.

"There's been a slight mess made outside, the boy next door should be willing to clean it up for a few notes," he said. Then, as quickly as he'd entered, he was out the door and hailing a taxi. I stood at his side, knowing once we were on our way to our next destination, wherever that may be, he would explain. Hopefully. The taxi pulled up, and as we took our seats, Hull handed a slip of paper to the driver.

Once we'd been moving for almost a minute, I nudged him. "You've known since the start?"

He sighed. "Think. A facility with that level of security is broken into? Hardly. Someone had to let the thief in, and that is exactly what happened. Rodgers told Cain about a security upgrade, knowing that Cain would take the information and try to turn it into a profit, which he did. Rodgers then disabled the security as soon as he saw the thief arrive at the facility and watched as they stole the fake serum and forged documents that he'd placed."

"Rodgers set Cain up?"

"No, Rodgers covered his tracks. The actual serum wasn't stolen by a thief, it was taken by him. He planted the fake serum and documents to make it look as if the real ones had been stolen. He has them."

"Then why call you? The best detective in Newfield?"

"Because he wanted time. Not much, but enough. He wanted to prove a point."

"A point?"

"Yes, but not to us, to the others. Possibly even to the country. He wanted to prove the serum was perfected, but he didn't want it used on the highest bidder. He wanted it for himself."

"He's going to take the prototype?"

"I'm counting on it."

"Then what do we do?"

Hull leaned forward, tapping the taxi driver's shoulder and pointing down a road. "We get Dr. Williams."

*

We arrived at Selecan Genetics, Dr. Williams having joined us. Hull had explained the situation on the drive, and the doctor had been more than willing to help. He even said he'd expected it of Dr. Rodgers. The three of us stepped into the elevator and waited as Williams pressed the necessary code to take us down to the central lab. We hoped Williams still had clearance to access the Project Superman room. Hull said that was where we would find Rodgers, patiently waiting for us to put the pieces together.

The elevator opened. The three of us ran across the room, Williams moving shockingly fast for a man in his late eighties. We reached the security checkpoint to access Project Superman.

"All right, Doctor, this is your field," Hull said, glancing around the rest of the lab. Williams looked over the thumbprint recognition scanner, then up at the sensors above the doorway. I could tell something was giving him a cause for concern. He looked over at me.

"The security's already overwritten. The door's unlocked," he said with confusion.

Before I could respond, the door slammed open, much faster this time than the first time we had been here. A loud *bang* echoed from the room, and Williams flew back a meter, landing on his back. His mouth was open and his eyes were wide as a pool of blood started to accumulate on the floor beneath him. I saw his chest rise once, twice, three times before ceasing.

"Excellent analysis, Seymour," a voice said from inside the room. "I always appreciated your input."

Hull and I looked in to see Alan Rodgers, gun in one hand and the other propped against the testing table. He dropped the gun, then grabbed a syringe from the tabletop. He jabbed the syringe's needle into his waiting arm, then looked forward at us with a sneer. Hull made no motion to enter nor run, so I stood still as well. But then again, what happened next probably would have paralyzed me anyways.

First Rodgers' injected arm, then his free arm started to... shake, I suppose. It looked like ripples of water moving underneath his skin. Then it started on his face. He held the sneer for as long as he could before snapping his neck to the left, then right. His skin continued to ripple, but before long, it started to *grow* as his muscles received an impossible burst in size. His head stopped throbbing and he resumed staring at us, his sneer even wider. His shirt tore in several places and his pants seemed to shrink as his legs grew. He moved up over a foot in height.

I wasn't sure how to respond. I wasn't even sure what we could do. I didn't know if Hull still had his pistol or if he even intended on shooting. I glanced at Hull, hoping for an answer. The eyes that met mine said one thing: *wait*. He looked back at Rodgers, and I had no choice but to do the same. It looked as if the man had stopped growing. He stood a head higher than Hull, which put him much higher than me. He breathed heavily, but wore his sneer proudly.

"Witness the power of science, gentlemen. With just a few lines of genetic code altered, I have become more powerful than you could possibly imagine. This is the future. I am stronger, faster, smarter than any man alive. I can and will use this power."

"Duck," Hull whispered.

"What?" I shot back as quietly as I could.

"*Duck.*"

I looked forward to see Rodgers tear the table from its roots in the floor and throw it with little effort at us. Hull shot to the right, I dived to the left as the table flew through the open door and slammed into the ground, about a meter away from Williams's body. Rodgers charged through the door, looking at me first, then at Hull. The detective glanced up at the large man, then through his legs at me.

"*Wait*," he mouthed before refocusing on the hulk of a man. Rodgers leaned down, grabbed Hull by the shirt, and threw him away, sending the detective flying across the laboratory and over a table of chemicals. The vials gave way, releasing their liquids, volatile or otherwise, onto Hull and the ground. Hull stood quickly, ignoring the chemicals on his coat and breathing quickly. I moved away from the doorway to a nearby table, grabbing the stool. I picked it up, turned, and tossed it at Rodgers, watching it bounce harmlessly across his broad back.

The man turned to me, his teeth clenched. He charged at me like a bull, head down and legs moving fast.

"Ohh, bad idea," I said as his head dug into my stomach, lifting me up and propelling me across the lab. My back slammed into some kind of refrigerator, and inside I could hear things fall and break. I looked up to see another stool soaring towards me. I ducked and rolled away as the stool smashed into the refrigerator, causing even more sounds of breaking from within. I looked up over a table to see Rodgers and Hull playing an impractical cat-and-mouse game, Hull feigning left, then running right.

Rodgers ran after him, catching up to him in a matter of seconds. He grabbed the detective by the waist, tossing him back. Hull slid along the ground, coming to rest about two meters from Williams. He looked up as Rodgers stood above him, pressing his foot into Hull's chest. Hull made a visible face of pain, but still stared up into the deranged scientist's eyes.

"It's been a pleasure, detecti—"

Rodgers froze. His eyes went wide and his back arched. He stepped away from Hull, his head starting to tremble. He collapsed to the ground, entire body seizing. I rushed to Hull, helping him stand, then together, we watched as the scientist seized for several more seconds before stopping, entire body going limp. His open mouth let out a horrible death rattle as his chest gave its final heave. Hull gave an audible sigh, eyes closed and chin high. I could see blood on his back, presumably from the shattered glass. The chemicals didn't seem to have an effect on him.

"Did you... know about that too?" I puffed, realizing how out of breath I was.

Hull took a moment to respond, no doubt slowing his own breathing. "When he took us in there, to the lab," he pointed to the Project Superman test room, "the chemical formula on the board. On just a single glance, I knew something was wrong. The chemical would yield what seemed like a successful test, but after long-term exposure, the compound would start to dissolve whatever organic substance it was near. As soon as he injected himself, it was only a matter of time. Once the formula had been properly dispersed and the time had elapsed, the chemical compounds broke down and tore away at everything. His heart, his lungs, his muscles, his brain. Everything."

"And you knew that?" I said, still taking in deep breaths. "All from one look?"

"It was all I needed," he replied, resting his weight against a nearby table. "I studied chemistry, remember?"

I laughed, then realized how much it hurt to laugh. I joined him against the table, looking over at Williams's dead body, then down at Rodgers. "You knew it would do that to him and let it happen?"

"Like I said when we left, I had theories. I wanted to confirm them. He would have injected himself with or without our presence. Though I suppose an audience made him feel more superior. As soon as we heard that Rodgers had told Cain of a security upgrade, I knew Rodgers still had the true prototype and that he intended to use it on himself. I knew the chemical would not work and that it would kill him."

I sighed, licking my lips with a smile. "You know Lennox isn't going to be happy when he hears that?"

Hull gave a short laugh. "Lennox can piss off."

BROTHERLY LOVE

"You made the paper."

Hull didn't bother looking up from his Sudoku puzzle as I perused the paper that Mrs. Hanson had only just brought up. From where I sat, it looked like he was on his fifteenth puzzle of the morning, the completed ones, all from inside newspapers over a month old, stacked haphazardly next to his chair. How he was able to just sit and do puzzle after puzzle without growing either bored or irritated, I would never understand. Personally, Sudoku puzzles did nothing but make me feel stupid when it came to numbers.

"Mm," he grunted, eyes locked forward and pencil moving across the paper rapidly.

"Fifth page in. 'Local detective brings end to 70-year genetic program.' Not painting you in the best light, but then again, two people ended up dead."

"Mm."

"You don't care at all what the paper says about you, do you?"

"Mm."

"Are you even paying attention to me?"

"What the press thinks about me is irrelevant," he said, eyes still focused on the puzzle. "The work matters. I get the job done. What happens along the way is secondary."

"Even when people die?"

He looked up. "People die every day, whether it be natural causes or a casualty of a situation. Do you expect someone to step in and prevent their death every time?" He looked back down at his paper. "The needs of the many outweigh the needs of the few. Without Dr. Williams, we would never have gained access to the facility, and Dr. Rodgers would be a threat to the rest of Newfield, or worse. I do not regret my actions, nor do I intend to."

"I never expected you to," I said, returning to my own paper. "God forbid you show signs of being normal. Like everyone else."

"Act like everybody else? Everybody else is so boring, where's the fun in being like them? I much prefer to act like myself."

"Of course you do."

He stopped his puzzle, staring at me with a half-glare. "You're upset with my actions?"

I set my own paper down. "I never said I was upset, but people dying is still a bad thing. It doesn't matter if it was natural or a casualty. Somebody died."

"The man had no family, you could tell that by the lack of photographs in the home. Nobody will miss him."

"Friends will miss him."

Hull scoffed, tossing his puzzle and pencil to the ground. "Friends."

I opened my mouth to retort, but a buzzing from below stopped me. Someone was at the door, and on a Sunday morning, the options were limited. I never received visitors, and obviously neither did Hull. Mrs. Hanson had family, but they were across the country. Hull evidently didn't care for the arrival, as he simply stared down into the hearth with an unattached gaze. I sighed, clasping my hands behind my head.

The sound of footsteps coming up the stairs caught my interest. They weren't quick, like that of a person seeking help. They seemed slow and casual, with a slight heaviness to them, that of a man's. So it wasn't Mrs. Hanson coming to see us. Whoever the visitor was, they were here for either Hull or me. Probably Hull. Though he still didn't seem to care. I watched the doorway with a small sense of anticipation. It opened to reveal a tall man, probably in his late thirties. He had blonde hair that was short and cut neatly and wore a black coat and dress pants. He looked in at Hull and me, turning his chin up and giving a very, very short smile.

"Hello, brother," he said, the slightest hint of an English accent showing. I glanced from him to Hull, my eyes widening.

Hull looked back at him, then rolled his eyes. "Oh God," he said, looking forward.

The man tilted his head. "Come now, is that any way to treat your older sibling?"

"What do you want, Malcolm."

"First to meet your friend. Dr. John Walker, is it?" the man, Malcolm, said. "I am Malcolm Hull, Sheridan's older brother. I would say I am surprised he has never mentioned me, but then I would be lying."

"No, he hasn't mentioned you," I replied, glancing at the younger Hull while I shook the older one's hand. "How did you know my name?"

"Well, you both are all over the newspapers, it seems only natural I pay attention."

"Liar," Sheridan said, eyes locked on the hearth.

Malcolm gave a quick sigh. "Sherrie and I have not always gotten along well."

"Haven't ever," the detective shot back.

"We need your help, Sheridan."

"Why."

Malcolm sniffed, eyes moving around the room. He moved to sit in the only open armchair, across from Sheridan and adjacent to me. He stared forward at Sheridan for a long moment before leaning back and pulling a folded piece of paper from his coat's inner pocket. He unfolded it, gave it a quick glance, then held it out for his brother. Sheridan's eyes had yet to move from the hearth. Malcolm sighed again.

"One of the FBI's Most Wanted, a man by the name of Wayne Fisher, has turned himself in to the Newfield Police Department. Two years ago, Fisher was charged with the alleged murder of two men, as well as the rape and murder of a woman. He then escaped arrest the evening after being taken into custody. Fisher has been gone for two years, and has only just decided to willingly turn himself in."

"Most Wanted criminals are not my field, Malcolm," Sheridan said, eyes furtively looking at the paper in his brother's hand.

"You will want this one, Sheridan." Malcolm held the paper steady. I watched as Sheridan glanced at the paper again, then up at his brother, before quickly snatching the paper from the second man's hand and opening it. His eyes moved rapidly over the contents. Malcolm shot a look at me before continuing. "Upon apprehension, Fisher made one request: to have a private meeting with Mr. Sheridan Hull."

"And?" Sheridan said, eyes still on the paper.

"And so we would like to acquiesce to his request," Malcolm replied, his voice cool.

"And?" Sheridan repeated. I looked at him with my brow furrowed, somewhat confused of as to why he was pressing further.

Malcolm pursed his lips and narrowed his eyes before responding. "And I would expect you to present yourself for this. It is not often that a fugitive of the country willingly turns themselves in, Sheridan. Even you could not have found him."

Sheridan scoffed. "It would have taken me two days."

"Hardly."

"Why should I comply with this? I don't exactly make friends with criminals."

Malcolm gave his own scoff. "You. Friends." Sheridan tossed him an accusatory glare. "Consider it a personal favor, for me."

"Because you are so deserving of those, aren't you," Sheridan snapped, eyes going back to the hearth. "I'll talk to him."

Malcolm smiled as he stood. "Excellent. We shall depart now and—"

"No."

Both Malcolm and I looked at Sheridan, but only his brother spoke. "Excuse me?"

"John and I will arrive later. You will leave now."

Malcolm gave a face of minor disgust, as well as irritation. He looked over at me. "It has been a pleasure, Doctor." He peered down at Sheridan before leaving the room.

I waited until his footsteps were faint enough to say he was off the stairs before I stood, moving to the other armchair. "What was that about?"

Hull gazed up at me, some slight sense of tension gone from his face. "Sibling rivalries that fail to pass with time. Since before I can remember, Malcolm has always been the man of propriety. I often suspect he was none too pleased when I was born, him having been an only child for thirteen years. Suddenly the attention was diverted." He looked back at the door before tossing the piece of paper Malcolm had handed him over his shoulder, leaning forward to rest his chin on his hands.

"What does he do?" I asked, looking down at the folded paper. "How does he have access to the FBI's Most Wanted?"

Hull breathed noisily through his noise. "Your government relies on the Federal Bureau of Investigation and the Central Intelligence Agency for its knowledge and security. Who do you think they answer to?"

"The president?"

"No. They answer to Malcolm Hull."

I looked from the paper to the door. "He's that important, huh?"

Hull coughed. "Hardly." He stood and walked to the window. From where I sat, I could hear the sound of a car starting and moving away. Hull stared out the window for almost a minute before I stood, moving to pick up the paper. I opened it to find a very detailed page of information on Wayne Fisher. His mugshot reminded me heavily of John Travolta's character in the movie *From Paris With Love*. His list of charges were exactly as Malcolm had stated: he had been accused of three accounts of murder and one account of rape, then with unlawful flight to avoid prosecution.

"I don't know him."

Hull's voice snapped me away from the paper. I looked up to find him still facing the window. "What?"

"I don't know the man." He turned. "I may be odd, but I do not associate with wanted criminals."

"I never said you did."

"You thought it." He walked from the window to his chalkboard, looking over its currently-blank state. His eyes traveled up slowly, looking at the terrace before moving to a relatively empty area in the room, that being the far corner that we'd used to initially put moving boxes. He licked his lips, eyes starting to move in their typical rapid fashion. "We should get a piano."

"I'm sorry, what?"

"I said it's time for us to go," he shot back, heading off towards his room.

I looked at his back, then at the open space. "A piano?"

*

We arrived at the Newfield Police Department to find a growing crowd. Most of them were reporters, all of them gathered at the barricades put up to keep people back. Apparently, an FBI's Most Wanted turning himself in warranted a big news story. Lennox stood at the top of the stairs, eyes surveying the crowd. When he saw us, he shouted something to two officers standing several steps down, then pointed at us. The officers pushed their way through the crowd, then escorted us up to the waiting inspector.

"Glad you two could make it," Lennox said, leading us into the department. "The last time we had any kind of crowd was when the mayor picked the new police chief."

"Has he said anything?" Hull asked.

"Fisher? No, won't say a word. Just keeps saying he wants to talk to you." Lennox held a door open for us, giving an odd look at the detective. "Looks like you've either got yourself a fan or an enemy in him. Can't really tell with these types." Hull ignored him, stepping through the door.

We found ourselves in a lobby of sorts, with three metal doors on the opposing wall. Inside the lobby was a collection of police officers, several upper men in the department, a man I recognized as Inspector Grayson, and Malcolm Hull, who was accompanied by a half-dozen others dressed in suits. Lennox walked across the room to the center door, then stopped. He glanced back at us.

"He's inside. We told him the room has no taps, but that was a lie," the inspector said.

"Disable them," Sheridan replied.

"What?"

"Disable them. He will know, and he will not speak until you have."

"How could he possibly know if they're—"

"Just do it."

Lennox looked at Hull for a long time, no doubt wanting to either retort or hit the detective. Finally, he sighed, looking over at one of the upper officers and nodding. The man moved to a computer console by the wall. Lennox looked back at Hull, who was moving towards the door with me in tow.

Lennox put his hand up. "Sorry, Doctor. Fisher wants Hull only. Said he wouldn't talk if anyone else was in the room."

Hull looked back at me, an almost-apologetic look crossing his face. I nodded. "No, it's fine. I can wait." Hull blinked, then returned his gaze forward as Lennox unlocked the door. He stepped through to a secure decontamination chamber, eyes set on the door ahead. Lennox closed the door behind him.

*

Hull stared forward at the closed door as a beam of light passed over him, ensuring he carried no weapons or potentially harmful items. He waited patiently, eyes locked on the sealed metal slab. After several seconds, a confirmation beep came from somewhere above and the door hissed open. He stepped through into a gray room with a single table and two opposite chairs. The chair that faced the opposing wall was open. The chair that faced him was occupied by a man, several years older than Hull but lacking any hair on the top of his head. Instead, it was all focused on his face, making up a large beard that stretched from his ears to his standard orange shirt.

"Hoped you'd show up," the man, Wayne Fisher, said, his voice hoarse. Hull moved slowly to the waiting chair, taking the seat and staring forward into Fisher's brown eyes. The criminal returned the gaze, a smile notable only from the disrupted facial hair. They stared at each other in silence for nearly a minute before the other man spoke. "Glad you had them turn off the wires. Heard the click." Hull remained silent. The man set his arms on the table, revealing them to be handcuffed. "Come on now, make this fun. I can't hurt you."

"That is hardly my concern," Hull said, eyes still on the man's own.

"So you do talk?" Fisher said, leaning back. "Good. It'd be hard to negotiate if you didn't." Hull didn't respond. The man resumed his forward lean, his head tilted to the side. He visibly licked the top row of his teeth, eyes narrowing slightly. "Not even gonna ask what we're negotiating?"

"Why waste my breath? You'll tell me eventually."

Fisher chuckled. "Smart man. I knew the boss wouldn't have me do this if you weren't."

"And your boss is?"

"You don't know him. But you will." Fisher smiled. "You will. You've been working against us for a while, you know. The higher-ups at Chimaera aren't too happy with you. That's why I'm here."

"You turned yourself in because you expect to leave here a free man."

Fisher nodded, pressing his tongue against his lip. "Good, yeah, good. I don't just expect it, though. It's gonna happen. And you're gonna help me."

"Why."

Fisher's smile disappeared, and a cold look fell on his eyes. "Ten children. All of 'em kidnapped, tortured, all sorts of things done to 'em. But they're alive still. Not for long. And if I don't get out of here, they'll die. Ohh boy will they die." The smile returned. "That's where you come in. You prove I'm innocent and I tell you where the kids are. The kids are saved and I walk free."

"Why would I ever agree to let a criminal walk free?"

"Because I've been wrongfully accused, Mr. Hull. All of that two years ago, they got it all wrong." He leaned even closer. "I know it. And you're gonna prove it to 'em. Or those kids are gonna die, and it'll be all your fault."

"People have died because of me before."

"Innocent people who weren't tied to what you were doing? Or people that put themselves in the fire?" Fisher licked his lips again. "These kids are innocent, Mr. Hull. The oldest one is nine. The youngest is four. And all ten of 'em are gonna die unless you get me outta here. I didn't pick 'em because they were criminals. They were just taken, practically right off the school bus. They've done nothing wrong. But they're gonna die. Unless you prove I'm innocent."

"And you think you're innocent?"

"Oh I know I'm innocent. I've known for two years." He leaned even closer, now with only about a dozen centimeters separating him and Hull. "I'm not a stupid man, Mr. Hull. A guilty man wouldn't turn himself in. But an innocent man? He's got nothing to worry about." He shook his head. "I got nothing to worry about."

Hull stared at his extremely close face, noting every tremble, twitch, and twinge to the man's skin. After almost an entire minute of the stare-down, Hull slid back, standing as he went. He cast no looks back at Fisher, moving directly to the door and pressing a button on the side panel. He stepped back as the door slid open, into the decontamination room. Just as the door behind him started to close, he glanced over his shoulder, seeing a very wide smile on the criminal's face.

*

I sat at one of the tables, softly tapping my fingers against the countertop. Hull had been in the meeting room for almost ten minutes now, and it was obvious people were growing curious. Everyone except Malcolm and his posse seemed to be anxious. Even Lennox had started pacing in front of the leftmost doorway. I scratched the side of my face, looking down at the table. The problem with these secure meeting rooms was, once the wires had been disabled, there was literally no way of knowing what was happening inside unless you went in physically. There were no security cameras and the doors and walls were so thick, sounds were contained to each individual room.

Finally, the center door hissed before opening, revealing the, and I use this word lightly, friendly detective face. Hull stepped out into the lobby, eyes locked forward and shaking ever-so-slightly. He took several steps away from the door, allowing it to close behind him. Everyone in the room now faced him. Lennox approached him, hands on his hips.

"Well?" the inspector said.

Hull turned to face the inspector. "I need the case files on Fisher. All of them."

"What? Why?"

"Because I need to visit the crime scene."

Lennox's brow fell. "You want to look at a crime scene from two years ago for a case that's been closed for just as long?"

"Yes. Will that be a problem?"

"What the Hell did he say?"

Hull looked forward. "Malcolm, I will need a copy of Fisher's case files. Forward them to my phone." He walked towards the doorway out. I glanced around, seeing Lennox watch the detective leave with an open mouth. Malcolm, however, had a look of disdain. I stood and followed the detective, who walked silently down the hallway, down the stairs and eventually to a taxi. We'd been driving for nearly five minutes when I decided to talk.

"So," I said, looking out the window.

"He wants me to prove he's innocent."

My head snapped to Hull. "He *what*?"

"He says he is innocent, and that I need to prove it. Otherwise, ten children will die."

I felt a wave of disbelief sweep through me. "He's extorting you?"

"He is doing what has been assigned to him."

"How does that work?"

Hull rubbed his chin slowly, eyes focused on the back of the seat ahead of him. "He works for Chimaera. Someone there has put him up to this. He would never have turned himself in if he didn't believe his innocence could be proven."

"And so you're just going to do it?"

"What was it you said earlier? I should act normal?" He looked at me. "There are ten children's lives at stake."

"When have you ever cared for lives at stake?"

"There is an interesting case attached."

I leaned back, jaw going slack as understanding replaced the feeling of disbelief. "It's not about the children. It's about being entertained. You think he's innocent."

Hull's pocket buzzed. He pulled out his phone and glanced at the screen. "We wouldn't be on our way to Los Angeles if I thought otherwise."

"Los Angeles?"

He showed the contents of the phone to me. "Fisher's file. The crimes were committed in Los Angeles. Therefore, we need to travel there."

*

I hadn't stepped foot on an airplane since arriving in Newfield almost five months ago, and it hadn't been nearly as large as the one that took Hull and me to Los Angeles. The flight was several hours, but the airport was large. I also hadn't visited Los Angeles since I was fourteen, and that had been over a decade ago. The airport was bustling with people, and since we arrived at about four in the afternoon on a Sunday, many people were in a hurry to get home. Hull and I walked casually through the crowds, his deep purple suitcase wheeling along behind him. I preferred to take a duffel bag that I could carry. I suppose it was a habit that had grown on me while I'd been overseas.

As we walked out of the terminal and joined the crowd of people waiting for a bus, I couldn't help but note that Hull was humming something. It took a while for me to recognize it, but once I did, I scowled.

"Please tell me you aren't actually humming that," I said, giving him a look of disappointment.

He returned the look with some actual shock. "What? It's fitting, isn't it?"

"You're humming a song by a teenage tra—" I stopped, glancing around at the people near us. None of them had heard the word I'd almost said, but Hull had certainly caught it.

"That's not very nice of you, John. For all you know, she could be a very pleasant individual and your opinions are misconstrued by the media."

I sighed. "Where are we headed?"

"A hotel. We'll start work tomorrow."

"You really think you can prove his innocence?"

"I have to. Giving up now would be pointless and expensive. Impromptu flights are not cheap."

"Your brother covered the flights."

"Did he?" He picked up his suitcase as a bus came to a stop in front of us. "That would explain the horrible seats." We took our place on the bus, and conversation would have been difficult on our current topic due to the proximity to other, unknowing people. Instead, I decided to try and make headway on another subject.

"What really fuels the rivalry between you and your brother?"

"Bets that were never paid off, fights that were never resolved. Challenges of intellect that were never won. The usual."

"Yes, but I talk to my brother."

"And yet here you are living with me rather than him."

The woman sitting next to Hull seemed to scrunch her nose in disgust, turning to look away. I held back the want to snap at her. Hull and I weren't involved, but an attitude like the woman's still pissed me off. "My brother also had two younger sons who were loud. It wasn't a good living environment."

"My brother has a daughter. Are we done comparing irrelevant facts about our siblings?"

I shrugged. "I just can't see why you two have so much hatred for each other."

"Not quite sure I can either. I still have no intentions of joining his family for Thanksgiving dinner this year." I recognized a pointless cause when I saw one, so I fell silent, instead electing to watch the scenery pass by. Los Angeles was much, much larger than Newfield, and even made Seattle, the city I had grown up in, pale in comparison. Many of the buildings stretched high into the sky, and the urban landscape itself spanned off into the horizon. I could see the faint etches of the Hollywood sign on a hill far off in the distance. Other than that, it was just a city.

The bus drove us around for nearly an hour, with the man sitting to my right nodding off twice and moving to rest his head on my shoulder. Hull had simply stared forward, not bothering to focus on anything in particular. Unfortunately, directly ahead of him was a woman and an arrogant child, and I had no doubt she assumed he was staring at her son. She left the bus in a subdued fury, but Hull didn't notice. Or at least, he didn't acknowledge it. Finally, the bus reached our stop, a hotel in Anaheim. The crime scene was about two miles away from where we were staying. Hull and I stood, paid our fare, and entered the hotel.

Our room was fairly nice, also paid for by Malcolm. I set my bags down on the bed closest to the window. We were on the tenth floor, so I assumed we would have some kind of view. I opened the blinds to find that the hotel looked out at a sprawling amusement park. It took no longer than a half-second for me to realize where we were.

"He picked a hotel that faced Disneyland?" I called over my shoulder.

"No, I did."

"Why?" But as soon as I'd asked, I knew the answer. His seeming obsession with Disney films was enough to explain, and he definitely knew I'd figured it out and didn't bother replying. He went about unpacking his things while I stared out the window. I'd always hoped to one day have children and take them to Disneyland. It had been my brother and I's favorite vacation spot when we were younger, though our parents would probably have preferred somewhere more tropical.

"The crime took place in an abandoned warehouse," Hull said, suddenly at my side. "Right over there," he pointed out to the right at a darker area.

"What do you think you'll find?"

"Something." He lowered his hand. "Anything."

"It's been two years."

"Time does not remove evidence, Doctor," he said, walking away. "People do."

*

We arrived at the warehouse early the next morning, toward the tail end of the early rush hour traffic. Hull had a jumpiness to him, not from nerves but from anticipation. It was always during a good mystery, I had noticed, that he became more and more excited and dedicated to what he was doing. It was like the deeper he went, the more adrenaline was pumped into his veins. He walked into the warehouse like a puppy chasing a thrown ball, feet moving quick and head craned forward. I walked alongside Lieutenant Collin Phelps, the officer assigned to assist us. The chief of the Anaheim district was not happy at all to hear the case was being re-investigated, but he was compliant.

Phelps and I stepped into the warehouse. Hull was already jumping from pallet stack to stack, head craning to look up at the ceiling. I stopped about three meters from the entry, as did Phelps. The lieutenant was about Hull and I's age, with short brown hair that he hid underneath a bowler hat. He wore a suit that matched his hair with a red tie and kept his hands in his pockets.

"From the pictures, it looks exactly the same," the lieutenant remarked.

"No one bothered to keep doing business?" I asked.

Phelps laughed. "Business? This place had been abandoned for about five years. Owners left town and didn't bother selling the place to anyone. It's been open since. Perfect place for the crime, I guess."

"Yeah. And what can you tell me about the crime?"

"Nothing more than what the files say," he said with a shrug. "I wasn't on the force for the case. It's just something every officer hears about from those who were around. The fact that another officer was killed tends to be the central bit."

"Ah." I looked over at Hull, who had jumped off the pallets and was now practically crawling across the ground. "What are you doing?"

"Investigating," he said, not looking up to check whether I was talking to him or not.

Phelps leaned in towards me. "Does he really think he's going to find something?"

"Yes," Hull answered. Phelps glanced at me, a look of curiosity on his face. I gave a short nod before moving to join Hull. He stopped crawling across the ground, now looking up at the ceiling once more.

"What've you got?" I asked.

He stood. "Three people. They disrupted the pallet there on the floor," he pointed to a lone pallet that was splintered in several areas, "and it's also where someone was shot. The blood was cleaned, but not too well. Traces of it remain on the pallets, deep in the wood." He walked over to the pallet. "There were two men present, the police officer and another man. The other man was more present on the pallet. I believe the woman was as well. It's hard to find exacts, though. Something's not right here."

"How so?"

"It's something with the second man." He walked over to the entryway, where Phelps stood. He looked down at the ground and started poking his feet in the darkness. He was eventually met with the sound of glass hitting the cement. He reached down and delicately pulled out a glass beer bottle. "He was a drinker. The police officer wouldn't have been carrying this."

"What about the woman?"

"Possible. But I doubt it. We will have to check the files to see where they all were before they ended up here. Especially Fisher." He looked back at the pallet. "But first we investigate the second man. The files give an address for his previous household. Says he had a girlfriend who may still reside there. She may be able to provide some information on her ex-boyfriend's previous.. activities." He walked from the warehouse. Phelps looked at me, curiosity painted on his face.

"Where now?" he said.

"Lampson Avenue," Hull shouted over his shoulder as he stepped into the squad car. He slammed the door, leaving Phelps and me to join him.

Phelps drove the police car while Hull and I occupied the back seats. The seats weren't designed for comfort, that much was certain. And I can't say I've been in many cop cars. Hull's attention seemed focus on the outside, meaning I was left to my own business. I pulled out my phone and realized I had received a text message from a number I didn't recognize. The preview message was simple:

What progress has Sheridan made?

I glanced down at the number for a long time. I didn't recognize the area code, but part of me wanted to say it was a government number. Something about it just rang official. I carefully formed my response before sending it:

We're investigating right now. Who is this?

I set the phone down, but only for a moment before it went off. I glanced at it:

Malcolm. Keep me updated.

"Did you give your brother my phone number?" I asked, looking over at Hull.

He peered at me through his peripheral vision. "I never gave Malcolm *my* number. He has his resources." His eyes returned to the outside. "Is he contacting you?"

"Texting me. Not something I'm exactly used to. My mother can't even send a text without hitting the enter key three times before the message is finished."

"If I were you, I would not even bother responding."

"Well he'd know I'd seen it and hadn't bothered to respond, wouldn't he?"

Now Hull turned his head. "How?" There was an actual hint of curiosity in his voice.

I held up my phone's screen. "That latest update for our phones allows timestamps on messages. Tells others when we received and read them."

"Oh." He pulled out his phone and accessed his messages. "Ohh. That would certainly explain how Malcolm knew I had read the messages."

The car came to a stop. Hull and I stepped out to find ourselves facing a condominium. Phelps walked around the car, joining us.

"Alright. This is where Christian Kaiser lived. His ex-girlfriend still lives here. Her name's Marie Swanson. She's not expecting us, and I don't know anything about her except—"

"Lieutenant, I think I am capable of gathering all necessary information," Hull interrupted, walking up the steps.

Phelps glanced at me. "Is he always like this?"

"Always," I replied coolly before following Hull.

It didn't take long for someone to answer the door. A young man, hair long and facial hair grown, greeted us, giving a look of surprise when his eyes spotted the cop car behind us.

"Is something wrong?" he asked.

"Is Marie Swanson here?" Hull shot back.

"Yeah, did Marie do something?"

"I'd like to speak to Marie and see the house please." Hull evidently had no patience for stalling, but given the circumstances, it was understandable.

The man looked at Hull with a minor sense of disgust before turning back into the house. "Marie! You got some people here to see you!" It took several seconds for a young woman to reach the door, clad in a loose shirt and pajama pants. Her black hair was tied up in a bun. After just one glance at us, a look of alarm fell on her face.

"What's going on?" she asked, her voice slightly tense.

"Ms. Swanson, we're investigating the murder of Mr. Christian Kaiser and would like to see the premises upon which he used to live," Hull said, hands clasped behind his back.

"Christian?" she replied, eyes peeled as she looked among us. "But he died over two years ago, why would you—"

"Ms. Swanson, I would appreciate your full cooperation so that we may be done with this promptly," Hull snapped. The woman looked at us for several more seconds before giving a quick nod, then opening the door. Hull stepped right on in, immediately looking around. He moved off into one of the closest rooms, vanishing from sight.

I extended my hand to the woman. "Dr. John Walker. That's Sheridan Hull, consulting detective. This is Lieutenant Phelps with the police."

She shook my hand with a sweaty palm. "What's happened? Did something about Christian come up?"

"His murderer turned himself in and said he's innocent. We're investigating the case further to reach a more sound consensus."

"Sound consensus?" Her eyes had a distant, pained look to them. "I saw Christian's body that night. He'd been strangled. You don't strangle yourself. I know that man did it."

"But you weren't particularly disappointed, were you, Ms. Swanson?" Hull said, sweeping back into the room. Her look at him was a broken one, her lips trembling.

"Excuse me?"

"There is not a trace of Mr. Kaiser having ever lived in this household," Hull replied, coming to stand by Phelps and me.

"Of course there isn't, it's been over two years."

Hull's eyes seemed to do a half-roll. "Irrelevant. A grieving girlfriend would have kept hold of something, mementos to remember a fallen lover. No, you purposefully purged his items from the house. No clothes, no personal items, not even a picture remains that hasn't had him removed. The pictures in your living room are all of you and your current boyfriend, as well as some family. One photograph, however, has been cut on the left, removing your right arm entirely. Now, either you have a twisted wish to be an amputee, or you cut Mr. Kaiser out of the photograph on purpose."

"How could you say that?" she barked. The man who had answered the door entered the room, moving to her side.

"What's going on?" he said.

"I can say that based on what I can observe," Hull said, turning his back and doing a walk around the entryway. "I know that Mr. Kaiser originally picked this place of residence when you and him moved here. He selected it not based on its affordability but rather its placement. There are approximately three different bars within walking distance of this residence, which would mean he could become as intoxicated as he wished and not have to worry about driving home and being cited. He'd only have to make the walk, and usually, being accompanied with friends, it wasn't difficult.

"His drinking habits weren't the only thing that led to your strained relationship, though, was it? A girlfriend who had lost the central man to her life would have been distraught, not so quick to find someone new, as you did. Only a month after Mr. Kaiser's death, too, if the dates on the photographs are correct. No, Mr. Kaiser had another habit that you disliked, something you knew of but would never accuse him of for fear of being right. Mr. Kaiser liked to frequent other parts of the darker districts here, didn't he? Occasionally find someone on the side of the road, willing to do the things you would never do for the right price?"

The man at Swanson's side stepped forward, but Phelps and I positioned ourselves between him and Hull quickly. The man's face was starting to go red in the cheeks. "You get him the Hell out of here, right now!"

"It's quite all right, I've seen everything I need to anyways," Hull said, turning towards the door.

"Wait!"

Everyone stopped, even Hull, to look at Ms. Swanson. Her eyes were rimmed with tears and her hands shook as they held her elbows.

"You're right," she said, her voice dimmed. "He cheated on me. So many times. He said that he didn't but I knew. He'd come home some nights and he'd smell like another girl. I just..." She gulped. "I couldn't take it. I was sad when he died, but I wanted out so bad. I couldn't take being hurt like that over and over again."

Hull didn't look back as he walked from the home. Phelps was quick to follow, no doubt avoiding the awkward moment that had just occurred. I looked from Swanson to her boyfriend, gave a nod, and followed the two men. We quickly made our way to the car, where Hull already sat in wait. Phelps started the car, then glanced back at us.

"Next stop?"

"Los Angeles Police Department." Hull's voice was resolute. Phelps nodded, looking forward. After a minute, I glanced over at Hull.

"Might want to work on your revealing skills, you know. Just because you don't feel emotions doesn't mean everyone else is so immune," I said with a half-smirk.

"I have emotions. I just choose to not let them control me."

"Ah." I paused for a moment. "So where does this put us?"

"Kaiser was an adulterer. It helps to explain his placement at the crime. Fisher was charged with rape, but it may turn out that he was not responsible after all. I will have to look at the information filed by the department. The police officer is our next focus."

Hull sat with his face glowing from the computer screen before him. The police chief had been extremely reluctant to grant us access to the files, but some coercion from Malcolm had easily pushed that aside. I was starting to see just how expansive a grasp the older Hull had. All it took was a phone call from him to give Hull and me access to some of LAPD's most sensitive files. Hull, of course, had zero interest in anything that wasn't relative to the case. He currently read over a very long entry in regards to the Fisher incident in October of 2009, over two years ago. Phelps sat at his desk next to us, eyes more focused on a stack of papers he needed to fill out.

"Curious," Hull said, the first words he'd spoken since we arrived. He hadn't even bothered phoning his brother to get us access; I'd had to make the call. And calling a man I had met the day before to give us access the sensitive files for a government employment was, to say the least, uncomfortable. "The emergency call was issued at 1:21 AM on a Sunday morning, but the caller never revealed their name. When additional forces arrived, everyone was already dead and Fisher was practically waiting."

"So Fisher was obviously guilty?"

"Not quite." Hull leaned back, pointing at some minor details noted on the report. "The police officer, Brandt Reaves, was not in his region of patrol. The warehouse is almost a half-mile outside of his assigned field. And he was not the officer dispatched to handle the call. Reaves did not request to leave his region, and therefore was out of line in being present. But because he ended up with a... slit throat, they disregarded it. And they found Fisher with the bloody knife."

"And you still expect to figure out he's innocent?"

Hull leaned in again. "The challenge is even more enticing. The red-handed man, after two years, turns himself in and pleas not guilty. Either Fisher was truly a victim of circumstance, or we have a genius on our hands. Or both." He went silent for another long moment before throwing a hand up. "Wait."

"Wait what? You're the one reading."

"Here." His finger touched the screen, another minor detail noted in the original findings section. "Only one person was shot. The woman, Victoria Ogi. No gun of any type was ever recovered from the scene. Not even Reaves had one on him, which is very unusual."

He scrolled up and down the report several times before pushing his chair back. "We need to see the scene again."

"What, again?" Phelps said, though I could tell he would rather leave than sit and continue staring down the paperwork. "One look wasn't enough for the consulting detective?"

"One look was more than enough, Lieutenant. But what I am after now requires more than just looking."

"And what's that?" the officer said as he stood.

Hull smiled. "*Observing*." With that, he turned and walked from the main office out into the stairwell. I quickly grabbed my coat as Phelps and I followed him. The lieutenant looked at me with an almost sorry tint to his eyes.

"Always like this. I can't imagine living with him," he said as he put his hat on.

"Oh he's far more unbearable when he's not on a case."

We were halfway down the stairs when my pocket buzzed at me. I pulled my phone out to find a new message from Malcolm:

What did the police records tell him?

I sighed, careful to not trip down the remaining stairs as I typed my response.

I don't know. Whatever it told him, it's in his head.

I pocketed the phone, not bothering to wait for a response. Phelps and I exited the building to find Hull once again waiting in the squad car. Phelps took the driver seat while I took my own, buckling as Phelps quickly took us away.

It was only a matter of seconds before my phone buzzed again. I pulled it out:

A place nobody truly understands.

Part of me felt like chuckling, but I knew it wouldn't be proper.

"Malcolm is texting you still," Hull said, his attention on me.

"He's curious of as to where we are in the case."

"He wants me to fail."

"What? Why?"

"If I prove Fisher is innocent, it makes both the Los Angeles Police Department and the Federal Bureau of Investigation look like idiots for pursuing an innocent man for over two years. The last thing Malcolm Hull wants to do is look like an idiot."

"But why help us if he wants you to fail?"

"He expects the evidence to affirm Fisher's guilty status. That they were thorough enough when the case occurred that nothing could have happened in two years to change."

"And what happens if you find out he is innocent?"

Hull smirked. "Then it will just be another thing to strengthen that rivalry."

We both were silent for the remainder of the ride. It only took about ten minutes to reach the warehouse, still as abandoned as before. Hull quickly entered and moved towards the shuffled pallet. Phelps and I followed, and I could tell the lieutenant was gaining more and more interest in the case. Hull seemed to have a very specific effect on people. Either he spurned you away or pulled you in with his intrigue. Phelps and I had taken the latter effect.

Hull moved around the pallet towards the bloody pallets, hands brushing over them swiftly. After a minute of searching, he slammed his arm between two pallets and moved his hand around the insides of the wooden supports audibly. Finally, he pulled his arm free to reveal a small, shining case. As I moved closer, a sinking feeling hit my stomach. It was a bullet case, and to a very specific weapon.

"A .40 caliber safe action shell fired from a Glock 22," Hull announced.

"The same type of gun carried by police officers," I finished, giving a sigh.

Phelps gave a sharp look between Hull and me. "You think Reaves shot the woman?" he said, his voice showing heavy signs of both disbelief and captivation.

"I know that Reaves shot his pistol before promptly disposing of it somewhere," Hull replied as he started climbing the pallets.

"You really think he was able to shoot her and hide the gun on top of a four-meter stack of pallets?" I shouted up as Hull reached the top. For a slim man, he was surprisingly fast at reaching the peak of the stack. "And didn't they find him with a slit throat?"

Hull's response wasn't verbal, but rather something that sent both Phelps and me away as a pistol flew down from the top, clashing into the cement and giving a small bounce. I held back several obscenities, looking up to see Hull staring down at us with a humored face.

"Relax," he said, holding a slender, black item in his hand for us to see, "I removed the clip." He glanced at the object. "It seems to be missing a shot, too."

"You think the gun itself wouldn't hurt?" I barked up at him. "You knocked a man out with a gun just a few weeks ago!"

"That was different," he said as he started down the pallets. "I meant to knock him out." He jumped from a meter up, landing softly on his feet. He stooped down, grabbed the gun, and brought it up, sliding the clip into its place and pressing the safety. "Reaves' gun was fired once, then disposed of. The question is, was he the one to fire and hide it? Oh what curious twists to this case."

"Do you think he shot her?" I asked, noting that Phelps was somewhat out of earshot.

"I'm not sure," he replied, looking down at the gun. "But I have an idea. And all we need to do is investigate one more aspect to complete the case. Ms. Victoria Ogi." He pulled out his phone. "Unfortunately, her home is no longer accessible."

"Why? The residents won't let us search?"

"There are no residents." He showed me the screen to reveal a building under construction. "It was torn down several months ago." He let his arm drop, sliding the phone into his coat pocket. He looked out around the warehouse, up at the ceiling, across at the pallets. "The police reports an eyewitness having seen both Fisher and Ogi at a nearby bar. We will have to check there, see if they have any remaining security footage."

"What do you expect to find?" I asked as we walked towards the exit.

"More clutter. This case has become far more muddled than a simple triple-murder and rape accusation."

"You call that simple?"

"Textbook."

"If I stick around you long enough to see a complicated case, I'll be amazed. Though I do recall you struggling on the Plyer case."

"There was insufficient evidence, it was hardly my fault. Such a simple case."

*

The night was growing late, as it was almost 8 PM by the time we reached the correct bar. It wasn't too busy, though, since it was a Monday night. Hull had taken a seat at the bar while Phelps and I had gone into the back security room to review the tapes from the night of the murders. The bar owner, Ray Bartley, kept security logs that dated back five years. Phelps and I sat watching the recording play from the night, waiting as Bartley fast-forwarded through the time leading up to the woman's arrival.

"We kept everything on tape until last year," Bartley said, hand on the remote to the small TV. "Not cheap, transferring everything over to DVD. And now they've got this Blu-Ray crap."

"Mr. Bartley, do you remember anything from the night of the incident?"

"Shit no. I don't remember a thing from last week. That's why I keep the recordings, whenever you police types come around looking for something." He hit the play button and pointed at a woman sitting at the bar. "There she is. She was a usual here, come to think of it. Every two weeks or so. Sometimes came with a man, I think. Never the same one, though. Don't think she ever left here sober, either."

"Thank you, Mr. Bartley, we can handle things from here," Phelps said. The man nodded, handed Phelps the remote, then returned to the bar. Phelps paused the recording and pointed on the screen. "There's Fisher. But he's nowhere near Ogi." He let the recording play. We watched for nearly five minutes, but Fisher never moved from his seat.

"Report said that an eyewitness saw him at the bar, but they never said he talked to her. This isn't looking too good for—"

"Wait," I interjected, pressing the pause button on the VCR that rested ahead of me. I pointed at a man that had only just entered. "That's Christian Kaiser."

Phelps leaned close, then sighed. "Damn. So he was here too. Now all we need is Reaves to walk in and this really looks bad." He pressed play and we watched as Kaiser came in and sat about three seats down from Ogi. Over the course of the remaining recording, Kaiser cast several glances at the woman but never approached her. About twenty minutes into the recording, Fisher stood and left. Eventually, Ogi stumbled her way out of the bar, and five minutes later, Kaiser also departed.

I turned the television off. "All of them gone and nothing to say who talked to who. Hull is right, this is becoming more and more cluttered the deeper we go." I rubbed the arch of my nose and shook my head. "How did the police and FBI not catch all of this?"

"If you found a man holding a bloody knife in the company of a dead officer, another body, and a raped woman, would you bother looking too far into it, especially if he went willingly at first?"

"When you say it like that, I suppose not."

Phelps and I left the security room to find Hull still at the bar, holding the top of a half-full glass and sliding it around the wooden tabletop. He stared forward at a row of different drinks with a glazed look. I came up to his side and grasped his shoulder.

"Please tell me you aren't drunk," I said, giving a slight shake.

He let go of the drink, looking over at Phelps and me. "Nowhere close. What did you find?"

"Fisher and Ogi were here, as well as Kaiser. None of them interacted."

"Interesting," Hull said distantly, placing a twenty dollar bill on the bar. He brought the glass to his mouth and downed the drink in one go, slamming the glass back down on top of the bill.

"What was that?" I asked.

"Vodka," he said, standing and moving towards the door.

"Now wait a second, why didn't you come back with us?" I questioned, keeping pace with him. "I know you didn't do it to get a drink."

He glanced back at the bar. "Someone had to talk to the other frequenters. The ones who would remember Ogi, and the night. I learned some curious things."

"Like?" I inquired as we walked out the door into the night.

"Ogi frequented the bar, like many of the others in there. Several of them said she had a bit of a reputation for occupying men's beds, including a few of the not-so-gentlemen in there. One of them said he was a family friend, and that she had been struggling for money for nearly three months before her death. He was here that night and said she left the bar without anyone, but someone had been buying drinks for her."

"That's a lot of different perspectives to this."

"Quite." We entered the car. "Take us to our hotel."

"We're done?" Phelps asked, a slight hint of disappointment in his voice.

"Yes. The doctor and I need to return to Newfield."

"You've figured it out?" I piqued.

"I have." He pulled out his phone, opening one of the saved documents he'd been sent. He panned through it quickly before arriving at the summary of events. "The official documentation says that somewhere around 11 PM, Wayne Fisher abducted Victoria Ogi from Ray's Place Bar and took her to the warehouse on Katella. There he took advantage of her drunken state and sexually assaulted her. A man, Christian Kaiser, stumbled upon the crime and attempted to intervene. Fisher attacked and strangled him.

"During the struggle with Kaiser, Ogi had the judgment to call 911, but the policeman to arrive was not the one called. However, Fisher attacked this officer, slit his throat, and proceeded to shoot Ogi in the head before being caught. Officers found Fisher with a bloody knife in hand and bruised knuckles, evidence of a struggle that they assumed was with Kaiser. Ogi had visibly been sexually assaulted, and after later autopsy results were received, traces of Fisher's DNA were found within Ogi."

"But that line of events doesn't make sense anymore. Does it?"

"It shouldn't. But at the time, it was incriminating. The bloody knife, the bruised fingers. A gun with a single discharged round. The seminal traces. Every sign pointed to Fisher being the criminal."

"But he wasn't?" Hull's response was a smirk. I would have continued the conversation, but once again my phone vibrated. I checked it to find another message from Malcolm:

The judge is growing impatient. What has Sheridan found?

I showed the screen to Hull. "Your brother's curious."

"His curiosity is unwarranted. We will see him soon enough."

We arrived at the hotel. Hull and I stepped out, and before we could leave, Phelps also exited.

"I just wanted to thank you both, for letting me accompany you on this," the lieutenant said.

"You were assigned to us," Hull remarked.

"I know. But this... well, don't tell anyone I used this wording, but this was the most fun I've had on the force. So thank you." Hull nodded to him, then turned, walking up the steps. I shook Phelps's hand and turned as well, following the consulting detective's stride.

*

Hull and I walked up the steps of the Newfield courthouse, with him not bothering to halt his strut. We'd slept for a short while and left the hotel at about 3 AM for the earliest flight to Oregon. Unfortunately, that had meant a redirect from Portland to Newfield, which put us at 10 AM by the time we made it home. Hull wasted no time in going to the courthouse, not even bothering to stop at home and drop off our luggage. Lennox stood at the top of the stairs, watching us approach with an absorbed gaze.

"Only took you a few days. You find out whether he's innocent or not?" the inspector asked as Hull passed him. The detective did not bother responding. Lennox looked back at me, but I merely shrugged. Despite everything, I was still in the dark. Lennox and I followed Hull through the central hallway, through the security X-rays, all the way to the pending courtroom. I had called ahead and informed them of our imminent arrival, so everyone should be gathered. The judge, Fisher, the police, Malcolm. Everyone.

We entered the courtroom to find exactly who I'd assumed and more. There was a significant crowd of reporters and other civilians, all with heightened interest to learn about the case. News had traveled fast that an FBI's Most Wanted had turned himself in. It had traveled even faster when they'd learned the local detective was off to prove his innocence. Hull came to stand between the tables where the attorneys would sit, but none were present. Malcolm had more than likely pulled the strings on that. He sat in the first row, eyes locked on Fisher.

Hull stopped his stride, allowing Lennox and me to catch up. Fisher stared down at him, his beard bushier than the mugshot and his face twisted in a very grim smile. I knew by the sour feeling in my stomach that he knew he was innocent. So did Hull. I think I did, too. Hull stood with his hands clasped behind his back, eyes on Fisher and nothing else. Once the attendees had settled down, the judge cleared his throat.

"Mr. Sheridan Hull, you have brought this court to order on request of Mr. Malcolm Hull to provide evidence in regards to Mr. Wayne Fisher's involvement in the triple-murder and rape case of 2009, in which Mr. Fisher was accused of said crimes and, prior to prosecution, escaped custody and has since been absent. What have you brought to present?" Hull stared at Fisher silently, and the man in the booth seemed to nod slowly. After almost ten seconds of complete silence, Hull looked forward.

"On October 12th, 2009, Ms. Victoria Ogi made her way to Ray's Place Bar, as she did on most weekends, and proceeded to intoxicate herself. Also present at this bar were Mr. Christian Kaiser and Mr. Wayne Fisher, neither of whom had direct contact with Ms. Ogi. After forty-five minutes, Mr. Fisher left the bar, shortly followed by Ms. Ogi and Mr. Kaiser. This is all the documented footage has to tell us.

"What is not documented, however, is far more interesting. Ms. Ogi, in her intoxicated state, managed to find herself two blocks away from the bar at an abandoned warehouse, where she hoped to take refuge until the morning. Upon her arrival, Mr. Kaiser identified her inebriated state and sought to use it to his advantage. He convinced her to engage in sexual intercourse within the dark depths of the warehouse and would have continued if not for a timely interruption.

"That interruption came from Mr. Brandt Reaves, a police officer on the Los Angeles Police Department who, in his boredom, had left the premises he was assigned to and started an independent search for any possible trouble. He stumbled upon the ongoing sexual activities and too noted that Ms. Ogi was intoxicated and proceeded to question Mr. Kaiser on his actions. Mr. Kaiser was reluctant to answer, but Ms. Ogi was disturbed by the interruption, having been accustomed to sex due to her new line of work, that being an informal prostitute. Ms. Ogi had found herself short on money and believed using her body to make her way to be the best option.

"Ms. Ogi's reaction to Mr. Reaves's interruption was less-than-pleasant. She lashed out at the officer, who proceeded to attempt and keep both her and Mr. Kaiser at bay by presenting his sidearm, a Glock 22 pistol. Ms. Ogi then resorted to a more violent method of repelling Mr. Reaves, and in the ensuing struggle, a round was fired from Mr. Reaves's pistol and Ms. Ogi collapsed backwards on a wooden pallet, a bullet having passed through her head, a round now lodged in the pallets behind her, and her blood sprayed across the wall.

"Mr. Kaiser witnessed the entire thing from a somewhat-dazed position, but upon Ms. Ogi's death, he retaliated, striking out at the officer and knocking his gun away. Mr. Kaiser eventually reached the gun and, rather than shooting the officer, proceeded to throw it on top of the nearest pallet stack, over four meters away and out of reach of the officer. Mr. Reaves then attempted to subdue Mr. Kaiser with physical force, aiming to cause him to pass out so that he could properly report the situation. His judgment of strength, however, was distorted as a result of the accidental murder, and Mr. Reaves inevitably caused Mr. Kaiser to suffocate and die rather than simply pass out.

"Mr. Reaves realized what had occurred and acknowledged that it had been by his hand. Knowing that otherwise, the scene would not be found, he called the police, then proceeded to slit his own throat out of guilt for the events that had taken place. Mr. Fisher arrived on the scene by chance before the police, and in a burst of confusion, picked up the knife Mr. Reaves had used to take his own life. The police then arrived and discovered Mr. Fisher with the knife and bruised knuckles, which had been bruised not from a physical ordeal but rather from his work earlier that day.

"Mr. Fisher was charged with the murder of Mr. Reaves, Mr. Kaiser, and Ms. Ogi, as well as the sexual assault of Ms. Ogi. Hours after being captured, he escaped custody, adding flight from prosecution to the list of charges. Mr. Fisher, however, was wrongfully accused. His presence at the bar was not tied directly to the murders of the individuals. His hands were bruised from his employment rather than a physical altercation. His discharged gun was a personal item of ownership, and not one used to fire the bullet found in the pallets. His possession of the knife was circumstantial. And the seminal traces were genetically tied to Mr. Fisher, but also to his twin brother, Mr. Christian Kaiser."

The entire courtroom was silent, save for the soft chuckling of Fisher. Hull held his chin high, his mouth slightly ajar.

"Mr. Fisher is innocent of the present charges against him," the detective said, his tone distant and unattached. He kept his eyes on Fisher, whose chuckling had increased in volume.

"Well done, Mr. Hull, well done," the former criminal said. "I told you I was innocent."

"Yes, well done indeed," Malcolm said from our right. "Good job at completely defacing two major faces of security and justice to this country."

"And now the children?" Sheridan said, disregarding his brother's snide comment.

"Ah yeah, the children," Fisher said, propping his feet up on the box. "You'll find all ten of 'em in an abandoned barn twenty miles south of town. Get there quick enough and you just might save 'em from dehydration." I glanced back at Lennox, who nodded and turned for the doorway. Sheridan's focus remained on Fisher, who was laughing heartily now.

"Sheridan, I think we should—" I started, but Fisher interrupted.

"Well, judge, I guess you better let me go. Looks like the sniffer dog found everything I needed to walk free," the man said, hands clasped behind his head. I could hear reporters and other people standing up and moving into the center aisle behind us. I glanced back to see Malcolm resting his head against his right hand, his thumb and index finger pressed against his cheek and temple, respectively.

"However."

The single word caused the entire room to go silent, Fisher to cease his chuckling, and the reporters to stop moving. Malcolm moved his hand away from his face. I turned to look at Hull, and even from the side, I could see the distinctive glint in his deep shamrock-colored right eye.

"On October 12th, 2009, Mr. Wayne Fisher set out with a very distinct goal in mind: to frame his twin brother, one he had despised from when they were very young yet kept his true feelings reserved. Mr. Fisher knew that his brother frequented Ray's Place Bar, and therefore went there to wait for him. He also knew his brother had a history of extra-relationship meet-ups with various women, and knew that, with the right timing, he could perfectly frame his brother, or better yet, kill him outright and remove the problem altogether.

"Mr. Fisher waited in the bar and quickly noticed the presence of a young Ms. Victoria Ogi, a woman who seemed promiscuous in nature and very accepting of anything that came her way the more intoxicated she got. Mr. Fisher silently paid a patron at the bar to keep anonymously providing Ms. Ogi with drinks, watching as she became more and more inebriated, and specifically, less able to hold proper judgment. Fisher then saw his twin brother arrive and, being the sex-driven heathen that he was, immediately attract to the woman, but not enough to approach her. He instead elected to silently watch and wait.

"It did not take long for the girl to become adequately inebriated, and eventually Mr. Fisher had his tip slip her a note along with a final drink. The note told her who he was and suggested she join him at an abandoned warehouse two blocks away for a promised enjoyable time. He then departed from the bar and waited until Ms. Ogi left as well, then watched as his brother, Mr. Kaiser, followed her the two blocks to the warehouse. Ms. Ogi arrived at the warehouse with Mr. Kaiser in tow, who initially spoke with her and, her being beyond judgment, assumed he was her liaison and proceeded to the promised 'enjoyable time.'

"Fisher left the warehouse, knowing his time was limited. He found a police car parked in a lot, the one belonging to Mr. Brandt Reaves who was parked in his assigned location. Mr. Fisher informed Mr. Reaves of what he believed to be a sexual assault in progress. Mr. Reaves departed with Mr. Fisher on foot, who, upon reaching the warehouse, elected to vanish into the shadows while Mr. Reaves confronted the two. Ms. Ogi lashed out at the officer, who had pulled his gun in an attempt to scare the two. The gun misfired, but did not make contact with Ms. Ogi. The bullet passed harmlessly by and lodged itself within the wooden pallets behind her.

"Simultaneously with Mr. Reaves' shot, however, was a second one, fired by Mr. Fisher from the nearby shadows. The shot was fired from a low point, passing through Ms. Ogi's chin, up through her brain, and exiting the top of her skull. The bullet then traveled up and into a dark corner of the warehouse ceiling where it remained. Mr. Kaiser lashed out at the officer, who in the process of defending himself, accidentally killed the former man. It should be noted, however, that Mr. Kaiser possessed an already-present heart murmur, one that was excited by the gunshot and worsened by the lack of air.

"Mr. Kaiser died not as a result of strangulation, but as a result of heart failure. Mr. Reaves, however, was unaware of this, and proceeded to slit his own throat and take his own life. Mr. Fisher emerged from his hiding place, quick to throw Mr. Reaves's pistol on top of the nearby pallet stack and ensure that Mr. Kaiser was dead. He then took up the knife and waited for the police that he knew would eventually arrive. Sure enough, officers found him at the scene, knife in hand, bruised knuckles. The perfect suspect."

All the while, Fisher's smile had slowly been disappearing. But Hull wasn't done.

"Fisher had planned it all from the start. A simple way to frame or kill his hated brother without personally getting his hands dirty. He knew of his brother's continued adultery and knew he would take the bait. He knew that with the proper scenario, his brother would seek to engage in intercourse with the girl. And he knew that, at the right moment, he would be able to frame his brother for sexual assault.

"The gun pulled by Mr. Reaves was an unforeseen circumstance, but Mr. Fisher quickly adapted by shooting the woman and ensuring that Mr. Reaves would assume he had done it. He also knew of his own brother's tendency for violence, and watched as Mr. Reaves and Mr. Kaiser fought, ending with Mr. Kaiser's death and Mr. Reaves's suicide. He was found and charged for all the wrong reasons. Mr. Fisher is, instead, guilty of the murder of Ms. Victoria Ogi, as well as the framing of both Mr. Christian Kaiser and Mr. Brandt Reaves."

The entire courtroom kept its silence. Fisher's face had gone pale, his legs had fallen from the box side, and his hands now rested in his lap. He stared forward at Hull with his mouth open, his bottom lip trembling and head subtly moving side to side. Malcolm's initial look of sadness was replaced by a definite look of pride. Even the judge had a look of genuine surprise at the turn of events. Hull gave a curt smile at Fisher before turning, nodding at me, then walking down the aisle way and out of the courtroom.

*

Hull and I stood in the lobby to the courtroom as Lennox escorted the ten children into the building. All of them looked weak, but none of them were hurt too bad. Lennox nodded at us as he passed by, Hull glancing down at the children with mild interest. I nudged him softly with my elbow, nodding down at the kids.

"You have to admit, helping them has to make you feel somewhat good about yourself."

"I proved a man's innocence and guiltiness all in the course of five minutes. That is enough to make me feel a sense of inner pride."

I chuckled. "I suppose so."

Once the children had left, Malcolm entered the lobby, followed by his posse. He came over to us, shaking my hand and merely nodding at Hull.

"Excellent work, Sheridan. I knew you would not let me down."

"You knew nothing, Malcolm. It's my job to deduce these things."

Malcolm smiled, then glanced back at the courtroom. "Bring him out."

The remaining members of his posse exited the room, escorting a once-again handcuffed Wayne Fisher. Fisher had a look of absolute hatred on his face, as well as... betrayal, I would say. They walked towards us slowly, and Fisher kept his gaze locked on Hull. Hull knew the man was watching him but still faced forward. Part of me was concerned the man may attempt and attack. When Fisher was within a meter of us, he stopped. Two members of Malcolm's posse drew their pistols.

"Calm down," Fisher barked, his voice cracking. "I just have something for the detective."

"And that is?" Sheridan asked, finally allowing his eyes to rest on Fisher.

The man looked over at one of the posse members. "Slip your hand down my shirt and pull out the envelope taped to my chest. Don't pull too hard, any chest hair comes off and it's your head." The man showed hesitation, first looking at Malcolm. The older Hull sighed and shrugged. The man slowly stuck his hand into Fisher's shirt, then gave a quick tug, pulling a white envelope from within. The exterior was completely blank. Fisher nodded at Sheridan. "That's for you, Detective."

Sheridan took the envelope from the man, then put it behind his back in his clasped hands and returned to looking at nothing. The posse escorted Fisher from the lobby. Malcolm gave a glance at us, a nod, then turned to follow. I looked at Hull, who now held the envelope before him, turning it over slowly.

"Careful," I warned, "you don't know what he could have put inside that."

"I doubt it's of any danger," he replied, peeling away the top of the envelope. He pulled out a single sheet of beige-colored paper, folded neatly and pressed with a red sealant. He softly peeled the sealant away, tucking it inside the envelope before opening the folded paper. It read:

To Mr. S. Hull,

Thank you for your regards. I'm quite the fan. Well done on the Fisher case.

-M

Hull looked over the letter several times before folding it and looking up.

"'M?'" I asked, eyes still on the paper.

"'M,'" he repeated.

"What does it mean?"

He remained silent for a long moment before gulping. "It means I have a fan." He tucked the letter into his inner coat pocket, then walked out of the lobby. I followed him, exiting the courthouse just in time to see the police car with Fisher inside drive away. Hull stood at the middle of the steps, looking down the long road that made up the spine of Newfield.

"Are you worried?" I asked, trying to match his gaze.

"I'm not sure," he said, his voice somewhat cold and distant. His mouth barely moved as he spoke. "I'm not sure."

THE CASE OF CAMPUS CRIME

Veronica Faith Daemon sat at the only chair visible in the dark room, eyes watching the constantly-changing array of computer screens ahead of her. There were nine screens in total, and right now, four of them displayed security cameras from an airport, two of them displayed information readouts, and the remaining three were screening televised news broadcasts. All of the screens were focused on one person: Wayne Fisher. She tapped a key on the illuminated console before her, maximizing one of the security camera screens. It showed the man, Fisher, being escorted by four police officers onto a military-issue plane.

She tapped the console again, reducing the screen's size. With a third tap, she brought up one of the information screens. It displayed a complete list of information in regards to Fisher, from his date and place of birth to his dietary habits. One of the top information options was "Status," and it currently read "Yellow." She tapped the option on a glass, miniature version of the maximized screen directly attached to the console with her finger, sending a pulse from the glass up to the screens. The word started to blink.

"Fisher is now en route to the Louisiana State Penitentiary," she said, glancing over her shoulder. Though she could see nothing, she knew there were two things hiding in the darkness behind her: a large table, and a man. The table's contents she had never seen before, and technically, the same could be said in regards to the man. He was always hidden underneath his cape and hood. She'd always seen it as dramatic, but her boss was not one to do things without making a show. He enjoyed watching people dance while he pulled the strings.

"Good," a hoarse voice replied from the shadows, sending the usual chill down her spine and bringing an icy feeling to her insides. "Let him arrive, then have the sleepers eliminate him."

"Yes, Sir," Daemon replied, giving a glance at the monitors. One word, one that had been specifically highlighted, stood out to her. "What about Hull?"

There was a long pause. The technology used by the console, the glass, and the screens that illuminated a small section of the room were completely devoid of sound. And the lack of any audible breathing from her employer was also somewhat concerning.

But only somewhat.

"He passed the test," the voice replied. Shortly after, a horrible sound came from the darkness, like someone taking a knife to a chalkboard and dragging it across the full length. "Let's conduct another."

"Yes, Sir," she said, turning to face the screen. With one keystroke, the word "Yellow" vanished, and was soon replaced with a very definite "Red."

*

"*No.*"

The word followed the sound of approximately ten keys on a piano being smashed at once. I glanced over my shoulder to the once-empty corner of the flat, now occupied by a very large and ornate piano that Hull had acquired about two weeks ago. He currently sat at the piano with a pencil above his ear, a sheet of notes in front of him, and his phone resting on the side of his stool. He took the pencil and erased furiously, removing an entire row of notes.

It had been one month since the Fisher case. Lennox had informed us a couple of days ago that the court processions had finally been wrapped up, and Fisher was sentenced to life in prison at Louisiana State Penitentiary. The space between that case and now, however, had not been filled by another case, and it started to show with Hull. I discovered just how plaguing boredom was to him, and how much the mindset really got to him. Where when I found myself bored, I could easily distract myself, Hull was much more complex. Much, much more.

In his month-long spree of boredom, he had decided to take up an array of new hobbies. The first had started a week after the Fisher case had closed, when the piano had arrived. I don't know where Hull had gotten it from, or how he had paid for it, or how he'd managed to get them to even deliver it. But he did. And since then, he was determined to spend half the day trying to learn to play it. The key word, however, was *trying*. For his skills as a detective, he had a lot of work to be done with the piano.

The second hobby was something I extremely disapproved of because of the obvious safety hazard it caused. Hull was okay with a gun, that much was obvious. But he found some level of fascination in a more archaic way of combat. I knew for fact he was damn good when it came to a physical entanglement, but the new hobby was more instantaneous. Someone had suggested he try archery, and from there, the walls of the flat had only degraded in quality. He preferred to pin his targets on the poor sides of our home and cover them with puncture holes from his arrows. And because his aim wasn't swell the first day, more than just the wall was hit. Mrs. Hanson was none too pleased to hear about the vase.

Today, I had managed to wake up before Hull and take the arrows, hiding them in the back of the pantry. The man rarely ate as it was, so I knew he wouldn't bother digging past the cans of soup and broth just to find the arrows. If anything, he'd find something else to shoot from the bow. He'd settled in to the piano and started transcribing the notes to different songs. So far, he had managed to somewhat-successfully transcribe both "My Heart Will Go On" and something from the country singer Taylor Swift. Now I had no idea what he was attempting to transcribe. I only knew that he was having little success, since he had exclaimed "no" and smashed the keys a half-dozen times in the past ten minutes.

"*No*," he said again, running his hands across the keys. I glanced away from my paper and over my shoulder at the man, seeing him start scratching away at the note sheet again.

"Exactly what song are you on now?" I asked. He slammed his phone up on top of the piano, swiped across the screen, and pressed play. The song "Clocks" started to play. Whatever he had just been playing was most certainly *not* that. "Yeah, you have some work to do."

"Shut up, John."

"Why do you keep transcribing other songs? Why not write your own?"

"I have nothing to provide to the musical world in regards to my own pieces."

"So you think."

"So I know."

"You always have to look on the 'I have nothing to give other than my deductive reasoning' side, don't you?"

"No." Once again he slammed on the piano, knocking the pencil from his ear. He rested his head on the keys, sending out another unpleasant noise.

"Maybe you could take a walk to clear—"

"*I need a case!*"

I looked over at him, slightly alarmed. He looked back at me, taking heavy breaths through his nose and staring me down with wide eyes. I knew he was agitated and not in the mood for poking and prodding. Unfortunately for him, I had to make up for his incessant, self-centered attitude by being snarky and sarcastic. It created a balance to the order of the flat. He rested his face in his hands, rubbing at his cheeks furiously.

"The time off is stagnating," he said, his lips presumably pressed together by his hands. "It's as if with each passing day, more and more of my mentality breaks away and every fleeting moment takes longer and longer. Not even the piano or the archery can suffice to distract long enough."

"Especially if you don't have the arrows," I said, a tone of pride in my voice.

"You hid them in the pantry."

My eyes shot back to him. "How did you—"

"I need a case, John."

My focus moved to the left, towards the pantry. "I swore there was no way—"

"I *need* a case, John."

"I know you weren't awake—"

"*I need a case, John.*"

"Unless you already checked—"

"*I NEED A CASE, JOHN.*"

I returned my gaze to him. It's not that I'd been ignoring him. I suppose it was me seeing the sense of him actually needing something in his life rather than himself. I cocked my brow at him before setting my paper down and picking up a stack of letters.

"Well, lucky for you we have plenty of people looking for help," I said, tearing the first letter open.

"I perused them, none of them caught my eye."

"How could you have looked at the letters? They weren't opened."

"I hardly need to read the letters to know their level of interest."

I looked over the first letter. "This one's a woman writing with concerns about her husband. She thinks his business trips are actually him cheating."

"She's right."

I peered at him with narrowed eyes before softly tearing the second letter open. "This one is a kid who thinks his... website coding is being stolen by another developer...?"

"It's not, though he is stealing his own code from another website."

"Two men found dead in an alleyway on Northern."

"Bar fight gone wrong."

"Dog ran off with a wedding ring and—"

"Buried it under the snapdragons."

I tossed the letters to the ground. "Are you joking me? How can you possibly know all of those?"

He gazed at me, a small hint of his signature glint appearing. "The woman's husband is cheating on her and she knows it, not by the business trips but rather by her own confirmation. She seeks my help to instead make it out as if I uncovered it and she is allowed to accuse him with true evidence rather than whatever she has found, resulting in her shaky handwriting and damp-from-tears envelope. The web developer obviously stole the code, because the only reason he would accuse someone else, and type his letter, is because he is afraid of someone else discovering what he has done, and sought not to write the letter by hand to prevent fictitious things like 'lie detectors' that scan your handwriting from finding him out.

"The bar fight is quite obvious, because it was on the news, and the letter was not sent by Lennox but rather by the concerned and completely oblivious girlfriend of one of the men, who had known of the tension between the two men and assumed one had murdered the other and then taken his own life. She is right and wrong, they had tension and killed each other in a drunken rage. She would have known that had she read the papers or watched the news, but judging by her inability to even write our address correctly, I highly doubt she is intelligent enough to keep watch of reliable, or otherwise, news sources.

"The dog is by far the easiest. The ring goes missing at the same time the man's girlfriend started planting snapdragons. Why? Because snapdragons are some of the only flowers that can survive the cold of March and are a popular piece of flora in this region. The girl would have been in the process of planting the flowers and would have seen the freshly-covered area from the dog's digging as a perfect place to plant. How do I know the dog buried it there? Because the man said the dog has a habit of burying things, but has no idea where to look. Obvious."

I ran my hands through my hair, glancing down at the remaining letters. "No point in opening any of the others, then. I took some of the lost posters from the market board, too, but I doubt you'll care for those."

Hull stood, walking over to look over the pile of paper posters. He sifted through them before stopping at one that had the words "LOST BIKE" written across the top. He held the paper for several seconds before bringing it close to his chest.

"I'll take it."

"What?"

"The bike case, I'll take it."

My jaw dropped. "Of all the things sent, you want to find some kid's *bike*?"

"Yes. Why not?"

"*Why?*"

"The kid would like his bicycle back. I am happy to assist." He ran off out of my line of sight, probably bound for his room.

"You're not seriously going to occupy your boredom by going on a bike hunt, are you?" I shouted back as I stood.

"But the bicycle is missing!"

"*Who cares if the bicycle is missing?!*"

*

Hull and I walked across the campus of Newfield University, the detective taking in deep breaths as if he were actually enjoying the fresh air. Granted, he hadn't stepped foot outside of the flat in two weeks, so this truly was his first burst of fresh air in a while. The campus was a beautiful sight, though. Despite the snow we had suffered from earlier in the week, the campus looked bustling with life, the trees all regaining their leaves and daffodils lining many of the walkways. I'd never visited the campus before, but I had heard good things about it.

Hull had made sure to call ahead and inform the kid, Carter Tyler, that we were on our way to investigate. The kid must have recognized Hull's name, because the excitement he expressed was audible enough for me to hear from across the taxi. He had agreed to let us come to his dormitory, where he would meet us at the doorway and take us to where the bike had been stolen. The campus was small enough to allow a casual walk from one end to another. And, of course, it wasn't hard to make the trek when we had to walk past the sorority houses.

We arrived at the dormitory to find the kid, nineteen years young and definitely showing the age. He had wide, hopeful eyes that had reminiscent bags under them from late night study sessions. He watched Hull and me approach with contained anticipation.

"Thank you so much for coming to help, I never thought of all people, you would see my poster," Tyler said, eyes locked on Hull, admiration pouring from his very essence.

"Yes, take us to where the cycle was stolen," Hull said, surveying the campus.

"Sure," the kid replied enthusiastically, starting off towards the center of campus. Hull and I followed behind him, Hull still observing the surroundings. There was something more to him taking this case, something he wasn't telling me. That wasn't exactly a new concept.

"What can you tell us about the situation?" I asked the boy as we walked.

"I was just getting some lunch from the cafe, and I thought it would be okay if I just left my bike on the rack. I didn't bring my lock, so stupid of me. I was inside for only two minutes, and when I came back outside, it was gone. Nobody saw it happen, and their security cameras don't face the racks."

I saw Hull keep from giving off a chuckle by choking it back. Obviously the theft was Tyler's own fault, and it took every fiber of Hull's body not to flat-out call the kid on it. We continued onward for almost a minute before reaching the cafe.

"Those racks?" he asked, slyly walking over to the black half-hoops in the ground and running his hand along them. He stopped at the center rack, then walked several paces to the left before reaching the sidewalk. He looked down the road, then up the road, then back down. He looked back at us, narrowing his eyes to stare at the racks. His gaze followed the sidewalk to the road, and finally, he locked his gaze on something down the road before smirking.

"What?" Tyler said, walking up to look down the road.

"I will need some time to finish my investigation, but I assure you," Hull replied as he started walking away, "I will find your bicycle." I moved past Tyler to catch up to Hull while the kid watched us, amazement and confusion no doubt overwhelming his feelings. Hull and I walked a block in silence before I decided to speak.

"Why did you take this case," I asked as we continued forward.

Hull sniffed. "Two days ago, there was a seminar held in the primary auditorium on campus in regards to the significant decline in coral life as a result of a certain, mutated strand of Alphaherpesvirinae. The virus has been spreading rapidly through the Caribbean and causing the death of over half the population of coral. In response, the scientists here at Newfield University set to working on finding a cure. This seminar was held to showcase the healing qualities of the cure and announce its imminent administration to the ocean waters."

"A strand of *herpes* is killing coral?"

"Yes, now pay attention. The scientists here found a cure and showcased it just two days ago. The boy's bicycle also went missing two days ago. I know for fact the two are linked."

"Why?"

"Why not?"

"I hate when you do that."

He stopped at a crosswalk. "I need you to go talk to the campus police, find out any information you can from the report the boy filed."

"What about you?"

He looked up and down the road before focusing on me. "I intend to ask around. Some of the best sources of information are unknowing eyewitnesses." With that, he marched off across the road. I watched him reach the opposite crosswalk and start forward, my mind at a halt. I had no idea where the campus police office was on the campus, but he didn't seem to care. I gave a sigh, looked up at the nearest building and, with some faith, started off in the direction I hoped would take me to the police.

*

Hull walked along the sidewalk slowly, eyes moving from person to person that moved on their own paths through the quad center of the campus. He held his hands in his pockets softly, tilting his head back ever-so-slightly and pressing his scarf against his neck. He could feel the slight breeze rolling into the canyon-esque quad brush past his ankles, offering a contrast to his far-too-hot upper body. The trees above him swayed gently, their branches sweeping across each other and creating a sound that was almost peaceful.

That was, of course, most certainly not the case.

He glanced up at one of the trees, watching a squirrel jump from the extended branch of one to another. From his peripheral vision, he could also see five figures moving in unison behind him. Four of them were engaged in conversation, two males and two females. The fifth, however, was not part of the group, nor did he belong on the campus. His horrible attempt to wear clothing that allowed him to "fit in" rather made him stand out like a neon sign in the dark. He walked directly behind the group of students, eyes locked on Hull.

Hull returned his vision forward, spotting the back of a familiar head. The person's hair was a fine strawberry blonde and reached just below her shoulders. She wore a gray sweatshirt and a presumably held a book, or phone, either of which currently occupied her attention. She was far shorter than Hull, but only younger by about six years. He increased his walking speed, not noticeably, but enough to catch up to her before she had turned the corner to walk along another road. He walked behind her for several seconds before clearing his throat.

"Decide not to go home for break, then?" he said. The girl turned with a slight jump, looking up at him with surprise. Her eyes were a brilliant blue, the same as her father's. The look of surprise quickly diminished to that of delight.

"Oh wow, Uncle Sherrie! What are you doing here?" the girl said, giving Hull a hug.

He first flinched at the contact, then very briefly returned the embrace. Bailey Hull was, after all, his only niece. "Something interesting is happening here. I like to put myself in the middle of such situations." He nodded forward. "You were heading somewhere?"

"Oh yeah," she replied, turning. He walked at her side, keeping his eyes forward. "Just going to meet up with a friend. What kind of interesting thing?"

"You have heard of Mr. Carter Tyler's missing bicycle, I presume."

"Jeez, you're here for that? That sounds so boring."

"You would think so. Would you happen to know anything about it?"

"Besides the fact that he's put up his fliers everywhere on campus and put it in the school paper?"

"So the cycle means a lot to him."

She laughed. "I guess. How's that guy you're rooming with? Dad said he's a doctor."

"Dr. Walker is fine. He is here with me, helping with the investigation."

"As he seems to do all the time, right? Dad said you guys worked together on that case a month ago."

Sheridan gave a short smile. "We do seem to make quite the team."

"So you're just here for a missing bike, huh? Nothing else?"

"Actually," Sheridan said, slowing his pace, "there is one other thing."

Bailey stopped. "What's that?"

Sheridan spun, grabbing the lunging arm of the man he had seen earlier as the attacker moved to stick a knife in Bailey's back. He twisted the man's arm and pushed him away, then spun to his niece.

"Stay back, call the police," he ordered before turning. The man had recovered from the surprise defense and was charging again, holding the knife ready to stab Sheridan now. The detective sidestepped to avoid the blood-hungry blade, sending his palm into the man's chin and knocking him off-direction. The man collided with the ground, his knife spinning away. Sheridan dove for the knife, but was too slow. The man scrambled to the side, kicking Sheridan in the gut and sending him back. Sheridan turned the energy into a backwards roll, coming up on his feet as the assailant reached the knife.

The man stood again, wiping a trail of blood from his mouth. He feigned left, then once again ran forward, this time going low. Sheridan jumped, shoving his foot out and catching the man's elbow. There was a definitive *snap* from the bone as the man collapsed to his back, knife flying into the air. Sheridan adeptly reached up, grabbing the knife's handle in the process. In just as swift a motion, he turned the blade in his hand and smashed it down, going clean through the man's palm and sticking into the crevice between the concrete panels. The man yelped in pain, giving a very minute pull to his hand before realizing how deep the knife was.

Sheridan took a step to the man's side, looking down at his face. There was nothing remarkably heinous about the attacker, save for the weapon that now protruded from his bleeding hand. He was young, maybe two or three years younger than Sheridan. He wore college-related clothes, but too much to be an actual student. He twisted and turned in throbs of pain, trying his best not to move his hand.

"Now," Sheridan said, clasping his hands behind his back, "you will explain why you followed me."

"You know why I was following you," the man replied through clenched teeth.

"Ah," Sheridan replied, walking around the man's figure slowly. "So, if my presumptions are correct, you are an employee of Chimaera, sent to follow me and attack my niece. How quaint, to know the depths your organization is willing to go."

"Just get the knife out," he shot back, the blood covering his entire hand. Sheridan stopped and looked down at him, eyes narrowed. He lifted his left foot and pressed it down on the butt of the knife. The man's back arched in pain as the knife was pressed maybe only a centimeter deeper into his skin.

"Who from Chimaera sent you?" Sheridan demanded, keeping pressure on the knife.

"You're crazy!" the man yelled. Sheridan glanced around, seeing that most students had left the area. Bailey sat against the wall several meters away from them, talking in to a phone and watching with wide eyes. He knew she wouldn't say what he was doing.

He pressed the blade deeper. "*Who* sent you?"

"*Stop it!*"

"*Who sent you?*"

"*Moriarty!*"

Sheridan's chin moved up slightly, as if he had gasped. He looked down at the man with wide eyes, taking his foot from the knife handle. He turned around, vision seeming to blur at the edges. Only two seconds passed before he spun again, foot coming up. His heel slammed down on the handle, pushing both blade and handle clean through the man's hand. The man jerked forward, free hand slapping to the bloody hand while he screamed in pain. Sheridan stepped back, eyes on the crimson knife still planted in the ground.

"Moriarty," he whispered, every detail of the weapon coming into focus.

"Uncle Sherrie?"

He turned, seeing Bailey's frightened face. She held the phone in her limp hand, watching him with shaking eyes.

"Did you call the police?"

"Yes, but—"

"Wait here for them." He looked back to see their assailant unconscious. "Tell them what happened and that I will be at the police station to answer questions."

"But Uncle Sherrie—"

"No, Bailey. Keep safe. Watch for any other potential attackers." With that, he started away, not acknowledging the blood on his shoes, or the bottom of his coat, or even his hands. Every essence of his thoughts was focused on one thing, a simple word.

Moriarty.

*

I was sitting in the lobby while an officer retrieved the theft file for me when Hull walked in. I haven't felt that level of fear upon seeing someone since my time in Iraq. When he walked in, blood was located in several places on him: his shoes, his coat, his hand. His eyes were wide, not with fear, but with... something. Realization. Revelation. The look someone gets during the climax of a movie, I suppose. And for something to have affected him to that point, I knew it was bad.

I stood and rushed to him, but one of the officers beat me to him.

"Sir, I'm going to have to ask you to come with me," the officer said, extending one arm towards Hull and another towards his firearm.

"Stand down!" I exclaimed, nudging the officer out of the way. "He's with me." The officer stepped back, giving me a nod. I moved in front of Hull. "What happened?"

"A man attacked my niece and me."

"Your niece? Is she okay?"

"She's fine. The man is injured. The police will have found him by now."

"What did you do to him?"

The wideness to his eyes diminished in size. He glanced at me, the hint of a smile appearing at the corners of his mouth. "I protected my niece and myself."

I sighed, knowing all-too well what he meant. "Why did he attack you?"

"Chimaera sent him. It makes sense now, Walker." He let out a rattling breath. "Oh how it makes sense."

"What makes sense?"

"Get the police report. Meet me outside." He turned to walk away.

"Uh, Hull?" He stopped, glancing back. "You're covered in blood. You can't just walk outside like that. I can't imagine how you even walked across campus." He shrugged, then continued out. I gave another sigh, waited for the report, and finally joined him.

"He said his employer's name," Hull said as we sat down in the taxi.

"Oh?"

He blinked a few times. "Moriarty."

I wrinkled my brow at the name. "Moriarty?"

"It will make sense when we get home."

"How?"

He took his time replying before turning his focus to me. "I have been expecting this for quite some time now." He remained silent for the rest of the drive.

Upon arriving at the flat, Hull immediately charged up into his room. I set the police report down on the table and started flipping through it. Of course nothing significant stood out; it was a bike theft, not some grand daylight robbery scheme. Still, it had attracted Hull, and I knew he wouldn't give up until he'd found the bike, or more importantly, solved some hidden crime I had yet to be filled in on. When he finally emerged from his room an hour later, he was cleaned and holding a bottle of pills. He set the bottle down on the table and moved towards the bookshelf. I grabbed the bottle and read the prescription.

"Did you just take these?" I asked, eyes still going over the information.

"Yes."

I set my elbows down on the table, pointing the bottle at his back. "This is Ambien. These are sleeping pills."

"They help me think."

"Think about what?"

Hull was now at the window. "He's making a game of it all."

"He?" I repeated, looking up. "He who?"

"Moriarty."

"And this Moriarty is the person who sent you the letter? The one Fisher gave you?"

"Without a doubt."

I ran my hands through my hair, knowing that if Hull was right, and he often was, this wasn't good at all. This man had called himself a fan in the letter, and Hull said the only kind of fan a man of his profession made was a lethal one.

"So what do we do?" I asked after an uncomfortable silence.

Hull seemed to spin something around in his hand before turning to me. "We head back to the university and we complete the investigation."

My jaw dropped. "Seriously? You still want to find the missing bike?"

"The investigation is in regards to the person planning to sabotage the aquatic Alphaherpesvirinae cure. The bicycle will come with its completion."

"...the what?"

"Someone stole the bicycle on their way to the seminar. They stole it because they were late. The auditorium was a straight shot from the bicycle racks, and there were minor signs of the tracks having gone in that direction. The thief was not in a rush solely because of their absence but because of their importance to the announcement, perhaps one of the creators of the cure. We will need to investigate the four professors behind the cure's inception: Charles Oake, Kenneth Elem, Torin Birsch, and Meredith Rowen."

*

Hull and I sat in the office of a Dr. Charles Oake, the first professor, and scientist, Hull had selected to speak with. The man had left us for only a minute, and shockingly enough, Hull had remained in his seat. I had taken the time to observe the room for myself from my seat. It was a standard office, several stacks of books lining the same wall as the window that looked out on one of the many fields on campus. The office was on the third story of the science administration building. Besides Dr. Oake's desk, there was a coat rack, a closet, several filing cabinets, and some very dirty boots.

Dr. Oake reentered the room from a side office, running a hand through his blond-silver hair as he took his seat. He looked to be in his early forties, but time and dedication to his work had certainly taken its toll. His fingers were frail, but when he went to write something, his hand went steady. He wrapped his fingers together, rested his hands on his desk, and smiled at us.

"So, what can I do for you gentlemen?" he asked, his smile revealing tainted teeth.

Hull sat with his left leg crossed over his right and his back relaxed. "We are conducting some research in regards to the cure recently announced for aquatic Alphaherpesvirinae. We know you held a significant role in this and would like to receive your own opinion on things."

"Did you attend the seminar?" the professor asked.

"Unfortunately, we did not."

"Ah. Well, I suppose that's for the best, the seminar could have been much better." He grabbed several pieces of paper from the side of his desk and handed it to Hull and I. "The Alphaherpesvirinae cure took two years to complete. When we realized what was killing off so many of the coral species, we set to the creation of the cure. Not only would curing the strain of the virus help the coral, we could use the development in a cure for herpes in other species.

"Drs. Elem, Birsch, Rowen, and myself have been working on the cure for so long now, the success was starting to look dim. But finally, we found our breakthrough and finished the serum. We knew the impact this would have on the world, not just for aquatic life, but everyone. We scheduled the seminar, organized our information, and prepared. Though as I said, the seminar could have been better. There were last-minute adjustments made without the consent of the entire group that caused some concern."

"Interesting," Hull said as he leaned forward. "What kind of changes?"

"Small changes that don't need to be aired publicly."

"I see. Were you late to the seminar, Dr. Oake?"

The man looked at Hull with a puzzled face. "I don't recall being late. Why?"

Hull smirked. "Small details that don't need to be aired publicly." With that, he stood. I joined him in leaving the office. We stepped into the elevator together, but he did not push the button to take us down.

"Contemplating something?" I asked, looking from the panel to my companion.

"Just adding some time," he replied before pushing the button to take us to the lobby. The elevator moved slowly to the bottom before opening. We walked out into the lobby, but still Hull took his time. As the elevator door closed, he seemed to slow his pace to a step every few seconds. I turned to stare at him when I was almost three meters ahead of him.

"Adding time for what?" I questioned, watching him move at a crawl. He smirked again. It took him almost a minute to reach where I stood.

"This," he said, turning to face the elevator. I peered at it and felt a hint of surprise when it opened to let Dr. Oake exit. That small sense of surprise was greatly strengthened when I realized there was a gun in the man's hand. Hull dove to the side, taking me down in the process. We both slid behind the receptionist's desk as the professor fired, his shot ricocheting off the ground and shattering the glass that made up the entryway. I pressed my back against the desk while the receptionist hid where her legs would normally go. Hull, however, was still smiling.

I would have questioned, but the answer came through the now-open entry. Five police officers, led by Inspector Lennox, charged in, guns aimed forward.

"Police! Drop the gun!" Lennox yelled. I popped my head up and watched Oake drop his pistol and put his hands behind his head. Two of the officers moved to handcuff the man as Hull stood, walking over to Lennox.

"Impeccable timing, Inspector. I hoped you would arrive at the opportune moment," the detective said, giving Lennox's hand a shake.

"I wasn't sure what to make of you saying some professor planned to completely sabotage a cure for herpes, but walking in to find a man holding a gun is incriminating."

"That it is. If you go upstairs and search his office, you will find a bicycle in his closet. It belongs to Mr. Carter Tyler. I am sure he would appreciate having it returned," Hull said as he walked from the building. I followed behind him, amazed at everything that had just happened. After only ten steps, he gave a short chuckle. "I did not expect to pick the right man on the first go."

"How, though?"

"Oake was one of four who created the cure, but at the seminar, he was left uncredited due to his absence. Accidental move on his coworkers' part, but enough to set him off. He intended to sabotage the cure and defame the other professors. It would harm the coral, but I doubt he cared for them as it was. He was late to the seminar and attempted to make up for lost time by stealing a bicycle. The mud on his boots had left definitive prints in the dirt by the cafe, and it has yet to rain since."

"You figured that all out by walking into his office?"

"No, I figured that all out when my niece and I were attacked."

I stopped walking. "Not possible."

"When the man who attacked us revealed he worked with Chimaera, I knew it was inevitable for them to have a presence in the creation of this cure. Where Chimaera can hold power and influence, they will. It only required finding which member of the team was a Chimaera agent. Oake was not necessarily the one who would do their work, though. He was placed on the project, probably by Moriarty, perhaps by someone secondary, but the other professors were paid to exclude Oake from the cure credit. They sought to anger him and cause the crime." We started forward again.

"Why?"

"Because it is a game to Moriarty. He knew what to do to make the right reactions."

"Aren't you worried about Moriarty?"

This time Hull stopped. "No. I am merely curious." With that, we continued forward, both of our minds drifting to try and discover the root of the new problem. If Hull was right, this Moriarty had a far wider reach than I had anticipated when he had delivered the letter. And with Chimaera at his fingertips, the possibilities for what he could do were insurmountable. The man was a force to be apprehensive of. What he did, who he was. Even his name was something that could inspire fear.

Moriarty.

*

Daemon walked into the central intelligence room, no surprise filling her at it still being dark. She walked over to where her chair waited for her, taking her seat and moving the nine screens out of standby. All of them changed to show security cameras that watched two men walking. One of the men had dirty blond hair and wore a long, gray coat that went halfway between his knees and his ankles. He walked with a definite sense of pride, arms moving back and forth. All of the camera angles changed to show the same angle of both men walking away from the camera.

"Mr. Sheridan Hull and Dr. John Walker," her boss's voice said from behind her. She glanced back in his direction. She knew the names of both men; they'd been under surveillance for almost seven months now, Hull even longer. Her employer had become seemingly obsessed with keeping tabs on the two. Hull was a detective, and an impressive one at that. But why would her employer be concerned?

The screens changed to show camera angles inside the building the men were leaving. Several police officers were currently escorting a man from the building while another man escorted a bike from the elevator.

"Oake is captured, Sir," she said, bringing the angle that looked at the professor's face to full size.

"Status change," the voice replied from behind her. She nodded and changed to Oake's status page. With a swift keystroke, the word "Green" changed to a vivid "Yellow."

"What of the cure?"

"Birsch will handle its dispersal. We have nothing to gain nor lose by having the creatures of the sea immune to a trivial disease."

"Yes, Sir."

"And Veronica."

"Yes, Sir?" she asked, turning. Now a hint of surprise reached her as she was met with a black shape, the front of her employer's coat. He stood, staring down at her with his hood completely masking all of his facial features. She felt a slight chill go down her spine as she stared up into the vastness of the hood.

"Mr. Hull and Dr. Walker," Moriarty said, his voice frigid. "Update their statuses as well."

She hesitated. "To what, Sir?"

He gave a deep exhale. "In play."

THE MAN IN RED

"Come up on his right!"

I pressed down on the accelerator, swiftly passing a small white car and coming up behind the speeding vehicle. Hull sat in the passenger seat beside me, one hand clutching the shoulder of my seat and the other holding the dash. Ahead of us, a burgundy-colored van veered through traffic on the two lanes of road that made up part of the freeway, the very freeway that made up the spine of Newfield. Hull and I were in our own vehicle, one we'd gotten just a month ago after the taxi had become too much for me.

I suppose now would be the best time to bring things up to speed. Three months had passed since the reveal of Moriarty, and in the time since, we had heard nothing of the man. Surprisingly enough, Hull had not dedicated his every waking hour to finding this illusive person. In fact, it almost seemed like he'd pushed it from his mind entirely. Or so I'd hoped, until I realized just why he was taking such odd cases. In those three months, Hull had taken on almost a dozen assorted cases, all of them minor, but at the same time, all of them involving the crime syndicate group Chimaera. In a way, Hull was still tracking down Moriarty. He was simply taking the most indirect route possible.

The latest case was one that even I saw some merit in. A man had come to us just three days ago, distraught and frantic about the theft of a very valuable diamond from his home. The diamond was a rare one that shined a brilliant cyan color, and it had apparently been stolen from right under his nose while he was in a different room than his safe. Hull had immediately set out to find the diamond, and instead, he had managed to find the thief at a fast food restaurant with a van full of stolen goods. The man wasted no time in putting as much distance between his bounty and us as he could. Naturally, Hull had demanded we chase him down. And that led us to here and now, going down the freeway at almost eighty miles per hour, chasing a van filled with stolen goods.

And to think I moved to Newfield to settle down.

I felt a soft wind suddenly enter the Ford Expedition we'd bought and saw Hull unrolling the window. He stuck his right arm out, securing it on top of the car.

"Come up alongside him. Keep steady," the detective said, quickly scrambling through the open window and somehow managing to situate himself on the roof of the car. I matched speeds with the van, trying to watch both the thief, Hull through the sunroof, and potential traffic hazards ahead. I glanced up to see what I assumed was Hull sizing up his odds of successfully jumping from our car to the van. Sure enough, just moments later, he leapt from the top, and if not for my having been close to the van itself, I don't think he would have completed the jump.

The van veered to the right, coming towards me. I mimicked the motion, but realized it wasn't aimed at me. Hull scrambled to secure a hold on the roof of the van, but failed. I watched him slide down, and thankfully, the van's windows were not tinted, so I was able to see him grab on to the racks on the van's top and flatten his body against the driver door. The thief, a man probably in his late thirties with a hat used to hide his baldness, looked up at Hull with a snap of his neck. Moments later, he produced a gun, and it didn't look as if he had any intention of bothering to roll down his window.

He fired once, twice, three times at Hull, who adeptly rolled and ducked to avoid the bullets. The fourth one, however, caused the window to shatter entirely. Hull's grip on the top racks gave way and I watched his head vanish for just a moment. That moment ended with him suddenly being at the back of the van, his feet actually skimming the pavement of the freeway. He quickly hopped up on to the rear bumper, using the back windshield wiper for support. What he did next, I can't say, as I was forced to nearly smash into the curb median rather than rear-end the unsuspecting car ahead of me.

By the time I'd caught up, Hull was slowly sliding his way across the top of the van, careful to use the racks to avoid another swerve. I paralleled my speed with the van, still careful to watch the driver's intentions. It looked as if he assumed he was relatively safe, but I knew that was not the case. It's hard to miss someone climbing onto your vehicle, even at eighty miles per hour. I watched as Hull drew his gun and carefully took aim down, not at the driver, but at the front windshield. He fired one bullet, directly through the center of the glass. Then, with a swift motion, he turned the pistol in his hand and smashed the butt down into the glass, causing it to implode. The shards of glass covered the thief, who released the wheel to shield his eyes.

This release, however, came too close to the center curb median. The van bumped into the curb, causing the entire vehicle to buck. Hull flew up and off to the right, barely managing to grab the racks and secure himself on the passenger side. He released one hand from the rack, causing his body to twist. His back slammed into the rear passenger door, and the minute look of pain that flashed across his face made me feel somewhat sorry for him. But then again, he was the one who insisted on climbing out of the window.

The thief appeared to have regained his composure, as he soon noticed Hull's disposition and decided to take advantage of it. The van curved to the right, coming towards me. I slammed down on the brakes, just in time to keep Hull from being smashed between the two cars. He looked back at me, a half-smirk on his face. Then his eyes traveled up, and the sirens coming from behind me confirmed my thoughts. I glanced through my rear-view mirror to see four police cars and two police SUVs coming towards us, with Lennox at the wheel of the front car.

Hull jerked his head at me, signaling for me to pull forward. I accelerated, but part of me was still worried of the thief's possibilities with Hull in such a position. Hull, however, had different plans. When I was within two meters of the van, he jumped, back crashing into the hood of our car. He rolled up to the top, hands catching our own vehicle's racks. He knocked rapidly on the sunroof glass. I quickly set it back, assuming he planned to get back in the car.

"Took the police long enough!" he shouted, his voice only slightly audible over the sirens and the car itself. He made no move to enter the vehicle.

"Is now really the time for jokes?" I yelled back up at him, but knew it was useless.

He took in several deep breaths before licking his lips, then speaking. "When you hear my gun fire, hit the brakes!" I nodded up at him, hoping and praying he had something in mind. He slowly raised his body from the top of the car, careful to keep one hand on the racks. With the free hand, he cautiously raised his pistol, aiming it at what I assumed was the driver of the van.

His bullet, however, found a home in something I did not expect. The bullet smashed through the passenger window of the van and made contact with the windshield wiper controls on the wheel hub. My foot slammed down on the brake, and it was only then that I knew why he'd advised it. A quick jet of washing soap sprayed out from the hood of the van, going right into the thief's face. He released the wheel involuntarily, sending the van smashing into the center median and subsequently out into my lane.

The only other thing in the lane besides me right now, was Hull's flying body. He soared off the car, tucking into what I think was a roll. The success of the roll wasn't visible, as not even a second later, the van careened over where Hull's body had been, then tipped up on to its side and started grinding down the road. My car had finally come to a complete stop, but my heart was racing. One, because I hadn't driven over eighty miles per hour in years. Two, because the chase had been absolutely exhilarating.

And three, because it was very possible Hull had been underneath that van when it had flipped.

I ran from the Expedition, the exhilaration fading to a very strong sense of fear. "Hull!" I shouted, seeing smoke start to fume up from the van. As I ran towards the turned car, I could hear the sounds of footsteps behind me as the police charged forward. So far, there was no blood on the pavement, so I had hope. A lot of hope. And a lot of faith in him being okay. I swerved around the overturned van to find the driver, still belted into his seat, unconscious. I looked around and saw no signs of my friend the detective.

"*Hull!*" I yelled, craning my neck as if it would make a difference.

"What?"

I spun around to find the man standing right behind me and looking completely unscathed. "How in the Hell did you live that?"

All he did was smirk.

It didn't take long for the police to get the area cleaned up and the man put away in one of the police cars. I glanced over the minor damage to our car, knowing that it could have came out a lot worse. Hull stood to my side, holding the stolen diamond in his hand and holding it up to the sun.

"So, another Chimaera employee?" I asked once I'd decided the car was okay.

"Mm," he replied, face shining from the diamond's refraction of light. From behind Hull, I could see Lennox approaching us, a slight look of agitation on his face, but also a small hint of relief.

"We'll have him locked up in no time," the inspector said, stopping and also eyeing the diamond. "Had at least half a million in different stolen things in the back of that van. It's a good thing your little stunt didn't damage them too much."

"I was hired to find the diamond," Hull said as he brought his arm down, holding the cyan jewel in his palm, "and as you can plainly see, I found it. Whatever else the man stole is irrelevant."

"Thought you might say that, "Lennox replied, looking over at the van before sighing. "Alright, I'll take the diamond now."

"No."

"What?"

"As I said, I was hired to find the diamond," Hull shot back as he pocketed the gem. "And I intend to complete my case, my way."

"That's evidence for the case, Hull, you can't just leave with it."

"Take it, then," the detective said, extending his arms. "I will make no move to stop you."

Lennox stared at Hull for a long moment before sighing. "Fine. Whatever. Just don't look so smug when you leave." With that, he turned and walked away. Once he was out of earshot, I nudged Hull.

"You didn't mention why you were so determined to get the man. It wasn't for a diamond, it was obviously for Chimaera," I said, eyes watching Lennox.

"He has no need to be informed," Hull replied coolly. "Besides, if Moriarty's connections are as thorough as I believe, trust may be a difficult thing to come by with officials in high places."

The two of us turned towards our car. "You don't really think Lennox is a Chimaera agent?"

"No. I have known Lennox far too long to believe he would be apart of such a syndicate. No, Lennox is just an inadequate inspector on a failing force. But it makes little difference for me." He cast one last glance back at the inspector before getting into the car.

"A successful police force would put you out of the job," I remarked as I started the car.

He smirked. "Because a successful police force is something tangible, isn't it?"

*

I wish I could say the next morning was boring, but then I'd be lying. I think it was about 5 AM that the song started playing, and it wasn't until four hours later that it finally stopped. Jumping from a moving car and nearly being flattened apparently had no effect on Hull, who was awake long before either of us should have been and immediately took to combining music with archery. And by this, I mean he decided to blare music while firing arrows off randomly in the main room.

At about 5:30, I had given up my hopes of him either turning the music down or simply going to sleep. It wouldn't have been all-too irritating if he would have played different songs. But no, he insisted on playing one song over and over. "Bangarang," the one, and probably only, song Hull enjoyed by Skrillex. I can't say I knew the song before, but now I knew every wub to it. And I hated dubstep. Not only did he listen to the song several dozen times, he also took to firing arrows around the room. Not at anything in particular. The wall, the paintings, anything he could hit from his armchair.

The fact that he was sitting in the armchair told me that he was at least suffering from the jump on a minor level.

I sat with my laptop propped up on the table beside me, different news articles opened in a group of tabs for me to look through. Hull walked back from the kitchen, finally having abandoned his bow and now eating a piece of toast with some brownish jelly-like substance lathered across the top. He took his armchair and brought his feet up to rest on the same table as my laptop. I shot a glance over my screen, only to see him staring up at the ceiling and audibly chewing.

"It's not going to fall," I said as I looked back to my computer.

"Just admiring my work," he replied, taking another loud bite from his toast. I glanced up and felt my jaw drop. There were over a dozen arrows shot into the ceiling, conveniently arranged to make the letter M.

"You're getting those down," I said as my eyes fell.

He gave a slight chuckle as he set his plate down and wiped his mouth with the back of his hand. He grabbed a small, black remote from the table next to him and pointed it over his head. Finally, for the first time in four hours, "Bangarang" stopped playing. He tossed the remote back over his head and resumed his toast consumption.

"The song get to you?" I asked as I closed the news links and opened my email.

"Music distracts thought. I had no need for thought earlier. Now I do."

"Why?"

"Our visitor should arrive soon enough."

"Visitor?" I clicked the only new email, something from one of the nurses at the clinic I worked at. I'd been there for quite a while now, and managed to work three days a week. That money, coupled with compensation funds Hull received from clients, had gone to buying our car, though Hull had insisted on not having his name attached to it.

"Yes," he replied coolly, refocusing his attention on the toast. I shook my head before clicking the link she'd attached. Her message simply said, "This is pretty weird. Give it a look, and see you on Monday!" The link took me to YouTube. I glanced up at Hull, suddenly smelling something sweet.

"What exactly did you put on that toast?"

"Vegemite."

"Vegewhat?"

"Vegemite. Australian jelly, essentially."

"Why do you have Australian jelly?"

"I tried it before and enjoyed it."

"When did you find the time to try it?"

"When I went to Australia."

"When did you—"

A slight knock at the door stopped me. I expected it to open and have the visitor arrive, but instead Mrs. Hanson walked in holding a medium-sized cardboard box. She looked tired and somewhat-disturbed, possibly by the early delivery. It was only 9:30 and usually deliveries weren't made until noon or later.

"This came for you, Sheridan," she said, her voice cracking. He practically jumped from his seat, toast flying from his hand. I lurched forward to catch it, preferring to have the jelly on my hands than on the carpet. As I set the half-eaten piece on his plate, Hull placed the box on the top of the piano and started clawing like a child at Christmas. By the time I'd wiped the minimal jelly from my hands, he'd successfully breached the cardboard.

From the box he pulled something that nearly made me laugh at assuming it was a joke. In his hands were a pair of shoes, mostly gray except for the laces and the lining between the bottom and sides. Those parts were a very bright neon orange. He beamed down at the shoes before sitting on the piano stool and trying them on.

"You're going to actually wear those?" I asked, still trying to resist laughter.

"Of course I am. I would never pay sixty dollars for a pair of shoes if I had no intention of wearing them."

I sighed, knowing that the shoes appealed to him and it wouldn't be my place to judge. "You never told me who the visitor is supposed to be. And I'd like to know." I took my seat. "Especially if it's a fan like Moriarty."

He tied the shoes and stood, doing a slight pace around the room before responding. "No, I overheard some interesting conversation on the police scanners. Seems something very important has happened and Lennox is in charge of solving it."

"So?"

"So if it is that important, Lennox will be out of his field of skill, as usual."

"He wouldn't have gotten so high in the police force if he was an absolute idiot."

"Idiots make it high and low, especially when they are surrounded by idiots who support them."

I glanced over at my laptop, seeing the video still pulled up. It was titled "The Man in Red is Watching" and was only about ten seconds long. There was a surprising number of views and comments, though. For a short video, it must have contained something of interest. I pressed play and at first wondered if my laptop's speakers were disabled. But alas, throughout the entire video, there was no audio to be heard.

There was, however, a very peculiar video to witness. Despite its shortness in length, it certainly was captivating. It showed a figure, most likely a man judging by the face, just sitting and looking at the camera. Effects had been used to alter the lighting, however, so all that was visible was the man's face in all red, with everything else black. There was an odd pulsating to the lighting, too, that seemed to fluctuate every second or so. Just as soon as the video had started, it was over, and I was left having no idea what I had just witnessed.

I scrolled down, finding a long list of comments all sharing my mindset. Nobody seemed to understand what they had watched, but some contained sentences in quotes. I scrolled back up to find a very, very odd description for the video. It was three lines, all separate, that read:

Gihwimttensniaadechnr.

Ogrcotetsncyustoehneohpdiianae.

Sednwtiheno.

I looked from the lines down to the comments and realized some were from people attempting to decipher the scrambled letters.

"How often do you go on YouTube?" I asked, seeing that Hull had taken his seat and finished his toast.

"Never."

"So you haven't seen this video, then?" I said as I turned the laptop towards him.

"I don't watch videos for pleasure."

"Well look at this. It's not normal." He rolled his eyes, then leaned forward. I pressed play and watched it again, but mostly kept my eyes on him. He stared intently at the screen, eyes illuminated by the pulses from the changing light. When it was over, he scrolled down once to get a full view of the description. Then he started typing. I craned my neck to watch as he typed "'The Man in Red is watching. There is nothing you can do to escape. The end is now.' How clever." He submitted the comment, and not even a second later, it was listed with the rest, the user's name as "Sheridan Hull."

"There," he said as he turned the laptop back towards me.

"How were you signed on to an account with your name? I thought you said—"

"Hardly a clever video, and the editing was poor. A simple filter."

"But what's it mean?"

"Nothing," he replied as he leaned back in his chair. "Just someone being stupid on the Internet. Oh the foreignness of such thought."

I turned the laptop back to just me, still wary of his name somehow being listed for the comment. "Well I thought it was interesting." With that, I fell silent and resumed my browsing of other popular videos. Hull looked at me, sighed, then stood up on his seat and started pulling the arrows from the ceiling. It only took him a minute to successfully remove the arrows, but I knew he wouldn't do a thing about the minuscule holes that still left a dotted M in the plaster. He tossed the arrows to the side of his seat before walking over to the window. After almost a minute, I heard him chortle.

"Our visitor has arrived," he said as he walked back to his seat. I stood and moved to the window to find a police car parked outside. As I turned, the door opened to admit Lennox, looking somewhat-winded.

"We've got a murder, body was just found an hour ago," he said, eyes locked on the back of Hull's head.

"And?"

"And I have no leads. Evidence is slim to none. I need you for this."

"And?"

The inspector's head gave a sharp snap back and a look of confusion crossed his face. "And what? I need your help."

"Perhaps my schedule is simply too full at the moment," Hull said as he grabbed his bow from the side of his chair and nocked an arrow.

"It's a teenage boy."

"Far too busy."

"It's the mayor's son."

Hull let the arrow fly, pinning it on the tiny line of wood that made up the center of the windowpane. The arrow shook slightly in its place, but my attention was most certainly on other things. I had met the mayor before, months ago, before meeting Hull. He had seemed like a nice enough man, and for his son to be dead, I could only imagine the pain the man was experiencing. Hull stared at the shaking arrow until it finally ceased its trembling before standing, his bow dropping to the floor.

"Mayor Montorum's son found murdered on a residential sidewalk," he said, more to himself than Lennox or me. "Now the case has some level of interest." He started forward, plucking the arrow from the wall and pointing it at the inspector. "Now I will go."

*

The police car turned on to a neighborhood lane that was at the heart of the wealthier residential area. Most of the houses were two or three stories tall, had long and elaborate driveways, and were worth far more than I had ever owned. The road had been barricaded at both ends to prevent unnecessary through traffic. Currently, two police cars blocked a section of the sidewalk, where a blue tarp lay draped across something, obviously the boy's body.

Hull and I stepped out to the sidewalk, the detective immediately removing the tarp. The boy was about sixteen years old, tall and spouting black hair that was, unfortunately, matted with dried blood. His eyes were open and mouth ajar. It looked like he had been shot directly through the heart. Hull leaned over the boy, eyes flickering like blurs.

"Nathaniel Montorum," Lennox said from behind us. "Aged sixteen, attended Filimore Preparatory. Dad is the mayor and mom is a stay-at-home wife. Neighbor found him and called us before realizing who it was." He did a small sidestep, as if making sure Hull was listening. Hull cast a short glance back at him. "We notified the parents. Haven't heard anything back from either of them."

"Curious," Hull said as he ran his finger along the side of the boy's body.

"What, that they haven't done anything?"

"No," Hull replied, motioning for me to help him. Together we carefully moved the body over to its side. "Curious that the bullet had an upward trajectory. Entered the chest, pierced the heart, but exited through the neck."

"Do you think he did it himself?" I asked.

"Not sure. To precisely shoot oneself from such a position would require astonishing accuracy. Accuracy I find hard to believe a teenager would possess. But given his history in athletics, perhaps it is possible."

"History in athletics?" Lennox prompted, coming to kneel beside us.

Hull pointed at the body's legs. "His legs are significantly more toned than his upper body. Not by chance, but by choice. His selection of shoes, socks, and jacket are also reflective of an athlete, a long-distance runner, to be precise, which gives us some insight on why he was out so late to be shot."

"How does this help us?" the inspector grinded.

"It gives us more to work from, things to inquire about. The cross country coach at his school. Fellow runners. It doesn't take a genius to see how little evidence there is here. The boy does not look like he was in a hurry, or his clothes would not be so neat, blood excluded. He purposefully went on a walk and ended up shot through the heart, possibly by himself. Whether he was suicidal or not, we will only learn through further inquiry. Right now, we have nothing to base our knowledge on to establish a case."

Lennox sighed. "Alright. So what do we do?"

"Inquire." Hull stood. "Go and speak with his mother. Search the house for anything that may help. Walker and I will head to the school and find out if he may have done this himself." Lennox gave a nod before walking away. I stood, but noticed Hull still looking down at the body.

"Something wrong?" I asked.

"Motive," he replied, turning to look down the full length of the sidewalk. "No signs of stress, no signs of theft. He willingly took a bullet through the heart. Suicide is not an option, though we are meant to think it was. Had he shot himself, there would be a gun, and even then, the gun could not possibly have had a silencer efficient enough to keep the entire lane asleep. Someone with access to very valuable weaponry did this. But the motive..."

"Political scandal?" I suggested.

He shook his head. "Keeping him alive would have been far more effective. I doubt the killer was aware of the boy's father. Though I also doubt he cares much."

"Why?"

"Isn't it obvious?" he said in that intellectual tone. When I gave no response, he sighed. "You have to observe. What sort of person shoots a young man through the heart in the middle of the night, leaving no evidence, no sign of motive?"

"I don't know."

He gave a thin grin. "The smart kind." He started walking towards one of the police cars. "The cunning kind."

We both remained silent on the drive to the school. Filimore Preparatory was an impressive enough facility, built on the easternmost property in Newfield. The school consisted of about five different buildings, three of them being three stories, one being four, and the fifth an amazing six stories. All of the buildings were a pristine white, as if they were made from the same marble as the pillars at the entryway to the central facility. Hull and I were escorted by one of the eight lobby receptionists to the district office.

It seemed like we had visited just as the students had entered a break of some sort. It was too early to be lunch, too late to be breakfast. It just seemed like leisure time. Many of the students took to the halls, pulling out their phones and texting or doing whatever they do freely. Several even had laptops that they revealed. We were approaching a set of doors with the words "DISTRICT" above them when Hull stopped. The receptionist looked back at him, a puzzled look on her face.

"Is something wrong, Mr. Hull?" she asked.

Hull, who was now staring into one of the rooms, took his time on replying. "This would be the computer lab, I presume?"

The receptionist glanced in, then nodded. "State-of-the-art equipment. Computers with some of the finest programs the district can afford."

"And the students use this room frequently?"

"Daily."

He stepped into the room, followed by a very confused receptionist and a very intrigued me. There were about ten students already in the room, a few of them grouped at two computers and the rest on their own. Hull walked the length of the room before reaching the row with the group. He approached them slowly, careful not to catch their attention. When he was within five meters, he stopped and looked back.

"And what kind of blocking methods are in place on these computers?" he questioned.

The receptionist bit her lip, not sure on where he was going. "Only the necessary firewalls. Many good websites will share classifications on what is 'inappropriate', so it's easier to trust the students to work when they need to work."

"Ah," Hull said, his voice entering its distant tone. He glanced back at the students, who had yet to even acknowledge our presence. I'd call them ignorant, but I remembered all-too well how it was to be in high school, and how much you treasured the moments when your teacher wasn't watching you with hawk eyes. He watched them for only a moment before turning to the receptionist. "Apologies. We can see the superintendent now, I believe?" With a somewhat-unsure nod, she led us out and to the district office, which was actually an elevator that took us to the fifth floor.

The superintendent had agreed to meet us prior to our arrival, and yet, he still took nearly twenty minutes to open the doors of his office and allow us in. He was an older man, probably in his early sixties, with thick, white hair and a face wrinkled from smiles. He shook our hands with a steady grip and invited us in. The office was decorated with awards the school had received, and even some the man had been given for merit and dedication. He took a seat at his desk and gestured for us to take the two open seats across from him. As I sat, I couldn't help but see the big, gold-painted nameplate that said "HARRISON F. COLLINS."

I'd never seen such a blatant display of wealth.

"So sad to hear about Montorum's son, the mayor and I are good friends, you see," Collins said. "He was real proud of his boy, you know. And the boy was a good enough student. Rough patches along the way, but we can't expect perfection. Just damn close." He gave Hull a short wink with the last statement. The curling of the detective's nose was enough of a sign of disgust.

"What can you tell us about the boy's personality?" Hull asked, no doubt trying to ignore the fluff Collins had said.

"Teachers said he was a smart kid, did his homework, participated in class. No real troubles, minus a few tidbits here and there." Collins looked down at a stapled packet of papers on his desk. "I actually had his current teachers send me just a sampler of his work, their opinions, the usual stuff we lock away in their permanent records and never see again. It looks like none of his teachers had any gripes." The man fell silent for a moment. I could tell from his eyes that something on the page wasn't fitting his description of the boy.

"What does it say."

Collins looked up, thoughts interrupted by Hull's monotonous question. "Pardon?"

"The footnote that has caught your attention. What does it say."

"Oh, it's nothing, really," Collins said, flipping the front page to its original place and setting the packet down. "Just one of the teachers noting some minor bullying citations."

"Ah," Hull said. Then, in a very flash-like motion, Hull's hand shot out and plucked the packet from Collins's desk. Hull flipped to the page while the superintendent stared at him, face going pink. "So it would seem the boy was not the star child you have made him to be. Fourteen different citations of bullying from the same teacher. How curious." Hull stood, taking a step away from Collins's desk.

"Now, Mr. Hull, those records need to be in the hands of—" Collins started.

Hull snapped his head back. "I do not care, Mr. Collins." He returned his focus to the page. "The class was a physical education course. The boy excessively picked on weaker students in particular, whether it be through taunting them or.. well well, physically assaulting. Not enough to constitute a referral, but just enough to be noticed. And to harm the individual." Hull was about to flip to the next page when his hand stopped, a slight spasm traveling through his fingers. I stood from my seat, coming to stand beside him.

"What?" I asked, looking down at the page.

Hull's grip on the paper seemed to tighten. "A large number of the weaker students were not weak by choice. Handicapped students. Physical and mental impairments." He threw the packet back, the papers sliding across Collins's desk. Hull didn't bother glancing over his shoulder when he spoke to the very flustered superintendent. "You harbor these disgusting individuals. And I would not doubt that the boy was treated with care, given his relations. You are no professional of education. You are a breeder of filth." With that, Hull stormed from the office.

By the time I'd caught up to him, he was already in the police car, sitting and waiting for me. He stared out the front windshield with pierced eyes and pursed lips.

"What was all that about?" I asked as our escort policeman drove us away.

He deeply inhaled through his nose before responding. "When I was eight, there was a young girl in my class. And one of the bigger students, a brute I never liked who ended up as a cabbie, would torture her. Day after day, he would steal her writing utensils, trip her, mimic her. Everything someone could do to upset a normal person. But she also lacked mental stability. Every time he tortured her, she would cry, and it would take her mother coming and taking her from school to make her stop.

"As soon as I saw that note, I could hear that girl again. Her wails as she hit the floor, her screams as he snatched the pencil away, how her voice would go higher and higher to try and make him cease his mimicry. I had never seen such evil. Such filth. And the teacher, that stupid woman, never did a single thing to help her. She acted as if nothing had happened, blamed the girl's instability. The boy was never punished." He smirked. "That was, of course, until he tried to shoplift when we were in our last year of school, and I turned him in. That was the closest he came to justice, and it was not even for the right reason."

There were no words for me to provide. But it was then that I saw another sign to prove Hull's humanity. Even though anger wasn't the best emotion to exhibit, it was there.

"We need to speak with the mother and see the house," the detective said after a very long pause. I nodded, knowing he expected no words of comfort from me. He didn't need them.

*

The boy's house reflected the family wealth as much as the school had. Tall, three stories in total, with a vast garden that bordered the cobblestone walkway to the doors. The woman who greeted us was tall, black hair that stretched down her back. Her eyes were red, and every several seconds, she would sniffle. Lennox had already done an efficient enough job at looking for evidence and, as Hull had estimated, he had found nothing. The boy's mother had said her son had left at around 11 PM for a jog, and she had trusted him enough to the point where she had fallen asleep before he came home.

Hull, Lennox and I currently sat on a couch with the boy's mother, named Carla, seated across from us. She watched us with her tissue at the ready.

"Mrs. Montorum, I have only a few questions about your son," Hull said, his voice sounding almost sincere in its condescending tone. "I know what you are going through is difficult, and I know you would prefer I not occupy too much of your time."

"Yes, of course," the woman said through a loud sniff. "Thank you, Detective."

"Now, your son, what was he like at home? And do you know how much it differed from when he was with friends?"

"He was always so focused on his sports or spending time with his friends that I hardly saw him. I always thought it was a typical teenager thing. Nathan was our only child." She gave a longing look at the fireplace mantle before continuing. "I know he was somewhat of a leader with his friends. A group of them would pal around town, sometimes visit his father. Jameson is devastated by this. Horribly devastated. I haven't spoken with him since the news. I wish he'd come home."

"Did your son seem depressed?" Lennox asked. From the corner of my eye, I saw Hull rub his own eyelid in an irritated manner.

"No, of course not! He was so happy, so determined. He never showed signs of depression. Not once."

"Was your son in contact with any individuals that you would regard with suspicion?" Hull questioned. Lennox shot him a curious glance, but did not pry.

"Not that I know of," she said, her voice giving a slight shake. "But he spent so much time on his phone talking or texting or emailing his friends. I could never keep up with everything he was doing, he was such a busybody. Like his father."

"Phone?" Hull said, leaning back. I could see his eyes start to tremble slightly as his brain kicked into overdrive. "Phone..."

"Well yes, his father and I got him a new one just this past Christmas."

Hull blinked once. "Phone." He stood, eyes wide. "Phone!" His eyes shot down to the woman. "Can you show me your son's room?" She stared up at him with concern for a long time before agreeing. She led us to a room decorated with sports paraphernalia, clothes, garbage, and other miscellaneous items. Hull immediately went to the boy's desk. There was a laptop, fairly new but still dirty on the keyboard, propped up and on. The screen was dimmed to probably preserve battery life.

"Is something wrong? Did Nathan leave something here for us?" the mother asked, a small sliver of hope in her voice.

"Possibly," Hull said ominously, tapping a key on the laptop. The screen came to life, revealing the YouTube homepage.

I came up beside Hull, kneeling close to hopefully prevent the other two people in the room from overhearing. "Phone?"

"Yes, John," he replied, giving me a quick side-glance. "Phone." He took the mouse and moved it around the screen before finding his target. He accessed the boy's account, and from there, his viewing history. It was then that I was forced to stifle a gasp.

Right at the top, where the most recently viewed video would be listed, was a very familiar title. "The Man in Red is Watching."

"But that's the video I showed you earlier," I commented, feeling like a tidal wave of understanding was just moments from hitting me.

"The same video the boy had recently viewed, in fact, the last video he watched before departing." He scrolled through the viewing history, pausing several times, before removing his hand from the mouse. "The same video that the students in the computer lab were watching at Filimore Preparatory. The same video students in the hallway were watching. Oh, now this is truly getting interesting."

"Why?"

"Because now we have a link. Now we have something to work from."

Hull turned to face the boy's mother and Lennox, both looking at him with puzzled faces. He didn't speak, but rather started a brief search around the room before stopping at the bedside table. He reached down, into the crease between the table and the boy's mattress, and pulled out a black cable. I recognized it as a phone charger.

"Has he lost it?" Lennox said, mostly in my direction.

"A standard phone charger, but no phone attached," Hull said, releasing his hold on the cable. "A charger that should have gone to a phone on the boy."

The tidal wave finally hit. "But there was no phone on the body."

"My previous analysis of nothing being stolen was wrong. Something was stolen, something that is the key to truly figuring this out." He walked around the boy's bed, pointing at the laptop. "He watched the video, received something on his phone, and promptly left. I would say he was murdered just minutes after departing. And the murderer contacted him on his phone, and took the phone to prevent tracing."

"What kind of phone did you get your son?" Lennox asked.

"The new Apple one," she replied, slowly looking from Hull to Lennox.

"Those can be traced," I added.

"He never would have kept it, he would have known the risk," Hull said, pressing his hands together.

"He?" Lennox prompted.

Hull pointed at the laptop screen. "The Man in Red. He is our murderer."

"The man in what?" Lennox said as he moved to the computer. Hull stepped away as Lennox attempted to navigate the page. I came up beside the detective, trying to grasp what he was saying.

"The man from the video is the murderer?"

"Yes, and how clever of a murderer he is. A serial killer who uses a video to find his victims." After a pause, he clapped. "Oh yes, this is definitely a clever case. We need to go home, there are some things I would like to check. Lennox!" The inspector looked over his shoulder, somewhat-alarmed at Hull having yelled. "There is nothing left to be found here. The case is out of your depth. I can handle it from here." With that, Hull left the room, leaving the woman, Lennox, and myself in a haze.

By the time I had exited the home, the detective was gone. He hadn't taken a police car. Odd as the thought was, I believe he walked. Lennox came up behind me, hands in his coat pockets and jaw slightly slack.

"I don't think I'll ever be able to get that man," he commented, looking out at where he presumed Hull to be.

I chuckled. "I've been living with him for over half a year and I'm no closer to understanding him."

He clasped my shoulder. "I'll keep my investigation going, but I don't doubt him. There's not much at all to work off of here. Little evidence. I don't get how some man in a video could be the murderer. But if he's found the connections I can't make, I won't complain." He started forward, but after five meters, he paused, shooting me a glance. "I know he's smarter than me. Hell, he's smarter than just about anyone. But I appreciate the help he gives, whether he means to or not. And he can be decent enough. Sometimes." With that, he turned and left, leaving me with a new impression of the inspector.

Because I took a taxi back to the flat, I arrived just minutes before Hull. I'd opted to wait outside for him to arrive, and when he did, he did not show signs of being tired or even mildly fatigued. He was impressive in that regard as well. Together we walked up the stairs to the flat, and once there, he immediately went to work on his computer. As I set my coat down on my chair, I noticed a red blinking from the table. It took a moment for me to realize what it was. The blinking came from a small black box with a speaker. The voicemail for the landline Hull and I never used.

"Hull?" I piqued, looking down at the blinking light.

"Mm."

"We have a message."

His head slowly moved up to stare out the balcony window before turning. His eyes froze when they saw the light. He stood and joined me, both of us staring down at the box and waiting, as if we expected it to play itself. Finally, after almost a minute, I reached down and pressed the play button. What came from the box was just ridiculous. It was a horribly distorted audio file, the audio increasing and decreasing in volume in a wave-like fashion. It lasted only about ten seconds before stopping.

"What the Hell was that?" I said after it had ended. Hull held out his own phone, pressed something on his screen, then pressed the play button again. The recording warbled out of the speaker once more, still making no sense whatsoever.

"Oh dear," Hull said as he stepped away.

"Oh dear what?"

He plugged the phone into his computer and waited. "Oh dear oh dear. The level of interest in this case just seems to increase with each passing moment, does it not?"

"It does?"

He brought up a folder within a program and went to work. I didn't quite know what he was doing, but it looked like he had taken a recording of the message and was now doing some kind of editing to it. After about five minutes, he gave a nod in success, then made it so his screen was split between the audio clip and another window.

The other window was narrow and black, with a large "Play" button in the center. Hull looked up at me. "Ready?" I was hesitant, but I nodded. He pressed the large "Play" button, then moved to the audio file and started it. What happened next was enough to send a chill down my spine, not just because of what it was, but because of what it meant.

The black window started to play a video, the same one I had shown Hull earlier, the one that had been on the boy's laptop. "The Man in Red is Watching." The audio file started playing a slightly-corrected clip of six simple words being repeated. The audio and video seemed to work in perfect synchronization, the fluctuations in the audio correlating to the visual pulsations. But of course, what was most important was what the recording said.

"The Man in Red is Watching. The Man in Red is Watching. The Man in Red is Watching."

THE RED HUNT

I leaned away from the laptop, an odd numbness coursing through my body. The dimmed face of the Man in Red still seemed to vibrate on the screen, with the audio waiting for another play that I prayed to God would never come. I glanced over at Hull, who was still in what looked like a petrified state. It wasn't that he looked scared. His eyes seemed to have glassed over, the typical glint when he was hot on the trail of a criminal not entirely there. Instead of the vibrant blue and green, they were dulled by a gray, as if fog had somehow manifested within his irises. And something about that look sent a chill down my spine. Like Hull had found a case more complex than he could handle. Or more dangerous.

"Poor Nathaniel," the detective remarked as he leaned away from the laptop.

"Nathaniel?" I asked. "The murdered boy?"

"He made a very grave mistake, if I am understanding this correctly." Hull clicked his tongue. "Very grave mistake indeed."

"What's that?"

"Nathaniel Montorum was known at his school as a bully. Being a bully does not earn you friends. Someone noticed the young man's actions and decided to take matters into their own hands. This

'Man in Red' contacted Nathaniel and carefully instructed him on where to go. Nathaniel received the same recording that we have, except his was not altered. The Man in Red then texted Nathaniel on where to go, and the young man complied. He feared for his life, though I doubt that was the only thing the Man threatened.

"When Nathaniel did arrive, I do not think the Man killed him immediately. I expect they spoke for a while, perhaps amicably. Nathaniel did not try to run. He made no attempts at attack or escape. He took the shot willingly, not by the act of suicide, though. Something the Man told him forced him into such a position."

"How did the Man in Red find Nathaniel?"

Hull maximized the screen with the video. "This video is surprisingly popular, but very few comment on it. Those that do tend to leave snide remarks, minus my own and a small amount of others. The Man uses these comments to find his victims."

"A serial killer?"

"That is where this becomes more interesting." He stepped away from the laptop, grabbing a stack of papers from the bookshelf. He brought them back and set them in front of me, a stack of printed news articles from a multitude of websites. Each of them described an odd suicide or unsolved murder, with the articles stretching from New York to California.

"A bunch of murders and suicides?"

"Serial murders and suicides. He has slowly moved across the country, killing people as he has traveled. Twenty-one deaths now. Curious thing to note, though, is the last article." I flipped to it to find two young men who were "Internet personalities" marked as murdered. "Both of them dead, no resolution ever found to the case. Not just Internet personalities. YouTube personalities. Possibly people who remarked on the video."

"Why?"

The foggy look became more prominent in his eyes. "I'm not sure. That, my friend, is what we must find out. And soon." He glanced down at the laptop. "It seems we have been targeted. It would be wise to keep out of harm's way."

"We can't just sit and wait for him to come after us."

"No, that would never do, would it?" He walked over to the balcony window, looking down at the street.

"So what do we do?"

He peered over his shoulder at me. "We hunt the hunter."

I stood. "We go after him?"

"It provides a challenge for all of us. And it should quicken the pace of the hunt."

"You *want* him to find us?"

"I want to solve this." He let out a deep exhale through his nostrils. "We need to find the boy's phone. And I'm afraid the only way we can do that is by getting some.. unwanted help."

"Lennox isn't that bad, you know."

"I don't mean Lennox."

I furrowed my brow. "Then who?"

He seemed to roll his eyes before answering. "The government."

"Oh." After a moment, it actually sunk in. "*Ohh.*"

Hull took out his phone and tapped away. Presumably he was going to his address book, and part of me had always been curious of how many names were actually listed. To be honest, I predicted two. Maybe one. Even one was a stretch. After a moment, he pressed the phone to his ear and waited. "Hello, Malcolm. Do you mind if Walker and I come for a visit?"

*

Malcolm's house was exactly as I had expected it to be: formal. It was like walking into a building that reflected everything Sheridan wasn't. The walls were adorned with paintings of people and landscapes, the floors were made of elegant carpet and linoleum panels that practically reflected my own face up at me. Malcolm's daughter, Bailey, led us to the family room, which was about two times the size of our flat. Malcolm currently sat in an auburn-leather armchair, a very large book in his hands and his attention on the nearest window.

"Uncle Sherrie is here, Dad," Bailey said, nodding at us before leaving. Sheridan and I took the couch that faced Malcolm's chair. He gave a sigh before setting his book down, then linked his fingers together and rested them on his lap.

"This must be important," he said, eyes locked on his brother. "You only come when Bailey requests you for dinner parties."

"I enjoy the company of my niece," Sheridan replied coolly.

"What do you want?"

"I am currently involved in a case—"

"Yes, the murder of Montorum's son."

"—and something has come up that requires further connections."

Malcolm grabbed a glass filled with a very dark liquid and took a sip. "You need my connections for your case?"

"Yes." Sheridan's reply was no doubt forced.

The older Hull set the glass down. "The man you are trying to find, this 'Man in Red.' We have been after him for several months now. Why do you think you will be capable of capturing him?"

"I proved the guiltiness of Wayne Fisher on your request. You owe me."

"Owe you? Now would not be the time to compare who owes who, Sheridan."

"The Man stole a phone from Nathaniel Montorum, and I believe he still has it. Unfortunately, I am not able to remotely activate the tracer in the phone without your assistance. Find the phone, find the Man."

"Is that so?" Malcolm said as he picked up his glass again.

"The Man in Red has targeted us now," I prompted. Sheridan closed his eyes, lips pursed in disappointment. Malcolm, however, had a slight shake to his hand when I'd spoken. "If we don't find him, he'll find us."

I knew that Sheridan would have preferred I didn't mention that, though I hadn't known why until now. I wasn't the best at reading people, but I recognized compassion and love when I saw it. As hard as Malcolm and Sheridan tried, there was undoubtedly the connection only brothers would share. The tremble that had passed through Malcolm's hand had been no coincidence. It had been the registering of his brother possibly being in danger, a danger that had avoided even him for months. And I think it was that knowledge that tipped Malcolm in our favor.

"Why has he targeted you?" Malcolm said, eyes on Sheridan.

"Irrelevant. Will you help us?" the detective shot back. So perhaps the willing compassion wasn't as two-sided as it could be. Nevertheless, Malcolm's opinion had no doubt changed. He stood from his seat, walking over to a desk that was pressed against the wall opposing us. From the desk he pulled a laptop. He returned to us while opening it, tapping at the keyboard with his free hand. After a minute, he set the laptop down on the coffee table in front of us.

"Input the boy's name and area of residence," the older Hull said, returning to his seat. Sheridan typed in Nathaniel Montorum and his address, then watched as the tracer homed in on the part of the globe that was Oregon. It took its time pinpointing the exact location, and when it did, it sent a chill down my spine.

"That's... the street outside," I said, my voice shaking. I saw Malcolm's eyes waver as he stared us down.

Sheridan shot to his feet. "Then he is here." He charged out, almost too quick for me to catch up. I could hear Malcolm shouting behind us, but my focus was on Sheridan. The detective ran forward, through the home's doors and out towards the street. Once I'd made it through the doorway, I saw him running down the pathway that led to the entrance, a black van parked against the curb in the other lane. As soon as Sheridan reached the sidewalk, the van sped away, leaving marks on the pavement.

Sheridan stared down the street as the van turned, removing it from our sight. I stood next to the detective, who was panting slightly and licking his lips.

"He followed us here," the man said, eyes still focused on the corner. "From the message onward, he's tailed us." He bit back an obscenity as he looked away.

"What do we do?"

He looked back at Malcolm's house, eyes moving from thing to thing. "I don't know. We have to find him, but he knew. Somehow he knew we would get someone to activate the tracer."

"But if he did that, wouldn't he—"

I stopped as my eyes fell on it. Resting on the sidewalk near the van's peel-out marks was a small, black object. It was thin, maybe a centimeter or two in width, and the reflective glare from the object's top confirmed my thoughts.

"The phone," I said, not even looking at Sheridan. He turned rapidly, feet seeming to skid along the ground as he did. When his eyes reached the phone, he gave an audible intake of breath. He moved across the street quickly, hand extending down to scoop up the phone when he reached it. I came to his side as he pressed the center button on the phone, bringing the screen to life. It brightly displayed a single message from a blocked number.

THER3 I5 N0THING YOU cAN DO TO ESC4p3.

"Well that's just great," I said, looking down the road. "Now he's taunting us."

"No," Hull replied, eyes wide. "He's not taunting us at all. He's shown us the way."

"How the Hell has he done that?"

"The message is a sham." He handed me the phone. "There are characters in the text that are prominent, whether they be written as numbers or lowercase letters. 350C4P3. The 350 is a time, 3:50, most likely in the afternoon. C4P3 is a word, with the 4 being an A and the 3 being an E. CAPE. The message is telling us where he will be next."

"And where is that?"

"Cape Bar and Grill at 3:50 PM this afternoon."

"Why would he meet with us?"

"He isn't. He's going to kill someone else."

*

Cape Bar and Grill was situated in a more populated part of town, about three blocks from the police station. It was on the second story of an older complex, with the first being completely closed off. It wasn't a formal place, but it was still nice enough to be a hotspot for locals. Hull and I currently sat at one of the booths, Hull's eyes locked on the door and mine on the menu. I figured if we were going to be here long, I may as well enjoy myself. And since we'd been here for almost a half an hour, with ten minutes to go until 3:50 PM, I would get just enough time to order.

"Why don't you ever eat?" I asked as the waitress walked away.

Hull sniffed. "Why stop to eat food in the midst of such an important case?"

"Food is important."

"Food is distracting."

I sighed. "At least we know why you're so impossibly thin."

He looked away from the doorway to stare me down. "What's that supposed to mean?"

"Well, you know." His resilient stare brought on an odd realization. Perhaps Hull was truly so focused on his cases that he neglected his own fitness. He was remarkably skinny for a man his age, but at the same time, surprisingly strong. He ate as much as he slept. I set my mug of coffee down and did a bit of a side-look, as if one of the patrons would help me, before continuing. "You never eat and it shows. You're thinner than the average teenage male and you have ten years on them."

"Average teenage males have more time to sit and stuff their faces with fat and sugar."

"Average people *eat*."

He scoffed. "And when did I last strike you as average?"

"Fair enough," I said as the waitress returned to refill my mug. Hull resumed his unwavering watching of the entry while I made my way through the black coffee. Coffee was something I'd grown accustomed to over the years, and I'd quickly learned that any additives lessened its taste and potency for me. Hull, on the other hand, drank coffee on a very rare occasion, and when he did, he buried the "coffee" under the cream, sugar, and whatever else he could possibly fit into the mug.

"Why are you so concerned about my eating habits?"

The question came after almost five minutes of silence. "You're my friend, I'd hate to see you die from starvation halfway through a case."

The look that crossed his eyes was new, one I can't say I'd seen before. It was a confused look, but more one caused by experiencing something completely unfamiliar. It shocked me to think that my friendly compassion for him was the first he'd experienced in a long while. But given the life he had chosen for himself, it was possible.

"...thank you, then. I think." I almost smiled at how delicately he chose his words. As if he'd never given meaningful thanks.

"You're most certainly welcome," I replied, taking another drink. He seemed to hesitate with his gaze before returning to the doorway. I looked down at my watch to see we had two minutes left until our meeting was supposed to occur. Hull saying the Man in Red was going to kill someone was unsettling, but the detective hadn't bothered to follow that up with any other information. In fact, he hadn't spoken in the time it took us to go from his brother's home to Cape.

Something his brother had said before we'd departed had stuck with me. His tone of voice had been so cryptic, so monotonous. He'd stopped us from pulling out, walked to the passenger window, and said, "Be careful, Sheridan. Do not dive into a case you may not be able to come up from." It had brought so many questions to my mind. Did Malcolm know something we didn't? Was he involved? Of course I wasn't able to obtain any answers, and Sheridan hadn't felt inclined to respond. He'd simply looked forward and ignored his brother's presence entirely.

And now we were here, possibly waiting on a serial killer to meet us for lunch. It was times like now I really questioned my choice of company. It didn't take long for my mind to remind me that the company wasn't forced on me; I *enjoyed* it.

"He's here," Hull said, giving a very slight jump in his seat. I turned subtly to see a young man walk in, barely eighteen in age, with balding black hair and a very fragile-looking posture. The boy looked around the room nervously before spotting us. A look of recognition crossed his eyes as he started towards us. I knew immediately that he wasn't the Man in Red. No serial killer would be so afraid to see us after scheduling the meeting.

"Are you Mr. Sheridan Hull and John Walker?" the boy asked, his voice trembling.

"Who wants to know?" Hull asked, eyes locked on the boy's face. I could tell by watching the boy's reaction that he was nervous. Something was very off with the entire scenario.

"I was told to come here. To meet you both." He looked from Hull to me, giving a gulp. "He said you both could help me."

"He?"

The boy looked around cautiously before leaning down, bringing his head to eye level with us and pushing his body forward. "The Man in Red."

"He told you we could help you?" I asked, shooting a glance at Hull. The detective's eyes were narrowed and piercing through the boy's weak gaze.

"He... he left me a voicemail. I don't even know how he could've gotten my phone number..." He glanced around. "But he called me. And said to be here." His eyes gained a sense of desperation. "He killed Nathan, didn't he?"

"You knew Nathaniel Montorum?" I questioned.

"We were best friends. We both played basketball, varsity team. We did stuff every weekend." He gulped. "We watched the video together. I was there when he made the comment on that video. And he sent me a text the night he died. He said he'd gotten a voicemail from him. The man in that video."

"Sit down," Hull said, pointing at me. The boy shook his head. "I can't. We can't stay here. I know he's here."

I glanced around at the other patrons, not seeing anyone who could have been the Man. I thought back to when Hull and I had entered, and suddenly, so many potential people came to mind. We'd walked by at least a dozen different people, some obvious contenders, others not even a possibility. A group of three homeless individuals in one of the alleyways, two of them covered in rags and the third in a wheelchair. Two people in business suits who watched Hull and me with mild interest. Three teenagers. One woman walking two dogs. Another woman yelling into her phone. And two other people who had been standing by a taxi with far too much interest in us than they should have.

"What would you suggest, then," Hull replied, eyes still on the boy. The boy leaned in even closer.

"I know who he is."

This undoubtedly grabbed Hull's attention. "The Man in Red?"

The boy nodded. "Nathan was able to send me a text with his identity. The Man told him before... before Nathan stopped. But he told me his name."

"And?"

"I can't say it here!" the boy said in an all-too loud voice. He looked around with shaking hands before returning his trembling eyes to Hull. "It's too risky. We have to leave."

"You are perfectly safe here, now tell me the name."

"I can't!"

"Tell me."

The boy looked around, and his eyes froze when he reached a booth. I followed his gaze to find the two businessmen who had been outside earlier sitting and talking, with the occasional glance in our direction. When they saw us observing them, they looked at each other, careful not to reestablish eye contact with us. I looked at Hull, who nodded. Together, we stood, and the three of us started for the door, just after I'd set down enough money to pay for our drinks. We were almost to the exit when the men stood.

I saw Hull's arm drop slowly to his side, no doubt to where he kept his pistol. I hoped he wouldn't make a violent scene in the restaurant, because the publicity that would come from it wouldn't be worth it. The men approached us, but the anticipation was too great for the boy, who bolted forward and through the door. The men paid him no mind, instead going directly to Hull. I held my breath as I waited for them to reach us.

"You're Sheridan Hull, right?" the one on the left, wearing a light blue button-up shirt, asked.

"I am," Hull replied cautiously, eyes looking down on both men. I will give Hull credit, for someone so thin, he was surprisingly tall. Maybe that contributed to the visual leanness. The man on the right reached into his coat, and for just a moment, I feared the worst of the situation.

When he pulled out a notepad, I finally let my held breath free.

"Can we get an autograph? We're new at the department and Lennox has told us all about you."

Hull looked over at me with wide eyes before sighing. "Autographs."

"Your work is phenomenal," the light blue shirted man said.

"Absolutely amazing," the coated man added. Reluctantly, Hull signed their notepads and, with a swift handshake, charged through the doorway.

As we moved down the stairs, I took the small opportunity to talk. "So you're famous now."

"Absolutely ridiculous thing," Hull remarked with a disgusted shake of his head. "What could Lennox have possibly told them to make them think anything of me?"

"Couldn't be that you're brilliant, could it?"

"No. In fact, I doubt Lennox even knows who those gentlemen are."

"What?"

"We need to find our informant, and fast."

We exited the flight of stairs to find a bustling roadway, oddly busy for almost 4 PM. Off to the left stood the boy, eyes locked on us with both excitement and fear spilling from his face. We went to him quickly, Hull glancing around before standing in front of the boy, his back to the street.

"Now," the detective prompted, "tell me who he is."

The boy gulped, doing a quick look around before nodding. "Nathan said his name was C—"

Bang.

I jumped back as the boy's chest exploded, blood splattering out towards us. The boy's head jerked forward, his eyes rolling up into his skull before his body fell to the ground. I looked into the dark alleyway and charged forward, pulling out my own pistol as I ran. Unfortunately, there was no assailant to be found. Whoever they were, they had made their escape in no time at all. I spit in anger before returning. The sight of the killed boy pained me, but what stood above him was even more horrific.

Hull had yet to move. The shot hadn't hit him; in fact, if I'd seen correctly, the bullet had come from an almost-impossibly low angle and had gone over Hull's shoulder. This did not, however, prevent Hull from being completely covered in the boy's blood. His face was painted with red spots, as were his coat and arms. He stared forward with fluttering eyes, his mouth slightly ajar and his lips moving in very minute motions. I could see blood on his lips and knew some had more than likely managed to hit his tongue.

"Sheridan?" I asked, standing in front of him with the hopes of breaking his current contact. "Hull!"

"I..." he muttered, eyes falling to the body. "We were..."

"Hull, we need to leave now." Sure enough, a crowd had gathered, and more than a handful of people were on their phones. I pulled out my own, dialing the police department and moving to the road to hail a taxi. After a minute of waiting, Lennox's voice chimed in.

"Dr. Walker?"

"Lennox, a boy's been shot. Hull and I can't stay here."

"Boy outside Cape? We've gotten six calls now. Nobody can identify an attacker."

"And nobody will. It was the Man, Lennox. The boy was just about to tell us who he is."

"What happened?"

"The boy's damn chest exploded in front of us, that's what happened. Hull's... gone quiet. I have to get him home."

"I'll handle things there. Is he hurt?"

"No. I..." With a glance back, I mentally confirmed that Hull had yet to move, despite multiple people trying to help him. "I don't know what's wrong with him. I'll get back to you." With that, I hung up the phone and returned to my friend. "Hull, come on, we need to go home."

"He just... So..."

I was no stranger to dealing with people in shock. I'd dealt with my fair share during my time in the Army, and had been in the position myself. To witness something so horrific, so atrocious, that every part of your mentality screeched to a halt. It was enough to destroy even the strongest man or woman. But what was overcoming Hull wasn't the same kind of shock.

And that was what made it more terrifying.

*

When we returned to the flat, Hull immediately went to the bathroom. Being the kind friend I was, I gathered a clean change of clothes from his room and set them outside the door, gave a knock to inform him, then returned to the living room. It was almost an hour later and I could still hear the water running in the bathroom. A small part of me was curious, but I knew better than to intrude on his privacy. Hull held privacy as one of the most important rules in the flat. And he didn't set many personal rules.

By the time the clock changed to 6 PM, I knew he couldn't possibly still be in the shower. The hot water only lasted at most forty-five minutes, and by now, he had to have used up the entire block's water. As I stood to go check on him, the sound of smashing glass sent a chill down my spine. I charged down the hallway and banged on the door.

"Hull?" I yelled, giving another two bangs. "Sheridan, open the door!" There was no response. I could still hear the water from the shower, and that was it. I reached up above the door frame and grabbed the metal key, quickly sliding it in and unlocking the door. I pushed the door open to find Hull standing at the sink, hands clutching the porcelain sides. He stared forward at the broken mirror, breathing heavily. He was fully dressed in the clothes I'd laid out for him, but his hands were still spotted with blood, and from a distance, I couldn't tell if the blood was the boy's or his own.

"We were so close, John," he muttered. "So close to finding him."

"Something else will turn up, Sheridan, it's only a—"

"No, John, don't you *see*?" he yelled, turning to look at me with eyes that looked bloodshot. It was then that I realized, Hull hadn't slept for almost four days. "It's a game to him, John, *a game*. He's smart. Everything he has done, he has done carefully." His head fell. "There is no conclusive evidence. There is nothing else to turn up."

"Are you giving up?"

"*No*," he bit back, eyes locking on mine.

"Then what are you doing?"

He seemed to simmer for a moment before spitting out a reply. "*Thinking*." With that, he returned his focus to the broken mirror, hands clutching the sink even tighter. I gave a sigh, tilting my head and staring at the very puzzling man. Whatever was going on in his head, I couldn't tell. I'd been covered in blood before. Human blood. When one of my squadmates had been stabbed in the neck, and I'd been right next to him. I'd held him as he'd died. I still had his dogtags, since he had no family.

There wasn't a night that went by that I didn't replay every single military death I had witnessed in my head.

It was about three in the morning when I woke from hearing something very loud scratch its way across a wooden floor. I stumbled from my bed, eyesight blurred from the sudden waking, to find one lamp on in the living room, its glow casting a flickering shadow on the balcony windows. In one of the armchairs sat Hull, except he sat with his legs jetting over the top and his head hanging where his feet would be. He stared forward, hands holding on to the wooden knobs that made up the end of the chair.

I looked down at him, turning my head to the side. "Everything all right?"

"The Ambien doesn't work anymore."

"It never made you sleep."

"It doesn't make me think, either."

"Ah." I leaned down to try and be more level with his eyesight, but he didn't seem to notice. He simply stared forward with a vacant look. "Maybe you could try actually sleeping."

"Dull."

I sighed. "You're human, Sheridan. You have to sleep. And death has an effect on you, whether you admit to it or not."

"It's not a matter of life or death. We were so close to solving it. To having the Man. He's played his hand so carefully. He is far more intelligent than the vast majority of my previous case criminals. Far more."

"Whether he's smart or not doesn't mean you can get away with five days without sleep."

He looked up, or I suppose down, from his perspective, at me. "What is it like, living in your world? Where trivial lives have such significant aftershocks when they are lost?"

I stood up straight. "I spent two years watching people I'd come to know as brothers get shot, die of disease, explode, or just go missing. There are some men I met in basic training that were never heard from again. I've seen friends mutilated, people left on a rooftop with their stomachs sliced open and their innards strung out like decorations. There is no such thing as a trivial life. All life has meaning, Sheridan. Maybe someday, you'll understand that." With that, I walked away, no stomping of feet, no added drama. Somewhere deep down, I knew I had left my mark.

As I lay in bed trying to drift back to sleep, I couldn't help but think of some of the men who were lost in the many months I spent deployed. We'd been moved from location to location, fighting different outcrops of terrorist syndicates. My time in Iraq had been short compared to the overall length of the conflicts overseas, but I'd seen too much in too little of time. One of my best friends growing up, James Kryack, had been one of four men who went missing that night. And I could remember his vanishing all-too vividly. The size of the moon in the sky, the sounds of bullets screaming over our heads.

It was April 29th, 2011.

*

Captain! Sir, wake up!

John's eyes snapped open, and immediately the sound of yelling men and explosions filled his ears. He lurched forward, throwing his blanket and grabbing his boots. To his left stood Sergeant Major James Kryack, one of John's oldest friends. He had a look of desperation to his face that stressed the urgency of the situation.

"What's going on, James?" John asked, tying his boot.

"They hit us hard, John. Patrol was taken out at oh-two-hundred. They sent a flaming jeep through the camp."

"Where's the Major?"

"At the forward bunker, trying to coordinate a counterattack."

John stood, grabbing his jacket from the foot of his bunk. "Casualties?"

"No idea yet. But it's bad, John." James looked him dead in the eyes, a shadow cast over the man's face. "Real bad." John nodded, then together, they ran from the tent, their direction focused on where the forward bunker would be, about thirty meters north of the bunks. As they ran, John could hear explosions ringing out from all around them. Ahead of him, a tent was in flames. Two troops did their best to contain the fire, to no avail. John grabbed the pistol from his holster, holding it at his side.

"Where did they come from? We cleared the outpost hours ago!"

"No clue. Probably a group sent to find out what happened to that outpost. I was just about to head to bed when the jeep came through." The man hesitated. "I think I could see someone inside it."

"Who was on patrol tonight?"

"Olsen and Jenkins."

"Damn. We have to regroup. Is everyone headed forward?"

"Mostly. Some people are going towaaaaaarrrrrrrrrgggggggghhhhh!"

John spun as fast he could to see an arm pulling James back into a tent. From the tent came two men, both hidden by the darkness. John's pistol was raised in an instant, one bullet going through the head of the left man, another through the leg of the right. He lurched forward, grabbing James' hand with his open arm and firing into the tent with the gun. James looked up at John with fear overflowing in his eyes; the pulling arm wasn't giving in.

"Let go of him, you son of a bitch!" John roared, firing two more shots into the darkness. A figure burst from the tent, smashing the pistol out of John's hand. John stumbled back as the assailant toppled on to him, rolling off and quickly standing. John turned to the man and, with a swift spin, sent his leg out and into the man's stationed feet, causing him to trip and fall in his charge. John stood quickly and with just as swift a motion, slammed his heel down into the man's face.

"*John!*"

The soldier turned to see the tent, but no sight of his friend. He snatched his pistol from the ground before running in, only to find it empty.

"James!" he yelled, running to the back of the tent and forcing his way through the polyester. He ripped through to an area of rolling sand hills, and still, his friend was nowhere to be seen. In the distance, he could see the outpost they'd attacked, the buildings burning with instigated fire. But those fires didn't matter to him.

His friend was gone. And he'd let him slip right out of his hand.

"*James!*" he screamed again, hoping, praying for a response. Nothing besides the sounds of gunfire and more explosions returned. It was remarkable, really. Despite the mesh of different noises of violence occurring, John's ears had tuned it all out. They patiently waited for the voice of his friend to call back to him. They waited through the silence for a response.

A response that never came.

*

When I finally woke from my night of sleeplessness, I couldn't help but groan. The aches and pains of my memories still rang through my muscles and joints. But what was even more shocking was the smell of cooking bacon that wafted from the kitchen to my room. Bacon that I knew I had not made. And considering Mrs. Hanson was a very firm-minded vegan, it was impossible she would have made it. Which left only one option.

I entered the living room to find the chalkboard covered in printed pictures of the Man in Red, all the same. Hull's laptop and my laptop were propped on the table that had been moved to be parallel to the board, both computers playing the Man in Red's video. Even Hull's phone was positioned so that the screen was between the laptops, and it was playing the video. Hull, however, was in the kitchen, wearing the same clothes as he'd donned last night, but with cleaned hands, which were currently handling a pan and spatula.

"Oh, good, you're awake!" he called out, not looking my way. "I just finished breakfast."

"You... finished breakfast?" I asked as I shuffled my way into the kitchen. Sure enough, the small table was filled with different breakfast items. Pancakes, sausages, bacon, toast, fruit. Even a glass of grape juice had been poured and waited by the only plate on the table.

"You were right, John!" he exclaimed as he added more bacon to the already-filled bacon plate. "I felt the need to thank you."

"I was ri— now hold on, since when can you cook?"

He smiled. "My mother was not the best chef. I learned to fend for myself at an early age." He turned back to the stove, switching it off and taking the pan to the sink. I shook my head, more confused than ever, but decided it would be easier for me to play along than question his seemingly-good intentions. I took the seat and started filling my plate. As I did, he moved out into the living room, pressing the play button on all three screens.

As I cut through one of the pancakes, I decided to press my questions. "How was I right?"

"You said that there was no such thing as trivial life. You were right, to an extent. A person such as yourself would think along those lines because you had witnessed the unnecessary loss of life. You hold that in value which you have seen taken unwillingly. And it made things click. The Man in Red must have a motive for his selections, else there would be no touch of genius to this. And the morality is the motive!"

"The morality is the motive," I repeated, dipping the pancake in syrup.

"The Man chooses his victims from a video, but more specifically, he picks those who comment. But the video had hundreds of comments, and yet, only twenty-two people have died. So what set them apart? Morality. Each of these individuals must have held some ulterior significance, must have done something to put them on the Man's radar. He only needed them to comment on his video, as if it were a green flag for him to continue."

He danced across the living room, picking up the pile of papers about the murders and suicides. He held one up for me to see. "The murdered YouTube personalities. Their account had over six hundred published videos that were aimed at comedic entertainment. They had well over two million subscribers. So what could they have done to provoke the Man in Red? And subsequently, what could the other twenty have done? What did Nathaniel Montorum do? What did the boy at the bar do?"

"I don't know, Hull," I said as I raised my glass of juice. "What did they do?"

The glint to his eye was impossibly indistinguishable. "Comment." He turned back to the computers, scrolling down. "Each and every one of them commented on the Man in Red's video. But this was not the only video they commented on. Only a short half an hour ago did I realize a video in particular was highlighted in the recommended sidebar. This video was made by the two individuals who were first murdered. The video is a comedic look at *bullying*. A satire on the issue. But not just that. Their sick sense of humor displays bullying of everyone. Boy, girl, supervisor, animal. *Handicapped students.*"

Realization dawned on me. "The Montorum boy had a reputation for bullying handicapped students."

"Precisely!" Hull said, his voice ringing with excitement. "I perused the comments and found a large number of people to remark on the humor in the abuse of the fake handicapped individuals in the video. It may be fake to them, but to the Man in Red? Perhaps he took it to another level entirely. This is what I believe." He pulled out his phone. After a very short moment, I heard a very soft response. "I need Inspector Lennox, now."

"Why are you calling Lennox?"

Hull ignored me. "Lennox, I need you here, and I need you to bring seven of your best computer specialists. Oh, and bring seven computers." He hung up. I gave him a look that screamed of curiosity. "My resources are limited, but I suspect that if we search the comments of both the bullying parody and the Man in Red's video, we will find the same people. And all of those people, will be those who have died."

It wasn't long before Lennox and his men arrived. While they set up the living room with seven additional laptops, I cleaned the kitchen as best I could. By the time I was done, they were ready. Hull had arranged them in a semi-circle, all facing him. In his hand was a sheet of paper, and on it, a list of names.

"All you need to do is link the names to one of the YouTube accounts from the video comments to 'The Man in Red is Watching.' From there, you will find that account and its accompanying comment on this video. Once all nineteen are accounted for, we will be ready to continue." The men, Lennox included, nodded and began working. Once I was sure all of them were deep in their searching, I came up beside Hull.

"Finally found that breakthrough, then?"

"Oh it feels so liberating, I cannot even begin to describe it. It all makes sense now. Now the hunt is in our favor."

"How will confirming the names to the comments help us?"

"It will give substantial evidence. I know who he is."

"What? You do?"

"Oh yes. And once we have gathered enough evidence, it will only be a matter of time before he turns himself in."

"I've got a confirmed link," one of the specialists announced before rattling off a name and account. Hull nodded, scratching the name off his list. One by one, the specialists found the people before finally, all nineteen had been accounted for.

"I thought you said twenty-two people had been murdered?" I asked as Hull ripped the pictures from his chalkboard.

"Two of them were the owners of the YouTube channel, and they did not need to comment, the Man targeted them anyways. One was the boy murdered yesterday. He did not comment, but did take part in the bullying with young Montorum." Once he'd finished ripping away, the words "THE MAN IN RED IS WATCHING" were visible in chalk, the only words written on the board.

"So how do we show this all as evidence?" Lennox prompted while the other specialists started packing their equipment.

"We show the correlations and—"

Hull stopped, his eyes locked on the chalkboard. I waited for him to finish his sentence, but he obviously had no intention of doing so. His jaw seemed to tremble as he stared at the chalk-written words.

"Hull? What do we do?" Lennox questioned.

"*Brilliant*," he finally said, even though it had no relation to his previous sentence.

"Brilliant what?" I asked, looking from the detective's face to the board.

"Absolutely brilliant." He looked at Lennox. "You really do think this is brilliant, don't you?"

"Hull, I have no idea what you're going on about," the inspector replied.

Hull gave a look of surprise. "Do you not see it?" he said with a gesture at the board.

"I see what you wrote. Am I supposed to see something else? Crop circles in the letters?"

"Isn't it obvious, it's all a—"

He stopped again, and this time I heard a distinct vibration noise come from his pocket. He reached down and grabbed his phone, swiftly bringing it up and reading the screen. After ten seconds of silence, he pocketed the phone and moved to the armchair.

"I have to go," he said as he stretched into his coat.

"You what?" Lennox and I both said.

"My attention is required elsewhere," he shot back.

Lennox was visibly irritated. "Sheridan, you can't seriously just walk out—"

Hull slapped the stack of papers about the murders and suicides into Lennox's hands. "Take these and the data found to the courthouse. I will be along shortly." With that, he was out the door. And none of us had even the slightest clue why.

*

THE END IS NOW.

The message that had shown up on Hull's phone was still burned bright into his inner eyelids. He'd expected it. He'd waited for it. And as soon as it had come, he had taken the opportunity. And now, as he exited the taxi cab and walked towards an old warehouse, he knew the hunt was over. He had found his target, here, in the district commonly called "the End" by warehouse owners and industrial corporations. His target, here, inside the building owned by the Newfield Organization of Workers. His target, here. Oh how clever he had been.

Hull stepped into the warehouse and followed the dimly-lit path. It led him through the empty warehouse towards the back offices, exactly where he expected his target to be. The Man in Red was smart, and knew when he was beaten. He knew that Hull had made all of the proper connections, and that the hunt was done. He was the victor. Of course the Man would want to meet him in person. Two men of such astounding intelligence should have the honor of meeting each other. Hull considered it a shame that the Man would dedicate his intelligence to murder rather than something more beneficial to progress. But then again, there were still parts of this case that were unclear. Parts that he hoped would soon become clear.

Before him was a single door with a distorted window, yet he could still see the light inside. He slowly turned the handle and entered to find a conference room of sorts. A large, bulky chandelier hung from the ceiling above a wooden table that stretched the length of the room. Only two chairs were at the table, however, both at the center and facing each other. The chair that faced the door, the one Hull had only just walked through, was empty. The chair that faced the opposite direction was occupied by a burly figure who had a slight hunch. What was more interesting was the wheelchair parked at the figure's side.

"Oh, of course," Hull said out loud, giving a slight smirk. "How could I have overlooked such an important part."

The Man looked over his shoulder, nodding his head towards the table. "Have a seat, Mr. Hull." Hull complied, moving around the table to take the seat. The Man in Red was a fairly normal-looking individual, probably in his late fifties, gray hair, some slight stubble. He wore a ragged shirt and aged pants, and currently rested his hands in his lap. He looked at Hull with avid interest, his amber eyes swirling.

"I must congratulate you, Mr. Hull," the Man said. "This has been quite the end of my mission. I could not have hoped for better."

"Your mission, yes. And now the motive makes even more sense. Now you make more sense."

"Put all the pieces together, then, I presume?"

"Of course. Only someone with plenty of connections could have performed as stealthily as you have. A former CIA agent, then. FBI would have been too unaccommodating. Your previous connections allowed you to stay under the radar while you performed your mission. A fascinating case, if I do say so, Mr. Carth Younger."

The Man in Red, or Carth Younger, gave a smile. "Glad you understood that part as well. You truly are an intelligent individual, Mr. Hull. I doubt anyone else could have understood my riddles."

Hull smirked. "Why, then? The riddles, the killings, the game? The hunt."

"You want me to tell you what you already know?"

"No, I want you tell me what you did, thus confirming what I already know."

Younger snorted. "Clever man. But I'd rather hear your take on it. Please, Mr. Hull. Enlighten me."

Hull paused for a moment before leaning forward. "Carth Younger, former Central Intelligence Agent, retired due to multiple circumstances in 1996. One circumstance was your preexisting handicapped state as a result of an early hereditary disease. At the age of five, you suffered from a steady disintegration of bone marrow that rendered your legs almost useless. You have been confined to a wheelchair since."

"You've done your research," Younger interrupted, giving a content shake. "Continue."

"Your motive was tricky, but now that I can see you for myself, it makes much more logical sense. To take a trip back into your history, we go to when you had a son. Charlie Isaac Younger, I believe his name was. Your son, unfortunately, inherited the same genetic disorder that caused you so much suffering, and at the age of six, he too was confined to a wheelchair. His experiences, however, were far worse than yours had been. A horrible new sensation had swept its way through the public education system. That sensation was bullying.

"Your son was bullied at a very young age, and the abuse continued up until his early high school years. Despite you and your wife's best attempts, the bullying persisted and caused your son much grief and distress. At the age of fourteen, your son could not handle the attacks anymore, and committed suicide. Found by your wife in the bathroom after having bled to death. As a result of this, you decided to seek justice. You had frequently heard names from your son, the names of the major bullies, and started a campaign to charge them with the murder of your boy.

"Your attempts were, unfortunately, unsuccessful. No justice was served on the young men, and soon enough, they had graduated and moved on with their lives, not giving your deceased son a second thought. You, however, were not so willing to let go. You wanted more to come from his death. Your wife, however, did not share this sentiment, and two years after the death of your son, she left you. The pain of her leaving was hard enough on you, but just three months after your divorce was finalized, she was in a fatal car crash. In the blink of an eye, both of your dearest loved ones were lost.

"In your sorrows, you resigned from your position with the CIA and started a new life, or at least tried. You found no happiness, however, as you felt justice had not been served for your son. Approximately seven years ago, you gained a new purpose when you were diagnosed with amyotrophic lateral sclerosis. This disease would not only destroy your body, but it would inevitably kill you. From there on out, you acknowledged that you were living on borrowed time. And that was when you put your plans into motion.

"It started with a video that you saw of two young men poking fun at victims of bullying. You were able to lure them away from the public and murder them. After they were dead, you realized that with your disposition, continuing your murders would be difficult. So you devised a new strategy in your intelligent, devilish mind. You created a video and used distortion effects to alter it enough to make the video interesting and, using a simple method of watching and searching, you waited for people to view your video, leave a rude comment, and move on to another video, like the one made by the YouTube personalities you'd killed.

"One by one, you were able to kill people, luring them away by scaring them and then talking to them. You told them of the dark, sinister evils they had performed, and as a result, they either committed suicide or begged you for death. The art of war fought with words is a delicate one, but can in fact be the most dangerous. By the time you had reached here, twenty people were dead, and only two of them had opted to take your bullet. The rest had willingly killed themselves. Little by little, a part of you believed that justice in the memory of your son was being enacted. Little by little, you believed that you witnessed redemption."

"Right on all counts, Mr. Hull," Younger said. "Right on all counts indeed."

"But the intelligence in your plans does not stop there, does it?" Hull added. "No, you see, you're not just an intelligent man. You're a proper genius. It was not until just an hour ago that I realized the true extent of your intelligence, locked away in a few simple words. 'THE MAN IN RED IS WATCHING.' Upon first glance, a simple title to a video, very self-explanatory. But when elaborated upon? When all things were considered, when your true character was taken into mind? Then it became so much more. Then your true intelligence became evident.

"In 400 AD, a poet whose identity is not known to this day published a piece by the name of 'The Missed Man in Red and Black.' The poem spoke of Oedipus, the Greek king of Thebes. A particular passage in the poem said, 'Redemption is at hand. The younger witch dies. The new hangs. I cannot, son. Oeci.' Curious bit of insight from the poet, but even more curious when a man like you, sixteen hundred years later, saw what the poet had done and created an anagram cleverly hidden in the text that came directly from the title.

"When the letters from the passage were rearranged, they created a new sentence. 'The Man in Red is watching.' You were able to derive a title for your video from a passage that held such deep meaning to you. Redemption, sought for your dead son. The younger witch, a reference to your wife, whom you loved so dearly, the woman of the Younger family, but also a woman who had become so rude, so vile in her personality, you viewed her as a witch. The New, referring to the original bully of your son, a young man who had the last name Newman. And of course, your inevitable acceptance of your inability to provide proper justice. 'I cannot, son.'

"The final four letters required to complete the anagram were tricky, but with the right amount of deduction, it made sense. Oeci was not apart of the original transcript to the poem, but it was added several hundred years later by a fellow who believed a word of Latin parting would do it well. You, however, took your own turn to it. OE was to reference Oedipus, the one the poem was written for. CI was to reference your son, Charlie Isaac, the one the anagram was created for. With this, the anagram was completed. Your intellectual prowess was peaked."

"Very good, Mr. Hull, very good," Younger said, leaning back slightly. "Now why did I bring you here?"

"To congratulate me. You observed as I solved the anagram through the many viewings of the video, the repeating of the words, the pictures. You watched as it fell together for me. You never intended to kill me. The only reason the boy outside Cape died was because of his relation to your cause. Otherwise, he would have lived."

"Well done. Truly, well done. You have been a pleasure to watch at work, Mr. Hull. You really have."

Hull smiled. "Oh, I'm not done yet."

"Oh?"

"You see, Mr. Younger, there is still a very significant issue at hand. Despite the string of murders and suicides, you still feel an emptiness, a yearning for justice in memory of your son. It's visible in the kills, in the video production, in your face, in your eyes at this very moment. You hold on to the memories of your son with what remains of your former self. But you know what you are doing is in vain." Younger's cheek twitched, and Hull knew he was on the brink of success.

"You grieve over the death of your son because you feel responsible. Like his weakness was your fault. You could not have stopped the bullies. You could not have prevented what happened. So much played into the death of your son, and alone, you could not have changed the events. You are a man driven by morality. You must see why you act in vain. The only way to truly do your son justice is to live on in his memory. To remember him. Not to avenge him. For his death is not one that calls for it."

"Who are you to say that?"

"A man who has come to know someone like you. Someone who has the subconscious need to cling to something in their past. A man driven by morality."

Younger's eyes trembled. "Those boys tortured my son, Mr. Hull. Physically. Emotionally. Mentally. Psychologically. They destroyed everything he was until there was nothing left."

"I understand, Mr. Younger. But nothing you do now will change what they have done. They must live on with their actions haunting their thoughts. You cannot." Hull leaned back. "I will admit, your cause was a noble one, and that is why I have no intentions of turning you in to the police. While I cannot condone your actions, I can observe and deduce that you did what you, and many others, would deem as right. Self-served justice. It is a shame the true courts would never see it that way.

"Mr. Younger, I am not a man of emotions, nor will I ever profess to be. I am a man of science, a man who is able to look at anything and understand it. And when I look at you, I see a very pained person. One who does not need to suffer as they do. You can find solace in the memories of your son. But you will never find peace in the murders of others."

Younger stared at Hull for a very long, quiet time before giving a small nod. Hull could feel that he had reached a part of the man that had long been sealed away.

"You're right," Younger said, nodding a few more times. He licked his lips. "You're right." He remained silent for nearly a minute before straightening in his seat. "Would you mind changing seats with me, Mr. Hull?"

Hull looked at the man with a slight hint of confusion, not expecting the request. Complying, Hull stood and moved to the side of the table. Once again confusing Hull, Younger did not enter his wheelchair, instead using the table for support as he hobbled to the other side. The shake to the man's legs were visible even through his pants. Once he had taken Hull's seat, the detective took the only open one and faced the man with his own avid interest.

"Thank you, Mr. Hull." Younger gulped, a cold sense of resignation crossing his eyes. He nodded once. "Thank you."

What happened next, Hull most certainly did not expect.

Carth Younger pulled a gun from the inside of his ragged coat, and instead of aiming it at Hull, he pointed it to his left. Hull quickly followed the man's aim and found a rope tied to the wall. Hull's eyes traveled up the rope, seeing it cross over the top of a supporting beam in the ceiling, then move horizontally to another beam before reaching the top hook of the chandelier. The chandelier which was now positioned directly above Carth Younger.

Without hesitation, the man fired the pistol. The bullet pierced the rope with amazing precision, causing its few threads to snap. The rope quickly flew up, flying over the first beam and giving the chandelier enough free reign to move. The mighty structure of glass and metal moved down, nothing to stop its path. Hull's vision seemed to slow down, all sounds and other things to see becoming dark. All that existed was the falling chandelier. Despite time having slowed to a crawl, the chandelier had gained its momentum. And just a moment later, it found its target.

Carth Younger was no more.

*

Lennox and I approached the warehouse with caution, a squad of policemen behind us with their pistols ready. The emergency call had come twenty minutes ago, about an hour and a half after Hull had left. None of us had followed him, but we knew he was here. And as we waited patiently, our eyes trained on the door, fear began to seep into all of our minds.

Fear that was quickly dispelled.

Hull walked from the doorway, his eyes showing their distinctive glint. He approached us with a slight bit of a stride, not one filled with pride but resolution.

"Send your men in, but have them lower the guns," Hull said to Lennox. "Have them delicately extract whatever remains there may be of Mr. Carth Younger."

"Who?" Lennox asked.

"The Man in Red. His body, or whatever is left, will be underneath the shattered chandelier in the back conference room."

"His body will... *what*?" Lennox demanded.

Hull clasped the man's shoulder. "In time, Inspector." He walked past a flustered Lennox and approached me.

"So," I said as we turned to walk away.

"Thank you, John. Your services were invaluable in this case."
"And exactly how were they invaluable?"
He smirked. "In time, Doctor."
In time indeed.

THE CASE OF THE MISSING KNIGHT

"The doctor will see you in a moment."

The nurse closed the door behind her before walking back out into the small circle of desks, where I currently sat with a pile of folders to my right and signed paperwork to my left. I scribbled my signature onto another file, signifying that I had seen the patient and cleared them for a certain prescription before setting it on top of the visibly-shorter pile and glancing up. The nurse, named Amy, came to me with a smile before handing me another folder.

"Got another one for you. He won't go into detail on his symptoms, so I have no idea," she said casually, leaning against the desk.

"Gotta love the silent ones," I remarked as I looked over the file. The patient's name was something foreign, presumably French. Jacques Retenue, mid-twenties, good health all of his life. In fact, his medical history was surprisingly empty for someone around twenty-five. "Well of course he's sick, he's due for it. Never been sick a day in his life, if this record means anything."

"He didn't seem very French to me," Amy added. "But I guess I'm just here to get their height, weight, and temperature."

I laughed. "But it's so much fun, especially when it's kids."

She smiled. "So, have any plans for the weekend?"

As it turned out, I didn't. In fact, I hadn't done anything but work in two weeks, since it had been that long since the Man in Red incident had been wrapped up. Sure enough, the body of a crippled man was found torn to shreds under a chandelier and there was no way to check if Hull had been the one to do it or not. Lennox had helped in that regard by sweeping Hull's involvement under the rug. Everyone just seemed to be happy the murderer had been caught. Even the mayor had given us a call and thanked us personally for aiding in the stopping of his son's killer.

I think the only person not happy with the case's results was Hull. He still won't tell me what happened inside that room, but I don't think it was all-too destructive towards him. He's the one that lived, after all.

"It just so happens that I have nothing this weekend," I replied as I closed the folder. "Why, do you happen to know of anything good happening?"

"I have tickets for *The Amazing Spider-Man,* if you'd like to go. Monica was going to go with me, but she bailed."

"I think I'd love to go."

"Great!" she exclaimed, her smile widening. "Then it's a date."

A slight flutter in my stomach made it hard not to try and match her smile. "Looking forward to it."

"Awesome, I'll text you the details." She glanced back at the door. "Right now, you should probably get to your patient. I'd hate for us both to get fired."

"True enough," I said as I stood, walking around the desk and towards the door, file in hand. My mind was now thoroughly distracted, so part of me was worried I'd completely mess up the minor diagnosis for this patient. Those minor worries very, very quickly dissipated after I entered.

The man who sat on the medical bed waiting for me was not in fact a French by the name of Jacques Retenue. It was Sheridan Hull.

"Why would you use a fake name, go through the appointment process, and sit here just to talk to me when you could've walked in the front door and asked?" I said as I slapped the folder down on the table.

"I didn't feel the need to disturb you in your working environment," he replied, legs rocking back and forth slightly.

"Are you actually here for a medical reason?"

"Oh no, of course not, I am here to get you."

"So you didn't want to interrupt me, but you want me to leave."

"It is of the utmost importance."

"It must be, since you created a false identity."

He looked towards the window. "I created Jacques Retenue years ago, the name comes in handy when I need it."

"And you need it now?"

"No, I need you now."

"Why?"

"Moriarty is back."

That was enough to stop my thoughts. It had been almost four months since we'd heard any direct mention of the illusive figure. For Hull to be making this level of a claim, he had to have some ground to his theory.

"How do you know?"

"I received a most urgent phone call from a Mrs. Angela Knight, requesting my presence at once. Her message told me that her husband had recently gone missing while on a trip to Venezuela and she would like me to investigate."

"And that leads to Moriarty how?"

"Easily. We need to leave now," he said as he stepped down from the bed.

"You do realize I'm working, right? That this is a job?"

He grabbed his coat from the back of the door. "Yes, I am aware. Though I do not see how you could fail to weigh the importance of the situation."

I sighed. "If you get me fired for this, I'll stop the Hulu subscription."

"Why would this affect me?"

I grabbed the folder from the table. "Don't you dare think I haven't heard you laughing at *The Office* around four in the morning. You went through at least half of season six alone last night."

*

Mrs. Knight lived in a somewhat-isolated home in the residential district, a blue two-story with a large window facing the front and a picket fence creating the perimeter. There wasn't another owned house for the rest of the block, which was probably due to the prices. The homes here were most definitely not cheap, or even relatively affordable on a high-paying job. You had to be very well-off to live here. And when you factored in the car that was parked in front of the house, it wasn't hard to tell the Knight family was most definitely well-off.

Hull and I currently sat in a furnished living room with two cups of coffee in front of us. Mrs. Knight was putting a tray of snacks together for us, giving Hull some time to examine the room. It was pretty straightforward, though. Leather furniture, paintings on the walls of landscapes and people, a fireplace with picture frames above them. The room looked like a typical living room for a typical family.

Except for, of course, the swords and knives.

In all of the blank spaces on the walls, swords had been propped into place with tiny plaques beneath them. Along the far wall of the room was a glass showcase, filled with knives and other sharp, pointed weapons. Mrs. Knight had warned us prior to our entering the room that her husband had been an avid collector of medieval weaponry. But this was something else entirely. If Moriarty really had a hand in this case, then this room was literally my worst nightmare.

Mrs. Knight reentered the room with a silver tray in hand. She looked to be in her late twenties, with bleach blonde hair pulled back into a bun and thick bags under her green eyes. Her complementary green dress was finely pressed, completing an image of a happy woman who lacked sleep. The lack of sleep no doubt came from the matter at hand.

Hull took his seat next to me as the woman set the tray down, gesturing for us to try the food. The tray was covered with crackers, cheeses, meat slices, and some kind of dip in the center. I constructed a small sample while Hull leaned back, eyes focused on the woman.

"Now, Mrs. Knight, please explain the situation, and do not exclude information you may believe to be unimportant," the detective said, nostrils flaring. The woman cleared her throat before beginning.

"My husband has worked as a business liaison for several years now, since before we were married. Most of the time his company would only send him around the state, but sometimes they would have him do international trips. I was able to go with him on a few of them, but after a while the international trips became more and more frequent, and I had my own job to worry about. I spent more time home alone while he was off in Europe or Australia.

"Four years ago, my husband went to Venezuela for a conference meeting to discuss the business he was apart of expanding to have a branch there. When he came home, however, the first thing he did was quit his job. He and I spent a lot of time together after that, and he even tried starting his own business from home. It was successful, I would say. It helped us buy this house, and fuel his want for these ridiculous swords. Everything seemed to be going well.

"About a month ago, he received a phone call from a private number. The very next day, he was on a plane to Venezuela, and when he came back, he was different. Everything about him just seemed to be off. And I assumed something had happened on the trip, and either he would tell me or he'd get over it. But he just seemed to get worse. A few days ago, he told me he was going to Venezuela again. He left the next morning and I haven't heard from him since. I don't want to think the worst, Detective, but I don't know what else to expect at this point. I believe my husband is dead."

Hull stared at the woman for a very long, silent time before standing. "Not interested."

Her eyes widened. "I beg your pardon?"

"Not interested." He turned away.

"Mr. Hull, you have to help me! I need closure!"

"You are assuming I do the work of a greyhound dog. I do not. If you want to find your husband, you will need to find someone who specializes in finding lost things."

"But Mr. Hull—"

"Mrs. Knight, unless you can provide me with sufficient reason to believe finding your husband holds any interest, I bid you a good afternoon." He started walking from the room.

"Wait!"

Hull stopped. I looked at the woman to see a newfound desperation in her eyes. Now the bags beneath her eyes were far more significant than the other features. Now it was obvious how in need of help she was.

"He mentioned something before he left," she revealed, looking around the room. "I wasn't sure what he meant, but there was a letter." Her eyes finally reached a stack of mail on the end table by the door. Before she could even stand, Hull had the stack in his hands and started filtering through. His hands ceased motion when they reached the designated letter. I could tell by the sudden rigidness to his back that whatever the letter contained was no good at all.

"Arthur Mallory Knight," Hull said as he turned. "Businessman, renowned author, philanthropist. And yet none of those titles matter in comparison to his true employer." He set the stack down, still holding the one letter. He came back to us, still standing but now facing Mrs. Knight and staring very sternly into her eyes. "Did your husband ever mention Operation DAGGER?"

She looked from Hull to me. "Operation what?"

"I thought not," Hull remarked, tucking the letter away inside his coat. "The case now has my interest. Mrs. Knight, I would like you to contact your husband's prior place of employment and have them tell you everything about his regular trips to Venezuela. Who he had dealings with, the purpose of the trips, those sorts of things. Be thorough. Dr. Walker and I will do our own outside investigation and return to you once we have substantial information." With that, he once again turned and this time left the room entirely. I had no idea what to make of the situation, but I knew better than to wait. I joined Hull outside the house, where he waited. He looked up at the sun, popping the collar of his coat as he stared.

"Operation DAGGER?" I asked.

"I haven't the slightest clue what it is. Unfortunately, neither does she. That makes things worse."

"Wouldn't your brother know?"

He scrunched his face in disgust before replying. "I do not think this is a government project."

"So what the Hell kind of leads do you have for this? What did the letter say?"

"'Operation DAGGER must be continued. -M' was the exact wording."

"Moriarty. But why would Knight leave? Do you think he's still in Venezuela?"

"No," Hull said with a bit of a purr to his voice. "I think he's here, in Newfield. And I think he's dead."

*

Hull and I stood in the police station thirty minutes later, waiting for Lennox to get the proper clearance to get us the information Hull had requested. I wasn't entirely sure what Hull hoped to find, but he seemed determined enough. He wanted a background check done on Arthur Mallory Knight, no information withheld. A lot of this case was very foggy for me, but I suppose that wasn't anything new. Most of the cases went completely over my head until Hull took the time to explain, and even then there were times I was left perpetually in the dark.

Lennox returned to his office after about five minutes, giving Hull a nod. The detective accessed all records he could in regards to Knight. I watched as page after page flashed into view, Hull pausing for only a fraction of a second per page. At least three dozen pages had flashed by before he finally stopped, sitting down in Lennox's chair and pressing his hands together.

"Very curious," he said.

Lennox crossed his arms. "I hate when you say that."

"Knight is a very normal individual. Graduated from college with degrees in psychology and biology, as well as a minor in chemistry. He met his wife in his third year of college and married her ten months later. They have been married since."

"So nothing substantial," I noted as I leaned against the wall.

"One thing thus far." Hull scrolled back a few pages to show Knight's résumé. "Knight's place of employment is a name you won't recognize, simply because the company has been bankrupt for almost seven years. This application, however, was updated just three years ago, with the same company listed. I doubt he worked for this company at all. In fact, I believe he has been working for someone else the entire time."

"Anything about DAGGER?" I asked.

Lennox cocked his eyebrows. "About what?"

"Nothing comes up," Hull replied, eyes returning to the screen. Lennox stared at him, then glanced up at me.

"We're not quite sure what it is," I replied, being completely honest. The inspector shrugged, eyes going back to Hull. The detective scrolled through pages without pause for another minute before he stopped, eyes flashing.

"Interesting," he said ominously, the chair squeaking as he leaned back. "Knight wrote his masters' thesis on suggestive natures as a result of chemical influence. Quite the specific topic."

I gave a shrug. "Masters' theses usually require a specific topic. You'd know that if you—"

"If I graduated college, har har. As if that joke hasn't reached its point of weariness."

"I wasn't going to make a joke, but sure, let's go with that."

Hull scoffed. "It's what you were going to go with beforehand. Your sentence was lined up for it. You would know that if you had stayed in your first selected major." With that retort, I couldn't help but smirk. My first major had been English, for about two terms. It was the third term that I realized medicine was my true calling.

That, or English major-based jobs made nothing in regards to money, and I wasn't going to become a teacher.

"Nothing here can assist us. His information is either too vague or too specific to point us in the right direction," Hull stated as he closed out of the window. "Without a trip to Venezuela, I do not think we will make as much progress as I would prefer."

Before I could respond, a distinct vibrating started from Hull's pocket. He pulled the phone out and gave an odd look at the screen before pressing the answer button.

"Hello?"

*

"So boring, isn't it? When the case lacks the information needed to make it keep you going? When it lacks what it needs to make it fun?"

Hull stood, his eyes narrowed and face slightly flushed. "Who is this?"

"Come now, Sheridan, who do you think it is?"

Without ever having heard the hoarse voice before, he knew with every fiber of his body who was on the other end of the line. "Ah. You."

"Yes, me. A pleasure to finally speak to you in person. Or via telephone, I suppose."

"What do you want."

"A chat. Am I not allowed to call up an adversary for a simple conversation?"

"No."

There was a chuckle. "No, I suppose not. I called to push you on the right path. I'd hate to see you give up."

"Hull, who is it?" Walker said. Hull shook his head at the doctor, quickly pressing his finger against his own lips.

"Stop delaying, then. Give me the 'push.'"

"There's a reason the neighborhood was so empty."

"That's all?"

"Any more and it just wouldn't be fun."

"Fine."

Before Hull could hang up, the voice continued. "How challenging did you find the Man in Red before your big revelation?" A slight pause. "Before you dismantled the code?"

"Six."

"What a low rating when your adversary was a genius. Curious, how he was able to do everything with just his mind and a not-so-able body. He entered my radar after the third murder, but I recognized how futile his efforts were. How misguided his plan was."

"I would say he was far from misguided."

"His plans didn't align with my own. But no matter. There isn't much longer left now."

"Until what?"

"It's going to happen very soon, Sheridan. The pieces are in play and the world is in motion. Quite fun, though, isn't it? Watching the lesser ones dance? So clueless, so yearning for clarity. They'll never understand like we do, Sheridan. They simply never will. Until my plans come to fruition. Then, finally, order will be brought to the chaos."

"Then it is my job to ensure your plans do not come to fruition."

"Of course. You don't understand. Not yet. Perhaps you never will. You will either submit to my eventual rule, or you will die. And I know you are not a man to submit, Sheridan Hull. So you shall die. And when that day comes that you do die, and trust me, it will come, I will ensure that I am there to witness it, if I am not the one killing you myself."

Hull stepped out of the room and into an empty hallway, closing the door behind him. "If I were assured of your eventual destruction I would, in the interests of the public, cheerfully accept my own."

Another chuckle. "I thought so."

Click.

*

"What the Hell is going on?" I questioned as Lennox and I exited the office. Hull stood in the hallway, phone in his hand and screen off. He stared down into it with glazed eyes and a slight twitch to his cheek. "Hull?"

"It was Moriarty," the detective said, flipping the phone over slowly in his hand.

"What? He just *called* you?" I prompted.

"Who the Hell is Moriarty?" Lennox interjected.

"He said there's a reason the neighborhood Knight lived in is abandoned. Nobody lived within two houses of theirs." Hull pocketed the phone. "Which means something is inside one of the houses. And I think I know exactly what."

"How did he get your number?" I asserted as Hull started down the hallway.

"*Who* is Moriarty?" Lennox added.

"The leader of a crime syndicate group here in Newfield. With a network as vast as his, I would be surprised if he wasn't able to access my number."

The first sentence froze Lennox. "The leader of *what*?"

"A crime syndicate group, Inspector. Called Chimaera."

Despite Hull's tone of voice, I was impressed. In telling Lennox this, it showed he had some level of trust for the man. A level higher than the one he held for his own brother.

Lennox ran his hands through his hair. "Jesus.. I know that name. We've had it come up in questionings but we've never given it a second thought."

"It would be wise to give it a *first* thought, then," Hull said as he stepped into the stairwell. Lennox and I followed him down to the lobby, where I finally found the words I'd been struggling to garner.

"Exactly what are we going to find?"

"You'll see. You both will."

Lennox stopped. "Both?"

"I would assume you would accompany us, Inspector." Hull gave a very short smirk. "You seem to have a vested interest in this case. Independent from the department." With that, he was out the door, and sure enough, Lennox walked at my side as I followed the detective from the building.

Another half-hour passed, and by the time we reached the neighborhood, the sun was starting to set. Part of me was growing more anxious about my date, but I knew better than to get distracted now. We pulled up quietly to the empty house directly next to the Knight home. It wasn't too late, but the lights were already off in the windows, presumably meaning the woman had gone out. The three of us moved quickly towards the house, Hull and me keeping watch while Lennox picked the lock.

Yes. The police inspector was the one to pick the lock.

"Got it," Lennox announced as he opened the door. As soon as we entered the house, a very foul stench permeated my nostrils. I recognized the scent all-too well: death.

"Find it, but do not disturb it," Hull said as he stepped forward into the dark living room. I moved off into the kitchen while Lennox went up the stairs. As he walked, I could see his hand drop to his waist, his palm resting on the top of his pistol. As much as I wished otherwise, I knew what he was doing was smart. Too bad I hadn't brought my pistol.

The kitchen was fairly empty, except for a refrigerator. My curiosity was too much on how convenient the appliance's placement was. I threw the door open and felt a slight sense of disappointment seep into my mind. The fridge was completely empty. Even the light didn't turn on, meaning the house was probably not powered. I started back into the main room when Lennox called out.

"I've, uh... I found something."

Hull came back into the main room, and together we moved up the stairs. We found Lennox in one of the bedrooms, this one also empty, except for what he'd found. Lying on the floor was a body, arms and legs splayed out in a star shape. It wore a bloodstained button-up shirt and brown dress pants, with neon tennis shoes similar to Hull's. I say it about the body simply because easy identification wasn't possible. A very important thing missing from the body was the head.

"Is that him?" I asked. "Arthur Knight?"

"Unclear," Hull said as he leaned over the body. "Without the face, it will have to be genetically identified. Your area of expertise, Lennox."

"I can call it in, have the boys pick it up and get to work," the inspector replied, looking down on the decapitated body with a tilted gaze.

"Please do," Hull said, grabbing the body by the shoulders and slowly lifting it.

Lennox shifted uneasily where he stood. "Are you sure that's a good idea?"

"Just making sure of something."

"What?" I questioned.

"There was a lot of blood lost, but the blood on the shirt couldn't have come from the wound. Someone else was injured in the ordeal."

"Someone else had to hide the body here," Lennox added.

"Mrs. Knight said her husband left for Venezuela before going missing," I said, looking out the window to see the woman's house.

"Many aspects of this are still unclear," Hull concluded as he stood. "We will have to wait for the genetic confirmation."

"I'll make the call now," Lennox said as he left. I moved to stand next to Hull, casting a long glance at the body.

"What part does Moriarty play in this?"

He sighed. "I'm not sure." His gaze moved to me. "This is why we must be cautious." We lingered only a minute longer before leaving, knowing that Lennox would keep in contact. And when I checked my watch, I saw that it was almost eight at night. I pulled out my phone and found that Amy had texted me twice almost three hours ago. With a depressing sigh, I pocketed the phone. I knew the chances of me actually going on a date were slim.

When we reached the flat, Hull immediately went to his laptop while I took a shower. By the time I'd finished, Hull had managed to cover the chalkboard with different theories. Something new, however, was a little glass vial, and inside the vial a black knight chess piece. I picked the vial up and turned it over, finding it impossible to get the knight out.

"How did you manage this?" I asked, giving the vial a shake.

"I didn't. Knight did, however."

"Arthur Knight?"

"Yes. One of Moriarty's, I suspect. His Knight."

"How many 'Knights' can Moriarty have?"

"Two."

"How do you figure?"

"How many knights are on a chessboard?"

I paused, glancing back down at the vial. A distant memory clicked as I looked back up. "This is what you told me when we first met. About the pawn, and the king." The glint in his eyes was enough of an answer for me. After a moment, he returned his focus to the laptop, then turned it to face me. On the screen was a flower of some kind, white petals with a red spot on the inside and an frayed core.

"A very rare kind of opium poppy found only in Venezuela. This certain type was used in anesthetic drugs until about ten years ago due to the plant's rarity. That rarity would give it a very high price today, and all transfers of funds and items would be in person."

"Knight's frequent trips to Venezuela," I said with confidence.

Hull nodded. "Knight became involved in something far larger than he may have anticipated." He looked back at the screen, then out at the balcony. "It's getting late. Lennox texted me and said they would not get the results back until morning. It'd be best if you rested." That was the last he said before he returned to his computer, eyes illuminated by the screen. I gave him a nod before heading off to my room. I was asleep within a minute.

*

We didn't delay in leaving the very next morning. I don't think Lennox had even contacted Hull about the results of the tests when we left, but the detective was determined. Prior to leaving, he'd told me we had a meeting with Mrs. Knight. That was all. And by now, I'd grown to simply trust his cryptic sentences, especially when he was on the brink of solving the mystery. At least, I assumed he was. His personal progress was something far beyond everyone else's when it came to these cases.

We pulled up to the house at around eight in the morning, the sun shining brightly on the horizon and the woman's house amiably waiting for us. Mrs. Knight greeted us at the door, the bags under her eyes even deeper and the paleness to her skin more notable. Her health was in a steady decline as a result of this case. I could only hope that Hull had figured everything out and would be able to help the poor woman. She led us to the living room and sat us down. The room looked exactly as it had when we'd been here yesterday, except there was no tray of food for us this time.

"I'm hoping you've made some headway with the case?" she asked once we were all settled in.

Hull pressed his tongue against his cheek before responding. "We will receive key information here shortly."

"Did my husband die in Venezuela?"

"Yes."

I cast an odd glance at Hull. "He did?"

The detective nodded. "Curious case. A shame for someone as intelligent as your husband to die. His scientific advances would have been greatly beneficial to the world of medicine."

Mrs. Knight titled her head, a slight twitch appearing in her left eyelid. "I'm sorry?"

"Businessman, renowned author, philanthropist... and scientist. You were of course aware of your husband's scientific endeavors, were you not?" Hull asked as he leaned forward.

"My husband never told me of any scientific interest. He's worked with the same company since we met."

Hull smirked. "That he has."

Before anyone could speak, a loud vibrating sound echoed from the table, where Hull had set down his coat. He reached his slender hand into the coat pocket and pulled out his phone, gave the screen a quick glance, then smiled as he put the phone away. Before he resumed speaking, he stood.

"Arthur Mallory Knight was a skilled scientist, a very skilled one indeed. At the age of twenty-four, he was discovered for his talents by a crime syndication group called Chimaera. He was immediately recruited into their organization and put into a new project for the syndicate, called DAGGER. This specific subsidiary of DAGGER was focused on the development of potential chemical weapons. Very powerful, very potent chemical weapons.

"Knight was extremely proficient in the development of drugs, finding new and innovative ways to use preexisting drugs for different means. One of them was taking opiates and making them into half-anesthetics, half-hallucinogens. To make this very peculiar effect, a certain mixture was required from a certain species of opium, one only found in Venezuela. Knowing he would have to obtain the drugs on his own, he set out to Venezuela four years ago to conduct trade.

"The individuals he met with, however, were not as interested in a fair trade, and upon his arrival, Knight was captured, tortured, and eventually murdered. His body was sent back to the United States in pieces. Chimaera took the body and made a very prompt, very sick decision. Knight's research was too valuable to let pass with his death. They had the opiates. Now they simply needed to test if Knight's creation would work. They needed a viable test subject. The drug, if successful, would make an individual completely susceptible. They would believe anything they heard with only minor evidence to support it.

"They chose you, Mrs. Knight. You were to be their live test subject for the experimental KT01 suggestive influence drug. But the drug was very temporary unless regularly administered, which required a constant presence in your home. Chimaera employed a doctor to deliver your first dosage and sent you back home to await the arrival of your husband. The man that arrived at your door was not Arthur Mallory Knight but was, in fact, a young Jason Fieldman, a man who bore a very close resemblance to your late husband. A resemblance that would be close enough for the drug to trick you.

"Fieldman assumed the identity of your husband, moved in to your house, slept in your bed, and ensured the continued administering of the drug into your system. So long as you were drugged, you would believe he was your husband, and Chimaera would get all of the results they needed. Four years they conducted this test on you. But young Fieldman was beginning to grow doubtful. He began to question what he was doing. Why he was doing it. Four years of lying, of giving you an illegal drug. It became a moral conflict within his mind.

"One month ago, Fieldman came to a very sad realization, one he had been warned about. Before taking the job, he had been told to keep his mindset professional. To not allow his emotions to get in the way. But masquerading as your husband, and you believing it wholeheartedly, showed him that you loved him, or who you thought he was. And he started to reciprocate that emotion. It took more and more precedence within his mind before he made a decision. He would return to Venezuela, tell the suppliers to end the trade relations, and stop giving you the drug.

"Fieldman made the decision to stop working with Chimaera, to cease the drug administering, and to be true to you. He understood the consequences of what would happen once the drug had worn off. You would return to your senses and realize you had been living with a different man for over four years. But he continued with his decision because his emotions were his motivation. Because he now felt something for you that he should never have felt."

Hull stood, walking to stand beside the couch. "Love. A dreadful bond, and yet, so easily severed."

As I glanced from the detective to the woman, I knew what was coming.

"Upon your coming to, you realized you had been lied to, and you were none too happy with it. Fieldman attempted to calm you, attempted to profess his developed love for you, but the KT01 drug had a unique side-effect, one I had not expected until I had observed the chemical makeup for myself. With extended use came prolonged deterioration of the frontal lobe, specifically the area where your reasoning is controlled. Deterioration of this particular area would eventually lead to a significant loss of sanity. As it did.

"In a fit of rage, you took up one of the weapons from your husband, whom you knew to have died long ago, and attacked Fieldman. He was able to avoid your first strike and draw his own weapon, managing to get a single cut across your abdomen. The blood from his attack ended up on his shirt when you tackled him and knocked the sword from his hand. He was given no time to beg for mercy, and you no time to reconsider. With the sword in hand, you severed Fieldman's head from his body, dousing the carpet right here with blood, which you promptly cleaned with bleach, leaving a very noticeable mark. You cleaned the sword, but not efficiently, as the blood is still visible on the blade. And you tended to your own wound, but not before you had lost a significant amount of blood.

"Your sanity, your husband, and your husband's imposter gone, you knew your options were running out. You hid Fieldman's body in the next house and spent the next two days recuperating before making the very foolish decision of calling me. Though I suppose that could have been whatever sanity you still have making a final plea for help. Help you will not receive from me, Mrs. Knight. You murdered Mr. Jason Fieldman, and for that, you will be held accountable."

The woman stood, her eyes wide and lips trembling, not in fear, but in white hot rage. "He deserved that punishment for what he did to me. Sitting there and knowing he was tricking me, but still willingly participating. He deserved to die!"

"You are not one to determine who deserves to live and die," Hull snapped, his chin rising. What the woman did next, I never would have expected.

Her hands flew like lightning, smashing through the nearest glass panel and pulling a long knife from the case. In just as fluid a motion, she sent the knife spiraling towards Hull, who dived behind the couch. I jumped to my feet and, in a quick moment of decisiveness, grabbed one of the swords from the wall directly to my left. I held the sword cautiously with the tip aimed at Mrs. Knight, who tilted her head at me with a look of both interest and hatred.

"Keep her distracted," Hull called from behind the couch as he scrambled away.

"For *what*?!"

"*Just do it!*"

My retort was drowned out by the sound of metal hitting metal as Knight brought up a sword of her own, almost managing to throw mine to the side. I was not experienced at all with sword combat, or any kind of melee combat save for my fists. This woman, however, seemed to be very skilled in the usage of a sword. She pushed me back over the couch, then somehow managed to send the couch back as well. I rolled to avoid the falling white furniture, shuffling to grab my sword before she plunged her own into the carpet next to me.

I stood as quickly as I could, trying my best to stab at the woman. She jumped up and back, deftly pushing my blade to the side each time. She rolled away from me, grabbing a knife from the end table as she went and throwing it my way. I managed to side-step with not even half a second to spare as the blade found a home in the wall behind me. I glanced over at the blade as it shook in the wall, then back at the woman.

"Now that wasn't very nice," I said as I pulled the knife from the wall. Instead of throwing it back at her, I simply dropped it to the ground. This woman had done nothing against me and didn't deserve death. And, Hull had told me to just keep her distracted. So that was what I would do. Why I was distracting her, though, I hadn't the foggiest. Of course, it seemed like she was doing a far better job at keeping herself distracted. Or entertained. I couldn't quite tell the difference, given the sneer on her face.

I dropped again as another knife carved its way through the air, hitting almost the exact same spot as the first. I crouched behind the overturned sofa, and barely realized my mistake in time to avoid the woman's blade plunging through the couch to nearly pierce my stomach. I jumped over the top of the couch, catching her in the chest and sending her back onto the center table. Together we rolled back into the single seat she'd occupied before, causing this one to also fall backwards. As we both struggled to stand, I found that my sword was missing. It was now in her hands.

She kicked out viciously, sending me back into the wall. She promptly kicked against the chair, pushing it along the ground and forcing it against my legs, effectively pinning me against the white plaster. She poked the tip of the sword under my chin and held it there before arcing it back.

"You will not forestall my judgment!" she screamed in my face as she plunged the blade forward.

Luckily, Hull's arm caught hers before the blade came anywhere close to me.

The detective pulled back, sending the blade from the woman's hand and spinning her to face him. His free arm lashed up, elbow pointed, and smashed the woman in the nose, forcing her down onto the floor with blood gushing from her face. Hull softly brushed his pants off and shook his head.

I clasped him on the shoulder once I'd freed myself from the chair. "You have a knack for timing."

"I do my best," he replied, eyes still on the woman.

*

"So what, you just came here on a hunch and hoped my message would prove your hunch right?"

Hull and I now stood outside the house while Mrs. Knight was escorted away by three police officers. Lennox was in front of us, no doubt wanting answers.

"I do not make hunches, Inspector, I make deductions. I knew the body we had found could not have possibly been Arthur Knight and decided to act before Mrs. Knight found some sensibility and fled."

Lennox shook his head as he glanced towards the house. "I don't know how you do it, Hull. I really don't. But.. keep it up, I guess." With that, he turned and walked away, leaving us to marvel the sight. Once Lennox was far enough away, Hull opened his coat and pulled out a small, green book with the letters "AMK" imprinted vertically on the cover.

"Arthur Mallory Knight?" I asked.

"A private journal of his life. Detailing his time with Chimaera. His work with DAGGER. I have only perused a few pages, but I have already made some very interesting finds."

"Like?"

"Moriarty is mentioned. A figure by the name of Daemon. Chimaera has been around for almost fifteen years, according to

Knight's sources. And something else. Something he only alluded to without further discussion, presumably because he personally had no further knowledge. A very high-priority project within Chimaera called ENDGAME."

"ENDGAME. Doesn't sound good at all."

"No, I imagine it is quite horrible. Especially if the likes of Moriarty created it. Just as he created this entire scenario."

"What, the case?"

"No." He tucked the journal away inside his coat, eyes traveling to the ambulance where Mrs. Knight had been taken. "He needed a proper testing environment for Knight's drug, but he knew Knight would never test it on his own wife. So he framed Knight for stealing from the contacts in Venezuela, thus resulting in Knight's death. I also suspect he was aware of the insane side effect of the drug, but he held no care for it. He simply wanted to ensure the primary purpose of the drug would happen."

"He has no care for life."

"No, that's just it. He does. But it is only for the life of himself."

I gulped. "So how do we beat him?"

He inhaled deeply through his nose. "How do you win a game of chess, John?"

"You get the king."

He smiled. "That's how we beat him." With that, we started walking away, and we would have gone silently had a thought not crossed my mind.

"You both quoted *Pirates of the Caribbean*."

"What?"

"You and Mrs. Knight, you both quoted it. You both said lines from Davy Jones."

"Why would you suggest such a thing?"

"Because I know the lines! Because you said them in sequential order."

"And?"

"And because it was on last night and I know you watched it."

He smiled again. "I'm glad you pay attention."

*

The security camera feed watched as the three police officers carefully helped the bleeding woman into the back of the ambulance before closing the doors. It watched as Inspector Lennox knocked twice on the back of the ambulance, signaling for it to leave, before he walked back to his own police car and drove away. It watched as John Walker and Sheridan Hull quickly looked over a small, green book with an indistinguishable cover.

Moriarty paused the feed on the book, the static from the traffic camera fizzling across the screen. He stared at the screen from beneath his hood for several very long minutes before leaning away. He stood and killed the power to the single monitor, staring down at the screen as its light dimmed.

This complicates things.

He walked away as the monitor's light finally died, leaving no trace of his presence. It wouldn't matter, though. Soon, none of the privacy would. Soon, privacy would cease to exist. Chaos would cease to exist.

Order to the chaos.

Peace.

BURN

Tyler Belt walked casually from his bedroom towards the stairs, his hands fumbling to untangle the knotted mess of wires his earbuds had managed to become while in his pocket. Downstairs he could hear a collection of sounds, from the kitchen sink to the television to his screaming siblings. There was never a quiet moment in the Belt house, that was guaranteed. He reached the first floor and entered the kitchen, finding his mother peeling the husks from corn cobs and his youngest sister banging the head of a doll into a cupboard.

"Nice, corn for dinner. Just like last night. And the night before," Ty remarked as he walked by. She glanced back at him, no doubt preparing a retort she wasn't given the chance to say.

"Mommy!" a shrill voice cried as another little girl ran into the room, taking cover behind her mother's legs. This was also Ty's sister, only a few years older than the youngest and two years younger than—

"Give that back!" another voice yelled. Ty barely managed to sidestep as his younger brother charged into the kitchen.

"MOMMY!" the girl repeated.

"Jacob and Alexandria, you both stop it right now!" their mother bellowed, trying to pull her daughter from her legs. Ty's brother ran forward, bringing a scream from the girl.

"Well this is fun," Ty said as he moved towards the bathroom.

"Mark!" his mother shouted, pointlessly trying to get her husband's attention. Ty put the earbuds in, stepped into the bathroom, and closed the door. He could dimly hear his brother yelling something, but only a second later, all outside noises were gone, replaced by the sound of Dragonforce.

I gotta write that speech up soon. I think they want it done next week. But how do I start it? "Gentlemen, this will be our..." Nah, too cliché. What about, "Today, we will fight for tomorrow as one!" Blah, too Churchill. "We stand and fight as one!" Ack, too 300. "If we can't protect the Earth, you can be damn well sure we'll avenge it." No no, too spoilerful. Dang, this is hard. Ha, a double-entendre. Maybe I should take a shower, that always helps me think. Meh. Well, at least this song is awesome.

Finally, the song was over and his business was done. He washed his hands slowly, noticing the lack of any yelling coming from the kitchen. *Nice to see things settled down*, he thought. He took the earbuds out and walked back into the kitchen, only to stop short. The sink was still running, but no one was at it. The TV had been muted. His baby sister's doll had somehow been thrown across the room, now underneath the dining table. He looked down and frowned at the new, black scuff marks on the linoleum floor.

"Mom?" he asked, raising his voice to reach the entire house. No reply came. "Dad?" He stepped out into the living room. The TV had indeed been muted, but his father's recliner was devoid of life. He ran up the stairs, finding that his bedroom door had been forced open. Not a living soul was on the second floor of the house.

He walked back down to the kitchen, stopping in the center and looking around. Never before had he been so afraid.

"Guys?"

*

It wasn't often that Hull went out on his own. I suppose the boredom had to be getting to him by now, since it had been six weeks since his last case. It's always so interesting, watching the steady chain of events that follows him not having a case. For the first week or so, he's usually fine, but after that, the decline becomes more and more sharp. The experiments start in the kitchen, the walls become more and more perforated. It becomes almost unbearable at times. Almost.

In the aftermath of the previous case, even Lennox had taken a more alert status in regards to all things Chimaera and Moriarty. It was nice, to say the least, knowing that we had someone on our side whom Hull held some level of trust for. I didn't know how much work Hull had done with the police force prior to our meeting. Lennox had mentioned in passing that his own time with the department had been eight years, from the day he graduated high school onward. I'd often wondered where Hull had spent his two terms of college, but judging from the random school paraphernalia I occasionally found, I would narrow it down to either Oregon State University, or the University of Cambridge.

Moriarty, however, had gone silent once more. Even activities from Chimaera had dropped off the radar. That, or no case had struck Hull as interesting enough to take on. Nonetheless, the constant presence of our foe was there, hovering somewhere in the shadows beyond our field of vision. Going about our days as usual wasn't easy with that thought. Or it wasn't easy for me, I guess. Hull never seemed to let anything show in regards to how he really felt about Moriarty, or Chimaera, or everything.

Today, Hull had left around noon, according to Mrs. Hanson. I'd been at work and got back around 2, and he had yet to return. When he did walk in, he returned with an object I can honestly say I had never seen in the flat before, and was therefore very curious. He held over his shoulder a metal bat with a green logo across the side, and as he stepped into the room, he gave a heavy sigh.

"What were you doing?" I asked as I looked up from my book, a particularly interesting selection my uncle had recommended to me a couple of months ago.

"Nothing," he replied, doing his best to avoid my gaze. He walked casually to the piano, opening the top and placing the bat inside, then took his seat facing the keys. Within no time, he was tapping away on a piano cover of another song. I quickly recognized this one as "Rolling in the Deep" by Adele. An interesting choice for him, since I'd never heard him listen to her music before. But he was full of surprises. And he was getting much better. He only slammed the keys once per song now.

I opened the Saturday paper and started flipping through, eyes skimming the titles of multiple articles before stopping on a military-related issue. Despite my having been discharged, I still made a point to keep up with the ongoings overseas. We were supposed to have been effectively pulled out of the Middle East by now, but from where I watched, progress on that moved slowly. Very slowly.

"Got any plans for the weekend?" I asked when Hull reached a stopping point.

"Have I ever had plans for anything that wasn't a case?"

I shrugged, eyes still on my paper. "You never know. You might have changed your mind."

"Minds don't change. People don't change."

"That's the spirit." Once I'd finished the article, I resigned hope in there being anything left of interest in the paper and set it aside. "So just what were you doing? Why did you have a bat?"

"Went for a walk."

"Where?"

"Somewhere I could think."

"And the bat, that helped with the thinking, yeah?"

He glanced back at me. "When you stop to think, you cock your head to the side, and if you continue, your neck will eventually become so worn from the sudden motion that when you have aged to where your muscles can no longer support your skull, your head will lull to one side. You also tend to put more weight on one leg to pause and consider your thoughts, which will have a similar outcome. And yet, despite these, you will continue to do these things when you think because it works." He turned away. "I do not seek to judge your way of thinking, so I would hope you would not judge mine."

"Well then," I said as I walked into the kitchen. "Sounds like someone really needs a new case."

"Oh God, you have no idea." He jumped from the piano and moved to the balcony, running his finger softly along the glass. "Six weeks is far too long. Stagnating. It fuels my insanity."

"Something will come up, I'm certain of it." I grabbed one of the beakers from the table and took a whiff. Immediately it felt like my nostrils had been set on fire. I slammed the beaker down, hands grabbing my assaulted nose. "What the Hell is this?"

"A concentrated mixture of ammonia and urine."

"*But why?*"

"It's an experiment."

I shook my head in disgust, holding my nose closed while I took the beaker to the sink. "Pick less odorous experiments, please. For the love of God, Sheridan, we have to live here."

"The smells have no effect on me."

"Liar."

"Would you like me to point out another flaw in your everyday actions?"

"I'd like you to either rent a lab or just stop doing these ridiculous experiments in our *kitchen*."

A knock from below stopped his retort. I heard Mrs. Hanson shuffle to the front door and admit someone, a familiar masculine voice which she soon led up the stairs. I walked into the main room as the door opened to admit Lennox.

"Inspector," Hull said without turning.

"I need your help. This one's important."

"They always are with you," the detective replied as he walked towards the piano.

"A boy just charged into the police station and said his family is missing. Dad, mom, three siblings, all taken right out of his house in the span of ten minutes. I stopped there before coming here. It's bleak. I'd rather have you there now than later, in case something happens."

Hull sat down at the piano, but instead of facing the keys, he put his back to them and stretched out, his head resting on the top of the instrument. "The most that amounts to is a five."

"A what?" Lennox asked, glancing from the detective to me.

"Nothing," I replied, stepping past the inspector. I stood above Hull now, noting that his eyes were moving in their rapid-like motion. "Some kid's family was abducted, do this for him."

"And why should I consider him any different? What good would I be to all of the countless other abducted individuals scattered across the globe?" Hull shot back.

"Just because you can't help them all doesn't mean you shouldn't help one."

He rolled his eyes. "Oh how fallible your logic is."

Lennox sighed. "Fine. Don't help, then." With that, he started back out the door and down the stairs. I looked down at Hull for a very long time before scoffing.

"Are you happy with yourself?"

"A case with no interest is no case at all."

"Then I'm going to help him."

Now he looked up at me, a very small sense of surprise on his face. "You, the army doctor, and him, the inept inspector, taking on an abduction case?"

"If you think we're so incompetent, you take the case."

"Fine."

"What?"

"The case is mine."

I stepped back as he stood up, still very confused at his change of mind. "*What?*"

"The case," he repeated as he moved towards the door, "is mine." And with that, he was through the door and down the stairs, hot on the heels of Lennox. I gave a heavy sigh, rolled my eyes, and followed suit.

*

Hull, Lennox and I now sat in one of the smaller conference rooms at the department with a young man sitting across from us. He looked to be about fifteen years old, dark blonde hair that was similar to Hull's, with green eyes hidden behind a pair of glasses. From the damp marks on his shirt, I could tell he had been crying, and he had every reason to. For someone to have their entire family go missing... it was a thought I couldn't bear to take in. I only hoped we would be able to find the boy's family before it was too late.

"It all happened so fast, it's only just sinking in. My family was in the house, like a usual Saturday morning, nothing out of place. I left my room, closed the door, headed for the bathroom. My mom and baby sister were in the kitchen, my other sister and brother were chasing each other, and my dad was in the living room. I went into the bathroom, came out seven minutes later, and they were all gone. Scuff marks on the floor, TV muted. It just don't know what happened."

"Did you hear anyone?" Lennox asked.

"I couldn't have if I wanted to, the song I was listening to was way too loud."

"Was anything stolen?" the inspector continued.

"Not that I could tell, no. I didn't look too hard, though."

Hull stood. "Then it would be wise of us to return to your home and look."

"Already?" Lennox asked, looking up at the detective.

"It is quite obvious there is little information to be garnered from the boy. The more physical evidence we can find, the better chance we have at finding the family," Hull said as he walked back.

The boy stood, looking from Lennox to me. "Is he going to find my family?"

I shot a glance back at Hull before returning my gaze to the boy. "I would expect so, yes. Your name is Tyler, correct? Tyler Belt?"

"People just call me Ty. You're Dr. John Walker, right?"

I felt a ripple of surprise pass through me. "I am. How did you know that?"

"Mr. Lennox said he was going to get you both before coming back. Said that Mr. Hull is the best there is."

"Really now," I said with a look at Lennox. He shrugged before following Hull out. "Well I hope the detective can live up to your expectations."

A look of desperation came to the boy's face. "I just want to see my family again, Dr. Walker. My mom. My dad. My sisters. Even my annoying brother. I just.. I can't even think of trying to—"

He stopped, and I immediately saw tears well up in his eyes. I gestured towards the door, and the boy quickly ran forward, no doubt trying to hide his face. I followed him out to the road, where a police car waited for us, Lennox at the wheel and Hull in the back seat. The boy took the front passenger while I slid in next to Hull. Within moments, we were on our way.

The boy's house was in the southeastern area of Newfield, a white two-story home that looked to be several decades old. Two police cars were already parked in the driveway, which was also occupied by a small red car and a large truck. Lennox parked along the sidewalk in front of the house, and as a group, the four of us walked in. The house itself was well-furnished, showing that the family had made the most of their money. Children's toys were scattered about, bills on the table. Everything pointed to it being a typical family. But it couldn't be so simple.

Hull immediately entered the kitchen and crouched, his nose hovering several centimeters above the scuff marks on the floor. He followed the scuff marks to the door, which led to the living room, then walked out of sight. Lennox took to the upstairs while I glanced around the kitchen. Today must have been a good day, because after one glance at the floor, pieces of the event were able to fall into place for me. I could see where his mother had stood, where his sister had sat, and where the intruders had intervened.

Like a video, it played out for me. I watched in my mind as the mother returned her attention to the sink, explaining why it had been left on. The intruders had come in through the door to her left and had immediately grabbed the children. The youngest had screamed and started thrashing the baby doll around, resulting in it being removed from her possession and thrown across the kitchen. When a man went for the woman, she resisted and caused him to plant his feet and drag them, resulting in the scuff marks.

The scuff marks leading to the living room were confusing, though. Why would the attackers take her farther from the door? Unless, of course, they had planned to use her as leverage to get the husband to come willingly. The TV had been muted, which hinted at conversation having occurred. From there, the family would have been taken away. And all of it had to have happened in the span of seven minutes. The motives were still unclear. A lot of the case was unclear for me.

Then again, that wasn't new.

What I found on the kitchen table, however, was definitely unusual. I could tell by its placement that it hadn't been there long, probably placed during the scuffle. The pen next to it was missing its cap, and the notepad strewn to the side had matching paper as the note. Scrawled on the paper in crude red ink was a short message.

They will all burn.

I picked the note up carefully and walked out into the living room, finding the young man sitting on the couch and Hull poking around the recliner. "Hull?" I prompted, holding the note up. The detective glanced over at me and did a slight double-take before walking over to me and briskly taking the note. He read over it several times before looking up, his eyes moving rapidly.

"They will all burn," he repeated, the latter R having a growl to it. He spun and walked towards the boy, holding the note out for the young man to read. "Did you see this in your initial passing through the house?"

The boy grabbed the note and looked at it with disbelief. "I know it wasn't here, I would've seen it and brought it with me."

"Lennox!" Hull yelled as he tucked the note away in his pocket. The inspector charged down the stairs, stopping at the foot to give a slight heave. "We need to leave. The abductors will have the family at Burns Tower in the city center."

"What, how?" Lennox asked as he walked into the room.

"I can explain while we drive, but we have to go immediately." Hull made no point in delaying. He was gone and out of the house before any of us could react. Things felt like they were going far too quick with the case, and part of me wondered if Hull may have been going on a guess with this rather than factual information. Nonetheless, the three of us made our way back out to the police car and awaited the explanation. Once Lennox had started toward the city center, the detective started.

"The case in and of itself is very boring, lacking any and all methods of creativity or cleverness from the abductors. A simple run in, take all they can and demand ransom scenario. I presume they will have the building locked down to prevent them being killed without receiving their pay, but even then the plan is faulty. In writing, 'They will all burn,' they too aptly left a ransom note. Really, it's quite obvious what they intend to do. No creativity or cleverness whatsoever."

"And you're sure?" I asked, a slight sense of wariness seeping into my mind. Hull's state from earlier didn't seem to have dissipated entirely, and I couldn't shake the feeling that this was all a guess without evidence. Something seemed off here.

"Absolutely certain."

"I don't know," I said, my tone hushed. "I feel like you might be rushing this."

"You doubt my abilities?"

"Yes," I replied sternly. The gaze he shot at me would normally have cut through anyone's resolve, but something was so off with the conclusion to the case. "This can't be so clear-cut. You know that more than I could possibly know. But you're having us charge on to some random tower in the city center just because they left a warning, and you saw it as a ransom note."

"These criminals are only looking for a quick and easy source of money. They put no effort into their crimes except the most textbook of operations."

"Do you really believe that, though? After all you've seen, all we've seen? With Moriarty being a constant threat, you think this case is simple?"

"What do you want me to say, John?" he snapped, causing both Tyler and Lennox to look back at us. "Do you want me to say, 'Oh, I must be wrong because the evidence we found is only so substantial and there must be something more to this case?' I said at the flat the case was a five. I hold to that statement."

"You said the Man in Red case was a *six* to Moriarty, how good does that make your rating system?"

"My 'rating system' is perfectly fine, as it accurately rates each case I take part in. I absolutely refuse anything below five, and anything above seven is too good to let pass. The in-betweens are just time-passers, things to occupy my mind before it rots from the inside out."

"I think you're wrong," I said, looking out the window.

"About my own rating system?"

"About this case, Sheridan. I think you're wrong about this case being so simple. It doesn't feel right, none of it feels right, and there's no way it's as simple as showing up at a building and getting them back."

"I am never wrong."

Lennox's timely interruption was more than enough to stop the conversation.

"What the Hell?"

*

Hull and I looked forward to see what the inspector had remarked on. In front of us was a very, very large traffic jam. Cars were stretching on for at least three blocks. Even with the police car's lights on, there was no way for us to get through. Hull opened his door and stepped out, walking in front of the police car and standing on the front bumper. I stepped out as well, walking to join him.

"Backed up for almost four different lights, with intersecting traffic also on hold," he declared as he jumped down.

"So we walk?"

"No," he said as he returned to the car, "we use the police vehicle to our advantage." He tapped on Lennox's window and waited. "Hand me the radio."

Lennox looked up at him reluctantly. "I'm not allowed to let you use that." Hull gave him a look that truly did say, "Oh *please*." The inspector sighed and, after a slight moment of hesitation, handed Hull the radio microphone.

"Attention traffic. This police vehicle needs to have a clear lane immediately. Your cooperation is key to the survival of a family. That is all." He tossed the radio back into Lennox's lap before returning to the back seat. I retook my seat and watched as cars slowly scrambled to make a path, which Lennox instantly took. Our pace was definitely slower than preferable, considering the space at which the other cars had to operate within. But after about ten minutes of maneuvering, we were finally clear of the traffic and on our way to Burns Tower.

The tower stood at a surprisingly tall fifty-five stories in the heart of Newfield, with its large ridge-like roof giving the look of flames when it was night and the special floodlights were turned on. Now they just looked like sharp, gray blobs jutting out from the top of the building. The four of us ran into the lobby, Hull immediately going to the receptionist.

"Where are they?" he demanded, his face leaned in close to the poor woman's.

"I'm sorry?"

"Where are they keeping them? They never would have selected this building unless they had connections, so tell me now, where are they?"

"Sir, I don't know what you're—"

"Hull, I don't think she—" Lennox started.

"They have to be here!" Hull said as he turned. "The abductors clearly said—"

He stopped. His eyes were looking between Lennox and me, back at the doors we had just come through. The look on his face was a sudden transition, from determined to shock. And shock was not an emotion Hull showed often. I turned to see flashing lights in the distance, and with a bit of squinting, I was able to catch the tail end of a firetruck before the flashing lights disappeared to the right, heading west.

"Oh no."

I looked back at Hull, whose face had paled slightly. There was a slight tremble to his left eye, and his lips seemed to move in a very diminutive way, as if he was talking but only in a very dim whisper. Before I could speak, Lennox's pocket started wailing at him. He pulled out the source, his phone, and listened intently. After only five seconds, he returned it to his pocket.

"Warehouse fire five blocks over," he said as he started back towards the entrance. "They aren't sure yet but they think there's people inside."

"What about my family?" Tyler prompted.

"They aren't here," Hull said, his voice monotonous and distant.

"What?" both Tyler and I said.

"They are not here. They never were. They never were going to be here." He looked down at the floor, lips still trembling, then sharply looked up and ran after Lennox. Tyler and I joined him and found the inspector and detective climbing back into the police car. I jumped into the back seat, conflicting emotions starting to swell up in me. On one hand, I think I may have been right, and that Hull had been wrong.

On the other hand, this meant I was right. And Hull was wrong.

And that meant the family was more than likely dead.

Lennox wasted no time in getting us to the scene of the fire. Two firetrucks were pulled up alongside a blazing warehouse, their hoses doing their best to keep the flames from expanding. Lennox parked us against the sidewalk opposite, where a small crowd had gathered to watch the fire. Hull slowly stepped out of the cop car, leaned his back against the metal, and watched as the blaze encompassed the entire facility.

I came up beside him, trying carefully to pick the right words to say. "I think we should go home."

"No," he replied coolly, eyes glowing as a result of the fire. "Not yet." That was enough for me to stop. I too leaned against the cop car and watched, a growing sense of dread taking over. Once the fire was tamed enough, the firefighters would be able to move in. But by then, it would be too late. Whoever was inside and didn't escape had a very small chance of survival. And something told me that chance had been diminished by whoever had put the victims inside.

It had been four hours since we arrived when the blaze was finally put out. The majority of the building structure had been demolished as a result of the fire, with only a few metal struts still standing. Firefighters picked through the burned wreckage, looking for any survivors. At least, that was what Lennox had relayed. What he had meant was, of course, entirely different. They were looking for remains. And when they finally did find the remains, the pit in my stomach finally hit its lowest point.

With Tyler at our side, Hull and I stood and waited as a firefighter stomped in our direction. The young man stood with his chin held high, but his fear radiated like pure energy. I too was afraid, my thoughts actually hoping for someone else to have been inside the inferno. Hull, however, was stoic. No emotions found their way to his person. Not yet.

"Two people were inside," the firefighter said. "We don't have any confirmed identities yet, but a Mark Belt made the call. And we found this." He extended his gloved arm to reveal a golden-lace necklace. Tyler gave an audible gasp, but was careful to keep his lips pursed. The firefighter closed his glove and slid his hand back. "I'm sorry."

Tears had started streaming down the boy's face. I gave his shoulder a reassuring squeeze and turned to Hull, only to find the detective had started walking down the sidewalk, somewhat in the direction of our flat. I looked at him for a long time before turning away and walking towards Lennox. He was my ride home, after all.

Hull didn't get home until around nine. When he did walk in, I was busy going over a file on the Belt family, as well as watching a nightly news segment. He sulked across the room, plopped down into his armchair, and propped his feet up against the bookshelf. I let the news segment end before muting the television, then set the files down.

"I'm sorry," I said with a gulp. His eyes were locked on the outer balcony, which was currently illuminated as a result of the shining moon.

"You have no reason to apologize. You were right." He sighed. "I was wrong."

"You can't always be right."

"But I should be. I strive to be correct. Peoples' lives depend on my being right."

I tilted my head to the side, knowing there was something more to this. "How many times have you been wrong in the past? Not on small assumptions, but on everything involved in a situation?"

He took his time before responding. "Once. It was enough for me to learn."

"What happened?"

The twinkle in his eye from the moonlight seemed to dim in the minute it took him to respond. "It was my first year of university. First month of being in such a foreign environment. And first day of truly being on my own. I had gone to a social gathering out of boredom. I quickly discovered the 'campus life' was not suited for me. While everyone else was enthralled by the flashing distractions, intricate drug mixtures, and copious amounts of alcohol, I was bored.

"And yet at this event, I made a friend, a girl my age. Realize that by this time, I had already discovered my passion for logic and deduction. That is what makes this occasion such a gem. I made a friend, and for this particular instance, I abandoned logic for emotion. Some foolish part of me invested my effort into creating a significant relationship with this girl. So when it all came crumbling down, I learned from my mistake.

"And from that decision on, I have never repeated that mistake. Emotions are trivial, fueled by their own misguided drive. People are liabilities, willing to take all that one can offer, but never compensate."

I knew I was finally making some progress. And now I could understand why he had been so distant earlier, if something like this was on his mind. "Why did it crumble?"

"She lied." He rolled his tongue around inside his mouth and let out a loud sigh. He closed his eyes and remained silent for another minute before continuing. "Some people said I looked too far into it all. But they were wrong, just as ignorant as ever. She was different. Unique. I'm not one to believe in intangible things, John. Destiny, fate. Creations of creativity to give the masses hope. She was the closest I came to believing in someone special.

"But while, at the time, I would have devoted my all to her, she was ignorant. She was ignorant, she was forgetful, she was stupid, and she was a liar."

He stopped again, his eyes open and locked on the outside window. A slight tremor ran along his left cheek, and for a moment, I couldn't help but wonder if the additional glint at the bottom of his eye was actually the glare from a tear.

"She said she would always be there. That she cared. But even as the words spewed from her mouth, I knew she was lying. Because here we are now, and she isn't here. And she doesn't care. I don't believe she ever did. That, John, is the one time I have ever been completely wrong. And it was a wrong that was rightfully deserved."

That was all he said for the rest of the night. I left him sitting in that chair around one in the morning, his eyes still locked on the balcony window, the moonlight still making his pupils look like silver spheres.

*

The next morning, Lennox called to see if we would be rejoining him to continue the investigation. He said they'd found some vehicle tracks leading away from the warehouse and may be able to backtrace them from the tire imprints. Today was an oddly rainy day for late August, so I decided to wear my coat. As I stretched my arms into the thick jacket, I looked around and found Hull exactly where I'd left him, feet still propped up, eyes still on the window.

"You coming?" I asked once I'd gotten my hands to reappear.
"No."
"What? Why not?"
"I am removing myself from the case."

I walked over to him, staring down at his stone-like face with a furrowed brow. "You know Lennox needs you on this, those criminals are still out there." He offered no response. I stood there for several seconds before sighing in resignation. If he wasn't willing to help, I was. I drove to the police station and found Lennox in his office, paperwork strewn across his desk. He sat with his head buried in his hands, not looking up until after I'd closed the door.

"Where's Hull?" he asked.
"He's not going to help. I'm sorry."

He rubbed his face and sighed. "We might not need him. Those tire tracks have a match. We've even got an ID."

"And?"

"Van owned by a Ronald Callahan. It was spotted on a security camera heading towards the warehouse just before we received the 911 call. We've got his address on file."

"So what are we waiting for?"

"Nothing. We can go now." He led me from the office, and together we took a police car to the listed house. It was on the fringes of the southern districts, where the homes were less-than-impressive. This one in particular had a large trailer parked in the front, axles resting on cinderblocks. The screen that would have separated the front door from the world was torn open. The van was nowhere in sight. Lennox and I approached the front door cautiously, the inspector's hand hovering over his pistol's grip.

"Don't we need a warrant for this?"

He smirked. "We're investigating the premises under suspicions of abduction and murder. We can worry about the paperwork later."

"Fair enough." I too rested my hand on my pistol and waited as Lennox knocked on the door. When no response came, he tried the handle and found it to be unlocked. He slowly opened the door to reveal a dark living room, minimal furniture, no television, some pizza boxes on the ground. We walked carefully across the room to the kitchen, which was just as disgusting as the living room.

"He can't be living here, not with all of this crap everywhere," Lennox said, opening a cupboard and quickly closing it. "Shit, I think there was a raccoon in there."

"Maybe the van was stolen from him and used for the abduction?"

He carefully stepped over a broken glass to the fridge. "Unlikely. Cameras matched his profile as that of the van driver."

I shook my head. "It doesn't add up. Some guy who lives in these conditions decides to take a family hostage, then kill the parents? What about the kids?"

"I don't know. This is why I get the consulting detective. These damn cases are so confusing these days, it's like they're tailored for him."

I moved into the hallway, using the flashlight Lennox had provided me with to light up the path. "What, the day-to-day at the force getting you down?"

"Oh no, it just feels like more and more crimes are becoming a higher caliber. The petty crimes still happen, and I still spend half my workday in a police car. It's that these types of things keep happening. The weird murders, the missing people. The weird cases." We stopped to glance into one of the rooms, which was completely empty. "You write them all down, don't you? His cases?"

"I've kept some notes from the cases. He doesn't really care for review, so they sit in a box in my room."

He shrugged, pointing at the next room. "You could put them together and let people read them. People like a good mystery, and Hull seems to always be in the thick of them."

A slight smirk crossed my face, but quickly vanished when I remembered the cryptic messages Hull's newest adversary had given. If Moriarty truly did intend to be Hull's rival, it would practically guarantee a bad ending for either, or both, of them.

In the last room, we found a broken bed, a dresser stuffed with papers, and a closet missing its door. The closet had been emptied, but there were two garbage bags ripped open on the floor. I stepped over a piece of the bed's mantle to look at some of the papers on the dresser. Most of them were newspaper clippings, some of them dating back as far as 1990. I sifted through one pile in particular before I recognized a pattern.

"These papers all have articles about fires," I said, handing a few to Lennox.

"Discothèque fire from Aragon, Spain... Happy Land fire in the Bronx..." he read as he flipped through them.

"Hold on, I remember this," I said, pointing to one in particular. It showed a large building in Los Angeles engulfed in flames. "Yeah, this happened when I was five or six. Entire building burned down, everyone inside died."

"There's two more copies of this article, from different papers. Whoever was using this house had a particular interest in this fire."

"So we're dealing with arsonists. Great."

Lennox sighed. "I'm really not sure. Reports are starting to suggest the fire at the warehouse may have been caused by an electrical surge. Other facilities on that block said they experienced some power troubles when the fire started."

"But the note."

"That's the only thing we have to go on. And the bodies being in there." He gulped. "DNA tests came back positive for Mark and Patricia Belt."

"What about Tyler?"

"He's staying at the station until we get things sorted out. If we are dealing with arsonists, and they try to get him, he's much safer with over a hundred officers at his side."

I scoffed. "Worked so well in *Terminator*, didn't it."

"I've never been a fan of that movie for that exact reason."

I grabbed the stack of papers and walked towards the door. "I guess now we try and find all the local arsonists and work from there."

"And hope another ping comes up on Callahan."

As we walked back to the police car, I couldn't help but note that Lennox seemed to be building up to something, but he was cautious about it. Once we were in the car, I was sure of it. And I knew exactly what it was he was curious about.

"He's fine," I said ominously.

"Oh don't tell me he's somehow rubbed off on you," he replied sarcastically.

I chuckled. "You've worked with him longer than I have. Has he ever screwed up like that before?"

"No, and that's why it caught me off-guard. My having him help tends to be off the record, since the police chief doesn't like us bringing freelancers in. He's never let me down before."

"He was.. distracted, I guess. Other things on his mind. Despite his infinite wisdom, even he gets caught up in his thoughts."

"I guess so. Didn't look like he took being wrong too easily. I've never seen a man just sit and watch a fire burn for so long. I don't think he even blinked." He shook his head. "Sheridan Hull's an odd man, but he's a smart one. And a good man. Somewhere inside that deductive shell." I nodded and smiled, and would have responded had the radio transponder not start screeching. Lennox grabbed the radio and clicked it. "Go ahead."

"We've got a hit on the van. It was spotted about a half-hour ago at a gas station. 39th Street."

"We'll be right there."

*

We reached the gas station quickly and found no sign of the van. Knowing our time was limited, I went in to the general store to hopefully get some information from the clerk. The store was surprisingly humid despite the downpour occurring outside, and the man who sat on a stool behind the main desk was dozing off. He was fairly well-built, his head shining from baldness, and some slight stubble on his face. He watched me with feigned interest as I entered and was relatively slow in responding.

"Did a white van just pass through here?" I asked as Lennox came through the doors.

"I don't really keep track of the cars, man," the clerk replied, "I just make sure they pay for their gas."

"Don't you have security tapes?"

"Nah, boss abandoned that a long time ago."

"Dammit," I barked, turning to Lennox. He looked from the clerk to me. "No use."

The inspector shook his head and charged past me. He presented a picture for the clerk. "Did this man just come through here?"

The clerk looked at the paper for a long time before giving a slight nod. "I think so, yeah. Came through about half an hour ago. Filled up, bought a drink, left."

"And did he say anything?"

"He said keep the change, man, do you think I make conversation with every guy who comes through the station?" With that, the clerk turned away, grabbing a magazine from the desk and plopping down on another chair. Lennox turned to me, his brow furrowed in anger. We walked out to the gas pumps, where the inspector found skid marks on the curb.

"Tracks match the van. Guy inside said he filled up. He might be on his way out of town, and he might still have the kids."

Lennox and I were staring down the road when the clerk came out of the building.

"Hey, are you guys cops?" he called out to us.

"Of course we are," Lennox shouted back.

The clerk held up a phone. "You guys got a phone call. Won't say who he is."

Lennox and I exchanged glances, both of us thinking the same thing: Moriarty. We cautiously returned to the clerk and took the phone, then activated the speakerphone option.

"Hello?" Lennox asked.

"The children will not be harmed if you comply with my request," a deep voice replied. Instantly I felt like this did not match the description Hull had given of Moriarty. This deepness seemed faked.

"What request?" Lennox questioned.

"You will wait for my next call. When I do call you, I will provide you with the location of the children. You will go, you will leave a notarized letter of neglect in regards to my actions, and we will consider everything square. Understand?"

"And if we don't?" I snapped.

There was a slight chuckle. "They will all burn." The resounding click that followed the chilling voice seemed to echo, even in the rain. The clerk was first to break the silence.

"That's some messed up shit, man," he said as he took the phone back. "Seriously twisted shit right there."

I looked at Lennox. "So what do we do?"

He bit his lip before replying. "We wait. It's all we can do."

The wait was spent in the confines of the police station. Minutes turned into hours as we sat in the inspector's office, knowing that at any moment, we could receive a phone call. Lennox had received the notarized letter an hour after our return. The criminal was certainly covering his bases with forcing us to get the letter, but it was still an odd request. In this occasion, however, odd was better than risky, such as if he'd demanded money.

"So I'd assume when Hull isn't on a case," Lennox started while sifting through his own paperwork, "he's damn near unbearable?"

"He has his moments. Plays music. Shoots arrows. Does experiments. So long as he doesn't shoot me or put me in a test tube, I'm relatively okay with it."

He chuckled. "His brother stops by the station every once in a while to talk to the chief. I've talked to him a few times before. They're a lot alike, I would bet."

"I haven't gotten to know Malcolm very well, but that'd be a safe bet. Two proper geniuses."

"Isn't that the truth." He tossed his pen across his desk and leaned back. "I think I'm fine being the 'incompetent inspector.' I've got a nice balance between work and personal time. Been engaged for almost a year now, I should probably get around to tying the knot there. What about you?"

"I've never had the best luck," I said shortly.

"Eh, we all have that. Crap luck that lasts up until the day we meet that special someone, you know? The one who proves all the others wrong, the one that makes those disappointments pale in comparison."

"True enough. Hopefully someday I find that special someone."

"We've all got one. I bet even Hull has one. If his brother could get married and have a daughter, why can't he?"

I gave a slight nod, more to myself than Lennox. "Sheridan prioritizes things differently than his brother. Much differently. He sees emotions as a distraction, and therefore they should be disregarded. I know he still has them, though. He smiles, he laughs, he gets mad. He holds his niece in fairly high regard, so he loves in that way."

Lennox leaned forward to check his phone. "Well maybe the proper genius just needs to find another proper genius. One that isn't trying to kill him."

I laughed. "Unfortunately, I think he'd rather attract those ones than the ones who are just looking for love. That's why his cases are so high-caliber. These crazies rally to each other, making competitions on who can outsmart the other. I haven't seen Hull lose yet. Hopefully I won't."

He nodded. "He's a good man. Somewhere in there."

The next couple of hours passed in silence. Soon, the sun started to set, and I began to wonder if we'd been tricked and the arsonist abductor had taken the opportunity to run. It was around seven at night before a call finally came. Not from the abductor, though; from Logistics.

"We've got another ping on the van. It's parked outside an old apartment complex on the corner of 25th and Haring. Cameras saw Ronald Callahan and several other men taking three children out of the van and into the complex."

"Got it," Lennox said as he stood. I quickly wormed my way into my coat and joined him as we walked for the police car. Once we were seated and in motion, he spoke again. "Think we should try and get Hull onboard?"

I sighed. "We can try. But that's probably all we can do." We drove, lights flashing, to the flat, where I quickly jumped out and charged up the stairs. I expected to find Hull still in his armchair, but was surprised to find him kneeling by the fireplace, poking at the hearth with a stoker.

"Yes," he said monotonously, not bothering to look up.

"We're going to get the kids. Do you want to come?"

He seemed to hesitate in his poking before replying. "No. It seems the case has been put in capable hands. Well done, Doctor." I sighed, knowing this had been a lost cause, and ran back down the stairs. Lennox frowned when he saw me return alone, but still drove onward with haste. The kids' lives were in our hands now.

We reached the location within ten minutes of leaving the flat. The sun was probably starting to go down, but since the rain had yet to stop today, all we could see above us was gray. The building was three stories tall, exterior made entirely of brick. Lennox parked the car across the street from the building, grabbed his pistol, and started forward. I walked at his side, my own pistol up and ready. We didn't know what to expect. The main door to the complex was unlocked, allowing us easy access. We walked through a dimly-lit hallway that led to a common room of sorts. There on the couch, tethered and gagged, were the three children.

Lennox rushed to their aid immediately while I checked the perimeter. I suppose it was a military habit of mine, and a useful one at that. Once I'd determined that nobody seemed to be on the same floor as us, I returned to the group. Lennox had unbound the older siblings and was carefully removing the rope that had tied the baby girl's legs together. The other two children were crying, but their cries were stifled. The gags were a tainted yellow color, suggesting they had been in their mouths for far too long.

"Now we leave," Lennox said, holding the baby tenderly. I nodded in agreement, grabbing the other two children's hands. Lennox carefully set down the letter and joined me, and together we walked towards the exit.

Slam.

The exit vanished from sight, cutting off all light in the hallway. Lennox and I stumbled our way to the door and discovered it had somehow been locked from the outside.

"Hey!" Lennox yelled as he banged on the door with his free hand. "Open this right now! That's an order!" I walked back towards the common room, looking for a light switch as I walked. As I walked, I noticed a new, stinging smell coming from above me. Once we'd reached the common room, my fears were confirmed. The smell was most definitely smoke.

"Lennox!" I yelled, eyes glued on the ceiling. My sight had somewhat adjusted to the darkness, and although I couldn't see any smoke, I could certainly smell it. Lennox returned to the common room and immediately picked up the scent. He came to my side and sniffed several times.

"Oh no," he murmured, setting the baby down next to her siblings. I looked around and found that all of the windows had been boarded up. The only entry or exit was the front door, which was designed to never be locked from the inside in case of a fire. We'd walked right into the arsonist abductor's trap.

And now, we were going to die.

I pulled out my phone, praying I'd be able to call Hull so he could help us. My heart sank at the sight of the words "NO SERVICE" blinking on the top of my screen. There was a glow coming from the top of the staircase now, and just from touch I could tell the inner walls were all made of wood. All three of the kids were crying now, their screams only barely masking the sound of the fire above us.

"Greg!" I roared, seeing the man stumbling around near one of the windows. He ran to me as fast as he could. "We need to get the door open!"

"But how!"

I looked around and, lo and behold, found the perfect battering ram. A small wooden end table that would work perfectly for slamming against the door. Together we heaved the table up and charged back into the hallway, noting that the smoke was growing thicker and the flames were visible on the stairs now. For almost two minutes, we desperately smashed the table into the door, with no luck. I could tell by the reverberations that some large piece of metal had been jammed into the handles from the opposite side.

We dropped the table and moved back into the common room. I stripped my coat from me and wrapped it around the children.

"Cover yourselves in this and breathe in as little smoke as possible!" I ordered. The oldest child nodded before making a small hut out of the coat, giving him and his siblings some form of temporary protection. As I stepped away from the children, I felt Lennox rest his hand on my shoulder.

"There's no way out, John," he wheezed. I could tell the smoke was affecting him far more than it was affecting me. "They did a damn good job at boxing us in."

"There has to be a—"

My voice was cut off as the ceiling above us cracked. Lennox and I dove to cover the children as the ceiling collapsed, allowing a chunk of burning floor to fall through and smash into the area where we'd just stood. We crawled away from the burning patch carefully, trying our best to keep the children protected. I knew, though, that our efforts would be in vain. Without a way out, the fire would engulf the building. And we would most certainly die. It took a miracle in that moment to save us.

And this is one of few times I will ever call Sheridan Hull a miracle.

The sound of a wall imploding is a sound you don't often hear, unless you work in cinematography and therefore witness special effects constantly. The sight of a large vehicle smashing through said wall is even more unusual. But to the group of us, huddled in the center of that common room, the sight of the front door vanishing and being replaced by headlights was the most welcome surprise possible. The vehicle backed up as Lennox and I stood, carrying the kids in our arms past the burning floor and out onto the street.

The vehicle that had saved us was parked on the sidewalk, headlights shining brightly. It was some kind of jeep, one I couldn't recognize. Standing by the driver door was Sheridan Hull, a smirk on his face and a glint to his eyes.

"Get in quickly. I'll drive," he said as he climbed back into the seat. I nodded to Lennox, and together we put the children in the back seats, made sure they were secured, and lastly climbed to the front. I took the center hump seat while Lennox buckled himself in. Hull gave the car a sharp turn to the right and started down the road. After almost a minute, my coughing had stopped enough for me to speak.

"You want to explain?" I said with an interjecting cough.

He glanced at me. "Gladly."

*

Hull waited until he heard the door close on the floor below before jumping from his seat. He scrambled towards the balcony and watched as Walker entered his car and drove away. As soon as the vehicle turned the corner, Hull leaped backwards, barely missing his armchair in the process. He charged onward to his room, going for his dresser with rushed intent. He rifled through the drawers quickly, throwing several articles of clothing over his head and onto his bed. Once he'd collected a hefty amount, he slammed the drawers shut and observed the collection.

One shirt in particular stood out as something ordinary. In fact, it looked like one of Walker's. He threw this shirt through the door, then moved on to the pants. Once he'd selected an entirely new attire, he grabbed the clothes from the floor and changed. When he was finished, he looked nothing like his usual self. A baseball cap, an Avenged Sevenfold T-shirt, and pants that had the knees torn. He put his hands in his pockets and walked around the confines of the bathroom, making sure the disguise was efficient enough.

"God, how can he wear clothes like these and not feel like an absolute idiot?" he remarked to himself before running from the bathroom and grabbing his cell phone from the piano. He barreled his way down the stairs, narrowly missing Mrs. Hanson, and threw the door open to reveal the street. A taxi sat in wait for him, the driver giving him a nod.

He had a hunch.

Ten minutes passed before he arrived at the site of the burned warehouse. Smoke was still rising from the charred structure, but this was hardly his concern. As soon as he was out of the taxi, he moved to the opposite side of the road, eyes going close to the ground. He walked cautiously along the edge of the sidewalk, right where it changed to dirt. Finally, after a minute of searching, he found a deep imprint in the mud, not watered down as a result of the gutter above the area.

He pulled out a measuring tape and checked the length: thirty-five centimeters. He measured the width, then ran his hand along the pattern inside the imprint. It was that of a very large industrial boot, that much was certain. He stepped back from the imprint and closed his eyes, allowing the events from the previous night to repeat.

He could see the blazing fire. He could see himself, and Walker, and Lennox, and the boy. But his attention right now was focused on the crowd of people who had gathered to watch. He allowed the events to move at a quickened pace, watching the crowd slowly dissipate until just one figure remained, a fairly tall man who lacked hair and wore heavy boots. He tossed an empty cigarette box from his pocket before walking away, the last cigarette hanging from his mouth.

Hull opened his eyes and looked to the spot where the man had tossed the box. Sure enough, it still rested there, untouched by the rain. He stooped down and scooped up the box, turning it over once. Even though you couldn't tell now, he'd smoked quite frequently in his late teenage years. He knew cigarettes, or more specifically, tobacco, very well. And he knew that this brand of cigarette was offered at one location in Newfield. Only one.

He returned to the taxi, handed the driver a $20 bill, and nodded forward. "Take me to 39th Street." The driver nodded and started off.

When the taxi reached the street, the driver stopped. "Where exactly do you want to go here?"

"Wait here for a moment. Pull off to the side."

"Will do."

Hull watched as Walker and Lennox spoke to a man inside the general store, one he couldn't distinguish from here, but still knew the exact identity of. After a few moments, the two men stepped outside and walked around a bit before the clerk exited the store. Sure enough, it was the tall, bald man, and in his hand was a phone. Hull's eyes traveled down the road to where a black car was parked, much like how the taxi was currently. He watched Lennox and Walker speak into the phone for only a short while before giving it to the clerk and returning to the cop car.

"Wait for the police car to depart, then pull in to the station. Fill the tank. I can cover the cost," Hull said as he leaned back.

"Gotcha."

The cop car passed by without pausing, and instantly the taxi moved forward, pulling into the gas station. Hull stepped out and started for the store, looking as casual as possible. From his peripheral vision, he could see the black car also pulling into the station. He stepped into the store, nodded at the bald man, and started browsing an aisle filled with different kinds of chips and candies, and not even the good kind of chips. Why Americans insisted on calling their potato and tortilla wedges "chips" was beyond him.

He grabbed a bag of odd ring-shaped chips, called Funyuns, from the rack and sulked his way to the front counter. He dropped the bag on the tabletop and pointed behind the clerk.

"Can I also get a pack of the Mountain Indians?" he asked as he pulled out his wallet.

"Sure thing," the clerk said as he turned, swiftly grabbing a pack of cigarettes from the rack. "These are my favorite. Damn good cigs."

"That they are," Hull replied, and as he handed the $5 bill to the clerk, his eyes spotted a pair of muddy boots stashed in the corner of the man's area. From a simple glance, he knew that they were fourteen inches in length. As the man handed Hull his change, the detective's ears perked up at the familiar ring that meant someone else had entered the store. "Do you guys have a bathroom?"

"Sure do," the clerk replied. "Turn around that corner, doors are at the end of the hall."

"Thanks," Hull said as he pocketed the cigarette box. He walked to the corner, turned just enough to be out of sight, then stopped. He looked up and around to make sure no security cameras could see him before he pressed his body against the wall and listened.

"The longer belts are thrown out. Now we've got the three small ones left." That voice was Bald Man's, he knew that. The next voice was new, but he was certain it belonged to the man who had been inside the black car.

"We forgot to buy one," the new voice said. "We'll have to go back for it."

"What about the others?"

"Retailers want them. We'll give 'em back on the corner of 25th and Haring."

"And then?" asked Bald Man.

"Close up shop, make our way to Ash's Cross."

Hull stepped down the hallway quickly, pushed one of the doors open, then started down the hall again. The sound of the door closing behind him was convincing enough. He rounded the corner to find Bald Man behind the counter and the new voice belonging to a man who had a fairly large burn mark across his neck. He wore a golfer's cap and shaded glasses, and upon Hull's arrival, gave a nod to Bald Man and left the store. Hull passed the clerk, gave him a nod, and made his way to the taxi.

Longer belts thrown out, Belt mother and father killed. Three small belts left, three Belt children in their grasp. Missed belt, Tyler. Retailers want the belts, Lennox and Walker. 25th and Haring, abandoned apartment complex. Ash's Cross, northernmost bus station in Newfield.

Danger.

"Take me back to the flat."

"Gotcha."

Once back at the flat, Hull changed into his previous attire, stashed the clothes he'd worn, and took to playing the piano. He played a good four songs before his phone chimed. He glanced down to find that there were three hours until the latest bus departure from Ash's Cross. Which meant the abductors would be giving the children back soon. Which of course meant they intended to kill them.

He walked over to the fire and grabbed several wooden sticks from the side, then began propping them up in the hearth. He carefully arranged them to create a structure-like appearance, giving the image of a three-story building. He then reached up onto the table behind him and grabbed a drink saucer, one of a metal design he'd never cared for. He propped the saucer up against the front of the wood and stood back. Once he felt he was an appropriate distance away, he grabbed the lighter fluid from underneath his armchair and applied it to only the top floor of the mini-structure.

As soon as the bottle was empty, he tossed it aside, managing to slide it under the piano. He then pulled the cigarette box from his pocket, as well as his old lighter. He carefully selected one of the cigarettes from the box, lit it, gave it a few puffs, then smirked.

"Burn," he said as he tossed the cigarette into the hearth. The top floor of the structure burst into flames, the tips of the fire almost stretching out to him. He sat back and watched as the fire worked its way down, and when it had reached the first floor, he grabbed the stoker from the side of the fireplace and jammed it into the saucer. The saucer shot forward, not collapsing the structure around it. He smiled in success, then leaned back and watched the rest of the structure burn.

By the time the structure had burned and the saucer had been sufficiently melted, the sun had set and two more hours had passed. Behind him, his phone chimed, telling him there was only one hour until the bus departure. As if on time, he heard the door below open and the patter of someone running up the stairs. He waited and timidly poked at the remains of the fire with the stoker.

"Yes," he said once the steps had ceased.

"We're going to get the kids," Walker replied from behind him. "Do you want to come?"

25th and Haring. Abandoned apartment complex. Danger.
"No. It seems the case has been put in capable hands." He minutely jabbed at the glossy remains of the saucer. "Well done, Doctor." He heard Walker sigh before running back down the stairs. Once the door had closed again, Hull jumped, grabbing his phone from the piano and looking out the window. Once the flashing lights had vanished, he ran

down the stairs, hoping the taxi driver would be on time. He, of course, was there, ready and waiting.

"Back to 39th," he said promptly.

"Gotcha."

They reached the gas station just as a white van pulled out, driving in the opposite direction. Hull threw another $20 at the taxi driver before jumping from the car and running to the gas station's parking lot. The black car from earlier was there, and had only just arrived. He could hear sounds from the engine as it cooled down inside. He looked in the back of the car and shook his head in disgust. *Too small.* He turned rapidly and spotted a jeep parked towards the back of the lot. With a grin, he went to work.

Only minutes later, he was driving the hotwired jeep in the direction the van had taken, trying his best not to break too many laws while driving without a license. He swerved down roads, barely braked to turn, and had a hard time stopping for every stop sign. He knew his destination well enough, but he'd taken longer than expected to get the jeep working. Bald Man and Burned Man had a head-start on him, and that time advantage could mean the difference between life and death for Walker, Lennox, and the three children inside the abandoned apartment complex that was more than likely burning at that very moment.

He turned the corner to see the apartment complex in flames, the fire just now reaching the first floor, judging by the windows. He pressed down on the accelerator and watched the yellow arrow go from 50 to 60 to 70. He'd need to be going at 78 miles per hour in order to cleanly break down the metal door to the complex. The meters between him and the door decreased rapidly until finally, the front wheels of the jeep ramped up the stairs and the front bumper made impact. The jeep slammed through the door, forcing it and a good area around it forward. Just as quickly as he had made impact, he backed up, knowing his companions would be running to escape the fire and smoke.

Sure enough, just as he climbed out of the jeep, Lennox and Walker emerged from the building, both holding the three Belt children. They looked at him with absolute disbelief, and all he could do was smirk.

*

Once Hull had concluded his retelling of events, I couldn't help but whistle.

"Absolutely amazing. Why didn't you help us sooner?"

"I could not risk revealing who I was, else the men would not have been so conversational in my presence."

I nodded, recognizing the logic behind it. "So now where? Ash's Cross?"

"Ash's Cross. I expect we will find all four of our men there waiting for us. Or for their bus, I suppose, but the bus was conveniently canceled."

"Four men?"

He chuckled. "You think one or two men could have successfully abducted five people from their own house without more sign of struggle? No, there had to be at least four men. And a convenient discovery you made at the home of Mr. Ronald Callahan helps to confirm this thought."

"How did you know about that?"

"One of the articles fell out of your coat pocket when you came before leaving for the apartment. I gave it a quick glance and understood perfectly. Now, the case made all the sense in the world."

I paused for a second, knowing he was waiting for one question in particular. "And?"

"Seven."

The only appropriate response was to laugh.

Within twenty minutes, we had reached the bus station, Ash's Cross, quite literally at the northernmost tip of town. There was a small group of people waiting on the benches, most of them scattered. I checked to make sure the children were safe before joining Hull and Lennox. Together the three of us walked along the crowd and, sure enough, we found a group of four sitting at a table, one wearing a golfer's cap and another completely bald.

"Gentlemen!" Hull shouted, causing the four men to jump. Each of them turned to look at us, and once the bald man saw Lennox and myself, a bolt of fear shot through his eyes. "I would not hold out hope for your bus. You have a previously scheduled engagement."

Lennox cuffed the four men to the table. We learned their names pretty quickly: the bald man was Ronald Callahan, which we'd already known; the man with the neck burn was George Everrard; the man with the gimp leg was Peter Depp; and the last man, surprisingly shorter than the rest, was Kevin Milo. The men sat with their heads down and their arms bound, an ever-present aura of fear and disappointment hovering above them.

"Well, Mr. Everrard," Hull said. The burned man looked up. "You seem to be the leader of the group. How about you enlighten us on the situation?"

"I know who you are," Everrard replied coolly. "The detective. I told them to keep an eye out for you." He snorted. "That damn disguise shouldn't have fooled me, but it did. Damn it did."

"Tell us why you are here," Hull demanded.

"Why? So I can just tell you what you already know?"

"No, I want you to tell me to confirm what I already know. And to fill in the others," Hull added with a glance at Lennox and me.

Everrard looked between the three other men before giving a hefty sigh. "It all started back in early 1990. Callahan, Depp, Milo, Mark Belt, and myself had just entered our second year of law school, and damn did we get lucky. A local law firm, down in L.A., was taking interns. Five interns. We all got the jobs and thought everything was swell. Damn were we stupid, stupid kids. We should've seen that kind of corrupt son of a bitch from a mile away.

"The guy who hired us was as bad as a lawyer could get. Working with the gangs, funneling money, if it's been featured in some stupid Hollywood movie, he did it. He was shit if we ever saw it, and we decided to take things into our own hands. The five of us were smart, law students interning for a local firm, and we knew what to do and how to do it. We knew how to get this man off the map and try and do some good for the world.

"Things didn't work out like that, though. Because dipshit here," he elbowed Callahan, "didn't get the right goddamn schedule. We were supposed to hit it when the building was empty, everyone off on vacation. But no, we hit it when it was filled to the fuckin' brim with lawyers and lobbyists and receptionists. I had a thing for one of them, too, she was a good piece of ass. But dammit, Callahan got the wrong schedule, and the five of us set fire to that firm in '92. We didn't know the people were in there until half the building had gone up in flames, and by then, dammit, it was too late.

"Building crashed in on itself and just like that, eighty people were dead and their burned blood was on our hands. We swore to ourselves we'd keep our mouths shut, just try to get over it, but Belt couldn't do it. He always was the weak one of the group, always pussying out of the harder shit. The police found him, and then us. All five of us were arrested and charged with arson and murder. But Belt, that fuckin' ass, he was able to sweet-talk his way out of it. He talked the investigators into believing he was just a victim of circumstance. He got five years of parole. We all got life in prison.

"Belt didn't say a goddamn word to us after that. He avoided that prison like the plague, moved an entire state away. Came up here, met his wife, settled down, had kids. I bet after the fourth kid, he'd forgotten completely that eighty fuckin' people had died and four other deadbeats were rotting in jail because of him. But we waited. We were smart, we knew the right things to do, the right things to say. And it worked.

"Twenty years later, all four of us were let go on good behavior and lack of substantial evidence to support the ruling of our guiltiness. We were free men, and we wanted to get back at Belt. Twenty years of our lives had been spent in cells while he had lived like a goddamn king. That wasn't okay with any of us. So we were going to make him pay, just like he'd made us pay. We were going to put him through what we all, together, put eighty others through. We were gonna burn him. And his wife. And his kids. All of 'em.

"We planned for weeks. Staked out his house, his job, all of it. We knew the exact schedule of his house, we knew every time him and his stupid wife were having sex while their kids watched a goddamn Disney movie. We picked our date and hit. Don't know how the fucking teenager avoided us, but we took who we could grab. We told Belt what was gonna happen, and he asked us, he *begged* us, to let his wife and kids live. And you know what, we were in an understanding mood. They didn't sell us out.

"That stupid bitch, though, she wouldn't leave his side. So we decided to burn 'em both and use the kids as our leverage. We burned the warehouse with them bound and gagged on the floor. I remember the look on his goddamn face as we closed the doors. The smoke had just started flooding the room, his eyes were tearin' up. He looked so pathetic lying there. Callahan stayed behind to make sure everything burned, and that's when you asshats started poking your nose in our shit.

"I knew we'd have to move fast, so we decided to bargain the kids off quickly, burn the building and take whatever police with it. You'd all be so distracted with the fires you wouldn't catch one bus headed for Portland. But you, damn you, you smart as fuck detective, I knew coming here that you would be a problem if you got involved.

And dammit, you got involved, and now we're all fucked. I don't know how you fucking did it, but you did. So damn you for that, you son of a bitch."

Hull stepped back, a large smile on his face. "All correct. As I expected." He turned to Lennox. "I'd get them to the station. The doctor and I can take the children to the nearest hospital." Lennox nodded to Hull, then to me. Hull shot me a glance and started back towards the stolen jeep. I followed slowly, mind still reeling.

"I don't know how you do it," I finally said once we'd reached the vehicle.

He breathed in. "Sometimes, neither do I. But I do at the same time. Wonderful thing."

"So," I said as I opened the driver door, knowing he wouldn't drive now that it wasn't necessary, "still a seven?"

He waited until he was seated before replying. "Seven and a half."

THE COMBUSTIBLE CABINET

And yet, I do, don't I.

The shrouded man slowly lifted his chin, his facial features masked by the shadow of his hood. His gloved right hand scratched pointlessly at the metal armrest while his breath emanated from under the hood in rattles. With his left hand, he grabbed the top of a metal cane from the edge of the closest table, only just visible in the naturally-lit room. The light crept in from a tiny dome some dozen meters high, while the room echoed with a song from The Ink Spots.

The man struggled to his feet, using the cane for support. It always seemed to be during the darker periods, the periods where things were not advancing as he would like, that he found need of the cane. It wasn't that he was physically impaired; if anything, the cane gave him mental comfort. Some kind of crutch that wasn't a person to rely on. One that could never betray him, or get the upper hand. The perfect object of support.

Indeed I do.

He stepped away from the chair, walking through the darkness towards one of the seven corners of the room, all hidden in darkness. Once he'd reached the right amount of steps and the music had increased significantly in volume, he stopped. Before him, the distinct noises of a record needle scratching over a record that predated him pierced his eardrums. The cold silence from the rest of the room was nothing but reassuring.

He grabbed the needle from the pitch black, stopping the singing voice halfway through the final word. He held the needle for a long moment before sliding it to the side and flicking a switch on the edge of the player, causing the sound of the rotating record to cease. He stared forward into the blackness for at least two minutes before scoffing.

My one desire is no one person. It is them all. To do what must be done, to provide direction.

Moriarty stepped away from the record player and started towards the doorway. He entered the dark hallway that had only two doors that faced each other, around twenty meters apart. He quickly advanced to the second door and stepped into the central room, where his right-hand woman, Veronica Daemon, sat and worked, eyes glued to the array of glowing monitors before her.

"Veronica," he said, his voice a growl. The blonde woman looked up sharply, a slight sense of surprise crossing her face.

"Yes, Sir?" she asked in one of the most petty voices he had ever heard.

"Hull ensured the detaining of the arsonists. Xaphon is displeased with the loss of one of his most skilled agents. We must work to rectify this."

"Of course, Sir."

"And Veronica."

She paused, a slight twitch appearing for only a second under her left eye. "Yes, Sir?"

"Hull possesses the diary. We need to retrieve it. Immediately."

"What would you suggest, Sir?"

He walked past her, moving into the shadows behind the monitors. "A distraction."

*

"They paint me in a good light this time."

I looked up from my laptop to see Hull slide into the room, his purple robe billowing behind him. He tossed the paper towards my face, my hands barely catching the flying bundle. I turned it over to reveal a very large, very different headline from the last time Hull was in the news.

"'Local detective solves decades-old arson story.' Well, that's not bad at all," I replied as I skimmed over the article.

"I still could not care less about their opinions of me."

"Of course you don't. But at least they seem to be on your side here."

"*At least.*"

I glanced up at Hull to find him scaling the bookshelf, climbing higher and higher. The shelf itself was around twelve feet tall, and instead of using a conventional tool, like a stool, he preferred to climb. He reached the top shelf, grabbed a dusty book from the row, and tossed it over his head. The book soared over my own head and slammed into the revealed soundboard of the piano. He jumped from the shelf, deftly landing on his armchair.

"If I didn't know better, I'd say you were bored after just one day of being done with a case," I commented as I set the paper aside.

"The last case had intrigue, I cannot deny that. This point of the year has always made my mind restless."

"So I can see."

He retrieved the book from the insides of the piano, then scooted back to his armchair and propped it open. The book was *The Adventures of Tom Sawyer*, judging by the cover. It looked to be an original print, surprisingly. He flipped through the pages before reaching somewhere near the middle. He ran his slender finger down the page, then back to the top.

"Last year around this time, my brother was so concerned for my health, he sent me to a counselor," he said as his eyes read the pages' contents at record speeds.

"And how did that go?"

"Waste of time."

I chuckled. "Let me guess. They told you everything you already knew?"

"Of course. I know everything of importance in regards to myself. One who does not know themselves is in no position to attempt to understand others."

"Well," I said as I returned my attention to my laptop, "that's one way to think of it." We both remained silent for several minutes before he chuckled.

"Clever man, that Twain. Very clever indeed."

"How's that?"

Before he could reply, a short knock came from the door ahead of me. Mrs. Hanson slowly pushed it open, peeking through to make sure it was okay to enter. She stepped in with an envelope in hand.

"This came for you boys," she said as she handed me the envelope. I nodded to her before she left, then carefully looked the mail over. It was simply addressed to the house rather than any individual person, meaning the mail person had more than likely specified. I gently peeled the envelope open to reveal two thin pieces of paper with removable stubs.

"Tickets," I announced, "to the evening showing of Thomas the Trickster at the Lawson Concert Hall." I looked the tickets over a few times before shaking my head. "Thomas the Trickster?"

"Expert magician. Well-versed in the arts of illusion," Hull said as he set the book to his side.

"We were anonymously sent tickets to a magician's show?" He gave no response. "Well, unless you suddenly have plans tonight, I suppose we could go."

"A slight distraction may be in my best interests," he added. "Besides, it will keep my mind occupied for minuscule moments at a time, deciphering the science to his trickery."

It was one of few times Hull had ever accepted any kind of offer to go out for entertainment or leisure. But I wasn't in a position to complain. I knew that if he didn't go, he'd just sit in the room and eventually start firing arrows, or mixing chemicals, or adding chemicals to the tips of his arrows. Preventing that inevitability was worth an evening watching magic tricks. The show wasn't until later in the evening, meaning we had a good ten hours to spare. I spent it organizing my thoughts from the previous case. I'd aptly titled it "*Burn.*" I suppose it just seemed fitting to me.

Oh, and Hull passed the time by writing on his chalkboard in Latin.

*

Hull and I arrived at the concert hall about a half-hour before the show was scheduled to start. We'd both dressed appropriately, Hull adopting a nice coat and dress pants, with the collar of the coat popped. I wore my usual formal attire, a suit I'd used for many occasions with a red tie. Upon our arrival, I immediately sought to find a familiar face in the crowd. I knew Hull wouldn't care, but I liked to have company. Fortunately, one face did stand out.

Lennox stood at the edge of a group, his attention focused on the other members. He surprisingly looked like he normally did, his tan coat, blue tie, and shirt appearing to be slightly tugged at. Hull and I cut our way through the crowd towards him, and when he noticed us, he signaled for us to join him. When we did, I found that he was with three other men, only one that I recognized. The three men turned to face us with smiles.

"Sheridan Hull, John Walker," Lennox said with a nod, "I'm sure you know Mr. Jameson Montorum." The tallest man of the group, Montorum, shook our hands. I'd met him once before, months ago, and Hull and I had helped solve the mystery behind his son's death. Other than that, I knew little about the man. Lennox gestured to the man directly at his side, a balding, older man with a hardened gaze. "This is the chief of police, Mr. Lamont Conn." This man was supposedly friends with my brother.

Lennox gestured to the final man, an intimidating fellow with black hair, similar to Montorum's, except his was persuaded to move to the right. His face was gaunt, pale-skinned. His eyes were both a dark brown, almost so brown they were black. Neck-down, he was thin, and wore a black tunic and pants in no attempt to disguise his weight. His right hand was hidden beneath a black glove that stretched nearly to his elbow.

"This is Mr. Ross McNair," Lennox said, "one of our political liaisons to the capital." McNair extended his left hand rather than his right, and I couldn't help but feel awkward when I shook it. Hull's eyes were somewhat narrowed as he shook the man's hand.

"I've heard a lot about you two gentlemen," McNair commented, his voice having a purr to it, almost metallic. "Your handling of the arsonist case was admirable."

"These fine men helped bring my son's murderer to justice," Montorum added as he clapped my shoulder. "Newfield would be far worse off without them."

"Oh no," Conn said, his first time speaking. "God forbid the police department do their job." He shot a glare at Lennox with the last word. The inspector was careful to avoid the man's gaze. My attention, however, was focused on Hull, who had yet to remove his sight from McNair. Or, more specifically, his gloved hand. I too found it odd that the man would wear such a noticeable glove on only one hand, but Hull was making no attempts to hide where his attention was focused.

A voice over the intercom told us it was time to take our seats. The group of us started moving towards the entryway, and as we did, Hull made a point to stand between me and McNair.

"Injury, then?" Hull commented, his voice directed at McNair. I watched Lennox glance over his shoulder at Hull, a slight tremor of disdain crossing his face.

"I prefer to keep it out of sight," the man replied with a cool sneer. He entered the room without another word. Hull kept a cautious watch on the man as we took our seats in the seventh row, center seating area. In no time at all, the lights dimmed and a figure walked out to take the stage.

He certainly looked the part of a magician. With the black hat, the wand, the twisted black mustache, and the waiter-like suit, he walked with the spotlight hovering above him to center stage, then gave an illustrious bow. He looked back up at us all with a wide grin, his arms spread wide to encompass the crowd.

"Welcome, ladies and gentlemen, to 'An Evening of Magic,' courtesy of yours truly, Thomas the Trickster! Tonight, I vow to bend the laws of reality, twist the fabric of nature, and show you the true meaning of magic!" A round of applause followed. "With the help of my lovely assistants," three young women stepped out from the shadows, "we will leave you fascinated. Let the festivities... *begin!*"

With the final word, a puff of smoke shout up from underneath the man, and once it had cleared, the Trickster was gone. Another round of applause erupted from the crowd around us. Even Lennox was giving a casual clap. Hull just scowled.

The show went from act to act, each wowing the majority of the crowd, some tricks sending waves of laughter, other tricks throwing a blanket of silence. I often found myself more entertained by the presence of the three assistants rather than the Trickster. One of them in particular had caught my eye. She looked to be about my age, with blonde hair that reached her shoulders and a glistening smile. Her slender figure was complemented by the leg-revealing costume each of the assistants wore. And if I didn't know better, I could've sworn she had smiled in my direction more than once.

Time started to move fairly quickly during the show, and in what felt like minutes, we had reached the final act. The single spotlight had returned, and the Trickster stood, hands clasped behind his back, the three assistants standing in line behind him. He looked out at us, his grin wider than ever.

"Well, ladies and gentlemen, we are rapidly approaching the end of our show, but fear not! The final act is always saved for a reason. This act in particular has been attempted by many a magician throughout the course of time, and only few have lived to perform it again. An act birthed in the times of ancient witchcraft and wizardry, the magic of survival, levitation, and disappearance. I present to you, ladies and gentlemen... *the combustible cabinet*!"

He threw his arm back, signaling for the lights to come to life. Behind the Trickster's assistants was a large wooden cabinet, almost eight feet tall. Next to the cabinet was a table, and on the table, eight different swords. The Trickster walked to the side of the cabinet, opening the door to reveal the inside.

"Carefully watch and ensure that you are not fooled. The cabinet contains no hollow spaces, no points of escape." He tapped it twice with his wand, and suddenly the cabinet lifted into the air, rotating slowly to show us the bottom. He pushed against it with his free hand. "There is no false bottom, no way of falling through to safety." He tapped it again, causing it to reverse its rotation and return to the ground. "In just a few moments, I will step into the confines of this cabinet and have my lovely assistants insert each of the eight swords on the nearby table into the cabinet.

"Then, once each sword has been placed, my assistants will step away from the cabinet, and you, ladies and gentlemen, will watch as this wooden container is lifted into the air, just as I have shown you, higher and higher before the boundaries of reality and magic have been broken. The cabinet will erupt into flames before your very eyes, and only once the entire cabinet is charred and black will it return to the ground, and I, Thomas the Trickster, will emerge unscathed."

I glanced over at Hull, who was now leaned forward slightly, a look of genuine interest on his face.

"Are you ready, my friends?" the Trickster asked. A chorus of affirmations answered. His grin widened once more. "Then let the final act, the act of the combustible cabinet, begin." He slowly stepped into the cabinet, and once he had turned to face the crowd, the blonde assistant closed the door and, with the other two assistants, stepped over to the table and grabbed the swords. One by one, they jammed the swords into the box, and not a single scream in pain came. Once all of the swords had been placed, the three stepped away. They stood nearly three meters away, their hands clasped. Slowly, the box rose into the air, moving centimeters at first, then rising to be almost two meters in the air.

What happened next made even me gasp.

The box erupted into flames, first starting at the bottom and working their way up. Within seconds, the fire had taken the entire cabinet in. Still no sounds came from inside. The assistants turned and smiled at the crowd, creating a roar of applause and cheering. I found myself clapping in amazement, part of me believing the magic I was seeing. With a quick glance at Hull, however, I felt my insides chill over. His eyes were starting to tremble, his skin whiter than usual.

I'm sure my skin went the same shade when the first scream came.

It was a horrible noise, like a herd of animals being tortured. It was gargled and muffled, but it was most certainly a human scream, and it was coming from the cabinet. The screams increased in pitch over the course of just five seconds. People in the crowd stood as the assistants turned and frantically started signaling to someone to the side of the stage. The box slowly began its descent, but after a second of movement, the thin, almost invisible ropes holding the cabinet in the air snapped, the fire having weakened their strength. The cabinet smashed to the stage, and as it did, the screams ceased.

People from behind the curtains rushed out, fire extinguishers in hand. The three assistants were ushered off the stage by several figures. Lennox and Conn had started pushing through the crowd, Montorum was staring forward in shock, even McNair appeared horrified. Hull was nowhere to be seen, but I knew where he would be shortly. I started after Lennox, knowing that pandemonium had just broken loose in the concert hall. By now, someone had called 911. Everything was in complete disarray.

And I had no doubt in my mind that Thomas the Trickster was dead.

*

Hull, Lennox, Conn, and I stood around the smoking cabinet, firefighters moving around us and other officials of the concert hall standing off to the side. No one had opened the charred door to the cabinet yet, but I could tell Hull was anxious to. Two firefighters gave Conn a crowbar, who handed it to Lennox. Together, Lennox and I pried the door from the cabinet, and immediately we stepped back as a wave of smoke poured out.

Once the smoke had cleared, the insides were exactly what we expected. The charred remains of an individual, contorted by multiple glowing swords sticking through the burnt remains, were all that was left of the magician. All of the skin had been burned of the fire, and there was nothing left to even slightly suggest it had been a smiling, cunning man before. Lennox ran his hands through his hair at the sight, and Conn had a very sullen look to his eyes. Hull, however, was intrigued and alive.

"I hoped for something of interest to occur this evening, but never in my wildest dreams could it have been this captivating," he commented with a glimmer to his gaze.

"Captivating?" Conn said with a look of disgust. "You think this is captivating?"

Hull smirked. "If you disagree, then your profession as a police chief must be extremely boring."

Conn's jaw dropped slightly, the bridge of his nose crinkled. With a swift turn, he shifted his eyes to Lennox. "This case is officially under the jurisdiction of the Newfield Police Department. I want no outer involvement." His last sentence was no doubt directed at Hull. The detective kept his chin high and eyes forward, not acknowledging the presence of the chief. With a huff, Conn walked away. Lennox cast me an apologetic glance before focusing his attention on the burned body.

Hull and I walked up the steps towards the lobby, and once we were out of earshot from Lennox or any other individuals of importance, I spoke. "So what's the plan?"

"Lamont Conn is an idiot, but he holds significant power. Power I am in no position to cross."

"So..."

"So we operate outside the jurisdiction of the Newfield Police Department. Work independently to solve the mystery."

"And that mystery is?"

He paused once we'd entered the lobby, glancing over at the poster for the show. "Renowned magician suffers a fatal accident performing a trick he has done countless times before? Body burned beyond recognition? Oh, this is most certainly a mystery, Doctor. The mystery of the failed magician, why he failed... and who he wanted to kill."

I stopped and shot a glance at the detective. "Who what?"

He looked up and down the road in front of the concert hall, no doubt searching for a taxi. "The body inside the cabinet was not the body of Thomas the Trickster. So we need to find out who Thomas the Trickster really was, and who he wanted dead."

We returned to the flat, since the hour was late and Hull seemed determined to do some research on his own. When we walked into the doors of our area, Hull stopped, eyes surveying the room. I walked in slowly, glancing back at him.

"Something wrong?" I asked.

He finished his survey before blinking. "No."

"Alright then. How do we learn more about the man?"

He moved to his laptop, taking it to the piano and propping it up on the top. "We find out who Thomas the Trickster really is. And we find out how he made the switch."

"Switch?"

"Thomas was the one to step into the cabinet, and yet upon its burning, he was no longer the occupant. And he did not lie when he said there was no method of escape. The bottom was secured and the stage possessed no pitfalls underneath the cabinet. He stepped into the box, yes, but he did not step out. So we must figure out how."

The online research did not take long. Thomas the Trickster was definitely renowned, as Hull had said. He did shows from New York City to Las Vegas year-round, and had been an active magician for almost eight years now. An enthusiastic reporter had even managed to get an interview with him, in which he listed his original name as Thomas Kneeler. Born in Florida and discovered he had an aptitude for magic. His largest inspiration had been Harry Houdini.

The deeper our searching went, the more information we found. In the first two years of Kneeler's career, he had worked as an apprentice magician to a once-well-known man who called himself Melvin the Magnificent. Melvin had been in the magic business for over a decade prior to working with Kneeler. Melvin's name had been Melvin Hartford. He had left the business six years ago, and had given a substantial amount of money to assist Kneeler in his solo career.

"These little details from his past don't do a damn to help us right now," I said after closing another tab.

"On the contrary, the littlest details are by far the most important." He turned his laptop to face me, even though I was sitting some few meters away. "Take note of how Hartford left. No mention of retirement or possible future career. The man was in his late fifties and had practiced magic for sixteen years. The job of a magician is not one that pays heavily, no matter how good their acts are. Without a proper plan, Hartford surely would have failed after leaving, and yet he was somehow in a position to leave Kneeler with a substantial amount of money.

"Something else to take note of is something Kneeler said in his show. The final act was something many had attempted, yet few had succeeded. This is a lie. The act of the combustible cabinet was one designed by Hartford in 1995, and he only performed it once in his final show. He succeeded at it, and since then, it has only been done by Kneeler in shows. This is a result of the danger in the trick. But I believe that danger is feigned. I doubt Kneeler was in any danger at all during the act."

"But that doesn't explain who was in the cabinet, or how he got out."

"We can make the assumption that the person inside the cabinet was Hartford, but how he came to be inside the cabinet, and why, is yet to be determined. How Kneeler escaped is a mystery indeed that will require further investigation, which we will have to continue in the morning. We will have to hope for Lennox's cooperation in minor glances at the scene, though I doubt our attention will have to be focused there."

I watched as his eyes shot from the laptop to the bookshelf, stopping at the top shelf. He stared at it for a very, very long time before sighing.

"What's wrong?"

He glanced down at me. "I need to speak with Mrs. Hanson about the cleaning. Something is amiss in the room." He looked back up at the shelf before giving another sigh. "It is irrelevant. Now is best if we rest."

*

The next morning, Hull and I returned to the concert hall, where a line of police cars prevented all public access. Lennox was wary at first to grant us access, but Hull ensured that he only wished to speak with the three assistants. He had no want nor need to see the actual scene of the crime again. Quietly, Lennox led us to a crew conference room on the third floor of the concert hall, where the three assistants sat in chairs, hands trembling in their laps and eyes focused on the ground. My eyes paused on the blonde woman momentarily before Hull spoke.

"We'll start with the brunette," he said as he entered the conference room. Lennox nodded to the brunette assistant sitting closest to the door, then gestured inside. The woman stood with shaking legs and entered. I nudged Lennox before entering myself.

"You're allowing this?" I asked with a glance at the remaining women.

"He'd find a way to talk to them otherwise. Might as well help him out." He shrugged. "Besides, I can't do a damn thing until the genetic results get back to us. I know he doesn't need those results to work, but Conn won't authorize any other investigation on my part without physical evidence." The two of us followed the young woman in and took the seats beside Hull. The detective clasped his fingers before him and stared forward.

"Name," he said, his monotonous voice piercing the silence that had fallen in the room.

The woman glanced at the three of us before gulping. "Carla Goldstein."

"What can you tell us about Mr. Thomas Kneeler?"

Lennox furrowed his brow. "Who?"

"Thomas Kneeler, Thomas the Trickster, names are irrelevant. What can you tell us about him?"

"I only started working for Thomas in March. He saw me at a show in Vegas and asked if I wanted to join him."

"Did Mr. Kneeler ever allude to any preexisting conflicts he may have had with other individuals?"

"No?" She looked between us again, her eyes starting to shake. "Was Thomas murdered?"

"How was Mr. Kneeler to escape from the cabinet?"

At this, Goldstein looked completely shocked. "He never told us. None of us knew how he could get out, and we'd checked. The cabinet had no way out once the door was closed. We knew the ropes levitated it, but we didn't know how he got out. He's always been able to. But not this time."

Hull stared at the woman for a very long, quiet time before rolling his eyes. "Done. Send in the next one."

Lennox glanced at the detective before giving a sigh and standing. He led Goldstein out and nodded to the blonde woman. I felt my insides twist as the beautiful woman entered the room. Her blonde hair was in a ponytail now, her makeup not as illustrious as the previous evening's but her beauty in no way detracted. She took her seat and looked at me, her eyes screaming for care and attention. Once Lennox had returned to his seat, Hull continued.

"Name."

"Cassidy Claypool."

Hull seemed to be somewhat taken aback by the name, but it was only visible in his eyes. "Ms. Claypool, what can you tell us about Mr. Kneeler?"

"I've been working with Thomas for three years now. He's always been very happy, his mind set on his goals. His purpose was to entertain people, to make them feel like the magic was real. That was all he ever wanted in life."

"Were you ever aware of any conflicts Mr. Kneeler may have had with others?"

She bit her lip for a moment before responding. "He said he and his old partner didn't end on good terms, but he'd never mentioned anyone else. He never stayed in one city long enough to make enemies."

"How was he supposed to escape the cabinet?"

"I don't know. None of us did. I've even seen the recordings of when his partner did it and I couldn't figure it out. He steps in, the ropes lift the cabinet up, the entire thing bursts into flames, and once it's lowered to the ground, he steps out, no sword wounds, no burns."

Hull narrowed his eyes at the woman. "You watched the recording last night, didn't you."

"What?"

"You watched it last night. After the chaos had ended and the police had dismissed you three, you returned to your hotel, found the tape in Mr. Kneeler's belongings, and reviewed it."

Nothing but pure amazement filled her eyes. "I.. I did, yes."

"Get it and bring it back."

"Hull," Lennox interjected, "I can't just go dismissing people without—"

"Then go with her. I can interview the third assistant in the time it will take you to walk across the street and retrieve the tape."

Lennox opened his mouth to object, but instead sighed. He stood once more and walked around the table. As Claypool stood, she looked at me and gave me a smile, just like the ones I was certain she'd given me during the show. I felt my cheeks start to grow red and nodded before looking at Hull, trying my best to distract myself.

"So Kneeler and Hartford didn't have an easy departing of ways," I said once the door had closed behind Lennox. "That contradicts the claim that Hartford gave Kneeler money."

"Or Hartford gave Kneeler money under strenuous circumstances."

"Extortion?"

"Possibly. Can you get the third assistant?" I nodded and moved for the door. The girl was waiting at the farthest seat, hands holding her elbows. She looked up at me, her lips shaking. I gave a short nod towards the room before reentering. She followed slowly after, closing the door behind her and taking her seat. I could tell that she was taking the situation far worse than her counterparts.

"Name."

"M-Melissa Kielenhon."

"What can you tell us about Mr. Tho—"

"*I swear I didn't do it!*"

The girl's scream caught both Hull and I off guard. I glanced at the detective, who had his brow furrowed.

"Never once did I assume you had—"

"But they think I did and they're going to turn me in and I swear to God I *didn't do it!*"

"Who's going to turn you in?" I asked.

"The others," she said as tears started streaming down her face. "Carla and Cassidy. I was in charge of getting the cabinet on stage. They both think I did it, that I tampered with it somehow."

"How would you have tampered with it?" Hull questioned. "Were you aware of how Kneeler would survive?"

She shook her head frantically. "I don't even know how it catches on fire. I've seen the trick dozens of times and I still don't understand how he does it. I think..."

"Think what?"

"Sometimes I think it actually is magic."

Hull scoffed. "That is the most preposterous thought you could ever have."

"Then you tell me how he does it!"

"Oh, I intend to." He shooed in the door's direction. "You can leave now. I need to think." The woman looked from Hull to me before standing and leaving. Once she had closed the door, he glanced at me. "Find a television and working VCR. Wait for Lennox to return before bringing it in."

"Why wait?"

"I need the space."

"You need the—"

"Please." With a sigh, I stood and left the room, and immediately after closing the door, I heard the distinctive *click* of the lock.

*

It was about twenty minutes later that Lennox and Claypool returned to the concert hall. I'd been waiting outside the conference room with a television and VCR sitting on a cart. The two other assistants had sat in their seats and kept to themselves the entire time, not a word being spoken by either. Claypool held the tape in her shaking hands and watched as Lennox and I tried the door. It was, of course, still locked. I banged on the door and sighed.

"Hull, we're all back," I said with a final pound. "Let us in." The door clicked open. What we stepped into was mind-blowing.

Somehow, someway, Hull had managed to create and suspend his own version of the cabinet. It wasn't on fire, but it was about the same size and was hovering in the air with the use of several dozen wires, no doubt pulled from the walls that had been viciously torn at. Hull was currently inside the cabinet and softly swaying it side to side.

Lennox was first. "How in the Hell...?"

I glanced down at the door. "How did you unlock it without going to the door?"

"Time is of the essence, gentlemen," the detective replied as he hopped down from the cabinet. From a glance, I could see that he'd used parts of the table, the chairs, and the walls to create it. It was a mesh of different textures and materials, and yet, it looked exactly like the cabinet Thomas the Trickster had stepped into.

"This is going to cost a fortune to fix," Lennox said as he took in the room.

"I do believe I have figured out the key to understanding Kneeler's success, but we must review the tape to provide the facts to confirm my theories," Hull prompted. Claypool held the tape out for his retrieval, her attention no doubt on the room. I gave a slight shake of my head before moving to the wall and plugging the TV and VCR in. Once everything was in place, Hull softly pushed the tape into the VCR and stepped back.

The taping was from 2005 and showed a stage similar to the one in the concert hall. Front and center was a man, about the same height as his counterpart, who I immediately recognized as Thomas Kneeler. The man, presumably Melvin Hartford, was addressing the crowd and proudly displaying the cabinet behind him. A chorus of *oohs* and *ahhs* followed as he lifted the cabinet into the air and showed the bottom. Then, with a nod at Kneeler, he stepped into the cabinet and closed the door.

The act played out just as it had the previous night. The box lifted itself into the air and soon burst into flames. This time, though, there was no blood-curdling scream. The box burned in the air for almost a minute before lowering itself to the ground. Once it touched the ground, the flames immediately vanished. Kneeler approached the door slowly, unlatched the front, and stepped back as the door swung open to reveal an unharmed Hartford.

Hull stopped the tape there, leaning forward to examine the contents of the screen. He moved his eyes up and down the television's screen before stepping back, his eyes narrowed and pupils dilating. After a long moment, he pressed the power button on the television and turned to face his own cabinet. Lennox, Claypool, and I watched as he stepped into the cabinet and caused it to lift up into the air. It hovered there for several seconds before softly touching down on the ground.

Hull stepped out of the cabinet, the all-too familiar glint to his eyes.

"Perfect," he said, a tone of finality very noticeable to his voice.

"Perfect what?" I asked.

"Perfect illusion. We need to see the concert hall."

Lennox crossed his arms. "I'm already pushing my luck having you here, and now I'm going to definitely get my ass roasted."

"I know where Kneeler is."

Even Claypool's attention was grabbed now. "You do? Where?"

"The doctor and I need to visit the concert hall, alone. Inspector, I need you to take the three assistants elsewhere."

"Why?" Lennox questioned.

"I do not expect Kneeler to come compliantly. And I would prefer to avoid further casualties to the case. We already have one dead magician."

And finally, things clicked in my head. "Hartford was in the cabinet."

"Correct," Hull said as he started towards the door. "Now it's time to find out how."

Hull and I walked away from the conference room with the concert hall directly ahead of us, its entry doors closed to prevent unnecessary access. As we walked, I couldn't keep from glancing over my shoulder to catch one last look at Ms. Claypool before she was gone. A small part of me wished I'd said something, but I knew I had a tendency to idealize and romanticize. Odds were, she only saw me as one of the people solving the case.

"What did you see in the video?" I asked once we were within a hundred feet of the door.

"The trick to the illusion. So simple, it upsets me that it took this long for it to make sense. Such a simple illusion."

"And that is?"

"The illusion of an empty cabinet."

We stepped through the doors into the dimmed concert hall. The stage was still relatively roped off, with the burned cabinet sitting in the center. I suppose it was only now that I realized what other props had been on the stage at the time. Lined up at the back were eight coffins, each of them black and sealed. To the right of the cabinet was a metal cage, its hinged door open. Somehow these had slipped my view when we had been here last.

"We must move cautiously," Hull said as we walked towards the stage. "Kneeler will no doubt be expe—"

The gunshot that rang out was enough to finish the sentence.

Hull and I ducked in different directions, both of us taking cover in the seats. I had no idea where the shot had come from, but I prayed that where I'd jumped would put me out of sight. I crawled forward towards the center aisle, carefully glancing back to see if I could find Hull. Once I reached the aisle, I scrambled to my feet and followed the auburn carpets to the stage.

"Hull!" I yelled as I looked around for the detective. As I yelled, however, the lights began to flicker. I stepped back to avoid the spotlight's strobe effect and yelped as a heavy hand pushed my chest back. My feet gave way when they made contact with what felt like a metal bar, and my back soon smashed into the wooden floor of the stage. I heard the loud smash and click of a metal door and lock, and only then did the lights quit their flickering to reveal where I was. Somehow I had made my way to the metal cage, and now I had no means of escape.

Another gunshot rang out, but I could tell this one wasn't directed at me. I watched Hull jump up onto the stage and cast a glance in my direction. I shook my head frantically, knowing he wouldn't be able to open the gate before he was shot. He gave a sharp nod and ran forward, his destination the row of coffins. When he was just a meter away, the lights went off altogether, and all I could hear was the opening and closing of one of the coffin doors.

The lights shot to life once more, this time with no flickering and no subsequent gunshots. Standing next to the charred cabinet was a figure clad in a black robe, the hood drawn to hide his face. He glanced over in my direction, and for a brief moment, the worst sensation of death passed through me. A hand reached out from inside the robe to reveal a pistol, but instead of firing, it let the weapon go. The gun fell harmlessly to the ground, bouncing once before coming to a stop. The free hand reached up and pulled the robe clean from the body, and revealed the perfectly unscathed Thomas Kneeler.

"Excellent work, Dr. Walker," Kneeler bellowed as the robe dropped to his feet. He wore the same clothes he had donned when he'd stepped into the burned cabinet at his side. "And to you as well, Mr. Hull." He started towards the eight coffins, but averted his path slightly to instead reach a table I had not seen before. The table was covered with what appeared to be swords, just like the ones that had been jammed into the cabinet.

"Now, gentlemen, are you ready for the true final act?" Kneeler grabbed two of the swords from the table. "I call this one the Flight of the Magician. It's where the conscientious doctor and the arrogant detective are found dead, and the amazing magician who survived death is never seen nor heard from again." He stepped over to the caskets, holding a sword in each hand. "Now, to be logical, the arrogant detective would never use the two on the left or right." He kicked out furiously, knocking one, then two caskets back into the curtain on the left, then moving to do the same to the coffins on the right.

Kneeler stepped back to stand front-center from the remaining for coffins. "And that leaves these. Now the fun truly does begin!" He walked over to the leftmost coffin. "Oh where, oh where has my Sheridan gone?" He stabbed the coffin with the sword, stepped over to the table and retrieved a new blade, then moved to the second coffin. "Oh where, oh where can he be?" He stabbed the second, and I could feel my heart begin to pound. "With his hair so short and his coat tail so long..." He stabbed the third, and now I could barely keep a grip on the metal bars of the cage. Kneeler walked to stand directly ahead of the fourth and final coffin.

"Oh where, oh where can he be!" He stabbed the last sword into the coffin and stepped back with a heavy sigh of victory. My insides felt as if I'd been stabbed, though. But that feeling soon dissipated when both Kneeler and I realized the same thing. No sound of pain nor wound had emanated from any of the four coffins. Kneeler took another step back to take in the four caskets. "Where the Hell is he?"

A loud bang came from the charred cabinet, and out of the burned door stepped Sheridan Hull. He jumped from the cabinet to Kneeler's back, bringing the unsuspecting magician down in one swift movement. Kneeler struggled against Hull, but the detective gave no lenience. He pulled a pair of handcuffs from his pocket and quickly clapped Kneeler's hands together.

"You should really keep from leaving handcuffs around like that," Hull said as he pulled a long key, the key to my metal cage, from Kneeler's pocket. "You never know when an arrogant detective might use your own magic tricks against you."

*

Hull, Lennox and I stood on the stage with Kneeler propped down in one of the audience chairs, his hands secured behind the seat. The three assistants had not returned, but the police department was no doubt on their way, Conn included. Lennox had yet to mention Hull's involvement, and if I had interpreted Hull's intentions correctly, he planned to be gone before the chief of police ever arrived. Lennox would most certainly be commended.

"It was confusing at first, I will credit you for that," Hull said as he paced along the stage. "Your mistake was in thinking I would believe in the illusions. I will admit that I was perplexed of as to how you would survive being burned alive in a suspended cabinet, but once I reviewed the tape of your predecessor doing the exact same trick with your assistance, I realized where I had failed to pay attention.

"The combustible cabinet trick is really an illusion on multiple levels. The box is simple in design, the only point of entry or exit being the doorway. There are no pitfall panels, no walls that push through for escape. Once you stepped in, you were secured. Except for, of course, the hidden compartment at the back of the cabinet, cleverly disguised to appear as if it did not exist. The way the box was designed made it so even when closely scrutinized, detection of the hidden compartment would be almost impossible without the proper method of opening it.

"This method was, of course, the tapping of the side using your wand. The wand's tip has a special metallic alloy in it, one that would trigger a magnet within the hidden compartment and cause the door to slide open, the door being made of a very flexible metal that would resist the burning of the cabinet. With the compartment now open, yet still looking no different than before, you would step into the cabinet, close the main door behind you, step into the compartment, and use the magnet to close the door. Once the cabinet had been sufficiently burned using a similar trigger within the compartment that started a spark at the bottom of the wood, you would emerge from the compartment unscathed, and your magic would be unquestionable.

"It was difficult to notice at first, but in the taping of your mentor, Mr. Melvin Hartford, the doorway to the cabinet was not entirely closed, and from the certain angle the camera was kept at, one could see the minute opening of the secret compartment as Hartford tapped the side of the cabinet. People were too focused on the seemingly-levitating cabinet to ever notice the compartment's opening."

Hull stepped over to the cabinet, tilting his head to look inside before continuing. "When you performed the trick last night, you had ulterior motives. Your mentor had wronged you in the past, prior to his retirement, and in retaliation you had blackmailed him. If I read correctly, he had a tendency to be very flirtatious with his assistants, usually at the same time. You used this knowledge against him, forcing him into early retirement and requiring him to pay you a monthly amount of money to keep your voice silent.

"Hartford, however, grew tired of the extortion and told the assistants of his polygamous actions. Angered by the loss of funds, you murdered Hartford. You knew that you would be caught... unless you could cleverly dispose of the body. And what better way to dispose of it than to make it your own? With the money, you could start a new life, and everyone would assume Thomas Kneeler had died in a tragic magic accident. You hid Hartford's body in the back of the compartment and, instead of unlocking it from the outside, you unlocked it from the inside to make sure nobody saw the body when you entered.

"You quickly moved the body out to the main area of the cabinet and sealed yourself in. Your assistants stabbed the body, had the cabinet lifted into the air, and from the safety of the compartment, you set fire to the outer cabinet, and subsequently to your former mentor's body. What caught me as odd was the screaming, but upon finding the recording device in the compartment, it made sense. One of the blades had passed through the burned body's voice box, making it physically impossible for him to have screamed in agony upon the starting of the fire.

"Another thing that gave you away was your wand. Your wand, such a delicate and important tool to a magician, that somehow vanished from the inside of the cabinet. Had it been with you upon your burning, it would have remained at the bottom of the cabinet, as all wands are made with a special wood that does not burn easily, so as to make your fire-related tricks more believable. The wand was not present in the cabinet once it had been searched, meaning you still had it, and would need it in order to escape from the hidden compartment.

"Your illusions were executed in the best manner possible, but even the best illusions cannot best me. You will be tried for your crime, Mr. Kneeler, and found guilty." Hull looked to Lennox with a nod. "And you, Inspector, will receive all the necessary credit for the discovery. It seems you could use the positive enforcement from your employer."

With that, Hull and I left the concert hall, and only just minutes before the rest of the police arrived. Hull was in a surprisingly chatty mood, and talking with him on the taxi ride home was enlightening. He had built his own replica of the cabinet, but had not known of the hidden compartment until watching the video. To think he was able to observe all of this continued to amaze me. It was nothing short of astonishing.

When we reached home, I couldn't contain my excitement. *The Combustible Cabinet*, I would call the case. Part of me actually felt compelled to seek out a medium to allow others to hear about Hull's endeavors. Lennox had suggested it before, but I had never taken it seriously. I sat down at my laptop and watched as Hull walked into the room and stopped again, just as he had the night before. I watched his eyes peruse the room slowly, his nostrils flaring.

"What is it?" I asked when his eyes stopped on the bookshelf again.

"Someone's been here. Someone who should not have been." He jumped over to the bookshelf and climbed it again, this time stopped at the fifth shelf. His hands ran along the book's spines before stopping at an empty space. "The diary. It's gone."

"Diary, what diary?"

"Arthur Mallory Knight's diary. The one with the green cover. It's been stolen."

I stood from my seat and walked around the room, my senses alert. "Who could've just walked in and taken that? And why?" My eyes stopped when they reached the piano. Sitting on top of it was a very small, black object. I approached the piano slowly as the item came into focus. It was a piece from a chessboard.

Hull stepped beside me and scooped the piece up with his hand. He held it in his palm before us, and when he spoke, his voice was more monotonous and distant than I had ever heard.

"The king."

*

"You performed well, Veronica."

Moriarty looked over at the blonde woman, who had only just walked through the doors into the control center. She undid the ponytail from her hair and took her seat, then held up a small, green-covered book. Moriarty took it from her with his gloved hands.

"I provided your distraction, as promised, Sir," she said as she began typing.

"And you have started to earn the trust of the doctor," Moriarty added, his voice becoming a whisper.

"I've started, Sir."

"Be mindful, Veronica. To meddle with emotions is to risk them becoming your reality. I would hate for you to end up as Fieldman did."

"I would never consider it, Sir."

"Good."

"What of Kneeler, Sir?"

"Kneeler's capture was a necessary loss. The acquisition of the diary was our priority. Had Hull discovered the true intentions of ENDGAME, it would have made our position far more... complicated." He stepped back into the shadows, out of Daemon's sight. "We must enter the second phase. Contact Xaphon and inform him."

"Yes, Sir."

Our time is rapidly approaching.

"And Veronica."

"Yes, Sir?"

"Ensure that the PHE-1 is functioning. I suspect we will need it soon."

"Yes, Sir."

"*...A flame in your heart...*"

"I'm sorry, Sir?"

"Nothing, Veronica," Moriarty called back as he reached the door. "Nothing at all."

THE CASE OF THE ANGERED MEN

This case was one of oddity for the first-half, mainly from my lack of involvement. It's not often that Hull will give me a complete recap of his endeavors when I am not present, but this time he insisted on filling me in. I suppose his own ego may be growing now that he knows I publish his stories to be read. He doesn't like the attention so much as he conceitedly enjoys seeing his name strewn across the pages. I usually prefer to accompany Hull on his cases, but this one was literally impossible for me to be there. And it all started with the receiving of a letter from the county.

"Oh you have *got* to be joking."

I glanced from my armchair at Hull, who had only just returned from getting the mail. He held one letter away from his body with a look of absolute disdain.

"What?" I asked as I set down my morning cup of coffee. Or, I suppose, my fourth cup.

"A jury summons. Me, on a jury."

"That'll be the shortest case ever."

"Is it even legal for me to be on a jury?"

I smirked. "If you're a citizen of the United States, I would say yes."

"For the love of God, this is the last thing I want to waste my time doing. It restricts all productivity."

"Comes with being here."

He tossed the letter across the room before falling into his seat. "What a joke. Relying on twelve men and women to decide the fate of an individual based on evidence collected by a failing force."

"Two weeks without a case and you're already insulting the police," I replied as I picked up the letter and read the details. "Starting next Monday. They have you scheduled for the entire week. No mention of the case."

"I know exactly what the case is."

"How?"

"Because it's the only one scheduled to be in session. Young man, age 20, convicted of murder on the 21st of June, trial postponed until the week of September 11th. Lennox mentioned it on his dinner visit last weekend."

"What about his wedding announcement, did you pay attention to that?"

"Of course not, why would I?"

I gave a heavy sigh before standing. "Sometimes I wonder about your mental organization methods."

"Everything of importance receives such classification and is properly stored," he snapped back. "All else is discarded."

"Makes sense," I said as I stepped into the kitchen. I lowered the volume of my voice to a murmur. "For a computer..." I poured myself another cup of coffee before returning to the room. "You have to attend, you know. By law and such."

"I know. That doesn't mean I have to enjoy it."

I clapped him on the back before returning to my seat. "Think of it this way. It'll keep you distracted for at least a day."

He scoffed. "At least." His eyes fell to the letter, and for a moment, I thought I saw a smirk cross his face. "At least indeed."

If only I'd known then just what he was getting into.

*

At promptly seven in the morning on the following Monday, Hull awoke and wasted no time in preparing for his visit to the courthouse. He wore a suit that he usually preferred to keep in the closet, left his coat and scarf on the hook, and made his way towards the city center. He had visited the courthouse many times before, often for different reasons but all centered on his detective business. His familiar taxi picked him up at 7:45, and by 8 o'clock he was on the courthouse steps.

Jurors were told to go through security and meet outside the courtroom fifteen minutes prior to the hearing's start, which was at 8:15. Now, Hull sat alone at one of the benches, his eyes casually passing over the eleven other jurors. Six males, five females, each wearing business attire similar to his own. Three wore glasses, all but one man cleanly shaven. These were, of course, the obvious details, the ones anyone could notice without bothering to look. What Hull observed was far more important.

First male, teacher, elementary school, presumably first and second grade. Worked with the same school district for nearing thirty years. Second and third male, construction workers. Fourth male, upper business management, upset by his preoccupied state from being here. Fifth male, factory worker. Sixth male, unemployed, recently departed college, degree in engineering, plenty of job opportunities but no willpower or confidence to search.

First female, also teacher, high school, several statements made against, promiscuous in nature, no doubt slept with at least four students in current class, all in their last year. Second female, office assistant, pen ink still smudged on her right hand. Third female, student at college, studying in journalism, aspires for little, evident by closeness and apparent interest in second female's topic of conversation. Fourth female, mother of two, never attended college, no intentions of trying. Relies on partner for household income. Fifth female, also upper business management, possibly director of public relations.

He breathed in deeply through his nostrils before focusing his gaze on the wall ahead of him. None of the people were near interesting enough to be given more than the second glance he had already provided. He looked up at the clock to see it was only 8:03. He let the intake of breath out through the slits of his clenched teeth before clasping his hands together and closing his eyes. Even without seeing, though, he could hear everything. And just by hearing everything, he could see everything.

"...three times, he said it, I just couldn't believe..."

"...we tried to keep the stocks up but they kept..."

"...and they actually managed to get the all-time..."

"...fourteen-point-three-seven was the correct..."

"...no idea how hard a time it was keeping it..."

Chair grinding along the linoleum floor. Hand scratching at gelled hair. Popping of neck. Feigned laughter. Clearing of throat during awkward pause. Readjustment of standing position. Fly in nearby potted plant. Upset individual on phone in private room. Vibration of cell phone. Completion of conversation. Opening of door.

His eyelids shot up. The clock now read 8:04.

"Hey," a voice said from above-right. He looked up to see the fourth male, the upper business management one, gazing down at him with a look of curiosity. "You're that detective, right? Sheridan Hull?"

Hull gave a long blink and a smug grin before nodding. "That would be me, yes."

The man extended his hand. "Absolute pleasure to meet you, name's Kyle Richy, I work with Plyer Incorporated. You helped us out of a tight bind a while back."

Hull looked the man over as he returned the handshake. *Late thirties, odd physical emphasis despite business job, face familiar, one of the board of directors. Irritable status result of missed stockholder meeting for jury duty. Competence level: high.* "Pleasure to meet you as well, Mr. Richy."

"Please, call me Kyle," the man said as he took the space on the bench next to Hull. The detective sidled away minutely, his jaw popping as he rolled his chin. Richy looked at the group of other jurors before shaking his head. "Waste of time, these things. People with jobs like us shouldn't have to put up with this kinda thing."

"I can't but agree," Hull said shortly. *Intelligence level: high.*

"I had to miss a stockholder meeting for this. Can you believe that? You'd think being one of the people in charge of one of the biggest companies in Newfield would get me some kind of alibi to miss this. But nope, they're adamant. You get your summons and you show up."

"So the system has been since before our births."

Richy chuckled. "True enough. So, I gotta ask. How do you do it? We got a full rundown at Plyer on the steps you took and it just blows my mind. You pieced it all together like it was nothing."

"Some things just come easier for individuals."

"You got that right. I can do math like no other, but I could never do what you do."

No one can do what I do. That is why I do it. "It took time, practice, and dedication to hone my observational skills. Theoretically, someone else could do the same, just as one could become as proficient in math as you are."

"I think some people are born good at things."

Like you were born "good" at being arrogant. "It's possible."

Richy shifted slightly in his seat, not in an uncomfortable manner, quite the contrary. The man actually seemed to be getting more comfortable in Hull's presence. "I hope this goes quick. I know the kid's guilty, it was obvious back in June and it's obvious now."

"Is it?"

"Oh sure. You've been keeping up with it, right?"

"Can't say I have."

"Whole rotten mess the kid's in. Got into a bar fight, ten minutes later the other guy's found dead in an alleyway. Caught the kid on security tapes. Not only did he stab the man three times, he took his wallet. They found the kid with the knife in his bag and the wallet in his coat pocket. I don't even see why we need a full jury. Like I said. It's obvious."

Hull cocked his head back slightly as he pressed his tongue against his cheek. "I suppose things will become more clear through the trial, won't it."

Richy snorted. "I don't need a trial to tell me he's guilty."

And at that very moment, the doors to the courtroom opened. A police-like man stood in the doorway now and gave the jurors a nod. "We're ready for you."

*

The trial itself took the entirety of the first day and half of Tuesday. The evidence presented was no doubt convincing of the accused's guiltiness. The defense attorney provided very little in regards to actual defense. The boy's face throughout the trial had become progressively more sunken, and most of the spectators had come to the conclusion that he was without a doubt guilty. At around noon on Tuesday, the judge dismissed the jurors to their private meeting, and there they now sat, just moments away from deliberating the verdict.

Hull sat at the opposite end of the table from the foreman, the first male who was the teacher. From his left and going around, it went the upper business woman, Mr. Richy, the first male construction worker, the unemployed male, the female office assistant, Hull, the second male construction worker, the female teacher, the female college student, the male factory worker, and the only mother of the group. With just a quick glance around the table, Hull could see exactly what verdict each person had in mind. And from the first glance, he could tell it was almost unanimous.

Almost.

"Well, I suppose we can begin now," the foreman said with a nod at the other jurors. "I thought we could start with a quick introduction from everyone, just your name and what you do, before we begin." He gulped. "Uh, my name's Will Copper and I am an elementary school teacher at Churchill Elementary."

The upper business woman gave a curt nod. "Elizabeth Caughell, district relations manager for Regal Entertainment."

"Kyle Richy, director board member for Plyer Incorporated."

"Daniel Whittaker, I'm a contractor with Whittaker Construction."

"John Welsh, recently graduated from Newfield U, still in the job market."

"Karen Davis, personal assistant to Mr. Robert Lloyd of LLD Markets."

"Sheridan Hull, consulting detective."

"John Portman, construction site manager with Andersen Construction."

"Babette Hall, middle school teacher."

"Courtney Sykes, student at Newfield University."

"Tyler Forth, production line supervisor for Warmack Chemical."

"Sadie Katwell, full-time mom."

The foreman smiled. "Now that we're all introduced, let's get, uh, right to it. I think we're all mature enough to just vote it out, right? So, can we do this by a show of hands?" A silent chorus of nods followed. "Alright, so... all those who believe the accused is guilty?"

One by one, the hands of the jurors rose into the air. It took only five seconds for the hands to be presented, and as Hull had expected, the people he had deduced to vote guilty had indeed voted guilty. The foreman pointed at each hand as he counted vocally.

"So, one, two, three... seven, eight, nine... ten. My vote is also guilty, so eleven... eleven votes guilty..." He glanced at Hull, whose hands were clasped tightly in his lap. The foreman rubbed the back of his neck and cleared his voice. "And, uh, all who think the accused is innocent?" Hull's hand slowly raised into the air. The eleven other jurors looked at him, some with confusion, some with anger. Mr. Richy looked at him with pure disbelief in his eyes. The foreman sighed. "So, one vote innocent... and we need a unanimous vote to reach a verdict."

"That we do," Hull said as he lowered his hand.

The production line supervisor, Forth, gave Hull a sideways look. "You really think the guy's innocent? After everything that was presented?"

"I do not *think*, I know he is innocent."

"How so?" Portman asked.

Hull glanced at him. "Evidence is used to either prove an individual's guilt or innocence. The evidence provided proved his innocence."

The college student, Sykes, shook her head. "I don't get it, you think he's innocent after all of that?"

"I do."

Whittaker threw his hands in the air. "Well, isn't this just great. Here I was thinking we were all level-headed people who would reach a conclusion quickly."

"There's always one in the bunch," Portman added.

The personal assistant, Davis, looked up at the foreman. "So what do we do?"

"Well, we, uh... debate it, I guess," Copper replied with his eyebrows raised.

"Debate? Debate what?" the unemployed graduate, Welsh, barked. "We try to convince the detective that the man's guilty? If the damn evidence didn't do it, what difference can we make?"

"Well, I don't know," the foreman said cautiously as he looked around the table. "I suppose the best thing we could do is, uh, just go around and get everyone's opinions. Why we think what we think and such."

"We all think he's guilty because the evidence says so!" Welsh snapped back. "He's the one who thinks differently, make him talk!"

Hull ignored the man's jab. "I would like to hear the group's opinions."

Copper gave a nervous nod before returning to his seat. "So, uh, I guess I'll begin. It's really pretty simple for me, I guess. The kid was found with the knife used in the murder, as well as the dead man's wallet. Security tapes show the boy at the dead body. Witnesses inside the bar overheard death threats. Everything just speaks against the boy." He gulped and nodded at the woman to his left.

"I have to say I am of the same opinion as Mr. Copper," Caughell said, her eyes narrowed to slits. "The boy is plainly guilty, and I feel no need to repeat what Mr. Copper has stated."

Richy stood to provide his opinion. "Even if we didn't look at the evidence, there's the history between the dead man and the boy. The boy even testified and said the man had slept with his girlfriend. That's enough to make any guy pissed off, but Hell, the kid was messed up enough to say he'd slit his throat inside the bar. And what about his alibi? 'I got mugged in the alleyway and stumbled on the body.' My four-year old nephew could make a better lie than that."

"Kid's guilty," Whittaker said without offering anything else.

"I may have a degree in engineering, but I know knives," Welsh said as he rested his chin on his hand, propped up by his elbow on the table. "Three stabs and they all went deep, and that knife had a long blade. Wouldn't have been hard at all for him to draw the knife in the dark alleyway and get three stabs in to the handle before the drunken man could fight back."

Hull's eyes settled on Davis, who hesitated before speaking. "Well, I think everything just makes sense that he would be guilty. I mean, I guess it's possible that his story was true, but that's really unlikely."

All eyes fell on Hull, since it was technically his turn to speak. He blinked twice before giving a curt smile. "I think it would only make sense for everyone who believes the boy is guilty to speak before I provide my opinions." The group nodded in agreement, then turned their focus to Portman.

"What do you want me to say? Everyone's said it already. The kid is guilty, his hands are red. There's no getting by it," the construction site manager said flatly.

The middle school teacher took her time before speaking. "The boy fits the three aspects of guilt. He had the means, the motive was clear, and the opportunity presented itself perfectly." She paused, casting a glance around the room before giving a solemn nod. "That's all."

"He didn't say enough to defend himself," the college student said as she twirled her hair. "I don't see how he can be innocent. He looked guilty."

Forth cleared his throat. "All things considered, the boy is guilty. It's a simple look at the surface of the case and make a call."

Katwell did not seem keen on speaking. Hull noted that her hand had been slow to lift, not out of laziness but out of uncertainty. The foreman looked down at her expectantly before she finally gave a short nod. "I think the boy is innocent."

"You what?"

"You've gotta be kidding me."

"Innocent!"

"I do!" the woman shouted, causing the uproar to cease. "I think there's a considerable level of doubt in the case. Some things just don't make sense to me."

"But you said he was guilty!"

"You raised your hand, dammit."

"Enough!" the foreman yelled. Once the group had sufficiently quieted down, he gave a nod at Hull. "I guess we've moved into the innocent opinions, so it's your turn."

Hull smiled before turning his attention to Caughell. "You say the boy is plainly guilty. Why is it plain?"

Caughell looked taken aback by his homing in on her opinion. "Well, the case is hardly one that is complicated. Murder brought about by anger, alcohol, and revenge."

"And you do not think that those three motives can be more than plain?"

"I do not."

"Well I do." Hull stood and stepped away from the table. "About seven months ago, I took part in investigating a case where a man was 'plainly guilty' for the crime he was accused of, and upon completing my investigation, it turned out the man was in fact innocent of the crime, but guilty of a subsequent crime. That which was plain was incorrect; that which was complex was true." Before Caughell could respond, Hull turned his attention to Richy. "The evidence, according to you, dictates the boy's guilt."

"It does," Richy replied shortly.

"Let us, then, take a look at said evidence." He stepped over to a small box, which currently contained the knife used in the murder, the stolen wallet, and the security tapes on a DVD. Hull gently pulled out the knife and held it delicately in his left hand. "A light knife, not easy to conceal but certainly sharp enough to pierce an individual's skin, organs, with enough force, it could even scratch a bone." Hull pointed the knife at Welsh. "You said you know knives. And you are sure this knife was used to commit the crime?"

"Yes."

"Why."

Welsh furrowed his brow before standing, walking to Hull, and taking the knife. "Blade's definitely long enough to go deep into the dead man's chest."

"And why would the accused have kept the knife?"

"To kill the man."

"Wrong."

Welsh leaned back and looked at Hull with apprehension in his eyes. "How do you figure?"

Hull carefully took the knife. "This kind of knife is difficult to conceal, correct? And if I am right, this knife in particular is often used by fishermen to help efficiently gut a larger fish, possibly a tuna or salmon."

"So?"

"The accused is not a college student, but is of that age. A look at him shows a tough upper body, but no tan. Calloused hands, eyes used to avoiding salted water. The boy is a crew member on a commercial fishing boat that frequented Siuslaw Bay. The knife was not for murder but for his job, and was not found on his person but rather in the duffle bag he had with him at the bar and on the security tapes."

"Big deal if it's used for fishing," Welsh snapped back. "It could still be used for the murder."

"Could it?" Hull ran his finger along the blade. "Serrated blade. A knife like this, upon piercing the skin, would have left a very definitive mark, wouldn't it? A serrated blade would cause a significant amount of blood loss. But the autopsy of the man revealed his death did not come from loss of blood but rather from the pierced heart."

Welsh scoffed as he moved back to his seat. "That means jack shit."

Hull smirked. "Indeed." He returned his knife to the evidence box before turning to look at Richy. "Your coveted evidence, you see, can be used to prove the boy's innocence."

Richy gave a short laugh. "You're a cocky, confident one, I'll give you that."

"You," Hull said, his eyes on Whittaker, "provided no opinion whatsoever to explain why the boy is guilty. So, I can easily tell that you actually believe the boy is innocent, and would rather say guilty and allow yourself to believe the lie."

"Oh yeah?" Whittaker said. "Prove that."

"Of course." Hull moved to be within a meter of Whittaker, leaning down to look him directly in the eyes. "Four years ago, you were also in a court case, but the accused was you. You have a history of violence, not one you are proud of, but the scars are not so easily hidden from your face. Bruises, scars, all of them show as clearly as a ledger of your personal history. You knew you were innocent, and the evidence provided clearly stated it as well. And yet, the other man's attorney fought valiantly and did a phenomenal job of convincing the jury that you were guilty."

"How do you know that?"

"Because your case took four days, and you would prefer to avoid that elongated process, both for yourself and for the accused. A quick and easy verdict is your preference. You have spent your time in the courtroom, you have spent your time in the fights, and you know the field better than most of us here. But it is this extensive experience that tells you, death is a very rare end result of a bar fight. Death is the most rarest of end results."

"And that makes me believe he's innocent how?"

"Because the fight that supposedly ensued after the bar fight is where the murder occurred. And you, despite being a contractor, are also a film enthusiast, and a fan of cinematic continuity. You reviewed the security tapes and the fact that the actual murder was not caught on film disturbed you. All we see is a dead body and the accused."

Whittaker leaned away from Hull, a look of caution on his face. "How do you know I like films?"

"The shirt you wear underneath your business attire is a shirt obtained only at the South by Southwest film festival in Austin, Texas, the hub of independent film discovery." Whittaker was no doubt shocked by the observation, which was obvious by the silence that followed. Hull walked back to his seat and observed the other jurors with vibrant eyes. "I propose another vote. So we know where we all stand now."

The foreman coughed. "I, uh, suppose we could call another vote. Do we want to do it by hand or...?" A similar chorus of nods followed. "Okay, so... all who find the accused guilty?" Once again, the majority of the hands rose. However, this time, Katwell's hand remained down, as well as Whittaker's. "So.. nine guilty... and all who find the accused innocent?" Katwell, Whittaker, and Hull rose their hands. "Three innocent... so we are now at nine guilty, three innocent. That's... great.."

*

A short break followed the second vote. Hull had made his way to the bathroom, just to wash his hands. He knew how things would pan out. In fact, something about the way the guilty-voting jurors had looked at him confirmed his suspicions. While in the bathroom, he quickly pulled out his phone, selected Walker's name, and sent a simple text: "Please bring me my coat."

"Pretty interesting thing you're doing in there," Richy's voice said from behind him. Hull pocketed his phone and looked in the mirror to see Richy approach the sink next to him. "Weaving everything to change their minds. You really think you can change everyone's?"

"It should not be a matter of changing anyone's minds," Hull replied. "It is a matter of sifting the truth out from the tainted lies."

"Tainted lies, huh?"

"In this case, we are presented very objective facts, but the fallacy of the common jury is the temptation to twist facts to suit theories, rather than theories to suit facts. Quite obviously the evidence could be seen in a way to make the boy guilty, and as such, the majority of the jury will take those facts and make them fit their individual theories. I, however, acknowledge that the evidence can be seen to prove both the boy's guilt and innocence, and as such, I am changing my personal theories to match the provided facts."

"Is that so."

"Yes."

Richy clasped him on the back. "Well, good luck to you with that. I can't say you'll change my mind anytime soon."

Hull smiled. "I didn't expect to." *Competence level: low. Ulterior motives are present.*

280

The jury reconvened twenty minutes later, everyone resuming their seats. The foreman gave a quick glance around the room before nodding at Hull. "I, uh, suppose you can continue what you were doing."

"Thank you," Hull said courteously as he stood. His eyes turned to Davis, passing over Welsh completely. "You said you think it is possible for the boy to be innocent. Why?"

Davis looked shocked at having been spoken to directly. "Well, it's just that I remember watching a movie when I was in college. It was about a jury, just like us, who almost decided a man was guilty when he was in fact innocent. The only person who believed he was innocent believed it from reasonable doubt. And I guess that's what I have."

"Why do you have this reasonable doubt?"

"Well, it's like you said about the knife and tapes. The knife doesn't really match the one that could stab the man, and the tapes don't actually show the boy murdering the man. It's those little things that make me a little doubtful, I guess."

"I see. Thank you." He looked to Portman. "Of the evidence provided, which do you believe is strongest in proving the boy's guilt?"

Portman looked up at Hull for a long time before clicking his tongue. "The witnesses. All the people in the bar who heard the kid say he was gonna kill the man. How do you beat that? Over a dozen people heard it."

"Yes, the witnesses. Tell me, Mr. Portman, with your heavy interest in video games, how many times on a daily basis do you hear a death threat?"

"How the Hell do you know I play video games?"

Hull tilted his head to the side before nodding at the man's hands. "You are a construction site manager, yet your knuckles are significantly swollen from carpal tunnel syndrome. I estimate your age to be around thirty-six or thirty-seven, which means you would have been around ten years old when Nintendo released Super Mario Bros. Since then, your interest in video gaming has only grown, meaning you have had extensive strain on your hands from the different controllers over the past three decades. The elastic band on your arm has a golden star and a red and white mushroom, two common symbols from the Mario saga.

"Now, although I cannot speak for myself, I have done my own research on the fallacies of studies done in regards to connections between violence and violent video games. A common occurrence in any violent video game is a short, temporary burst of rage when the game does not go in your favor. Obscenities, threats, anything of the sort is the norm in a video game environment. So, I will ask you once again. How many times on a daily basis do you hear a death threat when playing a video game?"

Portman gave Hull a wary glance before murmuring out a reply. "Probably once or twice a game."

"Ah yes, and each game would be about ten to fifteen minutes. So I would wager that in an hour, you hear around six to ten threats on someone's life. I would estimate you spend at least three hours in your video game environment, so... you hear a death threat eighteen to thirty times a day. Now, what sets this one in particular apart? The difference in location? One could theorize that the anonymity that comes from the Internet allows for a more free flow of verbal language, but I do not believe that in the long run. The same anonymity comes from a person in a bar."

"What's your point?" Portman barked.

"My point is fairly obvious. The witnesses stated that they heard a death threat, but in today's society, that means nothing. As such, the witnesses cannot be considered viable evidence." Hull looked to the middle school teacher. "You stated that the boy met the criteria for the three aspects to a crime. Means, motive, and opportunity. Can you elaborate on that?"

The woman gave a short nod. "The means would be the knife, the motive would be the existing tension, and the opportunity was the time alone in the alleyway."

"Excellent. Let us take these and disseminate them. The means are quite plainly not so plain, as I think we can all agree that the presented knife could not have been the one to murder the man. The motive, now. We were told by the accused of a preexisting resentment between the two men, and for what reason? The accused once dated a woman who left him for the murdered man. Now, I am no expert on relationships, but it seems to me that jealousy can be a motive for murder, but really, you all saw the accused. When he gave his accounts of the event, no tell was visible. The boy did not lie when he said the jealousy had passed soon after his relationship with the woman had ended.

"Let us assume, then, that the jealousy was not the motive for the murder. What does that leave us with? Stirred emotions as a result of a bar quarrel? It seems unlikely to me that whatever emotions rose during the confrontation would have remained and been strong enough to constitute murder. At this point, I would say the boy lacked motive for killing the man. That leaves us with opportunity." He walked over to the evidence box and quickly pulled out the security tapes. After some slight fiddling with the television, he had the tapes paused and ready for viewing. "Without even having to watch this clip, we can note that the time of the clip starts at 11:05 PM."

"We can read the clips, thanks," Welsh said.

"The clip starts at 11:05 PM and shows the accused standing over the body of the dead man. However." Hull ejected the disc and revealed another one from his pocket. "In my spare time this previous evening, I made a point to visit the bar and receive the security tapes that displayed the interior of the bar." He inserted the disc and paused it. "This clip begins at exactly 11:04 PM. The accused is sitting there, at the bar, a drink in hand. The murdered man is nowhere in sight. The previous security tape started just one minute after this current clip. I personally find it unlikely that the boy had time to attack and murder the man in the minute before arriving on the security tape."

The woman looked shocked, but the face was soon replaced with one of understanding. "So the three aspects do not apply. It would seem I was mistaken."

"I would like to call for another vote," Hull said.

The foreman looked at him with weary eyes before sighing. "I suppose we can vote again, sure. Um... all those who believe the accused is guilty...?" Caughell, Richy, Welsh, Portman, and Forth raised their hands. "Okay, and I also vote guilty... now... all who believe the accused is innocent?" Katwell, Whittaker, Hall, Davis, Sykes, and Hull raised their hands. "Okay... so six guilty... six innocent... we're, uh.. split right down the middle now."

Richy sighed. "I think that's enough for now." He stood, hands in his pockets, and looked at the foreman. "I'd like to speak with Mr. Hull privately." The foreman nodded and walked towards the door. Some members of the jury followed promptly while others bore confused faces. Hull nodded at those who remained, who slowly stood and followed the other jurors out. Once they had all left and closed the door, Hull's eyes turned to the window while Richy gave a heavier sigh. "So."

"So," Hull repeated.

"Guess it wasn't too hard for you, huh?"

"Hardly a challenge."

"Go on, then."

"Gladly."

*

Hull pushed his chin up and took in a deep breath before starting. "I found it quite interesting that the county would send me a jury summons, though that interest was quickly replaced by understanding when I realized exactly what the case would be. Everything about it had seemed very off until I took it upon myself to do my own research on the case. Convenient, I suppose, that such a flawed case would be delayed for so long. Until such time that exactly two years had passed since I had moved to the United States, thus meaning I could be on a jury.

"The trial itself was quite boring, but I was able to pass the time by observing my fellow jurors and how they reacted to what was being said. I found it surprising that three jurors in particular had elected to complete ignore the trial altogether and were, to put it aptly, mentally checked out. Elizabeth Caughell, John Welsh, and John Portman, three people who would seemingly have no correlation, yet they had all chosen to not devote any attention to the one job they had that day. This raised the question of as to why.

"It did not take long for the pieces to fall together. When we were dismissed that evening, I went to the bar and reviewed the security tapes and found a very familiar-looking armband on one of the patrons, the same band that Mr. Portman was wearing. I found that immediately after the murdered man left the bar, Portman followed him, and two minutes later, the accused left. The dead man was found by the accused, and from there, our case was made. Curious, though, that Portman had been there. Curious, and obvious.

"Mr. Welsh had a self-professed expertise with cutlery, one that would have helped him had he coordinated with Portman on the type of knife to use when he killed the man, and what knife they would plant on the accused. Upon some further investigation, I found that the murdered man had in fact attended Newfield University until one year ago, just a few months before his graduation. He was in the same class as Welsh. He was also once a close friend of Welsh's. In fact, they almost became business partners.

"Welsh's thesis discussed an architectural business concept that would be managed by two individuals, yet he worked alone. This was a result of the murdered man's departing college, abandoning their partnered project, and taking what money they had garnered for himself. Welsh decided to target the man and went to an old family friend who had a history in the bloodier market: Elizabeth Caughell, née Welsh. John's older sister. Caughell was able to find a hand for hire willing to kill: John Portman.

"Portman was instructed to wait at the bar that the murdered man frequented and pick the opportune moment to strike. That moment came when the man, fairly inebriated, departed from the back door of the bar into an alleyway. Portman promptly followed him and stabbed him three times, then left his dead body in the light and sight of the camera. Soon after, the accused entered the alleyway to apologize and found a dead body. Portman reported the identity of the accused to Welsh, who waited until the accused had gone home, found a knife he would see as suitable for the murder, and placed the murdered man's wallet in the accused's coat.

"It was all quite the show, very well done. Once again, part of me was curious of as to how someone had managed to get all three perpetrators on the jury. But, naturally, curiosity is soon replaced by knowledge. Of course it all had to be the workings of Moriarty. Caughell had no doubt gone to you, Kyle Richy, *former* member of the board of directors for Plyer Incorporated. You resigned just two weeks after the arrest of one of your fellow Chimaera agents. Poor timing on that one, and I humbly take full responsibility.

"Caughell approached you in need of help, for she feared that Welsh and Portman would link the crime back to her. You went to your employer, and he generously arranged for their placement on the jury. What I doubt your employer also told you, however, was that he would put me on the jury. Another test in his game. Now, of course, I will be more than happy to report to the police what has transpired, and I am certain you will enjoy your time spent in jail for murder."

Richy gave a slight smirk. "Well done. Now I'm impressed. Got it all right, except for one thing. My employer didn't keep your presence on the jury from me. In fact, he told me you'd be here. That's why I was put on the jury."

"And why is that."

Richy leapt over the table and grabbed Hull by the shoulders, spinning around as he moved. Hull made no attempt to resist as Richy turned him and slammed him on top of the table, lifting him from the ground with surprising strength. Hull struggled slightly as Richy pulled leather straps from under the table and secured them around Hull's wrists and ankles. The last strip he tied around Hull's neck. Once the detective was completely unable to move, Richy walked over to the evidence box and pulled out the slender knife.

"I was put on the jury so that when you started turning everyone else to believe the boy was innocent, I'd be able to step in and show you exactly what happens when you meddle with Chimaera's affairs." Richy took the knife up high into the air before slamming it down into Hull's palm, pressing it through the skin, through the table, all the way until only the handle remained. Hull lurched forward but managed to keep from roaring. "That's for the courier on Newfield University's campus."

"I never would have guessed," Hull spit back.

Richy gave a devilish smile before pulling the blade clean out. He set the knife down on one of the chairs before grabbing the edge of the table and flipping it completely. Now Hull's face was smashed against the wall as Richy pushed forward with his foot. "This is as close as I can replicate the car flip you put Wygant through."

"Hardly a comparison," Hull groaned back against the pressure of the wall.

"Oh really?" Richy pulled the table back and peered over at the detective. "Convenient, isn't it? Caughell, Welsh, and Portman will have led all of the other jurors away. Even if you were to scream, no one would hear you. Doesn't that concern you at all?"

"Not in the slightest."

"Good."

Richy flipped the table back up on its legs and patted Hull on the head before pulling a very long, very unpleasant-looking needle from his coat pocket. He tapped the tip of the needle a few times before smiling.

"I wondered why you insisted on wearing your coat indoors," Hull commented.

"Had to protect the delicates," Richy replied before jamming the needle into Hull's inner elbow. He pulled back quickly on the plunger, drawing 100cc of blood in only a few seconds. Richy pulled the needle clean out and stashed it in his coat. "For Cain, the poor, unsuspecting sap."

"Tell me," Hull said through gritted teeth, "do you truly have torture devices for every Chimaera agent I have brought to justice? Because that number is upward of thirty by now."

Richy smirked. "Guess we'll keep going until you lose consciousness. Boss doesn't want me to kill you."

"How fortunate. Would you mind fetching me my coat?"

"You can't wear it, but sure, I can grant you that decency." Richy turned and walked towards the coat rack, then stopped. He chuckled a few times before glancing over his shoulder. "You didn't bring a—"

His response was stopped when the door to the jury room slammed open as two figures charged in, both holding guns. The one leading aimed the gun directly at Richy's head.

"Get down on your knees, now!" Inspector Gregory Lennox yelled as he stared down the man. John Walker came in as well, one hand holding a gun aimed at Richy and the other holding Hull's coat. Richy looked from Lennox to Walker to Hull before smirking.

"You clever bastard," the man said before diving towards Hull. Lennox fired his gun once, the bullet planting itself in the wall where Richy had stood. The man clambered over Hull and forced himself through the open window, vanishing from sight completely. Walker rushed to Hull's side and started untying the straps.

"Glad you got my message," Hull said as he helped free his stabbed hand.

"I'm guessing we made it just in time," Walker replied as he spotted the wound.

"It's nothing. We need to catch that man, preferably *alive*," Hull said with a glance at Lennox, who was staring out of the window.

"He got into a car, I got the plate number."

Hull slid off the table and gently took the coat from Walker, using the sleeve to cover his wound. "There isn't any time to waste, then, is there?"

*

The car chase that followed was surprisingly short. The man Hull was pursuing took a route directly out of the city, nearly five miles to an old farm. I suppose by the time he reached the farm, he had resigned to his fate. He made little attempt to hide, in retrospect. Now, Hull and I stood several meters away from the barn while Lennox escorted the man, Kyle Richy, to the police car. Because Hull had been far too vague, Lennox had taken all of the other jurors into custody. The three who were charged with the crime were already in the car, while the seven others waited near us for a taxi.

"Good fun, then?" I asked as Hull let a paramedic wrap his hand and arm.

"It took some interesting turns, but it was fairly predictable when the man took a liking to me. People do not take a liking to me in the manner that he did."

"At least you enjoyed yourself."

"It made for quite the two days. Appeased my boredom for a short while."

"So now what?"

"I may do a professional review of the United States Judicial System. Or figure out how Moriarty was able to hold such sway with the courts and get five people onto a jury." He coughed. "Or find a place to eat shrimp."

"...shrimp?"

"Believe it or not, I quite enjoy shrimp."

"Ah. Good to know."

"Indeed."

A short silence followed that ended with Hull giving me a nod and walking away, his path going down the nearby gravel road. When he was only about four meters away, one of the jurors, a teacher by the name of Babette Hall, approached me. I'd spoken with her on the drive over, but only regarding simple pleasantries.

"Why does he do it?" she asked.

I shrugged. "He's bored. It distracts him."

"Ah. Well, I'd be careful, Doctor. What if one day, the cases don't distract him?" She paused, sending a glance at the detective. "What happens to him when the boredom wins?"

I looked down the gravel road at Hull and felt a peculiar feeling. I'd never considered what would happen if he was actually overwhelmed by his boredom. Part of me figured he would always be able to play the piano or fire his arrows. But if the boredom did overcome his entirety... what would happen?

And more importantly, why had this woman even mentioned it?

I looked back to answer her and gave a short jump when I realized she was gone. I glanced around in an attempt to find her, to no avail. Somehow, the woman had managed to vanish completely. And that scared me more than it should have. I looked back down the road at Hull and couldn't keep from hearing the woman's final question replay itself in my head.

What happens to him when the boredom wins?

I didn't have an answer. And that was what worried me the most.

HAUNTED

. . .October 6th, 1902

The storms are progressively worsening in their severity, and I cannot imagine the waters will calm themselves before it is our time to depart. I have made the unfortunate mistake of becoming far too comfortable where we are, despite having known what would eventually come. Our departure from this area is at hand, and there is work to be done in the west. There is much money to be gained from this work as well. The captain will not tell us what it is we will be doing. He simply says we will do our job and return home when we have finished.

But the concept of home, it is such a foreign one to us now. So many of us have spent the previous few years of our lives at sea, traveling

from port to port. Familiarity of location only
comes from your resting place and the endless
sights of the sea. There is no true home to us in
these dark and dreary days. But alas, in our time
spent here, I have found myself an acquaintance.
The light with which we have used for the month of
fishing comes from Heceta, just three leagues south
of port. And the daughter of the keeper is a fair
one to be had. It saddens me to think that soon I
will depart, and with the life I possess, I may never
see her again.

Yet our bond has grown strong. Never before
have I known a woman as this one, the sweet taste
of her breath, the deepness of her sapphire eyes.
She is the goddess of my sea, and for this I have so
rightfully decided to return for her hand. Though
it will certainly take time. The captain is illusive
in what information he provides. Our latest
endeavor may last longer than I would prefer. Even
so, I love my sweet so dearly that I shall remain
ever hers, and her ever mine.

The time soon comes when we shall depart, out
into the darkened seas with our destination lying
far across the abyssal plains of aqua. But we shall
reach there in time, and we shall do our duty. And
once our duty is done, we shall return.

. . .October 20th, 1902

Our time has come. The storms have not ceased
and the captain has grown restless. We are to
depart as soon as the ship has been stocked. And it
is with this time that I have slipped away to see
my love once more. I told her to wait for me by the

fence, just ahead of her home looking out at the sea. With the light of Heceta as my guide, I steadily tread the path to where she waited, her nightgown billowing in the fierce wind, her hair matted across her face. Never before had I witnessed such pure brilliance from the hands of God.

"My dear Rue," I said, "I cannot thank you enough for seeing me one last time before my departure."

"But Walter," she replied, "when will I see you again?"

"When our work has been finished, my love," I assured. "The captain will not lead us astray."

"But the captain has spoken with Joseph. You and I both know Joseph is not a man to trifle with."

"Have faith, my love. We shall soon see each other again." I held her trembling hands for so many moments before pressing my lips against hers and standing there, the rain on our backs, the constant flicker of Heceta above. She was my everything, my all, and when the ship had traversed far beyond Heceta's reach, she would be my light.

"Please, Walter," she begged, "be careful."

"I will, my love."

*

In all of my time with Hull, only one case stands out as peculiar. It is peculiar because I would say it is the only case in which Hull has not had all of the answers. It is the only case that was not completely solved. And I would associate that inability to solve it with a very simple thing: the unsolvable.

"You know, I've been reviewing my notes," I said to Hull as I perused through a large stack of papers, "and something's struck me as odd."

"Here we go," he replied coolly, not removing his eyes from his microscope.

"Exactly what does Moriarty want? Why does it seem like all of the cases you're involved in have him? What's it all for?"

"If I knew, I would tell you, I can promise you that."

"But you do know," I snapped back as I set the papers down. "You do know and you never tell me because you're afraid it'll go right over my head."

He gave a short laugh. "Afraid. That is most definitely the reason."

"Well fine, then, what is it? Why is he doing it?"

He gave a short glance to his right, where I was, before returning his focus to the microscope and replying. "Moriarty is the head of a criminal organization that has a very wide reach, and evidently is involved in far more than just crime. While Moriarty seems to take on the role of a 'consulting criminal,' the syndicate that is Chimaera does far more. Scientific research, weapon advancements. It's an underground army of outcasts, criminals, and miscreants. And Moriarty has no doubt made me a central figure because of what I am."

"And what are you to him?"

"His exact opposite. Consulting detective. I am that which destroys everything he has worked so hard to achieve."

"And what's he working to achieve?"

"Now that," Hull said as he stepped away from the microscope, "is the true mystery, I would say."

I sighed. "Well, glad to see you're in such a chipper mood."

Truth be told, Hull had been in an exceedingly good mood as of late, and I couldn't quite put my finger on what it was. Unless his favorite holiday was Halloween, which would sort of make sense, given that the evening of haunts and horrors was only three nights away. But even then, he had been without a proper case for over a month and had yet to resort to his normal spouts of arrow-shooting or bad-music-playing. He continued his experiments, of course, but nothing too rancid.

I suppose in retrospect, I had nothing to complain about from the past month. And that struck me as very, very odd.

"And I suppose you aren't worried at all about Moriarty?"

"Nothing to be worried about."

I would have given a retort if a slight buzzing noise hadn't started from downstairs. I moved to my armchair and watched as Hull pulled the petri dish from his microscope and licked the contents. I stared at him with wide eyes as he approached me. "What in the—"

"Can you taste this for me?" he asked as he held the dish out.

"God no, I'm not going to taste that."

"I guarantee it is completely safe to consume, now please, just take a lick."

"No."

"Lick it!"

"No!"

"Am I interrupting anything?"

Hull and I both glanced over to see a man, probably late thirties and dressed in clothes suited for somewhere much colder. He held a rounded hat in his gloved hand, which had more than likely hid his balding head, while the other hand seemed to rub nervously at his side.

Hull stepped away from my chair. "Just an unwilling doctor."

"Ah, that's not.. really the way I would put it.." I murmured.

The man looked to my companion. "Are you Inspector Sheridan Hull?"

"*Detective*. What do you need?"

"Apologies. My name is Nelson Regis, I am the head inspector with the Florence Department of Investigation. I was sent your way by Inspector Lennox."

"So you have a case that requires my attention?"

"It's one of the most peculiar nature."

Hull looked the man up and down before nodding to the open armchair. "Have a seat." Regis shuffled slowly across the room before carefully taking his place in a chair. A distinctive squeak had followed him as he walked, and it was only then that I noticed his wet boots. Hull jumped up on the edge of his piano bench, resting on it like a bird observing its prey. He glanced forward at Regis for a long moment before giving a nod. "State your case."

"Florence sees its fair share of petty crimes, but rarely do we have something of significant nature arise. Murder, I would say, is a rarity that strikes our little town once every several years, if even that. And yet, at a very early time this morning, the department received a very stressed phone call from a group of young men, in their late teenage years, all very desperate for help. They told us simply that they had found something and that they were at Heceta Head Lighthouse.

"Now, of course, this immediately drew questions from us, as the lighthouse has been closed for renovations now for several months. We made the assumption that the boys had broken in and found something unpleasant. Two cars made their way, and the time was only around 3:45 in the morning. The weather has been particularly unsettling as of late, so it took us quite some time to navigate the winding path up to the lighthouse. We found the three boys standing as far from the structure's entrance as they could be without falling from the cliffside.

"The boys told us they had broken into the lighthouse on a dare from their colleagues, but what they had found inside had horrified them to no end. They would not take a step closer to the building, so my sergeant and I entered the fenced off location, our flashlights forward and our guns at the ready. I had no idea what to expect. The entirety of the lighthouse had been completely deconstructed and was in the recreative process, but most of the outer shell had been put into place. The sergeant and I passed through the doors without harm... until they closed behind us.

"At first I assumed it was the wind, but I soon learned that was not the case. The wind could not have blown the door from inside the lighthouse. Cautiously and carefully, the sergeant and I moved farther in. I will inform you now that I have lived in Florence my entire life, and have become very familiar with the primary tourist attractions to the lighthouses. Everyone comes in search of haunted spirits, and I personally had never given them any serious thought. But this was something bizarre, something different.

"There was an initial chill that seemed to emanate from the optic section far above us. The reconstruction of the facility had rendered it powerless without the running of the nearby generators. The only light we had came from our flashlights. And one would theorize that the only sounds we would hear, were sounds created by us and the winds outside. But there were other sounds. At first it was footsteps from one of the nearby rooms. I thought it to be my sergeant, but he was just as confused as I. Then the crying started.

"At first I thought it was the wind passing through the open spaces in the tower walls. But I could soon tell the difference between wind... and a woman. It was a soft crying from someone distant. The sergeant and I searched two rooms in desperate search for the source, but our efforts were in vain. And after a while, the weeping went silent. And the silence that followed was so eerie, so chilling, that I personally considered leaving and coming back in the morning. That was, of course, when the scream came.

"It was so perfectly timed. The wind had died down, the weeping had been silenced. Even our own breathing had fallen to a barely audible sound. The scream brought a sense of fear to my stomach that I had not felt since I was a child. The hair on my arms, the back of my neck, all of it stood on end. A horrible chill crawled its way down my spine, and I will not lie to you, gentlemen. I whimpered and felt a tear begin to well up in my eye. And as soon as the scream had began, it ceased.

"The sergeant and I wasted no time in charging for the exit, and had I not been sweeping my arms to gain speed, my swiveling flashlight would never have caught sight of the body. A woman lay in the center of the main room, her body in a position as if she had fallen from the optic section. She looked to be around twenty-five years of age. She wore a white dress, one you would expect from a bride, and her face was twisted in a scream of pain. The front of the dress, however, was not white. It was a very, very deep shade of red.

"We immediately departed from the lighthouse and had the owners of the property down at the keeper's house come to activate the generators. We took the boys into custody and illuminated the crime scene as best we could. I had expected the case to go quickly, that we would identify the young woman and find out which of the boys had murdered her. But a few things were amiss. Why would the boys have called us if they had murdered the woman? It would have been futile for them. But this was minor compared to our later discovery.

"Identifying the woman proved difficult. At first I thought she may have been foreign, but I soon realized the difficulty in identifying her came not from her place of residence, but rather her time of death. Our medical examiner was able to find in his preliminary examination that the woman had been dead far longer than just the evening. And when we finally did identify her, we realized something quite astounding. She had been dead for almost one hundred years."

Regis handed Hull a folder with aged documents inside. "Her name is Ruth Virgil. Born in 1887. She was the daughter of the lighthouse's keeper. In late October of 1912, her and a small group of her companions boarded a boat to go fishing just off the shore from the lighthouse. A horrible storm hit the coast while they were at sea, and the boat was never seen again. Ruth Virgil and her three friends, Margaret Grahn, Joseph Belial, and Mathew Aslinger, were presumed dead at sea. No wreckage nor bodies were recovered.

"At this point, I am not sure what to do. The body is most certainly that of Ruth Virgil, and yet it does not appear to have suffered from the hundred years it has been gone. We have no information to explain how she could have appeared inside the lighthouse. And... personally, I am still uncertain on the source of the noises. And what closed the door. The scream. All of it has left me very cautious. I am not a superstitious individual, Mr. Hull, but I am also not one to deny the facts. Those events were not trickery of the environment. My sergeant can attest to that."

Hull had leaned forward little by little as Regis had explained the situation. When the inspector had completed, Hull slowly drifted away to rest his back on the piano and gave a very loud exhale. "This case has interest indeed. And I will gladly assist you in solving it."

"You have no idea how relieved I am to hear you say that, "Regis replied.

"It will be my pleasure to help," Hull said as he shook the man's hand. "Dr. Walker and I will be along shortly. Heceta Head Lighthouse."

"That is correct. I look forward to working with you," Regis said as he left.

I watched the man leave until his footsteps had faded from the stairwell before turning my attention to Hull. "So you find something of interest in this case."

"I do."

"Why?"

"You heard the account as I did."

I leaned out of my chair and gave him a skeptic look. "It's a silly ghost story. They probably just misidentified the girl."

"Possibly. Though I would still like to investigate."

With a sigh, I stood from my chair and grabbed my laptop, knowing I had little time to pack. "Of course you do."

The weather on the coast was unforgiving. Immediately upon arriving at the parking lot for Heceta Head, I had gone to the back of the car and retrieved my coat. Hull, being his usual self, had worn his coat, collar popped, and started straight for the group of police cars and other vehicles. I could tell a few of them were news reporters hoping to be first to get information on the big story. Like Regis had said, it wasn't often the small town of Florence had a murder. Especially one like this. Hull and I eventually reached Regis, who was surrounded by police officers and news reporters.

"Gentlemen, right this way. We can talk at the keeper's house," Regis said with a gesture towards a winding path that moved up into the hills. The three of us walked slowly, the wind pounding at us from the side. Even without seeing, I could hear the waves of the Pacific crashing against the cliff walls that we walked so dangerously close to. The police officers moved behind us cautiously, their eyes focused up on where the lighthouse was. The entire situation would be frightening, yes, but I had long ago learned not to believe ghost stories. They were just that, after all: stories.

"Now, the keepers of the grounds are descendants of one of the individuals who went missing with Ruth Virgil. The elderly man is Morgan Belial. His grandfather was Joseph Belial. He has told us that Joseph was far more sexually active than his counterparts, resulting in the impregnation of a woman whose identity Morgan is unsure of. When Ruth died, her mother and father left and the grounds fell into government ownership until the Belial family obtained it. Mr. Belial will be able to explain the history of young Virgil and his own grandfather," Regis told us as we walked.

"Has the body been moved?" Hull asked.

"No. And we have had four officers stationed within the lighthouse at all times."

"Reluctantly, I presume."

"It's been difficult."

The house that came into view was certainly a sight to behold. The weather did not do it justice, and it had no doubt undergone many renovations in its time, but the home was as authentic as the lighthouse in the distance, and still managed to look its age. A man stood on the deck with two police officers, looking to be about sixty or seventy years in age. He stood taller than Hull and me, his arms crossed as he watched us approach.

Once we had all taken cover inside the house, our current arrangement in the living room, Hull began his questioning.

"I would like to know, before we begin," the detective said as he walked around the inner circle of the room, "where your wife is."

Belial looked somewhat disgruntled. "My wife passed away several years ago. Cancer."

"Ah. I sincerely apologize." Hull stopped when he reached the window, his eyes no doubt falling on the lighthouse. "Tell me about the renovation efforts."

"The Parks and Recreation Department started work on it in April," Belial stated. "The completion is scheduled to be in mid-December. No one except the construction crew and other authorized individuals have been allowed within a certain radius of the site. The lighthouse has been dismantled and fixed piece by piece to ensure its survival throughout the years."

"And this recent event, what opinion have you on it?"

Both Belial and Regis looked at Hull with confusion before the prior man spoke. "My family has lived in this area for a very, very long time. As such, I am very familiar with the tales that you younger folk will disregard without a thought."

"And that tale is?"

"The tale of the Gray Lady." The older man glanced around the room before continuing. "People have spoken of her for as long as I can remember. A woman in a gray fog walking the halls of this home. Some say she wanders the premises searching for her lost daughter. But given recent circumstances, I would have reason to believe the Gray Lady is in fact the late Ruth Virgil."

"And you believe that after almost one hundred years, the young woman's body should turn up after being lost at sea, yet her spirit has wandered this building."

"I do not know what I believe. But I know what I have seen. The Gray Lady does indeed walk these halls. And now... now her body has surfaced in the house."

"How did it get there, I wonder."

I looked up at Hull, who had yet to take his eyes from the lighthouse. I couldn't quite understand what he meant, but I feared that he somehow suspected this old man of having a hand in a hundred-year old mystery.

"There were rumors of my grandfather and Ruth being involved," Belial said through narrowed eyes. "And it would only be affirmed by their consecutive demise. And her wish to remain here in spirit."

"Yes, about that," Hull said and he finally turned. "What can you tell me about—"

A quick knock on the door stopped the detective. All of us turned and watched the door open to admit an officer and a smaller figure, mostly hidden by a rain cloak. The officer looked to Regis, his chin shaking slightly.

"Sorry to interrupt, Inspector. We found one of Virgil's descendants."

Now my interest was most certainly caught. The small figure walked around the officer and pulled back its hood. Beneath the cloak was a young woman, probably around twenty-five years old. She had beautiful brunette hair that moved in waves to her shoulders, and her eyes were a deep blue that seemed to swirl.

"A descendant?" Regis asked.

The woman nodded. "My name is Olivia Virgil. Ruth was my great-grandmother."

Belial looked from the woman to Regis with a furrowed brow. "Ruth was an unmarried woman when she disappeared. For her to be this woman's ancestor is impossible."

"And yet it is true," the woman assured. "It is as my mother has told me, and her mother to her, and so on. We are a line of very proud women. It is why I still wear the Virgil surname, and why my mother does, and my grandmother did."

I glanced around the room to see how people were reacting. Most of the officers were neutral, but some wore faces of horror. Regis looked at the woman with trembling eyes, and Belial seemed to have gone even paler than he already was. Hull looked at the woman with the fiercest eyes I had ever seen on the man. A long silence seemed to follow the woman's arrival before Hull clicked his tongue.

"Can we see the lighthouse now?" he asked, eyes still on the woman.

Regis stood from the couch with shaking legs. "Of course. Ah, Arcan and Roloff, please stay here with Mr. Belial and.. Miss Virgil."

"If it's fine with you," the woman added, "I would like to see the body."

301

Regis's eyes seemed to widen at the thought. "I, ah, suppose we can manage that." She nodded in thanks. Regis gestured to the door. "This way."

The inspector led us up another winding path, this one seeming to take longer as the weather grew more bleak and dismal. The lighthouse was still kept hidden behind large tarps, but the top was poking out as a result of the weather blowing some of the coverings from the scaffolding. As I looked up at where the optic section was, I could not help but feel a very small, very quick chill shoot down my spine. For a brief moment, I had seen something.

And I wasn't sure what it had been.

Regis led the small group of us, those being the inspector, Hull, the woman, and myself, past the gates and into the lighthouse. Several generators were running outside with cables draped into the doorway, providing a substantial amount of light in the main chamber that led up to the optic section. Four officers sat in chairs at perpendicular ends of the room, all of them turned to face the center. Lying in the center was the body of Ruth Virgil, just as Regis had described, but with a more unsettling quality. Her body was pale, but not in any way deteriorated. Her face was most certainly twisted in a mixture of fear and rage. But the unsettling aspect came from her overall look.

Hull glanced from the body to the young woman accompanying us. "Remarkable. Your likeness to your ancestor is astonishingly close."

The young woman moved to look at the body, tilting her head as she observed. "We do look alike, don't we?"

To me, alike was an understatement. If someone were to give the body and the woman one glance each, they would think they were one and the same. Hull stooped over the body, his face hovering a few centimeters above the dead woman's. He tilted his chin up to look down the bridge of his nose at the open eyes, and for another brief moment, I saw Hull's eyes widen. It was a very, very small change in their size, but it had been there. And I knew I was the only person who had caught it.

"Curious," he said as he rose. "No evidence of deterioration. The body has been perfectly preserved for one hundred years. The blood on the chest is the result of a stab wound, no doubt, but there is a certain paleness to the body that suggests a more aquatic resting place. Somehow, she was both stabbed and drowned, and despite it being impossible, I would deduce that this body has spent a significant amount of time at the bottom of the ocean."

"We both know that's impossible," I commented as I looked down at the body. "Unless there's a vacuum of some sort where her body fell, it would have been reduced to nothing by now. It would've been buried in the sand, or predatory fish would have eaten it. There's no way it would come back this preserved. And there's no way it would have just hopped out of the water and come up here."

"So we can deduce a range of options. One, the body was retrieved from the waters and placed here. Two, the body never left the lighthouse."

"But neither of those explain how it's here."

"And that is what we must figure out." Hull looked down the dark hallway that led to the oil rooms. He cast a side-glance at Regis. "You said you and your sergeant heard noises. Precisely where did you hear them from?"

Regis walked around the body to point down at one of the doorways. "The footsteps came from that room. And when we moved towards them, they seemed to dim. That was when the moaning started, from the room across the hall. As we were walking across the hallway, the moans stopped and the scream came from right here."

"What can you say about the footsteps?"

"They weren't even. That's how I knew it wasn't me, or the sergeant. It was like someone was pacing back and forth inside the room, slowly. And it stopped as soon as we got there."

"And the moans?"

"They were a woman's. I know that for certain. It was like she was at the tail end of a long spout of crying. When you can't quite cry anymore, but you still want to. It had an echo to it and came from the room across."

"And the scream."

Regis shuddered. "It sounded like it came from all around us. The more I think about it, the more I feel as if it came from the optic section. The sound just echoed through the halls. But it couldn't have possibly come from the body. There was no sound of impact. And the officers outside did not report having seen anyone. And..."

"And what?"

Regis took in a deep breath before continuing. "And those who were outside did not hear a scream."

Hull glanced back at the doorway before looking down the hall, into the darkness. "What kind of living accommodations were made inside the lighthouse?"

"There were none," Regis replied. "All living accommodations were in the keeper's house. It would have been too inhospitable for anyone to stay here."

"Interesting." Hull took several steps towards the darkness before stopping. "Inspector, I will need two air mattresses, two sleeping bags, a portable heater, and a plethora of blankets."

"Hold on," I interjected. "Why."

"We are going to spend the night here and see if we can't recreate the previous night's events."

"We?" I shook my head. "Hell no. I am not sleeping in a lighthouse that isn't even complete."

Hull looked back at me with a smirk. "Are you scared, Doctor?"

All I could do was sigh.

*

I assumed the sun had long since gone down, but the weather outside made it difficult to properly tell. If not for my watch telling me it was almost 1:45 AM, I would have thought it was early evening. There just seemed to be this odd glow that came from the horizon. At least, that's what we could see through the open doorway. Hull had set up the air mattresses and sleeping bags side by side in the once-dark hallway. The portable heater was to our side and the blankets were still piled neatly beside the mattresses.

Hull's eyes were currently focused straight ahead, at the body of Ruth Virgil. The generators were still running outside, which allowed us to keep on the lights that watched the corpse. What we were expecting I wasn't sure, but as the night went on, I couldn't keep from feeling a chill. And one certain moment was approaching that neither of us were looking forward to: refueling the generators. Regis had told us that around 2 AM, the generators would need to be refueled, otherwise all power would cease to the lighthouse. Judging by how intently focused Hull was on a body that I believed had no intention of moving, the job fell to me.

A small one-room building was used to keep the tourist information when the area was open, but now it contained the gas

304

tanks for the generators. I slowly dredged my way from the lighthouse to the storage room, seeing lightning flash off in the ocean distance several times before reaching the door. As I fumbled with the keys, I noticed the wind pick up significantly, and a horrific howling noise started from behind me. I glanced over my shoulder to find nothing but emptiness and the sight of the ocean.

And I could have sworn I saw what looked like a large boat of some sort about half a mile offshore before the lightning flash had ended.

The lock clicked for the storage room, and I found myself in a thin but long room that was filled with orange fuel cans. The ones to my right were placed under a sign that read EMPTY while the ones to my left said FULL. I grabbed two of the full cans and started back out the door, the generators placed in a small enclave next to the lighthouse. Regis had said it would take four cans to refuel all of the generators. The first two were easy enough, but by the time I had finished and started back to the storage room, the lightning had made its way to the shore.

And for those who do not know, lightning that strikes close to you can be particularly horrifying.

I wasted no time at all in getting back to the storage room and grabbing another two cans. As I was walking back, I started to hear a very distinct and familiar noise. It was only when I was walking past the entrance to the lighthouse that I realized what it was.

"*Doctor!*"

I dropped the cans and charged back into the lighthouse, and as soon as I had passed through the doors, they slammed closed behind me. I glanced back, and as I did, I heard a loud zapping noise and watched the glow of the lights behind me disappear as the bulbs shorted out. I turned again and ran towards the small orange glow of the portable heater, forgetting completely that there was a body in the center of the room.

Or, at least, there had been.

"Hull?" I called out as I approached the mattresses.

A hand shot out and grabbed my wrist, immediately pulling me down. My eyes adjusted enough to reveal Hull's face, hiding in the darkness behind the heater's glow. His eyes were wide and almost manic in their appearance. He pointed back towards the center of the room.

"It's gone," he said, his voice shaking.

"Gone? The body?"

"Yes, the body, it's gone."

"How can it be gone?"

"I don't know!"

Thud. Thud. Thud.

My spine went rigid. Hull managed to pull me to his side and prop me against the wall as we stared to the left, down the dark hallway towards where the sound of footsteps had come from. It only lasted a few seconds before ceasing, the footsteps being fairly spaced out. Even the wind outside had seemed to die down, for all I could hear was our breathing, as well as the distant pitter-patter of rainfall.

Thud. Thud. Thud.

"How is this happening," I whispered through chattering teeth.

"I don't know."

"How is this happening."

"I don't know."

Thud. Thud. Thud.

"Hello!" Hull called out.

The footsteps ceased.

"Oh my God what have you done," I said with a trembling voice. We both waited in absolute silence. The pitter-patter of rain had either stopped or was simply too light to be heard. There were no more footsteps, and I could tell Hull and I were forcing ourselves to breathe as quietly as possible.

Then, of course, the moaning began.

It was that of a young female, of that there were no doubts. She sounded far off, distant, but her cries were still prominent and loud. After a few cries, she would stop to sniffle, then continue with her crying again.

"Your turn," Hull whispered to me.

"No."

"Say something."

"Say something to *what*?"

"It!"

"It what?!"

"Hello!" Hull called out again.

The moaning ceased.

"This isn't happening," I said as I pushed myself up the wall in an attempt to stand. "This cannot be happening."

"Sequential order."

"What?"

"Sequential order. First, the door. Then, the steps. Third, the moans. Last..."

We turned to look at the center of the room. And in that moment, I would have preferred to be anywhere else. I can honestly say I would have rather been in the middle of Iraq than in that lighthouse. I wish we had turned and seen nothing, or Hell, I wish we had turned and heard the scream, and the body had returned to its resting place. But we were not so fortunate.

For when we turned, we stared into the lifeless eyes of Ruth Virgil.

And only then did she scream.

It was exactly what I would expect all of the most tortured souls to sound like if they were to scream in unison. It matched the fictitious descriptions of a banshee's wail. The sound was ear-piercing and heart-stopping, and made it impossible for Hull and me to move. We could do nothing but stand and stare at the Hell-born abomination that levitated before us. She was about half a meter off the ground, with blood dripping from the tips of her dress to the floor. Her brunette hair was matted to her face, but not enough to cover her eyes, which I had recalled being a nice blue color.

Now they were swirling masses of gray.

As soon as the scream ceased, the body twisted its neck to the left, then the right, before staring straight at us, the mouth opening and revealing an abyssal black hole that could somehow conjure words.

"*FIND THE BOAT*," she screamed at us. I could feel my legs start returning to life. "*FIND THE BOAT.*" Now my legs could work. I turned and charged backward, grabbing Hull as I went. He stumbled as we moved, his eyes still locked on the floating corpse behind me. I ran mindlessly towards the darkness of the end of the hallway, recalling having seen a back doorway that would lead us to the outside. I ran as fast as I could, considering Hull was making no attempt to run at all. Finally, after what felt like a dreadful eternity, I found the handle in the darkness, gave it a twist, and emerged into the storming openness of the outdoors.

*

We ended up stumbling our way down to the keeper's house and sleeping on two of the couches. That was where Regis and his officers had taken up residence during the case. We offered them no explanation until morning, and when we had, none of them looked happy. In fact, they looked almost as petrified as Hull and I had when telling the tale. It was interesting for me, to say the least. I was still skeptic as ever, thinking someone had done a fine job of scaring Hull and me away. I had no intention of believing anything that took place last night was real.

Hull, however, was different. There was a dark caste to his face, a certain paleness to his already-pale cheeks. He even seemed to have a bit of a tremor to his hands as he slowly drank a cup of coffee. Hull was one of the most factual and logical people I knew, so it absolutely confounded me to think he may have started to buy into what he was seeing. And yet, he seemed genuinely afraid, even though he was working his hardest to hide it.

"Find the boat," Regis said after the long pause that followed the finishing of our story.

"That's what.. it said, yes," I replied, casting a quick glance at Hull. He offered no comment.

"I suppose it could be in reference to the boat Ruth Virgil was on when she disappeared. But all accounts we have recorded say it was a small paddle boat, nothing significant. If the Gray Lady expects us to find a paddle boat at the bottom of the Pacific, she'll be sorely disappointed."

I looked at the inspector with a furrowed brow. "I'm sorry, the Gray Lady?"

"Of course," Regis said, returning the furrowed look. "No doubt she is the one who spoke to you."

"You can't seriously believe in some old ghost story."

"Well then, Doctor, you kindly explain what happened to you gentlemen last night."

I sighed. "It would look to me like something you'd expect from a Scooby-Doo cartoon. Someone is trying to keep people away from the lighthouse, or stop the renovations, or something. The real mystery we need to solve is who killed the woman. Or if that's even Ruth Virgil's body." I looked over at Hull, who was staring down at the ground. "Help me out here."

He pressed his hands together and brought it up to his mouth, his eyes trembling before he spoke. "I think.. I believe we will.. I.."

"You've got to be kidding me!" I exclaimed as I stood. "Am I the only person here not buying into this? Ghosts are not real, people."

"Spirits walk these halls, mister."

I turned to see Mr. Belial enter the room, his hands currently cleaning the inside of a glass mug.

"And if you continue to speak against them," he warned, "they may soon turn their sights on you."

"For the love of God," I said with a turn towards Hull.

"Did you say the body vanished?" Regis asked.

"It wasn't there when I walked in, but.. well, *something* was there when we left."

"It would be wise of us, then, to go and check." The group of us stood, except for Hull. "Detective?"

"I, um.." Hull said carefully, eyes still on the floor. "I need to make a phone call."

Regis shrugged. "Let us move, then."

I looked down at Hull as the group exited the house. "What's wrong?"

"The sounds, the sight. It was there, John. I work based on logic, based on the ability to deduce using the five senses. And they were there. The sounds. *The sight.*"

"There are so many explanations for the sounds and the body talking."

"But only few make sense."

"Ghosts do not exist, Sheridan."

"You cannot say that for certain, John. The existence of something else... is improbable. But it is not impossible. And when you have eliminated the impossible, whatever remains, however improbable, *must be the truth.*"

"Fine then," I said as I started towards the door. "You sit here and be afraid of your ghosts, make your phone calls, and I'm going to continue with the case." Once I was outside the door, I scowled. "Whatever that case may be." I eventually reached the lighthouse and found that none of the officers, or Regis, had taken the initiative to enter. I truly could not believe this ghost had managed to get into everyone's heads. Especially Hull's.

"So, ah, Doctor," Regis prompted. "If you'd be so kind as to lead us through what happened to you last night."

I gave a short nod and pointed at the storage room. "I had just left the room with the third and fourth cans of fuel when I heard Hull shouting." I led the group through the doors and to the main chamber, where we found the air mattresses, the blankets, the sleeping bags, and the portable heater untouched, and the body still in its place, as if it had never moved. "The door slammed behind me as I came in and the lights went out. I walked right over where the body would be, nothing was there, and found Hull hiding behind the heater, in the dark.

"He told me the body was gone, which I had already figured out, and I assumed he'd seen something happen. Then the footsteps started from the room on the other side of the wall. They would've kept going, too, but Hull called out to them, and they stopped. The moaning started short after, and he called out to that. They stopped as well. About then, we both turned and saw the body of Ruth Virgil, floating in the air. And she screamed at us to find the boat."

"And that's all?"

"That's all."

"And this boat, did anything happen that would explain that?"

"Not that I can think—"

Only then did it sink in. I had seen a boat, when I'd first gone to the storage room. In a quick flash of lightning, the boat had appeared off on the horizon, and if my memory was right, it had looked similar to one you would expect to see in the bayous of Louisiana. A ferry boat of sorts, not something you'd expect to see off the Oregon coast at almost 2 in the morning.

I walked back through the doors, Regis and the officers watching me with confusion. I walked to the metal rail that prevented anyone from rolling down the cliff into the waiting waters and looked out. In my mind, I could see the boat again, the waters far more rough than they were now. The storms had subsided slightly since the previous evening. Regis came up beside me, his eyes perusing the ocean waters.

"Are there any ferries that come along this shore?" I asked.

"None come this far up from the bay. Any boats that would be out there would be private, and most if not all ferries that still operate on this coast are for tours." The inspector followed my gaze to a particularly dark patch of water, the same patch the boat had been in. "Why?"

I licked my lips. "I think I know what boat she meant. But..." I blinked several times, knowing that if I completed my sentence, I would turn myself to the side of believing in these ghosts. Or at least I would start down the path. It was impossible for that type of boat to have been there one moment and gone the next.

Wasn't it?

"But I don't think it's going to be anywhere above shore," I finished.

"You think it sank out there?"

"Yes."

"We've done SONAR readings of this entire coastline, if something was there, it would've come up before."

"In the same manner that a woman's body would have turned up before inside an aging lighthouse, and yet that managed to avoid detection."

Regis and I turned to see Hull standing a few meters to our left, his eyes focused out on the same blank spot. The inspector took a step away from the railing and put his hands on his hips. "You really think we're going to find something out there?"

"I do not think, I know for certain. I had suspected that the boat Ruth Virgil wished for us to find would be in fact the one she died on, but I could not know at the time where to look. That clue she instead planted in the good doctor's mind. A ferry-like boat to be found out in those dark depths. And we would require more than just SONAR technology. In fact, we will have to visit the ship's resting place itself."

"And just how do you plan to do that?" I asked.

The detective held up his phone. "Two scuba suits are being taken to Siuslaw Bay. A Coast Guard boat will escort us out to the spot, and we will dive down to find what it is Ruth Virgil wants us to find. What makes the boat so significant."

"Who did you call that would have access to scuba suits?"

"The United States government."

I sighed. Hull turned and started down the path, but first paused to cast a wary glance at the lighthouse before continuing. Regis nudged my elbow as we walked.

"What did he mean when he said that?"

"Surprisingly enough, he meant exactly what he said."

Indeed, when we reached the harbor in the town of Florence, the Coast Guard ship was ready and waiting, the two scuba suits in the crews' quarters. Regis was the only other officer allowed to come on deck. As the boat was taken from the bay, I found Hull standing near the front of the ship, his eyes out on the western horizon, which was growing significantly more darker as time passed.

"So, which did you swallow," I said when I reached his side," the pride or the fear?"

"Neither. When I took the moment to analyze the situation objectively, I realized we were misinterpreting things the entire time. And I will admit, you were right. The possibility of the body reanimating is far too much. There seems to be a darker past to this case than we may have realized, and it may turn out that we are solving two cases rather than one. But whoever the mastermind is behind the haunting of the lighthouse and the message to us wants us to find something."

"The mastermind?"

"Someone who is smart enough to use the already-existing legend of the Gray Lady to help keep people away from the area so that we could properly investigate. The body of Ruth Virgil does indeed complicate things, but I presume the facts will become clear in time."

"I've been saying that all along."

"Saying what?"

"That someone else is doing this. None of it's real."

"So we can hope."

"What did your brother think when you told him you needed two scuba suits to investigate a possible derelict ship from over a hundred years ago?"

"I told Bailey that you and your girlfriend wanted to go snorkeling off the Oregon coast, and she should convince her father to loan us two suits."

"I don't have a girlfriend. And I definitely do *not* want to go snorkeling off the Oregon coast."

"Irrelevant. Malcolm would be far more willing to grant use of the suits if it was to you rather than me." He swayed forward slightly, gaze falling to the water. After a moment, he shook his head.

"What's up with you?" I asked as I watched him drum his fingers against the railing.

"I, um..." He gulped. "I do not do boats."

"Of all things, you get seasick?"

"I do not get seasick. My body simply disagrees with the concept of a.. fluid surrounding."

It took about twenty minutes for the boat to reach the shore of the lighthouse. From where we were, I could look up and see the officers, as well as Mr. Belial and the young Miss Virgil. There were also several more news teams gathered to get the latest scoop. The ship's crew had brought the suits up, which now sat and waited to be used. I moved to the suit on the left and started shedding layers of clothing to climb in. I'd snorkeled before, several years ago on a family trip to Hawai'i. Hopefully I wasn't too rough.

Once I had completely suited up, I glanced to my side and found Hull had made no move whatsoever to put his suit on.

"You gonna suit up or not?" I asked as I adjusted my air tank.

"I am afraid I will have to sit this one out."

"What? What do you mean?"

"I am personally not a fan of having my life in the hands of a small tube connected to a tank of oxygen."

"This whole thing was your idea."

"And you will perform to the letter, as you always have."

"How am I supposed to communicate with you guys?"

He revealed a camera from his coat and secured it to my head, then tapped the lens twice. "This will allow us to see everything you see. The depth is approximately twenty-five meters. You will have twenty minutes of oxygen in your tank, so move wisely. When you find the wreckage, look for something, anything that may have been moved purposefully to be found." He started pushing me backward.

"Wait, what are you doing?"

He pushed the breathing apparatus into my mouth and smacked my goggles down from on top of my head. "The boat's name is the *S.S. Anna*." With that, he pushed forward, sending me over the boat's edge and plunging into the cold, dark waters.

While I wish I would have had time to gather my bearings, I knew oxygen was short, and immediately I oriented myself and started downward. With light coming from my shoulder and my head, a good two or three meters was illuminated ahead of me. Twenty-five wasn't too far to swim, but I knew that after a while, the light would only go about a half-meter ahead of me. And if there really was the wreckage of a ferry down here, I would have limited moving space.

The seconds started to feel like minutes as the darkness grew more engrossing. Only when I lost all sight of the surface completely did something appear ahead of me. It was a long piece of wood sticking out from the black, the wood ancient and fairly withered away. The closer I got, the more wood became visible around it. At first it was only broken pieces coming from the dark, but then I could see large pieces of a structure, as well as the coarse sand. After sifting through the wreckage for only a minute, I found an intact part of the previous side with the name of the ship on a plaque still nailed in place. *S.S. Anna.*

I glided up over the wall and into what looked to be the largest part of what remained. I slowly drifted into the darkness and found what looked to be a dining table firmly placed on the ground with the chairs floating off in the corner. How these objects had survived the past hundred years was beyond me, but they looked almost perfect, as if the ship had only just sunk. I continued through the dining room into a hallway that curved down, to what seemed to be underneath the sand.

I followed the hallway down into a bedroom of sorts, and as soon as my eyes fell on the room, I felt a horrific chill crawl up my spine. Carved into the wall was a very crude BELIAL. I looked around the room a few times before checking the time and seeing I had ten minutes left. I turned back to the hallway, deciding I had seen enough to confirm our thoughts.

I only wish I'd made it farther than the door's arch.

A strong pull from the water forced me back into the room, flying at an incomprehensible speed all the way to the bed. My back slammed against the wood of the hull, causing the wood to implode. The water pushed me through into a room that had somehow managed to avoid the water entirely. My body slid along the wooden floor of the hidden room before coming to a stop. Because of how the bedroom had been positioned, only a little water poured in after me before coming to a rest.

I glanced around the room nervously, my mouthpiece having come out. I had no doubt smashed through the BELIAL on the wall and now found myself in a room that had no visible entry or exit. There were no items in the room, no lights, no portholes. In fact, the only thing that seemed to be in the room was what hanged on the wall opposing me. At first I couldn't quite make it out, but once I'd turned the full extent of my two lights on it, I felt my heart stop.

Pinned to the wall was a body clad in a white dress with a harpoon jutting out through the upper chest. The head was tilted down, with long brunette hair that reached the body's shoulders. Without seeing the face, I knew that I was staring at the same body of Ruth Virgil that was supposed to be laying on the floor of the lighthouse, the same body that had levitated the night before. I stared up at it with fear pumping through my veins, my legs having given up on moving.

"I... I don't know if you guys can hear me... but that's her body... and the wall outside said Belial..." I glanced back at the wall and heard a slight shuddering from around me. "I think I know who killed her."

The shuddering grew in its intensity. I looked around and saw the walls start to crack. I jammed the rebreather into my mouth and looked back at the hole I had fallen through, only to fall back against the wall, almost hitting the body. Somehow, the entirety of the ship was moving, with me locked inside. The ceiling began to splinter in several places before a large section gave way, letting a massive wave of water pour in. The sudden rush slammed me back against the wall, and I found that I was completely unable to move.

I struggled against the current, trying to get myself somewhere near the center of the room. But it was no use. Escape was looking more and more bleak. And of course it was then that the rebreather was knocked from my mouth. I clamped my lips shut, my eyes desperately searching for a way to escape. The water was still pouring in from the ceiling, slowly filling the room. The light attached to my head flickered twice before dying, shortly followed by the one on my shoulder.

The bright light that poured through the open ceiling, as well as the outline of a diving suit, were the last things I saw before everything faded to black.

*

When I finally came to, I was greeted by Hull's face, with swirling gray storm clouds behind him. I coughed a few times as I sat up, looking around to find us on the deck of the Coast Guard boat.

"Careful," Hull said with a slight pat on my back. "You inhaled far too much water on your ascent."

"What happened?" I said through a fit of coughs.

"The part of the ship that you found was resting on an underwater crest. You walking set it off balance and started a downward slide, which caused the room you were in to implode."

I coughed twice more before looking up at him. "Who found me?"

"She did." The detective pointed behind me. I turned to find the younger Virgil woman in a wetsuit of her own, not the one we had brought.

"How did she find me?"

"She says that she is a frequent diver in this area. She followed you carefully and watched the derelict begin its descent when she intervened and found you. She had to strip your oxygen tank from you in order to rise quickly enough, and she performed cardiopulmonary resuscitation once you were both onboard."

I gave a quick shake of my head. "Hull, there's something very wrong, the body was down—"

"I know. We watched it all happen. The etching on the wall, the body. Things are starting to make sense."

I coughed again. "They are?"

"Yes. We will need to return to the lighthouse tonight, so I can confirm my thoughts. But I believe we have successfully solved two very interesting cases."

"Two?"

"Yes. The murder of Miss Ruth Virgil and the mystery behind her initial disappearance."

"But Hull, it doesn't make any sense. How could someone be murdered one hundred years ago and only turn up now? And how did you know the name of the boat?"

He presented a very tainted newspaper for me to read. "The *S.S. Anna* was a ferry that operated out of San Francisco from 1856 to 1872. It was in 1872 that the ship went missing. Its captain was named Sir Francis Belial."

"So that's why the name was etched on the inside of the bedroom?"

"Wrong."

"Then why?"

"It's obvious, isn't it?"

"No. With you, it never is."

The rest of the day passed fairly quickly. Hull wanted to stay one more night inside the lighthouse, and Regis had been happy to oblige. Virgil had requested if she could stay with the officers at the keeper's house, and it had been quite obvious that Mr. Belial had been reluctant. The uncanny resemblance between Olivia and Ruth Virgil definitely made it difficult to be in the same room as her after having just seen the body. But she had also just saved my life, and for that, I was grateful.

Now the sun was setting, the weather was getting worse, and Hull and I had barricaded ourselves on the floor, the lights focused on the body. This time, however, we had brought the required gas cans inside, which now sat near the entry. As well, Hull had placed impromptu tripwires at both entryways to help discover whoever entered. He was taking no chance in letting whoever was coordinating all of this escape.

"I know how you felt now."

Hull glanced over at me, the words having broken a very long silence. When he gave no inquiry, I continued.

"When the body spoke to us last night. I knew it was fake, but there was still a small part of me that was truly afraid. And that fear was... multiplied when I was down there and found the body."

"Fear is a curious thing."

"But something I don't get. How can there be multiple bodies? How did the one get inside the boat? How did it vanish from the floor and talk to us?"

"There are many possibilities. Some theories that I would like to explore, given time."

"It just feels like something is really off about all of this. We're trying to solve, what? A hundred-year old murder mystery? Or are we simply trying to figure out how the body got here? How it got in the boat?"

"I believe, my friend, that you will soon realize all of those aspects create one case."

I leaned back and gave a heavy sigh. "So why are we here again? Do you really think whoever's doing this is going to come back and try it again?"

"So I would hope."

"Because that's the logical thought."

"Because that is sensical enough. Someone is seeking to keep people away from this lighthouse, but why? What have they to gain from fleshing out an ancient ghost story? The risk of us finding whatever this building hides is too great for the person to ignore. They will come for us again, as they did the previous evening."

The next four or five hours passed without cause for concern. I think it was nearing 1 AM when Hull sat up from his mattress and started pacing the room. I'd personally grown tired of sitting and staring at a dead body, so I had taken it upon myself to do an actual medical examination. The cause of death had indeed been blood loss as a result of a stab wound through the back, which matched with the harpoon from the boat. The body had also been thoroughly saturated, also linking it to its place in the boat. But despite all of the factual evidence, the explanation for the body's arrival was still to be found.

"This makes no sense," the detective said as he paced, his hands clasped behind his back. "They should have come by now. The later it gets, the more time we have to investigate."

"The last event didn't happen until 2 AM. We have an hour to go."

"Irrelevant. The person will be desperate."

"Maybe you're just—"

"*Hush!*"

We both froze as a slight sound started from above us. It sounded like a soft tapping on glass, and it made sense that it would have come from the optic section. Hull walked out into the center and looked up the spiral staircase, being careful to avoid the body. He stared with his head arched back for almost a minute before he flinched and started towards the stairs. I jumped to my feet and stumbled forward.

"Hull, where are you—"

"*Wait there!*" I watched as he charged up and around, eventually moving completely out of sight. From where I stood, I could hear the echo of his footsteps on the metal stairwell as he came ever-closer to the top. After almost a minute, the footsteps ceased, and I stood there in absolute silence as I waited for any kind of sign.

"Sheridan?" I called out.

"John, the boat is out there!"

"The *what*?"

"The *Anna*! I can see it!"

I moved around the body and towards the door, careful not to set off the tripwire as I opened it. The weather was fairly decent compared to how it had been, but there was no moonlight to help see what looked like the dark mass of a boat drifting out in the water. I let my eyes adjust for a while, giving me a better view of what was most definitely the boat that had been drawn in the newspaper article. I also recognized the large metal plaque on the side. *S.S. Anna.*

And just as quickly as the mass had been there, a flash of lightning that struck far too close to the lighthouse hid it completely, sending my eyes into a frenzied state. Once the dots had stopped blocking my view, I found that the boat was gone. And it was only then that something Hull had said the night before came back to my thoughts.

"Sequential order," I whispered as I ran back into the lighthouse, carefully jumping over the tripwire and slamming the door. "Hull!"

"John, someone is coming from the house!"

"Who?"

"It's far too dark. Watch the door!"

I took a few steps away from the door and felt my insides twist as a familiar zap came from above me as the lights went out. I knew better than to turn around and look to see if the body was still there. I had a good feeling it wasn't. A certain calmness had fallen outside, too, the sound of rain ceasing on the walls and rooftop. All I could hear now was the sound of my own breathing. But then, little by little, I could hear what sounded like footsteps approaching the doorway. They had a certain irregular pattern to them, like the one we'd heard in the room.

"They're almost to the door!" Hull's voice called out from above. Sure enough, I could tell by the sound how close the footsteps were. And when it seemed like the sound was about to come through the door itself, they stopped. And I truly do wish that had been the last of it.

Bang.

"John!"

Bang.

"Sheridan!"

Bang.

"*RUUUUUUUUUUUUUUUUUUUUUUUUUUUUUUUUUUUU UUE.*"

I stumbled back away from the door, my feet tripping on the still-present body of Ruth Virgil. I fell back onto the air mattresses and, with help from the portable heater, watched Hull come flying down the stairs towards me.

319

"What was that?" he asked.

I pointed at the door with trembling fingers. "T-t-t-t-the d-d-d-d-door!"

"The what?" he said as he glanced back.

"*The do—*"

"*RUUUUUUUUUUUUUUUUUUUUUUUUUUUUUUUUUUUUUUUU
UUE.*"

Hull bounced away from the door as fast as his feet could carry him, jumping over the body, over the air mattresses, over me. I watched as he disappeared into the darkness that was the end of the hallway.

"What about the person!"

"*Bollocks to the person!*"

I didn't need any other motivation to return to my feet and chase after the man. Anything was better than sitting there and listening to the banging on the door and the horrible moan of a voice that was outside. In fact, Hull and I didn't even bother taking the designated path towards the keeper's house. We ran straight up the hill, right in the direction of the highway. And we didn't stop until we had reached it.

*

"So Rue."

It was about seven in the morning when the group of us had reconvened at the keeper's house. Regis, his officers, Mr. Belial, Miss Virgil, Hull, and I sat in a circle, with the detective and me trying our best to keep steady hands on our cups of coffee.

"Rue was the name the voice kept repeating," I replied before taking a very long swig of my drink.

"I suppose it could be a nickname for Ruth Virgil," Regis said with a glance at Olivia. "But I know for fact none of us heard anything from the lighthouse. No one screaming like that. No one walked by, either. If this was all happening at around 1:30 AM, Mr. Belial would have been up, as he said he was awake then because of the storm. Mr. Belial?"

The old man gave a nod. "Lightning always wakes me up. I went to get a glass of water and there was no one walking by, and I could not see anyone near the lighthouse. I did a quick walk around the inside of the house and found that Miss Virgil was no longer on her specified couch. She was also not in any of the bathrooms."

All eyes fell on the woman, but Hull seemed to regard her with something other than suspicious interest. She blinked a few times as she took in the others. "I enjoy the ocean breeze when I cannot sleep. I took a walk, but not towards the lighthouse."

"I find that hard to believe, given the circumstances," Belial retorted.

"I believe her wholeheartedly," Hull said. Now all eyes fell on him. Even I felt a hint of surprise at having heard him say that. "In fact, I believe her enough to say I have solved this case."

"You what?" I said, confusion thoroughly drowning out my other emotions.

"I believe we would all benefit from visiting the lighthouse this evening so I may convene this case. However, with your permission, Inspector, I would like to be able to tour it once more, by myself, with the guarantee that everyone else, even my own companion, is kept here."

Regis glanced around the room, locked eyes with me, then back to Hull with a nod. "We will meet you tonight at eight, then."

I caught Hull just moments before he walked from the house. "What are you doing?"

"Disproving the existence of the ghost." With that, he was gone from the doorway and headed towards the path. I watched him walk until he was hidden in the trees. It was only then that I realized Miss Virgil was standing at my side, her eyes also having been following Hull.

"Do you think he has solved the case?" she asked with a touch of hopefulness in her voice.

"With the confidence he displayed there? Yes. I think he has."

She smiled. "Good."

"Thank you, by the way," I added as I looked down at the woman. "For saving my life."

She looked up at me, her eyes a very definitive sapphire color that reminded me of the ocean on a nicer day than this. "You are very welcome, Doctor. It would have been improper of me to sit back and allow a man to travel to his death. I do have one question, however."

"Of course."

"The voice that cried for Rue. Was it a man's?"

I furrowed my brow. "I would suppose so."

She smiled. "As I thought. Thank you, Doctor." With that, she walked away. I watched the woman walk for a long while, part of me still disturbed by her likeness to the late Ruth Virgil. But I also found myself admiring her appearance, and for only a moment, my thoughts returned to the woman from the magic show, and how I wished I had made some kind of attempt to speak with her. Unfortunately, that opportunity was long past. It no longer mattered.

I was able to pass the day by spending time in the town of Florence, trying some of the food, exploring a few of the shops, and eventually making my way back to the keeper's house after having dinner at a quaint little place called Mo's. It was a quarter to seven when I arrived, and the group had congregated in the front yard. Together, Regis, four of his officers, Belial, Virgil, and I made our way up the path, to where the dark, tarp-covered lighthouse lay in wait.

When we arrived, we found Hull standing in the doorway, his back propped against the wooden arch and his feet pressed against the opposing side. In his hand he held a slender, aged envelope, one that he kept tapping against his palm. He glanced over at our group with a smirk on his face and a glint burning in his eyes.

"Glad you all could make it. Now, if we may begin." He gestured into the doorway, then moved through to grant us access. We passed through to find the body of Ruth Virgil had been tampered with. Instead of wearing the bloody white dress, she now wear a lilac-colored dress, her hair pressed back, no blood visible on her skin. Her hands were clasped on her breasts, her eyes were closed, and her mouth was no longer twisted in a horrible tear but rather curved in a slight smile.

"Did you do this?" Regis exclaimed, his tone frantic.

"Have no fear, Inspector. I have in no way altered the body to where it affects the case. In fact, the body will prove to have no importance besides being the catalyst for our investigation," Hull said as he stepped around the body, then turned to face us.

"Go on, then," Regis said with a slight nod.

Hull smiled. "1872. A large storm sweeps into San Francisco Bay, and one boat is lost, the *S.S. Anna*. The ship went missing with only its captain onboard, Sir Francis Belial. In actuality, Mr. Belial took his boat up along the coast of California and eventually arrived at a point between the Siuslaw Bay and the Yachats River estuary. It was here that he met Mr. Frank Virgil, a local seaman who had taken up residence on a cliffside by the coast.

"Belial and Virgil became good friends quickly, and started a small business among themselves. They were able to find a surprising amount of gold in the poorly-searched mountains near the coast, and with this gold, they made themselves a substantial amount of money. They elected to keep the money, continue to build on it, so that one day their families would be able to bask in their fortunes and not work another day. The money they collected, bills by the hundreds, receipts that would be eligible at banks for years to come, were all placed in a location only the two men knew of.

"The men coexisted peacefully until Virgil fell deathly ill with a horrendous strand of tuberculosis. This was in 1892. In just a few short weeks, construction of a mighty lighthouse would begin on Virgil's property, titled Heceta Head. Virgil's dying request, to his oldest daughter, Isabel, was for her to hide the money within the lighthouse and retrieve it once Belial had passed on. Virgil passed unto her the envelope, and she soon hid it within the incomplete structure of the lighthouse.

"Belial was aware of the actions Virgil had taken against him, and as such, he sought to receive all of the fortune. Knowing he would be unsuccessful without assistance from Virgil's daughter, he had his son begin a very archaic method of winning the woman's heart. Unfortunately, Isabel Virgil passed away in 1898, leaving only one member of the Virgil family: young Ruth. She had no knowledge of the fortune, but Belial still sought to find it, and the lighthouse properly belonged to the woman. He ordered his son, Joseph, to pursue her.

"In 1902, a young man by the name of Walter McMullen was working for the trading companies, and his ship took stop at Heceta Head. Young McMullen quickly grew fond of young Virgil, and a relationship soon sparked. Virgil found solace in her new partner, telling him of how Mr. Belial had always watched over her, not in the protective manner, but in one that disturbed her. McMullen's boat, however, was quick to depart, and he bid his love goodbye, saying he would one day return for her.

"That day, unfortunately, never came. Young Virgil would not know, but in 1904, the boat on which McMullen was posted sank off the shore of northeastern Russia. All hands were lost. McMullen would never return to his love. Virgil, however, held out hope. And at the same time, the younger Belial held out hope for winning the affection of the woman, and in doing so, unlocking the lost fortune. His attempts were all unsuccessful, and the elder Belial eventually passed away, the fortune still not found. Joseph Belial swore that he would find the fortune and live on in his father's name.

"October 30th, 1912. Joseph Belial, Ruth Virgil, Margaret Grahn, and Mathew Aslinger all set sail on the *S.S. Anna* to enjoy the wedding of Grahn and Aslinger. Belial intended to either win Virgil's heart or kill her and find the fortune himself. His attempts were in vain. Virgil would not take his advances, and in the struggle that followed, Belial forced Virgil onto a harpoon his father had used years ago to fish, and killed her instantly. He hid her in one of few compartments he knew of onboard the ship and started a fire in the dining room. The three remaining individuals jumped ship and watched as the *Anna* sunk to the depths.

"Ownership of the lighthouse fell into government hands, until our present Mr. Belial's father was able to obtain the rights just a short thirty years ago. He immediately began plans to deconstruct the lighthouse and find the lost riches. Regulations from the state, however, prevented him from making any action, and he passed away before being able to find the fortune. That responsibility fell to Mr. Morgan Belial, grandson of Joseph Belial. Morgan Belial was fortunate enough to have the state offer to renovate the lighthouse, giving him the perfect opportunity to gain access to the lost fortune.

"Unfortunately, by the time of the deconstruction, the envelope within which the fortune was kept had fallen into the cellar walls below, which required a significant amount of digging to locate. In time, though, I did find it. The amount of money within this envelope would amount to some several million dollars today. Money that will not find its way into Mr. Belial's hands, who has used the preexisting ghost story of the Gray Lady to steer people clear from the lighthouse."

"But what about the body?" I asked.

"That is where our true mastermind comes into play. Mr. Belial did not, in fact, create this entire debacle in order to distract us. The timing of the finding of Ruth Virgil's body was convenient for him. It created a physical enough ghost story to steer tourists away long enough for him to find the treasure. The true mastermind intended to use the ghost story to steer Belial away. And that mastermind, is none other than our own Olivia Virgil."

Everyone turned to see the young woman. Not a word was spoken until Hull elected to continue.

"Miss Olivia Virgil had been long aware of the fortune, but had no interest in finding it for herself. She instead sought to keep the greed of the Belial family from obtaining it. Using the legend of the Gray Lady, she was able to recreate a woman who could bear a passing resemblance to Ruth Virgil, portray her as having been recently murdered, and go through all necessary scientific steps to make the body appear as if it was one hundred years dead.

"In order to truly make the haunting authentic, she had to use her ability to sneak to her advantage. At night, Miss Virgil would sneak into the lighthouse and become a puppet master. She would cut the power using a remote transmitter to interact with the generators, she would dredge around the oil room with heavy boots, and she would create the moaning in the spare room. Miss Virgil sought to bring authorities into the picture to locate the fortune and prevent Belial from obtaining it. To do that, she needed a good murder.

"On our first night here, I had noted another presence. That would have been her. She created the sounds and the circumstances, and when she had us at our weakest, she herself dressed similar to that of the dead body and gave the image of herself flying, then spoke to us, pointing us in the direction of the *Anna*. There, she had placed another body, one that would help point to Belial's guiltiness. She watched from a distance as my companion entered the boat and found the body. Then, when the time came, she arrived and assisted in the doctor's retrieval."

"But what about the boat?" I questioned. "We both saw the boat."

"No, we both believed we saw the boat. But that was impossible."

Regis shook his head. "Absolutely astonishing, Mr. Hull. I can't thank you enough for helping." He glanced at Belial, then at his officers. "Now to figure out what to do with you." With that, the officers and Belial left the lighthouse, leaving only Hull, Virgil, and myself.

"It truly was a clever effort on your part," Hull said, his compliment directed at Virgil. She gave a slight smirk. "Though I do not understand the point in screaming the name 'Rue' at us."

She looked up at him with peered eyes. "You are a very smart man, Sheridan Hull, and for that, I must thank you. But I am afraid you may be mistaken on some parts."

He looked down at her with authentic confusion. "And what parts would those be?"

She cocked her head slightly. "You do not admit to having been even slightly afraid? When the Gray Lady herself told you to search the boat? Or when the good doctor found the Gray Lady's original resting place?"

"Fear is a fault found in those who are weak," Hull snapped back.

"Maybe," Virgil replied with a look down at the body, then towards the door. "But from where I stand, fear is by far the most powerful weapon. When one has lost their resolve to doubt, their strength will topple not long after."

"Very poetic," Hull said as he walked past the woman.

"Didn't you wonder about the circumstances under which the hauntings occurred? The sinking of the ship? The dragging of the foot?" Hull stopped as the woman continued to speak. "The moaning of the woman. And the scream?"

"Clever ruses to deceive the foolish."

She chuckled. "They say Ruth was so lovesick when Walter left. That she would just sit in the spare room of the lighthouse and cry. That some nights she would go up into the optic section and watch, hoping to see his boat on the horizon. But he was never to return. Poor Ruth."

"Indeed."

"You know, only one person ever called her Rue, if I remember correctly."

I felt a short chill go down my spine as Hull glanced up at me. "And who was that?"

"Walter McMullen. He used to call her that in his journals. And when they were together." Virgil walked to stand at the end of the hallway. "I heard rumors that he survived the crash and returned here. But because he had to work for his rite, he did not return until after she had passed. I heard that his leg had been injured, and he walked with a limp."

Hull and I both looked at her, my eyes starting to tremble. She smiled back at us, the smile not lacking sincerity but still managing to horrify me.

"But I suppose those are just stories," she finished. She turned to look down the hallway, which was now completely illuminated. "Though it would have been quite the love story, wouldn't it? If the spirit of the lost sailor were to find his way to the Gray Lady Rue."

Hull stared at the back of her head for a very long time before giving a short nod. "That would be a story, yes." He turned to face me, giving his head a jerk towards the door. Together he and I walked past the body and towards the waiting, open doorway. Just as we were about to exit, Hull stopped and started to turn. "What do you mean he was the only—"

He stopped, the next few words getting caught in his throat. With just a small glance to my side, I could see his eyes were frozen on a spot within the lighthouse, no doubt the hallway, where Miss Virgil had just stood. But I knew that if I continued to turn my head and join him in looking, I would find only an empty hallway, where Miss Virgil had previously stood, but had now vanished from entirely. Only her disappearance could explain Hull's complete lack of vocabulary. Something had happened that he could not explain.

And it no doubt came as a result of having the mastermind of the case, be the hundred-years-dead victim.

MYSTERY AT THE VATICAN

In the short period of time that followed the lighthouse case, I found Hull locked in some sort of inner battle, constantly spending days at a time scribbling away at his chalkboard, only to erase it moments later in a fit of rage. His encounter with the paranormal had most certainly left its mark. It was peculiar, to say the least. Watching the most logical man I know try and figure out the woman's disappearance, when deep down he knew there was no logic to its explanation, was fascinating. Although I believe what he was doing matched the definition of insanity.

There's only so many times you can write down "camouflage cloak" and try to recreate it before you realize your theory is impossible, after all.

Thankfully, now that it had been a full ten days since the case, he seemed to be returning to normal. Or, at least as close to normal as Sheridan Hull could reach. He currently sat in his armchair with his feet propped up on the coffee table and a large, ornately-covered book in his hands. I had my own laptop to my side, one of my more interesting news websites pulled up. Granted, nothing was too interesting on it at the moment. Everything was focused on the presidential election that had only just passed. I can't say politics have ever been high on my list of things I care about.

"Curious," Hull said with his nose in his book.

"Curious what," I replied, my eyes still on the screen.

"Reviewing. Studying."

"For what?"

"Moriarty."

I peered away from my screen to read the spine of his book. It was titled "Ireland: An Extensive History," and looked to be at least a century old. "You think the man behind Chimaera is going to use that book as a reference?"

"Why else call himself Moriarty if not to keep the game in motion and pay homage to some ancient meaning?"

"I still don't understand why he calls himself Moriarty in the first place. Or why we assume he's just 'called' Moriarty. What if that's his actual name?"

"Unlikely."

"Why?"

He raised his brows at me from behind his book, the only thing visible to me being his eyes. "When was the last time you met or heard of someone named Moriarty?"

"I haven't heard of anyone with that name."

"And you think that's simple coincidence? No. That is convenient. And convenience is not coincidence."

"How insightful of you."

"It's a game to him, Walker. A very large, very sophisticated, and very complicated game. My question is, why. Why has he taken an avid interest in me? A man who runs a crime syndicate group would take enough interest to kill me and prevent me from interrupting the flow of his plans, as I have done so often as of late. Yet here we are, alive, and not once has Moriarty done something to harm us without us being on a case, and even then his underlings always seem to fall short."

"He called himself a fan in that letter to you."

"I do not have fans."

"Oh, I wouldn't say that."

He set his book down on his lap, his eyes peered at me. "What do you mean?"

I nodded at my laptop with a smirk. "I publish your cases. You've gained quite a following."

"A what?"

"Fans. People who enjoy hearing about the cases."

"Why would anyone find any interest in reading about solved cases from the past?"

"Because not everyone's like you. You're a... crime junky, and they're just normal people who find entertainment in a good mystery."

He scoffed. "Good mystery. Everything we have done has been simple, once the facts have been properly analyzed. It has been a long time since I could reflect back on a previous case and call it 'good'."

"I also wouldn't say your opinion matters much. I'm not writing them for you, I'm writing them for everyone."

He shook his head and glanced down at his book. After a short moment, however, he glanced back up. "What do they think of me?"

"The occasional remark on your deductive abilities. But most people think you're inconsiderate, since so many people seem to die during your cases."

He brought his book back up and did not say another word. I couldn't keep from chuckling to myself, not at the thought of people dying but at the clear evidence of his ego not being so thoroughly stroked. We sat there in silence for maybe thirty minutes more before the flat phone started ringing. I looked over at Hull and felt no surprise that he hadn't bothered to acknowledge the ringing. I set my laptop down on the coffee table and moved over to where we kept the phone. I didn't recognize the number, mostly because of the format. Whoever was calling, they were most certainly not in North America.

"Hello?" I asked.

"I am attempting to reach Sheridan Hull, is this him?" The voice was an elderly man's.

"This isn't, but I can try to get him for you."

"Yes, please do."

I pressed the phone against my shoulder and glanced at Hull. "It's for you."

"Who."

"May I ask who's calling?"

"Ah, I would prefer to answer that to Mr. Hull. I apologize for the inconvenience," the voice replied.

I rolled my eyes and covered the phone again. "He won't tell me." The detective reluctantly held out his hand, his eyes still locked on his book. Once I'd given it to him, he glanced at the caller ID, narrowed his eyes, and pressed it to his ear.

"This is Hull." The pause that followed was long, meaning the man had stated his name and was presumably now discussing his business. The longer the other voice's monologue went, the more Hull's focus was pulled from his book and towards listening. After two minutes, Hull gave a solemn nod and licked his lips. "I will need to bring my companion, Dr. John Walker, with me." Another slight pause as the voice replied. "Excellent. We will see you then." He clicked the phone off and closed his book.

"Who was that?" I asked as I took the phone and returned it to its holder.

"The Pope."

I rolled my eyes. "No, really, who was it, and where are we going?"

His gaze was still locked forward. "Pope Benedict XVI. And we are going to the Vatican."

"...You're serious?" I said as I took my seat.

"Very. A most pressing matter has risen in the Holy See and the Pope has requested my presence in assisting them."

"So the Pope just.. *called* you and asked for your help."

"Yes."

"I call bullshit."

His eyes finally looked to me. "You can call whatever you would like. I will be departing in the morning for the Vatican, and I would greatly appreciate your presence on the case."

"So we're actually going to just go? To the Vatican? Tomorrow?"

"Why do you waste breath asking such idiotic questions?"

"Because if this is some stupid joke, I'd like to actually go to work rather than miss it, not be able to pay our rent this month, and have that problem to worry about."

"I am certain our hosts will provide substantial compensation if we help them."

"You'd better be right."

"Have I ever steered you wrong?"

I gave him a sideways glance. "And you think I'm the one wasting breath with stupid questions."

*

The flight to Rome, the closest airport, was almost a day long, starting in Portland, Oregon, taking us down to Los Angeles, then all the way across to London. It was the first time I had actually gone to London when not on duty, but of course, there was no time for tourism. Our layover was only two hours, and before long we found ourselves departing from the Rome airport at a little after four in the afternoon... the next day. I enjoyed sleeping on the main flight to London. Hull probably never even blinked.

He had elected to not inform me in regards to the case until we were sitting in the back of a cab heading to the Hotel Alimandi Vaticano. At first I didn't believe him when he explained the case, but I also had found it difficult to believe that the leader of the Catholic church had called our flat to talk with some random consulting detective. Things made much more sense after his explanation.

"Approximately four days ago, Archbishop Victorius Judas was reported as missing by his fellow members of the church. The first two days since then were dedicated to searching for him within the boundaries of the Vatican. They had no luck. On the third day, the Pope contacted an 'old friend' of his, Malcolm Hull, to receive assistance. Of course, Malcolm referred him to me. They do not know what happened to Judas, and they are relatively unable to make any accurate guesses. His disappearance has caught them all unawares, and the Pope believes he may be in trouble."

"Why does he think that?"

"There have been talks within the College of Cardinals about significant misconduct from several archbishops. There is no evidence to support their claims, but several of the cardinals have taken very strong stances against certain archbishops, Judas included. The Pope would not like to believe that his own Holy men would perform such sinful acts on each other, but he cannot find any other plausible explanation for Judas' vanishing."

"And so you're being called in to play greyhound."

"On the contrary, I believe this may be a case of significant importance. With the conflict rising in the College, authoritative figures within the church have been coming to the Holy See from across the globe. Many believe a papal conclave will be called to session, not for its usual purpose of electing a new pope but rather for the purpose of dissolving this conflict. Imagine over five thousand of the world's bishops, archbishops, cardinals, and other religiously significant individuals gathered in one building, and when only one person absent is enough to suspend progress within the conclave, one archbishop goes missing."

"So it really is a mad hunt to find him."

"Precisely. And his vanishing does not come without interest. For the Pope to have placed a call to us when it was nearing eleven at night for him means that he is certainly worried. I cannot say I avidly follow the ongoings of the Catholic church, but I can say that if an issue exists, the Pope has made a wise choice in hiring a private consulting detective to find an archbishop who may very well have gone missing by the hand of a fellow colleague."

"Because if you find him and figure things out, he'll trust you to keep silent about it rather than cause more flak for the church."

"Precisely."

"And you won't say a word, even if it's the largest conspiracy in the history of the Catholic church?"

"Why should I? Their business is hardly my own. I am merely here to find a missing archbishop."

I glanced out the window at the passing buildings before giving a response. I will admit, usually I am not one to find beauty in structures, but something about the Italian architecture was visually pleasing. The buildings were so pristine and well-crafted that it felt like I was driving in some kind of movie-created set rather than an actual place. "So once we drop everything off at the hotel, where do we go?"

"St. Peter's Basilica. The Pope wishes to speak with us in person so we may learn more about the archbishop. Learn information that may help point us in the right direction." He looked over at me with a slight smirk. "For the time being, you may as well enjoy the vacation. I know I am quite thrilled to be here, since I have never traveled here before and the city itself is filled with such history."

"Thrilled, huh? What if the archbishop's dead?"

"Then we will truly have an interesting case on our hands, and the thrill level will be significantly increased."

I sighed. "This may be why some of your fans are disturbed by you."

It took about an hour for us to reach our hotel, unload our luggage, and make our way to the Vatican. The hotel was actually very close, but I don't think there are any actual hotels within the perimeters of the city. Immediately, we could see the lights of the basilica as we were escorted into the city, directly to St. Peter's Square.

The building itself was a marvelous sight to behold. Large pillars for the entryway, statues lining the rooftop. Everything about it was so serene and peaceful. It made sense how someone could find a spiritual connection in this place. Hull and I were led up the steps and into the building, then back into a separate area that looked very out of place in comparison to the rest of the structure. The room we sat in was a meeting room of sorts, presumably used when official delegates came to visit the Pope.

After only a few minutes of waiting, the door at the back of the room opened to admit the elderly man. He looked far less impressive than normal, but I had only seen him in pictures and videos from religious celebrations before. Now, he wore very standard evening clothes, a white robe that no doubt doubled as a nightgown. His eyes were sullen but he smiled when he saw us and shook our hands with frail fingers.

"Such a pleasure to meet you gentlemen," the man said as he took our hands, the hint of a German accent sneaking through.

"Likewise," Hull said with a firm shake.

"And the companion doctor, John Walker, of course," the Pope said as he took my hand. I must admit, shaking the aged hand of the head of the Catholic church was somewhat exhilarating. It was like meeting a celebrity for many people, even if you weren't a fan of them. You still felt excited because almost everyone knew the person, and you were shaking their hand at that very moment. After that, the man took his seat, with Hull and me sitting at adjacent sides. The elder cleared his throat.

"There is not much I can say about Archbishop Judas that will be beneficial, but I believe a summary of his life prior to his appointing may assist you in ways I cannot fathom. He was born in 1965 in Tuscany to a family of wealthy, devout Catholics. He was largely religious throughout his younger years, and upon completing secondary school, he began a mission tour to many locations. His first stop was in the United States.

"I do not know much of his escapade there, but I know he worked for a small corporation as a human resources supervisor in New York. He spent two years there, then moved to Britain, where he spent another two years as a cab driver. After that, he relocated to Germany, where he found a fascination studying the histories of different religions, how they had spread, and how they had developed since. He remained in Germany for almost four years before departing for Russia.

"His activities in Russia are, unfortunately, unknown to us. We only know that he spent five years there, cut off from civilization. We believe he spent those years in a northern town that we have never been told the name of. He reentered the world of civilization in 1996, when he lived in the capital of India for a year before traveling through Romania, Croatia, and Greece before returning to Italy and beginning his time officially with the church.

"I cannot say anything substantial in regards to him other than this. I know that in Romania, he met a young woman whom he has not seen since. In Croatia, he made a small group of friends, who he lived with. In Greece, he simply explored the ancient Greek ruins before returning. Nothing he has done would warrant his disappearance."

Hull had nodded several times through the Pope's summary, and had even taken to a notepad at one time and listed the different locations Judas had traveled to. Once the Pope was done, Hull clasped his hands and peered his eyes.

"Do you believe it is possible that the Archbishop's disappearance may be a result of a fellow religious individual?" the detective asked.

The Pope's lips seemed to tremble as his eyes surveyed the room before returning to Hull. "This is not to leave this room. I truly do tell you in the utmost confidence. I have not been blind to the growing dissent between the College of Cardinals and certain bishops and archbishops. I have paid great attention to the words of wisdom and disdain spoken by all of those who have expressed their minds. This is not something a man of God *should* do, but as we all know, man is capable of sin, so it is something a man of God *can* do."

"Is there anyone in particular you would suspect of performing this act?" I asked.

He shook his head. "No name reaches my thoughts. No cardinal would be so bold. It is not my place to entertain thoughts of group efforts, especially in this regard. But I truly have no other options to believe. He has not been taken hostage, for we have received no demands of ransom. I can only pray that he has not been killed, as no body has been found in the city limits. An inside job, as one would refer to it, is the most logical option in my mind."

Hull gave a solemn nod. "It is most certainly a logical option, though it may not be the most logical. There is insufficient information, and as such, the doctor and I will need to be able to explore the city without much interruption. We will begin as soon as we can in the morning."

"Of course, I will be able to contact the Inspector General immediately and have two identification cards sent to your place of residence. It will grant you access no matter where you need to go, save for a handful of locations that are far too sacramental to be intruded on by anyone."

"Understandable. We will be at the Alimandi Vaticano, room 1434. I will find the archbishop, but I cannot guarantee the results to be to your liking."

"I would appreciate a high level of confidentiality from you gentlemen while you are here."

"Of course."

With that, Hull stood up and extended his hand, shook the Pope's, and walked towards the door. I gave the man a handshake and followed the detective out to the still-waiting cab. We rode in silence back to the hotel room, where Hull immediately went to work on his laptop with his notepad set to his side. By the time we had returned and settled in, it was past seven in the evening, the sun had set, and the effects of flying between timezones was most certainly setting in. Also, I cannot admit to being a fan of sitting in planes for more than three hours.

"We have found ourselves in the middle of a very interesting mystery, my friend," Hull said as he closed his laptop.

"Find something to help?"

"Some leads. Tidbits of information that may be beneficial tomorrow morning."

"What's tomorrow morning?"

"You and I are going to attend church."

"We are?"

"We are. A very nice location, I would say. The Santa Maria in Transpontina cathedral. If my research has garnered anything of value, it would suggest that we may find something about our missing archbishop while we are there."

"Have you ever attended church?"

He looked shocked. "Of course I have. What do I strike you as, a heathen?"

"Is that to suggest people who don't attend church *are* heathens?"

"Well, with how you put it, I wouldn't be surprised if that was your belief." We both chuckled for a moment before he grabbed his coat from the back of the desk chair and started wrapping himself in it.

"Where are you going?" I asked as he wrapped his scarf.

"Short walk. Shouldn't be long, I would like to get a sense of the area before we depart."

I watched as he slipped a number of items into his pocket from the desk before leaving the hotel room. I sighed as I stretched out on my bed and looked at the TV. I knew my odds of finding something that interested me while still being in Italian were low, but I was willing to give it a shot. I looked around the room for a remote and found it odd that there was none to be used. With an even heavier sigh, I laid my head down on the pillow and let my exhausted mind rest.

*

We were at the church fairly early the next morning, seated about ten pews back on the right of the chapel. The church was filled with people, most wearing very formal attire. In fact, it didn't take long for me to notice that Hull and I were fairly underdressed in comparison to everyone else. Nonetheless, we managed to hide ourselves in the crowd when the service began. I found myself tuning in and out of what was being discussed. I had never been a religious individual, except for my time overseas. There were plenty of times when I begged for mercy from God when bullets were flying over my head.

Unfortunately, certain events can take place in a person's life that make them question the existence of someone allowing so much torment and chaos to happen without intervention.

About an hour into the service, I glanced over to find Hull intently staring at the front. In fact, for the two minutes I stared at him, he did not blink nor adjust his gaze. He was firmly interested in what the preacher was saying.

"And so we turn our focus to the Book of Luke, Chapter 22, Verse 22. 'And truly the Son of man goeth, as it was determined: but woe unto that man by whom he is betrayed!' To betray is to—"

"See that group of young men, just to the side of the altar?" Hull asked in a hushed voice.

I glanced to the side of the preacher, my eyes falling on a group of eight or so men in black robes. "Yes. Please tell me you're not about to make a—"

"That is disgusting. No, I have something else in mind."

"What?"

"You'll see."

He fell silent for another hour or so. While he was silent, I watched him as his eyes traveled along the decorated ceiling of the cathedral, then to the back of the room, then back up to the altar. He watched the preacher for a good five minutes before giving a slight nod. As he nodded, a bell rang far above. I glanced around as people starting shifting in their seats before the preacher announced that today's session was finished.

"Tell me, Doctor," Hull said, not yet having moved from his seat. "How do you weed out someone who is not supposed to be present, yet has been ordered to do so no matter the circumstances?"

"I don't know, how?"

"Simple. You remove everyone who *is* supposed to be present."

I watched as he pulled out a slender, black object from his pocket. It only took me a second to realize it was the television remote from the hotel room. "What's that for?"

"It is the tool with which we shall commit an international felony." His finger hovered over the power button for only a moment before pressing down.

And oh how I wish he hadn't done that.

Immediately, a deafening noise ruptured from far above the altar, followed by the sight of the rear wall of the cathedral crumbling and flying in shrapnel-size pieces towards the crowd of people. The people who had stood started shouting and running for the doors. From a single glance, I could see that nobody had been significantly injured. Hull's eyes, however, were on the front. The preacher and the men in robes had started into the crowd.

All except one, who was still standing near the altar, his gaze carefully avoiding eye contact with anyone else.

"There's our man," Hull said as he pushed his way through the crowd. I followed behind him carefully, keeping one hand on his shoulder so as to not lose him. The majority of the people had managed to evacuate by the time we reached the young man. He looked to be about twenty years old, with combed, brown hair and significant stubble. He gave Hull a quick, nervous glance before looking away. I could tell he was guilty, but what surprised me more was his complete lack of shock at the explosion.

Even I hadn't fully recovered from that.

"Shouldn't you be evacuating with everyone else?" Hull asked, his head tilted slightly to the side.

The man looked at him with wide eyes before licking his lips. "Ja ću reći ništa."

I furrowed my brow. I knew Italian, and that most certainly wasn't it. If anything, it sounded more Russian. "What did he say?" I asked as I glanced to Hull.

The detective, however, appeared to be just as confused as I was. "I'm not sure. But I doubt he can understand us either." He pulled a pair of handcuffs from his pocket.

"Where did you get those?" I questioned.

"Sir, I am going to need you to come with us," Hull said to the man as he pulled an authentic-enough badge from his pocket.

"And where did you get that?"

As Hull clasped the cuffs on the reluctant man's wrists, he replied. "I believe it's necessary to be prepared for any scenario at any given time." He pushed the man forward gently.

"And the badge?"

The detective opened the badge for me to read, and it took every fiber in my body to keep from bursting out laughing. I lowered my voice to the quietest tone. "Have you ever *read* what that badge says?"

"No one else does, so why should I?"

"But where did you get it?"

"I stole it from a man in Florida."

I bit my finger and closed my eyes for a moment, truly having to snort back laughter. Here we were, evacuating a cathedral that Hull had just half-destroyed, and I was fighting back a giggling fit all because of his official badge. Once we had exited the cathedral and started in the direction of the police station, Hull finally cast me a sideways glance.

"Why? Should I be concerned about it?"

I snorted, still trying to subdue the burst of laughter just dying to emerge. "You should read the badge yourself."

He glanced down at the badge, and I had never seen the man's eyes go so wide. He immediately returned the badge to his pocket and shook his head, blinking a few times as he went. Now I truly couldn't keep from laughing, which drew attention from passersby and our captive.

It's hard not to laugh when your detective friend's fake badge reads Miami Vice Pussy Inspector.

*

It didn't take long for us to reach the Corpo della Gendarmeria dello Stato della Città del Vaticano, or simply put, the Vatican police. Once Hull explained what had happened and why we had a man handcuffed, Hull and I were escorted to the office of Damiano Gatti, the Inspector General, while the handcuffed man was taken to a cell in the back of the facility. Gatti was a tall man, his head bald and his eyes stern. He looked between us from behind glasses and spoke with a heavy Italian accent.

"So let me get this straight. You just knew this man was going to set off an explosion, you waited for him to do it, and then you managed to apprehend him and bring him here?" the man said with a sigh. "You have to see why I find this hard to believe."

"The Pope has hired my companion and me to investigate the missing archbishop," Hull stated, "and I believe firmly that this man has something to do with his disappearance."

"I know why you are here," Gatti retorted. "What I can't figure out is, if you knew an act of terrorism was to be performed, why did you not stop it before he set off the explosion and caused us millions upon millions of euros in damage? As well as the loss of historic, irreparable artwork and architecture?" I cringed when I realized the extent of the damage caused. I suppose having spent so much time in war led you to forget the things that came with culture.

"We had no way of determining who the man was prior to the explosion," Hull said calmly. "To call him out prematurely would have resulted in the partial destruction of the cathedral. I only took the necessary steps to ensure people were already able to evacuate in the event of the cathedral's collapse. Had I interrupted earlier, he would have no doubt set off the explosives early and caused the deaths of dozens."

Gatti gave him a wary glance before nodding. "I'll see your logic, but not for long. What do you expect to get out of him?" He glanced down at a stack of papers. "You told the front officer he doesn't even speak English. How do you plan to get anything out of that?"

"There are many languages understood on an international level, Inspector," Hull shot back as he stood.

Gatti tossed up his hands. "Fine. Interview the man, find out whatever, but don't kill him. We have laws against that, even for people here by order of the Pope." With that, he returned to his paperwork, leaving Hull and me to find the room with the man. Once we'd received directions from an officer outside Gatti's office, we were on our way.

"How did you do it," I said in a low tone as we walked down the halls.

Hull kept his eyes level while he responded. "While on my walk, I observed many different cathedrals, but the Santa Maria in Transpontina was most certainly the one that would be suffering a major calamity, as I first observed on our initial drive to the hotel. Scaffolding was put against the outer rear wall of the cathedral, and when I walked past, there were three men still at work, adding a coat of sealant to the brick wall. I overheard them speaking in the most peculiar language, similar to that of the current captive.

"When the three had left, I quickly climbed the scaffolding and chipped away at the brick, and found a crawlspace that had been filled with explosives, all of them wired to a remote detonator. In the time I had, I was able to direct the detonator to respond to the same signal as the television remote. When the time came, I would trigger the detonation and reveal who they had planted. Why they wanted to cause the explosion, I have not yet figured out. Hopefully our meeting will reveal more information."

"But you triggered it."

"Of course I triggered it."

I felt a lump start to sink in my stomach. "So you really did commit an interna—"

"No, I was a catalyst for a planned explosion. I did not plant the explosives, nor did I intend to use them for mischievous purposes."

"—Practically an act of terrorism—"

"Hardly an act of terrorism, because nobody is terrified. Now shut up, we have to talk to the man."

"But you *blew up a*—"

He grabbed me by the shoulders and gave me a shake. "John, right now that is *completely* insignificant. We will deal with the formalities later."

"Please tell me you aren't going to blow anything else up."

He released my shoulders. "I can't make that promise."

We walked into the room quietly and found the man, hands bound behind his chair. He stared up at us with a mixture of anger and confusion in his eyes. Hull grabbed a free chair, spun it around, and sat in it backwards, resting his chin on his arms and staring forward at the man with peered eyes.

"So," Hull said calmly, his head tilting slightly as he spoke. "I assume you can understand me, or you would not hold such contempt in your eyes upon seeing me. Now we will see if this understanding can be reciprocated. What was the intention of planting the bombs?"

"Ja ću reći ništa," the man shot back.

"Ah yes, the same statement you made earlier. Judging by your repeating it, I would assume you are probably telling me that you will remain silent. Or, you are telling me to kindly leave your presence. Am I correct in these assumptions?"

"Vi ste bagra."

"There is something new. Now, the explosion was not set to cause damage to the structure, else it would have been placed in the floor. Its positioning was to cause a scene. A statement. But from who?"

"Budite tihi, da američki guzica."

"That is where you are wrong, my friend." Hull stood from his chair and moved it to the side. I, having taken another free seat, watched with curiosity as the detective flexed his fingers. "I am not American, in fact. I am British."

Hull spun where he stood, his once-flexed fingers changing to a fist and coming in contact with the man's nose. The chair in which the man sat flew up on its legs and fell over, the man's head smacking into the floor. I stood immediately, looking from Hull to the captive with shock.

"What the Hell did you just do?!" I yelled as I looked around the room.

Hull leaned down. "Speaking the international language." He grabbed the man's shirt sleeves and pulled him upright. Blood had started pouring from his nostrils, and the look of anger that had been in his eyes had now been thoroughly replaced with searing rage. "Now, let's try this again, shall we?" He leaned in close to the man's face. "The explosion was to be a warning, if I am right. The recipient would not be the police, or any minor person. It was not directed at the church entirely... so the explosion was to be a message for the Pope."

"Možete govoriti gluposti."

Hull pushed his nose against the man's and spoke in a language similar to the one spoken by the captive. "Kto vy rabotaete?"

The man chuckled. "Silly man. I do not speak Russian. But you will learn." The man pushed his tongue back into his mouth, then bit down. Within moments, foam was appearing at his mouth. Hull pushed himself away, his nose crinkled in disgust.

"Cyanide," he said as he crossed his arms. "This complicates things."

"What did you say to him? And since when do you know Russian?"

"I knew enough to ask who he was working for, but I believe I already know the answer."

"You do?"

"Yes. We need to speak with Gatti."

*

Once the body had been removed from the room and the general level of chaos had been settled, Gatti brought us back to his office for questioning. It looked bad, I knew that, but Gatti recognized the evidence of cyanide and quickly ruled out our involvement. Still, I could tell the man was not pleased at all with our presence.

"We weren't able to identify him while he was alive," Gatti scolded, "and now we'll have an even more difficult time identifying him while he's dead. He's not from here, so now we have to put out a genetic test call to the rest of the damn continent. This had better be worth your investigation."

"Oh it will be," Hull replied smoothly, his hands clasped in his lap. "What do you intend to do next?"

Gatti gave him a glare. "What do I plan to do? I plan to figure out who the Hell died in my holding room and what correlation he has to an explosion in a church that's several hundred years old. Then I'll get enough paperwork to keep me in this office until the next Pope is elected, and mind you, that may be a very long time."

"I see. I hope you don't mind if my companion and I continue our investigation, then?"

"What say do I have in it?" Gatti snapped. "The Pope has spoken. Go finish your investigation and stop finding your way into the middle of crime scenes. And stop having suspects bite pills and fall out of their chairs." With that, he dismissed us. Once we had exited the building, I gave Hull a slight nudge.

"'Fell out of his chair,' huh? That's the excuse you gave?"

He shrugged. "They have no security cameras. There was no way to tell whether I was lying or not."

"I see. Now, you think you know who was behind the explosion?"

"Oh, I do not think. I know exactly who it is."

I sighed. "Of course you do. And who is it?"

He stopped. We now stood in St. Peter's Square, with a sizable crowd in motion around us and fire crews over near the cathedral we had been in just hours ago. Hull looked from the cathedral to the main basilica and gave a nod. "Someone who is supposed to be missing."

"The archbishop?"

"Observe. An individual who is vital to the progress of an important meeting goes missing, yet all of the individuals who would be suspected of having been involved would not make such a move because they are also vouching for progress. None of the cardinals could have abducted him, else their own time would have been wasted in the eventual wait, search, and replacement process. Logic would dictate that the man is not so much missing as he is simply not wanting to be found."

"Judas is behind his own disappearance?"

"Precisely."

"But why?"

Hull breathed in deeply and held it before exhaling slowly through his nose. "That is what we must find out. One thing is certain, though. This case is going to prove very, very interesting indeed." With that, he started forward towards the basilica, with me in tow.

*

Veronica Daemon watched as Sheridan Hull and John Walker started their walk towards St. Peter's Basilica. Only one screen was dedicated to them. The rest were displaying maps and tactical readouts of any and all information in regards to the Vatican. She toggled the controls for the camera, having it pause as Dr. Walker glanced back. She then carefully zoomed in, not too close to sacrifice quality, but close enough to get a good visual. He was a very handsome man, and she had enjoyed her time spent with him.

Unfortunately, the circumstances in which they found themselves made it almost impossible for her to consider anything besides his attractiveness. After all, his accomplice was her employer's most valuable target.

"Is the PHE-1 ready for usage."

Daemon zoomed out to a normal view when Moriarty's voice pierced the silence. "Yes, Sir."

"Good. Prepare it for deployment. We will be needing it very soon."

"Yes, Sir."

"Veronica."

She turned in her seat to glance back into the darkness from where the voice resonated. "Yes, Sir?"

"Keep your emotions in check. Do not fall victim to them."

She felt her cheeks start to burn as she turned. "Of course, Sir."

*

"And it came to pass after forty years, that Absalom said unto the king, I pray thee, let me go and pay my vow, which I have vowed unto the Lord, in Hebron." - 2 Samuel 15:7

TROUBLE AT THE VATICAN

We had only been in the Vatican for three days, and yet we had managed to cause more panic than I thought possible. With the "act of terrorism" on a cathedral just five hundred meters from St. Peter's Basilica, security had been significantly increased for nearly all of Rome, making our endeavors all the more difficult. Still, the Pope's clearance was enough to get us in to most locations, so long as they were within the boundaries of the Vatican. If we moved outside of those borders, though, we were at the whim of Rome's police force.

Just yesterday, everything had taken its turn, too. Hull and I had spent the evening poking around the Basilica, and even now I wasn't quite sure why. After that we had gone to see Gatti one more time to receive an information update. Nothing had been garnered about the man whom we had caught within the cathedral, but Gatti had noted that evidence had been found linking the man to the explosives that had reduced the rear wall of Santa Maria in Transpontina to rubble. That was reassuring, I suppose. It meant Hull and I were less likely to be held accountable.

Now, he and I found ourselves at the doorway to the home of Victorius Judas, our missing archbishop. Gatti had been able to grant us a key without police escort. I wasn't sure what Hull expected to find here, but then again, I'd learned to expect Hull to find everything I, or any other person, could never find. I watched as Hull stooped down to examine the lock, then pulled out a long metal wire and started twisting it.

"You know we have a key, right?" I told him as I watched him start creating teeth for the makeshift key.

"There's no fun in doing things the standard way," he replied as he tightened the metal.

"Can you even pick a lock?"

"Of course I can pick a lock."

He slowly slid the wiring into the lock and turned. I watched with mild satisfaction as the lock resisted and made no resounding click. He pulled his makeshift key out and started retightening it.

"You're sure you can pick a lock."

"Anyone with a competent mind can pick a lock."

He pushed the key back into the lock, only to have it resist once more. He pulled the metal free, but had too much of a tilt to his tug and ended up snapping the metal, leaving half of his makeshift key still in the lock.

"Ah. Well, that complicates things."

I leaned down to look at the lock, then gave a shake of my head. "'Anyone can pick a lock.'"

"Don't mock me."

I pulled my wallet from my back pocket and grabbed a gift card, then proceeded to slide it into the space between the door and the frame and thrust it down. Instantly I heard the click of the lock being pressed back into its place and the door opening. I gave the door a slight push and stood back. Hull licked his lips before entering the room, with me in tow and chuckling all the way.

We found a home that looked to have had its occupants rudely uprooted. Papers were strewn across the floor, furniture had been upended, even some of the lights looked to have been smashed. A sofa had been overturned and covered a hearth, the kitchen was an absolute mess, and the dining table had been cracked in two. A small staircase moved up to the second floor directly ahead of us, and a smashed wooden chair lay at the foot of the case.

"How quaint," Hull commented as he stepped over a shattered picture frame. "Judas did not help in the removal of his possessions, that much is clear. Whoever did it for him was very sloppy, not bothering to grab personal mementos and instead focusing on what would be seen as vital to their operations. All of these pictures," he glanced down, "show him on his trips. He would never have left them behind."

I glanced down at the picture, seeing the man for the first time. He looked to be in his mid-forties, with a yellowish-blonde hue to his hair and beard. He was both smiling and squinting at whoever was taking the photograph, with a large, snow-capped mountain behind him. Hull carefully pulled the picture from the broken frame, folded it carefully, and tucked it away inside his coat.

"I can handle down here. See if there is anything of interest upstairs," he said as he moved toward the nearest desk. I hopped my way up the stairs and found only two doorways, one leading to a bathroom and the other to a cramped bedroom. I was surprised to find a half-packed suitcase, mostly filled with clothes but also containing some crumpled sheets of paper. I unfolded one and gave it a careful look. It wasn't something I recognized, but it did seem familiar. It looked to be a very straight-edged C with an outline, possibly shaded where the letter wasn't present. This was, of course, a pencil sketch, so it was lacking color.

I tucked the paper into my pocket and searched the rest of the suitcase, but nothing else was of interest. The room had been efficiently cleansed of anything that could be helpful, so after about five minutes of searching, I started towards the bathroom. This too was fairly empty, except for a toothpaste bottle that had been squirted and smeared across the mirror. I ran a finger across the mirror, finding that the paste was hardened to the point where it cracked and fell in shards. I grabbed a ripped towel from the nearby rack and ran it along the entirety of the mirror. The toothpaste crumbled to the counter and sink, revealing a very smudged mirror and my own reflection.

Something didn't feel right about the mirror. I couldn't imagine why someone would smear toothpaste over the glass, but I had a feeling there was more to it. I tugged slightly at the side of the mirror and found that it in fact opened. I let the glass hover out enough so that I could see the contents, and was shocked to find it filled with empty prescription drug bottles. Not just a handful of them; several dozen. Little orange bottles piled upon each other. I gave the cabinet a leery glance before closing it and heading for the stairs.

When I reached the first floor, I found Hull crouched by the hearth, the sofa returned to its legs. His head was currently inside the fireplace, his fingers delicately prodding the ashes.

"Still hot," he said, no doubt hearing my footsteps. "Most of them were documents, but there were a few pictures. The pile of contents had to stretch to the top of the hearth, and there were folders with tough covers. Their contents took longer to burn and the metal rings are still present." He stood from the hearth and glanced around the room before focusing on me. "Find anything?"

"A bathroom cabinet full of empty pill bottles and this," I said as I unfolded the paper. He looked it over briefly before nodding.

"Familiar."

"My thoughts exactly. What did you find?"

He raised his chin. "Over the past ten days, five people, excluding us, have been here. One was no doubt Judas, as he would have been the one to use the telephone on the wall, but his departure was rushed, explaining why the phone was off its hook. Three more were sent to clean the location up and begin the purging of the documents. A fifth was sent to extinguish the fire and make one last check of the premise." He pointed back to the hearth. "Most of the top layer was damp, but the fool only sprinkled the ashes. Hardly enough to extinguish."

He moved over to the desk and showed a small pile of papers. "These were left not because of their lack of value but because of oversight. Each of them documents business ventures done by Judas on his trips. One of them was far more interesting than the rest." He handed me the top sheet. It was a ledger, of sorts, documenting different personal purchases made in different locations. "Observe his travel pattern."

I read the different locations. "Phoenix, Arizona... Los Angeles, California... Newfield?"

Hull nodded. "Quite some time spent there, too. Three months. I find that quite curious."

"What about the other papers?"

"Just some things I believe may assist us," he said as he picked them up. He looked around the room and licked his lips. "Not much to use for our advantage, though. I think we can confirm that Judas did not vanish on someone else's accord. He ensured his own disappearance, and whoever he is working with cleaned the home of anything that could be a risk."

"Who do you think he's working with?"

"I don't know. But the man we caught at the cathedral was with them. As were the men placing the explosives."

"Russians?"

"Can't be. The man laughed at me when I tried to communicate with him. And I cannot say I recognize the language."

"So where do we go from here?"

"I need you to return to the police station, see if they have identified the man. Our progress rides on that."

"What about you?"

"I am going to take another look at the cathedral. Maybe find more information about the accomplices to Judas."

"Alright. Where do we meet up when we're done?"

"The hotel. If I am not there when you return, take these." He handed me the papers. "Find what you can that is important in those. Why he was in Newfield for so long. Where he could have found his new allies."

With that, we left the house, making sure to close the door and use the actual key to lock it when we were done. I started in the direction of the police station while Hull moved off in the shadows of the buildings towards the cathedral.

*

Hull stood at the edge of the police tape, his eyes locked forward at the open doors to the Santa Maria in Transpontina cathedral, which was currently occupied by firefighters. One officer stood on the other side of the tape, hands on his hips and head shaking.

"I'm sorry, Sir, but I can't let you through. Inspector General's orders," the officer said.

Hull flashed the badge he'd received from the church. "I have clearance from the Pope. That should overrule any existing order."

The man shook his head again. "I'm sorry, Sir. The entire structure isn't faring well. They don't know how stable it is and we want to keep anyone from being injured if it does collapse."

"Fine," Hull said with a sigh as he turned away. This was unsettling, and kept him from continuing. He had wanted to gain access to the area where the men had planted the explosives, hoping to find some kind of foreign item or any trace of the explosive. Anything had the potential to be helpful, and the closer he came to identifying the language spoken by the men, the closer he came to learning why Judas had gone into hiding.

He took three steps forward and stopped. The nagging sensation at the back of his neck had yet to cease, and it wasn't caused by the police officer behind him. It was someone else, someone nearby, who was watching him. He had always been able to just *feel* when someone had their eyes, and their attention, focused on him. He glanced around and quickly found his target.

There was a man leaning against a nearby wall, his hat tucked low to hide his face but his eyes glowing from his cigarette. He wore a black suit and tie, dress pants, and shoes that were so deep a black they seemed to be purple. He watched Hull with unblinking eyes, and despite having a cigarette hanging from his mouth, he still managed to have a smirk. Hull looked over the man once more before feeling a creeping sensation.

Black hair, hidden beneath hat. Gaunt face, illuminated by cigarette light. Dark eyes, full suit. Hand.

He looked down to find a long, slender glove hiding the man's right hand, with the left being completely bare.

Ross McNair.

He approached the man slowly, not moving in a manner that would be threatening. He was almost certain it was the same man he had met in August, during the case regarding the magician. The nose had the same crook, the eyes had the same slant, and the sneer was undoubtedly the same curve. Hull stopped when he was within a meter of the man.

"Long way from home," he commented.

The man used his gloved hand to remove the cigarette. "That can be said for the both of us."

Hull gave a side-nod. "Fair enough. But what is a political liaison from Newfield, Oregon doing across the road from a bombed cathedral in Rome?"

McNair scoffed. "Liaison. Those fools in Newfield wouldn't recognize a liaison if he slapped them in the face and pulled the rug out from underneath them. The whole lot of them, idiots." He extended his free hand. "You can call me Xaphon."

"Xaphon?" Hull repeated, not making any motion to accept the man's hand.

"Just one of many names. Have to be versatile in my line of work, after all." He kept his hand up.

"And what line of work would that be?"

He lifted his chin with his mouth slightly ajar, his tongue visibly running along the tips of his teeth. He brought his free hand back and removed his hat, letting it fall to the ground. He ran his fingers through his slick hair before biting down on nothing. "You and I both know the answer to that."

"Ah. So Chimaera is involved here, then."

"Chimaera is involved everywhere." He gestured to the road. "There's someone waiting for you, just a few doors down. He's been wanting to meet with you for a very long time."

Hull looked down the road, feeling a slight chill slowly spindle its way down his spine. He knew exactly who waited for him, just a few doors down. Whether he was prepared for a face-to-face meeting was another matter entirely. He looked back at McNair, or Xaphon, as he seemed to prefer, and nodded. The man pushed himself away from the wall and started forward. They only walked about twenty meters before he stopped and gestured at the black door to his right. Hull moved to it slowly, pushing it open and finding himself facing a dark room. He took three steps in and flinched when he heard the definitive slam of the door behind him.

His eyes had a difficult time adjusting, as the room was unnaturally dark, but once they had, he could see it was a large room, wooden floors, a podium at the far end, and a cross on the opposing wall. The darkness vanished, however, as soon as a bright blue light shot up from the center of the room. He watched with unyielding eyes as the light took shape, eventually becoming the three-dimensional image of a person, clad in a cloak and face completely hidden. The figure stood facing Hull, his hands clasped on the metal ball top of a slender cane.

"Sheridan Hull. An absolute pleasure to finally meet you. I was worried we would be forever locked in a game of cat and mouse," the figure said, his voice having a metallic tinge to it. Hull glanced at the transmitting feed at the man's feet, then back up to him.

"Moriarty."

"Are you impressed?"

"With you?"

The man gave a hoarse chuckle. His voice was as sinister as it had seemed over the phone. "With everything. Because I am. In fact, this piece of technology here," he said as he tapped in the direction of the transmitter with his cane, "is most impressive to me. Developed by Xaphon, of course. Our technological and strategic genius." He cleared his throat. "A portable holographic emitter. Similar to something you would see in a science fiction movie, brought to life. Absolutely marvelous. Allowing me to speak with you, like this, even when we are continents apart."

"How innovative."

"Isn't it?"

"Your presence here would be unnerving..."

"If...?"

"If I were a man to be unnerved. I am not. Your presence here indicates activity from Chimaera, and given the circumstances, I feel comfortable in deducing that Archbishop Victorius Judas is one of your operatives. You have a knack for placing your agents in high places."

"Don't I?"

"Why you would elect to speak with me like this, however, escapes me. I do not require your petty clues to keep the game going for your sake. I know enough about Judas to be able to build a substantial case and locate him on my own."

"Do you now?"

"Yes."

"Feel free to fill me in, then."

Hull hesitated, but knew that whatever he said, Moriarty would no doubt already know. Plus, there was a certain sense of excitement building in him at speaking to someone who had been nothing but a ghost with a voice for so long. "Judas traveled the world before attaining his position, which Chimaera no doubt assisted in. He became one of yours when he visited Newfield, and has been faithful since, or so I can assume. Somewhere in his travels through Asia and eastern Europe, he became allies with a group, whom you no doubt assimilated, and now he works from the Vatican."

"What makes you think he works for me?"

"Your insignia. Dr. Walker found a sketch of it inside Judas' home, and I recognized it as the same symbol etched into a pin that was worn by Kyle Richy. A red letter C, softly outlined, with a golden-irised eye in the center. A reference to a lion, no doubt, since a mythological chimaera had the head of one."

Moriarty nodded. "Your observations continue to impress. But where do you plan to go from here? I can't imagine Judas' men left much for you at his home, and the good doctor will more than likely find that they have yet to identify the man who killed himself to protect his information."

Hull repressed the concern that grew at seeing just how much the man knew. "Judas is hiding here, in the city, and it will only be a matter of time before we find him."

"I'm counting on it. In fact, that is why we are speaking." The hologram took several steps to the side, his arms stretching out to place the cane on an invisible surface. His hands returned with what looked like a folder, his hood focused on its contents. "Victorius Judas was a valuable asset, but he has made himself into an unnecessary liability. The men you call allies, the ones you believe we assimilated, are in fact his own hired hands, thugs brought in from another country to help him with his new plans."

"And those plans are?"

"You tell me, Detective. Judas has become far too independent. He no longer operates under Chimaera's wing. In fact, his newfound independence is precisely why I am here. I know you were requested by the Pope to locate him, and I know the Pope assumes someone within the College of Cardinals is behind his disappearance. I have no doubt you didn't believe that for a second, and thus focused yourself on simply finding the archbishop. I want you to find him."

"Oh really."

"I do. When Chimaera's assets become liabilities, they must be dealt with accordingly. From where I stand, we can both benefit from his capture. Find him, turn him in, do whatever it takes to bring him to justice, and you will do me a great service. But of course, when I say that, it no doubt encourages you to leave the country. Why help me?"

"My thoughts exactly."

"Well, just imagine you aren't. Because Judas is powerful. His influence is strong with his followers. They are not religious, though. Purely a business venture, or perhaps more. His personal ventures were not of my concern. Judas was with Chimaera for a considerable amount of time, and for him to depart and feel safe in doing so means he is a threat to everyone near him." He walked back to stand above the emitter. "And he just so happens to be in the heart of the Catholic religion."

"I will find him on my own terms, not yours."

"For just a moment, consider that Chimaera is not your enemy. Because we aren't, Sheridan. You know that as well as I do."

"You are a criminal organization bent on chaos. You are the definition of my enemy."

"We are focused on *order*. Our means may be different, but our end results are the same." He scoffed. "So many believe that a trip is not about the destination but rather the journey. I disagree. The destination you and I seek, Sheridan, is a world that does not live in fear, where the average family does not need to lock its doors and enable its security alarms just for their safety. We seek a world where chaos no longer exists, where order has been established."

"You seek order through chaos. And that is paradoxical."

"Perhaps. Nonetheless, I will let you return to your investigation. And even though you asked otherwise, I will give you some assistance. Judas never worked from home when doing Chimaera business. He operated from a private hostel just five kilometers south of the Vatican. If he isn't there himself, I'm sure you'll find something to assist you in your.. deductions."

Hull turned, noting his shadow on the door as the blue behind him shimmered. "We will see."

"I look forward to hearing from you, Sheridan Hull."

Hull gave a short glance over his shoulder before opening the door and stepping back out into the light.

*

Hull returned to the hotel about an hour after I'd gotten back. He didn't offer much detail on what he'd found while at the cathedral, or if he'd found anything at all. My attempts had been just as successful. Nothing had been found on the man, but the forensics team under Gatti were hard at work trying to find out where he had come from. Once they had a country of origin, finding his identity would be far easier.

"So we're no better off now," I concluded while Hull shuffled through the papers he had gathered earlier.

"Not quite," he said silently, his eyes on the contents of the pages.

"We still have no idea who the guy is and you didn't find anything at the cathedral, or you did and you're holding out on me. Either way, we're no closer to finding Judas."

"Not quite."

"Will you stop repeating that?"

"Here." He turned to me, his finger pressed against the paper. It was another business entry, this one here, in Italy. "The address of the shipment. It's south of the Vatican. One of Judas' hideouts."

"How do you know that?"

Hull paused halfway through his turn back to the desk. "I found mention of it at the cathedral."

"What, something left by one of the workers?"

"I'm not sure. We would be wise to investigate sooner rather than later. We may be timely enough to catch him while he is there and bring this all to an end now." He grabbed his coat and started for the door.

"Hold on," I said as I stood. His hand hovered over the doorknob, a slight shake to it. I stared at the back of his head for a long moment, knowing he was deliberately keeping something hidden. And while it was normal for him to not state all of his observations to me, this was different. This was something else. "What did you really find at the cathedral?"

He glanced back over his shoulder. "Everything I need to assist me."

"I hate it when you answer like that," I shot back as I grabbed my bag and filled it with what we'd collected.

The location he took us to was quite the walk. I know he was aware of exactly how far, but of course he'd neglected to fill me in. We found ourselves at what looked like the door to an apartment complex, but the building had been closed for quite some time due to structural integrity weakness, according to a sign in the nearest window. Hull did a quick glance up and down the street before grabbing and twisting the doorknob. The door wasn't locked, allowing us swift passage to the interior.

The room we entered was less than impressive. A considerable amount of dust had accumulated over everything, that being some furniture, a main desk, some cabinets, and a decorative table to the side. Hull immediately fell to the ground, his nose just inches from the floor and his breathing ceased. I crouched down and took no time to catch what he'd found: faint footprints in the dust, leading towards the door to our left. Together we stood and approached it slowly, my right hand resting on the handle of my pistol.

Hull pushed the door open, the creaking echoing throughout the entire complex. It opened to a lounge of sorts, with furniture arrayed in a semi-circle around a table and an unlit fireplace. The window that held the sign was curtained to our left, and a full-wall coat cabinet was to our right. The footsteps moved in a very inaccurate way, swaying to the window, then to the doorway again, back to the window, to the furniture, to the cabinet, then just vanishing entirely.

"That's no good," I said as I moved over to the furniture. Hull, however, had his attention focused on the cabinet. I glanced over and watched him open it and slide its contents to the side. He knocked once, twice, three times on the wooden back of the cabinet.

"Hollow and an echo. Something is behind this panel," he said as his hands started feeling around the edges of the cabinet. I moved over to the cabinet and found that the cabinet was stuck solid to the wall. I felt around on top of it, only managing to cover my hand in dust. Hull started pushing around on the roof of the cabinet before smirking. "Lever. Flip it and..."

The wooden back of the cabinet slid over into the wall next to it, revealing a dark passageway. I pulled out my phone and activated the screen, then pointed it forward. About two meters ahead, I could dimly see another doorway.

"Do you think he's in there?" I asked as I put my phone away.

"If he is, he'll be expecting us," Hull said as he started forward. "But the footprints would suggest no one is present except for us."

"But the footsteps only led to the cabinet, none left."

"Which means he had another point of exit. The unnecessary movement around that lounge was not to throw someone off but rather Judas gathering items from the room before entering. He had no intention of going back the way he came." We reached the door, and by now, my heart was pounding in my chest. Hull was probably right, but there was always room for error. Especially at a time like now. He slowly turned the knob and pushed the door open. When no shouts or gunfire came, he nodded, and together we entered the next room.

What we found was definitely out of place. It looked to be a tenant's typical room, except the door had been completely boarded up, as had the two windows. Pushed against the opposite wall was a large desk, and on it were two computer screens, both of them blank. Several other desks were arranged around the room, most of them covered in different books, textbooks, notebooks, and other things that would be expected in a college professor's office rather than a religious leader's. To the left of the main desk was indeed a doorway with no boards, which was how Judas had more than likely left.

Hull moved to the computer first, reaching underneath to find the system's tower and turn it on. I walked around the room and looked at the different books. Sure enough, a few of them were textbooks. The titles were nothing substantial to me, but they fit their owner: "Experiencing the World's Religions," "Living Religions," World Religions: A Historical Approach," and "Eight Theories of Religion." All of the books were spiritually-based, I quickly found. One, however, caught my eye, as it looked to have had an entire section ripped out. It was titled "The Field," and even though it didn't appear to be a religious book, it had certainly offended the owner.

"Password, of course it prompts for a password," Hull snarled as he turned away from the screens. "Everyone needs a bloody password now, don't they."

"Can't be too hard to guess, can it?"

He glanced at me, an inspired gaze in his eyes. "Precisely that, Walker. Now you really are starting to observe rather than simply see." He moved around the room swiftly, doing little spins as he did, no doubt taking in every single book title as he went. He stopped when he reached one table, the one I had yet to see. He picked up the top book and turned it over several times before pointing back at me. "That book, the one with the ripped pages, who is the author?"

I looked down. "Lynne McTaggart."

"Same author as this one," he said as he turned to show me the book. It was titled "The Bond." He opened the book to where an entire section, maybe forty or fifty pages, had been torn. "He is either a very dedicated advocate against her works or he was taking specific pages. Find any other books by her." We set the two down by the computer screen and started our search. Immediately, I found another somewhat-torn book, by the same author and titled "The Intention Experiment."

"Found another," I said as I moved towards the desk.

"As did I," Hull announced from behind me, coming and setting down "What Doctors Don't Tell You." All four of the books had been torn at about the middle, each losing anything from twenty to over sixty pages. Hull looked over the titles of the books, turning them to stand with the spines up. He pushed them over and gave his chin a scratch before nodding. "Arrange them in order of publishing." Together we checked the dates and set them up.

"'What Doctors Don't Tell You,' 'The Field,' 'The Intention Experiment,' and 'The Bond,'" I listed once we'd set them up.

"In Judas' business ledgers, I noticed a frequency to round up. He would never make a business deal that worked without exact change, and he would never receive payments that did not operate in the same manner. Check the number of pages per book remaining," Hull stated as he opened the first book. I opened "The Field" and did the mental math from the two closest pages.

"Thirty-eight pages were removed from this one," I said as I returned it to its spot.

"Sixty from 'Doctors'," he added.

I flipped through "The Bond" and gave a short nod. "Thirty-six from this."

"And sixty-two from this."

The books were returned to their place and my mind was racing. "So.. that would be one hundred and ninety-six. That's not exact."

"No, it's not," Hull said as he moved to the computer. He quickly typed in four characters and watched as the password was confirmed and the computer's programs became visible.

"What was the password?" I asked as he started accessing files.

"Four. The remaining quantity to obtain exactness."

"How did you know that would be it?"

"People always make passwords somewhat relative to them, but also being obscure enough to keep the average person from figuring it out. He chose the spelled out version of the number because it helped appease the inner perfection after he tore the pages from the books. It's just the same with you and your password."

"You don't know my password."

"It was hardly a challenge. The name of your first dog and your high school lunch number."

"How could you *possibly* have worked that out?"

"First, you have it enabled to provide a hint. Second, you have mentioned your dog before, Cody. Third, you keep your old high school identification cards in the same box as your yearbooks and baseball cards."

"What are you doing going through my stuff?"

"We're in."

I looked at the computer screen and found a spinning icon, the same as the one on the sketch from earlier. Now, however, it was three-dimensional and colored. It was a red C with what looked like flames in the red, with smaller red lines as a distant outline. A bright, shimmering eye was in the center, the pupil large and the iris a golden color.

"That's from the sketch, but—"

"Chimaera."

I glanced at Hull. "What?"

"Chimaera. That is their logo. I have seen it before, associated with Chimaera operatives. Like Judas."

I felt my stomach sink. "Judas works for Chimaera?"

"Yes. I had suspected it, but my suspicions are more than confirmed. He *worked* for them. He operates on his own now."

"How can you be sure?"

"Because he left all of his data here, rather than following what I would assume would be standard procedure and clearing the console of all information." He pulled up a video and let it play. Immediately, Judas' face appeared on the screen, far younger than the pictures we'd seen, with the background being that of the room we occupied.

"October 14th. Moriarty has ordered the immediate relocation of the terror cell. He says he needs them for some kind of manual labor project in the states. He won't give me details." I noticed immediately that Judas had an accent that seemed to blend both British English and Italian. "It'll be difficult, but we can manage. We've almost completed the room in the chapel. Hopefully then I can start my own work."

The video ended. Hull brought up the information panel to check the exact timestamp. "1992," the detective said with a frown. "Chimaera couldn't possibly have been around for over twenty years."

"Couldn't it? Wait, how old do we think Moriarty is?"

"Difficult to tell when he goes around wearing a cloak and hood."

"I suppo— wait, how do you know what he wears?"

Hull slowly lifted his head from the screen, a slight tremor of anxiety passing through his eyes. "Irrelevant. There's another video." He pressed play. This one showed Judas' face again, looking older, but it seemed to be even more illuminated.

"I want results, Victorius, not delays," a voice said. I didn't recognize it at first, but the way Hull's eyes narrowed suggested he knew it.

"I apologize, Sir," Judas replied, avoiding eye contact with the camera. "Xaphon has forwarded the schematics to me and construction will begin as soon as we receive the next shipment of supplies." My fears were confirmed. Judas was speaking to Moriarty.

"Don't disappoint me again, Victorius. I want the construct as soon as possible."

"Of course, Sir." The illumination faded, leaving just Judas' face. He glared up into the camera. "And once the Construct is done, I'll make a point to leave you, and Chimaera, behind." The video stopped.

"Construct," Hull repeated, eyes moving around the room.

"Some kind of building? Vehicle?" I suggested.

"Whatever it was, it must have been large, and they must have constructed it in secret. Impossible for something of a vast size to be built here without drawing attention."

"But what could it have been?"

"Anything. But Moriarty wanted it promptly, and he wanted it done..." He brought up the information tab. "Two years ago."

"Are there any other videos?"

He shifted through windows for a moment before shaking his head. "Nothing else noteworthy. Except..." He opened a document titled "ENDGAME?" Listed in the document were dozens, possibly hundreds, of different bulleted points, each being what I can only guess were theories. Judas had no doubt tried to figure out what ENDGAME was, and it was definitely the same ENDGAME that had been referenced in Arthur Knight's notes.

"Do you think ENDGAME was the Construct?"

Hull reached under the desk and deactivated the computer. "I think it may relate to it. But I do not think it was all that ENDGAME entails." He gave a quick glance around the room. "Remember the trouble Moriarty went through to retrieve Knight's journal from our possession? That journal contained individual points regarding ENDGAME. How Knight had been brought onto the job, and how he became involved with the DAGGER initiative. There was never any mention of a Construct, though."

"What did Judas specialize in? If anything?"

"People. His charismatic skills seem to be his strength. We see it at work in these videos, in his ledgers, and here, in the city. Those men who work for him, the foreign ones. His ledgers have no mention of hired hands. They are loyal to him for something."

I looked from the computer to the room, then to Hull. "So where do we go from here?"

"The chapel he referenced in the first video. In the possessions we recovered from his home, I found a map, of sorts. It detailed the Sistine Chapel and specifically highlighted areas that were not in use at all. One of them had been circled. This is where he will have gone, and it is where we will go next."

*

We entered the empty chapel with the permission of Gatti, who said he was extremely close to receiving the data he needed to identify the man, and that when he did learn, he would call Hull. The chapel was empty not by request but by the timing. It was getting late and the sun had most certainly set. Tourists had been cleared out some hours ago. Hull unfolded a piece of paper from my bag and showed its contents to me.

"The chapel. Judging by this.. the room we are looking for should be.." His voice trailed off as he looked to our right. "Should be just through that door." He glanced around the room, eyes going directly to the ceiling. I glanced up, and for just a moment, I forgot the matter at hand and remembered where we were. Michelangelo had certainly created a phenomenal work of art when he'd done the ceiling of the chapel some five hundred years ago.

"It is nice, isn't it," I said, my voice somewhat distant.

"Look at them," Hull noted. "They're marvelous."

"What?" I asked as I followed his gaze.

"Those cameos, covering that tapestry. Fantastic."

Bang.

I fell to the floor as the familiar sound of a gunshot echoed through the chapel. Hull joined me as several more shots rang out above us, one piercing the nearby wooden bench and splintering it. Hull immediately started crawling forward, in the direction he'd pointed to initially. I crawled slowly after him, a continuous echo of gunshots coming from just a meter above our heads. I couldn't even tell where the shots were coming from, only that they were being fired frequently and freely.

We reached the closed doorway and found it conveniently under an arch, giving us a chance to stand and still be out of sight. We both pressed our backs against the arch while he fiddled with the door, eventually breaking the padlock from it and allowing us in. The gunshots ceased as we closed the door behind us. We glanced around the room and quickly found a side table with cupboards. Together we pushed the table in front of the door, hoping it would delay our attackers.

"We need to find his hidden room, check the walls," Hull said as he moved towards the farthest wall. I immediately went in the direction of the only wall-length cabinet in the room. Sure enough, I repeated the steps Hull had taken, first giving it a knock and finding it hollow, then locating the lever on the ceiling of the cabinet. With a flick of the lever, I watched the wooden panel slide out of sight. Hull came up behind me and clasped me on the shoulder. "Well done, Walker."

"They were waiting for us," I said as we entered the narrow chasm.

"Irrelevant."

"No, not irrelevant. If he's in there, he'll have heard us, and either he's running or he's ready to shoot us when we walk in."

"He won't shoot us."

"How do you know?"

He gave me a sneer when we reached the door. "Because he's an archbishop." He pushed the door open. And what we entered to, I most certainly did not expect.

The room matched something you would see in a conspiracy theory movie. It was an office of sorts, with a desk against the wall opposite us and several bookshelves lining the adjacent walls. Everywhere else, however, was either occupied with papers or pictures, most of them connected with white string. The string moved across the room, forming a very intricate web.

"Well now," Hull commented as he carefully kneeled to avoid a set of strings. "This is interesting."

I moved over to one of the walls and started reading the papers. All of them were news snippets, cut from newspapers in multiple languages. I could see English, German, Spanish, Russian, Italian, Greek, and even one that looked to be in Japanese. I quickly realized that all of the articles were in regards to religious leaders of multiple faiths. One article would discuss a Mormon priest, the next a Hindu god. The ones that had strings attached to them, however, were all of one religion: Catholicism.

I followed the strand pinned to the picture of a cardinal, running my hand along it until I reached the opposite wall, where an article discussed the sudden onset of cancer in a cardinal of the Catholic church. The picture next to it showed an elderly man in an elegant robe, which moved to an article describing an American preacher who had been sent to jail for molestation. Another string moved from his article, going to a picture of a young man, also in a priest's suit. His string moved to a group photograph of the College of Cardinals.

"This is just..." I murmured, my eyes looking at the dozens of strings coming from the group photo. "Unreal."

"John."

I turned to see him standing at the wall opposite, his eyes glued to a photo. As I came closer, I saw that it was a picture of the previous Pope, John Paul II. The picture was one I actually recognized, as it came from when he was diagnosed with Parkinson's disease in 2001. Several strings moved from his picture, but Hull was focused on one. We followed it to a nearby article that discussed his ailment, with another string moving to a picture of a young man, long blonde hair, some facial hair, and a bright smile on his face. I would say this young man had the second-most strings attached to his picture.

"Victorius Judas," Hull said with a sigh. I looked at the picture and felt a mental slap. The picture was indeed of a very young Judas, maybe in his late teens.

"What does it mean?"

Hull gulped. "I don't think you require my explanation."

I looked from the picture to the string that led back to John Paul II, then saw the picture above the desk. This one had the most strings attached to it, and one very long one came from Judas' picture. I tapped Hull on the shoulder and pointed to the central picture. I knew by the deep exhale that he had predicted who the picture would be of. Bright, white hair. Bagged eyes. Deep wrinkles.

Pope Benedict XVI.

"This isn't good at all," I said with a step closer to the picture.

"The conspiracy theory so many people yearn for," Hull said with a strain to his voice. We stood at the desk now, and only then did we notice the letter. I picked it up carefully and read it aloud.

"'Mr. Agneza. The plans are in effect. We will be abandoning currently-used posts and beginning the first phase of our operation. When we have concluded, we will reconvene at the Zagreb Cathedral. Signed, Mr. Victorius Judas.'"

"Zagreb Cathedral. The tallest building in Zagreb, Croatia," Hull said.

Before I could reply, a loud buzzing started from Hull's pocket. He pulled out his phone to find an incoming call. He activated the phone and held it close between our faces.

"Yes?" Hull asked.

"Hull, this is Gatti. We have a positive identification on the man. He comes from—"

"Croatia."

Hull and I turned to see six men aiming large rifles at us and one man standing in the center with his hands clasped behind his back. He wore a black cloak that reached the ground with the hood down. His golden-blonde hair reached his shoulders and his beard was very well-kept. We found ourselves face-to-face with Victorius Judas.

"Yes," Hull said as he ended the call and pocketed his phone. "Croatia."

*

"The desert owl and screech owl will possess it; the great owl and the raven will nest there. God will stretch out over Edom the measuring line of chaos and the plumb line of desolation." - Isaiah 34:11

CHAOS AT THE VATICAN

"I will give you gentlemen credit," Judas said as he stared us down, his eyes narrow and his lips pursed when he didn't speak. "I was at first puzzled. Why would the Pope call in an American detective to find me? Was he truly so desperate? But I see I underestimated him, as well as you both."

"I have that effect on people," Hull said, eyes locked on Judas. My eyes, however, were moving from Judas to the armed men. Croatians, apparently.

"Going to my home, I expected that, but going to the hostel?" The archbishop made a *tsk* noise as he shook his head. "Someone had to have informed you. I never made mention of the hostel, except when doing my private research or communicating directly with him."

"I was duly informed of its location, yes." I glanced at Hull with curiosity, not entirely sure who could have informed him of anything in the time we had been here. But I also remembered his wariness to inform me of what he really did when he traveled to the cathedral.

"Find anything of interest?" Judas asked.

"Only what we need."

"And what do you need?"

"Nothing, anymore."

Judas turned his head to the side, giving Hull a longways look. "I researched you as well, Mr. Sheridan Hull. Renowned detective in Newfield, no doubt. I remember visiting there. That would have been 1985, I would say. How interesting, to think neither of you would have been alive yet."

It was only then that I realized the true scope of Judas' involvement with Chimaera. The video we had watched had been dated in 1992. But if he had joined them in 1985, and it had already been a well-established crime syndicate... just how long had Chimaera existed? How long had Moriarty been in charge?

And how old was Moriarty?

"I would say your endeavors in Croatia are far more interesting," Hull commented, his hands moving behind his back. From where the others could see, it looked to be him simply clasping his hands together. But my peripheral vision said otherwise as a small, rectangular object slid down from his sleeve.

"Yes, of course, the clever detective wants to know all of the details," Judas said with a glance at the men accompanying him. "I didn't elect to travel, I was told to. Gather what people I could to be sent back as henchmen, you could say. Croatia just so happened to be my primary recruitment location. The loyalty between me and these men became strong, so naturally they joined me when I... departed from the ranks of Chimaera operatives."

"Understandable. Though for you to depart such an organization takes bravery." Hull's eyes seemed to flash as he spoke. "And extreme confidence in your own plans."

Judas gave a feigned look of surprise. "What, he didn't tell you?" I glanced from the archbishop to Hull, seeing the detective's face give a slight tremor.

"He was just as in the dark as I am."

"Ah, so you are working for him."

"*No.*"

I cast Hull a very concerned look. "Working for who?"

Judas smirked. "You didn't even tell your friendly doctor who gave you the best information to find me?" Another *tsk* noise.

"The friendly doctor did not need to be informed of our source."

"But his look says otherwise."

Hull cautiously glanced over at me, and I knew that my face was splashed with distrust. But I had to trust him in this moment, because with six rifles aimed at us, it could potentially be our last.

"No," I said, much to Hull's happiness. "I didn't need to be informed. Because we have you now." I drew my pistol from its holster and leveled it with Judas' head.

"For a doctor, you seem quite violent."

"And for an archbishop, you don't seem very peace-loving."

Judas chuckled. "Well played, Dr. Walker." He glanced at the men around him before sighing. "As fun as this has been, I do have business to attend to of the utmost importance. Since you gentlemen have already seen my fine arrangement, I feel no fear in telling you that the Catholic church is close to entering a new, revolutionary regime." He looked down at a thin, silver watch on his right wrist. "And it would seem many of the officials are about to step down from their positions." He looked around the room, giving his chin a slight stroke. "Shame we couldn't have met here in the chapel, but the floor needed major renovations. Precisely why I made the renovation request some two weeks ago. Precisely why there were no tourists to be caught in the crossfire of your arrival."

"I had my presumptions," Hull commented.

Judas gave a slight nod. "I'm sure you did." With that, he turned and took a few steps away before pausing and glancing to the Croatian man at his right. "Pričekajte da se vrata zatvoriti, a zatim ih ubiti. Možete ostaviti tijela ovdje. Nitko neće ih naći u sobi." He walked further away and out of sight. The Croatian nodded to the six other soldiers, who all disengaged the safety on their rifles.

"Got any plans to get us out of this one?" I asked as I adjusted my aim to one of the soldiers.

"One or two," Hull replied.

"Tri!" the leader of the men yelled.

"Which one seems more useful?" I questioned.

"The third one."

"You only said you had one or two."

"Dvije!"

"I came up with a third one."

"Now may be a *very* good time to start it."

"*Jedan!*"

Time seemed to slow down as the next sequence of events took place. Hull's hands moved like blurs, his left immediately coming forward and releasing what turned out to be a Bible. The book spun through the air viciously before making contact with the trigger hand of the leader, who lurched back in pain, and accidentally fired three rounds in the process. One round found a home in the leg of another soldier, who doubled over. In the momentary distraction, I fired off two shots, both into the legs of two other soldiers. They each hit the ground, their ability to fight removed.

This left three soldiers who were maybe a second from opening fire, the only cause for their hesitation being our element of surprise. Hull was on top of them, literally. Despite Hull looking completely inept at physical combat, he was capable of extreme movements and attacks. He first started by throwing what looked like ashes from his pockets, causing the men to shield their eyes. In a simple leap and tuck, he was in the air above the three men, his left arm swinging down and grabbing one man by the chin and pulling back as he landed. The man's head smashed into the wall, knocking him unconscious. One soldier started firing at me while the other turned to aim at Hull. I was able to shoot the man's hand and throw his aim off completely while Hull first grabbed the rifle, then the arm, then the torso of his assailant.

My attacker dropped his gun and charged forward, catching me in the chest and forcing me back against the wall. I felt the blunt tops of the tacks used to keep the pictures and strings in place dig into my skin as the man pushed me farther up the wall. My pistol had been knocked clean out of my hand and was now resting on Judas' desk. The Croatian pulled a knife from his belt and brought it back, preparing for a full-on stab into my skull.

A pale hand grabbed the man's arm and wrenched it back, causing the man to lose his grasp on me. He toppled back onto the floor, Hull grabbing the knife as he went. I quickly scrambled to my pistol and checked to ensure I still had three shots before aiming it at the man's head. He scuttled back against the opposite wall, watching us with utter fear in his eyes. All of the others had been incapacitated.

"Knock him out. Our time is short," Hull said as he dropped the knife. I took two steps forward and smashed the butt of my pistol into the man's temple, sending his limp body back against the wall, his head lulling to the side.

"Done," I replied as I holstered my gun. I turned around to find Hull at the archbishop's desk, his eyes scanning for anything that could be useful. I gave the men on the ground a quick glance before joining the detective. "Where does this leave us?"

"He says the church is about to enter a new regime. If his web tells us anything, it's that he plans to assassinate the Pope. But the odds of him being elected would be astronomical. There are over a thousand candidates." He flipped over several papers before reaching what looked like a schematic of the city, with certain areas drawn with green ink. "But where is he heading next..."

"When did you talk to Moriarty?"

"When I traveled to the cathedral. They would not let me in, but one man was there, one I'm sure you will be familiar with. Ross McNair."

"The guy from the magic show?"

"That's the one. He works for Chimaera, operates under the name Xaphon. He took me to a room where a... hologram, I suppose, spoke to me. It was Moriarty."

"What did he say?"

"He said that Judas had gone rogue and was dangerous, and it would be in our best interests if we captured him soon."

I rubbed my forehead slowly. "As much as I hate to say it, he's probably right. If Moriarty thinks Judas is dangerous, we have to catch up with him fast."

"I know. What he said, what he has here. He has something planned. We simply need to figure out what it is." He ran his finger along the green-ink line for a moment before pausing. "I'm... sorry I left you in the dark."

"I know why you did it."

"I hoped you would." He flattened out the map and stood back, no doubt trying to get a different perspective. I looked and found that the green lines would end at very irregular areas. After a while, I realized that these irregulars were when the lines hit the rivers.

"They stop at water. The lines are sewage pipes," I pointed out. He jumped forward and started tracing them.

"Yes, yes! Sewers under the city, pipes stop at the water, cut off to prevent pollution." He ran his finger south before tapping at one point in particular. "Santa Maria in Transpontina."

"The drain would've been underneath the scaffolding outside the back of the cathedral."

"Which explains how they were able to transport heavy explosives without catching the attention of the public. But where else would this lead..." His fingers ran along several paths before stopping. "Oh no."

"What?" I asked as I looked down. He brought his two fingers, which were currently at opposite sides of the map, along a straight path that went directly to the center. I leaned close to read the faint text labeling the building: St. Peter's Basilica.

"He said many of the officials would be stepping down from their positions. But that did not guarantee their removal was voluntary." He tore the map from the desk and started folding it. "He's going to blow up the Basilica."

"But how would he get everyone?"

He started for the door, only responding once we'd checked the next room for waiting attackers. "Papal conclave. A gathering of the highest leaders of the Catholic church, all under one destructible roof to discuss religious politics."

"The papal conclave meets here in the Sistine Chapel, though."

"And they normally would, but remember what Judas said."

I gave a slight inner gasp. "He made a request for renovations. He closed the Chapel."

"Which meant the conclave would have only one other location to meet."

"St. Peter's Basilica."

"And now that he's used the sewers to place the bombs..."

"All it takes is the meeting for him to wipe out the entirety of the Catholic church's leadership, and leave him as the sole survivor."

"When is the conclave meeting?"

He checked the outside before we walked out onto the street. "I haven't a clue. But we need to find out."

*

We returned to the police station to find Gatti angrily expecting us. Hull hanging up on him had not left him happy. It was almost nine when we did. Hull, however, had no intention of wasting time.

"The papal conclave is scheduled to meet, correct?" he asked.

Gatti gave a flustered look. "They are, but what does this—"

"*When?*"

"They're meeting right now." Hull and I exchanged very dark glances. "Why? What happened at the Chapel?"

"Inspector, we need to leave for the Basilica *right now*," Hull asserted as he turned for the door.

"Hold on, *bastardo*," Gatti barked at us. Hull gave him a short glance.

"The entire papal conclave is in danger at this very moment, Inspector, and every second we delay is another second Archbishop Victorius Judas has to detonate a very large tonnage of explosives cached beneath the Basilica and effectively wipe out the leadership of the Catholic church." He charged forward and opened the door, then shot the same glance back. "Now is hardly the time to resort to names."

I watched the detective fly through the door, his coat billowing behind him. I started after him, but Gatti managed to grab me by the arm.

"What does he mean by that? He can't be serious. Not the Basilica," Gatti said, a new tremble added to his voice.

"He's completely serious, Inspector. Judas plans to destroy the Basilica and be the highest-ranking official in the church remaining."

"He's an *archbishop*, not a terrorist! How could he have explosives of that caliber!"

"That man you identified? He's one of many." We started out the door, and I could see Hull moving at a jog towards the Basilica. "Judas has a small militia of Croatian men he's been using. The explosion at the cathedral was caused by them, and you'll find six of them, incapacitated, in a side room hidden in the Sistine Chapel. They've been using the sewers."

"But Judas put in a requisition to— *cazzo*! He made the requisition for repairs in the sewers!"

We'd managed to catch up to Hull when he spoke. "Which means he has been planning this for a very, very long time."

"But *how?*" Gatti grilled.

"You tell me, Inspector General," Hull snapped back, not breaking his stride. "How did a band of men manage to smuggle enough explosives to nearly destroy one cathedral and potentially completely destroy St. Peter's Basilica? How were they able to do this under your *studious* watch?"

"Explosives of that caliber could never have been simply brought here."

"Unless Judas has had adequate time to prepare and the labor force to assemble the explosives here while bringing supplies in to the city piece by piece," I suggested.

"How would he get away with it? If he was the only person left, everyone would be suspicious!"

"Simple," Hull commented. "You'd do the job for him. You already found evidence linking the cathedral explosion to the man, and now you know he is Croatian. A following explosion of a much higher caliber, with more evidence to link it to Croatia, would bring about a demand for justice against the entire country. Dispute would break out and Judas, working alongside his Croatian cohorts, would be able to diffuse the chaos and come out a hero in the public's eyes."

Gatti gave a disgusted cough. "This is the kind of *merda* best left to films and novels, not my city!"

"With any luck, Inspector," Hull said as we rounded a corner into St. Peter's Square, "you won't have to clean up a crater."

The Basilica looked as it had just two evenings ago, when Hull and I had first arrived here to speak with the Pope. Everything still looked as peaceful and serene as before, but now, with the thought of seeing the building in ruins nagging at the top of my thoughts, I felt an acute sense of fear and despair. The building was a cultural and historic icon. For it to potentially be destroyed for a man's personal gain...

The thought was absolutely sickening.

Hull stopped and turned to face Gatti. "Check the perimeter of the building and call for others. Walker and I will go inside and warn everyone."

Gatti gave a short nod and brought his arm forward, presumably to shake Hull's hand. The detective extended his hand. I heard the slap of metal and looked down to see a pistol in Gatti's hand, now being transferred to Hull's.

"Keep the Pope safe," Gatti said before releasing Hull's hand and running off. We watched the man for only a moment before charging in the direction of the Basilica. My blood was racing and heart pumping now, the thought of the floor blowing up underneath our feet giving me an endless supply of energy. We ran up the steps, skipping as many as we could without tripping. We passed through the doors and, using what recollection we could, continued onward towards where we assumed everyone would be convened, that being around the altar.

The main room was large, and it took me a moment to truly gain my bearings. The ceilings were so far up and the pillars so thin it seemed to visually alter the actual height, making it look taller. The altar was much larger than I had imagined, with four black, spiraling pillars holding up an ornate roof. Immediately, I could see hundreds, no, *thousands* of people sitting in seats around the altar, with Pope Benedict XVI seated in the center. All of them wore different-colored robes, presumably to help sort them. From where we were, I could spot red, white, purple, and gray robes.

Our feet made a loud, distinctive echo that soon caught the attention of the conclave, many turning to acknowledge us with disgusted looks on their faces. Once the Pope spotted us, however, he stood, a look of keen interest in his weathered eyes. We sidled our way past the sitting men, but once Hull was halfway to the Pope, he stopped and turned to face the majority of the crowd.

"Everyone needs to evacuate the Basilica immediately!" he yelled, his voice reverberating through the chamber. Many of the individuals just looked at each other, some giving scowls. "*Now!*" This sudden shout jolted a few into action. Hull turned again and raced up the altar to where the Pope waited.

"What's happened? Did you find Judas?" the elder asked.

Hull placed his hand on the man's shoulder and started pushing him gently towards me. "We need to leave now. Everyone inside is in grave danger."

"What danger? What did you find?" By now most of the gathered people had stood and were slowly moving in a mass towards the exit.

"The floor of the Basilica is going to detonate, and if we do not hurry, everyone is at risk of severe injury or worse," Hull warned. The look of fear that crossed the Pope's eyes were indeed a horrific sight to behold.

"Who would ever perform such an appalling act?" he asked as we made our way past the abandoned chairs.

"Your former archbishop. Victorius Judas."

I correct myself. The look of shock that crossed his face *then* was even more horrifying. "But Judas could never—"

BOOM.

Hull, the Pope, and I were thrown forward, our bodies slamming through several chairs. I glanced back to see the altar collapse in on itself, the pillars shattered. I looked around and watched as the ground started to fall away, the walls cracking and giving up, even the ceiling beginning to fracture. Hull threw himself on top of the Pope's limp figure while I struggled to remove a black marble slab from my leg.

BOOM. BOOM.

All around us the floor was exploding, and the cries of pain and terror that came from the thousands of cardinals and bishops were enough to make my heart stop. There was a severe amount of shaking to the room, no doubt caused by the walls that were falling in and crushing everything in their path. I finally freed my leg from the slab and moved over to join Hull, covering what part of the Pope I could. I spared a glance up and watched a large portion of the ceiling start its descent directly toward us.

"*Hull!*" I roared, trying to get his attention. It was no use. The explosions were continuing and the building's implosion was far too loud. I closed my eyes and braced myself for the extreme level of pain that was about to make contact with my back. Our chances of survival were slim. Very slim. When a loud cracking noise came rather than a burst of pain or the expanse of nothingness, I spared another glance and found that the piece had split into two pieces and wedged itself above us, making a tent-like shape. I gave a huge sigh of relief at our fortune.

From where we were, I could see statues in pieces, large slabs of marble and concrete scattered about, and bodies. Those red, white, purple, and gray robes were now found underneath large pieces of the destroyed Basilica. I leaned in as close as I could to Hull's ear before speaking.

"*We need to get out!*" I yelled. He gave a short nod. I wiggled my way from him, forcing myself through the small opening created by the collapsed ceiling. Once I was free, I turned back and extended my arms, grabbing the Pope's shoulders and carefully pulling him out. With Hull guiding the man and my strength, we had him free in seconds. From a quick glance, I could tell he was unconscious, but certainly not dead. Hardly even injured, in fact. The same could not be said for just a few of the men I could see when I turned. The explosion had been set off before anyone had even left the building.

The only positive I could find was that the explosives had been focused around the altar, meaning the farther you were, the less chance there was of you being injured. But when I looked up, an overwhelming sense of dread encompassed me. There was no ceiling anymore. I could clearly see the stars of the sky. A few chunks of the wall had managed to remain, but from a full panoramic view, I could see that the Basilica had been effectively destroyed. Not even a large repair effort would be able to help this atrocity.

"Will he be fine?" Hull asked me, his attention on the Pope. I leaned down and pressed my two fingers against the man's neck and found a slowed, but steady, pulse.

"He'll live. Only unconscious, but at his age, that can be risky."

Hull coughed, no doubt from the heavy cover of dust. "We need to find Judas."

"We need to get *help*," I retorted as we lifted the Pope and started forward. As we walked, I started mentally counting the number of absolutely-dead individuals I could see. By the time we were halfway to the exit, I was too mortified to continue keeping count. Because by then, the number was somewhere around forty. And I had barely scratched the surface on the number of people already dead. As well as the number of people left to die.

*

It took two hours for the police, the fire department, and citizen volunteers to clear out the wreckage of the Basilica as best as we could without additional equipment. The Pope was being taken to the hospital, as well as some several hundred others. A good majority of people had managed to evade any falling slabs, but not everyone had made it out. The tally right now was staggering. By doing a roll call of sorts, a number had been reached. 150 Cardinals, 7 Patriarchs, both of the Major Archbishops, 700 Archbishops, and 300 Bishops were unaccounted for.

In less than two minutes, almost a quarter of the Catholic church's leaders had been killed.

Hull and I now sat on one of the many benches in St. Peter's Square, with me facing the ruins of the Basilica and Hull facing the opposite direction. As I stared forward at the wreckage, I couldn't help but choke back a small tear. To see the remains of what had been such

377

a beautiful, historic, iconic building was heartbreaking. A fire had apparently started in the basements near where the explosions had gone off, and now smoke was rising from the ruins. With the moon shining off to my right, casting a ghostly hue across the remains...

It truly was the worst thing I had seen in a very, very long time.

"Judas could be anywhere by now," I said, breaking a silence that had fallen between Hull and I.

"But he will be close. He would have triggered the explosion himself and watched the destruction unfold. No man as self-confident as him would ever allow someone else to relish in that victory." The detective's voice had a dark tinge to it.

"Where do we even start?"

"Find where he goes from here. Trace him. The police know of his involvement."

"But we have no evidence to tie him to it."

"We will find sufficient evidence."

I turned on the bench, finding a large group of people gathered in the Square, all of them watching with tear-filled eyes as their beloved Basilica was reduced to nothing. There were at least two thousand people gathered. My eyes surveyed the crowd with sadness growing in my stomach. I couldn't even begin to imagine their feelings right now.

"We have to do it soon, Sheridan. We have to catch the person responsible. For them."

Hull sighed. "Were it so easy."

I looked back out at the crowd, the sadness flowing through me. Fathers were holding their wives and children. Elders observed with the most tired looks on their faces. A wave of depression and mourning had fallen over the crowd. The only sounds to be heard were the whimpers of those crying, the crackling of the still-burning fires in the depths of the ruins, and the occasional shouting of the firefighters and search-and-rescue workers.

My eyes continued around the crowd until I reached a blank area, presumably the lane they were keeping clear to allow emergency vehicles through. As my eyesight came into focus, I could see what looked like a man leaning against a far wall, his head bald, his face looking in our direction. The longer I stared at him, the more uneasy I began to feel. After almost a minute, I nudged Hull.

"Someone's watching us," I said with a nod in the man's direction. Hull looked off at him, peering his eyes. After a moment, he stood.

"Come on," he said, a newfound determination in his voice. I stood abruptly and followed him. We moved at a brisk walk at first, quickly closing the gap between us and the man. When we were within fifty meters, he pushed himself from the wall and started running. Hull started forward at a sprint, with me in tow. The man was fast, but we were fueled with adrenaline and a want for justice. The man was able to keep a minimum ten meters between us and him. He rounded several corners before reaching what looked like a bridge.

"*Stop!*" Hull yelled. The man turned to acknowledge us, smirked, then jumped clean off the side of the bridge, plummeting out of sight. Hull and I clamped on to the side of the bridge and looked down. To my surprise, there was a faint outline of a large ferry boat. I could see several figures, all armed, walking around on its top. None of them looked up at us, as if the person we had followed had yet to alert them.

"Plan of attack?" Hull asked.

"Oh, so it's my turn now?"

"Figured I would give you a shot."

"Still have that pistol Gatti gave you?"

"Of course."

"Let me use it. You work better with your fists anyways. We drop down, I take out the two on the deck, you move to the door."

"Perfect." He handed me the gun. "Ready?"

"Let's go."

We dropped without drawing attention, but as soon as our feet hit the deck, the two men turned. I shot one round into the closest man's chest, then a round from the other pistol into the shoulder blade of the far man. Both fell to the ground. I turned to see Hull moving swiftly to the nearest doorway. I pressed my back against the wall while he checked the door.

"Judas will be in the safest part of the ship, of that I have no doubt," the detective said as he grabbed the handle.

"Captain's quarters?" I suggested.

He shook his head. "Boiler room. It'll be guarded, but we have to find him. And when we do get there, we can stop the boat." I nodded in affirmation. He pushed his ear against the door before twisting the handle and pressing forward on the wood. I spun and aimed my pistols forward, finding a man waiting for us. Both of my rounds found a home in his chest. We stepped over his body and entered a main hallway, with many doors leading off to the sides. A map on the wall told us that the hallway led to a stairwell, which was how we would access the boiler room.

Hull led the way, even though I held the guns, his head moving back and forth towards the doors that bordered our path. One door flew open, allowing a bulky enough man to step out, a fairly large assault rifle in his hands. His body swung to aim at Hull, who had leapt up into the air, grabbed the chandelier in the hallway, and used it to swing his feet into the man's chest. The bulk of the man slammed back into the room from where he'd emerged. Hull grabbed the door and slammed it shut, then continued forward.

"You could have taken his gun," I said as we approached the halfway point to the stairwell.

"Me? Use a rifle?" He scoffed. "How uncivilized."

The doors to our left and right burst open, with two men inside each room. I fired off a shot and caught the first man to my left in the eye, and only barely managed to duck and avoid a followup shot from his friend. Hull had rolled into the other room, sweeping his legs to bring both of his assailants down. While down, I watched him kick one in the head, then jump back as the second man lunged for him.

Another bullet round brought me to my senses. I ducked and rolled to my side, immediately bringing the pistols up and firing a random shot, which found a home in the man's hip. He spun backwards, his head slamming into the wall as he went. I stood and turned to find Hull emerge from the room, giving his pants a slight brush.

I offered him one of the pistols. "Still uncivilized?"

He shot me a glare. "Still uncivilized."

As we approached the stairwell, I watched six more gunmen move quickly from the bottom up towards the top, in the direction of the captain's quarters. When Hull and I reached the stairwell, we looked both up and down with hesitancy.

"They were moving to reinforce the upstairs," I said.

"Could be to throw us off," Hull replied.

"Or it could be where Judas is hiding."

He looked down the stairwell wistfully before nodding at the stairwell's up direction. Together we climbed the spiral, reaching the second level in no time. The six gunmen had yet to establish themselves, giving me an easy chance to pick four of them off. The remaining two took cover near the captain's door. I watched Hull start forward, grabbing a potted plant from a nearby table as he went. He pulled the plant from its pot, then shoved both of his hands into the dirt. The pot fell and shattered on the floor, leaving Hull his dirt-filled hands.

He threw the dirt at each soldier, disrupting their vision for just a moment. He lurched for the man on the left first, sending his elbow into his chest, then up into his chin. As the man was falling back, Hull grabbed his assault rifle and fired several rounds into the man on the right. The opposing man slumped against the wall, one bullet having passed through his forehead. I reached Hull only as the action had finished. He dropped the assault rifle and looked at his dirty hands.

"Bulky weapons used for pointless murders," he noted.

"And you're not even bothered by the actual dirt on your hands," I pointed out as we reached the door.

"Dirt comes off."

As soon as we moved to open the door, the boat gave a mighty shudder. The shake was caused by what I could tell was a cessation in the boat's movement. Hull and I, being so close to the doorway, slammed into it with our bodies from the momentum, forcing it open and revealing an empty captain's quarters. Hull picked himself up off the ground and cursed.

"He'll be making a run for it now."

I holstered the pistols and pointed at an emergency exit, which I knew was a ladder going straight to the top. "We can still catch him." We charged the ladder, him going first. When we emerged, we found ourselves on the deck at the bow of the ship, which had managed to run aground. It didn't look like we'd gone far, as I could still see the smoke in the air rising from the Basilica, which was hidden by the walls of buildings.

"There!" Hull shouted. I followed his point and saw a figure, clad in a black cloak but without the hood, running towards the nearest building on the ledge next to us. His flowing blonde hair was enough to confirm his identity. Hull and I clambered to the side of the ship and made the jump to the ledge, putting us on the same level as Judas. He passed a corner and vanished from sight. We ran as fast as we could, Hull moving slightly faster than me. We rounded the corner and saw Judas swerve by the farthest corner, moving into an open area.

When we reached the open area, we found it to be a courtyard. About a dozen people were arranged in a circle, all holding lit candles. They were not looking, however, in the direction of the Basilica. Their focus was on the cathedral ahead of us, and judging by the slight parting of the crowd, I could guess that Judas had forced his way through. Hull and I followed his path, moving around the people and seeing the door to the cathedral, the San Bartolomeo all'Isola, close. We moved to the door quickly, Hull holding it open while I charged in.

We found ourselves in a dark cathedral, the only light coming from the moon shining through the stain-glass windows. Opposite us, at the altar, was a tired-looking Judas, his hands pressed against the podium and his head bobbing up and down in a heavy-breathing-like manner. I drew my own pistol and handed to other to Hull, who took it without question.

"It ends here, Judas," Hull shouted. The man looked up and, despite his heavy breathing, still gave a smirk.

"No, Mr. Hull. This is only the beginning."

"And just how do you see yourself escaping from this? More henchmen? The evidence is substantial against you, Judas. You will see no victory at the end of this evening."

"And you plan to stop me? You, a detective? Him, a doctor?"

"My plan to stop you is already in motion."

At this, I gave a short glance at Hull, somewhat confused by what he said. I was unaware of any plan. And it seemed Judas didn't believe him.

"Prove it," the archbishop cried out as he stood up straight.

Hull lowered his pistol. "The case had intrigue, and you performed well. Had I not been involved, I can almost be certain you would have been successful. The Catholic church would be in complete disarray, and all of Italy would be turning their sights, and their weapons, on Croatia. You, being the only remaining person of power, would have been able to create peace, and in doing so, you would have become an icon, a savior. A hero.

"It all started when you traveled to Russia, and experienced a taste of the collapsing Soviet Union. You saw power, you craved it, but you did not want it in the same fashion of politics. You knew you could obtain it elsewhere. Because where the sway of a political man can be lost due to a change in popularity, the sway of a religious man cannot be dictated by mere man. You wanted to lead. So you began your journey back, and that was when you met Agneza. Karl Agneza, a relatively unknown name to the general populace. But to someone like me? No, I knew it immediately.

"Karl Agneza was arrested in 1990 for drug trafficking and sex trade. But he was found to run a small group of soldiers, the Sovjetski Blade. Upon his arrest, the men went into hiding. You made contact with Agneza and made a contract: you would help break him out in exchange for his help, and his men. You broke him out. And you became partners. Agneza was wise in strategy, while you were skilled in communication. Together, you made the perfect hostile takeover.

"It took years to create your explosives, because you could only obtain so many supplies without attracting attention. You would transport the supplies via sewer, assemble the bombs in the sewer, place them in the sewer. You would purchase supplies from across the globe and keep a ledger to track of which vendors you used, so as to not repeat. You covered your tracks and ensured any and all potential connections were invisible. You even used your resources as a Chimaera agent.

"But you slipped up. Because you elected to go missing at too convenient a time, and you opted to not remove your personal belongings yourself. The Chimaera logo was enough to tell me you were behind your own disappearance. The business ledgers told me of your ulterior motive. And the books. Oh, how I loved the books. 'What Doctors Don't Tell You,' 'The Field,' 'The Intention Experiment,' and 'The Bond'. Obscure titles, all by the same author, all ripped in the middle. But why? Why the hatred for the books? Or was it directed at something else?

"Your drive for perfection in numbers, your insistence on organization, was *ruined* when you met Lynne McTaggart, author of the four books you destroyed, because she turned you away when you wanted assistance in achieving perfection. Because she told you that perfection was not something to be obtained by man, especially a religious man like yourself. In your rage, you insulted the woman, harassed the woman, and threatened her via email. And one of the emails was accidentally copied to another user, possibly unbeknownst to you. It was copied to a certain Malcolm Hull, a friend of McTaggart, who then forwarded it to me.

"Your biggest mistake in using email was your failure to acknowledge the existence of IP addresses. I knew you were here, in the city, the entire time. I knew you had never departed. Because you sent the emails from a smart phone, the one in your pocket right now. Had you left the city, I would have known. But you did not. And thus, I was able to stay, and wait. And I knew your plans would eventually begin. Had I known the scale, I would have intervened sooner. That was my mistake."

Judas had stared at Hull with the most abhorrent look possible while the detective had elaborated. That was the effect Hull usually had on the criminals he caught. But there was something different with Judas. Some kind of surprise that didn't come with being found out. It was almost like he had been wrong about something, but couldn't quite believe it. And I didn't understand why he would have this face.

Until he spoke.

"You aren't with him? You actually aren't with him?"

Hull furrowed his brow. "With who?"

"With Moriarty! Of course not, you'd never be with him, how could I have been so foolish, how could *you* have been so foolish!"

"I don't follow," Hull replied.

"He spoke with you, he helped you, but you're not Chimaera!" A pale look came over Judas' face. "He told you, didn't he? He told you their policy."

"What policy?"

"No loose ends."

I looked around the room frantically when the sinister voice joined the group. My eyes eventually returned to their altar, where a cloaked and hooded figure had appeared behind Judas, a black-gloved hand holding a pistol to the archbishop's head. One second later, a resounding *bang* echoed from the altar, and Judas' body flew forward, slamming into the podium and knocking it from the altar down to the ground. The hooded figure started off in a run towards a nearby doorway, and before I could respond to the situation, Hull had grabbed my sleeve and started forward.

"*Moriarty!*" he yelled as we ran. Some part of me had suspected the identity of the hooded figure, but I never imagined he would have been here, in person, in the right cathedral, ready to kill Judas at the right moment. How could he have known where Judas would choose to hide? How could he have gotten in before without being seen?

The hallway had led to a staircase, which moved up around a square room with a bell in the center. I could hear the *tap-tap-taping* of Moriarty's footsteps as he ran, which gave us inspiration to move. Second floor, third floor, fourth floor, all the way to the fifth floor. Hull and I rounded the bell to find ourselves on the roof of the cathedral, a thin, quarter-meter wide plank of wood moving forward towards the edge of the church. Moriarty was standing at the far end of the plank, his back to us. Hull moved forward slowly, not bothering to raise his pistol.

Just as we made it to within two meters of the cloaked man, a bright blue light erupted in front of us. Hull and I stumbled back to find a wall of glowing blue light blocking our way to Moriarty. We could see him clearly through the light, but when Hull tried to pass through it, he found it to be solid.

"More innovative technology from the heart of Chimaera," Moriarty mocked from behind the shield.

"Why!" Hull yelled.

"Because, Sheridan, it's exactly as you told Gatti. You did the job for me. Where I would have wasted resources on a manhunt, you were able to corral Judas here, to exactly where I needed him. Judas had become far too independent, you see. He needed to die." The man did some slight pacing on his side of the shield before looking back at us. "You performed well, Sheridan. And now, the exact outcome I required has come to fruition."

"What outcome?" Hull barked back.

"Without Judas, there is no one to blame for the acts of terrorism against the Vatican except for the Croatian terrorist cell. But because Judas is gone, there will be no one to coordinate a peace. Italy and Croatia will enter a state of tension, and all it takes is that tension to begin the domino effect. That domino effect will move little by little, bringing a call to action. Those who are weak, those who do not seek progress, will fall, and those who do will rise. Chaos will eventually be quelled, and peace will be achieved."

"You can't be serious!" I shouted. "Peace through chaos can't work!"

"I am serious, Doctor. I am very serious. The fire has started, gentlemen. All it took was a spark." He turned away, and I could hear what sounded like a helicopter suddenly come to life.

"You will fail," Hull said, his voice somber. "Everything you have worked to achieve will crumble beneath your feet. And you, with your organization, will fall."

Moriarty turned back, his hidden eyes no doubt falling on Hull. "You don't understand, even after so much. Chimaera isn't just an organization, or the people behind it. Chimaera is an idea."

Behind him, a large, black object rose into view, with a doorway on the side opening and a small ramp extending. He stepped back onto the ramp, his eyes still on us, while the ramp retracted into what I could distinguish as a helicopter, but with two blades inside metal casing on the top. Before the door closed, a metal cane emerged from the man's cloak. He grabbed onto the ball tip and pressed it down into the floor.

"That idea is not so easily destroyed."

His last words were said just before the door sealed shut. As soon as the door had closed, the shield keeping us back ceased. The helicopter moved up at an impossible speed, then jetted forward off into the horizon. Hull's eyes followed it until they could no more. And the stern look of determination on his face was one I will never forget.

*

The next morning arrived on the same note that the evening had left it on. A grim silence had fallen across the entire city, with people still gathered in the Square. None of the people who had been unaccounted for had survived. St. Peter's Basilica was effectively destroyed. And according to Gatti, a search was done on the sewers of the city, where an overwhelming amount of evidence was found proving that a Croatian terror cell by the name of the Sovjetski Blade had been behind the attacks. Demands for answers, and for justice, were already being sent by the Italian government. And there was no way to connect Judas, whose body had vanished from the cathedral, to the terrorists.

Hull and I had given all the information we could to Gatti and departed. The detective had insisted on one last visit to St. Peter's Square. We walked in silence, the only sounds to be heard being small ones at that. A shadow had fallen on the city in light of the tragedy. Everyone was thankful that the Pope was alive, and as such, Hull had received many thanks for his part. But the fact that over a thousand people had not made it out of the Basilica was devastating to the city, and to the church. The recovery process would be a very, very long one indeed.

We reached the Square and found a bench facing the ruins of the Basilica. We sat in silence for about ten minutes before a dove flew down and landed in front of us. Hull looked down at it for a long moment before gulping.

"He played me. He used me as a pawn. I was nothing more than a tool to help him reach his goal."

I shrugged. "You never could have predicted what he was planning. It's why he's the one in charge of a crime syndicate, and you're not. You're the one who's going to catch him, and bring this all to an end."

"Can I, though?" He looked over at me, his eyes a swirling gray. "Can I stop him? Can I stop Chimaera?"

"We've made it this far, haven't we?"

He gave a solemn nod before looking back to the dove. "I suppose so."

"And you're not alone. You have Lennox, and you have Malcolm. And you have me." I knew the first two names wouldn't make a difference to him, but I was curious to see how he would react for me. He blinked a few times before giving a deep sigh.

"It makes me wonder how long it will be, before he uses that to his advantage."

I nudged him. "We're all adults. We can handle ourselves."

He gave a smirk. "That you can."

We sat for maybe twenty more minutes before the dove flew away, joining what looked like five or six others in a group. Hull gave another sigh before standing. We were both sore from the previous day's events. As we turned to start walking towards our hotel, he cast one last glance at the remains of the Basilica and made a humming noise.

"Religion. A curious thing, inspiring individuals to do curious things."

"All because of a God who may not even exist," I added.

He smiled and looked at me. "I have seen far too much death, destruction, and misery to simply believe in a God. That is exactly why I do believe."

I furrowed my brow. "You believe because you don't believe?"

"I do not *simply* believe. I *fully* believe. Such a large amount of evil could not exist without an opposing side marching with reason. God created evil to give the rest of us purpose." With that, he cast one last glance before starting forward.

I, too, took a moment to observe the wreckage of the Basilica, the smoke still rising from the ruins, and suddenly, a burst of sunlight poked its way through the clouds above, shining down directly on where St. Peter's Basilica had stood just twenty-four hours ago. And in that moment, I understood what Hull had said. With a soft nod, I turned and followed the detective, off towards our hotel, eventually to the airport, and somewhere down the line, our next adventure.

*

"And the fruit of righteousness is sown in peace of those who make peace." - James 3:18

THE WOMAN

"No no *no*! You idiot! You grab the flag and run towards the *base*, not towards their spawn!"

And in a single sentence, the past twenty-four hours of my life was very, very accurately summed up. It had been well over a month since Hull and I had returned from the Vatican. As we'd suspected, the Vatican police had blamed the entirety of Croatia for the act of terrorism, and now a tension had formed with other European countries taking sides. Hull, however, didn't seem to care. Once Moriarty had escaped, the case was done. He truly had no interest in the politics of the world. To him, the case had been completed. That was that.

In light of this, however, everything else had seemed to bore him. Three potential clients had come requesting assistance after our return, and Hull had turned each of them away without even hearing their cases. I suppose I understood why he would find the day-to-day cases of Newfield boring. Things didn't blow up all-too often here. But even so, the fact stood that when Hull became bored, he became very difficult to live with. And since yesterday had been Christmas, I had started planning something that would maybe, just maybe, be able to distract his mind.

With a little assistance from his niece and her boyfriend, I was able to find a good video gaming system, an Xbox 360. With the console, I also obtained one game, Halo 4. I don't know why I thought video games might be a suitable distraction, but I guess I was also wanting something to do on the weekends. The gift was bought by me for the both of us. At first, Hull seemed absolutely disgusted at the idea of just sitting in front of the television, holding a controller, and dictating the actions of a pixel-created character. But once I explained the concept that was the Halo franchise to him, he changed. Completely.

We owned one Xbox 360 game at the end of Christmas, and seven by the middle of the day after. Hull had played maybe ten minutes of the campaign for Halo 4 the previous night before deciding to play through the *entire* series. Sure enough, he'd returned with the rest of the games this morning, all piled up and ready to be played. Before playing, however, he had asked what "War Games" was, and I explained to him that it was a way to play the game against other people.

What a huge mistake.

Immediately, he took to playing online, trying the different game modes, experimenting with different weapons. He discovered the element that is lag, and also discovered the horrible abundance of pre-teens online. I watched as the skillful detective, the calm, collected genius, devolved into a competitive, rage-fueled asshole who couldn't stand a hint of incompetence from his team. During his current game alone, he had managed to curse out three different individuals, one who had left the game. He had also managed to get twenty-five kills without touching the flag once. He didn't seem to care much for the objective. He preferred to boss everyone else around.

I pity the day someone tells him about online gaming communities.

"Oh *come on*! How hard is it to just *kill* the damn driver of the car!"

To spare the sliver of innocence remaining in the lives of the other players, I had discreetly disconnected Hull's headset when the game had paused for a host migration. It was probably the most productive thing I'd done all day.

"I swear to God above, how can any of these people manage to get a single kill when they are so disorganized?" he yelled from behind me. I glanced over my shoulder to see him staring at the post-game statistics, with him sitting at the top.

"Maybe it's not that they're disorganized so much as you're just too organized. Which is a lie, by the way."

He turned off the 360 and set down the controller before casting me a wary glance. "What do you mean?"

"I've met five-year-olds who had a better sense of organization than you. You barely remember to do your own laundry."

"I never do my own laundry."

I set the paper down and looked at him, my nose curled. "That's disgusting."

"Oh come off it, Mrs. Hanson does my laundry."

"Why does she do your laundry? She doesn't do my laundry."

"Because you do your laundry."

"But why does she do *your* laundry?"

He plopped down in the seat next to me and clasped his hands behind his head. "Because she knows that if she did not, no one would."

I opened my mouth to retort, but stopped when a buzzing came from downstairs. Mrs. Hanson had left a week ago to spend Christmas with her family, which meant Hull and I were the only people in the building. This also meant if someone came to the door, it was up to one of us to answer it.

In other words, it was up to me.

I reached the door and looked through the peephole to find Lennox, his gloved hands rubbing his cheeks. I opened the door quickly and gave him a nod before gesturing inside.

"Good to see you, Doctor," the inspector said as he stomped his feet on the rug.

"You as well," I replied as I closed the door. "Have a good Christmas?"

"Pretty good. Took the fiancée over to Bend for the extra long weekend. Got back early this morning and was immediately thrown on a high-priority case."

"Ah, and here I was thinking you just wanted to come visit."

He smiled. "Is he in?"

"Oh yeah. He's been playing Halo 4 all morning."

"Who loves him enough to get him that?"

"Apparently, I do."

Together we walked up the stairs, the sound of something scratching on wood coming from the floor above. I entered the room first and moved to my chair and watched as Hull threw the fire poker across the room and into the hearth.

"No, Inspector," he said with his eyes on the burning fire.

Lennox gave me a puzzled look before focusing on the back of Hull's head. "You don't even know the case yet."

Hull scoffed. "Easy to figure out."

"Then what is it?"

"Stolen equipment from Lawson Concert Hall. Heard about it this morning when I stopped at a café."

"Why won't you help?"

"Because I *won't*."

"All of the equipment's gone missing," Lennox said with a tone of desperation. "Half a million dollar's worth."

"It's a job for a search dog, not me." He pointed at the now-blank TV. "Or that fellow on the television show, he seems to enjoy finding things."

I gave Hull a confused glance. "You've helped people find things before."

"But I will not assist with finding *these* things." He looked over at me with a stern gaze. "Do I make myself clear?"

I furrowed my brow before looking over at Lennox, who sighed. He glared at the back of Hull's head before walking back down the stairs. Only once I'd heard the door slam did I step over and smack Hull's shoulder.

"What was all that about?"

He turned back to the television and picked up the 360 controller. "I have no interest in finding stolen goods today."

"What, too boring for you?"

"No."

"Then what?"

"I am simply *not interested*."

That was the last thing he said to me, except to ask when his headset had unplugged itself. For the rest of the day, he just sat there, eyes glued to the screen, hands on the controller, mind deep in the game.

*

The next day, Hull decided to take a break from playing Halo 4 and had opted to focus all of his attention on the contents of a small cardboard box. I'd made several attempts to see the contents, but every time, he had managed to hide them from me. Whatever was inside was important, to him or someone else. And once he'd finished with it, he made sure to lock his bedroom door after putting it back in its place. He came out into the living room, still clad in his purple shirt and sweatpants. He sat down with a heavy sigh and started flipping through different channels on the TV.

"Get tired of yelling at kids?" I asked as I signed a check for the month's bills. We'd received a very generous amount of money as compensation for our assistance in "bringing the Croatian deception to light." At least, that was what the Inspector General had told us. It made paying the bills much, much easier.

"Mm," he grunted back, still focused on the channels. I glanced over and watched his pattern. He didn't pause for even a half-second when he reached a channel, and he'd managed to loop through our arrangement of preferred channels about three times.

"Boredom is starting to set in, isn't it?"

"The boredom set in on November 14th."

"Maybe it's time to pick another case, then." I walked over to the table by the balcony, where a stack of letters waited to be opened. As I picked them up, I noticed a cop car parked on the opposite side of the street. It hadn't been there long, since it had snowed again last night and the car was untouched. Considering it wasn't your standard squad car meant we had a visitor.

The knock that came from downstairs verified that.

As Mrs. Hanson had returned home late last night, she was able to get the door. I held the stack lightly and watched as Lennox came up the stairs, a look of disdain on his face. Hull stopped flipping through the channels and glanced over his shoulder.

"How many times do I have to say no, Inspector, for you to understand the word's meaning?" Hull cast.

Lennox shook his head. "I can't take no for an answer. I need your help with this."

"The case has no interest."

"I don't care if it has no interest!" Lennox barked. "The concert is in four days and I don't have a damn clue where the equipment's gone. You know how important this concert is to the city."

"A concert's importance is hardly a factor to get my attention."
I sighed. "You need to take the case."

He looked over at me with narrowed eyes. "Why should I?"

"Because you need to get out of the house! You've left *once*
since we got back from the Vatican, and that was to buy six games
you haven't even played yet. You need a case."

His gaze screamed of anger, but there was also a hint of
calmness falling over his demeanor. "You have no idea what this case
entails."

"It's *stolen equipment*," Lennox interjected. "How much more
complicated can it get?"

Hull looked from the inspector to me before sighing. "Fine. I
will help."

Lennox gave a deep exhale. "Thank you. Meet me at the
concert hall as soon as you can." With that, he turned and left. I set
down the stack of letters and walked towards Hull, who was focused
on the TV once more.

"Why was that so difficult for you?"

He held his stare with the screen for ten seconds before
looking up at me. "You'll see."

Only an hour later, we arrived at the concert hall. Police had
blocked off the street and Lennox stood at the entrance with three
other officers. We trekked through the foot of snow to the waiting
inspector, who gestured for us to walk inside.

"Speakers, soundboards, light stands, the lights themselves, all
of it was stolen on Christmas. Estimated cost is a little over $500,000
for it all. How they got in, how they got it out, we have no idea.
Security tapes have been scrapped, even the stoplight cameras don't
have anything. We do know that whoever did it was able to clear out
the entire storage area in less than ten minutes," the inspector said as
we entered the hall.

"Couldn't have been just one person," I said.

"That's the thing. Whoever they were, they must've got caught
in some thick mud before coming in, because we've got a pair of
footprints. But there's only one. Unless everyone else had clean feet,
this was a one-man job."

We stepped into the main hall, which had obviously been
renovated since the magician mishap. Groups of people stood around
the room, some sitting in the rows, some standing. One group was on
the stage, and it was significantly larger than the rest. I glanced to my

right, where Hull had been just a moment ago, only to find him gone. I turned around and found him somewhat-hunched behind Lennox and I, his eyes glued on the stage.

"What are you doing?" I asked, careful not to trip as I walked backwards.

He flailed his hand at me. "Turn around, act natural." I cast him a wary glance before complying. We were about halfway to the stage now.

"Can you get anything from the footprints?" I questioned.

"He was wearing boots. But really, how much can you get from a muddy footprint?" From behind us, Hull scoffed. Lennox and I both stopped and glanced back. We'd reached the stage now, and Hull was making an active effort to have the inspector and I between him and the group before us.

"Is there a problem with those people?" I asked as I looked up at the group.

"No no no, please do not look at them, keep their attention away," Hull snapped back.

From where we were, I could see that there were about ten people in the group. Six of them were men, three were women, and one stood near the center that I couldn't quite distinguish. Their shoes were hidden but their pants looked most certainly feminine. One of the men in the group glanced over at us, then whispered something to the person in the center. The group parted to reveal the illusive tenth person.

My initial assumption was right. It was indeed a woman. But once I'd mentally established that, I was taken back by just how beautiful she was. Her hair was a flowing dark brown that went just below her shoulders. Her eyes were a very deep brown and her skin just pale enough to show collections of freckles on her nose and below her eyes. She wore a gray sweatshirt and white sweatpants, which somehow still managed to look phenomenal on her. And once her physical attractiveness had settled in, I realized something. I had no doubt seen her before, many times, but I couldn't quite recall where.

She kneeled down when she reached us and extended her hand to Lennox. "Inspector, so good to see you again."

"You as well, Ms. Duerre," Lennox replied as he shook her hand. That was when it finally hit me.

"Duerre. Caroline Duerre. You're the singer!" I exclaimed before feeling my cheeks go red. I'd handled myself far better when meeting the Pope.

She smiled at me and offered her hand. "That would be me, yes. Who might you be?"

"Doctor John Walker," I said as I shook her hand.

"Pleasure to meet you, Doctor," she replied. She tilted her head to the side and looked between Lennox and me. Both of us glanced back to see Hull, practically hiding behind his upturned coat collar. Duerre gave a wry smile before cocking her chin forward.

"Sheridan Hull. It's been a while, hasn't it?" she said. I looked back at Hull in surprise.

He flattened his collar and gazed up at her with stern eyes. "Two years, forty-six days, and seven hours. To be exact. It has been a while."

"Wait," I prompted, glancing from the woman to Hull. "You two know each other?"

"Hardly," Hull shot back.

"Oh come on, you can't be cold all the time," Duerre replied, her voice almost a purr. "Sheridan and I have met on a handful of occasions—"

"Three."

"—and he always acts so short and suspicious. What are you doing now, Sheridan?"

"Consulting detective," he replied, with a slight puffing out of his chest.

"Ah, very proper." She stood back up to full height. "Well I hope you're able to figure this one out quick. What with the concert being in four days and all." With that, she turned and walked back to the waiting group. Lennox and I both looked at Hull, who had watched Duerre walk away until she was hidden inside the group once more. I could've sworn I even saw his nostrils flare at one point.

"What the Hell was that?" I asked when he finally blinked.

"The Woman," he replied in a very platonic voice before turning and walking towards the storage area.

Once he'd exited our line of sight, Lennox looked over at me. "The Hell's that supposed to mean?" I shook my head in shared confusion and walked after the detective.

Lennox and I found him in the storage room, eyes glued to one of the muddy footprints. It had dried and cracked now, but the footprint was still somewhat visible. The room itself was completely empty, and there wasn't much to be found that could help in finding out where the contents had gone. This was, of course, from my perspective. I knew Hull would find far more. He pulled a small, gray object from his pocket and extended it, revealing a little magnifying glass.

"Hold on," I said as I leaned in close. "That looks familiar, where'd you get that?"

"Amazon," he replied offhandedly as he examined the footprints.

"No, as in why did you get it."

"Because it was a magnifying glass?"

"It's from something, I know it is."

He folded the glass back into its case and leaned away from the print. "Small feet, size eight and a half. Stands probably about two meters tall. Short gait, but a quick pace. Possibly from the lifting, possibly from something else." He stood and gave the room a glance before nodding at Lennox. "Not much to work with at all, what a pity. But I think I should be able to find the equipment before the concert."

He turned and started back towards the main hall. I followed him briskly, trying to keep pace. He was no doubt hoping to get out before Duerre could notice him, and part of me hoped she would. The curiosity was killing me. I had to know what connection he had to her, because whatever it was, he didn't like it.

We didn't even make it past the stage before she spotted us.

"Oh, Sheridan, hold on a moment," she called out before shooing away her entourage. Hull's feet skidded to a stop, his arms slamming to his side and his head looking forward. If I didn't know better, I'd think Duerre was his commanding officer and he'd just received an order to stand at attention. I came to his side and watched the woman silkily move her way to us. She hopped skillfully from the stage and landed in front of us.

"Yes?" Hull asked, his voice monotonous.

"I was wondering if you would like to attend a pre-concert banquet tomorrow evening. You are welcome to attend as well, Doctor."

"Time is valuable, Ms. Duerre, and I cannot be bothered to—"

I nudged him sharply. He looked over at me, his eyes wide and brow scrunched. "We'll go." He stared me down for a long moment before sighing.

"Fine. We will both be there."

She smiled. "Excellent. I'll see you then." She turned and walked away, and as soon as she had, Hull turned the opposite direction, grabbed me by the arm, and started pulling me up towards a different exit.

"I swear to God," he whispered as we walked, "if you do not come with me to that *banquet*, I will spike every single cup of coffee you drink with lemon juice."

"That cruel of a punishment, huh? What'd she ever do to you?"

"*Irrelevant.*"

"I have a hard time believing that."

He didn't speak again until we reached the street. Instead of walking towards the car, he started off toward the police barricade. I stopped and watched him walk a good meter before deciding to say something.

"Did you forget where we parked?" I shouted after him.

"I need to do some independent investigation. Chase a lead I have." He hadn't bothered to stop when he gave his answer, which meant he was too far away for me to get anything else out of him. I watched him walk to the other side of the barricade and climb into a cab before I went to the car. If we were doing independent investigations, I wanted to do some of my own as well.

But my investigations were on something other than the case.

*

I knocked on the mahogany door twice and took a step back, giving a quick glance at the garden. Such perfect hedges, perfect flowers, perfect saplings. Of course everything would be neat and tidy. Hell, it didn't look like anything had changed, except for the slight presence of snow. But even that had been shoveled and carefully removed from the more delicate plants. I paused for a moment and wondered just who took care of the garden, but considering the homeowner, it was probably a hired hand.

Or twenty.

The door opened to reveal a tall man, dark blonde hair and what could barely be classified as comfortable-casual clothing. He gave me a nice smile and nodded.

"John, so good to see you," Malcolm Hull said. He glanced up to look behind me. "And no Sheridan in tow? My, this is indeed a surprise."

I gave him a nod, remembering Sheridan having mentioned that he doesn't shake hands. "I don't think he'd have liked me coming, but I was hoping I could ask you some questions about someone. Someone who might be, uh.. important to him, I guess."

Malcolm gave a smirk. "This would be about Caroline Duerre, wouldn't it?"

"Right on the money."

He gestured inside. "Come in, come in. Bailey and my wife are out for the day but I should be able to provide you with ample information."

He led me to the living room, which had been decorated for the Christmas holidays. A large tree stood in the corner of the room, ornaments and lights giving the noble fir a rainbow-esque look. Two gifts were set to the side of the tree, neither of them opened. Malcolm sat down in his typical auburn armchair and offered me the white love seat that faced him.

"So Ms. Duerre is in town," Malcolm said, a chipper tone to his voice.

"She is. And I only know her as a singer, but Sheridan tried to avoid her as best as he could."

Malcolm gave a short laugh. "I'm surprised he was willing to see her at all. This would be in regards to the stolen sound and lighting equipment, yes? For the benefit concert this New Years' Eve?"

"Exactly that."

He clasped his fingers together. "And Sheridan, being Sheridan, would not tell you a single thing about his connection to her, would he?"

"Nothing."

"Of course not." He silently chuckled to himself before continuing. "Caroline Brooke Duerre is a world-renowned singer, songwriter, and philanthropist who spends the majority of her time traveling to lesser-endowed countries and assisting them through acts of charity. At the age of twenty-three, she has two platinum and two gold albums. She was officially recognized as a singer at the age of sixteen and has been hard at work since.

"However, Ms. Duerre also has a far lesser-known side to her. Lesser-known, that is, to the public. To the governments of every major country, she is very well-known. When Ms. Duerre is not traveling as Caroline Duerre, she is the finest thief of the 21st century. Everyone is aware of her hidden persona, and in fact, the United States government has consulted her on numerous occasions. She does not steal for herself, but rather for others, which is why she operates under the moniker 'Robyn'. She is the best of her time."

I leaned back in the loveseat and scratched my chin. "So how do her and Sheridan connect?"

He smiled. "Six years ago, Sheridan was sent to Seattle to assist in an abduction case. When he arrived, he discovered that the person abducted was one of Ms. Duerre's band members, which meant he would have to meet her. If I remember correctly, their first meeting went something along the lines of their eyes meeting and his knees giving way. He was so captivated by her appearance that he could not focus, and thus, he was unable to properly assist the police in locating the abducted individual. He was fine, by the way.

"Four years ago, the mayor of New York City requested Sheridan's assistance in finding a statue that had been stolen from the Museum of the City of New York. The statue was of John D. Rockefeller and had been taken from the fifth floor of the museum without any security cameras, any individuals, or any vehicles having assisted in its removal. His investigation slowly led him to find that the statue had been melted down and sold, with the money being given to the Harlem Restoration Project. Once he'd learned this, he went to inform the mayor and ran into Ms. Duerre once more. Realizing what had happened, he opted to return home and tell the mayor via telephone.

"Two years ago, Sheridan was asked to help with some stolen articles from the Winter Olympics. Upon arriving in Vancouver, he was immediately greeted by an entourage of people at the airport who were expecting Ms. Duerre. Within fifteen minutes, he was on a plane leaving the country. When he returned home, he found a sheet of paper slipped into his luggage that said, 'Sorry I missed you. -CBD'. So you see, Sheridan and Ms. Duerre have a very, very interesting.. relationship."

"Relationship?" I scoffed. "Sheridan doesn't have relationships. He barely has friendships."

"Which is why I use the term lightly. Their 'relationship' is not a standard one, but more of a level of rivaling admiration. Both of them are adept at what they do, and both of them can quite often work against each other. His admiration for her is quite possibly the only reason he will give her the time of day, and her admiration for him is why she has remained single since their original meeting."

"How do you know that?"

"Because it's obvious." He leaned forward slightly, unclasping his fingers and grabbing his legs. "He referred to her as 'the Woman,' did he not? The term, to him, is a label of both the deepest regard and deepest resentment. You see, to Sheridan, she is always *the* Woman. I have seldom heard him mention her under any other name. In his eyes she eclipses and predominates the whole of her sex. And to her, he is the same. She is a person of considerable fame. On a day-to-day basis, she is being regarded by men as a symbol of beauty, and talent, and sex. But she ignores them because she would rather have the man who both idolizes *and* abhors her than the man who only idolizes her."

I adjusted my jaw before speaking. "So if she's so well known as a thief, why hasn't she been arrested?"

"She's that good. It's a moment where you know someone has done something, but you have no way of actually proving it. A gut feeling will not convince a court. She leaves no trace, no prints, no possible way to connect the crime to her. And because she does not steal for personal gain, you cannot trace her bank records to show significant increase. The money she donates is all anonymous, and she goes to great lengths to ensure that. When I say she is the best thief of our time, I do not exaggerate."

"Is it possible that she's the thief for this case?"

"Oh of course not. Why steal from her own benefit concert, one in which she has personally paid for all the equipment? That would just be ridiculous of her. No, this is someone else, someone thinking they can make a quick buck from taking valuable equipment. I pity them."

"Why?"

He gave a cheeky grin. "Because they have the most formidable detective and the most illusive thief on their tail. Their odds of succeeding are very, very low."

"Ah. Makes sense, I guess." I stood from the love seat and felt my back pop. "Thank you. This definitely explains a lot. He's not normally so cold with people but he certainly didn't enjoy talking to her."

"Give it time. His true thoughts for her ought to reveal themselves."

I smiled. "We'll see, I guess. Have a good day, Malcolm."

He held his hands up. "Wait. Bailey wanted to ensure I got these to you." He stood and walked over to the packages. He picked them up delicately and handed them to me. "Christmas gifts from her. She sends her love."

I nodded at him. "And tell her we thank her and appreciate it." He led me to the door and closed it quietly behind me. As I started walking down the path, I couldn't keep from smiling. I knew Hull had held someone very high in his eyes during his first year of college, but that couldn't have been Duerre. This was someone else, someone much more important to him. Now I truly was curious to see how he reacted around her. And if we were really going to a banquet tomorrow night, with her present, I would get the perfect opportunity.

*

I returned to the flat and found that Hull had not only beaten me home, but he had found something in his private investigations. When I walked into the main room of the flat, I found him standing on top of a two-meter-tall speaker. He bounced softly on the top a few times before jumping to the ground. I watched him jump as I set my coat on my chair, the many different explanations for *why* he would stand on top of the speaker running through my mind.

"Glad your independent work paid off," I said as I sat down in the chair. I grabbed the newspaper from the side table and opened it to the local news. "Do I want to know why?"

"The thief had to have moved them without extensively touching the ground," the detective said as he circled the speaker. "I suspect that he jumped from speaker to speaker, as well as using the lighting poles for balance and redirecting his momentum."

"What, you think the thief is some kind of parkour expert?"

"Actually, that is exactly what I think. Otherwise I would not have spent my taxi rides watching different parkour videos."

"Good to know you didn't trust the only example of parkour from *The Office*." I tossed the paper to the side, knowing there wouldn't be anything worth reading in it. All it was these days were awards being given, people being disgruntled, and politics. Lots and lots of politics. "So how'd you find just one?"

"He left it at a gas station. He would have needed to change vehicles, so I presume he offloaded the equipment and transferred it there, but forgot the one. Purposeful or by accident, I can't say I'm sure of."

"How do you know it's a he?"

He walked over to his coat and pulled a sheet of paper from the pocket, then tossed it at me. I opened it to find a crudely-printed picture from a security camera. "Gas station cameras caught him for only a moment. Clean face, quick pace, tall, small feet."

"How'd you know to check the gas station?"

"Tracks in the snow. Trodden, somewhat covered, but still present. He used a U-Haul, the name was still imprinted in some areas of the snow. I was able to access the security cameras from traffic control and follow it there. Once he had transferred the equipment, though, he was more careful. I suspect he noticed the camera at the station and realized how well one could trace him via little snippets."

"Ah." I watched him continue to circle the speaker before I managed to muster the courage to move on to a more intricate topic. "I know about you and Duerre."

He smirked. "There is nothing to know."

"I talked to Malcolm."

He froze in place. From where I sat, I could only see the left side of his face, but I'm certain I saw a tremor go up his cheek, followed shortly by a twitch to his eye. He slowly turned to me and bit his bottom lip before replying. "Ah."

"So he wasn't joking?"

"He was incorrect, of that I have no doubt."

"But you really do—"

He stepped away from the speaker, turning his back to me. "I hold no hint of love, desire, or 'admiration' for Caroline Duerre. I simply cannot stand to be in her presence."

"Why?"

His head jerked back to glare at me. "What?"

"Why can't you stand to be in her presence? What did she do beside show you an equal?"

He turned his full body to face me now. "What did she do? She—"

"I'm sorry, am I interrupting anything?"

Both Hull and I turned to the doorway, where a figure now stood. They wore a white overcoat that stretched to their ankles and a red knitted beanie. It took only a fraction of a second for me to realize it was Caroline Duerre.

"Bwuh.. how did you..?" Hull muttered.

She smiled at him. "Phonebooks exist for a reason, Sheridan."

"Did Mrs. Hanson just let you..?" Hull continued.

"Oh she's such a nice lady," Duerre replied, her voice animate. "As soon as she opened the door she recognized me. Don't let me forget to sign a poster she has for her granddaughter."

"Why are you here?" Hull said, the stutter finally gone from his voice.

"I came to see how you were coming along." She looked down at the speaker. "And you didn't disappoint. Well, except for only finding one. Let me guess."

"No, please don't," Hull shot back.

"You figured out what vehicle the thief used to escape, tracked it with traffic cameras, and found the truck?"

The look that crossed Hull's face was an interesting mixture of both success and failure. "He transferred the contents to another vehicle but forgot this speaker."

"Mm. And I assume he's the one who stomped on its top?" she said as she ran her black-gloved finger across the speaker's cover.

"One of the people to, yes," I said, doing my best to avoid Hull's imminent glare.

"Well I can only hope it somehow benefits your investigation," she replied with a smile at Hull.

He, however, was working his absolute hardest to keep the cold, stoic lock to his face. "Why are you *really* here?"

She sighed and sat down in the armchair opposing me, the one Hull would usually sit in. "I want to help. I think that, given my experience, you could benefit from it."

"I don't need help."

"You never were a good liar."

"I'm not lying."

"What do you know of him so far?"

"How do you know it's a he?" Hull said, repeating my question from earlier.

She gave a smile that was both heart-melting and somewhat devilish. "No decent female thief would leave muddy tracks across a clean floor like that."

Hull opened his mouth to retort before biting his lip. After a moment, he blinked. "He is a tall, small-footed male who is adept at parkour."

"Which explains how he could leave so little trace."

He breathed in deeply through his nose. "He used a U-Haul truck to initially take the equipment to the gas station."

"I wondered why you were hovering a few inches above the snow on the curb earlier."

I have to say, the sexual tension in the room was so thick by then, I could've cut it with a blunt knife.

"I need to see the concert hall one more time," Hull said after a very long, very uncomfortable silence.

"We can leave right away," Duerre replied as she stood. "But I hope one of you has a car. I took a cab here and didn't realize how expensive they are."

Hull pounced on the opportunity. "Well you may just have to—"

"We have a car," I said quickly, stopping Hull before he said something that would undoubtedly be very rude. He looked over at me with daggers for eyes.

"Excellent!" she said with a bright smile. "We shouldn't waste time, then." She started her way down the stairs. I stood up slowly and put my coat back on, then turned to see Hull locked in place, eyes burning with fury and focused on me.

"You can't be serious," I said with a sigh.

"Why do you do this to me?" he shot back as he grabbed his coat.

"Maybe it's just a nice change, seeing you be the one squirming because you don't know what to do with yourself."

The three of us made our way to the concert hall without delay. Hull had opted to sit in the back driver seat, putting as much distance between him and Duerre as possible. She, however, had been positively delightful on the short drive, telling us about the upcoming concert, how pleasant Newfield was, and how great it was to see Sheridan again. He, of course, had not said a single word since we'd left the flat. When we reached the concert hall, we found Lennox standing by a sleek, black car, with an older man about to enter the door. Once we were parked, I recognized him as the chief of police, Lamont Conn.

The chief looked over at the group of us and gave an exasperated sigh. "Should've known better than to think he'd be too busy to help."

Duerre flashed a bright smile at Conn. "I personally requested the assistance of Mr. Hull. I hope that won't cause any trouble?"

Conn looked from Duerre to Hull to Lennox before letting off another loud sigh. "Like I could say a thing otherwise these days." He stepped down into the car and closed the door, which sped off within a matter of seconds.

I stepped over to Lennox and nudged his elbow. "I never did like your boss."

"He was your boss, too."

"For a *day*."

The four of us moved back into the concert hall, but instead of going straight to the storage room, Hull instead jumped on top of the seats in the center area and started scaling across them like an animal. Lennox and I must have been accustomed to this, because we simply kept walking. Duerre, however, had stopped, and was watching Hull with a tilted gaze. She followed his crawling until he reached the front row and stepped back down, his eyes going from the floor to the ceiling. He looked back over at us, then at her, and immediately away.

Once we'd stepped into the storage room, Lennox nodded back in the direction of the other two. "What's the deal there?"

I shook my head. "If I knew, I'd tell you. But I really, really don't."

"We ran the footprint and got a boot match," Lennox said, glancing back to see Hull tiptoe in with Duerre just a few steps behind him. "It's a brand made up in Seattle. Not cheap."

"So our thief has an expensive sense of style?" I prompted with a glance back at Hull.

"Or simply an expensive taste," Duerre piqued in.

Lennox nodded. "There's not much else besides that. I've got officers keeping watch on the roads leaving the city for any truck that could carry this, but nothing's been reported so far."

"They would never be foolish enough to leave so soon," Hull said, still managing to keep a minimum of five meters between him and Duerre.

"But they wouldn't be stupid enough to stay," Duerre shot back, her eyes narrowing and her lips curling into a smile.

"Biding their time, waiting for the opportune moment to leave," Hull spat. "They will leave when it is least likely a time for them to get caught. I would guess that they have no intention of leaving for at least two days."

"Brave guess," the woman said slyly.

"My guesses are all based on already-established information."

"So I've noticed."

"Alright then," Lennox said, bringing everyone's attention to him. "If you can handle this, I have another call. Keep me in the loop." He glanced between Hull and Duerre before nodding at me and leaving. Once he was out of earshot, Duerre let out a short giggle.

"Something tells me you won't keep him in the loop," she said as she stepped over to me, her eyes still on the detective.

"I never do," Hull said, his eyes instead focused on the entirety of the room.

I gestured down at the footprint. "So, boots made in Seattle. What a great tip."

Duerre gave a short nod. "I know exactly who we're after, thanks to that tip. A low-level thief, but he's clever, and fast. Tends to leave a calling card at the scene, but he didn't here." She looked around the room before focusing on Hull. "I'd be willing to bet if you took the screen off of the speaker you found, you'd find a card." Hull paused for only a moment to glance at her and acknowledge her words before returning his attention to the ceiling. She looked at me and shook her head slightly. "How can you two possibly work together as partners?"

"He doesn't treat me like an unstable nuclear bomb."

She gave a fake gasp and looked back at Hull. "Is that really what you think of me, Sheridan? A bomb waiting to explode?"

"Something of the like," the detective asserted. He gave one last look at the closest wall before walking over to us. "The room is clean, nothing left to find. Our best option is to start again tomorrow. I have a thought on where to start."

"As do I," Duerre said. Hull's mouth opened, but when his eyes locked with hers, his lips quickly pressed themselves together. I truly could not tell if he loved her or hated her, but it was certainly entertaining to watch.

"I guess we'll reconvene in the morning?" I offered. Duerre smiled and nodded, then cast one last furtive glance at Hull before leaving. I watched and waited until she was completely out of sight before turning to Hull.

"Why are you making me do this," he said in a voice that begged for mercy.

"The last time a girl looked at me like that was after my senior prom, and trust me, that was one Hell of an after-party," I said, my eyes still on the doorway.

"Then why don't you do us *both* a favor and garner her attention so it isn't focused on me."

"Something tells me you wouldn't like that."

He considered my sentence for a moment before scoffing and walking away.

*

When Hull and I returned that evening, he immediately went to the speaker, removed the screen, and found a small business card depicting a jail cell with it's door open. He'd then taken the business card, sat down at his computer, and gathered any and all information he could garner on this thief. When I left him at almost 1 AM, he was still hard at work. When I crawled out of bed at around 8, he was right where I had left him.

"You didn't forget about tonight, did you?" I asked as I poured myself a cup of coffee.

"How could I possibly forget," he replied with a dull tone.

"At least try to act happy. She likes you."

"Why?" I looked over to find him staring at the empty space ahead of him. "Why does she converge on me, why do we.. gah. Why does this happen to me, of all people? Shouldn't you be the one out there having women smile and giggle at you?"

I smirked. "Believe me, I've tried. I just don't have that charm of yours, apparently."

"What about the blonde woman from the magic show?"

"Cassidy Claypool? I haven't seen her since the show."

"No one to blame but yourself, then."

I sat down in my chair and took a swig of my coffee before replying. "So what have you got?"

He looked back down at his laptop. "She was right, the thief is from Seattle. The same card has been found on over a dozen separate occasions around the city. He is just as careful and articulate as she described, and he is a parkour expert."

"Come to think of it, she didn't mention that."

"She had no legitimate interest in assisting us, she was simply there to antagonize me."

"Maybe she was there to catch your eye."

"If she steals another statue and melts it down, then she will succeed in catching my eye. Right now, we cannot bear to have the distractions." He turned the laptop to face me. Currently his screen was occupied with what looked like a layout of a large room, with blue lines running across the floor. "A schematic of the storage room in the concert hall. Somehow, the thief was able to remove all of the equipment without leaving more than three muddy footprints. My first, and correct, thought was an aerial movement system."

"No wonder you spent so much time looking at the ceiling yesterday."

He nodded. "I was observing different points for harnesses to be kept in place. Sure enough, the upper walls had minute holes scattered around the room, all no doubt used for the movement of the equipment. Once he had tied them to the ropes, all he needed was to activate whatever system he had and watch as the speaker or light pole whizzed from the room to his waiting truck."

"And his parkour expertise is what helped him secure the harnesses."

"Exactly that." He clicked the mousepad and changed the screen to show a schematic of Newfield. "This took more work, but I was able to find four potential locations that he may have gone to once leaving the gas station. Because he has not left the city, he would need to hide the equipment somewhere obscure, but not so far off the path that it would attract attention if he were to visit. Once I had narrowed it down, I had the Deviants set out to see which one had—"

"I'm sorry, the what?"

He furrowed his brow. "The Deviants. Surely I've mentioned them before." I shook my head. "In the aftermath of the Man in Red case, I realized that the Internet could be a very powerful tool for investigation, rather than just a medium for that man to find his next targets. I started an organization of individuals here, in Newfield, who have an interest in criminal investigation, forensic sciences, et cetera.

The people who want to do what we do but would rather do it unofficially. I've grown fond of calling them the Newfield Deviants."

"Alright. Nice enough title."

"Indeed. I set them to work and about twenty minutes ago, one of them informed me that he had seen a loading truck, unmarked, parked near an old warehouse in the industrial district on Liberty Avenue. That is our best bet for finding the stolen equipment."

"So what are we waiting for?"

He nodded at me. "You."

I feigned a look of appreciation. "You waited up for me?"

"No, I waited up for a person capable of driving there." The smile that followed told me otherwise.

Within the hour, we arrived at the warehouse. It was old, probably from the late sixties, and hadn't been in use for around ten years. How these old buildings were able to go unattended for so long perplexed me, especially in a city growing as rapidly as Newfield. Nonetheless, this was where Hull believed we would find the equipment. We walked towards the sliding panel door to the warehouse slowly, my hand brushing softly against the butt of my pistol.

Before we'd even reached the door, Hull stopped, his eyes going to the ground and following the pavement back the way we'd come. He looked up at me for a moment before giving a heavy sigh.

"Too late. He came and left already," he said as he turned back to the door.

I looked down at the ground, confused. "How do you know?"

"Snowfall. It's been snowing heavily for the past three hours, but not heavy enough to cover up a fresh imprint leaving."

"Well couldn't we just follow the tracks?"

He shook his head. "Once he reaches the end of the road, the tracks merge. It would be near impossible."

"You specialize in near impossible." He smirked before sliding the panel door open. Sure enough, it revealed an empty warehouse, with trodden snow tracks leading in and out. We had to have just missed him by maybe an hour, probably less. Hull stooped down to examine the snowy prints before pressing his hands together and bringing them to his lips.

"Not enough data," he said. He stood and started pacing before looking back out the door. "The Deviant who spotted the truck should be able to identify it again. I will have to send them out, find where he has relocated to now."

"What do we do until then?"

He gave a groan. "Prepare for the banquet."

"The banquet's not until later this evening, we have at least twelve hours."

"You don't understand. It took me over twenty-four hours to be willing to leave the flat and risk running into *her*. Now you expect me to attend a banquet in which I will be in too close a proximity to her for a minimum of two hours. What do people even *do* at a, what? 'Pre-concert banquet?' What does that even mean?"

"It means it's a dinner of all the important people helping with the concert. We won't be alone with her, you know. I'm willing to bet Lennox will be there, probably the chief of police, the mayor, maybe even your brother."

He rolled his eyes. "You are quite literally listing reasons for me to *not* attend."

We started walking back to the car when I clasped him on the shoulder. "It won't be that bad. Consider me your anti-wingman. I'll make sure nothing any normal guy would want happens to you."

He gave a slight shake to his head. "What about attire? Do we have to look fancy?"

"Your normal choice of clothing is a purple button-up shirt, dress pants, a purple scarf, and a gray overcoat, and you're worried about looking fancy?"

"I also accompany that choice of clothing with a pair of handmade gloves and orange-laced shoes, thank you very much."

"Just wear what you normally wear. Minus the coat, scarf, gloves, and shoes."

"I don't own any other pairs of shoes."

"What the Hell is piled up at the bottom of your closet?"

"Evidence."

"You *keep* shoes that are from previous crimes?"

"No, I keep previous shoes of mine as evidence that I have in fact worn shoes that do not have orange laces."

I laughed and stepped carefully to avoid a large puddle. Even in the middle of a mystery, we found time to be humorous. And it was nice to see him not bored, or uptight. Or whatever it was that he got when Duerre was around. The more I thought about it, though, the more I realized how disappointed I would be if he decided to spend the evening with Duerre and leave me by myself. So in that moment, a little idea was hatched. One I hoped I could pull off.

As soon as we reached the flat, I grabbed a phonebook and started praying. And it seemed that today, luck was on my side, for when I reached the Cs, I found a "Claypool, Cassidy." And I really do think my heart skipped a beat when I made the phone call and got an actual female voice. One that was more than happy to accompany me to the banquet.

*

The group arrived at the banquet hall twenty minutes after the festivities had began. Hull was wearing his usual purple button-up shirt and dress pants, but had swapped his normal overcoat for a black one more suited for the occasion. On his feet were his normal orange-laced tennis shoes, but he had passed on wearing the gloves. He had also passed on wearing the scarf, but had managed to find a deep purple tie that nearly blended in with his shirt.

Walker had elected to wear a similar black overcoat with a white shirt underneath, a blue tie, and had also chosen to use gel in his hair to keep it calmed. His right arm was crooked to allow another arm, that of Cassidy Claypool, who had grown her hair to reach well past her shoulders. She wore an orange dress that stretched to the floor and held a sleek, golden-colored wallet. The trio stepped under an illuminated archway into the main center of the banquet hall, which was filled with men and women, all adequately dressed.

Hull looked around the room with a nervous glance. "It looks like a Men's Warehouse and every single dress store in Newfield exploded in one room."

Walker gave a smile. "I'd tell you to go socialize, but I know that can be difficult for you."

The detective glanced over at Walker with what could have been legitimate fear in his eyes. "Please do not leave me alone."

Claypool gave Walker a slight nudge. "Is he always like this?"

The doctor leaned in close to her ear. "Only when he's avoiding the woman he loves."

"I swear to God, the moment you two walk away, she will know and she will find me," Hull said with a cautious side-glance at the rest of the room.

Walker gave the detective a reassuring pat on the shoulder. "Maybe that wouldn't be such a bad thing." With that, he and Claypool walked off in the direction of the punch table, leaving Hull to stand very awkwardly by himself. Fortunately for him, or otherwise in his mind, Lennox soon walked through the door, sporting his own dress coat with a green undershirt.

"Look at that, you made it," the inspector said when he reached Hull.

"That I did," Hull said as he shook the man's hand. "Please do not leave me alone."

Lennox gave a look of surprise. "What, you're not shy, are you?"

"I am not one for large, formal events."

"Just grab a drink and enjoy yourself."

Hull cocked his brow. "If I were to properly enjoy myself, someone would have to die."

Lennox clapped his hands together quietly. "Alright, well, definitely didn't need to hear that. If someone turns up dead, don't be mad if I have to arrest you." He started away, presumably in the direction of the police chief. Hull helplessly watched the man walk away and disappear into the crowd before the hair on his neck stood on end.

"You know, you aren't that difficult to find in a crowd when you stand apart from it."

He turned to find himself face to face with a woman of absolute beauty. Her hair had been lightened from its brown to a blonde with dark streaks. Makeup had been applied to hide her natural freckles. Her lips were made infinitely more prominent by a deep red lipstick. But none of this could match her dress. A white dress that frilled out just above the knees, it seemed to have been made just for her. And as Hull looked her up and down, he knew what a horrible mistake he'd made in coming.

"I made no attempt to hide," he said, careful to breathe only through his nose. Somehow, she had managed to come within a quarter of a meter of his face.

Duerre smiled. "Shocking. I thought you'd be hiding under the tables by now."

"I have nothing to hide from."

"Oh you don't? That's even more shocking."

Hull opened his mouth to retort, but stopped when the lights dimmed. He looked around frantically before turning and staring in the direction of the DJ, who had just fumbled with his microphone.

"We're gonna slow things down for a song here. Special request by Ms. Caroline Duerre. Hope you all enjoy."

Hull felt something inside him freeze and curl up. He knew exactly what was about to play. He knew exactly what was about to happen. And despite everything, he knew he would be unable to stop what had been set in motion.

Duerre bumped his elbow. "I think this is the part where you ask me to dance."

The lights changed from their normal color to different shades of blue and green. Hull looked to his left, right into Duerre's deep brown eyes. The lights flickered across her face for only a moment, the lipstick looking to be a profound purple. He slowly extended his arm for her to take, and when she did, he led her out to the main floor, where at least a dozen other couples were already dancing. He turned to face her when they stopped, a slight quiver of confusion passing over his face.

"I, uh.." he murmured, but her smile shut him up. She took his left hand in her right and held it up, moved his right hand with her left so that his rested on her back, and softly pressed her free hand against his shoulder. She locked her eyes with his and, with a brisk step, put them into motion. At first they were out of sync, the detective still very unwilling to give in to the moment. But it didn't take long for their footsteps to mirror each other, moving them in a circular manner with the rest of the group.

"There now," she said with a smile, "that's not so bad, is it?"

The music had started moments ago, and only now did the lyrics begin. It was the exact song he had predicted. The very song that chorused through his mind whenever he thought of her. *So Close*.

"We both know better than this," Hull said, his voice fluttering.

"I know we do," she replied. "That's why we're doing it."

"Emotions influence action. You and I work in fields that cannot allow such influence."

"Maybe it's worth that risk."

"Unnecessary risks should not be taken."

She tilted her head. "You've never struck me as one to be overly cautious."

"Circumstances change. People change."

"I thought you used to say people never change."

He gave a slight smirk. "Whoops."

"So tell me, then, Sheridan Hull," she said as the dancers came to a halt and reversed direction, "have you changed? Or are you still the same Sheridan Hull I met all those years ago?"

"That depends entirely on who that Sheridan Hull was."

"He was a calm, collected guy with the mind of a genius and a rock for a heart."

"Sounds like me."

"I wasn't done." She dipped her chin slightly. "I was the one to break through the rock."

"Now I know you are fabricating your memories."

She giggled. "I thought you might say that."

The lights shifted again, starting to spin and creating a blue-green mesh of light that circled the room. The dancers shifted again, moving in the counter-clockwise motion. Hull and Duerre, however, managed to become the center of the circle, still moving but not joining the rest. Their eyes were locked on each other, barely noticing the world around them. As the song had gone on, their hands had slowly pulled each other closer. Now there was little space between them.

"What'll it take to convince you, Sheridan?" she asked before leaning close to the side of his head. "What does it take to change your mind?"

"The world must change before my mind will."

"Why?"

"Because there are people in the world who would use my changed mind against me, and you."

"Why should those people have a say in whether we can be together or not?"

"Those people will do everything in their power to turn our emotions against us. Because emotions influence action."

"Some of those actions are okay."

"But not all."

"But some."

"Not even some."

"This one is."

He had no time to react as she closed the space between them, pressing her lips against his and holding them there. Every logical part of him screamed in rage and horror, knowing he was making a terrible mistake, knowing that in a single motion, Caroline Duerre had endangered her life. The logical part of him wanted nothing more than to tear away from her and leave, right then, and right there.

But the smaller, stronger part of him, refused to budge.

The kiss lasted for only several seconds, but to them, it was an eternity, filled with dim blue and green lights, the blurs of motion that was the other dancers, and the soft ambience of the music. But as soon as eternity had began, it ended. She let her head move away, allowing their eyes to lock one more time.

"I can't."

The other dancers were stopping now and the song was coming to an end. Hull's eyes fell to the floor, but Duerre's remained locked on his face, her head tilting in minor confusion. The detective gulped twice before shaking his head ever-so-slightly.

"I can't," he repeated, giving a third gulp. "I'm sorry."

The other dancers had started to disperse now, and off towards the corner of the room, John Walker looked on with a touch of sadness in his eyes. He knew with just a glance, seeing Duerre's trembling hand clutching the detective's, and Hull's eyes focused squarely on the floor, that something had come so close to happening. He knew that Hull had held the utmost happiness in the palm of his hand, but let it go. And that pained Walker more than ever.

Hull and Duerre's hands returned to their sides. Hull's eyes looked up, over at Walker, then immediately to the door. He had no hesitation. He had no second thought. His feet started and within ten seconds, his hands pushed the doors forward, and he was gone.

*

Hull didn't leave the flat at all the next day. In fact, I can't recall actually seeing him in person. I could hear him moving around in his room, and I know there were a handful of occasions where his door would open and the bathroom door would close, and vice versa. But other than those sparse moments, he kept to himself. And to be honest, I wasn't sure how to react to that. I had dealt with Hull when he was wrong, but in the year we'd lived together, I'd never seen this. This was something new, and something sad.

I'd watched as he and Duerre had gone to dance. I'm no lip reader, but I'd been able to follow the conversation through their emotions. Well, mostly hers. It was when she kissed him that I thought she was making headway, that finally, we were going to see a truly human side to Hull. But almost as soon as the kiss had finished, his eyes had fallen to the floor, and I knew then that the moment had been lost. He'd left the room, left the banquet, Hell, I don't even know if he came back to the flat right after or just left Newfield for a few hours. All I know is, the night had left its mark.

Seeing him in such a state of confusion and sadness and despair had nearly removed me from my own date, but I'd been able to salvage what time remained. Cassidy was far more interesting than I first realized. We talked for almost two hours about my time in the war, her time in college, whatever came up. She'd been in a sorority every year and had graduated with a degree in new media communications. She truly was a fascinating individual, and it prided me to think I had a date with her the very next week.

At around 5:30 in the morning, on the day before the concert, Hull shook me awake. With half-opened eyes, I was able to see that he was fully clothed and ready to go.

"W..what's going on?" I said with a slight slur.

"I found him."

I blinked several times, watching the detective's face come into focus. "Found who?"

"The thief. I found him."

"How'd you do that?" I asked as I shook my head and sat up.

"The Deviants tracked the truck to an apartment complex. Two of them watched the building all of yesterday and saw him. Positive identification, verification of contents, everything. All that's left to do is go there and take him into custody."

I rubbed my eyes. "Then why didn't you call Lennox and just give him the address?"

"Oh forget him, he takes too long. Besides, it's too early for him to be at the station."

"It's too early for *anyone* to be doing anything." I glanced over at my clock and furrowed my brow. "Did you seriously wake me up this early on a Sunday?"

"For the love of God, will you *please* just get out of bed, throw some clothes on, and hurry up," he said before turning and leaving the room. I scowled at the doorway before throwing my covers off and stepping out of bed. After a very brief shower, I was roughly clothed and ready to go. I found Hull sitting in the main room, his fingers tapping away at his laptop keyboard.

"Don't you think he'll still be there in a couple of hours?" I asked as I put my coat on.

"No," the detective replied, stepping away from the laptop. "The Deviants reported that he left two hours ago and returned with the truck some twenty minutes ago. We have a very small window of opportunity, because I do not expect him to relocate another time."

"There's something more to this, isn't there?"

He closed the laptop and glanced over at me. "What do you mean?"

"You seem legitimately excited to be closing in on the thief, and you're never this excited about something like stolen equipment."

"Perhaps I simply want to put the case to an end and move on with myself."

"Or you think that by finding the equipment sooner, you can get it back to the concert hall sooner and be that much closer to never having to see her again."

This brought him to a halt. I watched his trembling hand feel its way towards his scarf, which had been resting on the top of his armchair. He carefully grabbed the scarf and wrapped it around his neck before giving me a very somber glance. "Perhaps."

I grabbed him by the shoulder before he could turn and start down the stairs. "What happened? Everything looked like it was going so well for you both. Why did you leave?"

He looked at my hand before gazing back at me. "John, you know how thick we are in the midst of Chimaera's operations. You know how powerful and devious Moriarty is. When we traveled to the Vatican, I believe we truly did bash the beehive. We have startled them, and he is not an individual to startle. He will use every available weakness to bring us down. And if I allow my emotions to dictate my actions, Duerre will become a weakness to be exploited."

"What makes you think he won't use me?"

"You are an equal variable, a matching piece in the game. He would rather strike from the bottom, weaken the structure, than attack the top and only injure the head."

I blinked twice and shook my head. "God I hope you're right. Because I won't like being his target if he decides bringing you down is more important than bringing us down."

"Nonsense." He started forward, then glanced back and gave me a wry smile. "I would be lost without my blogger."

We made our way to the car and off onto the main road, Hull providing turn-by-turn instructions on how to reach the location. The complex was in the western part of the city, practically on the opposite side from the concert hall. I could see the logic behind it, but at the same time, it was only a turn away from the highway, which was an easy path right out of the city. But I doubted the thief had intended to stay long.

We pulled up in front of the complex about a half-hour later. The sun had yet to start its climb into the sky, meaning the only light on the road came from the street lamps. Standing underneath one was a younger man, his arms clutching his sides. He glanced up at us and gave Hull a nod. The detective moved over to him, offering up what I actually think was a $100 gift card to iTunes.

"Which one," Hull said as the man tucked the card away in his pocket.

"8F," the man replied with a nod back at the complex. "One of the biggest rooms in the building. Registered under 'Scott Hardin'." Hull nodded at the man, who slowly walked off towards a nearby alleyway. I stepped up beside the detective and craned my neck to watch the man disappear from sight.

"Did you really pay him with a gift card to iTunes?" I asked.

"The Deviants consist of college-age individuals who would rather be paid in some form of online currency than actual money. Saves them the time of converting it themselves." We started forward towards the door to the complex. "The boy who first spotted the truck asked to be paid with a Steam gift card. And before then, I had no idea what 'Steam' was besides a form of gaseous liquid."

We passed through the door and started slowly up the stairs. The closer we came, the quicker we seemed to walk. Whether it was excitement or fear or just pure adrenaline, it only took us maybe a minute to climb all eight flights. We found ourselves directly in front of the door, a golden "8F" nailed to the black wood. Hull reached down and softly clutched the doorknob, then gave a very minute twist. When no resistance came, he glanced up at me and started a short countdown with his fingers. As soon as he hit one, his hand twisted the rest of the way.

The door flew open, allowing us to step in to a room filled to the brim with electronic equipment. Speakers were stacked on each other, light poles were lying across the floor, everything that had gone missing from the storage center of the concert hall was right here. But what we hadn't expected to find was the thief standing directly ahead of us with a pistol in his hand aimed at Hull's head.

"Don't take another step," the thief said. Hull straightened his back and lifted his chin slightly. "I knew as soon as you showed up my time was running out, and it wouldn't take long for you to find me."

"Intelligence and foresight. Good." Hull's words were far too mocking, and the thief was no fool to sarcasm.

"I'm not afraid to shoot you right here. Silenced gun, nobody would hear. I could take you both down right now and just throw your bodies into the truck with the rest of the goods."

"You know that'd never work," I said as I stepped forward, bringing myself parallel with Hull.

The thief turned the gun to aim at me. "I said not another step."

I lifted my hands into the air, then nodded at the thief's gun. "I hate that I'm saying this, but you're not gonna be able to do a damn thing with the safety on like that." The thief glanced down at the gun, giving Hull and I an opportunity to disarm him. But before either of us could move, two small arms wrapped themselves around the thief's neck, making his eyes bulge and his mouth open wide. From over his shoulder came the head of Caroline Duerre.

"Take the gun!" she barked. Hull and I snapped into motion, the detective grabbing the gun and me moving to secure the man's arms. As I wrestled to keep his arms under control, I couldn't help but notice that Duerre looked very, very different. She was now clad in what looked like a black cloak that was tied at her neck and reached down to the floor. Her hair was crudely tied back into a ponytail, with several different sections having come out. Once Hull had taken the gun, he pulled a pair of handcuffs from his coat pocket and secured them around the man's wrists. Once we were sure he was locked, Duerre and I released him.

Hull, rather than focusing on the thief, gave Duerre a very concerned look. "How did you even know where to look?"

She smirked at him. "I operate as the best thief this century since Stephane Breitwieser, and all he stole was artwork. You think I wouldn't be able to track down some low-life like Hardin?"

"If you knew where he was the entire time," Hull snapped back as he grabbed the thief's shoulder, "why not just arrest him then?"

"I didn't know *where* he was," she replied coolly as she reached behind her head and undid the tail. "I expected the thief to be someone from the concert hall, and chose to tail the suspicious guys one by one. I ran into one of your, what do you call them, Deviants? He was keeping a close eye on Hardin here. All it took was me sneaking in the back window last night and seeing the equipment, then walking back out and seeing the same Deviant, to know you'd be here soon."

"So you just waited?" Hull asked as he sat the man down.

"And waste my time? Of course not. I waited until you both left your flat before I came."

I glanced back towards the bathroom, which was the only possible entry for her. "How'd you even get in?"

She gave me a smile similar to the one Hull had given me not even an hour earlier. "I once broke into the White House just to get an autograph without the president knowing. You don't think I could get through a bathroom window?" She nodded back at the doorway. "And you're welcome for unlocking that for you. I'm sure that confused him enough to keep him from shooting. Also, nice touch with the safety. Hardin never was one for weapons, so of course he wouldn't think to just try shooting one of you before actually looking at the gun."

"You talk like you know each other," Hull commented as he started wandering the equipment-filled living room.

"In this line of business, you know *of* each other. Which is why I'm still so surprised he took the risk of stealing from me."

Hull tapped one of the speakers before turning and nodding at Hardin. "We'll take him in to Lennox, and have his boys retrieve the equipment. Which means you, Walker, can get some more sleep."

Duerre looked from Hull to me with a crooked brow. "Why do you call each other by your last names? You live with each other, you'd think it would be easier to just say 'Sheridan' and 'John.'"

"Formalities die hard," Hull said.

"Like you wouldn't believe," I added.

*

It only took a few hours for Lennox to relocate the equipment back to the concert hall, as well as have Hardin put in a temporary cell at the station. The concert wasn't until tomorrow but stage assembly had been going for days, and as soon as the group of us had shown up with the truck, the remaining stagehands and concert hall administrators had burst out in cheer. They were happy, to say the least. Before leaving the concert hall, Duerre had told Hull and me of a final get-together tonight, a tradition of hers, like a good luck toast for the concert. With a bit of encouragement from me, Hull had agreed to attend.

Because the rest of the day had been fairly uneventful, Hull and I had returned to the flat and simply passed the time by playing Halo 4. He returned to his raging self after barely two minutes in the first game. It wasn't until around six in the evening that we stopped playing and prepared for the event. Once we decided we looked formal enough, but not as formal as the banquet, we departed. When we were about halfway to the specified location, I decided to make a very great leap with Hull.

"I think you should go for it," I said, that being the first thing spoken since we'd entered the car.

"Go for what?" he asked ambiguously, his eyes on the passing cars.

"You know exactly what."

He sighed. "I do not take pleasure in endangering peoples' lives."

"Oh bullshit. You've put me through countless occasions where we both could've died."

"You can handle yourself."

"And you think she can't?" When he offered no response, I continued. "You saw her this morning, and you've known her far longer than I have. But I already know she's more than capable of looking after herself."

"But why take that risk when it is unnecessary?"

A distinct buzzing drew my attention down to the cup holder for only a moment. The screen of my phone was illuminated, and on it was a text message from Cassidy. It read:

I heard you guys found the equipment! Great job! Can't wait to see you next week!

I bit my bottom lip and refocused on the road.

"Y'know, there's something a good friend of mine used to always say," I added. "He would say that there is a significant difference between doing what is necessary, and doing what is right. And I think he had a good point. Sure, it might be an unnecessary risk... but sometimes it's not about necessity. It's about doing something because the chance is there."

And *that* actually made Hull fall silent for the remainder of the trip. I couldn't help but feel a small sense of satisfaction. I'd always wanted to use that quote, but the timing never really worked out. Still, it helped me pay James some justice. He always was the more poetic one.

We reached the location after about five minutes of wandering. It was, essentially, a high-class bar with a stage. Hull and I walked in to find the place filled with people, some there for the pre-concert event, some just there to be there. One of the larger tables was occupied by Lennox, the police chief, Malcolm, Duerre, and others. As soon as she'd spotted us, she signaled for us to join them. Hull gave one glance at the table's occupants, gave me a pensive look, and sighed.

Lennox gave us a nod as we sat down. "Good work today, guys. Glad everything worked out."

"They did a phenomenal job," Duerre said, her eyes on us. "Without the detective and the doctor, who knows what we'd be doing tomorrow night."

"We simply did our job," Hull said, his eyes focused narrowly on Duerre. "Nothing more."

She leaned back. "I wouldn't say that."

Before anyone could respond, the song that had been playing stopped and was replaced by some horrendous feedback. Everyone looked up at the stage with scrunched faces to see a man in a suit holding a hand up in his defense.

"Sorry about that, sorry. So, uh, it says here we have a special performance tonight by none other than Caroline Duerre. Uh, Ms. Duerre, if you could come to the stage, please."

Duerre turned and looked at us before standing. "Wish me luck!" We all watched her carve her way through the crowd before reaching the stage. It was only then that I noticed how drastically different her attire was from earlier today, as well as from two nights before. Her hair was up again, but now with a black studded band keeping it back. She wore high heels and gray laced socks that came up almost to her knees, a dark gray half-coat that was open in the front, and to cap it all off, a frilly, purple dress. She gave the man with the mic a nod before taking the stand and looking out at us.

"Hi everybody, thanks for being here. I know some of you aren't really here to see me perform, but there's a song I wanted to sing and felt like it'd be better suited here than at tomorrow's concert. So, with that, I hope you enjoy!"

The lights dimmed slightly, with a single spotlight remaining on her. She gave a slight gulp and turned her focus to our table. The music started to play, a tune I didn't recognize. Once she started singing, though, I knew exactly why she'd picked the song. I couldn't think of any other reason for her to sing "You Do Something to Me."

Now it made perfect sense.

I looked carefully to make sure her vision was locked exactly where I expected it to be.

I followed her gaze once more. Hull was the center of her attention. And from the way his eyes were unwaveringly holding her stare, I suspected she was the center of his.

The tune picked up, extra instruments coming into play. But part of me was content to just sit there and watch a second chance happen. Even though he wasn't smiling, Hull also wasn't trying to avoid her gaze. For over two minutes, they stared at each other, her singing in one of the best voices I'd ever heard, and him watching. Perhaps I was finally seeing another side of that admiration he held for her. Hull had never struck me as someone to be enthralled by a singer's talent, but I suppose she was, in his eyes, a multi-talented individual. Of course he would value all of the talents. Once she'd finished the song, the room erupted in applause.

And to my utmost surprise, Hull was also clapping.

The remainder of the evening went by fairly quickly. We all shared some stories, had one or two drinks. Everything was actually enjoyable. And why should it not have been? Tomorrow was New Years' Eve. 2013 was about to begin. Who knew what the year would hold, other than prospect? It was sitting there, surrounded by the most eclectic group of people, that I truly felt at home. Finally, Newfield was a place I felt comfortable in. Maybe now I would be able to go a week without a war-filled nightmare.

At around nine, the group started to disperse. I walked out to the front of the bar, holding the keys softly in my palm.

"Well that was fun, wasn't it?" I said to Hull, who had been behind me as we'd walked out. "Nice getting to see everyone. And she can really sing. Concert tomorrow ought to be great." No response came. I finally spotted our car in the parking lot and took a step forward, glancing over my shoulder to make sure Hull was paying attention. "You coming?"

But when I turned, I found myself to be alone.

*

Hull stepped out of the cab and handed a $50 bill back through the driver door. He stood facing the glass front doors of the Cher Restaurant, one of the most posh and expensive locations in downtown Newfield. He approached the doors slowly, waiting for the automatic sensor to push them out and allow him access. He stepped in, nodded at the server who came to greet him, and started towards the back of the restaurant. Towards the far corner was a booth, with what looked like a person wearing a wide-brimmed hat occupying one of the seats. Hull took the one opposite and picked up a menu.

"I knew you would come," Duerre said as she set her own menu down and removed the hat.

"Of course you did," Hull replied, still keeping his eyes on the menu. He started perusing the entrée section. "Your necklace is nice."

Duerre glanced down at it and smiled. "Thank you. It arrived for me anonymously about five years ago."

He changed his focus to the appetizers. "And the ring."

"Same situation three years ago."

He flipped to the back of the menu, bringing him to the beverages. "And the earrings."

"One year ago."

He set the menu down and clasped his hands on the table, giving her what looked like a forced smile. "You seem to have quite the admirer."

"Yes," she said as she reached her own hands across the table and placed them on top of his. "I do."

THE CASE OF THE BLACK TUNNEL

Jarrad Speed glanced up from his notepad just in time to see a wadded piece of paper fly over his head and peg the kid behind him. He looked forward and saw a burly-looking kid making rude gestures to the person behind him, but that was about the limit of how much attention he would give them. He didn't care much for the other kids in his Oceanography class, and he found it somewhat stupid that the entirety of his spring break had to be spent with them, and the Biology students, and the Marine Biology Students, and the Chemistry students. Four majors, six buses, three hundred students. What a great week.

He looked back down at his notepad, taking some time to admire his latest work. He'd taken to drawing during class to pass the time, and now he found himself drawing more than actually paying attention to any of the content. But then again, just how interesting could wave cycles be? He was only listed as an Oceanography major because it was what his parents expected of him. He hoped to become a recognized artist before the day he'd have to work as an oceanographer.

"Hey Speedo!" a voice yelled from ahead of him. He looked up to see the burly-looking kid's eyes on him. "Throw the paper back, would ya?"

Jarrad glanced down at his feet, where the wadded up paper had managed to find a home. He leaned down, snatched the wad up, and tossed it forward, not bothering to care where it went. He glanced out the window just in time to see their bus enter a tunnel, the lighting going from natural to a strobe-like orange. He looked down at his notepad again, smiled, and picked up his pencil to keep working.

The tip of the pencil only just reached the pad when the strobing orange outside stopped, as well as the lights on the bus. Everyone's voices went silent for a moment in shared confusion. Jarrad glanced out the window and found that he couldn't see any headlights, any light from the end of the tunnel, any light at all. And after a moment, he realized that the bus had stopped. It looked like everything in the tunnel had just ceased to exist. He shuffled his hand into his pocket, hoping to grab his phone and turn the screen on.

The single light at the front of the bus came to life, revealing a lone figure standing just a half-meter from the front row. The figure that stood there was a man, clad in a black suit and undershirt, dress pants, and shoes that were so deep a black, they could've been purple. The only thing that wasn't black in his attire was his tie, which was a pure white. The man's hair was black as well, stringy and looking as if it had gone a long time without being cleaned. It almost looked as if the man had been electrocuted, judging by his hair. He looked up at us with dark brown eyes that were wider than natural, and a sneer that revealed some of the most tainted teeth Jarrad had ever seen. The man held his hands to his side, the left hand being visible, the right hand hidden beneath a black glove.

"Hello, students of Newfield University! I am your instructor for today." The man's voice was like a purr with a metallic tinge to it. He stood with his head pushed slightly forward, his eyes surveying the students with eager anticipation. "I hope you've all had a fantastic trip so far, because it's about to get a lot more interesting. I don't want to waste anyone's time, so we'll get right to it." He lifted his chin and clasped his hands behind his back. "You won't be going to the beach. I'm sorry. We're going somewhere else, somewhere much more entertaining."

The bus gave a slight jerk to its side, everything outside still being completely dark. The burly student from before craned his neck to look behind the black-haired man before giving a slight jump. "What happened to the bus driver?"

The man glanced back to the now-empty seat, then forward at us, his sneer looking wider. "The bus driver had to leave. If you knew him, I'm sorry. He's not coming back. But you're in very capable hands!"

The student that had been sitting next to the burly kid jumped from his seat, his hands going for the man's neck. The man stepped back, his own arms coming forward. He grabbed the student by the shoulders and spun him to the side, slamming his back against the bus wall.

"At tut tut, now now," the man said, "that's not very nice." The student tried to struggle, but obviously the man was much stronger than he looked. "Why would you do something like that?"

The student jerked in the man's grip before glaring at him. "To stop a crazy man like you."

"Stop me?" The man gave a cackle, something that could've come right out of a horror movie. "You can't stop me! None of you can." He lowered his gaze but kept his sneer. "And you've done a good service, you really have. What's your name, boy?"

"L-Logan Hammel."

"Good for you, Logan," the man replied, bringing his chin back up. "Now I have someone to show off, someone to make an example of. Thank you!" The man released him and took a step back, leaving Logan with a surprised look. After a short moment, the man held out his hand and continued. "Now, with your cooperation, I need you to give me your wallet, your student ID, and your cell phone."

Logan looked the man up and down a few times before reluctantly pulling his wallet from his back pocket and his cell phone from his front. He handed the two together to the man, who snatched them from the student's hand and tucked them away in his suit pocket.

"Good, good! You take instruction well, that's good," the man said.

In a sudden move that shocked every student on the bus, the man grabbed Logan by the shirt and threw him towards the front of the bus. Logan staggered against the windshield, his arms spread wide.

The man turned to the rest of us. "I will expect you all to give me your wallets or purses, your ID cards, and your cell phones. If you try to hide the cell phone, I will know. You all have one, you're teenagers." He opened his coat and pulled out a small, metal object. After a moment, he flipped the top open, revealing it to be a lighter. He glanced over his shoulder at Logan, who had yet to move. "Here, hold this for me." He tossed the now-lit lighter back.

Immediately, Logan was engulfed in a bright flash of fire, as if his entire body had been soaked in gasoline. Screams started from all over the bus. But nothing, *nothing*, was more horrifying than the sound of cackling that came from the man, an evil laugh that started in his throat and slowly worked its way out, as he sneered at the rest of the students.

*

"And I am telling *you*, that movie was completely below par and not worth the amount we paid to see it."

I shook my head and tossed my hat across the room, watching Hull take his own seat and put his feet up. I gave a sigh before replying. "It's a modern take on the Wizard of Oz, it was phenomenal."

He scoffed. "Hardly."

Being Hull's roommate, I had been forced to take the brunt of what had been three months of no casework. We'd welcomed in the new year at the concert, with tickets given to us courtesy of Caroline Duerre. But after that, it was right back to normal. I believe Duerre left on an airplane at around five in the morning the next day, so I doubt Hull had a proper chance to say goodbye. The minor theft case that had accompanied her had been the last case he'd worked on. Almost three months had passed since then. And I have to be honest, those months had *not* gone easily.

I think that the longer I lived with Hull, the different stages of boredom I began to see. He was like an onion in how many different stages of boredom he held within his tall, deductive self. The first stage often revealed itself within the hour of completing a case. The glint to his eye would diminish, his shoulders would sink slightly, and his overall mood would begin a very, very shallow decline. After a day, he would resort to trying to occupy his time by playing music, shooting things, doing Sudoku puzzles, or performing the feat of doing two or more of these things at once.

After a month, the normal occupiers would lose their luster, and he would experiment with other things. This led to the random science tests happening in the kitchen, and the bathroom, and the bedrooms. But this time, the boredom was really chipping at him in a new, unusual way. For Christmas, his niece had gotten him an Amazon Kindle, as well as a few different books. One of them discussed the art of feng shui. And as soon as he'd finished the book, he had taken the art to heart and started rearranging *everything* in the living room. After about five different attempts, he found an arrangement that left him satisfied.

It was, of course, the original arrangement.

In a feeble attempt to distract him today, on my day off, we had gone to an early screening of a movie that came out a few weeks ago, "Oz: The Great And Powerful." I thought it just might stand a chance at keeping him entertained. I was wrong. He didn't say a word until we reached the car, at which point he stated everything that was wrong with the movie. By that time, I'd managed to just block him out, because I had admittedly quite enjoyed the film.

"Look at that," he said with a sweeping gesture at the clock on the wall. "Not even 10 AM and I am completely ready to sit here for the rest of eternity and allow the stagnation to take place."

I pushed my tongue against my cheek as I grabbed the paper. "You could always go out."

"Go out, yes, what a novel suggestion. Go outside, into the world, where everything and everyone is interesting. Oh, no, that's not quite right, is it. Because the world isn't interesting. There is absolutely nothing of interest or value beyond that glass door."

"That's the spirit."

A very long silence fell on the room before the sound of footsteps coming up the stairs brought me from an odd newspaper-induced trance. I glanced over my shoulder and furrowed my brow when I saw both Lennox and Malcolm Hull approaching the door, the latter looking very worried. As in, physically concerned about something.

"This must be important, if both of you are here," Sheridan said without glancing at the men.

"It is," Lennox said, his breathing heavy. "Six buses of students left for the coast yesterday and never made it. We didn't find out until today, when we got a package sent to the police station with no return address."

"How difficult can locating six school buses full of students be?" Sheridan snapped back.

"We have no idea where they went, no idea how they *could* have gone missing," Lennox replied.

"Sounds problematic."

"Sheridan, it's the liaison, McNair. He's calling himself—"

"Xaphon. So I've heard."

Lennox took a step forward. "He's burning people, Hull."

"Sounds extremely problematic."

"Sheridan," Malcolm interrupted, his voice weak, "Bailey was on one of the buses."

I felt my insides chill over. Bailey, Malcolm's daughter and Sheridan's prized niece. Probably the only family member of his he would admit to loving. My eyes drifted to the detective, whose face had gone morose and pale. His eyes trembled slightly in their sockets, both focused on the nothingness before him. He took a moment before blinking and standing, then gazing over at the two visitors.

"What have you got."

Lennox gave a sigh of relief. "He sent a package to the station. We weren't sure what to make of it at first. A wallet, a student ID card, a DVD, and ashes. It didn't take long for us to piece together what had happened. We started the DVD and saw him.. something's happened to him, it's real bad. We knew we'd need you, so we stopped it to come."

Sheridan glanced down at the floor before nodding at the door. "Let's go. All of us." He looked over at me. I gave a nod and grabbed my coat, joining the group as we left. The detective didn't object to riding in the police car. In fact, he didn't say a word the entire time. He sat and stared out the window, his jaw locked, his eyes still giving a slight tremble. And I didn't blame him. The thought of losing a loved one was not an easy thought to bear. I only hoped we could all find the students before something happened to put both Sheridan and Malcolm at the throat of Xaphon.

We arrived at the police station within ten minutes and immediately made our way to the screening room. Several other inspectors and officers were gathered, as well as the chief. He leaned against the wall and glared at Sheridan when we entered. I knew the detective had never done anything against the man on a personal level, but Sheridan had a knack for making the Newfield Police Department look extremely inadequate.

"Are we ready now?" Conn asked, the television remote clasped in his hand. Lennox nodded at him. Conn looked at the television, propped against the wall. He flicked the light switch to his left and pressed the play button.

The screen seemed to shuffle around for a moment before settling down and focusing on what I assumed was a room that was dark, save for a single spotlight. After a moment, a figure stepped into the light, and a very distinct chill crawled its way up my back. The figure had an essence of familiarity that was drowned out by an overwhelming essence of horror. The person was no doubt Ross McNair, the man we'd met over half a year ago. That was easily identifiable by the face and the gloved right hand.

The rest of him, however, had changed. His clothes were relatively the same. He wore a black suit, matching dress pants, and shoes so deep a black they could've been purple. Even the glove was the same color. The only thing that didn't match was his tie, which was a contrasting white. What had changed about him was more visible in his face and head. His eyebrows seemed to have an unnatural curvature, his nostrils were flared, and when he faced the camera, an evil sneer carved its way across his face. The combination of the three made for something reminiscent of the Joker.

His hair was the new, defining point. When I had met him, his hair had been neatly cut and persuaded to the right, carefully combed and formed to perfection. Now, it looked as if he had abandoned all hope in maintaining it, as well as going out of his way to make it even more aberrant. His hair was curled and twisted upward, like that of a mad scientist. It was like a bolt of lightning had passed through him and only left its mark on his hair. He sneered at the camera for a long moment before clasping his hands in front, the gloved one clutching the bare.

"This, oh, this is fun, good fun," he said, his sneer diminishing to a far more mild smile when he wasn't talking. His voice had a very odd metallic tinge to it, not a product of the recording. "I've been waiting a long time for this, I really have. Now that you've given me a grand opportunity, I've decided it's time to start. You're all very smart people, very smart, so it shouldn't take you long to figure out what I've sent. The wallet, the student ID, and the student. He was a brave kid. Stupid, but brave. Though I guess those can be very synonymous, can't they.

"Whatever thoughts you had of me before, you can quickly replace with the thoughts I intend to give you now. Did I really strike you all as a good-natured political liaison? Because if so, maybe you aren't so very smart after all. The only one of you who saw through that was the know-it-all detective. Even your mayor was too stupid to realize how horrible of a job I did. No, I'm no political liaison. I'm much more than that. I am Xaphon, and this, this is my stake at introducing you, the quiet, quaint people of Newfield, to something more.

"In the course of just five minutes, I was able to successfully abduct over three hundred of Newfield's future. So many students, so many hopefuls. All of them are now in my grasp. All of them are now in my merciless hands. I was kind enough to make an example of exactly what I plan to do with these students, until my demands are met. Newfield harbors and reveres an individual who has done too much in too little an amount of time. He has allowed his head to become so enlarged with his own fame that I think it's time he was brought back down to our level.

"Sheridan Hull, the boy wonder, the genius detective, must be dealt with. Something must be done about Sheridan Hull. You can excommunicate him, you can arrest him, you can kill him. I demand that action be taken against him. And I don't need any logical reason why. This is simply what I demand. And I think you'll find my demands important, because for every day that something is not done about Sheridan Hull, two Newfield University students will be burned alive. Any two, it won't make a difference to me. I will then kindly pack their ashes, their student ID cards, and their wallets or purses into a little baggy and send it to you.

"When I hear that Sheridan Hull has been adequately dealt with, I will release the students and be satisfied with the complying of my demands. And I will warn you right now, I will accept no bargain, no negotiation, no anything. I will also say that if you make the foolish attempt to 'find me' and stop me, you will fail. Because this, unlike everything else Newfield is used to, is not a game. The police department, and Sheridan Hull, must remember that they cannot always be one step ahead of the criminal. They cannot always win.

"There is no potential for the odds to be changed against me. This is not a circumstance in which I can be defeated. Why? Because I control the factors, I control the scenario. You've entered my world now, and my world is very, very violent."

The video cut with what sounded like a horrible, malevolent cackling noise.

A disturbing silence fell across the room as people looked between themselves. Once the lights came back, though, I immediately looked to the chief of police, who had his eyes square on Sheridan Hull. Lennox moved through the crowd quickly, but Conn was too quick.

"What the Hell are you all waiting for?" he roared, glaring out at the room full of flustered officers. "Arrest that man right now!"

"I'll take care of it," Lennox said, finally reaching the detective. He cast a furtive glance at Conn, not caring to get his approval, before gazing over at me and nodding to the door. I rushed to join him as he escorted Sheridan from the room. We turned left and started down a hallway, Lennox escorting Hull at the shoulder. Once we were in the hall that led to the front doors, Lennox grabbed both Hull and I's shirt elbows and pulled us off through another doorway, which led to a staircase moving down.

"What are you doing?" Hull said, genuine confusion in his voice.

"Disobeying orders," Lennox sharply replied as he started down the stairs. "Don't make me regret it." Hull looked at me with a furrowed brow before following the inspector. He led us down to a dimly-lit basement, with several doorways leading off in different directions. Once he'd closed the door behind us, he started across the main area. "This section of the basement's not in use anymore. We used to keep people in the cells across the hall temporarily, but it became too much of a liability."

"Why are we down here?" Hull asked.

"Nobody comes down here," Lennox shot back. "Ever. So I'm putting you in one of the rooms, and I'm going to help you as best I can. I'll tell Conn I transported you to Lane County Adult Corrections. But you can't leave here, at all."

Hull stopped walking. "My niece has just been abducted, inspector. I will do *everything in my power* to find her."

Lennox turned and pushed his face close to Hull's. "If you even so much as step outside, someone's going to shoot you. Conn will put out an APB on you and give every officer in a fifty-mile radius permission to use deadly force." He stepped back and opened a door, leading to a meeting room of sorts. "I'll bring everything of relevance down here and take over the investigation formally. I will do everything in *my* power to help you, but only if you cooperate."

Hull looked at the inspector, his eyes narrowed and trembling. I glanced from Hull to Lennox, hoping he would just agree for once. After a very long wait, Hull nodded in compliance. "I need the package and the DVD."

"As soon as I can bring it down, I will. I'll also slip food and water down, but you might be able to find stuff in the refrigerators."

"What about security?" I asked.

Lennox scoffed. "Cameras down here stopped working months ago. And since nobody comes down here, nobody bothered to fix them."

"Where do you want me?" I questioned, both to the inspector and Hull.

Lennox gave a slight shake to his head. "I can't have you stay here too. I can say you're helping me, so you can come down when I do, but if you drop off the radar as well, it'll attract attention." I gave a nod and followed him into the room. It was spacious enough, meaning Hull would have plenty of area to do whatever he'd need to do. I couldn't really imagine how he would figure everything out while stuck here, but I'd learned better than to underestimate him.

Hull walked over to one of the desks and ran his finger along the top before speaking. "Contact the Florence Police Department, work with them. Trace the route of the buses for any sign of the students." Lennox nodded. Hull looked over his shoulder at me. "I need you to speak with Malcolm. He will already know what we are doing, but someone needs to provide.. assurance. You are far more suited for that than I." With nods of agreement, I turned and followed Lennox to the outside hall. We started for the staircase together, only pausing to hear the door close.

"I'm investing a lot of faith in this one, John," he said as we started up the stairs.

"I know. He won't fail."

"Whether he succeeds or fails, something tells me I'll be out of the job."

"That's okay. Something tells me you'd operate better outside of the law anyways."

"Maybe I could work with you and Hull."

We stopped at the top of the stairs, looked at each other, and laughed.

*

I met with Malcolm around noon at a coffee shop several blocks from the police station. He'd changed from his casual attire he'd worn before to a more formal coat and tie outfit. His face was still somber, but he was conversational enough. I did note, however, that he was on his third cup of coffee in the past half-hour, and I couldn't recall having seen the man drink more than half a cup before. Crises truly did bring out our inner faults.

"I am guessing the inspector has hidden Sheridan away," Malcolm said as he raised his coffee mug.

I nodded. "He'll siphon him the information. He'll find her."

Malcolm chuckled. "You know I have the utmost faith in my brother's abilities. Sheridan is the best of his kind. I do not doubt he will be able to find the students, even when confined to a police basement."

I didn't bother asking how he knew where Sheridan was being kept. "Best of his kind. That's one way to put it, I guess."

"He is certainly the most intelligent in his field. I hate to insult the men and women of the Newfield Police, but in comparison to Sheridan, they are surprisingly incompetent."

"Intelligent, yeah. That can only get him so far."

"Oh, I would not say that."

"Why?"

"I would say Sheridan has reached a point in which he is able to confidently acknowledge his superior intellect, yet keep it restrained so as to survive in the world. He is able to 'dumb himself down,' as one would say."

"Is he really."

"Of course." He raised his mug. "My brother has taken four intelligence tests since he was sixteen. Do you know what the scores were?" I shook my head. "One hundred and thirty-six, one hundred and sixty-four, one hundred and fifty-two, and five."

I softly set my mug down, not quite ready to believe he would have dive-bombed so quickly. "Is five even possible?"

He finished his drink before replying. "I suspect by the fourth test, he knew that I was able to view the results."

"So he purposefully failed the test?"

"Oh, he did more than that. To achieve a score as low as five, you would have to deliberately answer every single prompted question in a way that would require no foresight or common sense.

Even for a person of very low intelligence, that score is not obtainable without a considerable amount of effort put into failure."

"Why would he do that?"

"To show that he could both exceed expectations and reach the lowest point of failure. That the test was at his whim, rather than he being at the test's." He gave a slight nod. "So remarkable, when you think about it. Cocky, but remarkable."

I shook my head slightly. "It's so odd, hearing you speak such high praise of him when he.. well, doesn't reciprocate it."

He gave a weak smile. "I do not expect Sheridan to ever reciprocate respect for me."

"Why is that, exactly? What really happened between you two?"

Malcolm breathed out heavily through his nose, watching me with unwavering eyes. "How often does he speak of me, if ever?"

"Not often."

"And what of our parents?"

I furrowed my brow. "I don't think he's ever mentioned your parents. I don't even know their names."

"Robert and Cynthia. There is a very specific reason why Sheridan has made such a desperate attempt to remove my parents and me from his life."

"And what is that?"

"I would say I am surprised he has not told you already, but then I would be lying." He set his mug down before continuing. "There is a member of the Hull family that you have not been informed of. My parents were both born in 1956, and my mother gave birth to me in 1974. In 1987, she gave birth to Sheridan, and in 1989, she gave birth to our sister, Lydia. Sheridan and I were not close due to the age gap, but he and Lydia were very close. Attached at the hip, you could say. He held her in the highest regard, protected her at school, all of the things expected from an older sibling.

"Now we must move forward to December 31st, 1999. By then, I was happily married to my wife and Bailey was seven years old. Sheridan was twelve, Lydia was ten. To celebrate the welcoming of the new millennium, my family and I returned to England. As my parents had never owned large cars, I was responsible for renting my own vehicle, which I transported my immediate family in. The two cars traveled from London to the celebration in Cambridge.

"At around one in the morning, our group decided to depart. My car was in front, my parents in back. About halfway through the drive, when going around a curve, we were met with an erratic driver. Thinking quickly, I swerved my own car into the ditch on the right, in the opposite direction of the railing and a subsequent steep hill. My parents, however, were not so quick. The driver slid into their lane and collided with the passenger side, and sent the car spinning into the railing and off the hill. The car rolled its way down the length of the hill before coming to a stop.

"When I was able to reach the car, I went for the back seats first. Sheridan was relatively unharmed, several scrapes across his face, but nothing serious. Once I had pulled him out, I went back in for Lydia. Her condition was far worse. I could tell she was unconscious and had lost a significant amount of blood. She had been sitting in the rear passenger seat, meaning the car had collided with her door. The window had shattered, and a disturbingly large piece had lodged itself in her upper chest. I was able to unwrap her from her tangled seat belt and remove her, but even then, I knew there was little hope.

"Emergency crews arrived within the hour and transported my family to St. George's Hospital. When I arrived, I found Sheridan sitting alone in a lobby for the emergency room, clutching Lydia's purple scarf. He told me our parents had gone back to see the progress on our sister. I sat with him for two hours as we waited for news. Around four in the morning, he turned to me with a pale face and asked why I had swerved when he knew our father was not one with quick reflexes, and would surely not be able to avoid the car. I had no answer to provide.

"At five-thirty, our parents returned, my mother's face white and my father's eyes glued to the floor. Lydia had passed away at approximately 1:45 AM on January 1st, 2000, as a result of her critical injuries. The funeral was held later that week. After that, our family noticed a significant change in Sheridan. I realize now that Lydia had a very bright and innovative personality for someone so young. When they would play, she would be the one to imagine the scenario. She was the one who came up with the ideas, she was the one who encouraged him to be more open with the world.

"Without Lydia, Sheridan lost his way. He became very introverted for a twelve-year-old, but also started to show signs of extreme intelligence. It did not take long, though, for my family to realize why he had become so cold towards us. In his heart, he held us all responsible for Lydia's death. He believed that we did not take the proper course of action to prevent her demise. And I will admit, my reaction was poor. I should have remembered my father's poor reflexes, but I did not. And not a day goes by that I do not regret that.

"I would also say that Lydia's death is what inspired Sheridan to become what he is today. A drunk driver resulting in her death led him to enter a field of work in which he upholds justice. And, though he will never mention it to you, I know for fact that when he was nineteen, he was able to successfully find that drunk driver and gather enough evidence to put him in jail for life. The man was quite the criminal, and had not been charged for the murder of Lydia. Sheridan changed that. To this day, I know Sheridan still holds my parents and I responsible, and it is why he makes such an effort to keep us out of his life. The only reason he speaks to me is because of Bailey."

The more he spoke, the more heavier the pit in my stomach became. Of course something like this would have happened. Now so many things made sense, especially his love for all things purple. Now Sheridan Hull was even more of a person than I'd thought before. He wasn't a machine, turned on to solve mysteries. He was a man who had a purpose. And now the current situation became even more dire. Because if I was right, Bailey had started to fill the void left by Lydia's death. And if Bailey were to die...

Well, I certainly did *not* want to imagine the result.

"Thank you, Malcolm," I said after a minute of silence. "For telling me this."

The man smiled, but I could see it was forced by the dim look in his eyes. "You deserve to know. You are Sheridan's closest friend. Perhaps his only friend."

"Lot of pressure there." I gave a short blink as a buzzing started in my pocket. I pulled out my phone and saw a text message appear from the detective.

Police checked route. No sign of buses. Check back tomorrow.-SH

I stood from my seat and nodded at Malcolm. "I'd best be off. He'll find them."

"I know he will," the man replied, his gaze shifting towards the window to his left. "I know."

*

I woke early the next day and made my way to the police station. For late March, the weather today was particularly dreary. Some would say the weather reflects the mood of the times, and to be honest, I would agree with that right about now. When I reached the police station, I found Lennox waiting in the lobby, a brown box in his hands. He looked up from it with doleful eyes, giving me a grim stare. I knew without looking in the box what its contents were.

Together we made our way down into the basement, and found that it had been slightly changed. The dust had been cleared, for one. Hull had never struck me as one to clean, but I imagine him sneezing every ten minutes from the absurd collection of filth would have gotten to him. We found him in the meeting room, a knife in his hands and a very jagged etching on one of the tables.

"Who is it today," the detective asked without looking at us.

"I don't know yet," Lennox replied as he set the box down. "I haven't opened it." Hull and I moved to the inspector's sides and watched him open the box. The inside had been stuffed with packing peanuts, but after a slight amount of digging, we found what mattered. Two bags of ashes and IDs, as well as another DVD. I grabbed a pair of rubber gloves from the nearby gear table and opened one of the bags, carefully fishing the ID and a wallet out.

"Robert Payne," I read once I'd cleared the ID.

"Ren A. Mizu," Lennox stated, his hands holding an ID and a purse.

"Two more students," Hull said as he grabbed the DVD and started towards the old box television in the corner. He hastily grabbed a DVD player from the desk by the TV and started hooking it up. After a minute or so, we were ready. The three of us gathered in front of the screen and watched with dreaded anticipation. Once again, the same setting appeared, a single-lit spot in a dark room. After a moment, Xaphon stepped into view, licking his lips and giving his sneer.

"Day two. I'm a bit disappointed. I thought the overzealous police chief would have done something about Sheridan Hull by now, but it seems I was wrong. And yes, I know nothing's been done. The advantage in working for Chimaera means I have eyes everywhere, at all times. I will admit, I don't know where you've gone, Sheridan Hull, but I know you've gone somewhere willingly. The city has yet to act accordingly, and for that, I have burned two students at random. I enjoyed these two. The girl in particular. The way she wailed as the fire burned.

"My demands are the same, but I will help provide a time to comply. Every day, at four in the morning, if I do not hear that Sheridan Hull has been dealt with, I will burn two more students. The contents will arrive in their neat packages and the cycle will continue. The police department will have to make a very serious decision, very serious. Do you continue to let the arrogant detective remain while innocent students die? Or will you make the right choice? It's up to you. But I wouldn't advise waiting too long to make your decision."

The video stopped. Lennox let out a heavy sigh before burying his face in his hands. Hull ejected the disc and examined it, then walked back over to where the bags of ashes were.

"One of the rooms down here contains a research lab, correct?" he asked as he placed the items back in the box.

Lennox glanced back, thinking for a moment before nodding. "Should be down the hall, to the left."

"I need the DVD and ashes from yesterday. Bring them to me there." He picked up the box and walked from the room. Lennox and I exchanged glances before going upstairs, finding the contents from the previous day, and taking them back down.

We found Hull in the research lab, three different magnifying glasses set up, as well as an older style computer turned on. He clicked through several windows before turning to face us.

"He prepared the DVDs with the gloved hand. No traces of DNA to be found," Hull stated as he took the new box from Lennox and removed the bag of ashes. "These are far more curious, however. Mizu and Payne were both burned in a very crude manner, but shortly after, their bodies were placed in a crematorium. He burns to kill them, and once they are dead, he reduces their bodies to the ashes he sends us."

"Torture and humiliation?" I prompted.

The detective shook his head. "Torture and death, then simple transportation. Were he to send full bodies to us, it would be easy to trace. A small bag of ashes can be moved without detection."

I looked at Lennox. "Who keeps delivering the packages?"

"No one," he replied. "They just find their way into the lobby. We can't figure out who leaves them, even on the security cameras."

"He's far too careful for that," Hull commented as he shook the ashes from yesterday, belonging to a Logan Hammel, onto a petri dish. He slid the dish under the closest microscope and went to work. He studied the ashes for almost ten minutes before leaning away. "Similar fashion. Crude burning before cremation."

"How are we supposed to find him when all we have to work with are ashes and untraceable DVDs?" I asked as I sat down.

Hull removed the petri dish and scratched his nose. "We wait for him to slip up."

"And how long will that take?" Lennox implored. "How many more of these students are we going to let burn?"

Hull offered no reply. He simply turned away and slid another petri dish under the microscope, then jotted down something on a notepad he'd found. I looked at Lennox, who gave me an exasperated shrug before walking from the room. I gave Hull a slight pat on the shoulder, remembering what Malcolm had told me, before following the inspector from the room.

"How long do you think it'll be before Conn finds out Hull never made it to Lane?" I asked as we started up the stairs.

"He won't. Malcolm Hull put in a call and forged documentation. Sheridan Hull checked into Lane yesterday at 1 PM. Now the chief just thinks this Xaphon is playing the police for idiots."

"That ought to complicate things."

"Conn hates the police being undermined. But now that he thinks Hull is imprisoned and can't do a damn to help us, he's feeling even more incapable."

"You could always tell him."

"The less people who know, the better." We stepped into the lobby, Lennox giving a cautious glance around the room before focusing on me. "We both know there will come a point when keeping him hidden won't work. If he can't figure this out soon... I'm going to have to break a lot more rules."

The day went by without anything of importance. In fact, I could hardly remember the rest of that day. It moved in a blur. The next day started as soon as the last. The weather was even more dreary and the news had finally caught full wind of what was happening. The morning newspaper arrived with the headline "DETECTIVE OR THE STUDENTS?" The article was so unbelievably biased, it made me sick to my stomach. This would certainly complicate things, and now, Hull definitely was not able to leave.

I arrived at the station and found the stairs filled with news reporters. A few of them recognized me and tried to get me for questioning, but Lennox was able to grab me from the crowd and take me inside.

"How'd they find out?" I asked once we were in the lobby.

"You didn't watch the morning news, did you?" he replied.

"I try not to."

"He sent a copy of today's video to the press. They've been running it nonstop. Conn's pissed and trying to get ahold of Malcolm. The biggest problem now is the parents. We've had at least three dozen of them come and demand answers, but everything's so sensitive we can't disclose anything."

"What did today's video say?" He gulped and nodded down the hall. Together we walked for the door, down the stairs, and into the meeting room. Hull was already waiting when we arrived. Lennox popped the DVD into the player and stood back. Within moments, Xaphon's person appeared on the screen, standing in the single-light spot.

"Jarrad Speed and Drew Jones. Two very fine students, very bright, full of potential in their futures. Two students who were promptly burned to death just a few hours ago. This is what's happened, Newfield. This is the result of allowing your petty form of order to go unchecked. These are the fourth and fifth students to be burned, too. And it's all because you aren't willing to give up Sheridan Hull.

"Sheridan Hull, the detective you all hold in such a high light. Sheridan Hull is a menace, a blight on your society. He has worked so hard to create a cushioned world of safety in Newfield, but you all know better. You know that no matter how hard Sheridan Hull, or the police force, or anyone, works to stop it, crime will always exist. Crime, and chaos, and anarchy. And I am here to make sure you all remember that. Because Newfield should not be allowed to fall into a state of denial, a state in which everyone feels safe when they should not.

"I have no intention of stopping. Not until Sheridan Hull has been dealt with. I have over three hundred students to burn and all the time in the world. See, that's the joy of being the one in control. You dictate how things pan out. And I don't plan to stop my fun until you start listening."

I leaned back and pushed my chin into my chest. "He really likes the sound of his own voice, doesn't he."

"Underground."

Lennox and I both looked to Hull, who was staring into the blackness of the screen with an intense gaze.

"Sorry, what?" Lennox asked.

"Underground. The videos are recorded underground," the detective said ominously as he took the disc from the DVD player.

"How do you know that?" I questioned, watching Hull run over to the computer.

"The acoustics, the echo to his voice," Hull replied as he inserted the disc into the computer. "It's caused by being in a large room that is surrounded by rock. He's either hidden himself away within a mountain, or he is underground."

"What good does that do us?" Lennox asked.

"It means we know how he was able to hide six buses, and how he evaded the police when you searched for him."

"So we know he's underground somewhere," I said, watching Hull grab one of the wallets from the box. "But that leaves a lot of space to search. Hell, that really doesn't help us at all." He opened the wallet and pulled a slim piece of folded paper from inside. He set the wallet down and unfolded the paper to reveal a pencil-written message that simply said "BT."

"BT.. BT.." Hull murmured, eyes moving left to right. "Blachly? No. BT..." He stared at the paper for a long moment before his eyes gave a slight shake. "Wait."

"Wait what?" I asked, moving to get a better look at the paper.

Hull pointed over at the nearby table. "Someone grab me a pencil." Lennox obliged, grabbing the writing utensil and tossing it to Hull. The detective scratched the tip of the pencil along the bottom of the paper, leaving long strips of gray. After a moment, faint outlines of letters started to appear. I watched as he scratched his way across the thin paper, revealing a message.

"'illic detinetur locum'," I read. "Latin?"

"It roughly translates to 'a place where they are kept for exhibition'. Jarrad Speed is trying to tell us where they are," Hull said as he moved to the computer. "What a clever student. We are close, gentlemen. Very close."

*

The next day came quickly. The news was still blown up with the video from Xaphon, and Conn had officially put out an APB on Sheridan Hull. It certainly didn't help when a bulkier package arrived that morning. Lennox, Hull, and I stood in the room, staring down at three bags of ashes instead of the regular two. The ID cards had identified the three as Heather Hall, Blake E. Price, and William S. Brown. But what was even more surprising was the presence of a VHS tape rather than the usual DVD. After some considerable digging, we found a working VCR, plugged it in, and watched.

This video was different. Now, the entire room was lit, revealing it to be nothing more than a white-walled, white-ceilinged, white-floored room that stretched on for maybe fifty meters. The camera was no longer propped up, but was rather in somebody's hand. Where Xaphon usually stood was now a wooden chair, occupied by a young boy with a face that had been burnt in several places. The camera fiddled around a moment before coming very close to the boy's face.

"Tell me again, Preston," a voice, Xaphon's, said. "Who is in your group?"

The kid looked up at the screen with drooping eyes and a heavy head. "I'm not saying... anything."

"Oh really?" The camera moved back a few meters, then revealed a long, sharp, glowing red rod, held by a black-gloved hand. After a short moment of showing the burning rod to the camera, it was immediately thrust into the boy's chest. The boy lurched forward, not moving far. His hands were presumably tied behind the chair, but I would also wager to guess that Xaphon had stabbed so deep, the rod had emerged from the boy's back and pinned him to the chair.

"*Bailey Hull*!" the boy screamed, his voice contorted with pain. The rod was viciously pulled from the boy's chest, then thrown off-camera. The angle readjusted to instead face Xaphon. He looked up at the camera with horribly stained teeth and eyes wider than I thought possible.

"So the niece of Sheridan Hull is here," he said, his voice lowered to a purr that made my stomach turn. "That makes this much more interesting." He let out a roar of a cackle before throwing the camera. The angle tumbled for several seconds before stopping. I looked over at Hull, expecting some kind of emotional reaction. Instead, he reached forward and started rewinding the tape. I watched the actions play back in reverse before he pressed play, right when Xaphon turned the camera to himself.

Hull pointed at the boy in the back, only just visible over Xaphon's shoulder. "Watch." We all watched the boy, doing our best to ignore Xaphon. Sure enough, the boy appeared to summon as much strength as he could muster, look directly at the camera, and mouth something before losing consciousness.

"What did he say?" Lennox asked as Hull rewound the tape again. We watched once more. The third time certainly seemed to be the charm for the detective.

"Black Tunnel," Hull announced, jumping away from the television and grabbing several items from the table.

"Black Tunnel?" Lennox repeated.

"There is a single tunnel between here and Florence. Petersen Tunnel. Somewhere inside the tunnel is a separate entryway to this underground facility. We go there, we find the students, we find Xaphon."

"What in all of God's green Earth is going on down here?"

I felt my heart freeze in my chest as I turned. Standing in the doorway, face turned a shade of red in anger and horror, was the chief of police, Lamont Conn.

"Sir, let me explain—" Lennox started.

"Shut your goddamn mouth, Greg." Conn turned to stare at Hull with daggers for eyes. "Are you happy? Huh? How many kids have died because you were too damn proud to go?"

Hull took a cautious step towards the table. "I apologize. But there are far more pressing matters than whatever you have in mind." He grabbed an empty box from the table and chucked it towards Conn, who instinctively reached up to protect his face. Hull ran forward and curled himself up into a ball, flying through the air with the box and colliding with the police chief. Both men hit the ground, Hull rolling to his feet while Conn rubbed his head.

I knew what we had to do. "Get the police to the tunnel," I said to Lennox as I started after Hull. "We'll meet you there!"

Hull grabbed a large bowler hat from a nearby rack before charging up the stairs with me in tow. We ran up the stairs and through the doorway, Hull careful to avoid eyesight with anyone in the lobby. We stepped outside and started down the steps. I was actually surprised at there not being any news reporters. This was the perfect time for them to leave.

"What's the plan?" I asked when we reached the bottom of the steps.

He glanced over my shoulder, mainly at the road, and smirked. "Borrow a police car."

We managed to turn a usual hour and a half-long drive into about forty minutes. It helped that Hull turned the police car's lights on once we'd exited Newfield city limits. The tunnel was less than thirty minutes from Florence, and since it was midday on a Thursday, it wasn't too busy. Then again, it was one of the only ways to reach the Willamette Valley from that area of the coast. We stopped the police car at the beginning of the tunnel, doing our best to keep from halting traffic. Together, we trekked along the very short sidewalk that led trough the tunnel.

"What are we looking for?" I asked, careful to keep a hand sliding on the wall.

"Some kind of triggering method," Hull replied, his eyes forward. "A switch, lever, anything to reveal where the buses may have gone."

"How could he have built this without drawing attention?"

"I'm not sure. But he is here, somewhere. They all are."

We continued along the inside of the tunnel before reaching a small dip into the wall. There was a small control panel in the dip, probably to manage the lights of the tunnel. Hull opened the panel and started running his fingers along the different switches. After a moment, he snapped his fingers and flipped one of the switches. Immediately, the tunnel went dark, losing both artificial and natural light. I could tell that something had sealed off the entrances to the tunnel, but I was more surprised at the electromagnetic pulse-like effect that took place.

There had been five or six different cars inside the tunnel when Hull had flipped the switch, and all of them had stopped. I could hear people start complaining, car doors opening, cell phone lights coming to life. How those had evaded the pulse, I wasn't sure.

Then the shaking started.

It was a small quake at first, but it was steady and continuing. I looked down and saw that the cement we were standing on was in motion, sliding further to the right and away from the road. I looked up and, with my eyes having adjusted to the dark, saw that a large section of the tunnel wall was moving with us. It continued for nearly a minute before stopping. The lights returned to life and revealed a metal platform now in the space that had opened with the moving of the wall. There were indeed six cars in the tunnel, but they were all on the opposite side from us.

"He closed the tunnel, moved the buses onto the pad, and just like that, over three hundred students went missing," Hull commented as he stepped out onto the pad. I joined him and glanced around, not really sure what to expect.

"How is any of this possible?" I asked. "This is a government-constructed tunnel, probably cut out decades ago. There's no way this has been here the entire time."

"Of course not. But with Chimaera's aid, I cannot imagine it being very difficult for him to close the tunnel for renovations, which would have given him ample time to create this." Hull glanced around. "The technology is surprising, but considering it came from Chimaera, that surprise is significantly diminished."

Before I could reply, another rumbling started, this one from below. I watched as the panel we were standing on began lowering itself. It dropped us down slowly, taking us at least thirty meters down before stopping and revealing a large, garage-like room, which was currently occupied by six school buses. I could tell from just a glimpse that none of the students were still in the buses, which was somewhat relieving. I doubted they were getting any better treatment outside of them, though. Hull pointed at a large, metal double-door on the far side of the room, prompting us to start running.

The doors slid open automatically, revealing another large room, this one definitely not for vehicles. It was smaller than the first one, but still large enough to hold what looked like three hundred people. The students were scattered in small groups, all huddled together and sitting on the cold, concrete floor. Their backpacks had been taken and thrown into a large pile in a corner opposite us. A lot of them were too weak to even stand when they saw us, and it was only then that I realized Xaphon had more than likely been starving them.

"That sadistic bastard," I said, my eyes surveying the crowd.

"She's not here," Hull said.

"Bailey?"

"No. I can see her backpack in the pile, halfway to the top, but she is missing."

I knew what that meant. "The metal floor in the last room didn't lower itself on its own."

Hull gave a long look at the room before turning to me. "I need you to do something for me."

*

Hull leaned over a control panel to the next doorway, tapping away madly at the console. Not even two seconds passed before he had accurately entered an access code. The door slid open to reveal a dark room, one that had no doubt been used for Xaphon's filming. He took seven steps inside before coming to a halt, listening as the metal door slid to a close behind him. He stared forward into the darkness, hearing two different sets of breathing, one coming from a throat, the other from a nose.

The lights burst to life above him, revealing a room of absolute white. Standing some thirteen meters ahead of Hull was Xaphon, his gloved hand resting on the shoulder of Bailey Hull. She was currently in a wooden chair, hands bound behind her back, tape across her mouth.

"Welcome to Black Tunnel, Sheridan Hull," Xaphon said, the sneer on his face growing. "My true home."

"What happened to you?" Hull asked as he clasped his own hands behind his back.

"Time happened to me," the man replied, twisting his neck to the side, sending off a resounding *pop*. "You think a level of intelligence like mine can come without cost? Insanity set in a very long time ago. It's all a matter of making yourself presentable when necessary. The same as wearing a mask. You wear a lie to convince everyone of a fabricated truth, and watch them panic when you remove the veil."

"Why all of this, then? Why the abductions, the murders?"

"To teach a lesson."

"Well you failed. I was not apprehended, and here I am, having found you."

Xaphon chuckled. "You're so witty, so quick to think you're right. You're not, Sheridan. This was never about getting the city to turn on you, no. That comes later. You have to truly hold their utmost respect. You have to hold their hope in the palm of your hand. And you don't have that. Yet."

"Then what was it about, then?"

"Does everything have to be justified, Sheridan? Must it all have a *reason*?" He stepped away from Bailey, spreading his arms wide to encompass the room. "There is nothing in this world that holds value in my eyes, but there is plenty within my mind that deserves to be shared. I don't need to operate with a plan. I don't need a purpose, or reason, or explanation. I don't have to explain *why* I do things. I just need to do them."

"Why?"

"Why!" Xaphon let out a gargled cackle. "Is there always a why with you? With all of your brilliance, all of your deductions, are you really not able to see that your fundamental question, your basis for investigation, holds *no* relevance to me?"

"I suppose not."

"If you really need something, something to make you sleep at night," Xaphon said as he brought his arms back in, slipping one of his hands inside his coat. "Consider me a fire. A burning fire that has no care nor consideration for the world. See, that's the joy about fire. It doesn't care who you are, or what you've done. It doesn't care if you're white, or black, or any color. It doesn't care what it burns, it just *burns*. It is the ultimate indiscriminate force of nature." He pulled a lighter from his coat and flicked it on. "I am most certainly a fire."

"Understandable enough," Hull replied, his eyes momentarily glancing at Bailey, who gulped, before returning to Xaphon.

"You know, all it takes is a force, like fire, to make us who we really are. Something to change us, morph us, shape us... create us. Something that sets us in the right direction." The man flexed his gloved hand. "Do you know why I wear this glove? Why my hand is masked?" Hull gave no response. "See, a long time ago, I was a stupid teenager, just like this girl here. I lived in the middle of the country in a state nobody cares about. And I had three friends, my best friends. We did everything together.

"One night we decided to explore an old house five miles from the nearest town. Nobody ever went to this house. It had been out there for fifty, sixty years, and nobody had lived in it while our parents had been alive. It was abandoned, it was wrecked, it was the perfect place for four teenage boys to be teenage boys. One of my friends liked to smoke. He lit a cigarette while we were in the downstairs living room and puffed it away until all that was left was a stub. Then, being a typical smoker, he flicked that stub into the corner of the room.

"The four of us went upstairs and looked around a bit, and none of us smelled the smoke. None of us realized we'd started a fire below us, and it was slowly working its way across the first floor of the house. Only when it was too late did we realize how hot it was getting. We ran for the stairs, and just as the four of us were working our way down, the aged, burning wood of the staircase collapsed. All four of us fell to the first floor. We were burnt, we were cut up, and we were afraid. Oh, we were very, very afraid.

"We tried running for the door, but the fire had spread to the ceiling. The second floor started to collapse, and a large portion fell right on top of us. One particularly heavy piece of wood landed across my forearm and pinned me to the ground. Another piece landed next to it, right by my exposed hand, and caught it on fire. I was only able to grab a piece of metal that had landed next to me and place it between me and the fire burning away at my hand to keep the rest of me from perishing. But I still had to sit there and watch that fire burn through my skin, burn through my blood, my bones. I felt every millisecond of that.

"But you know what really made it memorable? Once I knew I couldn't move, I realized my friends weren't better off. A large section of flooring had landed on them and pinned all three of them to one spot. And that spot was burning. So naturally, the fire, in its indiscriminate nature, burned through the wood and started burning through them. I sat and watched my three closest friends scream in pain and agony as the fire melted their clothes, melted their faces, to nothing. I watched my friends burn until their was nothing left that was familiar. And then, only then, I was able to pull the stub of an arm free.

"You don't get to see what's under the glove now. But that fire? That fire changed me. That fire made me who I am today. Now I see why the fire is such a perfect element, why it is such a perfect piece of nature. Fire is the ultimate, unbiased cleanser of life. Fire is what puts us at bay when we advance too far ahead. Fire is what keeps us in check. And it does not pick and choose what to burn. It simply *burns*."

Hull heard a very short noise from behind him, the sound of hollow metal touching the concrete floor. He reached his hand into his pocket and pulled out a lighter of his own, bringing it to life with a simple flick.

"Let us see how enjoyable your fire is when it is truly unbiased and indiscriminate," the detective said as he dropped the lighter.

The ground ahead of Hull burst into flames, rushing forward to completely engulf Xaphon. The flames went high, eclipsing even the tallest point of the man's wiry hair. Hull rushed towards his niece, cautious to avoid the spreading fire. He carefully removed the tape from her face and started unbinding her. Once she was free, he helped her stand, keeping his hands securely on her shoulders.

"Run for the exit, help the others, and *leave*," he ordered. She nodded rapidly before running off. Hull watched her go until she was clear of the room. His eyes slowly worked their way in a circle, observing the filled shelves that had been behind him, the quickly-diminishing fire path that led to him, and the still-burning circle of flames to his left. He waited a moment for that fire to diminish, revealing a completely untouched Xaphon.

"Very clever ploy," the man said, his sneer painted across his face. "But where you and everyone else may fear the fire and see it as a fierce, unstoppable force, I embrace it."

"*Embrace this.*"

From Xaphon's left came a small, metal can, which collided with the man's face and caused him to recoil in shock. Hull took advantage of that shock and tackled the man, forcing him down onto his stomach. Walker joined the detective in holding the man down while Hull pulled a pair of handcuffs from his pocket. Xaphon, however, made no motion to resist or struggle. They were able to secure the handcuffs, stand him up, and start towards the door without problem.

As soon as they stepped through the door, they were greeted with the sight of several dozen police officers helping the abducted students to their feet. Hull could see Lennox pushing his way through the crowd, them no doubt being his intended target. The inspector arrived and gave Hull a curt nod before taking Xaphon.

"Well done," Hull commented as he and Walker started forward.

"I wasn't sure if you were serious at first. Searching through the backpacks for cans of body spray just seemed stupid." The doctor gave a short smile. "Now it makes sense."

They joined a large group on the metal panel and waited as it lifted them to ground level. As soon as the panel stopped, a group of six or seven heavily-armed men started approaching the two, with Lamont Conn at the front. Lennox tried to steer himself and Xaphon into their way, but was unsuccessful.

"I want this man arrested *immediately*," Conn barked. Two of the SWAT troopers moved around the chief, guns aimed at Hull.

"That won't be necessary, Commissioner Conn."

*

Hull and I glanced to our left, a new voice having joined the mix. I was met with a tall man, black suit and matching hair that was significantly longer than the last time I had seen it. The man's hair now went down the back of his head, almost like a mullet. He stood almost a head taller than me and had a bright, shining smile on his face.

"Uh, Mr. Montorum.." Conn started.

"I don't want to hear it, Commissioner. These men are heroes." Montorum clasped Hull and I's shoulders. "Securing the capture of a horrible man like this. Wonderful job, men. I'll see to it that we have you recognized in a good way." The mayor glanced back at Conn, who gave a heavy sigh and signaled for the SWAT members to stand down. Montorum looked back at us, gave a nod, and started over towards a crowd of students.

"I'm not a fan of him," Hull said once the SWAT team had dispersed.

I gave a short chuckle. "What, you vote for the other guy?"

"I don't vote."

Together we walked over to where a single SWAT car waited, with Lennox making sure Xaphon was put into one of the seats. We stood behind truck and watched the inspector buckle the man's seat belt before stepping down. Xaphon glanced past Lennox, eyes falling on Hull.

"He provided the spark. I provided the flame." The sneer slowly crept its way onto the man's face. "This isn't over, Sheridan Hull. The fire has yet to rise."

"You assume I care for your meaningless threats," Hull shot back. "I do not."

Lennox closed the door before Xaphon could respond. I gave the inspector a nod and turned to Hull, who was gazing off in the direction of a group of students. I followed his gaze and quickly found Bailey, standing with a red shock towel wrapped around her. She met his gaze, gave a chipper smile, and looked back to her friends.

Hull made a slight humming noise before looking at me. "I'd say we're done here."

IN MEMORIAM EX

Things had most certainly seen a shift around Newfield in the aftermath of what was, as titled by the news, the "tunnel student hostage crisis." The day after we'd found the underground facility, Xaphon had been placed in a high-security cell in the police station; the basement was now back in use. Hull and I had been pardoned for our actions, and the mayor had held a public commencement ceremony in which he thanked the detective, Inspector Lennox, and myself for our hard work and diligence in bringing the heinous criminal to justice.

Because the SWAT team that had arrived was issued from Eugene and not Newfield, the city officials had deemed it necessary to create a more close-to-home special weapons and tactics system. In response to the hostage crisis, Mayor Montorum had created a new program, called the Emergency Response and Restoration Fund. This fund would allow the city to be better prepared for situations similar to the hostage crisis, as well as other potential scenarios.

The fund had also allowed the city to finally finish its construction of the McMullen County Jail, which had been undergoing work for some several years in the northeast part of Newfield. Because Lane County Adult Corrections was reaching a point of costly capacity, a large number of inmates were transferred, and reports had said that Xaphon was moved from the basement of the police station to a confinement cell in the new facility. This helped to put quite a number of people at ease.

The consequences for the crisis were not so easily solved. The day after the commencement, the chief of police put Lennox on a three-month suspension for insubordination and illegal actions in light of a municipal crisis. I'd seen him a few times since, and he seemed to be getting along fine. He did miss work, though. As well as this, there had been an almost-situation when one of the families of a missing student sought to sue Hull for unnecessary delaying of action. The lawsuit, however, held no ground when a "little birdie" by the name of Malcolm informed the parents that Hull had not ever been officially in charge of the investigation. That fell on Commissioner Conn.

That was not, sadly, where things ended. Once the students had been retrieved from Black Tunnel, a headcount was held. The students whose ashes had arrived at the police department were obviously not counted, but six other students were unaccounted for. After querying the other students, they found that the six still missing were all Chemistry majors and had not been seen since the buses were taken from the road. The whereabouts of the students were still unknown. But there wasn't much hope to be found when the only person capable of saying where they are was sitting in a padded cell, legs crossed, eyes closed.

As for things around the flat, there had been a very large bout of normalcy. I would say this is completely due to Hull deciding to take a trip to different countries in South America. He'd left in the first week of April and had only returned a few days ago. He told me the trip had been purely for leisure, but I suspected it had been advised by Malcolm. There was still a considerable amount of tension throughout the city. Even though we'd caught him, Xaphon had certainly left his mark. People were afraid.

I suppose that fear wasn't unwarranted. Although I had only lived in Newfield for a short while, just a month longer than how long I'd known Hull, I could tell it wasn't a city that was accustomed to things like these. In fact, to be honest, it seemed a rarity for any city to have such an unusual spree of criminal activity. Since meeting Hull, I had witnessed a multitude of different scenarios, some normal, others not so much. Newfield may have been just a sprawling city to the populace, but to Hull, it was a battleground. And it pained me to think that standing on the other side was Moriarty and his army of intelligent criminals.

As for Hull's trip, he'd neglected to give me any real specifics. He told me he'd had the opportunity to try a variety of things, like rock-climbing, bungee-jumping, and cave exploration. All of the things one could do on a vacation, I suppose. I'd spent my time working, really. I had the chance to see Cassidy twice during Hull's absence. I'd also taken some time to look through the case notes I'd collected over the past year and a half. Hull and I had been involved in some remarkable cases. And it felt like we'd been doing this for a lifetime, when in reality, we'd only met one year, six months, and three days ago, in a simple triple-homicide-turned-conspiracy.

That really did feel like ages ago.

Now, Hull and I sat, a typical Thursday morning in which I had not been called in for work. It struck me as sad, that I hadn't bothered finding a better job than a call-in doctor. But I suppose the cases were what I invested my time into, even if I largely operated as an observer. They were far more interesting than someone with a cold thinking they had a tumor. And, they paid a lot better. But money had never been my focus.

Except when we had none.

"Why do you suppose he really did it?"

I glanced over the top of my laptop at Hull, clad in his purple robe, his feet propped up, and his gaze focused on the balcony.

"Why do you suppose who did what," I prompted when he remained silent.

"Xaphon. There had to have been a motive. Even an insane person recognizes a goal. A crazed shooter enters a mall of people and opens fire, and even then, there was a motive, even if we are quick to assume there was none. But he did not do that. He made a show of it all. He claims to the public it was to have me removed, then he tells me that was a lie. So he was killing students to pass the time?"

"Maybe he was right when he said he didn't need a reason to do what he did."

"Illogical. Everyone has inner desires, something they wish to accomplish. It's innate."

I set my laptop to the side. "Have you ever watched *The Dark Knight*?"

"No."

"Maybe you should."

"Why?"

"I think you'd find a lot of familiarity with one of the characters." As I moved to stand, the home phone began ringing. I walked over and glanced down with a slight frown, not recognizing the area code at all. I picked it up and stepped back, showing the screen to Hull. "That area code seem familiar?"

He glanced up at me, then at the phone. I saw a very small, very subtle shift take place in his eyes. He delicately took the phone from my hand and answered.

"Hello?" he asked, his eyes closing. "Yes, this is him." He remained silent for a long moment before nodding. "Tomorrow morning." Another pause, another nod. "I will see you then." He hung up, placed the phone on the arm of his chair, and buried his face in his hands. I looked down at him with both curiosity and concern. Something was very wrong.

"Who was that?" I asked.

"Person." He stood up quickly, causing the phone to fall. He paid it no mind, instead turning to focus on the hallway.

"Well who?" I questioned as he started walking.

"Someone." He stopped and glanced over his shoulder. "I need to leave early tomorrow morning for Plainfield, Illinois. And it would mean a lot to me if you came along."

I grabbed the phone from the floor and matched his gaze. "Sure. But who was that?"

He started towards his room. "You'll see soon enough."

*

He didn't talk much for the rest of that day. Most of his time was spent in his room. At around 9 PM, he'd brought a suitcase out, nodded goodnight at me, and returned to his room, not emerging until early the next morning. I don't think he said a single world until we were at Portland International Airport, walking from where we'd parked our car to the terminal. I hadn't prompted the conversation, but he was good at judging when I had something on my mind.

"Early yesterday morning, 24-year-old Alice Parker was found dead in her apartment. Her neighbor found her door open, walked in, and discovered the body. Investigation started and the body has been transferred, but we are still being called to assist," he said as we passed through the sliding doors.

"Why is this case so important?" I asked.

"I used to know Alice Parker."

"Oh." I bit my bottom lip. "I'm sorry."

"No need to apologize. You did not kill her, and you did not know of my association to her." We reached the terminal and received our tickets, then started for the security line.

"How did you know her?"

"We met several years ago," he replied as he handed his passport to the TSA officer.

The officer glanced it over and handed it back with a smile. "Happy birthday, Sir."

I handed my passport to her, but my attention was focused on Hull. "Wait, what? Is today your birthday?"

"Irrelevant," he replied as he started untying his shoes.

"No really, is your birthday today?" I couldn't believe I had never known what his actual date of birth was. Somehow, that had never come up.

"May 17th, 1987, yes. Can we move on?"

I put my laptop bag in one of the security bins and glanced around the terminal. "Now I need to get you something."

He sighed. "If prior to one minute ago, my birthday held no importance, why should it be important now? A day dedicated to celebrating one's birth? Why are we celebrating? 'Congratulations, you involuntarily entered a world you will probably hate for a large portion of your life.'"

"Well, when you put it that way," I murmured as I removed my shoes.

The flight that followed went without conversation. He had that feeling to him, the one that said he held a personal connection to the case, and I knew he hated that. If the entire ordeal with Caroline Duerre had taught me anything, it was that Hull preferred to keep work and emotions as far from each other as possible. And if he had it his way, there'd probably be no emotions at all. We touched down in Chicago at around four in the afternoon and left in a taxi for the address of the woman. The drive was roughly an hour before we reached a complex, police cars parked on both sides of the street.

Waiting at the front of the complex was a woman, about my height with sandy brown hair that was tied in a bun. She was clad in a black blouse and jeans, a badge fastened neatly on her upper chest. Her attention was focused down on a clipboard, until we were within five meters of her, when she looked up at us with a nod.

"Glad to see you both made it okay," she said as she extended her hand. "Caitlin Ward. I'm the head of the Investigations Unit for Plainfield."

"Sheridan Hull," my companion said as he took her hand.

"John Walker," I said when she turned to me. I noticed a hint of an accent to her voice, but I couldn't quite place where it originated.

"I've heard a lot about you both," she spoke as we turned to enter the complex. "You were the guys who caught that creep burning students, right?"

"That would be us," I replied.

"Australian?" Hull added. Both Ward and I glanced at him.

"Yes," she said, a smile appearing on her face. "Most people don't catch it. Actually, most people assume it's British."

"I know that feeling all-too well," the detective returned as we started up the stairs.

"Now to what matters," Ward said as we reached the second floor. "Two floors up, first apartment to our right. Neighbor lady went to take her dog outside and saw the door open. When she looked in, she saw Parker's body on the floor of the living room. First officer on scene was Colleen Hershey, she's upstairs. Our evidence guys checked the area and had the body removed. We had to act promptly, the family was pretty distraught but they have some kind of tradition that requires the body be put in the ground fast. Funeral is scheduled for Sunday."

"Any ideas on the cause of death?" I prompted as we started for the next flight of stairs.

"Our evidence technician said there were signs of strangulation and foul play, but neither could have caused the death. Drug tests will be back tomorrow to see whether it was something internal."

We walked the next two flights and reached a section of the complex taped off with police marks. Two officers stood with a woman near a door to our left, but our attention was to the right. We walked into the open apartment and found one police officer, a female with light blonde hair, and a man dressed similarly to myself, his hair a dark blonde and his attention focused on an outlined spot on the floor. The officer and the man glanced up at Ward, then at us.

"Hershey, Rutland," Ward said as she pointed back, "this is Sheridan Hull and John Walker."

The woman approached us first. "Officer Colleen Hershey, first on scene."

"Nolan Rutland, head evidence technician," the man said.

Hull turned his eyes to Hershey. "Tell me how you found the body and what explanation the neighbor provided."

The officer glanced at Ward, who nodded. "The neighbor, Ms. Malinda Christion, made the call at 8:47 AM yesterday morning. She says she did not touch the body or anything in the room. Upon questioning, she mentioned that Ms. Parker had been out the night before with friends, who came to pick her up around 5:30 PM on Wednesday."

"And the body?"

"Lying on the floor, looking like she'd fallen off the couch. Hands were clutched around her stomach and her clothes were shuffled. Rutland found traces of semen on the skirt. She had blood in her mouth as well."

The detective's eyes moved to Rutland. "Your thoughts?"

"Internal bleeding as a result of drug overdose," Rutland started. "Her breath didn't smell of alcohol, but her throat had scarring, somewhat contributing to the blood. Clutching her stomach from pain. The seminal traces on her skirt were, ah.. well, for lack of a better term, leaked. It wasn't pretty."

"We have the three other women she was with the night of in custody at the station, but they all claim to not remember the events of the night," Hershey added.

Hull started around the room, moving to the window that looked out on the alleyway between this complex and the next. His eyes traveled from the window to where Parker's outline remained, his pupils seeming to shrink. He followed his vision-carved path to the outline, stooping down and examining the carpet. After about a minute of careful observation, he jumped to his feet and looked at the couch before speaking.

"I will need to speak with the three women in custody," he declared as he pulled his phone from his pocket.

Ward nodded at Hershey. "Go ahead of us. Make sure they're in individual rooms."

"That will not be necessary," Hull said, eyes locked on his phone's screen.

"You don't want to interview them individually?" Ward asked, her brow furrowed.

"I don't need to. Having them all together will make it far more easy."

Ward considered it for a moment before giving a short nod, then looking back at Hershey. "All together, then." Hershey gave a nod of affirmation then, with Rutland, left the room. Ward gave Hull and me a look before leaving the room as well. I walked over and stood by the detective, my eyes falling on the couch.

"What are your thoughts?" I asked.

"Unpleasant."

"Drugged, raped, left for dead?"

"Worse." He started towards the door, leaving me somewhat perplexed.

"How much worse can it get?"

"Much worse."

*

We arrived at the police station and were promptly taken to the doorway of an interview room. Ward, Hershey, and Rutland were standing in a line outside, their attention focused on the one-way window that revealed three girls, all twenty-three or twenty-four in age. The one closest to the wall had blonde hair similar to Hershey's, the center had black hair that reached her shoulders, and the farthest had curly brown hair. All three of them looked exhausted and scared.

"Taylor Ristich, Alexa Schneider, and Nicole Doyle," Ward stated, her arms crossed. "All three of them admit to having been with Parker the night of, but after a certain point, their memory seems to fail. They have no idea what could have happened to her."

Hull gave a quick glance through the window before clasping his hands behind his back. "I will be quick."

He walked around the corner with me in pursuit. I closed the door behind us and stood next to Hull as he took the seat facing the women. They looked from Hull to me with nervous eyes, the one on the left visibly more frightened. Hull pressed his hands together and rested them on the table, his gaze moving from woman to woman.

He closed his eyes. "I do not believe any of you had a direct hand in Ms. Parker's death," he stated, eyes still shut. Their postures became significantly more relaxed. "That does not mean, however, that I believe you held no indirect hand."

"What does that mean?" the girl in the center, Schneider, shot, her gaze going to me.

"It means that I believe you three were aware of something, and yet, you chose not to act."

"But we can't remember anything," Doyle, on the right, added.

"If you legitimately could not remember anything, none of you would be so concerned." He was using *that* voice now, the one that told you he knew everything there was to know about you, but you were too proud to admit it. "An innocent mind need not fear guilt."

A long moment of silence followed before the girl on the left, Ristich, spoke up. "Allie said she didn't feel comfortable," she said, her eyes fixated on the table. "She said it was like someone had been following her for weeks. And at the restaurant... she came back from the restroom and her makeup was smeared. Like she'd been crying."

"Where all did you go?" Hull asked, his attention on Ristich.

"We picked up Allie from her apartment and went to dinner. She picked the restaurant. La Dolce Vita. It was always her favorite. After dinner, we went bowling. Pioneer Lanes. It's where we used to go after football games when we were in high school. When we were done bowling, Nicole wanted to go to a nightclub. I think it was called Kegler's. After that... I don't remember. I'm sorry. I really don't."

"Did anyone strike you as suspicious when you were at any of these locations?"

"No," she replied, her eyes finally leaving the table and going to Hull. I could see tears welled up. "I don't know who would've done this. I don't know why anyone would have done this." She buried her face in her hands. My eyes moved to the other two girls, who had averted their gaze.

Hull stood. "That's all I need to know. Thank you for your time."

Doyle looked at the detective. "Can we go home now?"

"That is not my decision to make. I'm just a detective."

We exited the room to find the three Plainfield officials exactly where we had left them, except Ward wore a look that screamed for justice.

"Schneider and Doyle seem as guilty as you can get," she said with a pat on the handcuffs hanging from her belt.

"Seeming and being, I am afraid, are two very different things," Hull replied. His eyes traveled to the window. "They seem guilty because they do not know better. Ristich was somehow more fortunate than the other two, as she is able to remember far more details from the night. Because Schneider and Doyle are unable to recall the exact events, they cannot know for certain that they are innocent. The idea of guilt has festered in their minds, and we would be wise not to let it fester long."

Ward sighed. "So where do we go from here?"

"The restaurant," Hull responded, eyes going from the window to his now-revealed phone. "La Dolce Vita, not even ten minutes away. From there, we will retrace the steps of the women and, with proper time and deduction, we will learn who is responsible for Alice Parker's death." He switched to another program on his phone and pressed it to his ear. "Wait for me by the cars." He turned and walked away. Ward dismissed Rutland and Hershey, then turned to me.

"Your friend's quite the prodigy sleuth, isn't he?" she asked as we started for the exit. I offered no response.

Hull only took a few minutes before finding us in a waiting police car. He climbed into the back seat behind me and gave us the address of the restaurant before falling silent. The drive was short, as predicted. And it gave me a chance to get a feel for the area. Despite its proximity to Chicago, Plainfield was remarkably rural. It reminded me a lot of the outlying areas of Newfield. The weather was also surprisingly nice, which somewhat improved the overall mood. For me, at least.

"Thanks for everything, Jim."

The sentence had been spoken quietly, but I had most definitely heard it. Hull had murmured it behind me, the tone monotonous and sad. I glanced over my shoulder to see him staring out the window, his eyes doing their back and forth movement. His jaw was locked, and for the first time in a while, I could see a gray overcast to his irises. The last time I could recall that haze of gray was during the Man in Red case. It wasn't a good sign.

"Here we are," Ward announced as she turned to the right. I looked out to see a small outlet with our restaurant destination nestled in the center. She parked in front of the building and let Hull and me go first. Before we entered the restaurant, Hull opted to look around the outside, taking the time to walk across the parking lot and stand at the edge of the highway, eyes focused on the building. After five minutes of him scoping the building, he returned and nodded to the door.

We entered a dimly-lit and fairly empty main room, where a waitress immediately ran up and asked to serve us. I could see maybe six other people in the restaurant in total, and none of them together. There was room for probably seventy or eighty, on a busy day.

"I need to speak with a manager," Hull said as he stepped past the waitress.

She glanced from Hull to Ward and me, then gave a quick nod. "Of course, Sir. One moment." She left and headed for the back. Hull started around the room, sitting down at different tables and booths, eyes surveying the surroundings as he went. The waitress returned with a man probably the same age as Parker and her friends. The waitress pointed at Hull.

"Is there a problem here?" the manager asked, putting his hands in his back pockets.

"Two nights ago, four women came here for dinner. Hours later, one of them was murdered," Hull stated, jumping from one table to another. "I need to know what you served them and if you can recall anyone holding particular interest in their party."

"Hold on, murdered?" the man questioned, his jaw slack. "Who was killed?"

"Alice Parker. A regular here," Hull replied, craning his neck to see the window behind me.

The manager stepped back. "Allie is dead?"

"You knew her?" Ward inquired, her attention directed at the man.

"Well yeah, we graduated together." He moved carefully to the closest table, taking a seat with a heavy sigh. "She was here just a couple of days ago. She can't be dead."

"She is, Mr. Beckham," Hull interjected, reading the man's name tag. "And I need your full cooperation if we are to figure out who is behind it."

Beckham straightened up. "Of course. Anything I can do to help."

Hull clasped his fingers. "Parker was here with three others, do you remember who they were?"

"She was here with Taylor, Alexa, and Nicole," he replied, nodding with each name. "Oh, last names Ristich, Schneider, and Doyle."

"How many people were in your restaurant at the time?"

"For a Wednesday night, it was pretty busy. We even had people waiting outside."

"Did any of the patrons strike you as suspicious or having malevolent intent?"

He shook his head. "Nobody I can think of."

Hull nodded towards the ceiling space in the corner. "You have security cameras set up in five different locations around the main room. I would like to see the tapes from Wednesday night."

"Sure, of course," Beckham said as he stood, gesturing for us to follow. We walked across the restaurant and through the back door, entering a staff lounge of sorts. Beckham told us to sit by the television while he retrieved the recordings. After five minutes, he returned, plugged a memory stick into the TV's player, and stood back.

"What are we looking for?" I asked Hull.

"A distraction," he answered, his eyes fleeting across the screen. In the corner, we could visibly see Parker and her friends at a table. Nothing seemed noticeably out of place in the scenario thus far. We watched for maybe ten minutes before Parker stood and started towards a doorway to the right of the restaurant, with a female symbol on the door. Just as she was about to open the door, something dark raised up and covered the camera, eclipsing her from sight. The object remained in the way for several seconds before lowering. By then, Parker had no doubt entered the bathroom.

"Someone followed her into the bathroom and didn't want the camera catching it," Ward said as she leaned back.

"How would no one have noticed that?" I queried.

Beckham tapped where the time of the recording appeared on the screen. "I remember that. Someone bumped into a waitress and sent six plates and glasses to the ground. Everyone in the restaurant would've looked over."

I turned to Hull, lowering my voice as I spoke. "How many people are in on this?"

His eyes were still focused on the screen, the television's reflection making his irises look like a holographic gray rather than a dull gray. "I'm not sure." After a moment, he stood up. "That will be all. We need to leave for the bowling alley now." Ward and I nodded, following suit.

Beckham extended a hand to Hull. "Catch whoever did this. Please."

Hull shook his hand." I intend to."

We wasted no time in driving back up to the bowling alley. It was roughly 5:45 PM now, and the sun was starting its descent on the western horizon. The bowling alley was maybe five minutes from the restaurant, but the prior was far more busy than the latter. Only as we were walking towards the door did we learn that Friday nights were when local bowling teams came together for competitions. We avoided people as best we could, moving to the closest counter. A kid who looked sixteen or seventeen was sitting with his feet propped up and nose in a sports magazine. Ward smacked the kid's foot, causing him to give a startled jump and drop his magazine.

"Hey, what gives!" the kid yelled. His face quickly lost its instilled anger when he spotted Ward's badge.

"Were you working here on Wednesday night?" Hull questioned.

"Hell no," the kid replied, leaning away from Ward. "I only work weekends."

"Then who was working on Wednesday night?"

"How should I know?"

Hull shot his neck over the counter, bringing his face within ten centimeters of the boy's. "This woman will arrest you if you do not cooperate. Wednesday night, a group of four women came here. I need to know how they bowled and if anyone had interest in them."

The kid gave Hull a cagey look. "Why does it matter?"

"Because one of those women is dead."

The kid snapped back, eyes going wide. "Oh shit." He looked around before spotting someone behind us. "Hang on, that's my supervisor. Joe!"

I glanced back and saw a man probably ten years my senior hear the kid's shout and start walking towards us. He was dressed in a team uniform that matched the group of people he'd come from. He walked around the corner, propped his hands on the counter, and gave us a side-smile.

"Name's Joe Holliman. What can I do ya for?" the supervisor asked.

"Alice Parker was here with three friends on Wednesday night," Hull stated.

"Of course she was, she always came in Wednesday night." Holliman smiled. "That Alice has skill. Usually bowls hundred and fifty or higher."

"And how did she do Wednesday?"

Holliman glanced under the counter. "Well, gimme one sec and I'll know exactly how she did. Can't say I was here Wednesday." He rifled through a few things before pulling a logbook out. "Here we go. Alice always recorded her scores, and.." He crinkled his face. "Well that's odd. She only bowled one game and got a sixty-five. That's not like her at all. Don't think she's ever scored that low."

"Do you know if anyone else came with Parker and her friends?"

"No idea. Sorry." The man returned the book to its home. "Did something happen?"

"Ms. Parker is dead, Mr. Holliman. I am investigating her murder right now."

Holliman's jaw dropped. "That's a damn terrible thing to hear. One of the sweetest girls, that Alice. Some things just don't make sense in this world, do they? A good kid like that, dying so young." He shook his head. "If you need my help for anything—"

"No." Hull turned and looked over the bowling alley. "However, if you could tell me which lane Parker favored, I would be most gracious."

Holliman nodded forward. "Lane seven. Always lane seven with them."

"Thank you." Hull shot me a glance before walking in the direction of the exit. I nodded at Ward, who turned to follow. We found Hull standing a meter from the door, his eyes directed to the west.

"She was being stalked," Ward aired.

"Same person from the restaurant?" I added.

"Same person as before," Hull said ominously.

I stepped to his side and looked at him, and not just a glance; an actual look. Now his eyes had a blazing glow to their gray, but, the fact remained that the irises were still gray. How his irises were able to visually change depending on the man's mood was still unexplained, but with him, many things that should have normally been considered impossible were in fact quite possible. His eyelids were squinted slightly as he stared into the setting sun, the golden yellow light bringing all of his facial wrinkles, and even some scars, to life.

"Before what?" I asked.

He blinked once before licking his lips. "We need to see the nightclub."

*

The nightclub was significantly unimpressive, but then again, I'd never been one to enjoy clubs. We moved past a short line that had formed by the doorway, Ward using her badge to gain us access. The security guard had pointed us in the direction of the manager's office, where we found a woman, probably my age with a formal-looking suit and raven black hair. When we had entered, she'd been on the phone, angrily scorning someone for their failure to verify a booking of a DJ. Once she was done, she hung up, gave a heavy sigh, and smiled at us.

"How can I help?" she asked, the smile on her face looking like the product of a recent Botox injection.

"Wednesday night," Hull started. "What was the crowd like?"

The woman, Bridget Echols if her nameplate was correct, gave a smirk. "Full. Wednesday nights are Dubstep and Dollar Margarita nights. Always draws a large crowd."

"Other than the initial guard, what kind of security do you have in place?"

Echols raised her brow and turned to Ward. "Caiti, who is this guy?"

"He's a private investigator, Bridget," Ward shot back. "Answer his questions."

Echols sighed. "We have four cameras in the main room. One main entry, two emergency exits. We screen ID both at the door and the bar."

"The petty security is irrelevant," Hull interjected. "What do you have in place to keep someone from leaving with the wrong person?"

"We don't play babysitter. People come, people get drunk, people go home. We just make sure they pay and don't cause trouble."

Hull lifted his chin. "A twenty-four year old named Alice Parker was here Wednesday night with three friends. Her friends do not remember anything of their time here, but Parker is now dead. So, Ms. Echols, unless you are able to provide substantial evidence to point the blame elsewhere, your club will be held responsible for her death."

Echols's eyes widened. "Michael Parker's daughter?" she asked, the question directed at Ward, who nodded. "Oh God. I'm so sorry, I had no idea." She blinked and gulped in an attempt to regain her composure. "Wednesday night, there was a minor incident. A very small fight broke out at the bar, which was quickly quelled. The men involved were taken home by their dates. That's all I know."

"Do you have security footage to support this?" Hull demanded.

Echols nodded and turned to her computer. "All security data is copied to me for the week. Give me a second to pull up Wednesday night." She moved through a few windows before bringing up a video. After a moment, she leaned away, letting us get a good view. The feed showed four different views of the room, which was most definitely filled beyond capacity. The top-left feed showed one man take a swing at another, only to be knocked to the ground.

"The fight breaks out," Ward commented, her eyes narrowed. The two scrambled around on the floor before two women forced their way through the crowd and dragged the men apart. Hull slapped his hand across the desk to Echols's keyboard, pausing the video.

"Hey—" the woman started.

"Alexa Schneider and Nicole Doyle," the detective barked. Ward and I craned our necks to see that, indeed, the two women from earlier were the supposed dates who broke up the fight and escorted the men from the club.

"With Parker and Ristich nowhere to be seen," Ward added.

"Wrong," Hull shot back, his finger going to the bottom-left feed and homing in on a lone figure. It didn't take a second glance to see the trembles of Parker's body caused by crying. Hull's finger traveled to the bottom-right feed, revealing a very confused and drunk-staggering Ristich.

"Someone deliberately made it where Parker's friends would be out of the way," I said with a sunken tone. Hull pulled his phone from his pocket, nodded, and looked up.

"We need to leave. One last stop before I catch the murderer," the detective said as he turned.

"Wait, really?" Ward said, shock written on her face. "How could you have figured it out?"

"By paying attention." He stepped through the door and out of sight. I glanced back to find Echols staring at the doorway, her tongue pressed against her cheek.

"Who the Hell was that?" she asked.

Ward sighed. "Probably the greatest detective of the 21st century. Also one of the biggest dicks."

We walked out and found Hull once again staring into the west, catching the very end of the sunset. Even though it was dark, I could see that his irises had changed from the gray to a vibrant mixture of blue and green, with a certain, distinctive glint having made their home in the man's pupils. He gave a very minor smirk as the last of the sun disappeared from sight. His gaze fell to me.

"We have him," he said confidently.

"So it's a he?" Ward asked before I could reply.

"Indeed it is." Hull turned to the woman. "I advise you return to the department and release the three women being held. Then, with Ms. Hershey and Mr. Rutland, travel to this address." He handed her a piece of paper. She looked down at it, then back up at him.

"Where are you going?" she questioned.

Before he could reply, a bright light flashed on us from my right. Ward and I looked out to see a car stop in the spot next to us, the lights turning off a moment later. From the driver seat came a man, probably a few years older than myself, with dark brown hair that covered his ears and brows. He looked at us with sunken eyes, giving Hull a solemn nod.

"Hull," the man said after his nod.

The detective stepped forward and shook the man's hand. "Copper. Good to see you again." Hull turned to us. "Ward, Walker, this is Ryan Copper. An old friend of mine."

"Friends don't usually wait ten years before talking to each other," Copper commented. "But given the circumstances, I forgive you."

"John Walker," I added as I shook the man's hand.

"I've read a bit about what you two have been up to," the man replied. "Solving crimes like a classic Batman and Robin."

"I'll admit, that's a new comparison," I added with a smirk.

Hull looked at Ward. "Copper, Walker, and I will make our way to that address now. Please follow as soon as you can." Hull gave

Copper a nod, then one to me. I assumed it was my cue to enter the waiting car. I watched as Ward briskly made her way to the police car, heading back in the direction of Plainfield. Copper pulled out from the club parking lot and started in the same direction.

"So he finally did it," Copper said once we'd been on the road for about a minute.

"Unfortunately," Hull replied.

"Why'd it take him so long?"

"Certain circumstances stood in the way."

I leaned forward, having been put on the middle hump of the back seats. "Anyone care to fill me in?"

"You'll see soon enough," Hull responded, eyes locked forward.

"I hate when you repeat these cryptic things that just make me angry."

"Do you remember, all those months ago, when you asked me how many times I had been wrong on the entire situation at hand? I replied with one occasion." He glanced back at me. "This makes the second."

We drove for maybe twenty minutes before turning into a subdivision and slowly approaching a short driveway. Copper brought the car to a halt and turned it off. He glanced over at Hull, his lips pursed. Hull gave another short nod and opened his door. As we started walking towards the door of a house whose owners I had no knowledge of, the detective turned to me and nodded at my hip.

"Have your gun ready," he suggested. I nodded in compliance and pulled out my pistol, aiming it at the door. Copper took one side, Hull took the other. The three of us nodded in unison as I kicked just to the left of the handle, snapping the inner lock and forcing the door forward. It slammed against the inside wall and revealed a living room filled with about ten people. I could identify one older woman, one man who looked to be around my age, and eight others who were probably teenagers. Hull charged for the man in the back, who jumped over his seat and attempted to run for the kitchen.

Hull grabbed the man by the shoulders and threw him back into the living room, where Copper was waiting. The other man caught him and forced him against the wall, pinning him despite his vicious struggling. I aimed the gun at the man, who, once he realized just how pointless his struggling was, ceased. The man had short black hair, glasses, and stubble from a day or two without shaving.

Hull walked casually around the room before coming to face the man, his eyes fierce and his nostrils flared.

"George James Sankys," Hull declared. "An absolute pleasure to see you again."

*

It only took about twenty minutes for Ward, Hershey, and Rutland to reach the address. By then, the three of us had managed to get the man, Sankys, into an armchair while the elderly woman had taken the teenagers to the house next door. Hull waited for the three new arrivals to sit down on the couch to his left before he started pacing, his attention going from point to point in the room.

"This was not a case of finding the murderer, but rather in proving him. You, Sankys, have been on my radar for a very long time, ever since our first encounter. Long have I waited to see if you would lash out. And now that you have, I am more than welcome to be the hand that determines your judgement. Now, ten years later, I am finally able to enact the justice I should have enacted on you long ago.

"You held a grudge for almost ten years. As a result of one girl and one haphazard circumstance, your life slowly declined before you were put in jail for six months. Only one month ago, you were let out on good behavior. From the day you stepped out a free man to two days ago, you had been working to engineer this poor woman's death. Day by day, you would silently stalk her, making her more paranoid, more afraid. Two nights ago, you decided she was as vulnerable as she could possibly be, and you struck.

"At the restaurant, you watched and waited for her to use the restroom before following her in and telling her you would torment her until the day she died, but if she told anyone of your intentions, you would murder her then. You followed her to the bowling alley, where you sat silently at a bar behind her, engaging in conversation with one of your accomplices, but constantly keeping your eyes on her, explaining why she, a person who would regularly bowl a game of over one hundred and fifty points, did so poorly.

"You then followed her to the nightclub, where you organized the songs played to set her even more on edge. You had accomplices distract her friends with dances and expensive drinks while you targeted her once more, reducing her to tears but still not setting a hand on her. She left the club and retreated for her home, but was caught in a traffic ordeal orchestrated by your accomplices. You were at her home when she arrived.

"You had done your medical research and had gathered a volatile mixture of drugs that would slowly and painfully kill her without you doing it yourself. You told her she could end her life then or suffer for the rest of her existence. She killed herself, and it is your fault, Sankys. You murdered a girl who never once, not even a decade ago, did something to deserve the punishment. And once she was dead, in your newly-developed lack of sanity, you opted to take advantage of her lifeless state. I hope you have enjoyed your freedom, because it is now over."

Hull leaned in close. "You sick, filthy, cowering, *immoral imbecile*. Enjoy your time in Hell."

Ward, Hershey, and Rutland escorted the man from the home, hands cuffed behind his back. Copper gave Hull a nod before leaving the home as well. Hull, however, was focused on where Sankys had sat, the glint having disappeared from his eyes, the irises having lost their shimmer. He gulped, his vision unwavering.

"I know these aren't the words you want to hear," I said as I came to stand at his side, "but that was brilliant."

"Thank you," he said calmly, his gaze not willing to falter.

"There was a lot more to this than you let on."

He gulped again. "December of 2003. I made the acquaintance of someone who called themselves Alice Parker through an online chat program. The more I came to speak with her, the more I realized how wrong something was. The way she typed was unusual. The way she spoke of her activities was unrealistic. So I sought help. I was able to make contact with a person two years older than me, named Ryan Copper, who lived in the same city that Parker claimed to live. Plainfield, Illinois.

"The more we searched, the more we found, and the more disturbed we became. I had not been speaking to Alice Parker, but had in fact been speaking to a man named George Sankys. Sankys had opted to not only use Parker's name to his advantage, he had also been actively using her private and personal information for his own gain. The level to which he would go for this information was highly illegal. So I brought it to the attention of Michael and Allison Parker, Alice's parents. They acted immediately, notifying the police. Sankys, in his desperation, tried to make a deal with me.

"I threatened him with everything I had uncovered. He would be charged with theft, perversion, stalking, and pedophilia. Enough to lock him up for a very long time. I told him to never contact her again. Little did I know he had already fled the state. He gave me his word that he would not speak to her, or even come in remote contact with her. I, of course, did not trust him, and have kept active tabs on Alice Parker for ten years.

"From the moment I saw the area code for the phone call, I knew he had done it. I have been waiting for him to act out for ten years. It's unfortunate he went as far as he did, but that was a lack of foresight on my part. Sankys was a twisted and demented man. I knew he had done it. I held the investigation to clear the consciences of three girls who had no recollection of the evening. To prove their innocence. And to prove to him that, once again, I held the upper hand, no matter how cunning and devious he could be."

He stopped and blinked, his eyes falling to the floor. I bit my lip before speaking, but knew that my curiosity would overcome me.

"In the car, you said, 'Thanks for everything, Jim.' What did you mean by that?" I asked, watching him at the corner of my sight.

"When everything had been resolved, Alice got a restraining order against Sankys and contacted me personally. It was the first time her and I had actually spoken. We talked for a few hours, starting with what information he had used and ending with personal pleasantries. She was quite an interesting individual. Matured beyond her age of fourteen, but very conflicted. I know that inner conflict stayed with her throughout the years. Our conversation transitioned to that same chat program I had used to uncover Sankys. Her last message to me was, 'Thanks for everything, Jim,' with a smiley face at the end."

"What did she mean by Jim?"

He smirked. "My middle name. I was not one for Internet handles, so I used my middle name with a random assortment of numbers. James1175, I believe it was. Even though she knew my name was Sheridan, she grew to calling me Jim. A nickname that I would not care for, had it been anyone else." His eyes moved from the floor to the ceiling. "I've often grown fond of referring to that entire situation as my first case. The first time I truly used my deductive mind for the good of justice."

We fell silent. I'd heard everything I needed to, after all. And I could tell he wasn't back up to his normal self. I clasped his shoulder and walked from the room. Outside, I found that Ward had sent Rutland and Hershey back to the station with Sankys, and Copper was long gone. Ward was waiting by her car, her attention on the phone in her hand.

"That was amazing," she said I approached.

"It always is," I replied with a smile.

"Is it the same for every case he takes?"

I looked back at the doorway. "No. This one was different." I gave a solemn nod. "This one mattered."

Ward told me the processing of Sankys would happen quickly, and everything would be sorted out by Sunday. She requested that Hull and I remain in town until then. We took up residence in a nearby hotel, passing the time by exploring Chicago. All the while, Hull seemed off. His mind was elsewhere. He couldn't be bothered to focus on the present. Before I knew it, Sunday evening was upon us. Ward had invited the both of us to a dinner in somewhat-celebration. Sankys had been charged with first degree murder.

Hull and I made our way to the lobby, then to the front drive. Ward was waiting for us, no longer wearing her work attire. She was now in a white dress of sorts, with her hair tied up. Hershey and Rutland were visible in the car, waiting for us to join them. I gave the two a nod, then turned to Ward.

"We ready?" she asked.

"Absolutely," I replied, turning to make sure Hull was paying attention. But when my eyes reached where he'd been standing just moments ago, I discovered that Hull was gone.

*

It was several hours later before Hull returned. A group of us remained in the hotel lobby, many of them mingling among themselves. He walked in well after the sun had gone down, and there was something different about him. The glint to his eyes had dimmed from earlier, and his face looked somber. His hair was matted down, too, as if he'd been walking in the rain that had only recently ceased.

I tried to talk to him, but he wasn't looking for conversation. I knew that somewhere, deep in his well-protected heart, he was feeling pain. I had seen the look before so many times in so many others. I knew Hull wasn't normally one to display emotions, but something about this case in particular had knocked something loose. I assumed it was the close ties to his childhood, or as he had called it, "his first case."

Later that night, at about three in the morning, I woke to an odd noise. I carefully looked over my shoulder to find Hull at the room desk, pen softly scratching away at something. He sat and stared at the few words he had written for a very long time before sighing, crumpling it up, and throwing it away. That morning, I opened the paper while he was out. It simply said, "I'm sorry I didn't come sooner."

It was then that I knew, Sheridan Hull truly was both a complex and intricate human. One who had loved, and one who felt pain.

And one who held someone very dear in his memories.

CALM BEFORE THE STORM

A standard summer afternoon in Newfield would consist of crowded cars, people going to and from their lunch breaks, the sounds of construction, the sights of wispy clouds, and the essence of life. A day in which everything is ordinary, and usual, and normal. Where no one asks even once at the sound of a blaring car horn. Where no one gives a person standing at a street corner a second glance. Where not a single person would even remark at the oddness surrounding the eight figures that had been carefully positioned in eight places, each facing the same location. A standard summer afternoon would instigate no question.

But a standard summer afternoon was not what Newfield was in for.

Matson stood at the corner of Main Street that intersected with Highway 99E, passing directly through the heart of the city. Despite his being at a crosswalk, he had yet to move in any direction for one minute and thirty-six seconds. A group had just dispersed with the changing of the traffic signal, but he remained in place. He stared forward at a tall building, eyes lit with a burning need for victory. The building itself was white-walled with orange tiling, an analog clock facing forward, and a proud American flag flying high from the peak.

One minute, forty-five seconds.

Matson glanced over to his right, eyes resting on a crosswalk about half a block away. There stood another figure, like him, having not moved for almost two minutes. This figure glanced in Matson's direction, nodded, and returned his own gaze forward. Matson then looked to the left, spotting another figure, who nodded. Eight of them in total surrounded the building which housed the central authority figures of Newfield. And very, very soon, eight people would move into the same building and begin the plans their director had so carefully laid in place.

Two minutes.

"Move in," Matson ordered into his central microphone, masterfully disguised inside the pin on his lapel. From his peripheral vision, he could see the two figures from before start across the road. He looked up at the sky, patted his upper chest, and walked ahead, causing two cars to slam on their brakes as he moved into flowing traffic. When one car came too close, its front bumper imploded, the smallest field of energy having materialized before the vehicle. The car came to a jarring halt, the damage rippling its way up to the windshield. Matson didn't even blink.

He walked between two trees, following the sidewalk that led to the cement stairs. The two figures from before joined him, patting their hips. The three men were clad in black suits, black vests, and stark white undershirts. Matson gave a solemn nod, then started up the stairs. The three passed through the open white doors and found themselves at a security checkpoint. Behind the bulletproof glass sat an apathetic security officer, his attention focused on the contents of a book rather than on the doorway. Matson jerked his head slightly to his left, then forward at the officer. The man to his left pulled what looked to be a pistol from his hip and aimed it at the glass.

"Excuse me," Matson said with the clearing of his throat. The policeman looked up, giving a jolt when he saw the gun. He reached for his own pistol, but was far too late. The man to Matson's left pulled the trigger, and together, the three men watched as a glowing golden round shattered the once-bulletproof glass and made contact with the officer's throat. The dead body slumped against the wall at its back as Matson and his men walked under the metal detector, the minor alarms from the computer terminal not even registering in their ears.

The man on the right stepped forward, pulling his own pistol and aiming it at the double doorway ahead of them. To their left was a service desk, which was now occupied by a very scared woman.

"What are you doing?!" the woman bellowed. The man to Matson's left lunged over the desk and tackled the woman, forcing both to vanish from sight. The right man pulled the trigger to his pistol, sending out a fluctuating and growing wave of power that sent both doors flying from their hinges. Matson and the right man stepped through the doors, finding themselves in a large atrium, currently filled with people.

"Good afternoon, everyone!" Matson yelled, watching the people start huddling against the wall. "I apologize for the inconvenience, but it is my great pleasure to inform you that you are now hostages." He nodded forward, signaling for the right man to start tying people's hands behind their backs. Two additional men in suits emerged from a doorway to the left, backpacks bursting with their contents. Matson pointed to the room behind him, where there had been a staircase going to the upper levels, as well as down.

The two newcomers and Matson returned to the lobby, the prior going down the stairs and Matson moving up. He passed the second floor entirely, seeing that the man who had been on his left when entering was now busy apprehending all of the occupants of the level. He continued on his way to the third floor, carefully pulling his pistol from inside his coat. He reached the top of the staircase and found a single doorway with a portrait of the mayor, Jameson Montorum, to its left. He smirked at the picture before slipping a black ski mask over his face and kicking the door open, finding himself in a narrow office with about six others.

"This will be simple and quick, but I will say this right now," he said as he walked in, swinging his pistol to level with each person's head. "I don't want to hear a word from any of you. Do I make myself clear?" He glanced around the room, smiling at the fear etched across every face. His eyes came to rest on a man huddled in the farthest corner, making any attempt to stay out of sight. A coward through and through. Matson started towards him slowly, turning his pistol to the side. He stopped when he was halfway, doing a dramatic turn to encompass the others.

"Judging by your faces," he commented, "some of you may be wondering whether my gun is real or not." He showed the profile of the pistol to everyone. It certainly wasn't standard, with an elongated barrel and a small, circular object propped just ahead of the trigger. "It's not regulation, no. But it is powerful. Very powerful." His eyes went from the pistol to the man in the corner. "Would you like to see what it does?"

"N-No," the man stammered.

Matson cleared the space between the man and him in a matter of seconds. "What's your name?"

The man gulped. "J-John Michaels."

"Ah."

Matson pulled the trigger and watched as the man's skin was incinerated, a minuscule fire traveling across Michaels's body. He screamed in pain as the skin of his eyelids was burned away before going limp, his fully-revealed jaw hanging open.

"See that?" Matson shouted as he turned to see the other occupants. "That's why I want you all quiet."

Another suited man entered the room from the far door, holding what would've been a typical assault rifle, if not for the silver ball attached to its tip. He surveyed the group inside the room before looking up at Matson.

"Are the lower levels secured?" Matson asked. The man nodded. "Good. Tie these ones up, and give me your pistol." The man pulled the pistol from his hip and tossed it to Matson, who had holstered his own gun. He took the pistol, unchecked the safety, and started towards the doorway that led to the mayor's office. With a swift kick of his boot, the lock gave way and the door swung open to reveal a modest office, a single desk facing the doorway, two windows against the back wall, and a very confused-looking mayor rising to his feet.

Matson raised his pistol and fired a single round into the mayor's left leg, causing the man to spasm forward and fall to the ground. The gunman worked his way to the side of the mayor's desk, looking down as the older man struggled to contain the bleeding. Matson leveled his pistol with the man's head and gave a slight smirk, hidden beneath the cover of his mask.

"Moriarty sends his regards," Matson stated, "Mr. Mayor." *Bang.*

*

It was rare to hear the sound of so many different sirens going off in the distance without being at the heart of the problem. It wasn't normal, that many sirens. Sounded to be at least a dozen different vehicles. But for the past three hours, my attention had been focused on something else entirely. Or, more properly, someone. After a large number of dates, I felt comfortable in acknowledging Cassidy Claypool as my girlfriend. It was different, that was certain. I hadn't had a girlfriend since high school, and those really didn't count.

Since returning from Illinois, I had opted to spend the past month on myself and Cassidy. Being twenty-six years old, out of college, working a job, and having what I'd consider a part-time job of a hobby, there'd been a part of my life that just felt empty. Not really a want to settle down, but to have a person who wasn't Hull. Someone I could talk to, and have fancy dinners with, and see movies with. Someone who was a bit more social than the consulting detective. And of course, someone who had an interest in, ah.. relations.

Of course, Hull was still my closest friend. Even if our friendship was an odd one, it was strong. I trusted him and he trusted me. We had our own fun, we laughed. We enjoyed spending time together. But with Hull, it was almost like the stages of the moon. When at his brightest, he was quite enjoyable. But at every other time, part of him would be elsewhere, be it a case, or an experiment, or a Sudoku puzzle. One moment, he would be there, talking to you, and the next, he'd be so deep within his mind that speaking to him would be impossible.

For me, though, that was quite fine.

As I stepped out of my now-parked car and checked the road, I found a very sleek, very black car parked with its passenger side facing the doorway to the flat. I stepped around the car as the door opened, allowing a tall man, dark blonde hair and a midnight blue business suit, to step out. The man glanced over at me and nodded.

"John," the man said as he closed the car door.

"Malcolm," I replied, "always good to see you."

"You as well."

"How's the family?" I asked as I opened the flat door.

"Quaint as ever."

"I take it something bad's happened," I suggested as he stepped through the doorway.

"Something bad always seems to be happening, John," he replied as he started for the staircase. I gave a nod to Mrs. Hanson before following him up.

We reached the flat living room and found Sheridan lounging across the sofa, nose deep in another Star Wars novel. I knocked once on the cover of the book before moving to my seat.

"Visitor," I said as I sat down. The detective glanced over the top of his book, rolled his eyes, and lifted it once more.

"Busy," Sheridan said through the pages.

"Irrelevant," Malcolm snapped.

"Go away."

"No."

"*Go away.*"

"We need you."

Sheridan slammed the book shut and scrunched his face. "'We need you' is about the only thing you ever say to me. Find someone else to be your errand boy."

"At approximately 2 PM this afternoon," Malcolm started, his voice stern, "the mayor was attacked." I felt my jaw sink slightly, suddenly realizing why there'd been so many sirens. Sheridan rotated his body so that his feet touched the floor as he set the book down on the end table.

"Do we know who is behind it?" he asked as he clasped his fingers.

"Of course we know who is behind it."

"Then who?"

Malcolm inhaled sharply through his nostrils. "He was apprehended one hour after the attack. Legally known as Lucius Mendax. But I am sure you will recognize him by another name. Moriarty."

"Impossible," Sheridan said as he leaned back, his interest waning.

"And yet, possible." Malcolm ran a hand through his hair before continuing. "The leader of the crime syndicate came willingly and is being held at McMullen County with charges of first degree murder, attempted murder, and attempted acts of terrorism."

Sheridan smirked. "He would never willingly turn himself in. Can't you see why this is wrong?"

"You will have a chance to identify him yourself. His sole request prior to coming was that you meet with him."

I glanced at the detective. "This sounds bad."

"It's always bad," Sheridan replied, his attention drifting. It didn't make any sense to me, and I couldn't imagine how it would make sense to him. Moriarty, the man who had coordinated so much in the past several months, becoming a prisoner without problem? And after attacking the mayor?

"You have no choice in the matter of meeting with him or not," Malcolm stated. "He is completely unarmed and in confinement. He is being held for attempted acts of terrorism because eyewitnesses inside the city hall say they saw two gentlemen with backpacks filled with explosives heading for the basement, but neither men were arrested. The police took six men into custody and found Moriarty in their supposed escape vehicle."

"Something is still very off," Sheridan returned, his tongue pressed against his cheek.

"Sheridan!"

The detective raised his hands. "Fine, fine, I'll see him. But I know this is wrong."

The three of us rode together in Malcolm's car, silence falling over the vehicle. Outside I could still hear the sound of sirens in the distance, but we were headed away from them. Our destination lay in the industrial area of Newfield, where the tallest buildings were smokestacks rather than apartment complexes or the occasional skyscraper. Our destination was the newest building in the section, stretching five stories high and looking like nothing more than a solid block of concrete with black slits for windows.

Malcolm walked us through the doors and into the lobby, then stopped.

"This is as far as my jurisdiction goes," he said with a very minor, very minute gulp.

Sheridan narrowed his eyes. "Your jurisdiction doesn't end."

"Not today."

I watched the two stare each other down for several seconds before Sheridan leaned away, eyes fleeing towards the elevator. He glanced back at me and, with a nod, started for our pathway up. We were told to head to the fourth floor, third wing. The room at the far end was where Moriarty was currently being held. Even now, I refused to refer to him as whatever name Malcolm had stated. Lucius Mendax. Nothing felt right about that. Putting a name to the man beneath the hood just felt so very wrong.

The elevator came to a sudden halt, the door opening to reveal a long hallway, barred cells lining the sides. At the far end was a doorway with a small window that showed nothing but white. The hallway itself was very much the same as the exterior: bland, gray, concrete and metal. We started forward, our attention at first only on the doorway. But as we walked, my eyes started to wander to those who rose to their feet and clutched the bars, their eyes burning with an intense hatred. And only then did I recognize one of them.

"Hull," I whispered as we continued on, "was that Alexander Wygant?" The man's hair was a dimmed gray, ruffled and grown to something reminiscent of a homeless person. His wide eyes were a deep blue and his wrinkles were matted with scars and bruises. He certainly didn't look the same, but I knew that was the man I'd watched crawl from a flipped car almost two years ago. I looked away from the man, hoping to find some anonymity in a different inmate.

What I was greeted with was far more unpleasant.

The first figure who met my gaze looked to have been beaten to a pulp, but he was recognizable, to an extent. Benjamin Arnold. The man to his immediate right, a burn stretching across his neck, was George Everrard. I looked back and forth along the cells, quickly finding something that disturbed me to no end. A very large number of these criminals had been apprehended by Hull.

"That's unnerving," I said as we reached the doorway, casting a glance back at the cells.

"This jail is home to over eight hundred inmates, and yet, all of the ones I have enacted justice upon have ended up in the same wing." The detective scoffed. "Yes, that is quite unnerving."

He flashed the badge issued to us by the front desk over the scanner by the lock, which beeped in confirmation. The door before us slid open to reveal a plain white room, with a bed propped against the far wall, a metal pot opposite the bed, and a table directly ahead of us. The table had three chairs, one facing us and two waiting. Obviously, the man who sat in the opposing chair was our person of interest.

He looked to be in his late forties, judging by the hair color. It was a bright silver, combed neatly at the sides but frayed out on top, moving forwards. His upper lip and chin were hidden beneath a matching goatee, something I actually did expect of him. He stared up at us with deep brown eyes, made to look black by his bright orange inmate suit, with the numbers "43-11" embroidered on his left breast. He crossed his arms and gave a very slight smirk.

"Now this," he started, his voice exactly as it had been under the hood, "this is something I've been looking forward to."

"Turning yourself in now?" Hull replied as we sat down.

"Looks that way, doesn't it?"

"Why?"

Moriarty, or Mendax, smirked. "You tell me."

"Considering I just walked a hallway filled with your agents, I can only suspect malevolent intent."

"And what can you deduce from what you suspect?"

"You tell me."

"Clever, very clever," the man replied, his eyes narrowing. "There's no topping you, is there?"

Hull was clearly not interested in petty conversation. "No criminal mastermind would turn himself in without knowing that he would eventually escape. No genius would risk losing all that he had worked for. You are only in here because you know you can get out. The question is, why be taken in the first place."

The man leaned forward. "You tell me."

"This is one of the most secure facilities in the state. Even with the power of Chimaera, you would risk sacrificing what discreetness your organization possesses if you were to stage a full-scale assault on the facility."

"I had eight men attack city hall, you don't think I'd send an army to break me out?"

"Why get in if you can easily get out?"

"Because the time is at hand."

Hull's nostrils flared. "What time?"

"Almost a year ago, I told you the pieces were in play and the world was in motion. Everything has fallen into place. The world is ready to begin its journey to order. There are simply some minor things that need to be arranged."

"Like?"

The man chuckled. "Telling you wouldn't be fair. We both enjoy the game too much for that. There's nothing you can really do to stop things now, but you can try to catch up."

Hull stood. "Unless you plan to say anything of value, I can find solace in your being locked up and go about my business." He started away as I stood.

"The man of the memorial and the caretaker of the orphan meet." Hull and I both stopped as the man continued. "They will bear witness to the emergency's arrival and the pinnacle's fall. All it takes is the passing of the *solsticij* to bring about events to come." Hull paused for only a moment before holding the ID card over the door and stepping through.

Once we'd traversed the hallway and entered the elevator, I sighed. "What'd he mean by all that?"

"Irrelevant drivel," the detective replied.

"How often does a criminal mastermind resort to drivel?"

"Depending on how deep his insanity runs, potentially quite often."

The elevator opened to the lobby, and I was surprised to find a familiar face that wasn't Malcolm waiting for us. Standing with his hands in his pockets and attention on the plaque above the front desk was Inspector Lennox. The ding of the elevator drew his attention to us.

"Oh thank God, you are here," he said with a sigh.

"No breaks whatsoever," Hull commented under his breath.

"A break is by far the last thing you need," I snarled. "What's happened now?"

"Army veteran and his daughter were found dead in a graveyard this morning," Lennox reported. "Everyone else is busy with the attack on the mayor. Conn revoked my suspension early to put me on this. I don't even have petty officers to help me."

"Take us," Hull pitched, his voice going from uninterested to completely devoted.

I looked at the detective with a raised brow. "Really?"

"Yes, really."

"Alright then."

Lennox started for the door, but before Hull could go, I grabbed him by the shoulder. "Why the change of heart?"

"The man of the memorial," he echoed, quoting the mystic statement from Moriarty.

"You think this is connected?"

"I think it requires more investigation. If he was speaking in reference to an upcoming event, it would be wise of us to take caution and understand every variable."

*

The graveyard we found ourselves in bordered one of the university buildings, which I thought was quite creepy. I couldn't imagine being a Newfield University student, glancing out the window, and seeing a graveyard and just going about my day. Graveyards and I had never gotten along. Luckily, it was only about four in the afternoon and the sun was still high. The creepy factor had yet to really set in.

The two dead bodies were side by side, resting where they had fallen. The older man, looking to be in his late seventies, had one hand extended towards a flat headstone. The woman to his left looked to be maybe fifty, her hand clutching the older man's free one. On a quick glance, I could see that the veteran was shot through the back of head, while the woman was shot from the side.

"How do you know that's his daughter?" I asked Lennox, who was standing on the other side of the headstone.

He shrugged. "I guess I just assumed. Didn't really occur to me that they could've been something else."

"Astute assumption," Hull said as he lowered himself. "Father and daughter visiting the headstone of her mother, his wife. Passed away ten years ago." He pulled a pair of rubber gloves from his pocket, covering his hands before carefully moving the man's head to the side. "First bullet traveled through his skull, exiting his throat. Bullet would have decreased in speed..." He glanced up and pointed at a nearby tombstone. "And made a home there." Lennox started for the stone.

Hull gave a careful look at the inspector before lifting the dead man up and slipping his hand into the man's coat.

"What are you doing?" I whispered, keeping a watchful eye on Lennox.

"Getting this," he replied as he pulled a yellow sticky note from the insides of the coat. He quickly folded the note and pocketed it, then let the body rest. Lennox returned with the end of a bullet in his hand.

"Not your usual bullet," he commented as he handed it to Hull. "Custom bullet, custom gun. Won't be hard to find the owner."

"Not hard at all," Hull responded, his attention turning to the woman's body. He ran his hand deftly over her side before coming to a stop. He reached inside her pocket and pulled out a slim wallet. He opened the wallet and pulled out what looked like a business card.

"Ms. Anna Cartwright. Overseer of St. Jacob's Orphanage." He cast a quick glance up at me before looking back down, his head tilted. He opened the section where money would normally be and found another yellow sticky note.

"What's that?" Lennox asked as he leaned down.

"A note," Hull stated as he opened the paper. Scrawled in black ink was a single word: HELL.

"That's unsettling," I commented.

"Quite." The detective rose to his feet and handed the wallet to Lennox. "Our best option is to look into the bullet provider. Through them, we can find the owner of the gun."

"You don't think the gun's owner used it?" I asked as the three of us started back towards the police car.

"Right now, I cannot say. Too unclear."

As we walked towards the car, I couldn't keep from squinting my eyes. I stopped and glanced around, certain someone had been reflecting light at me. Only then did I catch the glimmer coming from a nearby bush. I walked over to the bush quickly, expecting to find some misplaced glass. Instead, I found the clean, studded handle of a very expensive-looking pistol.

"Found our gun!" I called back. Both Hull and Lennox stopped and turned. Once they'd reached me, Lennox took the gun and gave it a look.

"I recognize this make. Only one shop in the city that would sell it," the inspector announced.

Hull gave a confident nod. "Then that will be our destination."

It didn't take long for us to reach the gun shop, maybe ten minutes with the traffic. It was on the bottom floor of a four-story complex, with the upper floors looking more like apartments. The three of us walked in and found ourselves surrounded by an armory. It was unsettling, seeing so many weapons in such a small confinement. The thought of someone potentially walking in here and taking them was almost too much to bear.

The owner of the store came to greet us at the front desk, wearing a name tag with "LAWRENCE KING" displayed proudly. "How can I help the NPD?"

Lennox set the pistol from the graveyard down on the counter. "This gun was found at a crime scene east of campus. Custom made and used imported bullets, right?"

King nodded. "That's a Springfield Armory X-treme Duty 9x19mm. The XD-9. Better known as the HS2000. That one's been upgraded personally, though. Handle is different and the barrel's been changed. That gun can't fire your normal 9mm round. Takes something special."

"And what would that special round be?" Hull inquired.

"Well, if you give me a minute, I can pull up a book and find out," King said as he reached under the counter. He came back up with a book and started flipping through pages before reaching one that was half-empty. "Here we go. Custom XD-9, owner listed as Austin Abramovich. Ammo is—"

Hull slapped his hand down on the book. "Where does Abramovich work?"

King scowled. "How the Hell should I know?"

"You sell people handguns and other more potent weaponry on a daily basis," the detective spat as he turned to look across the store. "If you follow regulations, all customers must fill out a form, at which point you call the police and run a background check on the individual before giving them the gun. Those forms list their names, dates of birth, addresses, and places of employment." He turned again to stare the man down. "Now tell me, do you follow regulation?"

"Of course I follow regulation!" the man barked before rubbing his face. After a moment, he gave a deep sigh. "Give me a minute to find the records." He turned and walked into the back room.

"Abramovich," I commented, glancing between Hull and Lennox. "Russian?"

"Descendant, maybe," Hull replied, "but not born."

King returned from the back with a sheet of paper. "Austin Abramovich, age twenty-two, works as an emergency medical technician for Newfield General."

"Thank you," Hull shot as he turned and walked from the store. Lennox and I scurried to keep up, finding the detective standing by the police car.

"EMT shooting a vet and his daughter," Lennox said as he took the driver seat.

"It would never be so simple, something else is at play," Hull replied, his eyes going to the window.

"Someone could've stolen the gun and used it," I suggested.

"Yes, but why?" the detective questioned. I glanced over to see his eyes racing back and forth. "What does someone hold to gain from stealing an expensive gun and using it on an innocent veteran and his daughter?"

"Revenge?" I prompted, my own mind exploring the different possibilities.

"His riddle. I should have known better than to ignore it."

"Whose riddle?" Lennox asked.

"Moriarty," Hull said as he closed his eyes. "The man of the memorial and the caretaker of the orphan meet. They will bear witness to the emergency's arrival and the pinnacle's fall."

"Man of the memorial being the veteran," I added, "caretaker of the orphan being his daughter. The emergency's arrival could be this Abramovich."

"But the pinnacle's fall?" Lennox questioned.

"To be determined," Hull stated, his eyes opening. "We need to get to the hospital soon."

The hospital was nestled in the heart of the city, and was currently flooded with police vehicles and reporters. I was certain the mayor had been taken here. Newfield General Hospital was the hub of medical authority in the city; it was where all of our more severe patients at the clinic were transferred or recommended. The three of us parked the car with the other police cars and started our way past the reporters. As we walked, I caught a handful of their questions.

"Inspector Lennox, can you tell us more about the attack?"

"Is it true the mayor will be paralyzed?"

"The people behind the attack, are they the same group that abducted the students in March?"

"When will an official statement be given?"

"Is it true there are attackers unaccounted for?"

We eventually made our way past the police blockade, at which point I decided to ask my own questions.

"How are they able to get that much information without anyone saying a word?" I asked.

"People talk more than they should," Lennox answered, nodding towards the entrance to the hospital. It was partially eclipsed by a wonderful fountain that helped create the roundabout emergency parking area of the hospital. The fountain itself was a metallic look at a metropolis, with several large, rounded pillars moving up and a single, needle-like structure stretching the highest in the center. We walked around the fountain and into the central lobby, currently occupied by patients, visitors, and police. Lennox led us to the front desk, where a female receptionist sat, bags under her eyes and her hair unkempt.

"We're looking for an Austin Abramovich," the inspector said.

"One moment please," the woman replied, her hands flying across her keyboard. "We have no patient under that name."

"No no no, not a patient," Lennox stammered with a sigh, "he works here, we need to see him. Newfield Police."

"Oh," she responded, her cheeks getting a red tint. "I apologize. One moment." Her eyes illuminated as she brought up a secondary screen. "Mr. Abramovich just returned from an emergency call and is currently on the sixth floor. Would you like me to call him down for you?"

"Not necessary," Hull interrupted. "We will go to him."

The receptionist pushed her chair back slightly. "I'm sorry, Sir, but you will need proper authorization."

"That part about the Newfield Police?" Lennox stated. "That's our authorization." The three of us entered the elevator moments later and started up. When the number ticker dinged 3, Lennox turned to us. "Do we take this guy as a suspect or what?"

"We talk to him as civilized people," Hull retorted, clasping his hands behind his back.

"What if he is responsible?" the inspector buzzed.

"And what if he is not?" The detective turned his head to stare Lennox in the eyes. "There is something far more complicated at hand, not the work of a twenty-two year-old medical technician. If he were responsible, he never would have been stupid enough to come to work the next day. Those bodies were fresh. They were shot last night. If Abramovich is valuable in emergency situations, he could have been one of the people dispatched to the scene if the bodies had been found."

The elevator dinged again, telling us we'd reached the sixth floor. We stepped out into a fairly busy hallway, doctors and nurses scurrying about, with different visitors lining the wall to our right. We started down the hallway towards the wing desk, where two police officers stood speaking with the nurse. As we came closer, I could see more and more people in business suits, quite a few matching.

"I think Montorum is on this floor," I commented.

"Not just Montorum," Hull added, his eyes drifting to the doorways on our left. "All of the people involved in the attack. Dead and alive."

"I heard one of the guys was burned," Lennox said. "But only his skin. The fire burned the top layer away and just stopped."

"Xaphon was the technological innovator of Chimaera," Hull stated. "It would only make sense for him to devise a weapon capable of burning the flesh from a person's body."

We arrived at the desk as the police officers walked away, finding the nurse with a very tired look on her face. She glanced the three of us over before resting her hand on her hip.

"Yes, gentlemen?" she asked.

"We're looking for an EMT named Austin Abramovich," Lennox began. "The receptionist said he was on this floor."

She nodded to the hallway on her left. "Abramovich just brought in a gurney, room 4311."   Lennox and I started towards the path, but Hull remained in place.

"This is the sixth floor," he said. "Why are the rooms starting with four?"

"Bottom floor has no rooms and the second floor is used for ER," the nurse replied, turning to deal with other work. Hull stared at her for a long moment before coming to join us. The room we were looking for was only ten meters down the hallway, on the left. Before entering, I was able to catch the name of the room's new occupant on the door: Z. MATSON. We entered to find three different EMTs and one very burned body, presumably a man by the face. His right hand was desperately clutching empty air, looking for something, anything to hold on to.

"Keep him restrained," one of the EMTs ordered. The other two moved to secure the burn victim while the main EMT turned to us. "Can I help you?"

"Austin Abramovich?" Lennox asked.

The EMT on the left of the burned man looked up. "That's me."

"What happened to this man," Hull intervened.

The lead EMT looked from Hull to Abramovich, then furrowed his brow. "Who are you?"

My companion stepped forward. "Sheridan Hull, consulting detective. What happened to this man."

"Gun malfunction," the lead EMT stated. "He was one of the attackers at city hall. Just as they were putting cuffs on his wrists, his coat burst into flames, followed by him. We rushed him here as soon as we could and found the charred remains of a gun inside the jacket."

I stepped past the EMT towards the window, my own mind starting to work furiously. It was like Moriarty had remotely killed his own agent, or at least tried to. I glanced down towards the roundabout entrance of the hospital, the sun glinting off the metal structures within the fountain. I turned back around to see the man on the bed give one last attempt to struggle, only to go limp. The EMTs removed their shaking hands from the blackened skin and stepped away.

"What did you need me for?" Abramovich asked as the other two EMTs left the room.

"Do you own a custom XD-9 handgun?" Hull asked.

"I do, but I loaned it to my friend about two weeks ago," the man replied.

"And last night, say around ten, what were you doing?"

"I was here. I've been working since eight last night. Haven't gone home yet."

Hull gave a nod. "As I expected."

Abramovich scrunched his nose. "Wait, what's going on? Did something happen?"

"Nothing you need concern yourself with," the detective replied. "Yet." He walked from the room, pausing once to glance back at the burned body before continuing on. Lennox and I exchanged glances before moving to follow him. We met him halfway towards the elevator, his stride confident and chin held high.

"What'd you get from that?" I asked as we entered the elevator.

"Everything I needed. Moriarty is playing a game, and he is turning us into pieces," he responded. "It is time we stop being toyed with." We left the elevator and the hospital lobby and started our way across the roundabout.

"So what do we do now?" Lennox inquired.

Hull glanced down the road some distance ahead of us. "We find the pinnacle's fa—"

He stopped, as did our walking, when the sound of breaking glass and a subsequent scream drew our attention up. We turned and watched a figure come flying from a shattered window, their body flailing as they soared towards the ground. People around us started screaming with the figure, but I couldn't move. None of us could. We could do nothing but sit and watch the arms-swinging figure fall, fall, fall, right into the center of the fountain. The needle-like centerpiece pierced through the figure's stomach, pinning them in place.

The shock took a moment to fade before I started forward, my eyes soaring back up to the broken window. Some quick counting revealed my worst fear: the window was on the sixth floor. And the figure, dead and pinned for all to see, was Austin Abramovich. His blood was starting to work its way down the needle and into the water, turning it a horrible shade of red. Hull came to stand at my side, his eyes focused on the body.

"The pinnacle's fall," he whispered, his eyes trembling.

*

"Abramovich is dead."

Hull's words echoed through the white cell as he paced around Moriarty's smug figure, still sitting in his white metal chair, arms still crossed. Hull returned to the opposite side and leaned against his own chair, eyes narrowed and nostrils flared.

"But he did not work for you," the detective stated.

The man smirked. "Good, very good. Who did he work for?"

"Newfield General." The detective leaned in closer. "He was murdered. And your riddle has come to pass."

Moriarty leaned even closer. "Has it, though?" The smile on his face grew. "Because if my calendar is right, *solsticij* has yet to pass."

Hull remained almost nose-to-nose with the man for several long seconds before jumping away, back towards the doorway. He moved with tunnel vision, ignoring the admonishing stares of the men he'd help put behind bars. Into the elevator, into the lobby, into the taxi, he moved with speed and focus. Nothing was to distract him now. Not when Moriarty was still playing his game. He stepped out of the taxi at the doorway to the flat and ran upstairs, finding Walker sitting in his armchair with a newspaper open.

"What'd he say?" Walker asked as the detective grabbed his laptop.

"The *solsticij* has yet to pass," Hull mirrored, immediately bringing up a translation website. "*Solsticij*. No, Google Translate, it most certainly is not Spanish." He tapped away at his keyboard for several seconds before slamming his hands down. "Damn him, and damn his riddles. Why is he doing this? What's it all for?"

"Order through chaos," Walker replied, his attention drifting to the newspaper. "That's what he said at the Vatican."

Hull's head snapped up. "The Vatican." After a short moment, his eyes widened. "Oh of *course*! The Vatican! Judas!"

"What?" Walker piped as he closed the paper. "What is it?"

"*Solsticij*, Abramovich. Oh how brilliant. Malevolent and evil, but so brilliant, so marvelous."

"What are you rambling on about now?"

Hull turned his laptop to face Walker. "*Solsticij* is Croatian for solstice, Abramovich's name is Croatian. All of it ties back." He spun the laptop back. "The solstice has to be coming up." After a moment, he found his information. He leaned away from the computer screen, hands running through his hair. "June 21st. Tomorrow."

"So he's going to do something tomorrow?" Walker asked. "But what? Break out?"

"The emergency's arrival and the pinnacle's fall..." Hull muttered, eyes trembling. "Man of the memorial and the caretaker of the orphan. He said they will bear witness, but if they're dead..." He jumped to his feet, almost dropping his laptop in the process. "HELL."

"What?"

"HELL!" His eyes were bulging with excitement. "The word written on the sticky notes! HELL. Moriarty's inmate number. 43-11. The room number of the burn victim. 4311. Fours are Hs, threes are Es, and ones are Ls. HELL." He started pacing the room, his hands twitching behind his back.

"So they all correlate, but what good does that do us?"

"He's leaving a message."

Walker stood from his seat and sighed. "Well if you figure out that message overnight, tell me, because I'm going to bed." He started off in the direction of his room, but Hull paid him no attention. His mind was filling with information, with theories, with facts. The world around him was irrelevant; all that mattered was the data and the solution.

The man of the memorial and the caretaker of the orphan meet. They will bear witness to the emergency's arrival and the pinnacle's fall. All it takes is the passing of the solsticij *to bring about events to come.*

He opened his eyes and stared forward, not seeing the contents of the living room but rather his thoughts, his mind. He could perfectly visualize portions of his thoughts, isolating them into bursts that occupied the walls, the fireplace, the chairs, anything his brain could make into an easel. Words and images came to life, forming cohesive sentences, pictures, landscapes, everything. All of it was right there, before his eyes.

Man of the memorial.

He saw the back of the veteran from before, bullet wound through the back of his neck. The image of the man faded away to be replaced with a fog, the absence of the truth. He panned through different thoughts in a matter of seconds. *Man. Human. Veteran. Soldier. Leader. President.* The fog before him materialized into different structures now, each lined up in random order with their respected leaders.

Washington Monument. Thomas Jefferson Memorial. Theodore Roosevelt Memorial. Ulysses S. Grant Memorial. Lincoln Memorial.

LINCOLN.

He twisted his head to the side, cataloguing the president's name for future reference. All of the memorial images faded away, now being replaced with a single sentence.

Caretaker of the orphan.

He saw the murdered woman, the overseer of St. Jacob's Orphanage. She wasn't the true caretaker, though. There was something else to be found in the words. *Caretaker. Overseer. Watcher. Minder. Owner. Parent. Between parents. Foster parent.*

FOSTER.

His neck twisted again as the word soared its way to another part of his mind, going directly underneath the name of the president. Clarity was coming through the fog now, a sense of actual understanding. He focused his mind again, allowing another sentence to become corporeal.

They will bear witness to the emergency's arrival and the pinnacle's fall.

The two murdered bodies appeared once more, alongside a standing Austin Abramovich, no gun in hand. The vision faded to show Abramovich speared by the central part of the fountain of Newfield General. That vision too disappeared to be replaced with only two words. *Emergency's arrival. Emergency.*

911.

Emergency's arrival leading to pinnacle's fall. Pinnacle. Fall. Pinnacle. Fall. PINNACLE. FALL. Pinnacle. Apex. Apogee. Climax. Peak. Summit. Zenith.

ZENITH.

His eyes flew open as the words all came together. *LINCOLN. FOSTER. 911. ZENITH.* The words dissolved to create a map of the city, which quickly zoomed in on one particular location. The corner of Lincoln Avenue and Foster Road. The Zenith Tower, one of the largest skyscraper-like buildings in Newfield, stretching sixty-six stories high. The tower itself became the only thing he could see, all sixty-six stories highlighted. His attention went to the forty-third story, on the southern side. The room given the designation "Innovation & Integration." II. 11.

4311.

HELL.

The tower itself melted into the ever-clearing fog, replacing itself with a book, a very large, very well-known book with a golden cross on the cover. The book flipped open, pages turning so quickly they created a blur. Finally the pages slowed down, the name "ISAIAH" inscribed on the top of each page. The pages slowed down once more before stopping entirely, with the words "CHAPTER 43, VERSE 11" in the upper corner.

"I, even I, am the Lord; and beside me there is no saviour."

"John!"

He opened his eyes to find Walker standing in the kitchen, coffee pot and mug in hand.

"Did you even move?" the doctor asked as he poured himself a cup. "You're right where I left you."

Hull stood, feeling a slight ache in his back. He really hadn't moved in almost twelve hours. "John, he is going to bomb the Zenith Tower."

Walker's face went rigid. "Moriarty? But how?"

"The two attackers from city hall, the ones who supposedly had explosives," the detective said as he grabbed his coat. "They were never accounted for. Somehow they made their way to the forty-third floor, 'Innovation & Integration' room. The room is in a spot where it can collapse the upper twenty-three floors and bring the entire building down."

Walker set the mug down. "Even a controlled blast couldn't cause that much damage, could it?"

"We have to get there and defuse what they have set up."

"How do you even know where?"

"The man of the memorial is Lincoln and the caretaker of the orphan is Foster. The emergency's arrival is the bomb detonation and the pinnacle's fall is the collapse of the pinnacle building, the zenith. Today is the solstice. This is when it happens."

Walker watched the detective wrap his neck with his purple scarf before continuing. "Should I call Lennox?"

"Yes," Hull replied, his attention on his laptop. "Call and make sure the building is evacuated. Everyone has to leave now. He plans to kill as many people as possible."

"How do you know that?"

"HELL. 4311. Book of Isaiah, Chapter 43, Verse 11. 'I, even I, am the Lord; and beside me there is no saviour.' He is equating himself to God, and is deliberating saying no one other than him can change the fates. He is in control."

Walker grabbed the car keys from the nearby table. "So how do we stop him?"

"Defuse the bomb. Stop the explosion. Save the lives of hundreds."

"Hold on, *defuse* the bomb?" The doctor stopped and shook his head. "I was trained as a combat medic, not an IED professional."

"I can defuse it," Hull said as he started for the door.

"Like Hell you can. You can't just 'wing it' with a bomb, Hull."

"Trust me," the detective said, his glint-in-eye gaze resting on Walker. "I know what to do."

*

We reached the Zenith Tower at around eight, just a half an hour after Hull had awoken from his comatose-like stasis. I'd called Lennox as soon as we had entered the car, and by the time we'd reached the building, all of the people had been evacuated. The inspector was waiting for us at the main entrance, his foot tapping and fingers shaking.

"If he planted a bomb in here, why are we going in?" Lennox asked as we started through the revolving doors.

"A bomb going off and leveling one of the tallest towers in Newfield, and you think that would come without repercussion?" Hull prompted.

"There are people who are trained and paid to disarm bombs," Lennox spat. "And we aren't those people."

"It will not be an ordinary explosive," the detective shot back as we entered the elevator.

"How can you possibly know that?" Lennox piqued.

"Because Moriarty had it planted and Moriarty has been orchestrating events leading to this point. He knew I would go for the obvious and eventually figure this out. I expect he hoped it would take me longer, and the bomb would detonate before we could evacuate the premises."

"If he's doing it for you," the inspector said, a glare coming to his eyes, "how do you know this isn't just a trap?"

"I'm quite certain it is."

"Then why the Hell are we in an elevator going towards a *waiting bomb*?"

"He would never kill me outright. Not without being present. And unless he has broken out of McMullen in the time since I last saw him, he will have no way of being here." The detective matched Lennox's stare. "As long as I am here, you are safe."

The elevator opened on the forty-third floor. Our trio ran out, Hull immediately going right. Lennox and I followed about a half-meter behind. As we ran, I couldn't help but realize just how high up we were. Through the windows that lined the walls, I could see the entirety of the city. Zenith Tower was in the heart of Newfield, and looked out over the entire county. The direction I looked was the east, and I could see the mountains of the westernmost Cascades.

Hull turned another corner, bringing us down a narrow corridor. We ran for almost a minute before reaching a single door, with the words "Innovation & Integration" etched into the glass. Hull threw the door open and revealed a room devoid of anything except for a very large cardboard box. The detective rushed the box without hesitation and opened it. Lennox and I came to stand at his side, and in that moment, I felt my heart sink. The inside was indeed occupied by a detonation mechanism for a very powerful bomb.

"I have to remove all remote access, then disable the triggering mechanisms," Hull said as he went to work sifting through the wires.

"What's so important about Zenith Tower?" I asked. "Why pick here?"

Lennox shuffled a bit where he stood. "Zenith Tower is the hub of telecommunications on the west coast. Employing almost a thousand people who help manage, supervise, and coordinate all cellular, Internet, and land-to-space contact. Zenith Industries was at the forefront of creating satellites to provide Internet access to areas where standard methods were unavailable."

"So if Moriarty brings down the building, he can, what? Stop all communications on the west coast?"

"Not quite," Lennox stated. "But he could make it difficult for communications in Newfield. Cellular towers, phone lines, Internet lines, the works. Bring down Zenith Tower and you could throw the city into an information blackout."

"Got it!"

We both glanced down to see Hull split a wire in half. The three of us stared down into the cardboard box for a very long, very frightening moment.

Ding!

I jumped back and hit the floor instinctively, only to realize no actual explosion had gone off. Now that, *that* had brought back some very painful and horrific memories. I scrambled back to my feet and returned to Hull's side, finding that Lennox too had flinched away from the box. Hull's attention was centered on a little yellow sheet of paper that had popped out of the center of the explosive.

"No."

The detective's single word made the hair on my arms stand on end. "No what?"

"No, that cannot be possible."

"What can't?"

He pulled the yellow sheet from the explosive, revealing it to be a sticky note. Scrawled on the note, in black ink, was "YOU MISSED A SLASH."

"What's that supposed to mean?" Lennox asked as Hull rose to his feet.

"Missed a slash," Hull recited, his brow crooked and his eyes wide. "Missed a slash. Missed a slash *where*?" He glanced down at the box, then around the room. "Missed a slash, missed a slash, missed a—"

He stopped. I watched as he brow reset itself and his eyes instantly changed from their glinted blue and green to a very, very dark gray. I looked down at the sticky note, then at the box, then back at Hull.

"Hull, what does it mean?" I asked. The man offered no reply, his gaze moving from nothing to the window. "Hull!"

"I missed a slash," he whispered.

"But what does that *mean*? Sheridan!"

"Oh my God."

That came from Lennox. I looked over to find him staring at the same window as Hull, except his entire face had gone pale. I followed that gaze, trying to find what was peculiar about the window. There was nothing but the tops of buildings, the sprawling valley continuing to the south—

Oh my God.

It was only just emerging from the cloud coverage, but it was most definitely the content of my nightmares, the very reason I had nightmares on a monthly basis, the very *reason* I had been sent overseas. Soaring from the clouds was a very large airplane, and from its cockpit and engines burned a raging fire.

"I missed a slash because it was not in reference to the phone number, it was the date!" Hull roared as he grabbed Lennox and I by our shoulders. "*RUN!*"

I had no hesitation. My feet carried me as fast as they could, somehow keeping parallel with the detective and the inspector. We charged back down the hallway, to the left, back to the elevator. In any normal circumstance, the elevator would be strictly off-limits for escape, but this elevator traveled at a speed quick enough to have us on the ground floor in twenty seconds. I prayed that would be enough.

We watched the number tick down. 40. 35. 30. 25. I could feel the elevator, and probably the building, start to shake now. 20. 15. 10. My entire forehead was matted with sweat now. So many emotions were surging back to me, so many memories. So much in so little an amount of time. 5. 1.

The doors slid open, but before they could even reach their resting point, we had bolted, our destination locked. The sound of the incoming plane was deafening and the building itself was shaking so horribly, some of the glass walls had shattered. We knew the revolving door wasn't our choice of exit. All together, we increased our speed and braced our shoulders before smashing and breaking through the glass walls, falling a short meter to land outside. And we had done so at the perfect moment.

As soon as my shoulder hit the ground and my body slid me on my back, I blinked once, twice, three times, and watched as the burning plane, the symbol of terror to American's eyes, crashed into the forty-third floor of the Zenith Tower, taking not even a fraction of a second to vanish from sight. Fire and metal and wreckage burst from the building, the windows exploding, the structural integrity failing. Hull picked me up by the arm and started staggering away, Lennox already at the police car. The detective threw the back door open, chucked me inside, and closed it after tucking my feet in.

My eyes had yet to blink again. This small reminder, this action from the past, was all it took to release the floodgates and bring back every single memory of my time overseas. In a single millisecond, I relived every horror, every torturous moment, every single second, minute, hour, and day of Hell on Earth.

And then, as quickly as those memories had flooded me, they were gone.

*

Hull sat in the somewhat-dimmed cell room, fingertips pressed together and wrists resting on the table. Across from him, the smug smirk still in place, the pierced eyes still watchful, sat Lucius Mendax, or Moriarty. The unblinking, unwavering stare that created a sort of static between the two would've lasted long enough for every single star in the sky to burn to dust, if not for the detective's sniff and following words.

"Flight 4311. Departed Los Angeles International at approximately sixty-thirty this morning. Its intended destination was Portland. However. A chemical adhesive weaved into the glass of the cockpit window caused the viewport to shatter and implode, killing both pilots in a matter of seconds. Two subsequent explosions in both turbines reduced flight capability to nothing. The plane began its descent, and, with help from a remote assistive device, steered its way into the Zenith Tower, forty-third floor, 'Innovation & Integration' room."

Moriarty nodded. "That is correct."

"Three hundred and fifty-five people died in that airplane. No chance for survival."

"Again, correct."

"Why."

"Because the plane was not American, no. Quite the opposite, in fact. Once they recover the black box, they will find the plane was operated by Iranians. The communication logs will feature direct links with different resistance sectors inside the Croatian government." The man gave a single chuckle. "The fire of chaos will spread, and the wave of order will begin its trek."

"You murdered three hundred and fifty-five people to spread a lie," Hull growled through clenched teeth.

"I made a necessary sacrifice. The foolish will fight for righteousness while the wise will do what is necessary to survive."

"And now what?" The detective's nostrils flared. "More chaos, more tension, more panic? More death?" He narrowed his eyes. "You are so close to playing God with the powers of the world, pitting them against each other with no reason than to ease your boredom."

"Order from the chaos, Sheridan." Moriarty leaned back. "Order from the chaos. My boredom needs no appeasement. My time has come."

Before Hull could respond, the sound of an explosion echoed from behind him, presumably near the elevator shaft. He didn't bother turning. He wouldn't dare adjust his attention. The moment was far too important.

"What do you think happens next, Sheridan?" Moriarty asked as he rested his clasped hands on his upper chest.

"You escape and continue your defiled plans as normal."

The man chuckled. "No, I'm afraid that won't happen. In being caught, I became a liability." He pressed his hands against the table, leaning closer to Hull as he did. "A loose end. And Chimaera has a very strict policy." The man's eyes seemed to glisten with pride and victory. "No loose ends."

The door behind Hull slid open to reveal two men, both heavily armored and holding sleek assault rifles. The first man to enter slid to his right and fired three rounds past Hull, who had dived to the floor. In a swift motion, Hull brought the chair he'd been in around, causing it to collide with the second man who had yet to take aim. In the confusion, the detective rose to his feet and grabbed the barrel of the first man's rifle, twisting it in the man's grasp and causing him to let go.

Hull turned the rifle in his hands, then smashed the butt of the gun into the first man's head. He fell to the floor, his weak helmet not keeping him from receiving a concussion. The detective turned to make sure the second man had been thoroughly incapacitated before dropping the gun and returning to the table. His adversary had taken all three shots, one in the forehead, one in the neck, and one in the heart. Hull pressed two fingers against the man's limp neck and waited. No pulse was to be found.

Moriarty was dead.

*

By the time Hull had returned to the flat, the news had already gained a horrific amount of coverage on both the destruction of the Zenith Tower and the riot at McMullen County Jail. Nobody had been injured in the Tower's collapse, Lennox, Hull, and myself included, but all onboard the plane had perished. The jail, however, was not faring so well. Several inmates were dead, and even though the riot had been relatively quelled, a few inmates were still unaccounted for.

I admit, I was not holding up as well as I'd like to have been. The sight of the plane had stirred loose some very unsettling memories. Memories of days long gone. Days spent fighting, days spent watching some of my closest friends die. Days waging a war against an idea. The worst memory to resurface, however, had been the one of me at the age of fourteen. My family had been visiting New York City because of my dad's recent promotion. Our "vacation" was supposed to go from September 9th to the 15th.

We were at the top of the New York Times Building when it happened.

I looked over my shoulder and watched as Hull somberly stepped through the doorway, his face sunken, his eyes dim. He silently slumped into his own armchair and, after a long moment of silence, gave a very heavy sigh.

"They killed him," he said.

"They who?" I asked.

"Chimaera's agents. They caused the riot, and they killed him. They killed their own leader."

"They *killed* Moriarty?"

"A shot in the head, the neck, and the heart."

"But.. but *why*? That makes no sense!"

"I know. I wish I understood. But now, making sense of this is almost impossible." He licked his lips and let his head crane forward. "He wanted to kill us. All of us. You, me, Lennox. He wanted the three of us gone. He was willing to kill thousands of people just to make sure we died." He pressed his hands together, resting his chin on the tips of his middle fingers. "None of this makes sense."

I gulped, feeling my insides start to churn. "What now?"

He didn't reply immediately. He stared into the hearth for a long time, eyes trembling, racing back and forth. Then, after what felt like an eternity, he leaned back, his vision going from the hearth to the window.

"There is a storm on the horizon, John." His voice had gone cold, monotonous. Cryptic. "I fear that in light of recent events, things will only get worse." He paused, and when he did, I could see a slight tremor pass through his cheek. "Much worse."

ABDUCTION

"To Mr. Sheridan J. Hull and Dr. John F. Walker," I read aloud. "You are cordially invited to the annual Howitzer-Eccleston League Luncheon this Saturday, the 29th of June. All you need bring is yourself. Lodging, food and drink, and other amenities will be provided." I scoffed at the letter before turning it over. "We never get invited to anything."

"If that is the case, why should we start accepting invitations now?" Hull called from behind me.

It had been one week since the collapse of the Zenith Tower, the jail riot, and the murder of Moriarty. It had taken two days for things at the jail to return to normal, but the city itself was in a state of shock. The mayor was still hospitalized, so really, nothing had been done as of late. The area where the Zenith had stood was barricaded off, but flowers, crosses, pictures, all sorts of memorial items had started turning up. Most of the plane's occupants had lived in the Portland area, but about a dozen had come from Newfield.

Hull had told me about Moriarty's cryptic message. About the black box of the plane. And he hadn't lied. Three days after the crash, Malcolm had given us a heavy news update. The black box had been recovered with detailed communications logs between the pilots and an outside source hailing from southern Croatia. There were absolutely no signs of tampering. The evidence was too substantial, and the United States government was growing more and more anxious for answers. Answers that I suspected would not come.

Oh, and another reason the city was in a state of full alert? One of the unaccounted inmates was none other than Ross McNair.

"I think we should go," I suggested as I set the letter down.

Hull sighed. "Why do you always want to do these silly things? 'We should go see a movie,' 'we should go out to dinner,' 'we should go look at that new park'."

"We go and do things to keep you from being bored."

"Why is my being bored such a bad thing?"

"Because when *you're* bored, my life is miserable."

"I sincerely doubt that."

I pointed to a plastic bag next to the garbage can, with something charred and black inside. "Remember that product of your boredom? My old cell phone that you *microwaved* because of a video you saw on YouTube?"

"I did not microwave it because of the video, I did it to test the electrical properties of—"

"*You microwaved my phone.*"

"You were wanting to get the new phone as it was, why does it matter?"

I sighed and rubbed my face. "And then we had to replace the microwave."

"You wanted a new microwave, too."

"If I said I wanted a new car, would you drive the current one off the nearest cliff?"

He looked me dead in the eyes without a hint of recognizing my sarcasm. "Is this your way of saying you want a new car?"

I threw my hands up in defeat. "No. Whatever. We're going. Both of us. Tomorrow."

"Why!" he barked as he tossed his newspaper. "What did I say that gave you the slightest inclination that I had an interest in attending? These ridiculous banquets and luncheons, people wearing black ties and coats with tails. I have to look like a penguin!"

"The invitation didn't say you had to dress up."

"Compulsory preferences for any event. And what kind of league names themselves after people? The creators had to be horribly vain."

I chuckled. "You calling someone else vain. Now I've seen everything." I took a drink from my coffee mug. "If it's tomorrow night at the Sunriver Resort, we'll have to leave around noon. So you have time to pack."

He threw his head back with a groan. "These are wastes of time."

I stopped just before entering my room and glanced back. "You know they'll probably have shrimp there. Whole plates of it." His head snapped forward. I smiled and walked into my room, knowing I'd most certainly won.

*

Daemon sat with her hands on opposite sides of the keyboard, the nine screens illuminating the space around her. She stared into the center screen with sunken eyes and a disheartened mind. Things weren't going well at all. So many of Chimaera's finest agents were either dead or imprisoned as a result of Sheridan Hull. He hadn't directly killed any of them, but her employer had seen to that after they'd been obtained. No loose ends, he'd always said. But things had just continued to spiral. Xaphon was ordered to return to her after escaping, and he hadn't shown his face. She doubted he would.

And Moriarty.

She closed her eyes and let her head fall, her neck catching her before she made impact with the lit keyboard. She thought back to a simpler time, before her life had been changed in such a drastic way. Before deception became instinctive. Before crime was her field of work. But most importantly, before him. Because he'd made it all the more difficult. She never had to meet him, and she'd be better off not having met him. But she couldn't change that now.

Why did you have to be so cute, John?

She opened her eyes and focused on the center screen once more, its contents burning into the back of her head. Her reluctancy had grown over the months, but now it was reaching an unbearable peak. Now it wasn't just doing her job. Part of her job had become too influential in her life. She stared into the man's eyes of the center screen for ten more seconds before closing it down. She knew what came next, even if she didn't want to participate. The plans were laid out.

His plans.

She stood from the terminal and grabbed her keys, only stopping when she noticed three card-like objects resting on the table. She hadn't put them there, and the select few that could access the room were nowhere near. She picked up the cards and layed them out. After a moment, she recognized them as tarot cards, something she'd never taken a personal belief in. She had no idea what they meant, either. One was obvious in its meaning, but the other two mystified her.

The Chariot, The Hermit, and The Devil.

*

Hull and Walker entered the main banquet hall side by side, Hull adorned in the same suit he wore to the New Year's banquet and Walker in a gray coat, light pink undershirt, and black tie. The room was filled with people dressed similarly, men and women scattered about. They all looked to be about twenty or thirty years older than the newcomers, which was somewhat unsettling. Hull glanced out across the crowd with a wary stare, his eyes giving a slight quiver.

"If you leave me alone here like you did in December, I will never forgive you," the detective scalded as he looked to his companion.

"I don't have a date to abandon you for," Walker replied, a half-smile on his face. "And you don't have a woman to avoid. Yet."

"Because my purpose in being here is most certainly to find a woman."

"Seems like something any normal guy would be after. Oh, wait."

Hull scoffed. "Clever."

After about a minute of the two standing in the entrance, a woman finally approached them, her attire matching that of the rest of the resort staff. She smiled at them, her whitened teeth glistening. "Good evening, gentlemen. For security purposes, I will need to check you in. I will also need to see your identification. All attendees are assigned badges for the event." The two complied, and once she'd seen their IDs, she nodded and pulled two badges from her belt. "We are happy to have you. Dr. Walker, you have badge 11. Mr. Hull, yours is badge 43. Enjoy your time at Sunriver Resort." With that, she walked away. Walker neatly fastened the badge to his upper chest, but

Hull's attention was focused on the woman. Or, more properly, her clipboard.

"You'll want to put that on," Walker said with a nudge.

"Why would an event like this require badges?" Hull asked as he clipped the badge to the inside of his coat.

"Why do we drive on the right side of the road when plenty of other countries drive on the left?" Walker mocked.

Hull gave him a stern glare. "Both questions are valid."

The doctor shrugged. "Formalities? Attendance? I don't know. You're the genius detective, not me."

"You play that up far too much. Albert Einstein could have walked into this room and asked the same question."

"Albert Einstein would've been swarmed with fellow physicists. He wouldn't have had time to ask stupid questions."

Hull scoffed. "I ask why this requires badges and that is declared a stupid question, but when *you* ask *me* if they sell contraceptive items for men at the gas station on the corner across, it's not stupid at all."

Walker looked around the room quickly, eyes finally catching his target. "Right, well, I'm gonna pay the bathroom a quick visit. Why don't you go.. y'know, socialize."

"Please do not leave me alone."

"Do you really want to come with me?" Hull's lack of immediate response made Walker scrunch his nose in disgust. "*No. Just..* I don't know, wait for me to come back or something. It's not like I'll be gone long." He started away. Hull took two steps after him, then stopped. He would have to find a way to pass the short amount of time. His eyes passed over the throngs of people before reaching a table in the corner, currently occupied by a woman in very unusual clothing. The detective made his way across the room, carefully sidling between people before reaching the woman's table.

"Hello," he said.

The woman looked up, her black hair curled but not able to cover her large earrings. She smiled at him, her teeth not blinding like the woman's from before. "Hello. Would you like your fortune told?"

He furrowed his brow. "A fortune teller at an event like this?"

"My grandfather was Ludvík Howitzer. He came to America, but my father returned to Europe. He met my mother in Romania, and had me there. My uncle now runs the league and lets me work events as a fortune teller. He calls it adding a touch of my culture."

"Ah." Hull slowly sat down, leveling his eyes with the woman. "And what might your name be?"

"Claudia. Claudia Howitzer."

"Pleasure to meet you, Claudia. My name is Sheridan Hull." After a short pause, he nodded. "And yes, I suppose you can tell me my fortune."

She smiled. "Let me see your hand." With some slight reluctance, Hull offered his left hand. Howitzer turned it over and ran her delicate ringed fingers over his palm. He watched her face go from calm and mellow to a more concerned look.

"Is there a problem?" he asked.

Her eyes slowly closed. "I can see something.. I can actually see something. So many things. All in your future. I see the rise, and the shift. I see the dark. And a room of glass." Her eyes shot open, her lips trembling as she stared into the detective's dark pupils. "Oh my poor man. Your life. I can see the *Cădea*."

Hull slowly brought his hand back, his brows pressed down. "What do you mean by that? Rise, shift, dark? Room of glass?"

"I'm so sorry," she replied, her hands trembling.

"Why? What is that? What is the *Cădea*?"

"Excuse me, Sir?"

Hull looked up to find another member of the staff, this one a young man in his late teenage years, standing over him. "Yes, what is it?"

The staffer gulped. "Your friend asked me to find you. He said he wasn't feeling well and had to return to your room."

Hull stood, his gaze ignoring the staffer and focusing on the restaurant. "Of course he would vacate without telling me himself." He started off towards the exit, his concentration on finding Walker. Yet a small part of his mind couldn't forget what the woman had said, and he most certainly could not disregard the lack of dishonesty in her words.

The rise. The shift. The dark. The glass room.
The Cădea.

He did not take his time in returning to the room. All attendees had been given hotel-like rooms at the resort. Theirs was in the northernmost wing. He walked down the yellow-by-light hallway and reached their door, fiddling to grab the key from his pocket. As he fiddled, his mind returned to the woman in the banquet hall. Hull was not the person to believe in fortune telling. But the woman had been so sure of her words, of what she'd seen. So ambiguous in her wording. He glanced at the door with the key in his hand and felt a surge of understanding course through him.

They'd been given room 311. And now, a yellow sticky note had been attached to the door, with a large "4" in black ink drawn in the center, hanging just before the room number.

He slid the key into the lock and turned, only to find the lock jammed so that it would open with the slightest push. The door opened to reveal a dark room, with the outline of a person standing at the opposite wall. He stepped in slowly, closed the door behind him, and turned as the lights came on. Standing at the blind-hidden window was a slender figure, shorter than him with long blonde hair and a complimenting red dress. She looked up at Hull with somber yet determined eyes, but he didn't care. His ability to care about her emotions vanished the moment her identity became clear.

"Of course," he hissed, jaw popping. "An inside agent, playing to the emotions of the companion. John would be disgusted."

Cassidy Claypool looked down at the area between them, where a Chimaera-designed holographic emitter sat. "There's someone who'd like to see you."

The lights flickered, then turned off completely. The emitter sparked once, twice, three times before the image of a man, garbed in a black cloak, appeared. The man stood with his gloved hands clasping a metal cane, his hood down to disguise his face. Hull stood up straight and raised his chin, his eyes passing through the hologram to stare at the traitorous woman once more before focusing on the image.

"Still alive, then," the detective said.

"The end of the world couldn't keep me in a grave," Moriarty replied.

"I knew you would never be captured so easily," Hull stated. "And a person like you is far too vain to die."

"You knew that, but the rest of the world certainly didn't. Your endeavors against me were giving Chimaera too much publicity, and we aren't ready for that yet. We operated best under the streets, not under the scrutiny of the police. Now I am dead, and in being such, I am free to do as I please."

"And just what will you do, then?" Hull asked as he stepped to the side.

"Exactly as I have planned. Every event, every death, every action, every moment has gone as predicted. I told you how this ends."

"Of course you did. But you never could have predicted my actions."

"You've been a unique addition to the choreography, that I will not dismiss." The hologram had continued to turn with Hull, who had moved to the right side of the room, his footsteps slow. "Your inclusion has made certain things difficult, but everything is still going as designed. My intention is to create order through the chaos. And chaos is most certainly on its way."

"The order you would enact through operations like DAGGER and ENDGAME?" Hull shot, his jaw locking.

Moriarty made a clucking noise. "Knight was a nosy one, wasn't he? Always wanting to know what he was working for, didn't quite care who. I will admit to this as well: I panicked when I saw you with his book. I was worried he may have learned far more than he should have, and what you could do with it in your hands. Which is why I went to such great lengths to obtain it. How silly of me, to think someone like Arthur Knight could understand my true intentions."

"He was far more insightful than you may think," Hull snapped, taking another step.

"His insight is meaningless to me now. Yours, however, that's far more intriguing."

"Insufficient data."

"Too scared to assume?"

"Don't care to assume."

Moriarty adjusted himself again. "You know, for a long time I held you in admiration. Your talents were unrivaled, your abilities remarkable. But you quickly became as bad as the police force. Meddling in affairs far beyond your comprehension. This isn't about right or wrong anymore, Sheridan. It's not about enacting justice on those who do wrong. Everybody does wrong. Everybody lies, everybody sins. There are no saints to be found in the devil's world.

"Everything I have done has been for order. True order, an order that has not been seen by humankind. I strive to bring us above the petty conflicts, the trivial points of contention. I am the only thing that can save humanity from itself. But you? If you continue to persist as you have done, if you continue to interfere and meddle, I will make certain to show you how fierce and virulent I can be. Stand aside and let fate take its course, or my admiration for you will no longer outweigh my desire for your demise."

"You have been actively trying to kill me for months," Hull declared. "Why should you stop now?"

"Because I am offering you a chance to cease and desist. To step away from the chaos and let the order come about."

Hull leaped to the right, colliding with Claypool and bringing her to the ground. He quickly pulled her back up, wrapping his right arm around her neck and grabbing a pen from the nearby desk with his left hand. He held the pen tip to the woman's neck while she trembled in a mixture of shock and fear.

"Tell me where he is," Hull ordered, at both Claypool and Moriarty. "*Now!*"

"You think threatening one of my agents is going to be enough to spoil my fun?" Moriarty chuckled. "You wouldn't. No matter how hard you may try, you would never take her life."

Hull lifted the pen away. "In a single second, I could end her life. Quick strike through the jugular vein. She would bleed out before you or your *agents* could interfere. *Tell me where he is.*"

"I'm going to tell you," Moriarty chided. "That's the point. But if you harm Veronica, we will indeed have a very serious problem." Hull looked at the woman, foolish for not thinking "Cassidy Claypool" would be a pseudonym. Moriarty seemed to realize this as well. "Oh of course. Her name. Veronica Faith Daemon. Though she certainly enjoyed masquerading as Miss Cassidy Claypool, didn't you, Veronica?"

The woman offered no response. Hull could tell by her increased breathing and immediate perspiration, she was legitimately afraid for her life. And for him to be the one holding that in his hand...

Unacceptable.

"Where is John," the detective demanded as he released the woman.

Moriarty tapped his cane twice on his floor. "Let's do another riddle. I quite enjoy those. I take credit for Mendax's riddle, too. He was brilliant when I required a physical appearance, but his own creativity was far too limited."

"*Where is John.*"

"The man who does not run, with the world's best at his side, holds no victory to be won, for in due time, he will have surely died. The end to your world, it has begun, unless by my rules do you abide, for when all of it is said and done, even you will not be left with your pride. Ten strikes goes the clock, five past to seal his doom. No more shall the doctor walk. Forevermore shall he lie in his tomb."

Hull walked through the hologram, only stopping when he reached the doorway to glance back. His disturbing the feed had caused the emitter to release a static burst and fail. All he could see now was Claypool, or Daemon, as she was named. He stared at her with quivering eyes and pursed lips. He understood emotions well enough to know that this would ruin his friend, his companion. Learning the truth would destroy him. And now was a time when the detective needed Walker the most.

"I will not say a word," he said stoically. She gulped, her eyes wide. "But when I find him, *and I will*, I can promise you this. I will find you. And I will ensure that you tell him. Your fate will rest in his hands."

*

I opened my eyes groggily, feeling my head spin as I came to. I could remember leaving Hull at the banquet hall and entering the bathroom, but whatever happened immediately after was a very blurry, very painful splotch on my memory. I glanced around and found that wherever I was had no lighting of any sort. I was in a chair, cold and somewhat damp. The air was musty and cool, and I could hear what sounded like dripping water behind me. When I tried to move my hands, I discovered they were bound behind the chair with rope.

"Don't be alarmed, Dr. Walker."

My head snapped up, the eerily-familiar voice sending a chill down my spine. The voice was gravelly, and to be honest, my hearing it should've been impossible. Unless I was dead too.

"Who are you?" I called out, my eyes straining to adjust.

"Do you really need to ask?"

My eyes finally caught what I was so desperately hoping wasn't there. A tall outline standing two meters ahead of me. The figure was only distinguishable by the different shade of dark it appeared to be, caused by the full-body cloak. Hood drawn, metal cane in hand. Despite everything that had happened just one week ago, here I was in the same room as Moriarty.

"You're supposed to be dead," I said starkly, my chest aching.

"That could be said for the both of us," the man replied. "Head trauma, chest wound, blood loss. Any average man would have succumbed to his injuries by now." He took a step forward, and I could see his head lowered to be level with mine. "But you're no average man, are you, Doctor."

"Where's Sheridan?" I questioned, feeling my head start to wobble.

"Safe. For now."

"And where am I?"

"Right where I want you to be."

I gulped, tasting dried blood on the insides of my cheeks. "He said you were shot."

The man chuckled. "Lucius Mendax was shot and I ordered his death. That's how this works, you see. No loose ends and all."

"Then why am I here?"

"Because you and Sheridan need to learn. You have to experience firsthand what happens when you involve yourselves in matters far beyond your concern. I tried killing you outright. I was willing to kill over three hundred people and destroy a skyscraper just to try and send my message. Now it's time to make sure you receive it."

"What are you gonna do, then? Torture?" I spat. "Because I can tell you now, it won't get you anything."

Moriarty sighed. "What would I have to gain from torture? Torture is used to extract information, and there's no information to be garnered from you." He took another step forward. "No, you see, you and I are going to play a little game. I'm sure you're familiar with it. A card game."

"Might be difficult for me," I replied, giving a tug with my arms. The man stood up straight and nodded. I felt a slight tussling behind me, then the freedom of my arms being released.

In that moment, I could have done one of two things. I could have lunged at the man, attacked him, choked him, beat him, whatever. I could have finished the job and brought the head of Chimaera down. But my odds of reaching him were slim. I had indeed suffered major blood loss, and movement wasn't easy. Plus there was the addition of whoever stood behind me. The chances of my emerging victorious were slim. My only true option was to play his game. Whatever that may be.

"Okay," I said after a long pause. "I'll play."

A bright light turned on to my right, showing a small table between Moriarty and me. He still hid his face under the hood and now held the middle of his metal cane in his right hand. The light's source was a lamp without a shade, and the person that had freed me stood behind it. They also wore a cloak, this person's being orange instead of Moriarty's black. On a quick glance, I truly could not tell if it was a man or a woman.

"The game is poker," Moriarty announced as he sat down into a chair I had not seen before. "There will be a limit of 100 chips. The third party here," he gestured to the orange-robed person, "will deal the cards and give each of us 100 chips. We will play one round. If you win, I will not kill Sheridan on the spot, and with time, he will come to you. If I win, I will order my gunman to shoot Sheridan right now, and I will give you a drug that will paralyze you from the neck down and leave you to die."

"This isn't a game of skill," I stated.

"It is if you play it correctly."

"And how do you do that?"

"Poker isn't about the cards. It's about the mind, the willpower, and the foresight of the individual. It's the most simplest form of warfare. Knowing your enemy, knowing their honesty and their deception. Seeing the truth in their eyes, no matter the situation. To truly win a game of poker, you need more than just a strong hand. You need the utmost level of confidence in your own ability to achieve victory no matter the circumstances."

The hooded man leaned in close, and for just a hint of a moment, I think I saw what looked like his mouth, curved in the most devilish of smirks I had ever seen. "Now, are you ready to play the game?"

I licked my lips, knowing I had a severe disadvantage here. But all things considered, I suppose I didn't have a choice otherwise. I nodded to the man, who did a two-finger beckoning to the orange-robed person. They stepped forward, revealing two leather-gloved hands with a deck of cards and a stack of chips. They split the stack in half, giving one half to Moriarty and the other to me. Then, they shuffled the deck, quite professionally, I might add. Two cards came to me, two to Moriarty.

I picked up the cards with my hands, and only then noticed how scarred my wrists were. Whatever material that rope was made of was certainly not good for skin. The cards weren't bad at all, though. A King and a Jack, both of Hearts. But now I realized my extreme disadvantage. Reading your opponent was key in this game, and I couldn't read Moriarty at all. All of my faith was invested in the cards turning in my favor.

"You can go first, Doctor," the man said, holding his cards crisply in his velvet-hidden hands. I put forward a five-chip equivalent and looked forward. My opponent waited for maybe ten seconds before matching my amount. With that, the robed person put down five cards and flipped the first three. A Ten of Hearts, an Eight of Spades, and a Queen of Hearts. I felt confidence pour into me but did my best not to show it. With potential for a straight to King or even a royal flush, things were looking good.

"Tell me, Doctor," Moriarty started before I could make a move. "What do you know of the concept of true order?"

I knocked on the table and kept my eyes on where I presumed his were. "Impossible."

"Is it?"

"Yes."

He tossed a ten-chip in. "Why would you say that?"

The third person flipped the fourth card, revealing a Five of Clubs. "I fought in a war with no winners. That's how we are. We fight because we get bored."

"That's why a concept like true order exists. To bring us above those petty, groundless conflicts and allow us to focus on a better, more promising future."

"Conflict is innate. You can't get rid of it. It's practically conditioned into us to fight rather than seek a peaceful solution."

"That which is conditioned can be reconditioned."

"And you're going to do that?"

"Your move, Doctor."

I glanced down, realizing I hadn't done anything since the fourth card was flipped. I knocked on the table once more. "How could you possibly hope to 'recondition' everyone?"

He tossed in a fifty-chip and leaned back. "There are certain circumstances in which humanity recognizes its dire need for direction. The moments in which our independence ceases to matter, and all we want is a ruling hand. With the proper actions, I can bring about a circumstance that will show humanity what it needs. I will reveal to the world how far we have fallen, and I will provide us a guiding light to a better future."

I tossed a fifty-chip in and included a ten-chip. "A single country has enough difficulty accepting one person as their leader. You'd never be able to take the world in."

"The world may surprise you, Doctor."

"I've seen enough of it to know otherwise."

He matched the ten-chip. "Have you now?"

The fifth card was revealed. The Ace of Hearts.

Royal flush.

I was good at containing my excitement. I stared at him with unblinking eyes and a slight scowl. I knocked twice on the desk and leaned back. "Why are you trying to do it?"

"Some people are endowed with abilities. Born with talents that will benefit all of mankind." He leaned forward, clutching to the metal ball top of his cane. "I am one of those people. I have a vision of the world, a world in which chaos has been abolished and order is what remains. And I intend to see that vision become reality."

Moriarty set his cards down, signaling a fold. I looked from the cards to him, then back to the cards. Now things felt very, very off.

"Well done, Doctor," the man said as he stood. "Well done."

I put my cards down, face-up to ensure my victory. "What now?"

He turned and started off into the dark. "Now we see if the clever detective can find you. I said I wouldn't kill him and paralyze you. I never said I would let you go."

The person in the orange robe gathered the cards and chips from the table and tucked them away. They looked down at the light, then at me.

"I'm sorry," they said in a whispered voice, one that sounded familiar.

Then their hand came at my face with a damp cloth, and everything else ceased to exist.

*

Hull stepped cautiously over the metal gate preventing access to the Deschutes Memorial Gardens. It had taken him roughly four hours, putting the time at around ten at night, but he'd done it. Moriarty's riddle had been surprisingly simple, or so he hoped. The "tomb" bit had really made it clear that Walker was being held at a cemetery. All Hull had needed to figure out was which one. Only one cemetery in the area held a mausoleum, that being Deschutes.

Finding the cemetery hadn't been difficult, but getting to it had. It was as if every force of nature and man had stood in his way of reaching the location before five past ten, the time at which the riddle deemed Walker dead. The detective ran across the tombstone-riddled area, the mausoleum directly ahead of him. A lot of things didn't make sense to him about this. The riddle had been far too simple. Theatric, but simple. Moriarty was one to be dramatic, but not without cause. Something was off with the situation, that was very clear.

He stepped through the open door of the mausoleum, only to stop when a loud *thud* echoed from behind him. He turned as the room went dark, finding the entry and exit blocked. He felt a sinking sensation, as if he'd walked straight into a trap. But that made less sense. Moriarty wanted to teach a lesson. He'd tried killing them before, but not with much effort. Hull's death was not something Moriarty was truly focused on right now. His focus lied elsewhere.

But where.

The sudden brightness from behind him granted him some clarity. He turned slowly to see the hologram of Moriarty, just as he'd appeared several hours ago. He stood in front of what looked like a small table, his hands clasped around the top ball of his metal cane, his hooded face on Hull. The detective took two steps forward, careful to watch his surroundings.

"If you wanted to imprison me," Hull said cautiously, folding his hands behind his back, "you could have skipped holding me in traffic for three hours."

The man of the hologram chuckled. "Imprisoning you would be far too simple, Sheridan. I wanted to pass the time, surely. I knew it wouldn't take you more than ten minutes to solve the riddle, but how to keep you away? I had my own business to attend to."

"Surely." Hull took a step forward, eyes adjusting to the dark. He could make out the shape of a robed figure to his left, doing their best to keep in the shadows. "That business ensured you would be away, of course."

"Of course. I can't say I trust you, after your very rude treatment of Veronica."

"Yes, the traitor. Present once more, I see," he said as his eyes turned to glare at the robed figure. He could see them lower their head, no doubt ashamed.

"Without her, we wouldn't have a facilitator."

"For what?"

"Our game."

Hull lifted his chin. "And what makes you think I would want to play a game with you?"

"You'll play the game for two reasons. One, first and foremost. You love a challenge. You love the great game. So you will play. You will play because it grants you an opportunity to beat me, so to speak. You will also play because, if you do not, that slab will not move. You will die."

"My life has been put at stake before," Hull snapped. "I have long since learned not to let that keep me."

"Oh, but you wouldn't let the doctor's life go without trying, would you? He's here, as promised. But you have to play the game to save him."

Hull narrowed his eyes as he took another step forward. "What game."

The hologram sat down, setting the cane to the side and causing it to vanish from the feed. "Poker. One round. Each of us will be given one hundred chips to use."

Hull took another step forward, standing to the side of presumably his chair. "And what are we playing for?"

"That should be obvious."

"It is, but I want to hear you say it."

Moriarty looked up. "If you win, you and Dr. Walker will be allowed to leave this tomb with your lives. No harm will come to either of you. But if I win, that slab will not move, and you will die here. Both of you will."

Hull saw the robed figure, Daemon, shuffle where she stood. "But Sir, what about—"

"Silence, Veronica," Moriarty barked.

Hull glanced down at the empty table, recognizing the disadvantage, the circumstance, and what was at stake. Submission was not an option. Even with a game that, given the scenario, would only be won by chance, he had to play. He owed his friend that much. He sat down and clasped his hands on the table, staring forward into the holographic hood.

"Play," he said, his voice cold. Daemon stepped forward, her hands holding a deck of cards and chips. Hull's attention, however, was drawn to the trembling of her fingers, and the slightly damp parts just below her hood. Dampness caused by tears, no doubt. He watched her split the chips in half, then start shuffling the deck. When she moved to deal him his two cards, he saw her eyes. Visible signs of crying, from the smudged makeup. Not from pain, or fear of him. It was for John.

"Emotions, Sheridan," Moriarty stated, drawing Hull's attention back to him. "Emotions are the trivial thing that hold us back. They are such diminutive, simple concepts that can destroy everything."

"I would be inclined to agree with you."

"But you won't, because you are just as much attuned to your emotions as any other weak human being."

"Those emotions are what make us human."

"Do they now?"

"You can go first."

Moriarty glanced down at his cards propped against the table, then pointed at a 5-chip, which Daemon tossed forward. "Your lesson is obvious. I can destroy you with your emotions. Your companionship to the doctor. A strong bond, but just as much a weakness. One to be exploited."

"People in my life have died before."

"I know."

Hull's left hand gave a very short spasm as he tossed forward a matching chip.

"A curious thing, the way death changes us," Moriarty continued. "Shapes us into who we are. Who we will become. A single death can turn a person from who they once were into something completely new."

"Make your play."

The man glanced down once more, looking at the newly-revealed cards in the center of the table. A Four, a Three, and a Ten of Hearts. Moriarty pointed to a twenty-five-chip and two ten-chips. "Tell me about her, Sheridan. Tell me about that night, so many years ago, when the spirit of your soul died."

Hull tossed forward a fifty-chip. "Raise or fold."

"This can go quickly or very slowly, Sheridan."

"Yes, it can," the detective flared. "With the current cards, either one of us holds a good chance of having a flush. Because it was your peon who shuffled the deck, I can be safe in guessing that things will be turned in your favor, and your cards right now include at least one Heart."

"You'd be wrong, then. Because I play a fair game, Detective. Whether you believe it or not."

"Then make your play."

Moriarty tapped on another five-chip before leaning away. "If you won't tell me about her, perhaps we can look at the future."

"No."

"What would happen if the doctor were to die, hmm? I imagine you'd be quite troubled."

Daemon flipped the fourth card. King of Hearts.

"But why stop with the doctor? There are plenty of people who mean something to you. All I need to do is find them. Your emotions will do the rest."

"Why."

"What?"

"Why bother telling me everything?" Hull glared at the hooded man from over his cards. "In telling me what you plan to do, you enable me to do something about it, meaning you have no intentions of actually doing anything. Your words speak more than your actions because your actions are fabricated lies. You seek to distract me, not destroy me, else you would have done it long ago."

"There's an art to your destruction, Sheridan Hull." The man made a sweeping gesture to the rest of his chips. "An art that I would quite like to see in action. To strip you of everything that makes you who you are? To watch you slowly lose everything of value, everything of purpose in your life? I imagine most people would fall under the presumption that you are a machine, that you hold no goal in your life other than to solve crimes. I'm not most people. I know better. I know you, Sheridan. And I know you hold many people dear in your heart."

"Then do something about it," Hull snapped as he pushed the rest of his chips forward.

"Steel yourself, Sheridan. There is much to come in the future. And I fear you may not understand the true level of chaos that lies ahead."

Daemon flipped the final card. Four of Clubs.

"Steel *yourself*, Moriarty," the detective snarled as he stood. "You are correct in acknowledging that I am attuned to my emotions, but you fail to recognize the depth of them. Toying with my emotions is the equivalent of pulling wires from a bomb you know nothing about. Her death did something to me, Moriarty. Something far more volatile than you may believe. It introduced me to anger. Pure, unleashed anger. Anger that, with time, can easily be trained to focus on you."

"Good." Moriarty nodded at his cards. Daemon pushed them forward, revealing the Three of Spades and the Three of Diamonds. A Three of a Kind. Hull looked down at his cards, up at Moriarty, and smirked. He let the cards fall to the table, revealing his hand to be the Four of Spades and the Four of Diamonds. Coupled with two of the cards on the table, he had a Four of a Kind. And a victory.

"Open the slab," Hull ordered.

The hologram stood. "Do you know what we are, Sheridan?"

"*Open the slab.*"

"We're pieces. Cards to a game. You are quite obviously the Hermit. The man who would exist on his own, without contact to anyone. This would give you the utmost level of efficiency. The good doctor is the Chariot. A man of action. Of war. And I? I'm the Devil. The thing that brings about events to come. The harbinger of order. Order through chaos."

Hull turned away from the hologram, focusing his attention on the slab, as if his gaze would make it open.

"Your day will come, Sheridan. The day when you live up to your expectations." The hologram actually walked forward, moving through the table, something Hull didn't think possible. It came to stand behind him, and Hull watched as a glowing, gloved hand fake-rested itself on his shoulder.

"I will not ask again," the detective commanded.

"Can you feel that?" Moriarty asked, his voice practically in Hull's ear. "That sinking sensation as you stare forward into the blankness of nothing? That feeling that just seems to creep up on you, like water slowly pouring into a tub, and you're stuck inside without any hope for escape. You have no choice but to sit and feel the chilling, trembling water fill the space around you, covering you, encompassing you. And then, finally, in the moment when you look up and see that last glimmer of light, that last glimmer of hope. That is when the waters of isolation take you completely. That is when they eclipse your vision and show you your worst and most truthful fear."

The hand vanished, as did the hologram, but the voice remained for just a second more.

"You are, indeed, alone."

The slab which blocked the exit slid out of sight, revealing the last bits of light on the distant mountains. Hull pierced his eyes as he stared out, feeling a weight dissipate from his stomach. He turned to see Daemon, hood removed, staring at him with shaking lips. She took two steps forward, her orange robe dragging on the ground as she moved.

"He's in that room," she said as she pointed back. "He'll wake when you get to him." Hull gave her a solemn nod and watched as she passed him and started off towards the gate. He glanced back into the room, seeing the cards and chips still on the table, as well as the deck. His eyes traveled up from the table to the archway that led to the back, hopefully where Walker was.

He passed under the archway and found Walker in a chair, head lulled to the side and eyes closed. He moved behind the chair and started untying his friend's hands, which was evidently enough to wake him. His head stirred as he looked forward, and when Hull moved around to the front, the man's eyes widened.

"Hull! My God, I can't even begin to say how happy I am to see you."

"The feeling is mutual."

The doctor grabbed Hull's shoulders as he stood. "He's alive. Moriarty is alive."

"I know."

"The other man was just a double."

"I know."

"Well damn, how long was I out?"

"Too long."

Hull assisted the man in exiting the mausoleum, reaching the outer grass and finding a sky full of stars. Walker looked up and around, relief pouring from his eyes.

"I didn't think I'd get to see this again," he said with a smile. Hull offered no response. Instead, he furrowed his brow when his phone started to vibrate. He pulled it out and took a moment to recognize the number before answering.

"Yes?" he said. Walker watched him listen intently before giving a nod. "On our way." He hung up the phone and started forward.

"Who was that?" Walker asked.

"Inspector Lennox. Something is happening in Newfield."
Hull gave a very small gulp. "Something very bad."

*

Moriarty stood on top of the two-story bus, driving through
the night towards the glowing lights of Newfield. His cloak billowed
around him, the wind threatening to throw his hood back. But he
didn't care. That wasn't important now. It wouldn't be for much
longer.

Inside the confines of his mind, he could hear the tunes
playing once more. The Ink Spots never failed to appease his
subconscious.

"Newfield," he announced, though the only person who could
hear him was Veronica, who stood behind him with her head dipped.
She stood at the side of another figure, one also clad in a robe, but his
a crimson red. "Our equivalent of ground zero. Such an innocent
town. So many people yearning for proper leadership. For order.

"That's what we are, Veronica. We are the bringers of order to
the masses. The ones to quell the chaos."

"Yes, Sir."

"Don't take me for a fool, Veronica." He turned to face her,
but her eyes rested on the hood of the bus. "I know what you've been
considering. Take caution and remember that before me, you were
nothing more than a teenage orphan on her way to a juvenile
detention center. I gave you a purpose, and I can revoke it just as
easily."

"Yes, Sir. I'm sorry, Sir."

"Good. Go put all sectors on alert. Tell them we start in two
hours."

"Yes, Sir."

He returned his gaze forward, seeing a new light in Newfield,
from the top of the tallest building. A fire.

"No. No more showers. No more rain." He pulled his cane
from his cloak and propped it against the bus hood. "Only the fire.
Only order from the chaos. Only peace."

UPRISE

  Inspector Gregory Lennox stepped promptly from the passenger seat of the heavy-duty police SUV, careful to keep from catching his tie in the door as he swiftly closed it. Commissioner Conn walked around from the driver side, eyes narrowed, nose scrunched, and hand pressed against his hip. It was only 8:30 AM on a Sunday, and Lennox knew Conn to be a religious man who never came to work on Sundays. In fact, he was so devoted to his faith that he and his family would drive up to Portland every Sunday, just to be in the same church Conn had grown up in. But this matter was of the highest importance. This wasn't something the chief of police could sit out on.

  "Bring me up to speed, Inspector," Conn ordered as the two started through a crowd of civilians and reporters.

  "At about ten last night, several police officers stopped reporting in at their usual times. By 10:30, every car on patrol had dropped off the radar. We sent out a party to check in on one and found the officers tied up, gagged, and blindfolded. Guns and car gone," Lennox replied. "A half-hour later, the fires started."

  "First building?" Conn questioned, not-so-gently shoving a reporter from his path.

"Plyer Incorporated. Someone across the road noticed it."

"How many others?"

"Forty-three buildings in total. From an aerial view, the fires formed the number 11."

Conn grunted. "Continue."

"We couldn't find the police cars but we found every officer relatively unharmed. We were on high alert, and approximately an hour and a half ago, the explosions started."

The two walked past the police barricade and came to stand at the edge of a pit, which was part of a makeshift, waterless moat that surrounded city hall. Officers were working to create a lumber bridge to cross over for convenience.

"Arranged explosions cutting off any proper way of getting to the building," Lennox said as his eyes left the commissioner and perused the ditch. "Explosives were meant to harm only the immediate area. Short and small blast radius, but powerful. We believe the explosives are the same ones spotted with the Chimaera attackers last week."

"And what about that?" Conn asked as he pointed to the tail end of a black double-decker bus, something that would've been common in the United Kingdom, not here.

"That came about half an hour ago. Smashed through the police barricade, over the ditch, and into the building. License plates register as having been in use three weeks ago in Surrey. Reported missing on the 11th."

"Did anyone see who was driving the bus?"

"No, but there were at least two to three dozen people onboard, and they all departed once the bus had stopped."

"Then what are we doing, Inspector?" The commissioner turned and scowled at Lennox. "Stolen police cars and another hostage crisis in the city capital and we're just sitting here with a barricade, trying to keep the reporters away?"

"It's not that simple, Sir."

"Why not?"

Lennox nodded to the rooftops. "Snipers set up, six confirmed. Anyone steps foot on the other side and they fire."

Conn scoffed. "I'd like to see them try." The two watched as three police officers pushed a large slab of wood down, landing neatly on the just-built pillars in the ditch. A bridge had been made. Before

Conn could step forward, the doors to the building opened, allowing three figures to step out, all clad in robes.

The person to the left was clad in an orange robe, and stood shorter than the other two. The one on the right wore a rouge cloak and walked with their hands presumably clasped, judging by the way their sleeves linked. The figure in the center walked with a certain essence of pride, their metal cane tapping on the sidewalk path that brought them to the makeshift bridge. Once they reached the lumber slab, the three stopped, creating a very tense encounter.

"Commissioner Conn," the central figure stated in a raspy voice, giving an encompassing gesture. "So wonderful to see you."

Conn looked the central figure, a man, judging by the voice, a long look before replying. "Who are you?"

"Do you really need to ask?"

Lennox's eyes widened quickly when he realized just who he was standing opposite from. "You're Moriarty."

The central figure poked the balled top of his cane in the inspector's direction. "Finally, someone with the ability to think."

"What's this about, then?" Conn barked.

"It's about establishing order, Commissioner," Moriarty chided as he planted the tip of his cane in the dirt. "Order through the chaos."

"I don't like the way you see things, Mr. Moriarty," Conn admonished, pressing his hands against his hips.

The hooded man shook his head. "Please, forget the unnecessary addition to the title. Moriarty will do."

"Well, *Moriarty*," Conn replied with a frown, "I'm going to have to arrest you. Again."

"If you must, Commissioner," the hooded man responded, a splash of sarcasm in his tone. "But before you take me in, I have to congratulate you on a job well done." Moriarty extended a gloved hand.

Conn looked down at the hand before reluctantly extending his own. "A job well done on what?"

Moriarty took the commissioner's hand. "A job well done on dying."

Lennox tried to react, but the speed of lightning was far faster than him. White bolts of electricity shot from Moriarty's cloaked arm to Conn, coursing over the man's body for several long seconds before ceasing. The commissioner dropped to the ground, his body going limp. Lennox drew his pistol and leveled it with Moriarty's head, who, with his partners, had turned away.

"I wouldn't do that if I were you, Inspector," Moriarty's voice called back. Lennox glanced up to see the six snipers visible, all leveling their rifles on his head. Lennox kept his gun trained on the hooded head while the three walked back up the sidewalk path and into city hall. He only lowered his gun once the door had been closed. His attention shot down to Conn, who was swarmed with other officers now. It didn't take Lennox a second glance. He knew the truth. The commissioner was dead.

*

Hull and I had done our best to return to Newfield as quickly as we could, but things had proven difficult. My blood loss had come from a deep gash in my leg, not one caused by any kind of weapon, but rather from rough contact with a sharp and rocky surface. Hull had insisted we go to the emergency room and have the injury dealt with before continuing, which meant we hadn't actually left Bend until around seven in the morning. Thankfully, I was feeling better, and not just because of the painkillers the care center had provided.

He hadn't bothered to elaborate on what was happening in Newfield, but as soon as we had crossed over the pass, I'd been able to piece it together. The smoke was the first clue, long trails coming from multiple buildings. Numerous helicopters were hovering towards the center of the city, and off in the direction of the west, I could see what looked like fighter jets moving on a defensive perimeter. But the military wasn't involved in something pertaining to an individual city. It would have to be a threat on a national scale to warrant that.

"Has Lennox given an update?" I asked as we entered the city limits.

"One text, two words. 'City hall,'" Hull replied, his hands clutching the steering wheel. Yes, I let him drive, even though he had yet to get his license. I figured that the penalty for driving without a license would be less than driving under the influence of narcotics.

"Moriarty's staging another attack?" I suggested.

"Possibly."

I crossed my arms and stared forward, my mind still racing from yesterday's events. "He talked to me, during our game. His way with words.. it's no wonder he's heading a powerful crime syndicate. He said he would bring order by reconditioning humanity. That he would create circumstances which would force us to adapt."

"His greatest strength is creating an idea," Hull returned. "Ideas are the most powerful weapon anyone can possess. Birth an idea and it will never die."

"What did he tell you?"

"Exactly what he hoped would irritate me."

"Did it?"

The detective gave a sharp inhale. "Sufficiently."

We could only get within one block of city hall before coming to a stop, the number of cars and people in the street being too much. I carefully stepped out of the car, testing my leg. It seemed okay, but I knew better than to trust the initial feel. Hull and I carved our way through the crowd, eventually coming to a police barricade. I could see Lennox talking into a radio near one of the cars, and a large ditch creating a trench surrounding city hall, which currently had a double-decker bus sticking out from the side.

Lennox nodded to us, granting us passage. We walked to stand behind him, my attention on the central building. Now things were definitely getting murky.

"It's Moriarty," Lennox told us as he hooked the radio back into the car.

"I know," Hull replied, his eyes on the top of the building.

"We don't know how many people were inside when they took over. We don't even know exactly when they took over. First the fires on the buildings started, then the explosive-made moat. Bus came after, and about fifteen minutes ago... well, *that* happened."

I followed Lennox's finger to a wooden bridge, crossing the gap between the police barricade and the cement sidewalk that led to the building's entrance.

"Snipers along the rooftop keep from any potential advance," Hull noted, his gaze traveling down to other officers around the barricade. "Where's the commissioner?"

"Dead." Both Hull and I looked at Lennox with surprise. He gave a somber nod towards the bridge. "Fifteen minutes ago. Moriarty electrocuted him."

"Who's in charge now?" I asked.

"I am."

Hull pulled his phone from his pocket, checked the screen, then put it back. "Do your city proud, then," he said with a glance at Lennox, "Commissioner." He started away, towards the lumber bridge. I gave Lennox a nod and followed the detective, who paused when he reached the crossing.

"What's the plan?" I questioned, my eyes following the sidewalk.

"Go inside and say hello," Hull replied.

"*That's* your plan?" I echoed, my brow crinkled. "Just waltz past six snipers?"

"They have no interest in us."

"That doesn't fill me with confidence."

"Wasn't expecting it to."

He started across the bridge, his stride carrying him onward without hesitation. I followed with some qualm, but I knew that he'd never really steered me wrong before. As he predicted, the snipers did not pop their heads up to aim, as if we were on an authorized guests list. We followed the sidewalk to the double doors of the city hall entrance and, without any hesitation, Hull pulled the left door open and stepped in. I rushed to his side as the door closed.

"Now what?" I asked.

Hull opened his mouth to reply, but stopped when a sharp burst of static echoed through the atrium. I looked up and found a speaker in the corner of the room, linked to an intercom system that spread throughout the building. After the static, a bell-like noise echoed, followed by some very odd, very familiar deep vocals. Hull's attention went from the speakers to the doorway ahead of us, just beyond the security checkpoint. This door in particular would lead to the main hall.

"Good morning, gentlemen!" a voice bellowed from the speakers. Moriarty's voice. "Glad to see you here. I was hoping you wouldn't take long."

"Where is he?" I questioned.

"Through there," Hull replied, nodding at the main hall doorway. We ran forward, the music still playing through the speakers. The sense of familiarity had yet to dim. Whatever Moriarty was playing, it was something I'd certainly heard before.

"Come in!" Moriarty's voice called as we reached the doorway. "I have some people I'd like to introduce to you."

As we pushed the door open, the music shifted. A series of drum beats, followed by more vocals. Now the song was most definitely familiar, but somehow, the song itself evaded my thoughts. We stepped into the main room, a large hall that visibly showed the second floor. Standing on the second floor balcony, presumably facing us, was the dark-cloaked Moriarty, standing in front of an open double-doorway. He spread his arms wide, his metal cane held firmly in his gloved right hand.

"Let the events begin!" the man blared. I looked left as the doors to other rooms slammed open, allowing several people to walk in, one from each room. Hull's attention went to the right, where an equal number of people had entered. All of them wore black jumpsuits with the red Chimaera insignia on their chests.

"Be prepared," Hull muttered, his back pressing against mine.

"What?" I asked, my eyes focused on the four people approaching me.

"The song. *Be prepared.*"

Oh. Now that most certainly made things click.

"Eight on two," Hull stated. "Odds stacked. Unarmed, but lethal. Should be fun."

"I'm glad this is humoring you."

The man on my farthest left charged me, putting his head down in a ramming motion. I ran forward, grabbing his extended left arm and swinging it wide, sending him twirling into Hull's waiting kick. Before I could regain my balance, the next closest person lunged me, hitting me square in the chest. I toppled back and rolled, coming back up on my feet. *Now* I could feel my leg wound, and it most certainly did not feel pleasant.

Hull had gone from his quick kick into the first man's stomach to a full spin, his leg colliding with the hip of one of his own attackers. The assailing man slid to his side, making way for a woman to charge and grab Hull's arms. He pressed back against her strength, snapping his right arm out, hers attached, to catch the third attacker in the face. That man fell back, nose cracked. The woman gave a quick glance at her companion, which was all the time Hull needed to force her back and send her spinning.

My second attacker grabbed me by the scruff of my neck, pulling me up and throwing me forwards. I caught the ground and rebounded, sending my good leg into the man's groin. He collapsed backwards, legs snapping together. My third attacker barreled at me, his right fist arcing up above his head. I twisted to the side and shoved my good leg out again, catching him in the feet and bringing him to the ground. I jumped up and brought my elbow across the man's temple, knocking him out cold.

Hull's fourth attacker was actually not unarmed. He pulled a police baton from his back and swung, narrowly missing the detective's face. Hull arched his back and somersaulted away, going over the limp body of my first attacker. He pulled the body up and threw it at his fourth attacker, catching the man off guard. While the fourth attacker stumbled, Hull grabbed the baton from his hand and smashed it across the assailant's temple, spinning him to the ground with the first body on top. Hull glanced down at the woman, who was standing, then over his shoulder at me.

"Shift!" he yelled. I gave a quick nod and did a sideways roll in his direction, the same time as him. We'd definitely become a lot more coordinated over time, especially during physical altercations. I grabbed the baton from the ground as I rolled while Hull continued, bringing my fourth attacker to his knees with the momentum.

The woman pulled out her own baton, swinging it and catching my own. I batted her back, trying to keep my better leg planted. She wasn't a bad fighter, but at the same time, she wasn't that good. I brought my baton down on her right hand, causing her to lose her grip on the weapon. I smacked the other baton away, then brought my own back and crossed it with her knee. She collapsed to the ground, no doubt in pain but able to resist the urge to scream.

Hull jumped to his feet and turned, only barely catching my fourth attacker. The two held each other equally, no one able to gain the upper hand. Hull stared into the man's eyes, contorted in anger and rage. And fear. Hull tried to push forward, to no avail.

"John!"

I blasted the baton into the man's head, sending him to the floor. Hull looked down at the man, then up at me with a hearty nod.

Before I could move, an arm wrapped itself around my neck, pulling me back. Hull's first attacker was back on his feet and ready to fight. He threw me over, my body rolling on the floor. Hull pounced on the man, hands going for his throat. The man kicked out, forcing Hull away and onto his back.

I surged forward, wrapping my arms around the man's neck and holding on as he stood. He was a lot taller than I'd first thought, going so high my feet left the ground.

"Sheridan!"

"Working on it!" The man scrambled to grab me, managing to kick Hull away when the detective got too close. I held on with all of my strength, knowing that with just the right amount of pressure...

The man's squirming ceased as he lost consciousness, legs buckling and body falling to the ground. I released his neck and landed precisely on my feet. Hull gave a look around the room before looking up at Moriarty, who now stood with his hands clasping the balcony edge.

"Well done, well done!" the man barked. "Now for something more worthy of your time. I introduce to you, the Crimson Miles!"

The door beneath Moriarty opened to reveal a man cloaked like Moriarty, but his was a deep red rather than black. He too had his hood drawn, his hands clasped together inside the cloak.

"The what?" I asked, holding the recovered police baton up.

"Bad news," Hull replied, his gaze locked on the newcomer.

The cloaked figure stood still for a very long moment before looking up. The darkness of the hood hid any facial features, but I could still feel a pair of eyes locked on me. Now was a time where I would have greatly appreciated my pistol. The figured unclasped its hands and ran forward, at a speed I had certainly not expected. It jumped into the air, giving off a masculine grunt as it soared through the gap between us.

Hull dove away, leaving me with the baton aimed pointlessly at the figure. He touched down and rolled, leg snapping up in a very acrobatic manner and kicking the baton from my hand. I tried to catch the leg with my palm, but grasped empty air as the figure returned to his feet, throwing a very powerful punch my way. He caught me in the chest before I could act, and it had been a powerful punch indeed. I flew back, the wind knocked clean out of me.

The figure ducked as Hull's haymaker swung out, causing the detective to lose balance. Hull used his momentum to come down on top of the cloaked man, but was still too slow. The man, the Crimson Miles, as Moriarty had called him, rolled away, coming to his feet and taking an offensive stance. Hull threw sparse punches at him, each being deftly deflected. One punch was caught in the Miles's right hand, which he promptly twisted and sent Hull spiraling.

I swung the baton down, aiming for the figure's extended arm. He recoiled the arm and brought his other fist up, catching me in the chin. I spun and crouched, extending my arm to full length and colliding it with the man's legs. He jumped over my arm, cloak and all avoiding my attack. He landed and kicked out, catching the bottom of the baton in my palm and sending it flying. I brought my arm back and caught the man's foot, actually making contact. I yanked the foot, and for just a short moment, I had an advantage while the Miles struggled to regain his composure.

That advantage was quickly lost when Hull tackled the man, forcing both of them away from me. I struggled back to my feet and watched as Hull attempted to wrap himself around the man, only to be bucked away. The Miles jumped towards a nearby pillar, arms latching to it and giving him the ability to swing around it. He released himself and flew straight into me, legs colliding with my chest. I grabbed the man's feet as I fell back, throwing them to my side as I slammed into the ground. His legs flailed in my grasp, and were eventually able to wiggle free.

Hull hurled himself into the man, grabbing his cloak and using it to keep his own balance. The Miles wrapped his arm around the cloak twice, then pulled, bringing Hull forward. The man released the cloak and clutched the detective's throat, lifting him high into the air. His fingers tightened around Hull's neck while his legs twitched. He would've squeezed the life out of the detective had I not smashed the police baton into his arm, releasing his grasp and causing him to twirl away. I helped Hull to his feet, holding his shoulder while he stood.

The Miles charged at us, and even though we both braced ourselves, we weren't prepared for what he intended to do. When he had only a meter of space to close, the man jumped, flying over our heads like a bird and landing adeptly behind us. We turned and watched him charge through the doorway from which he'd come. I glanced up and saw that Moriarty too had left. Hull and I nodded to each other, then charged after the Miles, knowing he'd be our best bet at finding Moriarty. His path wasn't difficult to follow. He'd taken a door to the outside, judging by the open door on our right.

We flew through the door and caught sight of the Miles bounding across the courtyard towards the perimeter, where four police officers waited. They drew their guns on the man, but were hopelessly outmatched. The man jumped clear across the ditch, legs spreading wide to catch two officers in the necks. He caught the falling gun of one and fired it twice, one bullet into the head of the third officer, the other into the foot of the fourth. Hull and I only managed to claw our ways to the top of the ditch and see the Miles slide into the back of a taxi.

"We need a car," Hull said sharply, head spinning.

"Easy," I replied as I pulled the closest police car's driver door open. He nodded and ran around, jumping into the passenger seat. I started the car and pulled away from the barricade, moving in the direction of the taxi.

Boom.

My head smashed forward into the steering wheel as a very loud, very hot explosion occurred behind us. Hull and I glanced back to see city hall engulfed in fire, a plume of smoke rising high into the sky. The glass in the back window of the car had shattered from the explosion, but thankfully, the glass between the backseats and the front had held firm.

"He's really making a name for himself, isn't he," I commented as I floored the pedal, turning to keep the taxi in sight.

"By his logic, in order to receive order, one must first create chaos. Self-fulfilling prophecy," the detective replied, his hands clutching his seat and the dash.

"So who was that?"

"A Chinese myth. A legend from the fourteenth century, that amidst the Red Turban Rebellion, an orphan child was raised and trained in different martial arts, to fight as the perfect soldier. The child was named Zhan Shi Hongse. If my memory serves, the name translated to Soldier in Red."

"So this is what?"

"A person using the moniker. But also a myth."

"How so?"

"After my departure from college, I traveled. And while in Japan, I heard talks of a young warrior, an orphan trained in physical combat by some of the best instructors in Asia, being specialized in the arts of kung fu and a newer, more aggressive form called Kyokushinkaikan. He too went by the name of Zhan Shi Hongse, but had adapted to a more modern calling. The Crimson Miles."

I bit my lip. "Great. So Moriarty has one of the best physical fighters in Chimaera."

"So it would seem."

I presumed that the taxi driver was being held at gunpoint. His driving was more erratic than that of a drunk's. We followed him as he drove away from the city center, heading up towards the industrial section. I knew the Miles wouldn't lead us to any place of importance to Chimaera. He was just trying to get us away. But we had no better option than to follow him, even if it meant driving into a trap. We were good at that.

The taxi led us to an old warehouse, driving up onto the curb before stopping. As I opened my door, Hull tapped me on the shoulder with an object. I turned to see a pistol in his hand, as well as another in his lap.

"We may need them," he added. I nodded and took the gun, then stepped out just in time to watch the Miles glance back at me, then aim a gun of his own through the driver window of the taxi and fire.

"Stop!" I shouted, bringing my gun up. The Miles dashed away, into cover within the warehouse. Hull ran forward, focus not on the attacker but rather on the taxi. I ran to the warehouse door and peered in, glancing back to see Hull craning his neck inside the cab. I could see from where I stood the spray of blood. The cabbie never stood a chance. Hull pulled his head out slowly and turned, a look of absolute hatred on his face.

"Move," he growled, bringing his own gun up.

"Who was that?" I asked as I stepped to the side.

"Someone important."

I followed him into the warehouse, which was completely empty, save for the cloaked man standing at the other end. He faced us with his hands clenched in fists at his side. I aimed my gun at him and rested my finger on the trigger, but Hull had other intentions. He started pacing back and forth, eyes locked on the Miles.

"That taxi driver you shot?" Hull started as he paced. "The man you left for dead, head pinned to the steering wheel of the car he had driven to make a living? That is the same man and the same car that has driven me to almost every location in the entirety of Newfield. If ever I have needed a taxi, I called that man. Years of sitting in the back seat of that taxi cab, always with him as my trusted driver. And no matter my demand, he would comply. And each compliance came with a very simple, very affirmative statement. 'Gotcha.'

"And you know what? In all of those years, I never once asked the man for his name. Not once did it occur to me that this man had known me longer than the majority of people I had met in Newfield. This man had transported me from crime to crime. He knew my life better than almost anyone. And I never took the time to ask his name. And now, thanks you to, I will learn his name from an obituary in a newspaper. I will never get the privilege to hear his name spoken from his own mouth."

Hull brought his gun up. "You have denied me that privilege. And that is one opportunity I do not appreciate having been taken from me."

Bang.

The shot came from not my gun, but Hull's. The man who aimed to incapacitate, the man who fought for justice, had fired his gun, and the bullet had most certainly made contact with the Crimson Miles's chest. The man fell backwards with added force, and instead of landing on the concrete ground, disappeared from sight. Hull and I rushed forward, and only as we got closer did we see the unnatural pit in the floor of the warehouse.

From a simple glance, we could tell that the Miles had not been harmed whatsoever, and had quickly escaped from the pit into a tunnel at the far end. Any chance of pursuing him was lost. And I knew that Hull was angry. Very, very angry.

*

We went from the warehouse to the police station, per Lennox's request. The entire city was in disarray while the police tried to calm the citizens. Little by little, the city was doing exactly what Moriarty hoped it would do. It was falling into chaos.

"How many died in the explosion?" I asked when the three of us were seated in Lennox's office.

"None. Nobody was in the building. Everyone who would've been in there was accounted for. Only people who didn't make it out were with Chimaera, if any of them didn't get out."

"Where could they have gone?"

"Tunnels. Four of them leading out of the building basement and connecting to the sewers."

I glanced over at Hull, whose eyes were narrowed and focused on the window behind Lennox, before continuing. "So where does it leave us?"

"On a city scale? In a bad place," Lennox replied before sighing. "On a national scale? A much worse place."

"Why?"

"We caught some of the people who claimed responsibility for setting up the explosives that brought down city hall. None of them said they were associated with Chimaera, and a few didn't seem to even understand the concept of the group."

"Who were they with?"

"We think Chimaera did hire them, but not directly. Avoids the connection. Those that we recovered claimed to having come from insurrectionist groups in Iraq, Afghanistan, and Pakistan."

"Three more," Hull murmured, his nostrils flaring.

"Three more what?" Lennox asked.

"Countries." The detective stood. "Moriarty is deliberately turning small sections of countries into hostiles. Chaos on an international scale."

"Croatia," I said solemnly, my head tilting back.

"A tight network of different countries, all having fires started under the nests to ruffle the feathers of the higher birds," Hull commented. "The simplest way to achieve chaos on a colossal scale. War."

"He'd never be able to do that," Lennox said as he stood.

"But he could," Hull replied. "Because he knows that those decisions are not in our hands. He intends to start a wildfire, and all a wildfire needs is a spark."

Lennox rested his hands on his desk. "I have to start reorganizing. Twenty police cars still missing and a dead commissioner."

Hull gave the man a nod. "Do the city proud." With a glance at me, the detective and I left Lennox's office and started for the exit. We passed through the lobby and out onto the street, still swarmed with reporters. After pushing our way past the cameras and microphones, we found ourselves in our car, fatigue finally setting in for me.

"Where to now?" I asked as I started the car.

Hull cast a longing gaze out the window before turning to me, his eyes glassed over with a very sunken hue of gray. "There is something I need to tell you."

*

Moriarty stood with his cane centered and concentration honed on the nine screens of the command terminal, each screen showing news broadcasts of the day's events. Two of them were currently discussing the origins of the bombers. One of them discussed Chimaera, its known history, and all information on the illusive leader. Three screens focused on Detective Sheridan Hull and Doctor John Walker. The seventh and eighth screens were discussing the death of Commissioner Lamont Conn. And the ninth screen was a CNN broadcast.

A very, very important CNN broadcast.

The door to Moriarty's right hissed open, admitting the red-cloaked figure, the Crimson Miles. He walked confidently to stand at Moriarty's side, looking up at the screens as he clasped his hands.

"The evidence was recovered. Iraq, Afghanistan, and Pakistan are now on the list of suspicious countries," the Miles reported, his voice cold and stern.

"Excellent work. You've outdone yourself yet again," Moriarty replied, a Sam Cooke coming to life on one of the computers.

"And per your orders, I did not permanently injure the detective or the doctor."

"Very good. You follow orders to the letter. Strong quality to have." A pause. "You will note Veronica's absence," Moriarty commented as he turned away from the screens.

"I had noticed it, yes."

"And you chose not to inquire."

"I saw no purpose in doing so."

"Smart." Another pause. "Veronica will need to be dealt with. Promptly. If my insight is correct, she intends to betray me."

"Would you like me to take care of her?"

"No. I can think of two gentlemen who will handle her accordingly."

Moriarty stepped into the darkness, removing him from the Miles's view. "It is time the good doctor learned the truth about the love of his life."

"Of course. And if they do not react as you would like?"

"Then I will deal with Veronica myself. There is someone that requires your attention, though," Moriarty chimed as he took his seat.

"And who might that be?"

"We've struck at the heart of Newfield. But we must also be sure to damage the mind."

The Miles turned as the screens changed, now all synchronizing to show the image of a woman, with black hair that stretched down the length of her back. The Miles recognized her in an instant, but had never regarded her with importance.

"You are familiar with her?" Moriarty asked.

"Of course."

"She is your next target. But do not publicize her death. The one who will be most affected by her demise will know."

"Of course."

"Go, then. Ensure the death of Carla Montorum."

TURN

"Dead."

The Deviant, probably around the age of seventeen, nodded. "Found about two hours ago in her house. Didn't show up where she was supposed to be, coworker went to her house after calling her with no answer. Saw her through the bedroom window."

Hull pursed his lips and glanced down the road, eyes flitting over the numerous cars struggling to enter the rightmost lane. Pedestrians lined the sidewalks, making the best use of their lunch hour. Despite everything that had happened yesterday, people went about their days as usual, showing no signs of having been affected whatsoever by the events.

Life goes on.

"Who was sent?" the detective asked, returning his gaze to the young man.

"Couple of officers, an inspector. Not the usual guy," the Deviant replied as he ran his hands through his hair. "Looked younger. Black hair."

Hull pulled a small stack of plastic cards from his pocket. "So what shall it be today, GameStop, iTunes, or do we want to mix it up?"

The Deviant raised his chin to look at the selection. "Got any Steam cards? Supposed to be a sale starting tomorrow."

"City hall was destroyed yesterday and your primary focus is a sale of digital entertainment?" Hull asked as he handed the Deviant the specified card.

"I'm an emancipated high school dropout," the kid replied with a shrug. "My focus is getting enough hours in to pay for essentials. Not much time to worry about anything else."

"Evidently." Hull nodded at the boy as he walked away, heading to join the rest of the civilians with singular concerns. Hull turned his eyes up, looking at the dimmed horizon. For the first day of July, the weather was certainly murky. Storm clouds were working their way across the Oregon Coast Range, but the mood had already reached the city. Even though the people physically continued their days, mentally, they couldn't escape the truth. Newfield had become far more than just a city in the Willamette Valley of Oregon. Newfield was potentially the start of a very long, very dark period for not the state, or the country, but the world.

Hull had told Walker of the mystic gypsy woman, and her sincerity when stating what the detective could only describe as a prophecy. *The rise. The shift. The dark. The glass room. The* Cădea. All of it rested in his mind, plaguing his thoughts. And he had chosen to confide it in his only true friend, the person who had seen him through the strenuous events of the past year and a half. The doctor had dismissed it, not finding any credibility in a fortune teller. But Hull had seen otherwise. Because while he may dislike them, he understood riddles and veiled words.

The rise of Chimaera.

Upon rising this very morning, the doctor had found himself fairly weak as a result of his injuries from two days prior. Hull had received a call from the Deviant not a half-hour ago and had departed immediately, leaving only after having been assured that Walker would not "do anything stupid" while the detective was gone. He'd mentioned something about calling his girlfriend, the traitor whose crimes the doctor was not aware of, and asking her to go dancing. Hull had simply advised he be careful, as coming events may not bode well with him.

Hull now stood at the corner of 35th Street and Falcon Avenue, his destination being some three blocks south. The home was in a more tasteful part of Newfield, where your money and reputation spoke as loud as your words. He walked calmly along the sidewalk, seeing the police cars outside the three-story home just ahead. Gardens lining a cobblestone walkway to the front door, if he remembered correctly. And he always did. He'd visited the house once before, when a young man had been murdered. Now, here he was again, almost to the Montorum house. This time for the wife.

He followed the walkway with his hands tucked away in his pockets, eyes surveying the garden. It looked to have been severely neglected, notably the flowers in the front window. He arrived at the open door and glanced in, seeing three police officers in the kitchen and a fourth man, dressed in a formal attire that bordered on casual. This fourth man was tall, about Hull's height, with short black hair that looked relatively unkempt and a stern gaze that made him look intelligent.

The man looked up as Hull entered the room, walking over and extending his hand without a smile. "I was hoping you'd show up. Detective Bradford."

"Pleasure to meet you," Hull responded as he shook the man's hand. "What have you found?"

"We've got a few things collected that help," Bradford said as he walked back into the kitchen, Hull in tow. "Body's in the master bedroom, back of the house, hasn't been touched. If I've pieced things together well enough, her and the husband have been fighting for a while. The food kept here is only enough to really feed one, and the receipts on the counter show she's gone shopping for groceries once in three weeks."

"That all?" Hull asked.

"No." The inspector moved to the window. "Windows haven't been cleaned but the pantry is full of cleaning utilities that are fairly worn down. Well used, but not recently. Windows aren't clean, the flowers in the pots are dying, the garden's wilting. The laundry in the room through that door hasn't been done in five days. I don't know many orderly women who let that much pile up. All of the clothes are female, no sign of anything the husband would wear."

Hull resisted the urge to show his surprise at the astonishing level of competency. "Montorum is still in the hospital, correct?"

Bradford nodded. "My biggest clue on them fighting was in the study, across the hall and through the living room. Piles upon piles of letters and statements from about three and a half weeks ago. All of them discuss the mayor moving around a lot of personal funds to some outside source. They were rifled through, too, but nothing taken. I'd guess she went through 'em, got mad, and it went downhill from there."

Hull walked around the kitchen once, examining the receipts with a glance. "Cause of death?"

"Suffocation," Bradford said, but Hull could see the man hesitate.

"Just suffocation?" the detective asked.

Bradford grunted softly before nodding to the room. "It's a bit hard to explain."

Hull glanced in the direction of the bedroom and, with Bradford at his side, walked towards the room. He passed through a narrow hallway before entering a lavishly-decorated room with a large, ornate bed against the far wall. Lying in the center of the bed, dressed in evening wear, was the body of Carla Montorum, arms and legs tied with bristling rope to the four poles of the bed. As Hull came closer, he could see blood from the woman's eyes and ears, as well as two pieces of bloody cotton stuffed into the woman's nostrils.

"I've been on the force for five years," Bradford stated as he came to stand at the side of the bed, with Hull opposite him, "and I've never seen something that made me feel sick to my stomach before this."

Hull leaned over the body carefully, noting the strain to the woman's eyes and the cut marks on her wrists and ankles. "Forced asphyxiation.. but in one of the most brutal ways. The insertion of the cotton into her nose would effectively cut off any possible nasal oxygen, and a hand cupped over the mouth would completely remove any option for breathing. Her body would go into shock and pressure would begin accumulating in the brain, causing the blood. Had she survived, she no doubt would have gone deaf.. and her eyes could have potentially come out of their sockets."

"Thanks," Bradford said as he looked away. "That's exactly what I wanted to hear."

"Any sign of a break in?" Hull questioned as he stepped away from the body.

"Nothing. Whoever did it got in easy, and alone. Pair of footprints right outside the window," he replied as he pointed to the largest window in the room, "but they're completely bald. No way of tracing them."

"Hm," Hull replied, his attention following the tussled carpet to a desk against the adjacent wall, the top occupied by an array of folders. He stepped over to the desk and sifted through the folders, each of them labeled with what looked like dates. He stopped at 4-3-12, his heart giving a slight tremor. Then, in a quick burst, he flew through the folders towards the end of the pile before finding his target. A manilla folder with 4-3-11 written in a different style than the rest.

He opened the folder and found it empty, save for a single sheet of small paper, probably fifteen centimeters long and ten wide. Inscribed on the top of the page in a very fancy, very familiar handwriting was "An Ode From the Doctor." Hull's eyes moved down to the page itself, analyzing every single syllable to the poem that followed.

When the storm is done
All will cheer the light
Light that pours on one
Keeping all in sight
Err the man to shun
Receives the twilight

When the dawn has come
I will stand all right
Lest you abstain from
Letting me tonight

Does the private eye
In all things gone by
Expect me to die?

Hull folded the paper with one hand and set the folder down with the other, his jaw popping as he looked up. "I am afraid, Inspector, that your odds on finding the murderer may be very much stacked against you."

"That seems to be the case these days," Bradford replied as he pulled out his phone. He furrowed his brow before continuing. "But it looks like it doesn't matter. I've just been reassigned."

"Have you now?" Hull asked as he slid the paper into his pocket. "Something more important than the murder of the mayor's wife?"

"Text is from the new commissioner," the man said. After a short moment, his eyes went up to Hull, his nose scrunched. "Why would the odds be stacked against me?"

"How much have you been told about yesterday's events?"

"About the same as everyone else. Nothing."

"One of the people working for Chimaera is a very skilled combatant who goes by the title of the Crimson Miles," Hull stated as he stepped back over to the woman's body. "Killing a woman in so brutal, and so clever a way, is a calling card for him. If he is the one who murdered her, then any chance of finding him is very, very limited."

The inspector smirked. "Glad I've been reassigned, then. It seems one of the city commissioners needs help. He believes his brother has gone missing."

"And his brother is important?"

"Sure is. He's the Somalian ambassador to the United States."

"Ah."

Hull glanced back down at the body before feeling the buzzing of his phone. He pulled it out and sighed when he read who the caller was.

"This better be important," he said as he answered the phone, "I'm in the middle of something."

"Carla Montorum's death does not compare to this," Hull's brother, Malcolm, replied. "The Inspector you are with has been delegated to assist Commissioner Ghedi Rahim. His brother is the Somalian—"

"I know who he is," the detective interrupted.

"Then you understand the importance. Rahim is a coworker of mine. I trust you will not hesitate in assisting him."

Sheridan rolled his eyes before sighing. "I suppose the murdered woman won't be moving anytime soon."

"Good." The resounding click was the best part of the conversation, in Hull's opinion. He pocketed his phone and gave Bradford an optimistic grin.

"It seems I will be joining you, Inspector."

*

Hull sat in the passenger seat of a police car with Inspector Bradford at his left, taking them to where the brother of a supposedly missing man was waiting for them. The man, Rahim, was supposed to meet them at Covington Square, approximately ten blocks from where the two were now. Bradford was relatively silent while driving, which most certainly made Hull content. The lack of Walker was unsettling, though. He'd become so accustomed to the doctor's presence that not having him around felt wrong.

The detective slipped his index and middle fingers into his pocket and skillfully pulled out the folded piece of paper. He opened it and read it through twice more, not recognizing the possible author, title, or style of the poem. It had a standard enough rhyme scheme, five syllables a line, every other line rhyming, save for the last. And when he read it through without tearing it apart word by word, it didn't make much sense.

"Err the man to shun receives the twilight," he muttered, pressing his tongue against his check.

"Err the what?" Bradford asked.

Hull gave him a side-glance. "How familiar with poetry are you, Inspector?"

The other man scoffed. "I think I read *The Odyssey* once."

"Enough poetry to make anyone familiar," Hull remarked. "Tell me if this makes any sense to you. 'When the storm is done, all will cheer the light. Light that pours on one, keeping all in sight. Err the man to shun receives the twilight'."

"First part seems pretty obvious. When a storm passes, people are happy because it's clear. Light pouring on one makes the author pretty fond of himself, but the bit about keeping all in sight? Like the author is referring to himself in a plural form?"

"Possible. What of the last line?"

"'Err the man to shun receives the twilight'," Bradford repeated. "To err is to make a mistake, right? So the man who made a mistake receives the twilight... or something like that."

"Perhaps most of this poem is not to be taken in the literal sense. Twilight is often associated with the point between the sun's setting and the falling of night. But it can also be in reference to the ending of someone's life."

Bradford nodded. "So the man who made the mistake is on the path to his death?"

"Possible," Hull iterated. "It continues. 'When the dawn has come, I will stand all right, lest you abstain from letting me tonight'."

"Pretty straightforward, but I'd say that relies on 'twilight' actually meaning the time of day. Dawn would follow twilight, and the man would stand fine, unless you, whoever you is, abstained from letting them. So... whoever the author was, was directly telling them not to interfere, them being whoever they were speaking to?"

Hull rubbed his temples with his free thumb and middle finger. "This is why poetry and I do not have a good relationship."

"What's the poem called?" Bradford asked as he started slowing the car down.

"'An Ode From the Doctor'."

"Isn't your friend a doctor?"

"Yes." The detective sighed. "Which is why the poem worries me."

The car came to a stop by the park, a small patch of green in the urban environment, completed by the small pond in the center. Sitting in the bench facing the car was an older man, presumably in his late sixties, with a white cap and formal attire, complete with a frogged jacket. The man stood when Hull and Bradford approached, his wrinkled eyes narrowed not in suspicion, but from his smile. His circular spectacles helped to make his wise image perfect.

Bradford extended his hand. "Mr Rahim, I'm Inspector Bradford. This is my associate, Detective Hull."

"Dr. Ghedi Rahim. Thank you for coming so quickly," Rahim replied as he shook their hands. "My brother's disappearance is very much a mystery to me, and I hope I can assist in his finding."

"Where was your brother last?" Hull questioned.

"He was at my home," Rahim stated. "He arrived just last night and went out for a taste of the local cuisine. When he did not return, I became concerned, and when he had not come back by the morning, I called the police."

Hull nodded to Bradford, who gestured to the car. "Lead us to your home and we'll start investigating." Rahim nodded and took the passenger seat. Hull slinked into the back while Bradford moved around to the driver side.

"Does your brother usually leave home without a means of communication?" Hull asked once they were all seated.

"He had yet to receive a phone that could work properly," Rahim said. "I told him of its importance but he disregarded my advice before departing." The man pointed right at the stop before sitting back.

"You work with my brother?" Hull asked as they turned.

Rahim looked over his shoulder. "I knew you looked familiar. You are Malcolm's younger brother, yes? He speaks of you quite fondly."

Hull scoffed. "I bet he does."

The man returned his gaze to the front, then gave a bobbing of the head when he saw the poem Hull had left on the dash. He grabbed the paper slowly and read it once over before looking up at Bradford. "Where did you get this?"

The inspector glanced at the paper, then nodded back at Hull. "We found it in a murdered woman's home."

Hull leaned forward. "Do you recognize this poem?"

"This poem is old, far older than our ages combined. It is a very rough translation of a Swahili poem from no one knows when," Rahim declared.

"If it's a rough translation, what does it normally say?" Hull pressed.

Rahim looked the page over delicately before tapping it with his thumb. "In Swahili, it would read, '*Wakati vita ni kosa, yote jipeni mapambano. Amani hutoka kwa moja, kuweka wote katika, ila mtu kuondoka inapokea kifo*'. That would become, 'When the war is done, all will cheer the fight. Peace that pours on one, keeping all in warmth, except the man to leave receives death'."

"What of the second verse?" Hull continued, his focus engrossed on the man.

"In Swahili, it would say, '*Wakati amani umefika, nitasimama wote haki, isipokuwa wewe kutokupiga kuruhusu mimi kuishi*'. 'When the peace has come, I will stand all right, unless you abstain from letting me live'." Rahim tapped the page again. "This translation has been done in a very crude way. It deviates from the origins of the poem and changes it to suit another purpose."

"What purpose?" the detective asked, his head craned over the divide.

"I cannot say, for I do not know."

"And what of the last verse?"

Rahim shrugged. "That is where it deviates the most. The last three lines are not from the original poem. They have been added."

Hull held out his hand for the paper, which Rahim returned. The detective sat back silently, eyes looking over the page with intense ferocity. He focused on the paper for so long that when he finally did look up, they were parked outside the home of the man. The three stepped out and walked up the steps to the entrance, stopping only to let Rahim unlock the door. Once the man had entered, Bradford and Hull followed suit.

The room they found themselves in was as clean as physically possible. Hull's acute eyes couldn't find a patch of dust older than a day. Rahim huddled over to a coat rack, where he hung his hat, then looked to the men and clasped his hands behind his back. Bradford walked slowly and carefully into the living room, sniffing as he went. Hull looked from the living room to the opposing kitchen, noting every single pot and pan, cleaned like they were never used.

"Very interesting," Hull said as he stepped forward.

"What?" Bradford asked.

"I encountered a place like this before," Hull replied, his eyes falling on Rahim. "How long has your wife been deceased?"

The man made a sniffling noise with his mouth before gulping. "Ayanna passed away four months ago. How could you have known—"

"A clean house by a man who adopted the habit, not one who was accustomed to it," Hull stated as he stepped into the kitchen. "The pots are kept at a level not to accommodate your height, but that of someone far shorter. The array of cookbooks on the far shelf are highly recommended by last year's more popular television chefs, but you are not a man who finds enjoyment in television, explaining its new absence from the living room and replacement with a decorative vase, which has the Somali inscription '*Boji ku Nabad*'. Rest in peace. Not a vase, but an urn containing the ashes of your wife."

"Not just that," Bradford added as he moved around the coffee table at the center of the living room, "but you've got a row of photographs, all of a woman, too old to be a daughter, and the pictures are too well-kept to be a relative. You're not in any of the photos, though, not by choice, but by circumstance. Your wife didn't like having her photograph taken by anyone but you, meaning you couldn't be with her when they were shot. There is, however, a picture of you and her on the cover of the photo album, prominent on the shelf. Your wedding photos, I would guess."

Hull gave Bradford an impressed look. "Well done, Inspector."

"Not so bad yourself, Detective," the man replied with a wink. He turned to look around the living room once more before gazing up at Rahim. "Where was your brother going to be sleeping?"

Rahim, still in a slight state of shock, pointed up the stairs with a shaking finger. "The first door on your right." Hull and Bradford moved up the stairs and into the room, finding it to be a typical guest room with an unopened suitcase on the single-person bed. Hull stepped around the bed to the bedside table, eyes perusing its contents.

"Left his cell phone here," Hull noted, "as well as a set of keys and his passport."

"Didn't bother unpacking, except for whatever he had in the front pocket," Bradford added. Hull turned to observe the suitcase for himself. The front pocket had indeed been opened, and completely emptied, save for a torn piece of paper. Hull turned the paper over several times in his hand before dismissing it. Bradford moved to the cell phone, an older version of a Nokia flip model. He opened the phone and was immediately prompted with a password.

"Joy. Password to a missing Somalian man's phone," the inspector said as he showed the phone to Hull.

"Passwords are always a joy to figure out, Inspector," Hull replied as he took the phone. "All it takes is seeing the pattern. Unfortunately with a phone as old as this, determining it may be difficult, but..." He tapped away a five-digit code and pressed enter, then waited as the phone changed to the main menu. "Not impossible."

Bradford looked at the detective with sheer awe. "How?"

"Notice that the four key is the most faded, followed by the seven, then the two, and lastly the six. A phone that prompts a password would mean the most-used keys are the ones that include the digits of the code itself. A phone of this model would only accept a password consisting of no more than six figures, no less than four, and judging by the man and the key containing the letters G, H, and I, deducing that his password was in fact his last name, RAHIM, was no difficult feat."

"Amazing," Bradford exclaimed.

Hull smirked. "Funny, that was my friend's first reaction to seeing my deductive skills at work."

"I would be thrilled to meet him," Bradford said. "Everyone at the force knows of the great detective Sheridan Hull and his trusty doctor John Walker."

"I will be sure to introduce you at a more convenient time," Hull replied as he started accessing the phone's messages. The first to pop up was in, of course, Somali. "Dr. Rahim, could you assist us?" He waited as the sound of the man's footsteps came up the stairs, then to the doorway. Hull handed him the phone. "What does this say?"

Rahim lifted his glasses to read the message, his eyes peered. "It is a request, for Taban to meet with someone at a specific time. An address is provided, but the meeting time..."

"Yes?" Bradford piqued.

"It is for today. Within the very hour."

Hull nodded. "Then we may be able to catch him before something happens."

*

The police car pulled up on the specified address slowly, the three inside all staring forward with reluctance. The address had taken them to the farthest reaches of Newfield University's campus, where buildings were used for storage. The one they currently faced resembled a Victorian home, its spiked roofs stretching up like lightning rods. On the front steps sat a figure, their hands clutching their head.

The three exited the car and approached the figure slowly, Rahim leading them. When they were within ten meters of the sitting man, they stopped. Rahim, however, continued forward slowly.

"Taban?" the doctor asked as he sidled forward. "Taban, it is me, Ghedi. Are you okay?"

"No, Ghedi," the man uttered. "I am not okay."

Bradford stepped up to Hull's side, leaning in close so only the detective would hear him. "I don't like this."

"Neither do I," Hull whispered.

"What happened, Taban? Who were you to meet here?" the doctor asked, still moving closer.

"Turn back, Ghedi."

The doctor stopped and tilted his head. "What is wrong, Taban? Please, talk to me."

"I am doing what is right for our people, Ghedi," the man replied. Hull could see his fingers clutching his skull with even more strength.

"What are you doing for our people, Taban? Tell me."

The man looked up, his eyes going past his brother and locking on to Hull. He stood, his eyes going wide. "Are you a fan, Mr. Hull?" The detective met the man's gaze, searching for any sign of deceit or treachery. While he could not see anything, Hull knew that this man was certainly not here by choice. Everything that had transpired reeked of Moriarty.

"Fan of what?" Hull replied calmly, holding the man's sharp stare.

"Of the Doctor," the man replied. His next action was swift, his hand going to and from his jacket in a blur. He now held a small pistol, just small enough to go in the front pocket of his suitcase. Bradford brought his own gun up in as quick a fashion, evening it with the man's head.

Ghedi Rahim took one last step closer. "Taban, what are you doing?"

The man turned the gun to face the doctor. "I am so sorry, *abboowe.*"

Two shots followed: one from Taban's gun, the other from Bradford's. Both Ghedi and Taban fell, bullets having passed through their hearts. Hull raced to Ghedi's side as the man struggled for his last breaths. The detective lifted the man's head, cradling it and watching as tears started streaming down the old man's face.

"*Nabadeey, hoodaar,*" the man said, his voice going hoarse. "*Nabadeey.*" His head shifted to the side, his neck going limp. Hull softly set him down, crossing the man's arms across his chest.

"*Boji ku Nabad*, Ghedi Rahim," Hull muttered.

"Detective?"

Hull stood and looked to Bradford, who had gone to Taban. He'd removed the gun from the man's lifeless hand, but had found something else in his palm. He held a yellow sticky note, once crumpled but now open. He looked at Hull with a stern face, just like the one when they'd first met. Hull walked over to him slowly, and when he was in reach, the inspector held out the note for him to take.

"Some kind of riddle," Bradford said. "No idea what it means." Hull took it carefully, eyes going over the contents and instantly recognizing it. That recognition came with the most horrific feeling in the pit of his stomach. Taban's question made sense now. He looked over the note once more, feeling ashamed at having not realized what was happening earlier.

> *Tick tock goes the clock,*
> *He cradled and he rocked her.*
> *Tick tock goes the clock,*
> *Even for the Doctor.*

He clutched the note tight and closed his eyes, mentally smacking himself for his stupidity. *The Doctor. Not any doctor. My doctor.* He pulled the former poem from his pocket, holding it out for him to read. *When All Light Keeping Err Receives. When I Lest Letting. Does In Expect.*

W.A.L.K.E.R. W.I.L.L. D.I.E.

He crushed the poem in his hand, returning it and the sticky note to his pocket. He turned and started away, thinking of where Walker had said he would be. It made perfect sense, in hindsight. Distract Hull long enough to send in the perfect agent. Perfect perfect perfect. Before he could reach the street, he stopped and turned, eyes falling on Bradford, who had started walking as well.

"Tell me your name," Hull said as he approached the man.

"Matthew," the inspector replied.

Hull extended his hand. "It has been a pleasure working with you, Matthew Bradford. I now know that in times like these, we can overlook the details we deem as momentarily unimportant. I do not intend to make that mistake again."

Bradford shook the detective's hand. "Well, Mr. Sheridan Hull, it's been great."

Hull turned and started once again towards the road, knowing the competent, clever inspector would be able to sort everything that had transpired. Hull knew where he had to be.

Tick tock goes the clock.

He'd been a fool to think Moriarty wouldn't come after Walker now. He'd been even more of a fool to think the traitorous woman had changed. Now she was no doubt in the perfect position to strike Walker, to kill him, without him even standing a fighting chance.

He cradled and he rocked her.

The dancing. Of course it would be at the club. He'd come to know Walker very well, and knew that the man had a keen love of dancing. He would be at his highest, despite everything. Despite his injury, despite the current situation falling over the city. He would be with the woman he loved, and whom he believed loved him, and he would be partaking in a physical and social activity that he thoroughly enjoyed.

Tick tock goes the clock.

He could already be dead by now. The luring distraction of a complex, brutal murder, followed by a missing ambassador. All of it was too sweet an opportunity for someone like Hull to pass up, and Moriarty was very well aware of that. Hull had been a fool, the worst of fools. He had gone off and left Walker alone, even though he knew Moriarty intended to bring about destruction on them. Moriarty's focus was on Hull. But that focus, that determination to bring about the end, would expand. Certain doom would come for many.

Even for the Doctor.

*

I held the door open in typical gentlemen fashion, letting Cassidy exit the club with me in tow. It had been a long afternoon that moved into the night, but it had been absolutely amazing. What started with a wonderful dinner had moved to the dance club, a type of place I hadn't gone to in a very long time, perhaps since before my deployment. And spending it all with Cassidy, her blonde hair flowing over her shoulders, her inviting lipstick, and her figure-complementing dress all making her the most beautiful woman he'd ever seen.

"So, Miss Claypool," I said as we started towards the parking lot. "Where shall our next destination be?"

She smiled at me, but I could see something was on her mind, distracting her and keeping her from genuinely meaning the smile she provided. "Whatever you want to do, John. I'm open to anything."

"I suppose we can head back to my flat," I suggested. "Don't think Hull would be back yet, but even if he was, he wouldn't care."

"Yes, we can do that," she replied. I glanced over at her, noting the hesitancy in her voice.

"What's wrong?" I asked as we turned into the lot.

"It's nothing."

"Are you sure?"

Before she could reply, her eyes widened and she stopped. I looked forward to see a figure emerge from the dark shadows on our left, grabbing Cassidy and slamming her chest-first into the nearest car. I moved to hit the man, but before my fist could make contact with his chin, I realized who it was.

"What the *Hell* are you doing?!" I barked at Hull as he secured Cassidy's hands.

"I told you coming events would not bode well," he replied. "This is one of them."

"You're treating my girlfriend like a criminal!"

"Because she *is* a criminal."

"Stop!"

Cassidy's yell drew both Hull and I's attention to her. She'd made no attempt to resist Hull's restraint, but I could see tears in her eyes. Not from pain. From something else.

"Let me go," she said coolly, "and I will explain, if you will drive."

Hull held her arms together, but I could see him ease up on the force. "Who drive where?"

"You," she spat back. He let her go carefully, stepping back as she turned to face us. "I'm taking you to him. Unannounced." Hull nodded at her, then started for our car.

"Hold on, taking us to who!" I yelled as the two walked away. "Will someone explain to me what's going on?"

Cassidy glanced back at me as she opened the rear passenger door. "I will, John. Please get in the car." I stared at her for a long moment, not understanding *at all* what had just happened. The evening had gone from perfectly blissful to absolutely confusing, all with the arrival of Hull. How typical. I stepped into the back seat reluctantly and stared at the rearview mirror, right into Hull's eyes. He matched the stare until Cassidy took the seat next to me.

"Where am I going?" Hull asked stoically.

"Gold Bar Tower Club, on the corner of Onze and 34th," Cassidy replied, her eyes going to me. "John, I'm so sorry. But I haven't been honest with you about a lot of things."

My heart stopped for just a moment. "Like what? You know you can—"

"No," she interjected, closing her eyes. "Please, just let me explain. Don't talk until I'm done. It's easier that way." I nodded, folding my hands in my lap and giving her my full attention. "My name isn't Cassidy Claypool. It's Veronica. Veronica Faith Daemon. And I didn't work as a magician's assistant, or as a waitress now." She gulped before continuing. "I wasn't born in California, and I don't have a strained relationship with my parents. I was born in Russia, and have never known my parents. I spent the first thirteen years of my life living by myself with other orphans who had given up hope.

"When I was fourteen, I started becoming more brave with my thoughts on how much I could steal from local shops in Moscow. And I got caught taking the jewelry box of a very rich woman. On my way to being locked away, a hooded man stopped the car, claiming to be my father and that he would deal with me. But instead, he brought me here, to Newfield. He told me of an organization he ran, and how I would help him. He called himself Moriarty.

"He gave me a life. He paid for my college. He did everything. But then it all started going downhill in early 2011. He became obsessed with this consulting detective, and he worried that the man would interfere with his plans. He always had plans. Big, elaborate plans that he'd only tell me about when it was time to start. I swear, he's lost so much of himself to this. He didn't seem so bad when he brought me here. But I should've known better.

"I'm sorry, John. I lied to you about so much. But I've changed. I promise you, I have." She took my hands in hers. "Everything I've said. About you and me. I've meant it. You've helped me so much. And he doesn't understand that, and he can't understand that. He's wanted me to watch you and tell him of everything you both were doing, but everything I've told him has been a lie. I've helped you as much as I could."

"And what about tonight," Hull added, eyes locked on the road.

She shot him a glance before sighing. "He wanted me to come after you tonight. To kill you. But I wouldn't. I knew I would never go through with it."

I looked into her eyes, seeing the truth and sincerity. I wanted to be angry, I really did. But I couldn't. Because I knew she had been on our side. It made sense. So much sense. "It was you, in the tomb."

The car screeched to the side of the road, Hull's head turning to look at her. "How could I have overlooked that!"

"What?" I shouted, looking from him to the front windshield.

"You stacked the decks," the detective stated. "You stacked them in our favor. He would have demanded fairness but you ensured our victories."

I saw some color enter her cheeks. "I may have done that, yes."

He twisted his neck back around and tore the car back into traffic. "I knew it. I never win at cards."

She looked back to me with tears in her eyes. "I'm so sorry, John. I am."

Before I could reply, Hull brought the car to a screeching halt again. "We are here."

I glanced out the window, seeing the bright neon sign that read "GOLD BAR TOWER CLUB" above a two-story building. Hull jumped from his seat and walked around, tossing the keys to me as I exited. Cassidy, or Veronica, as she was apparently named, stepped in front of Hull, giving him a cautious gaze.

"You have to let me lead. They'll never let us into the right room otherwise," she stated. Hull matched her gaze, his own eyes narrowing to a glare. I gave him a slight nudge, a symbol of trust. We could trust her, even if I wasn't sure I could. She nodded at us, then stepped through the door, us following suit.

We entered a dimly lit room formatted like a bar, with most of the people at the far end tables. Daemon nodded at the bartender, who watched the three of us enter while cleaning a glass. She led us towards the side, where a doorway waited. Through the door was a narrow hallway that led us to a storage room of sorts. After sidling past several large crates, we found ourselves standing at the doors of a service elevator. Daemon pressed all three available options and stood back as the doors creaked open.

"Chimaera's center of command is located in the second story of a bar?" Hull asked as we entered the lift.

Daemon coughed. "Not the second story, no." The doors closed and the elevator gave a lurch, starting in an unexpected downwards motion. We stood in silence until the lift came to a halt and the doors opened once more, revealing a dark passage. She led us down the passage and to another door, this one sliding into the wall and revealing an even darker room. Daemon glanced back at us before stepping in. "I'm going to do something I've never done before." She reached her hand to the left and held it there.

I shielded my eyes as the lights in the room came on, revealing bright white walls, a desk and chair, an armchair behind them, and of all things, a pool table. Daemon moved her hand along the wall again, allowing the lights to dim to a more acceptable brightness. Hull and I stood at her side, my eyes focusing on the desk, Hull's on the pool table. With everything going on, I'd almost missed the sound of a small ticking noise.

Her and I went towards the desk while Hull moved to the table. She sat down at the chair and tapped on the desk, revealing an illuminated keyboard. Suddenly, nine screens burst to life above the desk, each currently acting as a separate-functioning screen. She typed in a password and browsed through the different options, her hands moving like a skilled artist's would at an easel.

"This was my job," she stated. "Any and all logistics of Chimaera, I oversaw. Keeping all of the operatives and agents coordinated in their respected fields. Anything they did came through me before going to him."

I leaned closer to her, my eyes on the screen. "Then what's all of this about? Why did he attack city hall? What's it all for?"

"Eleven countries," Hull announced from behind us. I glanced back to see his eyes on the pool table, his hand running softly along the edges.

"What?" I asked as I started towards him.

"Eleven countries. That is how he intends to do it."

"Do what?"

He looked back at me. "War on an international scale. Eleven countries. Romania. Croatia. Iran. Germany. Afghanistan. Iraq. Pakistan. Russia. North Korea. Venezuela. Somalia. Eleven countries with Chimaera-filled insurrectionist groups, all turning their sights on the United States to bring us into World War III."

I shook my head as I reached his side, looking down at the pool table. Instead of the usual green cloth, the table was filled with diagrams, lists, and statistics, all surrounding the names of eleven countries. "He'd never be able to do it. Not even with the full strength of Chimaera."

"It's not about the single strength of Chimaera, it's the unified strength of them all, each country individually spurned with a reason to be angry, each country poked and prodded with their own purposes to be hostile. He was creating the perfect environment for chaos."

I glanced down at the table again, my eyes falling to the very bottom, the part closest to us. Something had been scratched into the wood, probably recently. I ran my fingers over it, not able to quite make it out. "What's this?"

Hull looked down at it, his eyes going from peered to very wide. He looked at the rest of the table, and for a second, I swear I could see his ears move, as if they were attuning themselves to something in the room. He looked from the table to me, his cheek twitching.

"Tick tock goes the clock," he murmured. But I had no time to question. The lights in the room shut down, plunging us all into darkness. I looked to where Daemon had sat, but even the screens had died. I would've called out for her, but someone beat me to speaking. Someone I never wanted to hear from in that particular moment.

"No loose ends."

There were the sounds of a shot and a scream.

ENDGAME

You know that phrase some people use, saying two hearts beat as one? As a medical man who didn't care much for phrases, that never made sense to me. I suppose it seemed redundant. Of course it was possible for two hearts to beat as one; all they had to do was beat at the same time. Not that difficult, since a heart beats only so many times in a minute, maybe once a second or more. Synchronized heartbeats couldn't have been that rare.

And for a long time, that was my thought process. The literal interpretation of something that didn't mean anything to me. But now? Now I understand. Now I get it. Because I'd been at the side of a bed for coming on fourteen hours. I hadn't eaten, or slept, or even moved. I'd sat there, in the seat by the bed, my hand clutching hers, the only sound in the room coming from the heartbeat monitor. So, you could say that, for fourteen hours, two hearts had certainly beat as one.

Because with every beat of hers, my heart would beat, just to keep me going long enough to see her eyes open one more time.

I glanced up from her still face, looking at the heart rate monitor for the umpteenth time in the past hour. It just didn't strike me as fair, all of this. Despite everything that had been revealed, I felt obligated to be sitting here. Because what she'd said was the truth.

Because people like her, people who'd been caught up in the wrong situation fighting for reasons they didn't know otherwise, were allowed to be forgiven. I should know; I fought in a war.

Moriarty had disappeared before Hull and I could turn the lights back on, and we'd found her lying on the floor with a bloody wound in the center of her chest. We'd carried her back out to the car and brought her here, to Newfield General, where she'd been taken into intensive care for surgery. The lobby was the last place I'd seen Hull since, actually. He'd immediately departed, saying he had something very important to follow up on. I understood; she wasn't his responsibility. No, not responsibility. She simply wasn't important to him. But to me, even now, she was.

They let me help. During the surgery, I mean. I'd assisted with the trauma control once the surgeon had extracted the bullet. It had missed her heart by mere centimeters. Her following unconsciousness was a result of shock, blood loss, and sedatives. They wanted her to get a long, proper rest, giving the wound some time to recuperate. Even though it hadn't been fatal, the shot was certainly enough to incapacitate her. And once I'd had some time to truly calm down and consider the events, that was probably what Moriarty had wanted. Well, I'm sure he would have preferred her dead. But this was his target all along.

He knew, and that's what scared me the most about him. Here we were, noses pressed against the shield of a man equally as clever as Hull, and yet far more devious. I'd been with Hull long enough to know that he had rules. There were certain boundaries he would not cross, even for the sake of a mystery. He was one of the most emotionless people I knew, if not *the* most, but he still had morals. He knew the difference between right and wrong. And that was what set him and Moriarty apart. Moriarty was willing to do anything to bring his enemies to their knees.

He didn't want to kill us. He wanted to torture us.

Besides this, news had reached me of Carla Montorum's murder. I don't think it was public, but being who I was, people were more lenient on talking to me about sensitive matters. I'd imagine I was told around the same time as the mayor, who was apparently still a floor below. If the murmurs between the doctors and nurses were true, he hadn't taken the news well. His condition, however bad it may be, had worsened significantly. Some of the doctors didn't think he would leave the hospital for at least a month or potentially longer.

The only other thing that people seemed to be talking about was the storm. I'd seen it starting the day before, just clouds on the horizon, but now it was getting bad. Local meteorologists predicted this storm to last at the minimum a few days. Heavy rain, thunder and lightning. They were expecting it to be the worst storm to hit McMullen County in over four years. But I really wouldn't have anything from over two years ago to compare it to. My storms back then were very different.

I looked from the monitor to the door as it opened, allowing a tall doctor with a blue cap to enter. His hands were hidden beneath white latex gloves and the bottom half of his face behind a blue mask. He nodded at me before walking over to the monitor, pulling the keyboard to his front and tapping away. I didn't want to be suspicious, but I was. Every doctor who came in had some thing or another that made me worry. I expected Moriarty to try and finish the job, I guess.

"How has she been?" the doctor asked, his voice endearing and oddly high.

"Stable," I replied, still holding her hand. "Nothing substantial."

"Good, good," the doctor replied. He pushed the keyboard away and glanced at me. "And how about you, Doctor?"

I blinked a few times, my brow furrowed. "I'm doing fine, thanks. How'd you know I was a doctor?"

"A normal man wouldn't have known nothing substantial had happened to her, even though there are regular heart fluctuations," the doctor replied as he tapped the monitor. "A medical man would have recognized them as her pre-diagnosed cardiac dysrhythmnia and resulting tachycardia."

I narrowed my eyes at the man. "I don't think I caught your name."

"Dr. Jacques Retenue," the man replied. He glanced back down at her body. "She'll heal with time." He turned towards the door and started away.

"And what about you, Doctor?" I asked.

The man stopped and looked over his shoulder. "I have other patients who require my attention."

I gave a short nod and smirked. "Just tell me before you leave."

*

The doctor closed the door behind him quietly and started forward, going down the hall he'd walked just three minutes ago and essentially reversing the motions he'd made. He removed the latex gloves and tucked the blue cap from his head, ruffling his dark blonde hair as he went and folding the cap into the pocket of his scrub pants. Next he removed the doctor's coat, making sure to grab the falsified name tag as he hung the coat on a rack. On a cluttered table sat a blue wristband, which he scooped up with his hand and quickly squeezed over his fingers. He continued forward, throwing both gloves and his mask in the trash can to his left.

He nodded at a nurse and continued forward, grabbing two brown-with-blue-stripes gloves from another table and stretching them over his hands. He grabbed the coat next, long and gray reaching down below his knees, and slipped his arms inside. Lastly, he grabbed the purple scarf waiting for him on a doorknob, wrapping it around his neck in its usual fashion. He patted down his sides to make sure he hadn't forgotten anything, and when he was quite satisfied with the end result, Sheridan Hull continued with his stride towards the doorway at the far end of the hall.

He opened the door and stepped through, finding himself in a room similar to the one he'd just left, except the lights weren't on and the monitors had been turned off. Lying on the bed was a young man, maybe nineteen or twenty in age, with a large bandage wrapped around his forehead. His eyes were closed and his hands were clasped on his chest. Sitting on the couch against the far wall, windows blinded behind him, was a suited man, his focus not on the boy or on Hull, but rather on the unlit monitor that once displayed the boy's heart rate.

"Single shot, passing through the frontal lobe and exiting the occipital," the man, Malcolm Hull, stated. "No hope for a peaceful survival. His parents had the life support shut down one hour and fifteen minutes ago."

"And yet," Sheridan said as he closed the door behind him, "here you are."

Malcolm stood, hands going behind his back and eyes falling on the dead boy. "He was the last one to be with her. I would assume he attempted to stop the abduction and was shot by the attacker."

Sheridan came to stand at the opposite side of the bed, his gaze lowering as well. "They seemed quite happy together."

"I will be joining you in finding her."

"Too dangerous."

"Sheridan, she is my daughter." Malcolm's gaze was now locked on his younger brother. "No force of nature or man could stop me from finding her. I regret to admit, I have stood idly by and watched these events unfold with the hopes that you would not underestimate Moriarty. Now I see I was mistaken."

Sheridan's eyes shot up. "I did not *underestimate* Moriarty. I expected this."

"Absolutely, utterly irrelevant," Malcolm shot back. "I am coming with you, and we will find my daughter." Sheridan looked the man up and down, knowing that bringing another person into the mixture was dangerous, even if it was Bailey's father and his brother. Objectively speaking, he should have been able to trust the man without so much as a second thought.

But that was most certainly not the case.

"Where was he found?" the detective asked.

Malcolm stepped back, grabbing his umbrella from the couch. "He was on the ground next to his car, in the Regal 11 parking lot."

Sheridan started for the door. "I assume you have a car on standby outside?" He opened the door and gave a slight scoff. "Or five."

"No. I came in my own car. No one else."

"Good. That'll make it easier."

"For what?"

"I dislike being transported by your people."

The brothers left the hospital, Sheridan making sure he was one step ahead as they went. Malcolm stayed the step behind until they reached the hospital parking lot, when the older man took the lead towards a black car parked in a reserved section. Malcolm took the driver seat while Sheridan took the passenger, immediately diverting his attention to the window. The drive would have gone in complete silence, all twenty minutes of it, had a thought not started nagging at the back of the detective's mind. He gulped, blinked, and licked his lips before speaking.

"I'm sorry about your friend," he said, his eyes still on the window.

"Ghedi's death was not your doing. And I fear that if not for your involvement, we may have never known who his murderer was," Malcolm replied. Nothing more needed to be said.

The car came to a halt in a parking spot, with a taped off car parked against a building wall ahead of them. There were several evidence markers, none of them having any actual relevance, but there were no police officers, forensic investigators, or inspectors on site. Sheridan stepped out of the car and glanced around, his eyes peered.

"Why is no one conducting an investigation?" he asked as Malcolm stepped out.

"No one is available. The entirety of the law enforcement in this city has been thrown into disarray, and not as a result of Gregory Lennox's appointment. Your adversary has been far more versatile in his creation of conflicts than anyone could have predicted." The man sighed. "I have even had to take up the title of city commissioner as a result of Ghedi's passing."

"Not even a single person sent to help in the tracking down of the daughter of one of the most important people in the United States government?" Sheridan questioned as he stepped over the police tape.

"My importance is hardly of their concern. The city is at risk of total collapse," Malcolm responded as he lifted the tape with his umbrella. "The needs of the many outweigh the needs of the few."

Sheridan stooped down to look at the ground next to the car, where several watered down patches of blood remained. He pulled the collapsible magnifying glass from his pocket and glazed over the patches slowly before looking into the car. "Body found on the ground. Seatbelt is slack in the car, so he was pulled. Blood on the ground is minor compared to inside the car." He raised up and tilted his gaze, now looking inside the car.

"He had marks on his neck," Malcolm noted, standing in front of the car. "But the attacker would not have used both a knife and a gun in such a short burst."

"The marks came from the seatbelt," Sheridan replied as he tugged the seatbelt, causing it to snap back up into its usual place. "He was leaning over towards the passenger seat, probably the last motion he made. To shield Bailey from the attack." The detective turned to the steering wheel and tapped the keys in the ignition. "Key is bent. He tried to start the car but was shot before they could move."

"He made the mistake of unrolling the window to speak with the attacker," Malcolm stated, "and once he realized the person's intentions, he lunged to protect Bailey and attempted to start the car. The attacker fired his gun once, piercing the boy's skull and causing the spray of blood that is moving towards the passenger and back sides of the car without touching the dashboard."

"Her purse was left behind," Sheridan said as he pulled the purse up from where the passenger's feet would go.

"The only thing missing is her cell phone."

"Not sure I want to know how you're certain of that."

"Bailey possesses qualities you and I share. Do not carry what you do not need."

Sheridan stepped out of the car. "And I presume the cell phone is deactivated, otherwise you would have traced it by now."

"Correct."

The detective stepped around the back of the car, looking at the narrow space between the passenger door and the wall of the building. "His body was pulled from the car after he was shot and left on the ground. Bailey was then pulled from the driver seat, taking only her phone with her. She could not have been pulled from here because the door shows no signs of having touched the wall, and it never would have opened wide enough for her to be pulled free without having made contact."

He walked back around to the driver side, eyes surveying the primary seat. "If the attacker had pulled Bailey through, he would have set the gun down, probably on the seat. But Bailey would have made his job difficult, so grabbing the gun would have proven even more challenging once he'd freed her from the car. His time was short, so naturally, he would have left it behind. The gun is not on the driver seat and was not taken as evidence, leaving it..." He reached his hand under the driver seat and pulled out a sleek pistol.

"I recognize that model," Malcolm said as he walked closer. "It matches the one used by a Chimaera agent, capable of firing a round through bulletproof glass."

Sheridan pulled a plastic bag from his pocket and slipped the gun in, then tucked the gun and bag away inside his coat. He stepped away from the car, spinning slowly to encompass the parking lot. "Attacker would have been close enough to grab Bailey and move without too much time elapsing." He stopped when his eyes found the faint tire marks in a parking spot three plots over. The plot bordered a lamp post, with its base hidden inside a transplanted bush. "Tracks go to the left, and the distance between the axles would suggest a fairly large vehicle, a van with potentially four rows of seats."

"Most vans of that design have the back row entrance on the passenger side," Malcolm added.

Sheridan walked closer to the bush, his eyes and mind racing. "You were right. She does possess qualities like us. She's a Hull, and as such, she's clever. So, in the last moments for her, the last time she would have to leave something to help, what would she do? With limited resources and only seconds before the attacker sealed the door, how would she react?" He glanced back at the car, eyes going to where the purse had been. "Of course. The only thing missing was her cell phone."

The detective turned back to the bush and starting pulling the shrub branches apart, looking close to the ground for his intended item. It took him seconds to find the outline of a phone in the dirt, and only a second more to extract it. He held the phone delicately, showing it to his older brother for confirmation.

"That is hers, yes," the man replied. Sheridan brought the phone down and held down the power button. It took its time on coming to life, but when it did, it presented a picture of his niece and the boy from the hospital, smiling, happy, together. He switched past the welcome screen and was immediately taken to the messages, where an unsent text was waiting.

"REGALCAM," Sheridan stated as he stood.

"What?"

"It's what she left us," the detective replied, turning to face his brother and nodding at the building behind him. "REGALCAM." Malcolm turned to look at the building, seeing a security camera in the corner, set to rotate but currently facing them.

Malcolm cocked his head back. "Ah."

*

The brothers walked through the cinema doors and found themselves in a relatively empty lobby. It was early morning, so the emptiness wasn't too shocking. It was just another reminder of the state Newfield was in. Life went on for everyone, but there were still marks of how events had affected the city's society. Sheridan glanced at the nearby wall, eyes seeing the movies currently playing, a calendar, and other miscellaneous posters. There were only two days until Independence Day. He pulled out his phone and set himself a reminder, then joined Malcolm at the customer service table.

A young man, younger than the boy who'd accompanied Bailey, exited from the office and approached the table. His hair was similar to Sheridan and Malcolm's, a dark blonde that bordered brown. He had deep green eyes behind the lenses of his glasses. He wore the standard uniform of the cinema and held a clipboard, looking up at the visitors with some slight boredom. Sheridan, however, looked the boy up and down a few times, his eyes narrowed. The boy gave the detective a familiar glance before widening his eyes.

"Tyler Belt," Sheridan announced, extending his hand to the boy.

He shook the man's hand. "You're the detective who saved my life."

"Glad to see you're still living it."

"Still in school, a part-time job," Belt replied. "We've got the week off from school, actually. They said it's for the 4th, but I'm more willing to believe it's everything else going on."

"Unfortunately," the detective said as he crossed his arms. "How are your siblings?"

"Good. We live with my aunt and uncle now. It's been hard, but we get by."

"Glad to hear it. Hopefully you can help me with something now."

"Sure, anything."

"Last night, my niece was abducted from the parking lot outside. And if I'm right, and I usually am," he said with a nod at the office Belt had come from, "the security cameras will have caught her attacker in the act."

"Oh wow," the boy replied with a frown. "I'd heard about it, I'm so sorry. Here." He opened the half-door next to the counter. "Come on back."

Sheridan and Malcolm followed the boy into the office, passing through an employee lounge and leading them to a surveillance room. Belt sat down at the only chair and brought up a directory, filing through until he found the footage from the night before. He forwarded through the eventless parts and reached when a single black van pulled up and a man stepped out.

Events played out exactly as Sheridan had stated: the attacker fired through the driver window, pulled the boy's body free, then dragged Bailey to the van and out of sight. The van started and drove away, reaching the road and vanishing from sight.

"Take it back to the van turning," Malcolm requested. Belt rewound the footage to the time, then stopped. Malcolm pointed right to where the van's license plate was, completely visible and ready to be tracked. Sheridan pulled his phone back out and dialed a number, pressing the screen against his ear.

"Lennox?" he asked. "I need a license plate tracked. Plate identification T04 311. Text me the information." He hung up and stared at the screen for a long moment. "Of course those would be the digits."

The three walked back to the lobby, where Sheridan bid the boy goodbye. Together, Malcolm and Sheridan left, heading towards their car while the detective awaited a text message. They entered the car and sat in silence, the older brother staring at the taped-off vehicle and the younger focusing on his phone. With the spare moments they had, Sheridan pulled up his own messages and selected a new contact, one he hadn't bothered to message before. He gave Malcolm a quick side-glance and, once he was sure the older man wasn't watching, he started typing a quick message.

Happy Birthday. -SH

He sent the message and sighed, knowing that the acknowledgement of a birthday was pointless and stupid, but the message's recipient would appreciate it. He glanced back down as the phone buzzed with a message from Lennox.

"We have the address," he stated as he showed the phone to Malcolm. The older man nodded and started on their way. It led them to an old apartment complex, one that had been closed and was due for removal in about a month's time. The caution tape that had blocked the door was now torn, and the door itself was wide open. Sheridan and Malcolm walked up the steps and through the door cautiously, glancing around the dark stairwell as they entered.

"Search the upper levels," Sheridan stated as he started forward. "I can take the basement." Malcolm nodded and quickly started up the stairs. Sheridan watched and waited for his brother to reach the second floor before slowly moving to the elevator and entering. He waited patiently as the machine took him one floor down, the door creaking open to reveal a long hallway. He walked the length of the hallway without fear or hesitation, knowing exactly what was waiting for him on the other side of the oncoming doorway.

He stepped through the door and into a room with one lamp, hanging in the center. Below the lamp was a table, which was occupied by a chess set waiting to be played. Two chairs sat facing each other around the table, one close to Hull, the other near the only other occupant of the room. Hull stared at the hooded man for a long moment before he turned, giving a welcoming gesture to the detective.

"Glad you could make it," Moriarty stated.

"Would never have considered it," Hull replied as he closed the door. He clasped his hands behind his back as he stepped forward, Moriarty also taking a step and planting his metal cane on the concrete floor.

"Let's not stand on tense ground. We are both very intelligent gentlemen in our own regard." Moriarty extended his right hand. "It's only natural we acknowledge that." Hull reluctantly extended his own hand, which the other man grasped. Moriarty's shake was a single one, with a firm ending. He released the detective's hand and looked down. "Care for a game? I would wager to say your brother will take some time searching every room of the upper four stories."

"I can't think of an excuse not to," Hull replied as he took his seat. Moriarty set his cane down next to the table and seated himself, arching his shoulders and causing his cloak to expand. He rested his forearms on the table, his gloved fingers twitching. Hull's pieces were white; Moriarty's were black.

"Your move, Detective," Moriarty stated. Hull looked down at the pieces and board, all made of glass. He tried to focus on the reflection of his opponent, but even with the glaring light above them, it wasn't enough to illuminate the man's face. He reached out and grabbed the pawn on E2 and brought it forward two spaces, then returned his hand to his lap. Moriarty's gloved hand grabbed the pawn on C7 and moved it up one. Hull looked up to where the man's eyes would be, knowing that this would prove to be a very, very long game.

Pawn on D2 to D4. Pawn on D7 to D5. *Knight on B1 to C3.* Pawn on D5 takes pawn on E4. *Knight on C3 takes pawn on E4.* Knight from G8 moves to F6. *Knight on E4 takes knight on F6, enter check.* Pawn from E7 takes knight from F6.

"Have I ever told you the origins of my title?" Moriarty asked. *Bishop from F1 moves to C4.*

"No," Hull replied. Bishop on F8 moves to D6.

"It's Irish, actually. My family came from Ireland many years ago." *Knight on G1 to F3.* "My grandfathers of old were drawn to the seas. They quickly earned the title of 'expert navigators'." Rook from H8 to king, resulting in castling. "And of course, everything must have a proper title rather than just a combination of words, shouldn't it?"

Rook from H1 to king, another castling. "Mm." Rook on F8 to E8. *Bishop from C4 to D3.*

"The title, in Irish, was Moriarty." Bishop from C8 to G4. "A common family name, but it seemed to grow on us." *Pawn on H2 to H3.* "Many members of my family have since used the name. It was a personal favorite of mine." Bishop on G4 to H5. "Ironic, though. How it would come to mean more than just its translation."

Pawn, C2 to C4. "Indeed." Queen, D8 to C7.

"Not very chatty while playing, are you?"

Pawn, C4 to C5. "No."

"Shame." Bishop from D6 to H2, enter check. "Conversations always tend to keep things going."

King, G1 to H1. "I would certainly hate to end this early." Bishop, H2 to F4.

"Aren't you excited, Sheridan?" *King back to G1.*

"For what." Knight on B8 to D7.

"We've been building up to this for quite some time, you and I." *Pawn, B2 to B4.* "This game of ours." Bishop from F4 takes bishop on C1.

"Excitement is not the word I would use." *Rook from A1 takes bishop.*

Queen from C7 to F4. "What word would you use, then?" *Pawn, G2 to G4.*

"Expected."

Bishop from H5 to G6. "Of course, expected. Typical choice for you." *Bishop on D3 takes bishop from G6.* "You, the clever detective, the man striving to always be one step ahead." Pawn on H7 takes bishop. "You could see anything coming, couldn't you?"

Rook from F1 to E1. "To the best of my abilities."

"And how good are those abilities, would you say?" Pawn, F6 to F5.

"Very good." *Rook from E1 takes rook on E8, enter check.* Rook moves from A8 to rook.

"Tell me this, then." *Pawn, G4 to G5.* "If you knew your niece would be abducted, why not attempt to prevent it?" Knight, D7 to F8.

"Would an attempt at prevention have been successful?" *Pawn, H3 to H4.*

Moriarty chuckled. "You tell me." Queen from F4 to G4, enter check.

King, G1 to H2. "You are a patient man. Had I intervened, you simply would have waited." Knight, F8 to E6.

"You're a patient man as well, Sheridan." *Rook from C1 to C3.* "We would've been locked in a game of patience." Rook, E8 to D8.

"I would say that game has been in play for a very long time." *Queen, D1 to G1.* Queen from G4 takes queen.

King on H2 takes queen. "You'd be right." Knight on E6 takes pawn on D4. *King, G1 to G2.* Knight from D4 to F3, takes knight. "But you could have at least tried to save your kin from certain peril." *Rook from C3 takes knight.* Rook from D8 to D4.

"It was easier to let you act." *Pawn, A2 to A3.* Rook from D4 to H4, takes pawn.

"And now that I have," *Rook from F3 to D3*, "what do you intend to do?"

Pawn, A7 to A5. "Telling you would be playing fair." *Pawn, B4, takes pawn, A5.* "I can say we are past that point."

"I suppose we are." Rook from H4 to G4, enter check. *King from G2 to F3.*

It's not too late, you know." Rook from G4 to C4. "You could easily turn yourself in. Again."

Rook from D3 to D8, enter check. "That'd make things too easy." King, G8 to H7. "I'd hate to make things easy. Besides, I'm so close to achieving peace." *Rook, D8 to A8.* "To finally creating order from the chaos." Rook from C4 takes pawn, C5.

"You still find that plausible, do you." *Rook, A8 to A7.*

"Not just plausible. *Expected.*" Rook from C5 to C3, enter check.

King, F3 to E2. "Clever." Rook on C3 takes pawn, A3.

"In fact, I quite look forward to when things are said and done." *Rook, A7, takes pawn, B7.* "When order has been obtained. I may take a vacation." Rook from A3 to A5, takes pawn. "Find the certain sense of bliss that comes from standing at the tallest point and looking out over the world."

Rook, B7 to F7, takes pawn. "I can only imagine." Rook from A5 to A2, enter check.

"You hold such a negative view of what I do." *King, E2 to E3.* "Would you have acted the same had iconic figures such as Franklin Roosevelt, Martin Luther King, Jr., or John Kennedy preached what I strive for?" Pawn, C6 to C5.

"Iconic figures like those gentlemen would never have sought order through chaos." *Rook from F7 to C7.* "Iconic figures like those men would have recognized insanity at its most formal and refined."

Rook from A2 to C2. "Insanity is a delicate thing, Sheridan. Very delicate." *Pawn, F2 to F4.* "But I suppose that is an explanation for another time, isn't it?" Rook from C2 to C4. "I do believe, given the pieces remaining, we have entered our endgame phase." *Rook, C7 to C6.* "Wouldn't you agree?"

"No." Rook, C4 to C3, enter check.

"Then you would be an ignorant fool."

King, E3 to F2. "Ignorant is not quite the word I would use."

"And what would you use?" Rook from C3 to C2, enter check.

King, F2 to E3. "Clever." Rook, C2 to C4.

"Use whatever terminology you like." *Rook, C6 to C7.* "It's quite clear to me that we are nearing the end of all things." Rook, C4 to C3, enter check. "Game-wise, and in other regards."

King, E3 to F2. "You of course refer to your overall scheme. Your plan to bring about paradoxical order." King, H7 to G8.

"You could say that, yes."

"Then I would be inclined to inform you that you are wrong." *Rook, C7 to C8, enter check.*

"I don't believe you have much say on the matter at all." King from G8 to H7.

Rook, C8 to C7. "I believe otherwise."

"Tell me, then, Sheridan Hull." Rook, C3 to C2, enter check. "What is your brilliant plan?"

King from F2 to E3. "Ask me another time."

King from H7 to G8. "We have time now."

Rook, C7 to C8, enter check. "Not for long."

King, G8 to F7. *Rook, C8 to C7, check.* King, F7 to F8. *Rook, C7 to C8, check.* King, F8 to F7. *Rook, C8 to C7, check.* King, F7 to F8. *Rook, C7 to C8, check.* King, F8 to F7.

"And with that number of repeated moves," Hull declared as he stood, "we have reached stalemate."

Moriarty stood from his seat slowly, grabbing his cane as he did. Hull watched the man timidly, not entirely certain how he would react. Moriarty set the tip of his cane down on the floor and nodded.

"A well played game, Detective," the man said. "A well played game indeed."

"I don't suppose my prize for winning is knowing the location of my niece," Hull said amiably.

The man chuckled. "I already told you. That's the best part." He glanced down at the chessboard for a long moment before sighing. "It's coming, Sheridan. It really is. The moment in which order is achieved. And I will step from the shadows and let them know I have been the one to bring about a new era of humanity. They will all look up and shout my name." He paused. "It's what they need, Sheridan. Control. Order. Peace. And it's what people like us can bring them."

Hull snorted. The man looked up at him and sighed, giving a slight shake to his head. "No, of course. You use your knowledge for them. To help them in such petty ways. Your knowledge is wasted." He turned and started walking towards the darkness. "But that is why there are two of us." Hull waited for the resounding click of an invisible door before he turned, reopened the door he'd come through, and walked back to the elevator. He waited patiently as the lift returned him to the first floor, where he found Malcolm coming down the flight of stairs.

"Not a trace of her to be found," the man said as he reached the last step.

"It doesn't matter," Sheridan said as he started for the door. "I know where we can find her."

*

They arrived at the building owned by Plyer Incorporated, which was now the tallest building in Newfield as a result of the Zenith Tower destruction. Gaining access to the building hadn't been too difficult at all; because Sheridan was still recognized as the man who brought Benjamin Arnold to justice, most of the members of the board of directors were very much inclined to assist him. The brothers had gone for the only elevator that led to the highest floor, which would grant them access to the roof.

They stood in the elevator silently, Sheridan's eyes watching the floor ticker and Malcolm's the door. There were fifty-five stories in total, and the elevator had so far taken them as high as twenty-three.

"Sheridan," the older man started, his eyes closing, "I am sorry. I never thought..."

"Please don't," the younger man warned, but Malcolm shook his head.

"No. I have to do this." He gulped and blinked his eyes several times. "I should have known better. I should have known that by swerving, it would put your car in danger. But I did not realize that at the time, and I accept full responsibility. For everything. Especially for Lydia's death. Not a single day goes by where I do not think of her, and miss her dearly. Please remember that. She was my sister, too. And I completely acknowledge that she is not here with us now because of my actions."

Sheridan offered no response for the rest of the trip up.

At the ding of the thirty-fourth floor, Sheridan's phone buzzed. He pulled it out slowly, checking only the contents of the screen. Once he'd read the message, he slipped it back in, not wanting to draw an inquiry from his brother, especially with this message.

You don't know how happy I am that you remembered. -CBD

The elevator dinged at the fifty-fifth floor, the door opening to reveal a dim area that was probably used for storage. The brothers moved past them and towards the emergency staircase to the roof. Thankfully, the people downstairs had turned the alarms off for the top floor, making sure they didn't automatically call the fire department as soon as they pushed open the door. They climbed the stairs quickly, reaching a red door with the word "ROOF" above it. Sheridan slammed the door with both hands and stepped out.

The storm had gained significant wind strength, and almost stopped him from keeping the door open long enough for Malcolm to step through. The roof itself was plain, with an overhang typically used for cleaning platforms. Instead of a platform, it currently held a single chair, occupied by a tied and blindfolded young woman. The chair dangled over the open air, meaning the slightest cut of the rope keeping it in place would send Bailey Hull plummeting the equivalent of fifty-six stories to her inevitable demise.

"Bailey!" Malcolm called out as he walked closer to her. She turned her head quickly towards the source, unable to speak due to the gag tied around her head and shoved into her mouth. "Sweetheart, we are here, just give us a moment to get you!"

Before either man could act, the door behind them burst open, allowing three men to walk through. Sheridan immediately recognized their uniforms as those of Chimaera agents. He turned to face them fully, waiting for them to stop in formation. All three held guns, one aimed at him, one at Malcolm, and one at Bailey.

"Do you really think putting yourself between a man and his endangered daughter is a smart idea?" Sheridan mocked as the three stepped forward. They offered no response, instead all turning to focus their fire on the detective. Sheridan gave a deep sigh, mentally hitting himself for his stupidity. Of course Moriarty would send people. Of course he would seek to complicate things. Because that was what he did. He created chaos.

Bang.

Sheridan flinched, but felt no pain. He opened his eyes.

Bang. Bang.

The remaining two agents fell forward, making all three incapacitated. From behind the open doorway stepped an armed figure, his black leather jacket billowing from the wind and his gun at the ready.

"You were supposed to tell me before you left," John Walker stated as he lowered his gun. Sheridan gave another deep sigh, this one of complete relief. He turned to see Malcolm pull Bailey back to the roof's ledge and start untying her. Sheridan and John moved to help, making sure she wasn't harmed in any way. Once she was completely free from the chair, she gave all three men hugs, then, with her father's coat wrapped around her, started towards the doorway.

"I will take her home," Malcolm stated, avoiding his wind-flapping tie. "Thank you." He turned and walked to follow his daughter. Sheridan turned to look out at the city, eyes going from the grayish greenish clouds above to the blandness of the other buildings, all stretching to the city limit before becoming open fields. Walker came to stand at his side, his arms crossed and a smirk on his face.

"Impeccable timing," Hull commented. "As usual."

"I try my best," the doctor replied with a curt nod. They stood in silence for quite some time before Hull lowered his head, staring down at the moving traffic with complete disinterest.

"I'm sorry," he said solemnly, his throat dry. "I involved you in all of this. I never dreamt of ending up here. Despite how clever I may be, I never expected this. Not everything that has happened."

"Don't apologize. Not for this." Walker nudged the detective and nodded out at the cityscape. "If not for this, I'd just be one of them." He paused for a moment before smiling. "I wouldn't trade this for anything."

Hull returned the smile, but only for a moment. His attention was once again drawn to the storm, then to the mountain range that lay to the east. "It's drawing to a close, John. The game. The mystery. All of our pieces have been played. Despite having a crime syndicate for an army, Moriarty is alone. We have eliminated all other pieces on the board. All the remains is the King. The last bastion for Chimaera."

"Then let's take him down."

Hull sighed. "If only it were so simple. Here we are, so deep in the mixture. Here we are, standing on the brink. To our left, the prospect of peace, and order, and functionality, not by the cause of strenuous circumstance but by the flow of time. To our right, the looming dark. The possibility of a city, a state, a nation, a *world*, conditioned to understand a false concept of order. A world in which Moriarty is the keeper of the keys, the master puppeteer. I cannot allow that to happen, John. We cannot. But at a time like now, after everything that has transpired?"

He paused for a long moment, a very long moment, before continuing. "I'm not sure I am up to the challenge. The final fight."

John breathed out heavily through his nose. "People need heroes, Sheridan. Heroes like you."

And so there they stood, the city below and the storm above, a darkness like no other looming inside the depths of the clouds, and an indiscernible future lying on the far reaches of the horizon. There they stood, at the end of the penultimate. The future of not just a city, but a society in its entirety, could have very well been resting on their shoulders. The shoulders of two men. The clever detective and the honorable doctor.

There they stood indeed.

FALL

A few words may suffice to tell what little that remains.

It took me a long time to decide on those words. Eleven words that all-too accurately described my mindset in approaching this. We often find that we can waste our time away describing things rather than experiencing them. We search desperately for the words that fit our moment, and in doing so, we fail to actually express the most core essences to it. But I suppose that is detracting from the point. The point that is my last entry to a long volume. The end. The story of the fall.

It had been two days since the abduction of Bailey Hull. That made today the Fourth of July. A holiday that would normally be met with barbecues, parades, and an evening filled with family and fireworks. But after everything that had happened to Newfield, a normal day was too much to ask for. The weather had yet to ease in its ferocity, and torrential downpours were forecasted for the next three to four days. Evening festivities would be rather difficult.

After Bailey's abduction, Hull had taken the next day to himself. As in, I didn't see him at all. He left before I'd woken and returned long after I'd gone to sleep. His mind was in another place, one so far off and locked away from the rest of the world that I had no hope in penetrating the hardened barriers that kept him disconnected. He'd transitioned from the man who simply wanted to solve the case, to the man who felt lacking in his ability to save the city. He was too hard on himself, and it showed.

A very interesting turn of events had occurred yesterday, however. The mayor, who only a day earlier had been in a critical condition, had checked out of the hospital. Many believed that he was doing so because he felt the need to help Newfield. I'm sure when he was elected, he never would've imagined something on a scale like this. He'd dismissed his staff and decided to do his business from home until a more suitable location was constructed. I couldn't help but feel bad for the man. Coming back to a house that was once home to not only him, but his wife and son... it had to be taxing.

At about eight this morning, just after I'd finished making a pot of coffee, Hull had stepped from his room, fully dressed, and informed me of a very important robbery that had taken place the night before. Lennox had called him not even ten minutes ago requesting his help. The detective had given me time to prepare and, before long, we were on our way through the rainstorm to a location that brought back many, many memories. The robbery had taken place at Warmack Chemical, one of the first places I visited alongside Hull.

We moved up the long concrete walkway that led to the central building of the factory, its four smokestacks spewing their waste into the cloud-stricken sky. When we'd first come, we'd been directed to the visitor center; now our destination was towards the back, in the primary distribution building. Hull walked with his hands in his pockets, his coat collar up and his scarf billowing from the fierce wind coming from the west. I had my normal leather coat and jeans, an outfit I wish I'd planned out more accordingly. A police officer escorted us around the facility, following a driveway that led to the distribution center.

I could tell which building we were going to from the moment we turned the corner. The distribution center was tall, about half the height of the smokestacks, with squared windows up at the highest points. Six large garage doors lined the side facing us, as well as the driveway. And, the biggest hint: one garage door was torn free from its holdings, now lying in metal scrap pieces around the front of the adjacent door. Hull and I stepped into the center and found it lined with crates arranged in aisles, stretching up at least a hundred feet.

Lennox stood to our left, talking with one of the distribution supervisors. He nodded at us and held up a finger. I glanced around the center itself, taking note on whatever I could. Several crates had been brought down from their places, the tops open and the contents spilled. Tire marks led from where we stood back to the garage door, no doubt explaining its current state. It would've taken a pretty large truck to take the entire door down, which meant they'd gotten away with a *lot* of chemicals.

Lennox nodded the supervisor away and started towards us, now holding a clipboard in his right hand. He came to stand in front of us, giving us both a nod and a half-smile.

"Glad you guys could make it," he said as he tapped the clipboard. "Figured you'd want to be here for this."

"Who and what?" Hull asked, his eyes on the towering racks of crates.

"Chimaera," Lennox replied. Hull's attention moved solely to the commissioner. "We caught them on the security cameras. They just walked in, no problems with clearance, at about 2 AM. Six people, with your black-hooded friend leading."

"What'd they take?" I questioned.

"Chemical compounds. Lots of them." Lennox looked down at his clipboard and started listing. "After they ran inventory, they found that large amounts of iron oxides, calcium carbonates, calcium and sodium chloride, and sulfates were taken. Whole crates full of 'em, loaded into a truck and driven right through the door."

"Have you tracked the truck?" the detective asked as he stepped forward, moving towards one of the crates.

"We tried. Moriarty knows his way around the city. Not a single traffic camera could find that truck leaving here."

Hull glanced down into the crate before looking through the torn garage door. "And what of the offsite facility?"

Lennox gave him a wary glance before replying. "They've kept that under wraps, how did—"

"People talk," the detective intervened.

"Right. Well, yes. An offsite testing facility was also hit at exactly the same time. Smaller group, three or four people." Lennox perused the clipboard. "It was a joint location between Warmack Chemical and Selecan Genetic Studies, to test the biochemical properties of *thiobacillus* when introduced to chemical agents."

Hull stepped back to the group, fingers rubbing the bridge of his nose. "So Chimaera breaks into two separate facilities and makes off with a number of chemical compounds that hold no true significance when combined, as well as a bacterial experiment. Then, as quickly as they appear, they vanish. Magnificent."

"I know you don't like playing search dog," Lennox said, "but I remember you uncovering something with one of the scientists here. With everything that's been happening, who knows? Maybe your scientist was connected."

Hull's eyes shot open and soared to me. "Alexander Wygant was in the same wing as Lucius Mendax."

"Everyone on that wing was with Chimaera?" I prompted.

"Oh, of course, genius!" Hull cheered, turning to Lennox. "Commissioner, I commend you and your ingenuity. Well done. I need to speak with whoever is in charge." Lennox gave the detective a long look before nodding and leading us from the building, back around the main complex and into the central lobby. We were taken to an elevator, straight up to the administrative division. Through the relatively empty office we went, eventually coming to the door of the Chief Executive Officer, a scientist by the name of Dr. Kevin Somerville.

The three of us entered to find Dr. Somerville standing, hands clasped behind his back, eyes focused on the window behind his desk, which looked out at the smokestacks of the production facility. Lennox cleared his throat, causing the man to turn. He looked to be in his early fifties, but still chose to wear a lab coat rather than a suit.

"Gentlemen," Somerville said, extending a hand to us, "what can I do for you?"

"This is Mr. Sheridan Hull and Dr. John Walker," Lennox said. "They're helping with the investigation."

"Good to hear it," Somerville replied. "Have a seat."

"Actually," Hull interrupted, "I have only one question, perhaps some more, depending on the first answer."

Somerville gave a solemn nod. "Let's hear it."

"Alexander Wygant was a scientist here not too long ago, until my intervention prevented the deaths of many a political figure at his hand," Hull stated. "I know he was imprisoned, and I know what jail he is at. I want to speak with him."

Somerville shook his head. "Sorry, you might have a hard time with that. Wygant died in the jail riot."

"No loose ends," Hull murmured with a sigh. "Alright, if Wygant was killed, we take the next option. Wygant had an office here, I distinctly remember it having an overlook on the production line. Upon his detainment, all of his belongings would have been thrown out had he been less important, but since he was a head scientist, his research would have been kept, correct?"

"That's correct," Somerville replied. "All of Mr. Wygant's belongings were taken to storage. Haven't been touched since."

"Did you make record of this?" Hull asked.

"I don't think it was high priority. One of our scientists caught trying to murder a plane full of politicians didn't sit well with the board of directors. Boxed his stuff away and threw his name under the rug."

Hull smirked. "Good. Hopefully that means Moriarty would not have known to check there and remove any, shall we say, compromising information." He turned and walked from the office, leaving Lennox and me with our arms crossed. I glanced at the commissioner and shrugged.

"I guess that means he wants to see Wygant's stuff," I proposed.

"Spot on," the detective called back from the outer office. Somerville stepped around his desk and through his door with Lennox and me in tow, meeting Hull in the elevator and following the CEO from the central building to one of the more satellite structures, with part of it going down into the ground just before reaching the borderline fence. Somerville ran his identification card and stood back as the door slid open. The four of us walked in to a dark storage facility, similar to the distribution center but not as tall and, in my opinion, far less organized.

"It's supposed to be alphabetized," Somerville commented as he turned on the lights, "but I have a hard enough time trusting these workers with a 401k plan. If you find a box with a AW on it, that's what we're looking for." The group of us panned out, and it wasn't long before Lennox called to us with the box's location. We reconvened with the commissioner by a set of boxes in the farthest corner. Hull immediately started digging, pulling out thick stapled documents and other miscellaneous items. After about two minutes of rummaging, he stopped and pulled a single sheet of paper from the box.

"Perfect," the detective stated, the glint appearing in his eye.

"What?" Lennox asked.

"Wygant was sending shipments of chemical compounds to an offsite location, and each shipment was to be intercepted by Chimaera," Hull replied, handing the paper to the commissioner. "The shipments contained large amounts of iron oxide, calcium carbonate, calcium and sodium chloride, and sulfate compounds."

"If Wygant was already sending them shipments, why would they break in?" I questioned.

"Easy," Hull said as he started back towards the door. "They needed more."

*

We left Warmack Chemical fairly quickly, Hull no doubt walking about ten to fifteen steps ahead of us. He'd declared our next destination to be Selecan Genetic Studies, barely five minutes away from Warmack. Lennox had decided to accompany us, knowing that the officers would be able to clear up any issues at Warmack. Plus, he'd admittedly told me that anything involving Hull tended to be far more interesting than whatever paperwork would turn up at his desk back at the department. And so it was the three of us that marched up the steps to Selecan Genetics, Lennox and me walking just behind the detective.

"So," I started, noting that we had at least twenty steps to go, "Chimaera breaks in and steals a load of chemicals. But what for?"

"What for indeed, Doctor," Hull called back. "What for indeed."

"You know I hate it when you do that."

"You often remind me, yes."

"All this time, Chimaera's been causing destruction," Lennox added. "So taking chemicals like this would lead anyone to believe they're planning something big. What mixture of chemicals would be enough for a bomb?"

Hull stopped and glanced back. "Let me stop you there. The compounds they stole are not ones that can be combined to create some kind of weapon. Had they wanted chemical weaponry, they would have had easy access to it, but since they did not steal any, we can deduce that they do not want any."

I scoffed. "Don't worry. He was a chemistry major. Once."

We continued up the steps, but Lennox wasn't entirely convinced. "Then why are we here? That bacteria listed, *thiobacillus.* What's important about it?"

"I was a chemistry major, Commissioner, not at all interested in biology," the detective replied coyly.

"Lucky for you, I did take a few biology courses," I remarked. "*Thiobacillus* is usually used for pest control, typically for potatoes. I know that it's also found in acid rain."

Lennox sighed. "*That* could be weaponized."

"It could," Hull deferred, "but it will not be what Chimaera is doing."

"How can you be so sure?" the commissioner snapped.

"How can you not be?" the detective snapped back, turning once again. "You have to *think*, Commissioner. You have to get inside the minds of your opponents. *Think*: what could Chimaera possibly have to gain from acid rain? How do they benefit from that?" He spun and started back up the stairs. "They strive for order through chaos, not an environmental hazard." None of us spoke again until we'd entered the building. We approached the receptionist, surprisingly the same woman as when Hull and I first visited.

Lennox flashed his badge. "We're investigating the theft of sensitive materials from an offsite facility managed by Selecan Genetics and Warmack Chemical. My companion can do the rest." He stepped to the side and let Hull come forward.

"I would like to speak with one of the head researchers here," the detective stated. "I recall his name being Richard Cain."

The receptionist furrowed her brow at Hull and frowned. "I'm sorry, Sir, but Dr. Cain died over a year ago."

This definitely changed things. I watched Hull rock back and forth on his feet for a moment, his jaw working to form words. "How did he die?"

"Industrial accident, Sir. Fire in the lab caused by hydrogen sulfide."

"That would barely take a spark to set the room on fire," I commented.

"Which is precisely what happened," the receptionist replied. "Electrical shortage in one of the machines. We aren't quite sure how the hydrogen sulfide was spilled into the room, but we believe it was an error on one of the assistant's parts."

Hull scoffed. "That would be the sensible thing, wouldn't it."

The receptionist gave me a concerned look. "What does he mean by that?"

"Nothing," I replied quickly, watching Hull start back towards the doorway. I turned to the woman one more time before leaving. "Thank you for your help." Lennox and I exited and found Hull standing at the edge of the top step, his eyes peered and focused on the cityscape ahead of us. I gave Lennox a quick nod toward the car before coming to stand beside the detective.

"No loose ends," Hull muttered, giving his lips a lick.

"Cain said he did business with Chimaera," I reminded. "Doesn't mean it was just the one-time deal."

"I would wager to bet he was the individual overseeing the *thiobacillus* experiments. Testing a biological form with chemical compounds." He narrowed his eyes and shook his head. "But why? What could they possibly gain from biochemicals that have no correlation?"

"Not much of a case to be had when you hit dead ends," I said as I started down the steps.

"What are you doing," I heard the man whisper from behind me. "Why are you doing it." I'd made it halfway down the stairs when Lennox poked his head out from the car, his cell phone in hand.

"Guys," he yelled, "I have to be somewhere now!"

"What happened?" I asked as I hurried my pace.

"Remember those six students who were never found during the Black Tunnel crisis?"

"Yes."

"We found them."

I glanced back to find Hull behind me, his hands buried in his pockets and his jaw locked. With a nod, we circled around the car, him taking the rear driver side and me the wheel. With Lennox's instruction, we started on a rushed path to the given location. A van had turned up on the outskirts of town, with all six students inside. Unfortunately, it was southwest of Newfield, meaning it would take them almost a half an hour to get there.

"Alexander Wygant, Richard Cain," Hull stated from behind me. "Both Chimaera agents. Both killed in convenient means that removed them from the equation. Pieces eliminated from the board."

"Chimaera has agents everywhere," I reminded. "These two being connected shouldn't be that surprising."

"No, not surprising. But you are right. There are agents everywhere. Spread across the globe, in fact, but largely centered here. Alexander Wygant, Richard Cain. Alan Rodgers. Wayne Fisher. Thomas Kneeler. Lucius Mendax. Arthur Knight. Kyle Richy. Victorius Judas. Ross McNair. Veronica Daemon. Countless underlings. All of them focused in one place."

I ignored Veronica's name being mentioned and kept thinking. "Wygant provided the chemicals, Cain provided the bacteria. Do you think all of them have been helping some greater goal?"

"Difficult to say. Insufficient data."

"If this Moriarty has been wanting to make order," Lennox suggested, "he'd have to make a surefire plan. And order through chaos? That's what you guys kept saying, right? That's not too foreign a thought, is it? Making things so bad that people would accept any kind of order. If he had all of these agents spread out across the globe, that'd make it pretty easy to stir up the right amount of chaos."

"Yes, but *what* chaos," Hull jabbed. "He's already caused significant destruction to the city, but why here? What makes Newfield so important?"

"If we knew that," I said, "this would probably be a lot easier."

We remained silent until we passed the last building, now on a straight stretch to the van, which was reportedly found about a mile out of town. As we drove, I couldn't help but notice the mountain range reflected in the rearview mirror. With the swirling clouds above it and the occasional bolt of lightning, it looked positively horrifying. To think Hull and I had only just come over those mountains some four days ago after my abduction. Events were going by quickly; time, however, was not.

"With rain like this, it's a wonder the lake hasn't flooded," Lennox commented, the side of his head pressed against the window. "Normally about now there'd be a crew setting up fireworks and families claiming their spots along the shore. Lake Torrentem's pretty nice this time of year. Not with this weather, though."

"I've never been a fan of lakes," I replied. "My brother threw me off the boat too many times as a kid, I guess. And Puget Sound isn't a fun place to get pushed into. Not as an eleven-year-old who believed the stories of giant octopuses."

"Lucky. I've been here my entire life. I remember when I was younger, we used to get flooding around here all the time, until they built the dam in '93."

We eventually reached the van, with three police cars surrounding it. The officers were currently huddled underneath a large umbrella, about a meter from the van's side door. The three of us stepped out and walked to stand in front of them, Hull's eyes on the van, or specifically, its license plates.

"What's the story, boys?" Lennox asked.

The officer on the left spoke first. "Got the call about an hour ago about an abandoned vehicle. I was the first on scene. I saw what looked like a person in the back and opened the door. It was, uh.. pretty clear who they were."

Hull started moving towards the door while I gave the officer a narrowed look. "Why is that?" Before the officer could reply, Hull slid the door open. I recoiled as the stench of death hit me, coupled with a few other unspeakable smells. Inside the van were six bodies, all of them wet and very dead. A puddle of blood coursed out from underneath them, dripping to the freedom of the ground through the now-open door. Painted on the wall in what looked like blood was a very specific, and I suppose helpful, message.

"'Finished up our work. Thought I'd return them to you. -M,'" Hull read aloud.

I brought the neck of my shirt up over my mouth and nose, looking in at the pile of bodies with disgust. "What does he mean by that?"

Hull leaned into the van, left hand hovering above one body in particular. "Xaphon abducted a few hundred students, burned a handful, and was stopped, but six students were never found. Six students who were all, conveniently, chemistry majors. And now, the bodies turn up on the day after a significant amount of chemicals are stolen from one of the largest chemical production facilities in the state."

"He had the students do work with the original batches of chemicals," Lennox added.

"And now that they're dead..." I started.

"It means his plans are about to come to fruition," Hull said as he delicately turned one of the bodies over. It was that of a young man, tall with an unshaven face, not by choice. The detective immediately went for the man's hand, which was currently clutching a crumpled piece of paper. Hull pulled the paper free and opened it to reveal four letters: ERRF.

"...the Emergency Response and Restoration Fund?" Lennox suggested.

"We may want to start entertaining the notion that the city government is not all white knights," Hull stated as he stepped away from the van, still holding the paper. "We need to see the legislation." Lennox offered no response, and I knew why. I didn't know how long it would take Hull to remember city hall had been completely destroyed, which had no doubt taken the fund's legislation with it. The detective looked between the commissioner and I before sighing. "Of course. Electronic copies would have been sent to the capital, and today is a holiday." He turned and pulled out his phone, starting to walk down the road.

"I can make a call and see if we can get it today," Lennox called out.

"Even then, it will take too long, and it will be too late," Hull shouted back without turning.

"Where are you going?" I queried.

"*Home.*"

I watched him walk alone for at least three minutes, the wind blowing at his side and the rain pouring down, before a taxi appeared on the horizon. Then I sat there and watched him wait for the taxi and step in. Ten minutes had elapsed before the taxi had once again disappeared into the city. I knew he was puzzled, because he became more and more introverted when something didn't make sense. Moriarty was playing a game that spanned a field far larger than what we were looking at.

I only hoped he'd be able to expand his horizon in time.

*

I didn't return home until around 6 PM. I'd stayed with Lennox to help as best I could, but the only thing he could do was decipher the cause of the students' deaths. Each of them had been cut down the lengths of their chests, and each of them had bitten into cyanide pills. If not for the pills, they might have survived. But the bodies looked to have been in their spots for a while. Oh, and we figured out why Hull had been initially fixated on the license plate. He'd filled me in on his niece's abduction, but I was able to recognize what T04 311 meant.

I stepped up the stairs to our flat slowly, somewhat perturbed by the lack of sound coming from upstairs. Mrs. Hanson was out. In fact, now that I think about it, she'd been gone almost a week. I was starting to really miss her friendly presence in the building. I reached the middle point between the first and second floors and glanced up, seeing Hull's chalkboard propped up with a vast web of names and arrows. As I came closer, I recognized many of the names as people Hull had listed before as Chimaera agents. But some were new.

Benjamin Arnold was listed, and that was the first name to catch me off guard. He'd been with Plyer Incorporated, so long ago. Last I remember, he'd been arrested. But according to the chalkboard, he'd also been killed in a car crash not long after being sentenced. Charles Oake was also listed, him being the scientist who was helping to develop a cure for Alphaherpesvirinae. Below his name was a note that said he'd died from an overdose last July.

George Everrard. It took some thinking, but I eventually remembered that name belonging to one of the arsonists Hull had caught last August. His note dictated his death being in a building fire five weeks after his arrest. One name I didn't recognize, though. Zachary Matson. He, however, had been killed during the same riot that had taken both Alexander Wygant and Lucius Mendax. Many of the names linked to each other. Veronica's name was on the board. And in the center, no name, but enough of a moniker. A giant, chalk-written M.

"Fun fact," Hull's voice called from behind me. I turned to find him in the kitchen, elbows propped against the dining table and chin resting in his palms, with five empty bottles of wine making a semi-circle around him. Next to the dining table was an array of beakers and bottles, each containing different chemicals. "I suffer from a very rare genetic defect in my liver that immediately negates any physical or mental effects alcohol can have. No dampening of body or mind." He turned his gaze to me and knocked on one of the bottles. "I am physically incapable of getting drunk."

I walked into the kitchen and circled around the table, looking down at the bottles with a hint of astonishment. "Why would you want to?"

"People claim alcohol can open your mind," he replied with a shrug.

"You don't often do what people claim," I stated as I moved the bottles to the sink.

"He is doing something, John. Something absolutely devious, something abominably evil. But I have sat here and done my research, I have sat and looked up every convenient death to happen in the past two years, and I still cannot form a proper correlation. It's one thing, one tiny, minuscule thing, that is just on the tip of my mind, the one thing that connects them all."

"Well, your diorama pretty plainly points to that 'one thing' being Moriarty."

"He is the adhesive that bonded them together, but not the purpose. One purpose has united these people and many more. And all I have to work with are fifteen different types of chemicals, a bacteria that cost me a well-earned favor, and no results whatsoever."

"You'll figure it out," I said with confidence as I took the last bottle to the sink.

"Yes, but how long do I *have* to figure it out, how long will he take to put his final act into motion? He has been preparing for this singular moment for years. This is the paramount point to Chimaera's operations. My time cannot be long because this is all that remains between the current stasis and the chaos he so eagerly desires."

"I don't know what to tell you. I really don't. All of this, it's only ever made sense because I've had you to explain it. All of these connections and correlations, I never would've seen them if not for you."

He rose to his feet and took two steps to his right, coming to stand beside his beakers. "I read the entirety of the Emergency Response and Restoration Fund's legislation. Every single bit of it, all of the measurements, all of the precautions, everything. So much of it made no sense because it lacks correlation. Because of that single thing evading my thoughts."

"And what would that thing be?"

"*Why are these important!*"

I snapped around to find him hunched over the beakers, eyes moving like mad from subject to subject.

"Why, of every possible chemical concoction, has he elected to use these specific ones? Why, when after three hours of continuous testing, I have found no positive correlation, connection, nothing to explain why he would use chemicals such as these in his grand master plan. *The nexus is not there!*"

He lashed out angrily at the beakers, sending them all flying across the room and into the wall. Every beaker shattered, their contents spilling onto the concrete floor and mixing. I watched Hull clutch at his hair and bang his fist against the table, his anger building bit by bit.

"All of my life, I have found the links," he moaned, his hands trembling. I looked from him to the broken beakers and frowned, not quite sure at what I was seeing. "All of my life, I have been the one to see things others could not, because I knew to observe."

"Uh, Hull—"

"All of my life, I have been clever, but now what use is it!"

"Sheridan!"

His neck snapped and his eyes darted to me, his nostrils flaring and his teeth clenched. I met his glare and held it for a long moment before pointing at the pile of broken glass.

"Explain," I said sternly. He furrowed his brow at me before looking over.

The contents of the chemicals had mixed together, but no chemical reaction had occurred. Instead, something had started happening to the concrete. It was minor, but still noticeable. From a glance, it looked like the concrete itself was being disintegrated, tiny particles breaking off from the floor and disappearing into the mixture. Hull stepped around the table slowly, his hands shaking as he kneeled to look at the floor.

"My God," he sputtered, his head swaying back and forth. "How could I have possibly not considered this."

"Considered what?" I asked, taking a step closer to him.

He turned to look at me. No, correction, not *at* me, but rather in my general direction. "The chemicals do not combine, they have no combinative quality. But each chemical has a specific reaction to a certain material. Cement. Oh my God, of course. Iron oxides, calcium carbonates, calcium and sodium chloride, sulfates. All of them, individually, have the ability to deteriorate cement." He jumped to his feet, causing me to step back in shock. "And the bacteria!" I watched him run back into the living room, his destination the laptop in his chair.

"*Thiobacillus?*" I prompted as I followed him in.

"Anaerobic bacteria. *Thiobacillus*. When left in water, it creates hydrogen sulfide. Aerobic bacteria in biofilm on the surface of the concrete oxidizes it, and sulfuric acid is created. The acid can successfully dissolve carbonates in cement, thus deteriorating it."

"So all of the things stolen degrade concrete," I stated. "But why would he need them?"

"In such high quantities, the chemicals and bacteria would be able to individually deteriorate the state of a potentially large concrete body, perhaps a building's structure, an underground support system, or—"

He stopped, his jaw dropping and eyes going wide.

"Or what?" I asked forcefully, coming to stand directly ahead of him.

"Oh wow," he said as he closed his eyes. "Of course. A potentially large concrete body."

"*What* concrete body?"

His eyes snapped open. "The dam, John. The dam that prevents flooding in Newfield, the dam that created Lake Torrentem. If the dam were to be destroyed, if the entire structural integrity were to be weakened over time by chemical and bacterial agents, the structure itself would inevitably collapse and the water would be released. A flood, John. A *colossal* flood that would devastate the entire city."

He jumped from his seat and ran to the chalkboard, eyes skimming over every single name. After just three seconds of doing that, he bounded back towards his room, returning with his coat.

"Hold on, something still doesn't make sense," I piqued. "The student and the message, ERRF. You read the entire thing."

"The Fund contains a measure in the event of a flood. And not a small flood, but I quote, 'a colossal flood.' Something that would truly call for the use of a *restoration* fund."

"So he forced the students to help with the development of the chemicals?"

"No, he forced the students to help with the enhancement of the chemicals. They would take a very, very long time to deteriorate a dam, but if they were enhanced? With the proper amount of scientific endeavor, he would be able to collapse the dam on a whim."

"But even if he did do that, what good would it do him?" I questioned, watching the detective run around the room, picking up multiple things as he went. "He can't *do* anything with the fund."

Now *that* brought Hull to a screeching halt. He stared forward for several seconds, his eyes racing back and forth in his head.

"Oh my God," he whispered. He slowly turned his head to me, his eyes filled with more revelation than I'd ever seen before.

"Moriarty. I know who Moriarty is." He clasped his hands over his face and groaned. "My *God*, how did I not realize it sooner!" He threw his hands down and ran behind me, grabbing my keys from the kitchen and throwing them to me. "We need to leave now. We can still stop this."

"How? Where?"

"The dam is one of several city-owned facilities in the mountains. The control hub is above Dives Torrentem Falls, in the visitor center. He would need to be there to successfully add the chemicals and bacteria into the water, which would travel down the fall and into the lake." He wrapped his scarf around his neck and turned from the kitchen to the hall, the stairs his destination. "We are going to Dives Torrentem Falls."

*

The two men had wasted no time in departing. The falls were roughly an hour and a half's driving distance, but they'd gone with haste. Just an hour after leaving their home, they arrived at the parking lot of the visitor center. Walker brought their car to a halt at the closest spot, then nodded at the only other vehicle. Parked in the farthest place, up against the edge of the closest mountain, was a large truck with "WARMACK" written on the side.

"Found our missing truck," Walker said as he pulled the keys from the ignition. The two exited their car and started towards the glass doors of the entrance. "What's the plan?"

"Now is a moment to be very thankful there are two of us," Hull commented as they started up the steps. "We will need to split our tasks. One will confront Moriarty, the other will stop the chemical addition."

"You don't think he'll have any agents with him?"

"No. His *hubris* would never allow another person to be present in his moment of triumph."

They reached the entrance and found the motion sensors to be active. The glass doors slid apart to admit them, the lights in the lobby turning off at their presence.

"I'm going to guess you'll want to take Moriarty?" Walker proposed as they started towards the grand, circular stairwell that led to the rest of the center.

"I trust you will be more than capable in disabling the chemical distribution." The detective pulled a folded piece of paper from his coat pocket and handed it to Walker. "This contains all necessary instructions to stop the chemical's introduction to the water system. The control center will be at the topmost point of the stairwell. You will more than likely have to use an access code to enter. The code is also on the paper."

The doctor gave Hull a puzzled look. "How'd you get the access codes?"

"I contacted Malcolm on our way here."

"Ah. Of course." They ran halfway up the stairwell before reaching a stopping point. A large sign that read "OBSERVATORY" hung on the wall. Hull stepped from the stairwell and looked back at the doctor.

"He will be in the observatory. Perfect place to watch the administering of the chemicals. The waterfall's passage goes directly underneath it."

"Alright," Walker replied, showing slight hesitation. Hull looked at him with careful eyes, knowing the doctor was wary of the situation. "You're okay with this? You don't want me to go with you?"

Hull shook his head. "He will no doubt have a way of activating the chemicals remotely. I have to distract him long enough for you to disable it. If we both go, he will simply activate the chemicals. Newfield will be flooded."

"Right," the doctor replied. "Well, good luck."

"You too," Hull responded with a nod. Walker gave him one last look before starting up the stairs, eventually vanishing from sight. Hull waited at the sign for maybe a minute, listening to the echoing footsteps of his companion until they came to a halt. The sound of a door sliding open emanated down the long chamber, then hissed as the door closed. Hull's eyes fell, and inside, he felt a solemn *thud* as his heart stopped for only a moment. He pulled a thin remote from his pocket, one he'd reprogrammed on their drive up, and pushed the topmost button.

Thunk.

That sound, the most reassuring sound he'd heard all day, was the sound of the metal door to the control room locking. It would effectively prevent anyone from entering. Or exiting.

He slid the remote back into his pocket and walked slowly towards the double-doorway that would open to the observatory. If his memory served, and it often did, the observatory had been constructed with the intentions of giving people the perfect view of Newfield, Lake Torrentem, and Dives Torrentem Falls. As such, the ceiling, walls, and floor were made of heavy-duty glass. He was within a meter of the door when they parted, granting him access to the circular room.

He stepped through the doors with his hands at his sides, pausing only to hear the doors hiss shut behind him. He truly did have a great view of the city, and the lake, and the falls. He could even see the lights of Eugene in the distance. But none of that mattered. Not the city, not the lake, not the falls. None of it even compared to the man who stood at the other end of the room. His black cloak, his metal cane, his gloved hands. And, for the first time, the back of his head plainly revealed, with black hair that looked to have been recently cut. The man turned to face Hull, a devilish smile on his face.

"Here we are, Sheridan Hull," the man said.

Hull lifted his chin. "Here we are indeed, Jameson Montorum."

The man pressed his cane against the ground, leaning ever-so-slightly to the side and smirking at Hull. "Being as clever as you are, you have to tell me you figured it out before just now."

"Of course," the detective replied, blinking his eyes a few times. "I knew the true identity of Moriarty would have to be someone within the city's government, else they would hold nothing to gain from the restoration fund. Once I was sure the fund held significance, it took no time in remembering your handshake. A very peculiar one, unlike others. A single shake with a firm grip. You shook my hands after the detaining of Ross McNair, and again prior to our chess game."

"Good good good," Montorum cheered, puffing his chest out as he spoke. "Very good, detective, very good. Very clever. Have you pieced everything together, then? The great plan to bring order from chaos?"

Hull took a single step closer, bringing himself onto the glass floor. His eyes caught the motion in the reflection of the glass wall behind Montorum, coming from the security camera mounted on the wall at the detective's back. "There became a point in which I acknowledged that you intended to use Newfield as a ground zero for your motives. This would be the base of your chaos, and from it, you would spread a supposed order to not just the state, but as far as you could reach. Of course, there came the matter of creating chaos so groundbreaking and so devastating that society would suckle to the closest and most appealing source of nourishment available.

"Every law and piece of legislation is a reaction, requiring an action that drew a call for a declaration, something that was deemed necessary for the individuals of the future to acknowledge. So imagine my surprise when, while perusing the Emergency Response and Restoration Fund's legislation, I spotted a section dedicated to the necessary responses in the event of a flood. Not a small flood, mind you, but one on a catastrophic level. A 'colossal flood,' as you so aptly put. Legislation outlining this very specific event would normally have been a reaction to a prior catastrophe. But since no such event had occurred, it became clear to me that the legislation was not in fact a reaction but a premonitory action.

"In order to create such a state of chaos, you would first need an action. The catalyst to send people spiraling downwards. Your plans started long ago, far longer than I first anticipated. If I am correct, your age would be around fifty, meaning you would have been working your way up the political ladder in 1991, when the initial plans to create the dam, and subsequently Lake Torrentem, were drawn up. You were the spearhead of the project, but you required assistance from a significant number of people. This is where your other life, where your position as the leader of the crime syndicate group known as Chimaera, came into play.

"Victorius Judas, a young up-and-coming individual who held substantial weight with a particular group of Croatians, was your perfect recruiter. He was able to send free labor, people just begging for a way out of their home country. By early 1993, the dam's construction was complete, and you now had a way of bringing the city to its knees when the time came. But of course, that left the next phase of your plan to become reality. You had the bullet, but not the gun nor the hand to pull the trigger.

"You were elected as mayor of Newfield in 2008, thus enabling you to figuratively pull the trigger and be in a position to become a hero. As both mayor and the leader of Chimaera, you put plans into motion that would begin two separate, but connected, things. Chimaera would both develop the gun for your usage and create a growing sense of panic, discontent, and chaos in the city. You worked with multiple groups on multiple projects to create the perfect scenario, and it all started here, at the dam.

"Charles Oake, Alexander Wygant, and Richard Cain. Three brilliant men in the field of science who would help you create the perfect formula, the perfect concoction to create what would appear to be a natural disaster. The men worked individually on parts of a larger project, a series of chemicals and bacterial species that would break down the very foundation of the dam's concrete and eventually cause it to succumb to the pressure of the water, releasing the contents of Lake Torrentem and wreaking havoc on the city of Newfield. Not only would the entire city be flooded, the chemicals would still be active, causing significant damage to the buildings.

"Now that you possessed the bullet, the gun, and the hand to pull the trigger, you simply required one more important piece to finish your grand plan. You needed the handkerchief to clean the wound. That handkerchief took on the title of the Emergency Response and Restoration Fund, a piece of legislation passed in a moment of dire need following a student hostage crisis choreographed by a Chimaera agent. This legislation would enable you, the mayor of Newfield, to act accordingly and assist the city in the event of a catastrophic disaster.

"This fund, however, would require something very vital: funding. A budget would only allow so much of a percentage, and the destruction you had in your mind would require far more than what the state could give you. So once again, you used your powers as leader of Chimaera to generate a great quantity of funds through a variety of benefactors. Benjamin Arnold, a simple directing assistant for Plyer Incorporated. When his fantastic library plan was canceled, the money had nowhere to go. When the fund became legislation, Plyer Incorporated happily donated that money.

"George Everrard, presumably an underling to your pyromaniac agent Xaphon, was involved in a number of fires, one which engulfed an entire company and forced them into supposed bankruptcy. This bankruptcy was false, and the funds from the company were depleted to an unknown source, who, after a certain amount of time had passed, made the anonymous donation to the Newfield city's Emergency Response and Restoration Fund.

"Thomas Kneeler, a nationally-renowned magician working shows that would often generate several hundred thousand dollars when performed in cities like Los Angeles, Las Vegas, or New York

City. All proceeds were reportedly to be given to charity, but were in fact stored away and eventually given as a donation to the fund after Kneeler's death, per his request.

"Lucius Mendax and Zachary Matson, two individuals who had once been accused of having taken part in several very high-stakes heists in New York, Virginia, and Massachusetts. Their charges were eventually dismissed due to lack of evidence, but the immense amount of money that had been stolen was never seen again. However, an amount of money partitioned into two equal donations was received for the restoration fund, both coming from anonymous benefactors who had since passed away.

"Lastly, of course, Kyle Richy, the part businessman, part skilled assassin. He was the treasurer, the one who ensured all money came in accordingly. He managed all funds and, when the time came, ordered their individual movements. Each large amount coming as donations from benefactors, all assisting in the Emergency Response and Restoration Fund. The amount was staggering, surely enough to assist in the event of a catastrophic disaster. Everything was neatly in place. Everything was perfect. You were ready to begin your plans of bringing order through chaos."

Montorum's smile had not diminished in the slightest. In fact, it seemed to widen when Hull finished. "Very well done, Detective. I knew from the moment I saw you, years back, that you were something else. Someone who finally saw through the cloud, someone who could truly *observe*. Very well done."

"But you are a fool to think you will succeed."

The mayor raised his eyebrows and smirked. "Am I now?"

"Very much so. You made a very fatal error. Two, actually. The first came when you ordered the initial attack on city hall, in which Zachary Matson shot you. Not a feigned shot, mind you, as not a single member of Chimaera knew of your true identity. This was a real shot, one that passed through the top of your left lung. As a result of this, you were hospitalized. And that, that is where things become very complicated, very interesting, and subsequently very fatal for your plan.

"The second error came in the writing of the legislation. You see, each piece of legislation, be it the Constitution of the United States or the writings of the Emergency Response and Restoration Fund, will contain what we will call backup plans. It is why the line of succession exists. If the President of the United States is incapacitated, the Vice President steps in to make the decisions. Now, you carefully made it so, if the Emergency Response and Restoration Fund was to be enacted, the decisions would be made by you, and as such, you would be raised up as the great savior of Newfield.

"However. You made the grave mistake of forgetting the line of succession. With you in the hospital, it would pass control of the fund to the city commissioners. Even if you, as the mayor, were to abruptly dismiss yourself from the hospital, you would still be deemed unfit for significant decisions until a proper physician had cleared you. So, the city commissioners would be in charge. But as Moriarty, you killed both people holding those titles: Commissioners Lamont Conn and Ghedi Rahim. Naturally, these positions were filled rather quickly. The new city commissioners are Gregory Lennox and Malcolm Hull.

"As soon as I became aware of your intentions, I notified both gentlemen. I informed them that, if the fund must be used, they are to use it. You, as the mayor, would receive no public appeal. You would not succeed. You would ultimately, utterly fail."

Montorum's smile had certainly dimmed, but it had not disappeared. He gave a hearty cough and smirked. "The clever detective, thinking he has every outlet thought out. You didn't really think I'd just entrust all responsibility to the city commissioners, did you? You do me injustice, Sheridan. You see, once we have concluded our business here, and once the chemicals have been administered, I will ensure very creative and very agonizing demises for both of the new commissioners. Because that's what I do, Sheridan. I persevere. I have done so for many years. And to let a simple detective like you stop me would indeed be the ultimate failure."

Hull slid his left hand inside his coat and pulled free a gun, one he'd obtained not too long ago. He leveled the gun with Montorum's head, once again noting the adjusting of the security camera behind him. The inward and outward motion, telling him the chemical distribution had been disabled.

"It's quite interesting, your plan," the detective stated, staring at his adversary over the top of the pistol. "Your fantastic ladder. And how well-timed everything has been."

"I've always been good with time, Sheridan," Montorum replied, taking a step closer.

"I can see that. Although you missed the elections this past November, given the amount of damage you intend to do to Newfield, by the time you had completed your work, the next round of senatorial elections would arrive, and you would be the perfect candidate. The people of Newfield would praise you for your hard work and diligence in bringing this city up from its diminutive remains. Your influence would spread across the state, and just like that, you would become one of Oregon's senators. Jameson Montorum, the poster child from Newfield.

"And once you have obtained the position of senator, you will not stop. Your manic lust for power will drive you higher and higher. In a few short years, you would enter the presidential primary election, and once again, you will come out victorious. You will become the shining star in the presidential election and win by a monumental landslide. And in that moment, democracy as we know it will perish in the flames of your inevitable tyranny, your insane need for order through chaos. Diplomacy will crumble as your influence spreads across the seas like a virus.

"This country, followed by this continent and then the world, will succumb to your ever-tightening grasp. You will destroy and desecrate everything. Because you were *bored*."

Montorum clucked, his eyes closing as his chest beat with laughter. "You are clever, Sheridan. Clever indeed. But not enough. You have provided entertainment, and your value has been thoroughly exhausted. This has been fun, though. And I thank you for that. But I really do have to know, before we depart from this momentous occasion. I must know. Just how did you, a simple detective with hardly a friend to his name, plan to prevent all of this?"

"Simple. Very, very simple. If you do not administer the chemical, you do not have a catastrophe to fix, and you do not have the reputation to ascend. If you do not become senator, your foretold future will not come to fruition. And for you to not have even the slightest chance of succeeding, I must do one thing."

"What? Stop the chemical? Stop the flood?" The man chuckled. "Stop the relief effort?"

"No," Hull replied, his heart stopping and eyes narrowing, their very distinct glint shining brighter than ever before. "I only have to stop you."

His aim dropped, going from Montorum's head to the glass at the direct point between both men, the direct point at the center of the floor. He fired a single round, a single round in a gun designed to shatter even the strongest of glass. The round had no trouble penetrating the floor, sending dozens upon dozens of cracks out from the center to the walls. As soon as the first crack reached its last point of strength, the floor gave way, rupturing from the center and sinking outward. To Hull, it moved in the slowest of motions. The glass, piece by piece falling. Montorum's face changing from its smirk to utter shock. And fear.

He felt the glass beneath his feet split and gravity begin to work its law. He looked forward to see Montorum level with him, both men falling with the glass floor from the safety of the room. Slowly but surely, or quickly, he wasn't sure which, Hull watched the rim that had made up the perimeter of the floor pass. There was no surface of safety, no haven remaining. They were going in the sole direction they could travel now, the might of Dives Torrentem Falls roaring beneath them, the inevitable rocks and rapids at the farthest reach. He was finally here. He had seen the rise. He had seen the shift. He had watched the darkness spread over the city. He had stood in the glass room.

Now was the *Cădea*.

The Fall.

He glanced down at the roaring waters, then to his right. He could make out the faintest trace of a cliff edge. He put his strength into his left arm and threw the gun, watching it soar to the ledge and slam into the rock wall. The gun landed on the ledge itself, but he only had a sparse moment to verify before it vanished from sight. He quickly slipped his hand into his front pocket and pulled out the remote from earlier, once again pressing the topmost button. He glanced down at the dark depths, not able to see the ground. He could see the waterfall, though. And Montorum.

He adjusted his body accordingly, causing his fall to change trajectories. He was moving slowly but surely, closer and closer to the other man, who had abandoned his cane long ago and looked to be screaming in terror. Hull couldn't hear him; he couldn't hear anything, really. All sound had numbed itself away. All sound, and feel, and thought. Except for one thought. One singular, powerful thought. He reached out his arms and grabbed Moriarty, Jameson Montorum, the leader of Chimaera, the mayor of Newfield, by the shoulders, looking into his eyes with the deepest of gazes. He opened his mouth to utter one word, the only word that mattered.

"Checkmate."

And without even a second passing, both men made impact with the waterfall and vanished from sight.

*

No.

I stared at the terminal screen for a very, very long moment, my hands shaking, my heart and ears pounding, my eyes trembling. I'd done everything right. Every single thing I could have done, I did right. I followed his instructions and disabled the scheduled chemical distribution. I activated the security camera and watched as Hull confronted *Jameson Montorum*. The mayor, secretly the leader of a crime organization, going by the name of Moriarty. I watched it all. And when the confirmation came that the distribution was canceled, I did as instructed. I zoomed in, zoomed out, zoomed it, zoomed out.

I did everything right. Except for one very, very important thing. The one thing I never should have done, the thing I should have known better than to do.

I left Sheridan Hull alone.

I walked slowly from the terminal to the control panel once more, just to make sure I hadn't failed another instruction. The words were still on the screen, clear as day. "CHEMICAL DISTRIBUTION ABORTED." On that regard, I had managed to succeed. But on an ever more important regard, I felt like a complete failure. I used the walls for support, feeling my heart ache. I couldn't believe it. I simply could not believe it. Not after everything, not after *every single thing we had done*. It just wasn't possible for him to be—

I punched the access panel for the door and stepped through as it slid open, using the stairwell's railings to help guide me down. My brain was going numb, I could feel it. Around and around I went before reaching the level. I didn't bother giving the sign a glance. I knew where I was. I walked slowly, feeling the right side of my stomach pinch up. I reached the double doors that would take me to the observatory, where I would find him waiting, successful in having finally defeated Moriarty.

Because that had to happen. It just *had* to.

The doors slid open and revealed a very cold room with a very shattered glass floor. I walked up to the edge carefully, falling to my knees and looking down. The sound of water crashing on rock was all

I could hear. The waterfall was a flume of black and gray, the rocks below just shades. I stared down the length of that abyss for what could have been hours. When I stood, my knees were weak. My entire body was in pain. I failed.

I turned away from the shattered floor closing my eyes as I staggered back towards the stairwell. In that moment, I felt more helpless than I had in my entire life. Because I'd made a horrible, horrible mistake. And because of it, I had failed.

Because of my mistake in leaving him alone, Sheridan Hull was dead.

*

It is now Saturday, July 13th. Nine days ago, I watched as my best friend, Sheridan Hull, fell to his death. I now find myself in the driver seat of my car, the sun setting to the west, the back seats filled with all of my belongings. I'm on my way now.

We recovered his body the day after. Judging by how horribly his face had been damaged, I can only assume he landed headfirst. They had me recognize him. A crowd of faceless police officers, men who meant nothing to me, had brought me forward to a gurney. And on that gurney rested the body of a man, clad in a purple button-up shirt, black dress pants, tennis shoes with orange laces, a purple scarf, brown-with-blue-stripes gloves, and a long, gray overcoat. On that gurney rested the body of Sheridan Hull. They had me recognize him. They had me nod to say it was him.

Moriarty, or Montorum, or whoever he really was, never turned up. Only the one body was found. Conveniently, Mr. Jameson Montorum resigned from his post that morning, and had not been seen since. Malcolm had told me they were searching for him, but a very heavy issue held them back. When everything was said and done, even after searching the control center, there was no evidence that tied the identity of Moriarty to Jameson Montorum. My account was not enough to convict a now-missing man.

We'd arranged to have his funeral on the next Saturday. July 13th. Thankfully, the weather had changed. The sun had shined through a rough patch of clouds, down on the casket as it was lowered into the empty grave, with the tombstone firmly planted above. Malcolm and I had done the epitaph. We knew that he wouldn't have wanted something grand. We'd kept it simple.

SHERIDAN JAMES HULL
MAY 17TH, 1987 – JULY 4TH, 2013
THE MAN WHO SOUGHT TO DO WHAT WAS RIGHT, RATHER THAN WHAT WAS NECESSARY.

There were a surprising number of people in attendance for the funeral. It made me happy, to be honest. Considering one of the last things Moriarty had accused Hull of being was without friends, it filled me with happiness to see so many familiar faces, and unfamiliar ones, make an appearance. Malcolm was there, with his wife, and Bailey, of course. Two people I had never met before, who later introduced themselves as Sheridan's parents, had arrived.

Greg had been there, as well as a handful of police officers and inspectors. Despite what he had said about the force, they'd all held him in very high regard. It probably would've made him sigh, hearing that. The man we met in Illinois, Ryan Copper, was there. Mrs. Hanson had showed up, and was horribly stricken with grief. The attendance of Caroline Brooke Duerre was the one that meant the most to me. We didn't exchange words, but we did give each other a look. A very solemn look that spoke volumes to our thoughts. That was all we needed to exchange, you know? When you knew him as well as we did, that was all it took.

In total, I believe there were five dozen people gathered around that grave as the casket was lowered in. And little by little, they had eventually left, until few remained. Opposite me had been Caroline. To my right had been Greg, and to my left, Bailey. I suppose we were the four people closest to him. And now he was gone. Just like that, he was removed from our lives. And it hurt. All of us had our own personal connections to him, and now, those connections were severed. We'd lost something very important to our lives.

It's sad, looking back. Today marks exactly one year and eight months since the day I met him. How is it possible, that it had only taken him twenty months to become so important to me? Such an influential person, such a shining star even when he didn't mean to be. He was the hero Newfield needed, when it came down to it. He really was.

Now, as I sit and pen these last words, the words that have taken me nine days to complete, I can feel a sense of acceptance. I can accept what has happened. Can I cope with it? Can I really, truly come to terms with everything that has happened? No. I don't think I can. Not quite yet. But I will eventually. Greg repeatedly assured me that it wasn't my fault. He told me of how the doors had been locked while I was inside, and that any hope for helping the detective would've been met with failure. He knew what he was going into when he walked into that observatory. In fact, I bet he knew what was going to happen long before. But he'd never tell me. He'd never tell anyone, because that was *his* vice. The suspense and mystery fueled him.

If I glance out my window right now, ignoring the parked cars and the supermarket, I'm greeted with a beautiful sight. It's the sight of the setting sun, giving us the last rays of light before it disappears behind the Oregon Coast Range. For just a moment, I'm able to bask in that remaining light and feel like everything is going to be okay. But I know it won't be completely okay. It will be different. Very different. I knew it would be different, and difficult. And though I hate to admit it, I'm running away.

I've had my belongings packed since the day after his death. All of it just sitting in the back of my car. I knew that as soon as the funeral had been completed, I would be gone. I would set out on the road and start moving in a different direction. It hadn't been difficult to decide. Newfield was no longer a home for me, and going north to Seattle, my birthplace, wouldn't help. So I had to go south. My destination was Los Angeles. A new location. A new beginning.

I'm not alone, though. Despite everything, I'm not alone. Because right now, curled up with an orange blanket in my passenger seat, is the absolutely beautiful Veronica Faith Daemon. Even while asleep, I can't keep from admiring her. She'd been cleared from the hospital one week after his death, and she'd immediately come to me. We would be together, and for that, I was very grateful. And I suppose we were running away together. Because even though she had not personally performed the heinous actions of Chimaera, she was the only person left in the chain of command, a thought she was not happy to have.

So we were running, her and I, the two of us on a journey to leave our pasts behind and start a new future. Who knows what Los Angeles holds for us? I'm excited for it. I know it won't be anything like Newfield, because Newfield had something that made it special, and that something was gone now. That *someone* was gone. And though everyone, even Veronica, said otherwise, I know it was my fault. There had to have been something I could've done to stop it. But that was the past now, I suppose. That was history. And you know what? Despite everything, I'm not particularly upset. Because I know what happens when I allow myself to be upset. I know what that leads to. I refuse to regret anything that has transpired.

Regret is a horrible thing to have. Which is why I often make a point not to regret my decisions. I don't regret having moved to Newfield. I don't regret having taken a very temporary job as a medical examiner for the police department. And I most certainly do not regret having had the blessed opportunity of meeting him. A man who would quickly become my greatest friend. A man I would always regard as the best. The wisest man whom I have ever known. The clever detective. Mr. Sheridan Hull.

You were more than anyone could have ever thought. And the best part? You knew it.

—John F. Walker

The story of "Hull" continues. Visit our website at http://www.jameskryackltd.com/ for more information.

PLACET REDIRE AD NOBIS

About the Author

JT Phillips is the author of the "Hull" series, as well as the creator and content production manager of JamesKryack Ltd. When he is not operating as an author, he is pursuing a career in criminal justice.

JT lives with his family in the Willamette Valley of Oregon.

Made in the USA
Las Vegas, NV
25 August 2021